❦

Counterfeit Lady
Lost Lady
River Lady

JUDE DEVERAUX

Counterfeit Lady

Lost Lady

River Lady

Garden City, New York

This edition was especially created in 2004 for Rhapsody by arrangement with Pocket Books, a division of Simon & Schuster, Inc.

Published by Rhapsody, 401 Franklin Avenue, Garden City, New York 11530.

ISBN: 1-58288-132-4

Book design by Christos Peterson

Printed in the United States of America

Contents

Counterfeit Lady

Dear Readers,

Years ago, long before it was fashionable, I researched the family tree of both my parents back to the time when our ancestors arrived in this country, some during the American Revolution, some years before. Always a romantic, I was hoping to find a dashing highwayman or a disowned duke. Instead, what I found were generations, hundreds of years, of American farmers. There were no fascinating criminals that I could find, but only an embarrassing number of illegitimate children.

When I was older, I realized that passion that resulted in out-of-wedlock children was far more romantic than robbers, dashing or not. And when I started writing I began to think of all my farmer ancestors and their uncontrollable passions and wondered if a series of romances could be written about men who didn't control armies or fight with kings, but written, instead, about plain men and women whose lives revolved around spring crops.

I hope you like my stories about ordinary people with ordinary problems and the ordinary needs for love that we all have.

Jude Deveraux
Santa Fe, New Mexico
September 1983

Chapter 1

IN JUNE of 1794, the roses were in full flower and the lawns were of a green lushness that is known only in England. In the county of Sussex stood a small, square, two-story house, a plain house surrounded by a short iron fence. The house once had been part of a greater estate, an outbuilding for a gardener's or game-keeper's family, but the rest of the estate had been subdivided long ago and sold to pay off the Maleson family's debts. All that was left of this once great family was this small, neglected house, Jacob Maleson, and his daughter Bianca.

Jacob Maleson now sat before the empty fireplace in the par-lor on the ground floor—a short, corpulent man, the lower but-tons of his vest unbuttoned over the expanse of his large stomach, his coat carelessly tossed over another chair. His plump legs were encased in broadcloth breeches, reaching to just past his knees where they were fastened with brass buckles, his calves were cov-ered with cotton stockings, his feet were bulging from thin leather pumps. A large, sleepy Irish setter leaned against one arm of the old wing chair, and Jacob idly fondled the dog's ears.

Jacob had grown used to his simple country life. Truthfully, he rather liked having a smaller house, fewer servants, and less re-sponsibility. He remembered the big house of his childhood as a place of wasted space, a place that took up too much of his par-ents' time and energy. Now he had his dogs, a good joint of meat for dinner, enough income to keep his stables going, and he was content.

His daughter was not.

Bianca stood before the tall mirror in her second-floor bedroom and smoothed the long muslin dress over her tall, plump body. Every time she looked at herself in the new French fashions, she felt a touch of disgust. The French peasants had revolted against the aristocracy, and now, because those weak Frenchmen could not control their underlings, all the world had to pay. Every country looked at France and worried that the same thing could happen to them. In France, everyone wanted to look as if they were part of the commoners; therefore, satins and silks were practically banned. The new fashions were of muslins, calicos, lawns, and percale.

Bianca studied herself in the mirror. Of course, the new gowns suited her perfectly. She was just worried about other women less fortunately endowed than herself. The gown was cut very low, with a deep scoop across her large breasts, hiding very little of their shape and whiteness. The pale blue India gauze was tied with a wide ribbon of blue satin just under her breasts, the gown falling straight down from the ribbon to the floor where a row of fringe ran along the hem. Her dark blond hair was pulled back from her face and held with a ribbon, and fat sausage curls hung over her bare shoulder. Her face was fashionably round, with pale blue eyes like her dress, light brows and lashes, her little pink mouth forming a perfect rosebud, and when she smiled there was a tiny dimple in her left cheek.

Bianca moved away from the tall mirror to her dressing table. It, like nearly everything else in the room, was decorated with pale pink tulle. She liked pastels around her. She liked anything that was gentle, delicate, and romantic.

There was a large box of chocolates on the dressing table, the top layer almost empty. Peering into the box, she wrinkled her nose prettily. The horrible French war had stopped the manufacture of the best chocolates, and now she had to make do with second-rate English chocolate. She chose one piece of candy, then another. When she was on her fourth piece and licking her dimpled fingers, she saw Nicole Courtalain enter the room.

The inferior chocolates, the thin fabric of the dress, and Nicole's presence were all a result of the Revolution in France. Bianca chose another chocolate and watched the young Frenchwoman as she moved quietly about the room, putting away the gowns Bianca had strewn across the floor. Nicole made Bianca realize how very generous she and all the English were. When the French had been thrown out of their own country, the English had taken them in. Of course, most of the French had supported themselves economically; in fact, they had even introduced a new thing called a restaurant to England. But then there were people like Nicole—no money, no relatives, no occupation. That's when the English had shown their true generosity. One by one, they'd taken these waifs into their homes.

Bianca had gone to a port on the eastern coast of England and met a shipload of the refugees. She had not been in a good mood. Her father had just informed her that he could no longer afford to pay for her personal maid. There'd been an awful row between the two until Bianca had remembered the émigrés. She had dutifully gone to help the poor, homeless Frenchmen and to see if she could extend her charity to one of them.

When she saw Nicole, she knew she'd found what she wanted. She was small, her black hair hidden under a straw bonnet, her face heart-shaped with enormous brown eyes shaded by short, thick, dark lashes. And in those eyes was a great deal of sadness. She looked as if she didn't care whether she lived or died. Bianca knew that a woman who looked like that would be very grateful for Bianca's generosity.

Now, three months later, Bianca almost regretted all that she had given Nicole. It wasn't that the girl was incompetent; actually, she was almost too competent. But sometimes her graceful, easy movements made Bianca feel almost clumsy.

Bianca looked back at the mirror. What an absurd thought! Her figure was majestic, stately—everyone said so. She gave Nicole a nasty look in the mirror and pulled the ribbon out of her hair.

"I don't like the way you did my hair this morning," Bianca said, leaning back in the chair and helping herself to two more pieces of candy.

Silently, Nicole went to the dressing table and took a comb to Bianca's rather thin hair. "You haven't yet opened the letter from Mr. Armstrong." Her voice was quiet, with no accent, except that each word was pronounced carefully.

Bianca gave a little wave of her hand. "I know what he has to say. He wants to know when I'll be coming to America, when I'll marry him."

Nicole combed one of the curls over her finger. "I would think you'd want to set a date. I know you'd like to marry."

Bianca looked up in the mirror. "How little you know! But, of course, I couldn't expect a Frenchwoman to understand the pride and sensibilities of the English. Clayton Armstrong is an American! How could I, a descendant of the peers of England, marry an American?"

Carefully, Nicole tied the ribbon around Bianca's head. "But I do not understand. I thought your engagement was announced."

Bianca tossed the empty first layer of the candy box onto the floor and took a large piece from the second layer. Caramel was her favorite. With her mouth full, she began to explain. "Men! Who can understand them? I must marry if I am to escape this." Waving her hand, she indicated the small room. "But the man I marry will be far removed from Clayton. I've heard that some of the Colonials are close to being gentlemen, like that Mr. Jefferson. But Clayton is far from being a gentleman. Do you know that he wore his boots in the parlor? When I suggested that he purchase some silk stockings, he laughed at me—said he couldn't deal with a cotton field in silk hose." Bianca shuddered. "Cotton! He is a farmer, a boorish, overbearing, American farmer!"

Nicole straightened the last curl. "And yet you accepted his proposal?"

"Of course! A girl cannot have too many proposals; that only makes the bait more enticing. When I am at a party and I see a man I do not like, I say I am engaged. When I see a man I know is suitable for a woman of my class, I tell him I am considering breaking my engagement."

Nicole turned away from Bianca and picked up the empty candy papers. She knew she shouldn't say anything, but she couldn't help herself. "But what of Mr. Armstrong? Is this fair to him?"

Bianca walked across the room to a chest of drawers and tossed three shawls to the floor before she chose a paisley one from Scotland. "What does an American know of fairness? They're an ungrateful lot to declare themselves independent of us after we'd done so much for them. Besides, it was insulting to me that he thought I'd ever marry a man like him. He was a bit frightening in his tall boots with his arrogant ways. He looked more at home on a horse than in a drawing room. How could I marry someone like that? And he asked me after I'd known him only two days. He received a letter that his brother and sister-in-law had been killed, and suddenly he asked me to marry him. What an insensitive man! He wanted me to return right then to America with him. Of course I declined."

Not allowing Bianca to see her face, Nicole began folding the discarded shawls. She knew that what she felt too often showed in her face, that her eyes mirrored her thoughts and feelings. When she'd first come to the Maleson household, she'd been too numb to listen to Bianca's tirades about the ignorant, weak French or the crude, ungrateful Americans. Then, all that occupied her thoughts was the red horror of the Revolution—her parents dragged away, her grandfather . . . No! She wasn't ready to remember that stormy night yet. Maybe Bianca had explained before about her fiancé, and Nicole hadn't heard. It was highly likely. Only in the last few weeks had she seemed to awaken from her sleepwalking.

Three weeks ago, she'd met a cousin of hers in a shop while she waited for Bianca to have a dress fitted. Nicole's cousin was opening a little dress shop in two months, and she'd offered to let Nicole buy into it. For the first time, Nicole had seen a way to become independent, a way to become something more than an object of charity.

When she'd left France, she'd escaped with a gold locket and three emeralds sewn into the hem of her dress. After seeing her cousin, she sold the emeralds. The price she'd received was very low, for the English market was flooded with French jewels and the hungry refugees were often too desperate to quibble about price. At night, Nicole stayed up late in her little attic room in Bianca's house and sewed pieces for her cousin, trying to earn more money. Now she almost had enough, carefully hidden inside a chest in her room.

"Can't you hurry?" Bianca said impatiently. "You're always daydreaming. No wonder your country is at war with itself, when it's populated by people as lazy as you are!"

Nicole straightened her back and lifted her chin. Just a few more weeks, she told herself. Then she'd be free.

Even in her numb state, Nicole had learned one thing about Bianca—her dislike of the physical presence of men. She would allow no man to touch her in any way if she could help it. She said she found them crude, loud, insensitive beings. Only once had Nicole seen her smile with genuine warmth at a man, and he was a delicately boned young man with abundant lace at his cuffs and a jeweled snuff box in his hand. For once, Bianca had not seemed afraid of a man, and she had even allowed him to kiss her hand. Nicole was awed by Bianca, who was willing to overlook her aversion to the male touch and to marry in order to better her social status. Or maybe Bianca had no idea what went on between a husband and a wife.

The two women left the small house, walking down the narrow central stairs with its worn carpet. Behind the house was a small stable and carriage house, which Jacob Maleson kept in much better repair than the house. Every day at half past one, Nicole and Bianca rode together through the park in an elegant little two-seat, one-horse carriage. The parkland had once belonged to the Maleson family but was now owned by people Bianca considered upstarts and commoners. She'd never asked if she could ride through the wooded park, yet no one had challenged her. During this time of day, she could imagine herself the lady of the manor as her grandmother once was.

Her father refused to hire a driver for her, and Bianca would not ride in the same carriage as the smelly stablemen, nor would she drive her own carriage. The only thing left to do was have Nicole drive the thing. She certainly didn't seem afraid of the horse.

Nicole liked driving the little carriage. Sometimes in the early morning, after a few hours of sewing and before Bianca awoke, she'd go to the stables and pet the beautiful chestnut gelding. In France, before the Revolution had destroyed her home and her family's way of life, she'd often ridden for hours before breakfast. These quiet early mornings almost made her forget the death and the fire she'd seen since then.

The park was especially beautiful in June, the trees hanging over the graveled paths, shading them, making lovely little dappled patches of sunlight across the women's dresses. Bianca held a ruffled parasol at an angle over her head, working hard at keeping her pale skin that way. Glancing at Nicole, she snorted. The silly girl had put her straw bonnet on the seat between them, and the air was blowing through her glossy black hair. The sunlight made her eyes sparkle, and her arms holding the reins were slim and curved in places. Bianca looked away in disgust. Her own arms were exceptionally white and softly plump, as a woman's should be.

"Nicole!" Bianca snapped. "Could you for once act like a lady? Or at least remember that I am one? It is bad enough that I must be seen with a half-undressed woman, but now you have us nearly flying in this thing."

Nicole gathered the thin cotton shawl over her bare arms, but she did not put on her bonnet. Dutifully, she clucked to the horse and slowed it down. Just a little more time, she thought, and she would no longer be at Bianca's beck and call.

Suddenly, the quiet afternoon tranquility was shattered by four men on horseback. They rode large, big-footed horses, more suited for pulling a wagon than for riding. It was unusual to see anyone else on the path, especially men who were obviously not gentlemen. Their clothes were tattered, their corduroy trousers stained. One of the men wore a long-sleeved cotton shirt with large red and white stripes.

For a solid year in France, Nicole had lived in terror. When the furious mob had stormed her parents' chateau, she and her grandfather had hidden inside a clothes chest and later escaped under the cover of the black smoke that came from their burning home. Now, her reactions were swift. Recognizing the menace of the men, she used her long whip to flick the gelding's rump and urge the horse to a trot.

Bianca slammed against the horsehair carriage cushion, giving a soft grunt before screaming at Nicole. "Just what do you think you're doing? I will not be treated like this!"

Nicole ignored her as she glanced over her shoulder at the four men who had reached the path where the carriage had been. She realized they were quite far from any house, dead center in the park, and she doubted if anyone would even hear a scream.

Bianca, holding tightly onto her parasol handle, managed to twist around and look at what Nicole kept glancing at, but the four men did not frighten her. Her first thought was how dare such a rabble enter a gentleman's park. One of the men waved his arm, motioning for the others to follow him as he pursued the fleeing carriage. The men were awkward on their horses, holding onto the saddles as well as the reins, and they did not lift themselves in the posting manner but hit the saddle again and again with teeth-jarring hardness.

Looking back at Nicole, Bianca began to be frightened, too, finally realizing the men were after them. "Can't you make that nag go any faster?" she screamed, holding onto the sides of the carriage. But it wasn't made for speed.

The men, hanging on for dear life atop their slow, clumsy horses, realized the women were getting away. The one in the striped shirt drew a pistol from his wide belt and fired a shot that sailed over the carriage and went right past the horse's left ear.

The gelding reared, and the carriage rammed into its legs as it stopped abruptly, with Nicole pulling back hard on the reins. Bianca screamed once again and cowered in the corner of the carriage with her arm thrown over her face, as Nicole stood up in the carriage, her legs wide apart as she steadied herself, one hand on each rein. "Quiet, boy!" she commanded, and the horse gradually calmed, but its eyes were wild. Tying the reins to the front rail of the carriage, Nicole stepped down and went to the horse, running her hands along its neck, speaking softly in French as she placed her cheek against its nose.

"Look at that, mate. She ain't scared of the bleedin' animal at all."

Nicole looked up at the four men surrounding the carriage.

"You sure can handle a horse, little lady," said one of the other men. "I ain't never seen nothin' like it."

"And her just a little thing, too. It's gonna be a real pleasure to take you with us."

"Wait a minute," commanded the man in the striped shirt, obviously the leader. "How do we know it's her? What about that one?" He pointed to Bianca, who still cowered in a corner of the carriage, making an unsuccessful attempt to disappear into the cushion. Her face was white, terror draining the blood away.

Nicole stood quietly, holding the horse's head in her hands. To her, this was all a repeat of the horror she had known in France, and she knew enough to be quiet and look for a way to escape.

"That's her," said one of the men, pointing at Nicole. "I can tell a lady when I see one."

"Which one of you is Bianca Maleson?" demanded the man in the striped shirt. He had a strong jaw covered with several days' growth of beard.

So it was a kidnapping, Nicole thought. All the women had to do was prove that Bianca's father was not wealthy enough to pay a ransom.

"She is," Bianca said and sat up straight, her plump arm pointing rigidly at Nicole. "She's the bleedin' lady. I just works for her."

"What'd I tell you?" said one of the men. "She don't talk like no lady. I told you this one here's the lady."

Nicole stood very still, her back straight, her chin high, watching Bianca, whose eyes danced with triumph. She knew there was nothing she could do or say now; the men would take her away. Of course, when they learned she was a penniless French refugee, they would release her, since they would have no hope of obtaining a ransom.

"That's it, then, little lady," one of the men said. "You're to come with us. And I hope you got more sense than to give us any trouble."

Nicole could only shake her head mutely.

The man extended his hand down to her, and she took it, slipped her foot into the stirrup beside his, and was quickly in the saddle in front of him, with both of her feet hanging down one side of the horse.

"She's a looker, ain't she?" the man said. "No wonder he wants her brought to him. You know, I knew she was a lady as soon as I seen her. You can always tell a lady by the way she moves." He smiled in satisfaction at his knowledge. He held one hairy arm around Nicole's waist and awkwardly reined the horse away from the still carriage.

Bianca sat perfectly still for several minutes, staring after them. She was glad, of course, that her sharp wit had let her escape from the men, but it made her angry that the stupid men couldn't see that *she* was the lady. When the park was silent again, she began to look about her. She was stranded, alone. She could not drive the carriage, so how was she to get home? The only way was to walk. As her heel touched the gravel and the rocks bit into her flesh through the thin leather slippers, she cursed Nicole for causing her such pain. On the long, painful walk home, she cursed Nicole repeatedly and was so angry when she finally arrived home that she completely forgot about the kidnapping. Only later, after she and her father had shared a seven-course supper, did she mention the abduction to him. Jacob Maleson, half asleep, said they'd release the girl, but he'd talk to the authorities in the morning. Bianca made her way up to her bedroom, dreading having to find another maid. They were such an ungrateful lot.

The ground floor of the inn was one long room with stone walls that made it cool and dark inside. There were several long trestle tables set about the room. The four kidnappers sat on the benches at one table. Before them were thick stoneware bowls filled with a coarsely chopped beef stew and tall mugs of cool ale. The men sat gingerly on the hard benches. A day spent on horseback was a new experience, and they were paying for it now with their soreness.

"I don't trust her, that's all I'm sayin'," said one of the men. "She's too bleedin' quiet. She looks all innocence with them big eyes, but I say she's plannin' somethin'. And that somethin' is gonna get us in trouble."

The other three men listened to him, frowns on their faces.

The first man continued. "You know what he's like. I ain't

gonna risk losin' her. All I want is to get her to America, to him, just like he ordered, and I don't want nothin' goin' wrong."

The man in the striped shirt took a long drink of ale. "Joe's right. Any lady can handle a horse like she did ain't gonna be afraid of tryin' to escape. Anybody want to volunteer to watch her all night?"

The men groaned, feeling their sore muscles. They would have considered tying up their prisoner, but their orders about that had been very strict. They were not to harm her in any way.

"Joe, you remember that time the doc took them stitches in your chest?"

Joe nodded, puzzled.

"Remember that white stuff he gave you to make you sleep? Think you could get some?"

Joe looked around at the other patrons of the inn. They ranged from a couple of gutter rats to a well-heeled gentleman alone in a corner. Joe knew he could buy anything from such a group. "I think I can get some," he said.

Sitting quietly on the edge of the bed in the dirty little up-stairs room, Nicole looked at her surroundings. She'd already been to the window and had discovered there was a drainpipe outside and a storage shed roof just below the window. Later, when it was darker and the yard was quieter, maybe she could risk trying to escape. Of course, she could tell the men her true identity, but it was a little early yet as they were only a few hours away from Bianca's home. She wondered how Bianca had gotten home, how many hours it had taken her if she'd had to walk. Then it would take Mr. Maleson some time to get to the county sheriff and send out alarms and searches for her. No, it was too soon yet to reveal herself to the men. Tonight she would try to escape, and if that failed she would tell them in the morning of their mistake. Then they would release her. Please, God, she prayed, let them not be angry.

As the door opened, she looked up at the four men entering the little room.

"We brought you somethin' to drink. Real chocolate from South America. You know, one of us could of been on the voyage what brought this here."

Sailors! she thought as she took the mug. Why hadn't she realized it before? That's why they were so awkward on the horses, why their clothes smelled so strange.

As she drank the delicious chocolate, she began to relax, the warmth and creaminess seeping through her and making her realize how tired she was. Trying to concentrate on her plan of escape, her thoughts kept drifting, floating away. She looked up at the men as they hovered over her, watching her anxiously like giant, grizzled babysitters, and she wanted to reassure them for some reason. Smiling, she closed her eyes and let herself drift away into sleep.

The next twenty-four hours were lost to Nicole. She was vaguely aware of being carried about, handled as if she were a baby. Sometimes, she sensed someone was worried about her, and she tried to smile and say she was fine, but the words just wouldn't seem to surface. She dreamed constantly, remembering her parents' chateau, her swing under the willow tree in the garden, smiling at some of the happy times spent at the miller's house with her grandfather. She lay quietly in a hammock, gently swaying on a hot, close day.

When she slowly opened her eyes, the swaying hammock of the dream did not go away. But instead of the trees above her was a row of slats. Odd, she thought, someone must have built a platform above the hammock, and she idly wondered what it was for.

"So, you're awake! I told those sailors they gave you too much of the opium. It's a wonder you ever woke up at all. Trust a man to do everything wrong. Here, I've made you some coffee. It's good and hot."

Turning, Nicole looked up as a woman placed a large hand

behind her back and practically lifted her from the bed. She wasn't in a garden at all but in a bare little room. Perhaps the drug made it seem to sway. No wonder she had dreamed she was in a hammock. "Where are we? Who are you?" she managed to ask as she gulped the hot, strong coffee.

"You're still groggy, aren't you? I'm Janie, and I was hired by Mr. Armstrong to take care of you."

Nicole looked up sharply. The name Armstrong meant something to her, but she couldn't remember what. As the black coffee began to clear her senses, she looked at Janie. She was a tall, big-boned woman with a broad face, her cheeks looking to be permanently pink, reminding Nicole of a nursemaid she'd once had. Janie exuded an air of confidence and common sense, a feeling of safety and serenity.

"Who is Mr. Armstrong?"

Janie took the empty cup away and refilled it. "They surely did give you too much of that sleeping stuff. Mr. Armstrong. Clayton Armstrong. Remember now? The man you're supposed to marry."

Nicole blinked rapidly, drank more coffee from the pot set on a little brass charcoal brazier, and began to remember everything. "I'm afraid there's been a mistake. I'm not Bianca Maleson, nor am I engaged to Mr. Armstrong."

"You're not—" Janie began, sitting down on the lower bed of the bunk beds. "Honey, I think you'd better tell me the whole story."

When Nicole had finished, she laughed. "So, you see, I'm sure the men will release me once they hear the whole story."

Janie was silent.

"Won't they?"

"There's more to this than you know," Janie said. "For one thing, we're twelve hours out to sea, on our way to America."

Chapter 2

STUNNED, NICOLE looked at the room around her. A ship! It was bare, with oak walls, floor, and ceiling, and against one wall were two bunk beds. There was very little space from the bed to the other wall, which was bare except for a round porthole. A door was at one end of the room, and the other end was piled high with boxes and trunks held securely with ropes fastened to the wall. A low cabinet was in one corner, the brazier on top of it. Suddenly, Nicole realized that the rocking was the motion of a ship on a calm sea. "I don't understand," she said. "Why would anyone want to kidnap me—or Bianca, rather—to America?"

Janie went to one of the trunks and opened the lid, withdrawing a little leather portfolio tied with ribbon. "I think you'd better read this."

Puzzled, Nicole opened the packet. There were two sheets of paper inside, covered with a bold, strong handwriting. She began to read.

My dearest Bianca,

I hope by now Janie has explained everything to you. I also hope you will not be too angry at my unorthodox methods of bringing you to me. I know what a kind and dutiful daughter you are and I know how much you worry about your fa-

ther's health. I was willing to wait for you while he was so very ill, but now I can wait no longer.

I have chosen a packet boat for your passage to America since they are faster than any other. Janie and Amos have been instructed to purchase all the food you need for the journey as well as the makings of a new wardrobe since this haste has deprived you of your own. She is an excellent seamstress.

Even though I have you on your way to me, I do not trust that nothing will go awry. Therefore, I have instructed the captain to marry us by proxy. Then, even if your father did find you before you reached me, you would still be mine. I know I am being high-handed about this but you must forgive me and remember that I do it because I love you and am so lonely without you.

When next I see you, you will be my wife. I count the hours.

All my love,
Clay

Nicole held the letter for several moments, feeling that she was prying into something very personal and private that she should not see. She smiled slightly. She'd always heard that Americans were quite unromantic, but this man had gone through an elaborate kidnapping scheme to bring the woman he loved to him.

She looked up at Janie. "He seems like a very nice man, one who is obviously very much in love. I envy Bianca. Who is Amos?"

"Clay sent him with me to help protect you, but there was an illness on the passage over." She looked away, not wanting to remember the time when five people had died. "Amos didn't make it."

"I'm sorry," Nicole said as she stood. "I must find the captain and straighten this out." Catching sight of herself in the mirror over the corner cabinet, she paused. Her hair was a mess, tumbling about her face in short, fat, corkscrew curls. "Do you know where I could find a comb?"

"Sit down and I'll fix it."

Gladly, Nicole sat down. "Is he always so . . . so impetuous?"

"Who? Oh, you mean Clay." Janie smiled fondly. "I don't know if he's impetuous as much as arrogant. He's used to getting what he wants. I told him when he concocted this whole scheme that it would go wrong, but he just laughed at me. Now here we are in the middle of the ocean together. It's going to be me laughin' when Clay sees you."

She turned Nicole's head and tilted her face to the light. "On second thought, I don't think any man'd laugh at you," she said, taking her first good look at Nicole. The big eyes were striking, but Janie thought that what would intrigue a man most was her mouth. It wasn't very wide, but the lips were full and deep pink. What was so unusual was that her upper lip was larger than her lower. It was an extraordinary combination, one that Janie guessed would fascinate men.

Blushing lightly, Nicole turned away. "But of course I won't meet Mr. Armstrong. I need to return to England. I have a cousin who has asked me to be a partner with her in a dress shop. I have saved nearly all the money I need."

"I hope we can go back for your sake. But I don't like those men up there." Janie nodded her head toward the ceiling. "I told Clay I didn't like them, but he wouldn't listen. He is the stubbornnest man ever created."

Nicole glanced at the letter on the bed. "A man in love surely can be forgiven for some things."

"Humph!" Janie snorted. "You can say that, but you've never had to deal with him."

Leaving the cabin and climbing the narrow stairs to the main deck, Nicole felt the soft sea air blow through her hair, and she smiled into the breeze. Pausing, she was aware of several men staring at her. The sailors watched her avidly, and she pulled her shawl close about her. She knew her thin linen dress must be clinging to her, and she suddenly had the feeling that she was standing nude before the men.

"What is it ye be wantin', little lady?" one of the men asked, his eyes going up and down her body.

Concentrating on not letting her feet take a step backward, she answered, "I'd like to see the captain."

"And I'm sure he'd like to see you."

She ignored the laughter of the men around her as she followed the sailor to a door at the front of the ship, where he gave a curt knock. When the captain bellowed for them to come in, the sailor opened the door and half shoved Nicole inside, closing the door behind her.

After her eyes took a moment to adjust, she saw that the cabin was twice as big as the one she and Janie shared. There was a large window on one side, but the glass was so filthy that little sunlight came through. A dirty, rumpled bed was under the window, and in the middle of the room was a big, heavy table bolted to the floor, covered with rolled and flat maps and charts.

As a rat ran across the floor, she gasped. A low rumble of laughter made her look toward a dark corner to the man sitting there, his face dark with unshaved whiskers, his clothes rumpled, and one hand holding a bottle of rum.

"I was told you were a bleedin' lady. You better get used to the rats on this ship, the two-legged as well as the four-legged kind."

"Are you the captain?" she asked, stepping forward.

"I am. If you can call a mail packet a ship, then I'm her captain."

"May I sit down? I'd like to talk to you."

He pointed the rum bottle at a chair.

Nicole told her story quickly and succinctly. When she finished, the captain was silent. "When do you think we will be able to get back to England?"

"I ain't goin' back to England."

"But how will I get back? You don't understand. This is all a terrible mix-up. Mr. Armstrong—"

He cut her off. "All I know, girl, is Clayton Armstrong hired me to kidnap some lady and bring her to him in America." He squinted his eyes at her. "Now that I look at you, you ain't much like he described."

"That's because I'm not his fiancée."

Waving his hand in dismissal, he took a deep drink of the rum. "What do I care who you are? He said you might give me some trouble about the marriage, but I was to do it anyway."

Nicole stood up. "Marriage! You cannot think—!" she began but calmed herself. "Mr. Armstrong is in love with and wants to marry Bianca Maleson. I am Nicole Courtalain. I have never even met Mr. Armstrong."

"That's what you say. Why didn't you tell my men right off who you were? How come you waited this long?"

"I thought they would release me when they found out who I was, but I wanted to be far enough away from Bianca so I knew she would be safe."

"Is this Bianca the fat one the men said told 'em who you were?"

"Bianca did identify me, yes. But she knew I would be safe."

"Like hell she did! Are you expectin' me to believe that you kept your mouth shut to protect a bitch who would happily turn you over to kidnappers? I can't believe that. You must think I'm stupid."

There was nothing Nicole could say.

"Go on. Get out of here while I think about this. And on your way out, tell that man you came with I want to see him."

When Nicole was gone and the captain and the first mate

were alone, the captain spoke. "I guess you heard, since you spend most of the time listenin' at doors."

Smiling, the first mate sat down. He and the captain had been together a long time, and he'd learned how useful it was to know what the old man was up to. "So what do you plan to do? Armstrong said he'd see we were locked up because of that shipload of tobacco that disappeared last year if we failed to bring his wife to him."

The captain took a drink of rum. "His wife. That's what the man wants, and that's what he's gonna get."

The mate thought about this. "And what if she's tellin' the truth and she ain't the one he wants to marry?"

"I figure there's two ways to look at it. If she ain't this Maleson woman and the other one is, then Armstrong is askin' to marry a bitch that's a liar and who'd betray her best friend. On the other hand, that pretty little dark-haired lady could be this Bianca and she's lyin' just to get out of marryin' Armstrong. Either way, I think there ought to be a weddin' in the mornin'."

"And what about Armstrong?" the mate asked. "If he finds himself married to the wrong woman, I don't think I'd like to be around."

"That's what I thought, too. I plan to collect my money before he sees her and then be out of Virginia immediately. I don't think I'll even wait to see whether she is or isn't who he wants."

"I think I agree with you. Now, how do we go about persuadin' the little lady? She didn't seem taken with the idea of marriage!"

The captain passed the rum bottle to his mate. "I can think of several persuasions that might work on that little doll."

"I take it you couldn't talk the captain into returning to England?" Janie asked when Nicole returned to the little cabin.

"No," Nicole said, setting down on the bed. "Actually, he

didn't seem to believe me when I told him who I was. For some reason, he seemed to think I was lying."

Janie grunted. "A man like him's probably never told the truth in his life so he doesn't believe anyone else has. Oh well, at least we can enjoy the voyage together. I hope you aren't too upset."

Hiding her feelings, Nicole smiled at the large woman. Yes, she was very disappointed. By the time she sailed to America and back again, her cousin would have found another partner. And also, she thought of the money she'd saved, hidden in an attic room in Bianca's house. Rubbing her fingertips together and feeling the many little sore places where the needle had pricked her fingers because she'd worked by the light of one very small, very cheap candle, she thought of how hard she'd worked for that money.

But she wouldn't let Janie see her disappointment. "I've always wanted to see America," she said. "Maybe I can stay a few days before returning to England. Oh dear!"

"What is it?"

"How will I pay for my return passage?" she asked, her eyes wide at the thought of this new problem.

"Pay!" Janie exploded. "Clayton Armstrong will pay for your return, I assure you of that. I told him again and again not to do this but it was like talkin' to a brick wall. Maybe after you see America, you won't want to return to England. We've got lots of dress shops there, you know."

Nicole told her about the money she'd saved and hidden.

For a few minutes, Janie didn't say anything. In Nicole's version of the kidnapping, Bianca was innocent, doing what should have been done, but Janie heard more than the words, and she wondered if Nicole's money would be there when she returned. "Are you hungry?" Janie asked, opening a trunk on the top of the pile against the wall.

"Why, yes, I am. Quite hungry, actually," Nicole said, and

she went to look into the trunk. In those days, before ships catered to passengers, each traveler had to bring his or her own food for the long voyage. Depending on the skill of the navigator, the swiftness of the ship, the winds, the storms, and the pirates, a trip could take from thirty days to ninety, if it arrived at all.

The trunk held dried peas and beans, and as Janie opened another one Nicole saw salted beef and fish. Another trunk held oatmeal, potatoes, packets of herbs, flour, hardtack biscuits, and a box of lemons and limes. "Clayton also had the captain buy some turtles, so we'll have fresh turtle soup."

Nicole looked at the foodstuffs. "Mr. Armstrong seems to be an especially considerate man. I almost wish I *were* marrying him."

Janie was beginning to think that, too, as she turned and opened the doors of the corner cabinet and pulled out a tall, narrow hip bath. A bather could sit in it, knees drawn up, and the water would cover her shoulders.

Nicole's eyes sparkled. "Now, that is a luxury! Who would have thought a ship voyage could be so comfortable?"

Cheeks pink with pleasure, Janie grinned. She'd dreaded an ocean voyage in a tiny cabin with an English lady, thinking the English were terrible snobs and king-worshippers. But, then, of course, Nicole was French and the French understood revolutions. "I'm afraid we'll have to use sea water, and it'll take a long while to heat the water on that little stove, but it beats a sponge bath."

Hours later, after a delicious bath, Nicole lay in the bottom bunk bed, clean, fed, and tired. It had taken a long time to heat enough water for the two baths. Janie had protested that she was supposed to wait on Nicole, but Nicole had insisted that she wasn't Clayton's fiancée and therefore could only be Janie's friend. Later, Nicole had washed her only dress and hung it up to dry, and now the gentle rocking of the ship was lulling her to sleep.

Early the next morning, Janie pulled her hair back into a

tight little bun before she began to arrange Nicole's hair into a fashionable chignon. Producing an iron, she pressed Nicole's dress while Nicole laughed and said Mr. Armstrong had thought of everything.

Suddenly, the door burst open to admit one of Nicole's kidnappers. "The captain wants to see you—now."

Nicole's first thought was that he had decided to return to England after all, and she gladly started to follow the sailor, with Janie right behind her.

With one sharp shove, the sailor sent Janie back into the room. "He don't want you. Just her."

Janie started to protest, but Nicole stopped her. "I'll be all right, I'm sure. Maybe he's realized I was telling the truth."

As soon as Nicole entered the captain's cabin, she knew something was wrong. The captain, the first mate, and another man she'd never seen before were there. All of them seemed to be waiting for something.

"Maybe I should introduce everyone," the captain said. "I want to be sure everything's proper. This is the doc. He can sew you up or whatever you need. And this is Frank, my first mate. I guess you already met him."

The sixth sense Nicole had acquired during the terror in France made her aware now of a feeling of danger. As always, her eyes reflected her emotions.

"Don't back away," Frank said. "We want to talk to you. And, besides, this is your weddin' day. You wouldn't want it said you were a reluctant bride, would you?"

Nicole was beginning to understand. "I am not Bianca Maleson. I know Mr. Armstrong instructed you to perform a proxy marriage, but I am not the woman he wants."

Frank gave her a lascivious look. "I think you're about exactly what any man would want."

The doctor spoke. "Young lady, do you have any proof of your identity?"

Taking a step backward toward the door, she shook her head briefly. Her grandfather had destroyed the few documents he had managed to save in their wild flight from the terrorists, saying their lives could someday depend on people not finding out who they were. "My name is Nicole Courtalain. I am from France, a refugee, and I was staying with Miss Maleson. It is all a mistake."

The captain spoke. "We were talking, and we decided that it doesn't matter who you are. My contract says I'm to bring Mrs. Clayton Armstrong to America, and I plan to do just that."

Nicole straightened her back. "I will not marry against my will!"

After a crisp nod from the captain, Frank was across the room in seconds, grabbing Nicole roughly to him, one arm around her waist, the other about her shoulders, pinning her arms to her side.

"That upside-down mouth of yours has been drivin' me crazy ever since I seen it," he murmured, crushing her to him as he brought his mouth down on hers.

Nicole was so bewildered that she could not react quickly. Never had anyone treated her like this. Even when she had lived with the miller and his family, the people around her had been aware of who she was and had treated her with great respect. This man smelled of fish and sweat, a filthy, overpowering stench. His arms cut her breath off; his mouth touched hers in a way that made her want to gag. She moved her head away, gasping, "No!"

"There'll be more of that," Frank said, and he bit her neck quite hard, running his dirty hand over her shoulder. With one violent jerk, he tore her dress, the chemise tearing away along with it, and her breast lay bare to his touch and to the sight of the other men. His big hand cupped her flesh, his thumb roughly bruising her nipple.

"No, please," Nicole whispered, struggling against him, feeling sick.

"That's enough," the captain ordered.

Frank did not release her immediately. "I hope you don't marry Armstrong," he whispered, his breath hot and foul on her face, but he moved away from her, and Nicole clutched at her dress. With weak knees, she collapsed into a chair, running the back of her hand across her mouth, sure she'd never be clean again.

"Looks like she don't like you much," the captain laughed before turning serious and sitting down in a chair opposite Nicole. "You just got a taste of what's gonna happen to you if you don't go through with this marriage. If you ain't Armstrong's wife, then you're a stowaway and mine to use however I want. First, I'll throw that big woman Armstrong sent over the side."

Nicole stared at him. "Janie? She's done nothing to you. That would be murder."

"What do I care? You think I could ever go near the Virginia coast again if I don't do what Armstrong says? And the last thing I want is a witness to what I'm gonna let the men do to you."

Seeming to grow smaller in the chair, Nicole caught her lower lip between her teeth, and her eyes almost swallowed her face.

"See, lady," Frank said, "we're givin' you a choice, real kind of us." His eyes never left her dress, which gapped at her breast. "Either you marry Armstrong or you come to my bed. That is, after the captain here gets through with you. Then, when I'm done with you—" he stopped and grinned. "I doubt if there'll be much left after I'm done with you." Leaning over, he put a dirty finger on her upper lip. "I never had me a woman with an upside-down mouth. Makes me think of all the things I could make that mouth do."

Nicole turned her head away and felt her stomach turn over.

The captain watched her. "Which is it gonna be? Armstrong or me and Frank?"

Concentrating on breathing deeply and evenly, she tried to think. She knew it was important to keep her mind clear and working properly. "I will marry Mr. Armstrong," she said evenly.

"I knew she was smart," the captain said. "Come, then, my dear, let's get it over with. I'm sure you want to return to the—ah—safety of your cabin."

Nicole nodded and stood up, her hand holding her dress together.

"Frank here will stand in for Armstrong. It's all done legal-like. Armstrong had a lawyer draw up papers sayin' I could choose a man to act as his proxy."

Numbly, Nicole stood beside Frank in front of the captain, who would perform the ceremony, and the doctor, who would act as a witness.

Frank readily answered the captain's questions in the traditional ceremony, but when the captain said, "Bianca, will you take this man to be your lawfully wedded husband?" Nicole refused to speak. It was all so unfair! She'd been abducted, taken away from a country she was just becoming accustomed to, and now she was being married against her will. She'd always dreamed of her wedding, a blue satin gown, roses everywhere. Now she stood in a filthy cabin, her dress torn half off, her mouth bruised and tasting of a disgusting foulness. The last three days, she'd been thrown about like a leaf in a turbulent stream. But she would not give up her own name! At least she could hold on to that, even if everything else was out of her control.

"My name is Nicole Courtalain," she said firmly.

The captain started to speak, but the doctor nudged him.

"What do I care?" he grumbled, rereading the sentence and inserting Nicole's name for Bianca's.

At the end of the ceremony, he produced five gold bands of different sizes, pushing the smallest one on Nicole's finger.

The ceremony was finally over.

"Do I get to kiss the bride?" Frank leered.

The doctor firmly took Nicole's arm and led her away from the man to the table in the middle of the room. Taking a pen, he wrote something, then turned and handed the quill to Nicole. "You must sign it," he said, thrusting the marriage certificate at her.

Her eyes were filled with tears, and she had to wipe them away before she could see. The doctor had put her real name on the marriage certificate. She, Nicole Courtalain, was now Mrs. Clayton Armstrong. Quickly, she signed her name at the bottom.

She watched impassively, feeling numb, as Frank made his mark on the bottom of the document. It was legal now.

The doctor held her arm and escorted her from the captain's cabin. She was so numb that she was back at her own cabin before she realized it.

"Listen, my dear," the doctor was saying. "I'm very sorry about all of this, because I do believe you are not Miss Maleson. But, believe me, it was better for you to proceed with the ceremony. I don't know Mr. Armstrong, but I'm sure that an annulment can be arranged easily when you reach America. The alternatives were . . . much worse. Now, let me give you some advice. I know the voyage will be a long one, but stay in your cabin as much as possible. Don't let the men see you on deck. The captain isn't worth much, but he does control his men—to an extent. But you need to help him by making the men forget your presence, at least as far as that is possible. Do you understand?"

Nicole nodded.

"And smile. It's not as bad as it seems. America is beautiful. You may not even want to return to England."

Nicole did manage to smile. "That's what Janie says."

"There, that's better. Now, remember what I said, and try to look forward to your arrival."

"I will. And thank you," she said as she turned and entered the cabin.

For a moment, the doctor stood still. Personally, he thought Armstrong would be a fool to let a woman like that get away from him.

"You were gone so long!" Janie said when Nicole entered the cabin, her voice rising sharply. "What happened to your dress? What did they do to you?"

Collapsing on the bed, Nicole lay back, her arm across her eyes.

Suddenly, Janie grabbed her left hand and studied the shiny gold wedding band. "I was with Clay when he bought these. He got five sizes so he'd be sure one of them fit. I bet the captain kept the others, didn't he?"

Nicole didn't answer as she held her hand out and studied the ring along with Janie. What exactly did it really mean? Did this bit of gold hold her to the promise she'd just made to love and honor a man she'd never met?

"What made you agree to the ceremony?" Janie asked, touching Nicole's neck where an angry red mark was forming.

Nicole grimaced. It was the place where Frank had bitten her.

Janie straightened. "You don't have to tell me. I can guess what happened. The captain made sure he got Clay's money," she said, tightening her lips. "Damn that Clay Armstrong! Pardon me, but this whole thing is his fault. If he weren't so pig-headed stubborn, none of this would have happened. Nobody could talk any sense into his head. No, he wanted his Bianca, and he meant to have her. Do you know he went to four ship captains before he found one low enough to do the kidnapping? And now look at everything! Here you are, an innocent little thing rough handled by a bunch of filthy men, threatened in disgusting ways, forced to marry someone you don't even know and, after this, probably don't want to know."

"Please, Janie, it isn't so bad, really. The doctor said we wouldn't be bothered by the men since I'm married to Mr. Armstrong, and I know they won't hurt you. I'm sure it can be annulled once we get to America."

"Me!" Janie said angrily. "I should have known those scum would threaten you with me. And you don't even know me!" She put her hand on Nicole's shoulder. "Whatever you want from Clay—an annulment, whatever—I'll see that you get it. I am going to give him a piece of my mind like he's never heard before. I swear that he's going to make everything up to you—all the wasted time you've spent going back and forth across the ocean, the money you saved for the dress shop, and—" Suddenly, she stopped in midsentence and gazed amusedly at the trunks along the wall.

Nicole started to sit up. "What is it? Is something wrong?"

Janie's broad face broke into a grin of pure devilment. " 'Buy the best, Janie,' he said to me. There he was, standing on the dock, looking at it like he does everything, as if he owned it, and he was telling me to buy the very best."

"What are you talking about?"

Janie looked as if she were in a trance, staring at the trunks as if mesmerized. She took a step toward them. "He said nothing was too good for his wife," Janie said as the smile on her face deepened. "Oh, Clayton Armstrong, you are going to pay dearly for this."

Nicole swung her legs over the side of the bed and stared at Janie in puzzlement. Whatever was she talking about?

As Janie began to unfasten the ropes that held the trunks to the wall, she kept talking. "Clay gave me a bag of gold and told me to buy the very best fabrics available, the most expensive trims. He said that I could help his wife make dresses on the long journey," she chuckled. "The furs could be worked by a furrier in America."

"Furs?" Nicole remembered the letter. "Janie, those fabrics are for Bianca, not me. We couldn't make them up for me; they would never fit her."

"I have no intention of making clothes for some woman I've never seen," she said, struggling with a knot. "Clay said the clothes were for his wife, and as far as I know, you're the only one he has."

"No! It isn't right. I couldn't take something meant for some-one else."

Janie reached under the pillow of the top bunk and withdrew a large ring of keys. "This is for me, not you. Just once, I'd like to see something Clayton couldn't buy or have just for the asking. He has every girl and woman in Virginia making fools of them-selves over him, yet he has to pick some woman in England who I ain't sure even wants him." As she unlocked a trunk and carefully raised the flat lid, she smiled down at the contents.

Nicole couldn't help being curious. She walked beside Janie and looked down into the trunk, gasping at the loveliness there. It had been years since she'd seen silk and she'd never seen silk of such quality.

"The English are afraid of what they call the lower classes, so they pretend they're part of them. In America, everybody's equal. If you can afford to have pretty things, you don't have to be afraid to wear them." She withdrew a shimmering, delicate length of sapphire blue silk, twisted it around one of Nicole's shoulders, drew it down her back, and tied it loosely about her waist. "What do you think of that?"

Holding it to the light for a moment, Nicole rubbed it against her cheek and moved her body so she could feel it on her bare arms. It was a sensual, sinful pleasure.

Janie was opening another trunk. "And how about this for a sash?" She withdrew a wide satin ribbon of midnight blue and wrapped it around Nicole's waist. The whole trunk seemed to be full of ribbons and sashes.

Another trunk was opened. "A shawl, my lady?" she laughed, and before Nicole could speak she withdrew at least a dozen shawls—paisley from Scotland, cashmere from England, cotton from India, lace from Chantilly.

Nicole was gasping at the abundance and the beauty while Janie unlocked trunk after trunk. There were velvets, lawns, percales, soft wools, mohair, swansdown, shalloon, prunella, tammy, tulle, organdy, crepe, the delicate French laces.

Somewhere in the midst of all the lush wealth Janie was flinging about, Nicole started laughing. It was all too much. As she sat down on the bed and Janie started tossing the fabrics on top of her, both women started laughing, wrapping scarlets and turquoises, greens and pinks, around themselves. It was a silly, hilarious time.

"But you haven't seen the best yet," Janie laughed as she pulled long pieces of pink tulle and black Normandy lace off her head. Almost reverently, she opened a large trunk at the back of the pile and lifted an enormous fur muff from the trunk. "Know what fur that is?" she asked as she placed it in Nicole's lap.

Nicole buried her face in the long, deep fur, ignoring the six colors of silk wrapped around her arm and the transparent India gauze across her throat. There was only one fur that rich, that dark—so deep, so thick you could almost drown in it. "Sable," she said quietly, reverently.

"Yes," Janie agreed. "Sable."

Holding the muff, Nicole looked about her. The little room was full of colors that flashed or cried, shouted or lay still in sulky sexuality, all seeming to be alive and breathing. Nicole wanted to roll in them and hug them to her. There had been no beauty in her life since she had left her parents' chateau.

"Well, where do you want to start?"

Nicole looked at Janie and burst out laughing. "With *all* of it!" she laughed, hugging the muff to her and kicking six ostrich feathers into the air.

While she removed a chiffon shawl from around her legs, Janie lifted some magazines from a trunk. *"Heidledoff's Gallery of Fashion,"* she said. "Just choose your weapon, dear Mrs. Armstrong, and I shall show you my trunk of steel—pins and needles, that is."

"Oh, Janie, really, I can't." Her voice held no conviction as she rubbed the sable muff along her arm, thinking she just might sleep with it.

"I'm not listening to another word. Now, if you think you can spare one arm out of that thing, let's put these back and get started. After all, we only have a month or so."

Chapter 3

IT WAS early August of 1794 when the sleek little packet arrived in the Virginia harbor. Both Janie and Nicole hung over the starboard rail, looking with awe toward the dock that pressed against the dense forest's edge, feeling as if they'd been freed from prison. For the last week of the voyage, they'd talked of nothing but food—fresh food. They spoke of vegetables and fruit, all the many plants that would be ripening soon, and how they planned to eat some of everything, all of it topped with fresh cream and butter. Blackberries were what Janie wanted most, while Nicole just wanted to see green living things growing from the sweet-smelling earth.

They'd spent the long days of confinement sewing, and there were very few of the luscious fabrics that hadn't been made into a garment for either Janie or Nicole. Now, Nicole wore a frock of muslin embroidered with tiny violets, with a row of violet ribbon around the hem. Entwined in her hair was more violet ribbon. Her arms were bare, and she thoroughly enjoyed the warmth of the setting sun on her arms.

The women had talked while they sewed. Nicole had been the listener, refusing to tell anyone about the time when her parents had been taken and, worse, when her grandfather had been torn from her. She told Janie about her childhood in her family's chateau, making the palace seem like an ordinary country house, and she told of the year she and her grandfather had spent with the miller's family. Janie laughed when Nicole spoke quite technically about the quality of stone-ground grain.

But most of the talking had been done by Janie. She told of her own childhood on a poor little farm a few miles from Arundel Hall, as Clayton's house was called. She was ten when Clay was born, and she talked of giving the boy piggyback rides. Janie had been in her late teens during the American Revolution. Her father, like so many Virginia farmers, had planted all his fields in tobacco. When the English market was closed, he went bankrupt. For several years, he and Janie had lived in Philadelphia, a place Janie hated. When her father had died, she returned to the place she'd always considered home—Virginia.

She said that on her return she had found Arundel Hall greatly changed. Clay's mother and father had died of cholera several years before. Clay's older brother James had married Elizabeth Stratton, the daughter of the overseer of the Armstrong plantation. Then, while Clay was in England, James and Elizabeth had both been killed in a tragic accident.

The little boy Janie had known was gone. In his place was an arrogant, demanding young man who was a demon for work. While one plantation after another in Virginia went bankrupt, Arundel Hall thrived and grew.

"Look," Nicole said and pointed out at the water. "Isn't that the captain?" The heavyset man sat in a little rowboat with one of the sailors working the oars.

"I think he's going to that other ship."

Several yards away from the packet was an enormous frigate, its sides bulging with two rows of cannons. There were many men carrying bundles up and down a wide gangplank. As the women watched, the captain stepped out onto the dock, several minutes ahead of the packet, which was still slowly maneuvering itself into the harbor. The captain climbed the steep gangplank and stepped onto the frigate's deck, walking toward the aft end of the ship.

The women were quite a distance away, and the men on deck looked small. "That's Clay!" Janie suddenly yelled.

Nicole looked in wonder at the man the captain was speaking to, but he looked like all the other men from this distance. "How can you tell?"

Janie laughed. She was so glad to be home. "Once you know Clay, you'll understand," she said, turning away abruptly and leaving Nicole alone.

Straining her eyes to see the man who was her husband, Nicole nervously twisted the wedding band on her left hand.

"Here," Janie said and thrust a spyglass into her hand. "Take a good look."

Even through the glass, the men were small, but she could feel the presence of the man talking to the captain. He had one foot on a bale of cotton, the other on the deck. He leaned forward, his forearms on his bent knee. Even bending, he was taller than the captain. He wore snug trousers of light brown and black leather boots to his knees. His waist was circled by a three-inch-wide black leather belt. His shirt was gathered just past the shoulders, open at the throat, and the sleeves were rolled to his elbows, revealing brown forearms. She couldn't tell much about his face at that distance, but his brown hair was loosely pulled back and tied behind his neck.

Putting the glass down, she turned to Janie.

"Oh no you don't," Janie said. "I've seen that expression too many times. Just because a man is big and handsome is no reason for you to give in to him. He's gonna be awful mad when he finds out what happened, and if you don't stand up to him, he'll blame all of it on you."

Nicole smiled at her friend, her eyes dancing. "You certainly never mentioned that he was big and handsome," she teased.

"I never said he was ugly either. Now, I want you to go back to the cabin and wait because, if I know Clay, he'll be here in minutes. I want to get to him first and explain just what that scoundrel of a captain did. Now scoot!"

Obeying her friend, Nicole returned to the dark little cabin, feeling almost nostalgic about leaving it. She and Janie had become quite close in the last forty days.

Her eyes had just adjusted to the dim light when suddenly the cabin door swung open. A man who was unmistakably Clayton Armstrong burst into the room, his broad shoulders filling the space until Nicole felt as if she were standing in a closet with him.

Clay didn't wait long enough to give his eyes time to adjust. He saw only the outline of his wife. One long arm shot out and pulled her to him.

Nicole started to protest, but then his mouth found hers and she couldn't protest. His mouth was clean-tasting, strong, demanding yet gentle, but she made a weak attempt to push away from him. His arms about her tightened, and he lifted her so that her toes were barely touching the floor, his chest hard against her womanly softness. She could feel her heart beginning to pound.

The only time she'd been kissed like this was by Frank, the first mate, but there was no comparison! He turned his head, moved his hand to hold the back of her head, making her feel as if she were fainting, drowning. Her arms went about his neck and pulled him closer to her. His breath was on her cheek.

As he moved from her mouth to her cheek, she felt his teeth on her earlobe, and her knees turned to water. His tongue touched the cord in her neck.

Quickly, his arm swept under her knees, lifting her off the floor and wrapping her body around his. Dazed, Nicole was aware only that she wanted more and more of him as she turned her head back, offering her lips to him again.

He kissed her hungrily, and she returned his passion. When

he moved to the bed, holding her body next to him, it seemed natural. She wanted only to touch him, to keep him near her. He pulled her down on the bed with him, his lips never leaving hers, throwing one strong, heavy leg across hers, his hand running up and down her bare arm. When he touched her breast through her clothes, she moaned and arched her body toward his.

"Bianca," he whispered in her ear. "Sweet, sweet Bianca."

Nicole did not come to her senses suddenly; her passion was too strong for that. Only slowly did she become aware of where she was, who she was—and who she was not.

"Please," she said, one hand pushing against his chest, but her voice was weak and strained.

"It's all right, love," he said, his voice deep and clear, his breath warm against her cheek. His hair was against her face, smelling of the earth she so longed to touch again. Momentarily, she closed her eyes.

"I've waited so long for you, my love," he said. "Months, years, centuries. Now we will be together always."

The words were what made Nicole awaken. They were intimate words of love meant for another woman. She could believe that the caresses that had made her mind go blank were hers, but those words belonged to another.

"Clay," she said quietly.

"Yes, love," he answered as he kissed the soft skin around her ear. His big, strong body was beside her, half on top of her. Somehow, she felt as if she'd been waiting for this all her life. It seemed so natural to pull him closer to her, and it flashed through her mind that she should let him find out the truth in the morning. Instantly, she discarded the idea as selfish.

"Clay, I am not Bianca. I am Nicole." She hesitated about telling him she was his wife.

For a moment he kept kissing her, but his head jerked up, and she felt his body stiffen as he stared at her in the darkness. In one

41

movement, he was out of the low bunk bed. One minute he was in Nicole's arms, and the next they were empty. She dreaded the next few minutes.

He seemed to be familiar with the cabin, or one like it, because he knew where he would find a candle, and the little room quickly blazed with light.

Blinking rapidly as she sat up, Nicole had her first good look at her husband. Janie had been right about his arrogance. She could see it in his face. His hair was lighter than she'd thought, the rich brown of it streaked with sunlight. Heavy brows shaded dark eyes above a large, chiseled nose that thrust over his mouth, which she knew to be soft but was now drawn into a tight, angry line. His jaw was strong and hard, the muscles working.

"All right, just who the hell are you, and where is my wife?" he demanded.

Nicole's head was still foggy. He seemed to be able to turn their passion off rather quickly, but not so Nicole. "There has been a terrible mistake. You see—"

"I see someone else in my wife's cabin, that's what." He held the candle aloft and looked at the trunks along the wall. "Those are Armstrong property, I believe."

"Yes, they are. If you would let me, I can explain. Bianca and I were together when—"

"Is she here? You're saying you traveled with her?"

It was difficult to explain when he would not let her finish even a sentence. "Bianca is not here. She did not come with me. If you would listen, I—"

Setting the candle down on the cabinet, he moved closer, towering over her, legs wide apart, hands on his hips. "She didn't come with *you!* What the hell is that supposed to mean? I just paid the captain of this ship for performing a proxy marriage and for transporting my wife to America. Now I want to know where she is!"

Nicole also stood up. It didn't daunt her that her head

reached only to the top of his shoulder or that the tiny cabin pressed them close together, but now they were more like enemies than lovers. "I have been trying to explain, but your complete lack of manners prevents any communication; therefore—"

"I want an explanation, not a school teacher's lecture!"

Nicole was becoming angry. "You rude, boorish—! All right, I'll explain. *I* am your wife. That is, if you are Clayton Armstrong. I have no idea, since your rudeness precludes any form of conversation."

Clay took a step toward her. "You are not my Bianca."

"I am happy to say I am not. How in the world she could agree to marry an insufferable—" She stopped, not wanting to get angry. She'd had more than a month to adjust to being Mrs. Clayton Armstrong, but he'd boarded the ship expecting Bianca and had gotten a stranger instead.

"Mr. Armstrong, I'm sorry about all this. I really can explain."

He backed away from her, sitting down on a trunk. "How did you find out that the captain hadn't seen Bianca?" he asked quietly.

"I'm afraid I don't understand."

"I'm quite sure you do. You must have heard somehow that he didn't know her, so you decided to substitute yourself for Bianca. What did you think, that one woman was as good as another? I'll say one thing, you certainly know how to greet a man. Did you think you'd make me forget my Bianca by substituting your lovely little body for hers?"

Nicole backed away, her eyes wide, her stomach turning over at his words.

Clay looked her up and down critically. "I guess I could have done worse. I do take it you persuaded the captain to marry us."

Nicole nodded silently, a lump forming in her throat and tears blurring her eyes.

"Is that a new dress? Did you make Janie believe you? Did you by some chance create yourself a new wardrobe at my expense?" He stood up again. "All right, consider the wardrobe yours. The lost money will keep me from being so naive and trusting next time. But you'll not get another cent from me. You'll return to my plantation with me, and this marriage, if it is such, will be annulled. And as soon as it's ended, you'll be put on the first ship back to England. Is that clear?"

Nicole swallowed hard. "I would rather sleep in the streets than spend another moment near you," she said quietly.

Moving to stand in front of her, watching the candlelight make her features golden, he ran one finger firmly over her upper lip. "And where else have you been sleeping?" he asked, but he left the cabin before she could reply.

Nicole leaned against the door, her heart pounding, and more tears came to her eyes. When Frank had run his filthy hands over her she'd kept her pride, but when Clay touched her she'd acted like a woman of the streets. Her grandfather had always reminded her of who she was, that the blood of kings flowed in her veins. She'd learned to walk erect, her head held high, and even when her mother had been carried away by the mob, she'd kept her head high.

What the horror of the French Revolution could not do to a member of the ancient Courtalain family, one rude and overbearing American had done. With shame, she remembered her complete surrender to his touch, how she'd even wanted to remain in bed with him.

Even though she'd nearly lost herself to him, she would do her best to regain her pride. Looking at the trunks with pain, she knew they were full of clothing cut especially for her. If she couldn't bring the whole fabric back, maybe she could someday repay Mr. Armstrong.

Quickly, she removed the thin muslin dress she wore and donned a heavier, more practical one of light blue calico. She folded the delicate muslin and put it inside one of the top trunks.

The dress she'd worn onto the ship had been discarded by Janie after Frank had torn it.

Taking a piece of writing paper from a trunk, she leaned over the corner cabinet and wrote a letter.

Dear Mr. Armstrong,

I hope that by now Janie will have found you and explained some of the circumstances leading to our mistaken marriage.

You are, of course, right about the clothes. It was only my vanity that allowed me, in effect, to steal from you. I will do my best to repay you for the worth of the materials. It may take me a while, but I will try to get it all to you as soon as possible. For the first payment, I will leave a locket that has some monetary value. It is the only thing of worth that I possess. Please forgive me that it is worth so little.

As for our marriage, I will have it annulled as soon as possible and will send you notification.

Sincerely,
Nicole Courtalain Armstrong

Nicole reread the letter and placed it on the cabinet. With shaking hands, she removed the locket. Even in England, when she'd wanted money so badly, she'd refused to part with the gold filigree locket containing oval porcelain disks with portraits of her parents on them. Always, she'd worn it.

Kissing the little portraits, the only thing she had left from her parents, she placed it on top of the letter. Maybe it was better to break completely with the past, for now she must make her way in a new land—alone.

It was completely dark outside, but the big wharf was lighted with blazing torches. Calmly, Nicole walked across the deck and down the gangplank, the sailors too busy, still unloading the frigate, to notice her. The other side of the wharf looked black and frightening, but she knew she had to get to it. Just as she reached the edge of the woods, she saw Clayton and Janie together under a torch. Janie was speaking rather angrily to Clay while the tall man seemed to be listening silently.

There was no time to linger. She had so much to do. She needed to get to the nearest town, find a job and shelter. Once she was away from the bright lights of the wharf, the woods seemed to engulf her, the trees looking especially black, especially tall and formidable. All the stories she'd heard about America came back to her. It was a place of wild, murderous Indians, a place of strange beasts that destroyed people as well as property.

Her footsteps were the only sound on the forest floor, but there seemed to be many others—slithering movements, squeaks and groans, stealthy, heavy footsteps.

She walked for hours. After a while, she began to hum to herself, a little French song her grandfather had taught her, but it wasn't long before she realized that her legs wouldn't be able to carry her any farther if she didn't rest. But where? She followed a narrow little path, and both ends of it were nothing but black emptiness.

"Nicole," she whispered to herself, "there is nothing to be afraid of. The forest is the same during the night as it is in the day."

Her brave words didn't help much, but she used what courage she had and sat down by a tree. Instantly, she felt damp moss stain her dress. But she was too tired to care. Curling her body, pulling her knees into her chest, her cheek resting on her arm, she went to sleep.

When she woke in the morning, she was aware of eyes staring into hers, enormous eyes. Gasping, she sat up quickly, scaring off the curious little rabbit that had been watching her. Laughing at her silly fears, she looked around her. With the early morning sunlight coming through the trees, the forest looked friendly and inviting. But as she rubbed her stiff neck, and then when she tried to stand, she found her whole body was sore and aching, and her dress was damp, her arms cold. She hadn't even noticed yesterday how her hair had come unpinned and now hung about her neck in messy tangles. Hastily, she tried to put what pins were left back into her hair.

The few hours of sleep had invigorated her, and she set out on the narrow path with new energy. Last night she hadn't been so sure of herself, but this morning she knew she'd done the right thing. Mr. Armstrong's accusations were something she couldn't have lived with, and now she would be able to repay him and regain her pride.

By midmorning she was very hungry. Both she and Janie had eaten very little the two days before they reached America, and her growling stomach reminded her of this.

At noon, she reached a fence that protected an orchard of hundreds of apple trees, some barely ripe, and a few in the middle of the orchard laden with fat, ripe food. Nicole was halfway over the fence before Clayton Armstrong's voice accusing her of stealing made her pause in midair. What was happening to her since she had reached America? She was turning into a thief, a generally dishonorable person.

Reluctantly, she backed down from the fence. Although her mind felt good, her stomach gnawed at itself.

At midafternoon, she came to a steep-sided creek, painfully aware of the ache in her legs and feet. It seemed that she'd walked for days and she wasn't anywhere near civilization. The fence had been the only sign that a human had ever set foot on this land before.

Carefully, she walked down the side of the creek, sat down on a rock, unbuckled her shoes, removed them, and put her feet into the cool water. Her feet were blistered, and the water felt good.

An animal ran out of the bushes behind her and toward the

stream. Startled, Nicole jumped and turned around quickly. The little raccoon was as shocked to see her as she was to see it. Immediately, it turned and ran back into the forest as Nicole laughed at herself and her fears. Turning back to get her shoes, she was just in time to see them floating downstream. With her skirts over her arm, she went after them, but the stream was deeper than it looked and much swifter. She'd barely gone ten steps when she slipped and fell, her skirts wrapped around her, tangling her feet, and something sharp bit into her inner thigh.

It took several minutes for her to right herself and unwrap her skirts, and when she tried to stand her leg gave way under her. Grabbing at an overhanging branch, she used it to help pull herself to shore. On the bank at last, she lifted her skirts to survey the damage. There was a long, jagged cut on the inside of her left thigh, and it was bleeding profusely. She tore off the bottom of her chemise and gingerly daubed at the wound, gritting her teeth against the pain. With another piece of her chemise, she pressed harder on the cut, and after several minutes the bleeding stopped. Finally, she bandaged her leg with more linen.

The pain of her leg, her exhaustion, and the lightheadedness from her hunger were all too much for her. She lay back against the sand and gravel of the creek bank and slept.

The rain woke her. The sun was nearly down, and the woods were growing dark again. With a jolt, Nicole sat up, then put her hands to her head until her dizziness passed. Her leg ached, and she felt weak, her whole body aching. It was difficult to stand, but the cold rain made her realize that she had to find shelter. Her blistered feet smarted when she stood on them, but she knew it was no use looking for her shoes in the dark and rain.

She walked for a long time, and she was beginning to feel as if she were out of her body and the misery did not affect her. Her feet were cut and bleeding, but she kept walking. The rain had never gone beyond a cold drizzle, and now it looked as if it might stop. Long ago, she'd lost the pins from her hair, and it hung coldly and wetly to her waist.

Two large animals approached her, their lips curled back into snarls, their eyes firelight bright. Backing away from them, she pressed her back against a tree and looked at them in terror. "Wolves," she whispered.

The animals advanced on her, and she pressed closer to the tree, knowing these were her last moments of life, feeling that she was dying very young and there was so much she'd never done.

Suddenly, a large shape—a man—appeared on horseback. She tried to see if he were real or a figment of her imagination, but her head was spinning so badly she couldn't tell.

The man, or the apparition—whichever it was—dismounted and picked up some stones from the ground. "Get out of here!" he yelled, and threw the stones at the dogs. The dogs turned quickly and ran away.

The man walked to Nicole. "Why the hell didn't you just tell them to go away?"

Nicole looked at him. Even in the darkness, Clayton Armstrong's demanding tones were unmistakable. "I thought they were wolves," she whispered.

"Wolves!" he snorted. "Far from it. Just mongrels looking for a handout. All right, I've had enough of your nonsense. You're coming home with me."

He turned away as if he assumed she would follow him. Nicole didn't have the strength to argue. In fact, she had no strength whatsoever. She moved a foot away from the tree; then her legs gave out from under her and she collapsed.

Chapter 4

CLAY BARELY had time to catch her before she hit the ground. He refrained from a tirade on the stupidity of females when he saw that she was nearly unconscious. Her bare arms were cold, wet, and clammy. Kneeling, he leaned her against his chest and removed his coat, which he wrapped around her. When he picked her up in his arms, he was amazed at how light she was. He set her on his horse, holding her while he mounted behind her.

It was a long ride to his plantation.

Nicole tried to sit up straight to avoid contact with him. Even in her exhausted state, she could feel his hatred for her.

"Here, lean back, relax. I promise I won't bite you."

"No," she whispered. "You hate me. You should have let the wolves have me. Better for everyone."

"I told you they weren't wolves, and I don't hate you. Do you think I'd have spent so much time looking for you if I hated you? Now, lean back."

His arms around her were strong, and when she put her head on his chest she was glad to be near any human again. The events of the last few days whirled in her head. She seemed to be swimming in a river, and there were red shoes all around her. The shoes had eyes and were snarling at her.

"Hush. You're safe now. The shoes or the wolves can't get you. I'm with you, and you're safe."

Even in her sleep, she heard him and relaxed as she felt his hand rubbing her arm, the motion good and warm.

When he stopped the horse, she opened her eyes and looked up at the tall house that loomed over them. Dismounting behind her, he held up his arms for her. Nicole, somewhat refreshed by her sleep, tried to regain her dignity. "Thank you, but I need no help," she said, then started to dismount. The weakness of her exhausted, starved body betrayed her, and she fell against him quite hard, nearly losing her breath, but Clay merely bent and swept her into his arms.

"You are more trouble than any six females combined," he said as he walked toward the door.

Closing her eyes and leaning against him, she could hear the strong, steady beat of his heart.

Inside the house, he set her down in a large leather chair and pulled his coat closer around her before handing her a large glass of brandy. "I want you to sit there and drink that. Do you understand? I'll be back in a few minutes. I've got to take care of my horse. If you've moved while I'm gone, I'll turn you over my knee. Is that clear to you?"

She nodded her head, and he was gone. She couldn't see the room she was in—it was too dark—but she guessed it was a library since it smelled of leather, tobacco, and linseed oil. She inhaled deeply. It was definitely a man's room. Looking at the brandy glass in her hand, she saw he'd nearly filled it. She sipped it slowly. Delicious! It had been so long since she'd tasted anything. As the first sip of the brandy began to warm her, she took a deeper drink. The two days of fasting had emptied her completely, and now the brandy went straight to her head. When Clay returned, she was smiling devilishly, the crystal brandy snifter dangling at the ends of her fingers.

"All gone," she said. "Every drop gone." Her words were not slurred like those of an ordinary drunk but were heavily accented.

Clay took the glass from her. "How long has it been since you've eaten?"

"Days," she said, "weeks, years, never, always."

"That's all I need," he grumbled. "Two o'clock in the morning, and I've got a drunken woman on my hands. Come on, get up, and let's get something to eat." He took her hand and pulled her up.

Nicole smiled at him, but her injured leg would not support her. When she collapsed against him, she smiled apologetically. "I hurt my leg," she said.

He bent and picked her up. "Did the red shoes do it or the wolves?" he asked sarcastically.

Rubbing her cheek against his neck, she giggled. "Were they really dogs? Were the red shoes really chasing me?"

"They were really dogs, and the shoes were a dream, but you talk in your sleep. Now be quiet or you'll wake the whole house."

She felt so deliciously light-headed as she leaned closer to him and put her arms around his neck. Her lips were close to his ear as she tried to whisper. "Are you really the awful Mr. Armstrong? You don't seem at all like him. You're my rescuing knight, so you can't be that horrid man."

"You think he's that awful?"

"Oh, yes," she said firmly. "He said I was a thief. He said I stole clothes meant for someone else. And he was right! I did. But I showed him."

"How did you do that?" Clay asked quietly.

"I was very hungry, and I saw some apples in an orchard, but I didn't take them. No, I wouldn't steal them. I'm not a thief."

"So, you starved yourself just to prove to him that you weren't a thief."

"And for me. I count, too."

Clay didn't answer as he came to a door at the end of a hallway. He opened it and carried Nicole outside toward the kitchen, which was separate from the house.

Nicole lifted her head from Clay's shoulder and sniffed. "What is that smell?"

"Honeysuckle," he said succinctly.

"I want some," she demanded. "Would you please carry me to it so I may cut a piece?"

Closing his mouth on a retort, he obeyed her.

There was a six-foot brick wall covered with the fragrant honeysuckle, and Nicole tore off six branches before Clay said she had enough and carried her to the kitchen. Inside the large room, he set her on the big table in the center of the room as if she were a child and started the fire that had been banked for the night.

Lazily, Nicole toyed with the honeysuckle in her lap.

Turning from the fire to look at her, Clay saw that her dress was muddy and torn, her feet bare, cut, and bleeding in places. Her long hair hung down her back, the blackness of it playing with the firelight, and she didn't look more than twelve years old. As he looked at her, he noticed a darker stain on the light-colored fabric.

"What did you do to yourself?" he asked harshly. "That looks like blood."

Startled, she looked up at him as if she'd forgotten he was there. "I fell," she said simply, watching him. "You *are* Mr. Armstrong. I'd recognize that frown anywhere. Tell me, do you ever smile?"

"Only when there's something to smile about, which is not at the moment," he answered, lifting her left leg and propping her heel on top of his belt. Then he rolled her skirt back to expose her thigh.

"Am I really such a burden, Mr. Armstrong?"

"You haven't exactly added any peace and quiet to my life," he said as he gently pulled the bloody piece of linen from the cut.

"Sorry," he said when she winced and grabbed his shoulder. It was an ugly, dirty cut but not deep. He thought it would heal properly if it were washed well. He swung her around so her leg was stretched out on the table and went to heat some water.

"Janie said you had half the women in Virginia after you. Is that true?"

"Janie talks too much. I think we'd better get some food in you. You know you're drunk, don't you?"

"I've never been drunk in my life," she said with all the dignity she could muster.

"Here, eat this," he commanded, thrusting a thick slice of bread at her, the top liberally coated with fresh butter.

She gave her concentration to eating.

After filling a basin with warm water, Clay took a cloth and began washing the cut on her thigh. He was bending over her when the door opened.

"Mr. Clay, where have you been all night, and what are you doin' in my kitchen? You know I don't like things like that goin' on."

The last thing Clay needed was another lecture from a woman who worked for him. His ears were still ringing from Janie's tirade. She'd screamed at him for a solid hour because he'd been writing a letter of explanation to Bianca to be sent on the frigate that was just leaving while Nicole was lost in the woods.

"Maggie, this is my . . . wife." It was the first time he'd said the words.

"Oh," Maggie grinned. "Is this the one Janie said you lost?"

"Go back to bed, Maggie," Clay said with great patience.

Nicole turned around and looked at the large woman. *"Bonjour, madame,"* she said, and raised her piece of bread in salute.

"Don't she speak English?" Maggie asked in a stage whisper.

"No, I doesn't," Nicole said, her back to Maggie but her big brown eyes flashing.

Clay stood up and gave a look of warning to Nicole before taking Maggie's arm and leading her to the door. "Go back to bed. I'll take care of her. I assure you I am quite capable of doing so."

"You sure are! Whatever language she talks, she looks about as happy as any woman can get."

A glare from Clay made Maggie leave the kitchen, and he went back to Nicole.

"I guess we are married, aren't we?" she said as she licked the last of the butter from her fingers. "Do you think I look happy?"

He stood up, emptied the dirty water into a wooden bucket, and refilled the basin. "Most drunks are happy." He began again on her thigh.

Nicole touched his hair, and he lifted his head to look at her for a moment before bending again to his work. "I'm sorry you didn't get who you wanted," she said quietly. "I didn't really do it on purpose. I tried to get the captain to turn around, but he wouldn't."

"I know. You don't have to explain. Janie told me everything. Don't worry about it. I'll talk to a judge, and you'll be able to go home again very soon."

"Home," she whispered. "Those men burned my home." She stopped and looked around her. "Is this your home?"

He straightened. "Part of it."

"Are you rich?"

"No. Are you?"

"No." She smiled at him, but he turned away to get a skillet from the side wall of the enormous fireplace. Quietly, she watched as he melted butter in the skillet and fried half a dozen eggs, putting another skillet into the fire and adding several slices of ham. Buttered bread went onto a griddle.

Within minutes, he set a long platter of hot, steaming food beside her on the table.

"I don't believe I can eat all that," she said solemnly.

"Then maybe I can help you. I missed supper." Lifting her, he set her in a chair before the table.

"Did you miss it because of me?"

"No, because of me and my temper," he said as he dished out a plate of ham and eggs for her.

"You do have a terrible temper, don't you? You said some very unkind things to me."

"Eat!" he commanded.

The eggs were delicious. "You did say one nice thing," she smiled dreamily. "You said I know how to greet a man. That was a compliment, wasn't it?"

He stared at her across the table, and the way he looked at her mouth made her blush. The food was clearing her head somewhat, but something about being alone with him, the warmth of the brandy through her body, made the memory of the first time she'd met him very vivid. "Tell me, Mr. Armstrong, do you exist in the daylight, or are you only a nighttime ghost, something I've created?"

No answer came from him as he ate his food and watched her. When they were finished, he took the plates away and poured more water into the basin. Without a word, he put his hands under her arms and lifted her back onto the table.

She was very tired, very sleepy. "You make me feel like a doll, like I don't have any arms or legs."

"You have them both, and they're all dirty." He took one of her arms and began soaping it.

She ran her finger along a crescent-shaped scar at the side of his eye. "How did you do that?"

"I fell when I was a kid. Give me your other arm."

She sighed. "I was hoping it was something romantic, like you got it in your Revolutionary War."

"Sorry to disappoint you, but I was only a boy during the war."

She ran one soapy finger along his jaw line and then his chin. "Why haven't you ever married?"

"I did. I married you, didn't I?"

"But it's not real. It wasn't a real marriage. You weren't even there. That man Frank was. He kissed me, did you know that? He said he hoped I didn't marry you, because then he could kiss me some more. He said I had an upside-down mouth. You don't think my mouth is upside-down, do you?"

With his eyes on her mouth, he paused as he was washing her, and when he started soaping her face he still didn't speak.

"No one ever told me it was ugly before. I didn't know." Tears began to gather in her eyes. "I bet you hated kissing me. I know it felt funny, not at all like it was supposed to feel."

"Will you stop talking?" Clay commanded as he finished rinsing the soap off her face. Then he saw that more tears were gathering in her eyes and realized the food hadn't sobered her up much after all, or at least he hoped it was the brandy and that she wasn't so silly all the time. "No, your mouth is not ugly," he finally said.

"It isn't upside-down?"

He dried her arms and face. "It is unique. Now, be quiet, and I'll take you to your room where you can sleep," he said, swinging her into his arms.

"My flowers!"

Sighing, he shook his head and bent so she could get the flowers from the table.

He carried her outside, into the main house, then up the stairs as she snuggled against him quietly. "I hope you stay like this and don't become that other man again. I'm going to stop stealing, I promise."

He didn't answer as he opened a bedroom door on the second floor, and as he put her on the bed he realized that her dress was still quite damp. When he saw her eyes close in weariness, he knew she'd never be able to undress herself. Cursing under his breath, he began to undress her, aware that there wasn't much of the dress or the delicate chemise left. When the buttons gave him trouble, he tore the fabric away.

Her body was beautiful. She was slim-hipped and small-waisted, and her breasts lifted impudently. He went to the dresser to get a towel, all the while cursing the situation. What the hell did she think he was made of? First her thigh, and now he was supposed to treat her like a child and dry her. But she certainly didn't look like a child!

Clay's vigorous rubbing woke Nicole from her sleep. As she smiled at the pleasant sensation, he roughly pulled the light quilt back and put her under it, letting out his breath when she was out of view. He turned to leave the room, but she caught his hand.

"Mr. Armstrong," she said sleepily. "Thank you for finding me."

Bending over her, he smoothed her hair from her face. "I should apologize for causing you to run away. Now, go to sleep and we'll talk tomorrow."

She didn't release his hand. "Did you hate kissing me? Was it like kissing an upside-down mouth?"

There was a little light coming into the room, and Clay guessed it was nearly morning. Her hair was spread out over the pillow, and his memory of kissing her was far from unpleasant. He bent toward her, meaning to kiss her only lightly, but her mouth did entice him and he took her upper lip between his teeth and caressed it, running his tongue along its contours. Nicole's arms went round his neck and pulled him to her as she opened her mouth under his.

Clay nearly lost himself before he pulled away and firmly put her arms under the covers. Nicole smiled at him dreamily, her eyes closed. "No, you don't think it's ugly," she murmured.

He stood and left the room, closing the door behind him. He started to go to his own room, but he knew it would be no use to try to sleep. What he needed was a plunge in a cold stream and then a long, hard day of work, he thought as he left the house to go to the stables.

When Nicole woke in the morning, her first impression was

of sunshine and light. Her second was of a headache. She sat up slowly, her hand to her forehead, and as the bedcovers fell away she hastily pulled them up again, wondering why she'd slept in the nude. Looking over the side of the bed, she saw that her clothes lay in a torn heap.

As her mind became alert, she remembered seeing Clayton throwing rocks at the dogs and putting her on his horse. The ride was a vague memory, and the time after they reached his house was a blank.

She looked about her, realizing that this must be a bedroom in Arundel Hall. It was a beautiful room, large and bright. The floors were oak, and the ceilings and walls were painted white. Around the two doorways and three windows were carved pediments, simple and elegant. One wall contained a fireplace, another a deep window seat. The four-poster bed hangings, the curtains, and the window seat upholstery were all of the same fabric—white linen with blue figures. There was a blue wing chair before the fireplace and a white chippendale chair in front of a window, facing an empty rosewood embroidery frame. Another chair and a tall, three-legged tea table were at the foot of the bed. A matching wardrobe and bow-front cabinet of walnut inlaid with curly maple took up the rest of the room.

Stretching, Nicole could feel her headache leaving her, and she threw back the covers and went to the wardrobe. All the clothes she and Janie had made hung there. She smiled, feeling welcome; it was almost as if this beautiful room were meant to be hers.

She slipped into a thin cotton chemise, the top of the bodice embroidered with tiny pink rosebuds, and over it went a dress of India muslin, a wide velvet ribbon around the high waist. The low neckline was filled with transparent gauze. Hastily, she swept her hair back, curls falling forward to frame her face, and she tied it with a green velvet ribbon to match the one on her dress.

Pausing as she turned to leave the room, she saw that two of the windows faced south toward the garden and the river. When she looked out the window, she expected to see a garden like the English had, but what she saw made her gasp. It was closer to a village!

To her left were six buildings, one attached to the corner of the house by a curved brick wall. Smoke curled from the chimneys of two of the buildings. To her right were more buildings, including another one connected to the main house. Most of these buildings were hidden by enormous walnut trees.

Directly in front of her was a beautiful garden. There were paths bordered by high walls of English box. In the middle of the paths was a tile pool, and just to the right could be seen the corner of a little white pavilion, hidden under two great magnolias. There was a long bed of flowers and herbs, a kitchen garden walled by a brick fence covered in honeysuckle.

Past the garden, the land dropped away sharply to form low, flat fields, and she could see cotton, golden wheat, barley, and what she suspected was tobacco. Past the fields was the river. And everywhere there seemed to be barns and sheds and people going about their work.

Breathing deeply of the sweet summer air, catching the scent of the hundreds of different plants, she lost her headache completely and was impatient with a need to see the outside herself.

"Nicole!" someone called.

Nicole smiled and waved down at Janie.

"Come down and get something to eat."

Nicole suddenly realized she was ravenous as she opened one of the doors and went down the stairs. The hallway held several portraits, a few chairs, and two little tables. Everywhere she looked, she saw beauty. On the ground floor, the stairs ended in a wide central hallway, capped by a lovely, carved double arch over the stairs. She was standing there trying to decide which way to go when Janie appeared.

"Did you sleep well? Where did Clay find you? Why did you

run off in the first place? Clay wouldn't tell me what he'd said to make you run away, but I can guess it was somethin' terrible. You look a little thin."

Laughing, Nicole held up her hand in surrender. "I'm starving. I'll answer what I can if you'll show me where I can get something to eat."

"Of course! I should have guessed and not kept you standing around."

Nicole followed her to the garden door, which was covered by an octagonal porch with steps leading off in three directions. The right-hand steps, Janie explained, led to Clay's office and the stables; the center steps led into the shady, secret paths of the garden. Janie took the left stairs, which led to the cook houses.

The cook was named Maggie, a large woman with frizzled red hair. Janie explained that Maggie had once been an indentured servant, but, like a lot of Clay's employees, she'd decided to stay on even after her time of indenture.

"And how's your leg this mornin'?" Maggie asked, her blue eyes twinkling. "Not that I think it'd be anything but healed after the sweet tendin' it got last night."

Nicole looked at the cook blankly and started to ask her what she meant.

"Be quiet, Maggie!" Janie said, but there was an air of conspiracy between the two women as she pushed Nicole toward the table and wouldn't let her speak.

Maggie piled food on Nicole's plate—eggs, ham, batter cakes, tansy pudding, fried apples, hot biscuits. Nicole could not eat half of it and apologized for the waste. Maggie laughed and said that with sixty people to feed three times a day, nothing went to waste.

After breakfast, Janie showed Nicole some of the dependencies, as the outbuildings were called, of a Virginia plantation. Off the kitchen was a milk room where the butter and cheese were made, and next to the kitchen was the long, narrow loom house where three weavers were at work. Beside the loom house was the wash house that stored enormous wash tubs and barrels of soap. There were quarters above these buildings for the plantation workers, who were a mixture of slaves from Haiti, indentured servants, and employees working for wages. The malt house and smoke house stood near the kitchen.

Across a path from the kitchen was the produce garden, where a man and three children were weeding the vegetables. Janie introduced Nicole as Mrs. Armstrong to everyone. Nicole tried twice to protest, saying that her visit was actually temporary and should be treated as so.

Janie put her nose in the air and acted as if she were deaf, mumbling something about Clay being as sensible as any man could be and she had great hopes for him.

Across the family garden, which Janie said she'd let Nicole discover on her own, was Clay's office, a large brick building shaded by maple trees. Janie did not offer to show this to Nicole, but she smiled when Nicole strained to see inside the windows. Near the office, under cedar trees, were more buildings: workers' quarters, ice house, storage shed, gardener's house, estate manager's house, stables and carriage house, tannery, carpenter's shop, cooperage.

Finally, when they were standing on the edge of the hill where the land fell away to the fields, Nicole stopped, her hands to her head. "It *is* a village," she said, her ears ringing with all the information Janie had given her.

Janie smiled smugly. "It has to be. Nearly all the travel is by water." She pointed ahead, across acres of fields to the wharf on the river. "Clay has a twenty-foot sloop down there. In the north, they have towns like in England, but down here each planter is almost self-sufficient. You still haven't seen all of it. Over there is the dairy barn and the dove cote. A little farther past that is the poultry house, and you haven't met half the workers. They're down there."

Nicole could see about fifty men in the fields, including a few on horseback.

"There's Clay." Janie pointed to a man in a large straw hat astride a big black horse. "He was out there before sunup this morning." She gave Nicole a sidelong look, obviously hinting she wanted to know more of what happened last night.

Nicole could give her no information since she remembered so little. "What's your job in this place?"

"I take care of the loom house mostly. Maggie oversees the kitchen buildings, and I take care of the dye pots, the weavers, and the spinners. It takes a lot of cloth to run a place like this. We have to make saddle blankets, cheesecloth, and canvas, as well as the workers' clothes and blankets."

Nicole turned back to look at the house. The beauty of the house was in its simplicity and classic proportions. It wasn't large, only about sixty feet long, but the brickwork and the pediments over the windows and doors were what gave the house elegance. It was two stories high, with a pitched roof with several dormer windows. The simplicity was broken only by the lovely little octagonal porch.

"Are you ready to see some more?" Janie asked.

"I'd like to see the house. I really only saw one room this morning. Is the rest of it as lovely as that bedroom?"

"Clay's mother had all the furniture made for the house. That was before the war, of course." She started walking through the tall hedges to the house. "I'd better warn you, though, that Clay's let the house go in the last year. He keeps the outside in perfect shape, but he says he can't spare the help to look after the house. He's a man who doesn't care what he eats or where he sleeps. Half the time he'll sleep under a tree out in the fields rather than ride back to the house."

Once inside the house, Janie excused herself, saying she had to get back to the loom house since she was very far behind in her work.

Nicole was glad to take her time studying the house. The bottom floor consisted of four large rooms and two hallways. The center hall contained the wide, carpeted staircase and served as a reception area. A narrow hallway ran between the dining room and the morning room, the outside doorway leading a path to the separate kitchen.

Facing the garden was a drawing room and the morning room. The library and dining room faced away from the river, toward the north.

Making a quick survey of each of the rooms, she decided that whoever had decorated them was a person of taste. They were simple, quiet rooms, each piece of furniture an example of the cabinetmaker's art. The library was obviously a man's room, the dark walnut shelves filled with leather-bound books, an enormous walnut desk filling a large part of the room. Two red leather wing chairs sat before the fireplace.

The dining room was done in the Chinese chippendale style, the walls covered in hand-painted textured paper, a delicate design of greenery and gently tinted birds. All the furniture was mahogany.

The drawing room was exquisite. The south windows made the room bright and cheerful. The drapes were dusty rose velvet with the seats of three chairs upholstered in the same fabric. A couch sat perpendicular to the marble fireplace, its fabric of green and rose striped sateen. The walls were covered with paper of the palest rose, a border of darker rose at the top, and a little rosewood desk sat in one corner.

But the morning room was Nicole's favorite. It was yellow and white. The curtains were of heavy white cotton sprigged with tiny embroidered yellow rosebuds. The walls were painted white. A couch and three chairs were covered in gold and white striped cotton, and against one wall stood a thin-legged cherry spinet, a music stand beside it. A mirror and two gilt candle holders hung above the spinet.

But everything was dirty! The beautiful rooms looked as if no one had entered them in years. The polished surfaces of the wood were dull and dusty, the spinet badly out of tune. The curtains and rugs were choked with dust. It was a shame to see such beauty hidden and neglected.

Standing in the hallway and glancing up the stairs, she meant to explore the whole house but right now couldn't bear to see more rooms covered in dust and dirt.

With a glance down at the muslin of her dress, she turned toward the narrow hall leading to the kitchen. Perhaps Maggie would have an apron she could borrow and the wash house would have cleaning supplies. She remembered Janie saying Clay didn't care what he ate. In the milk house she'd seen something that looked as if it hadn't been used in years, or maybe never—an ice cream freezer. Maybe Maggie could spare her some cream and eggs and a child who could turn the crank.

It was quite late when Nicole began to dress for dinner. She slipped on a dress of sapphire blue silk with long, tight sleeves, the bodice cut very low—almost too low, she thought as she looked in the mirror. With one more hopeless attempt to pull the fabric up, she smiled. At least Mr. Armstrong would see her in something that wasn't torn and dirty.

At a knock on the door, she jumped. A male voice, unmistakably Clay's, spoke through the closed door. "Could I see you in the library, please?" Instantly, she heard his boots on the hardwood floors, then muffled as he went down the stairs.

Nicole felt strangely nervous at what would be their first real meeting. Straightening her shoulders, remembering her mother's words that a woman must always stand upright and look whatever fears she had in the face, that courage is as important to a woman as it is to a man, she went downstairs.

The library door was open, the room faintly lighted by the setting sun. Clayton stood behind the desk, a book open in front of him. He was silent, but there was no doubt of his presence.

"Good evening, sir," Nicole said quietly.

He studied her for a long while before he set the book on the desk. "Please have a seat. I thought we should have a talk about this . . . situation. Could I offer you something to drink before supper? Dry sherry, maybe?"

"No, thank you. I'm afraid I have very little head for alcohol of any sort," Nicole said as she took one of the red leather seats across from the desk. For some reason, one of Clay's eyebrows raised slightly at her words. In the light, she could see him more clearly. He was a solemn man, his mouth drawn too tightly into a straight line, a furrow between his brows making his dark brown eyes look almost unhappy.

Clay poured himself some sherry. "You speak with very little accent."

"Thank you. I admit, I must sometimes work hard at it. Too often, I still think in French and translate into English."

"And sometimes you forget to do this?"

She was startled. "Yes, that's true. When I'm very tired or . . . angry, I do revert to my native tongue."

He took a seat behind the desk, opened a leather folder, and removed some papers. "I think we should clear up some business matters. As soon as Janie told me the truth of what happened, I sent a messenger to a family friend—a judge—telling him of the unusual circumstances and asking for his advice."

Nicole nodded. He hadn't even waited until he had returned home to start annulment proceedings.

"Today the reply came from the judge. Before I tell you what he said, I'd like to ask you some questions. During the ceremony itself, how many people were present?"

"The captain who performed the ceremony, the first mate who was your stand-in, and the doctor who acted as a witness. Three."

"What about the second witness? There was another signature besides the doctor's for a witness."

"There were only the four of us in the room."

Clay nodded. No doubt, the name was forged or added later. It was another in a long list of illegalities about this marriage.

He continued. "And this man, Frank, who threatened you. Did he do it in front of the doctor?"

Nicole wondered how he knew the first mate's name and that he was the one who had threatened her. "Yes, it all happened inside the captain's cabin in a matter of minutes."

Clay rose and walked across the room, taking the seat opposite her. He still wore his work clothes, heavy dark trousers, tall boots, a white linen shirt open at the throat. When he'd stretched his long legs out toward her, he spoke. "I was afraid you'd say that." Holding the glass of sherry up to the light, turning it in his hand, his eyes came back to hers, flickering briefly over the low neckline where her firm breasts rose above the blue silk.

Nicole reminded herself not to act like a child and cover herself with her hand.

"The judge sent me a book on English marriage laws, which I'm afraid hold true in America also. There are several grounds for annulment, such as insanity or failure to be able to bear children. I assume you are healthy in mind as well as body?" Again his eyes flickered.

Nicole smiled slightly. "I believe so."

"Then the only other reason that would suffice is to prove that you were forced into the marriage." He wouldn't let Nicole interrupt. "The key word is *prove*. We must produce a witness to the marriage who can testify that you were forced."

"My word isn't good enough? Or yours? Surely the fact that I am not Bianca Maleson would carry some weight."

"If you had used Bianca's name instead of your own, then that would be grounds. But I have seen the marriage certificate and it is in the name of Nicole Courtalain. Is that true?"

She thought of her moment of defiance in the captain's cabin. "What about the doctor? He was kind to me. Couldn't he be a witness?"

"I hope he can. The problem is that he is already on a ship back to England, on the frigate that was being loaded when your packet arrived. I've sent a man to England after him, but it will take months, at the least. Until there is a witness, the courts will not annul the marriage. They call it 'putting the marriage aside lightly.'" He finished the last of the sherry and set the glass on the edge of the desk, and as he'd said all he wanted, he was silent, watching her.

Bending her head, she studied her hands. "So, you are locked into this marriage for some time to come."

"*We* are locked into it. Janie told me how you wanted to become partners in a dress shop, how you worked nights to save the money. I know an apology is little to offer, but I can only ask you to accept it."

She stood, her hand on the back of the chair. "Of course I accept it. But I would like to ask something of you." Looking at him, she saw his eyes were shaded, guarded.

"Anything."

"Since I'm going to be in America for some time, I will need employment. I know no one here. Could you help me find a job? I am educated, I speak four languages, and I believe I would make an acceptable governess."

Clay stood suddenly and walked away from her. "Out of the question," he said flatly. "No matter what the circumstances of the marriage, legally you are my wife, and I will not allow you to hire out like an indentured servant to wipe snotty noses. No! You will remain here until the doctor can be located. After that, we will talk of future plans."

Astonishment registered in her voice and looks. "Are you trying to plan my life for me?"

There was a hint of amusement in his eyes. "I assume I am, since you are in my care."

She held her chin up. "It is not by choice that I am in your care. I would like for you to help me find employment. I have many bills to repay."

"Bills? What do you want that isn't here? I can send to Boston for anything imported." Looking at her as she fingered the silk of the dress, he lifted a piece of paper from the desk. It was the letter she'd written him before she left the ship. "I believe you mean the clothes. I am sorry I accused you of theft." Again he seemed amused about something. "The clothes are a gift to you. Accept them with my apologies."

"But I cannot do that. They are worth a fortune."

"And isn't your time and inconvenience worth something? I've taken you from your home, transported you to a strange land, and behaved abominably toward you. I was very angry the first night I met you, and I'm afraid my temper overshadowed my reasoning. A few dresses are a small price to pay for the . . . hurt I've caused you. Besides, what the hell would I do with them anyway? They look a damned sight better on you than hanging in some wardrobe."

Smiling at him, her eyes twinkling, she gave him a full curtsy. *"Merci beaucoup, M'sieur."*

He stood over her, watching her, and when she started to rise he held out his hand for her. His palm was warm and callused as it swallowed Nicole's. "I see your leg's healed all right."

Nicole looked at him, puzzled. The cut was high on her thigh, and she wondered how he knew of it. "Last night, did I say or do anything unusual? I believe I was very tired."

"You don't remember?"

"Only that you chased the dogs away and put me on your horse. From then until this morning is a blank."

He studied her for a long while, his eyes staying on her

mouth so long that Nicole could feel herself begin to blush. "You were charming," he finally said. "Now, I don't know about you, but I'm hungry." Still holding her hand and seeming to have no intention of releasing it, he pressed it to his arm. "It's been a long time since I've had a beautiful woman at my table for dinner."

Chapter 5

WHILE NICOLE was dressing for dinner, Maggie had filled the big mahogany dining table with food. There was crab bisque, roast squab stuffed with rice, deviled crab in scarlet shells, poached sturgeon, cider, and French wine. The sheer abundance was amazing to Nicole, but Clay seemed to consider it ordinary. Nearly all the food had been grown or caught on the plantation.

They had barely sat down when the garden door banged open and some loud, excited voices shouted, "Uncle Clay! Uncle Clay!"

Clay threw his napkin onto the table and took two loping strides toward the dining room door.

Nicole watched in amazement. Clay's face, usually so solemn, had changed instantly at the sound of the voices. He didn't exactly smile; Nicole had never seen him smile, but neither had she seen such a look of joy. As she watched, he knelt on one knee and opened his arms to two children who fairly flew into them, wrapped their arms around Clay's neck, and buried their faces against him.

Nicole, smiling at the scene, walked quietly behind them.

Standing and holding the children close to him, he questioned them. "Did you behave yourselves? Did you have a good time?"

"Oh, yes, Uncle Clay," the little girl said as she looked adoringly at him. "Miss Ellen let me ride her very own horse. When am I going to get my own horse?"

"When your legs are long enough to reach the stirrups." He turned to the boy. "And what about you, Alex? Did Miss Ellen let you ride her horse?"

Alex shrugged as if the horse didn't matter. "Roger showed me how to shoot a bow and arrow."

"Did he? Maybe we can make you one for your own. What about you, Mandy? Do you want a bow and arrow too?"

But Mandy wasn't listening to her uncle. She was staring over his shoulder at Nicole as she leaned forward and said in a juicy, loud whisper that could have been heard in the dairy barn, "Who's she?"

Clay turned with the children, and Nicole got her first good look at them. They were obviously twins and she guessed about seven years old, with identical dark blond curls and wide-set blue eyes.

"This is Miss Nicole," Clay said as the children stared at her curiously.

"She's pretty," Mandy said, and Alex solemnly nodded agreement.

Smiling, Nicole held her skirt as she curtsied. "Thank you very much, *M'sieur, Mademoiselle.*"

Clay set the twins down, and Alex came to stand in front of Nicole. "I am Alexander Clayton Armstrong," he said quietly, putting one hand behind him and one in front, and he bowed, blinking at her several times. "I would offer my hand, but it is . . . what is the word?"

"Presumptuous," Clayton supplied.

"Yes," Alex continued. "A gentleman should wait for a lady to offer her hand first."

"I am honored," Nicole said, and held out her hand to shake Alex's.

Mandy edged beside her brother. "I am Amanda Elizabeth Armstrong," she said, and curtsied.

"Well, I see you two made it. You could have at least waited until I was ready so you could show me the way."

The four of them turned to look at the tall, dark-haired woman, in her forties, a stunning, large breasted woman with dancing black eyes.

"Clay, I hadn't heard that you had company. I'm Ellen Backes," she said, extending her hand. "My husband Horace and I and our three boys live next door to Clay, about five miles down the river. The twins were staying with us for a few days."

"I am Nicole Courtalain—" She hesitated, and looked over her shoulder toward Clay.

"Armstrong," he said. "Nicole is my wife."

Ellen stood still for a moment, holding Nicole's hand. Then she dropped it and exuberantly hugged Nicole. "His wife! I am so very, very happy for you. You couldn't find a better man unless you married mine." She released Nicole and hugged Clay. "Why didn't you tell us? This whole county could have used a wedding! And this house especially. There hasn't been any company since James and Beth died."

Nicole was very sensitive to Clay's reaction to Ellen's words. Visibly, he didn't move, but she felt a current pass through him.

In the distance, a deep horn sounded.

"That's Horace," Ellen said as she turned back to Nicole. "We have to get together. I have so many things to tell you. Clay has a long list of bad habits, one of which is being too antisocial. Now I know all that'll change." She glanced about the wide hallway. "Beth would be so glad to see this house come alive again. Now you twins come and give me a hug."

As Ellen hugged the children, the horn sounded again, and she ran out the door and down the path to the sloop at the wharf where her husband waited for her.

When she was gone, it seemed suddenly quiet in the hall. Nicole looked at the three who looked at the open door where their friend had just left, and she burst out laughing. "Come on," she laughed, and held out her hands to the twins. "I may not be Ellen, but I think I can put some sunshine back into this day. Do either of you know what ice cream is?"

The children timidly took her hands and followed her into the dining room. Nicole hurried to the ice house and back. When she returned, she carried pewter bowls that were so cold she had to use potholders. As the twins put the first bite of ice cream into their mouths, they looked at her with love.

"I think you've won them," Clay said as the twins dug into the creamy stuff. For herself and Clay, she topped the ice cream with brandied fruit.

Hours later, when the twins were in bed, she remembered that neither she nor Clay had eaten much supper. As she went down the stairs, Clay stood there, a tray in his hand.

"Personally, I'd like a little more for supper. Join me?"

They went to the library, and Nicole enjoyed the hastily contrived meal even if it was a little odd. Clay had made sandwiches out of thick slices of bread and smoked oysters, slathering both in hot mustard from Dijon.

"Who are they?" Nicole asked between bites.

"I guess you mean the twins." He sat in one of the red leather chairs, his long legs propped on the edge of the desk. "They're my brother's children."

"Is that the James and Beth Mrs. Backes spoke of?"

"Yes." His answer was almost hard in its brevity.

"Would you tell me about them?"

"They're seven years old. You know their names, and—"

"No, I mean your brother and sister-in-law. I remember Bianca mentioning that they died while you were in England."

He took a very long drink of beer, and Nicole got the feeling he was struggling with something inside himself. When he spoke, his voice seemed far away. "My brother's sloop capsized. They drowned together."

Nicole understood what it was to lose part of your family. "I think I understand," she said quietly.

Clay stood suddenly, nearly knocking the chair over. "You can't understand. No one could." He left the room.

Nicole was stunned at his vehemence and remembered Bianca saying that Clay didn't seem to care that his brother had been killed, that he went ahead and proposed as if nothing had happened. Yet Nicole had seen what happened at the mere mention of their names.

Standing, she started to clear away the empty plates but stopped. It had been a long day, and she was very tired. Leaving the dusty library, she went upstairs to the room Clay had given her, and it took only moments to undress and climb into bed, where she was asleep almost instantly.

The next morning, the early sunlight and the bright prettiness of the room made her smile. Maybe this room had been Beth's. As she went to the wardrobe, she thought that soon it would most likely be Bianca's, but she did not like the thought and refused to linger on it.

As she was looking into the wardrobes, she heard noises through the door. Yesterday, she'd had no time to explore the upstairs. One door led into the hallway, and the second door must lead to the twins' room. Still smiling, she opened it, only to be confronted by a half-dressed Clay.

"Good morning," he said, ignoring her blush.

"I'm sorry, I didn't know . . . I thought the twins—"

He reached for his shirt. "Would you like some coffee?" he asked, nodding toward a pot on a table. "I'd offer you tea, but we Americans aren't as partial to tea as we used to be."

Self-consciously, Nicole walked across the room to the coffeepot. It was obviously a man's room, paneled in walnut, the bed enormous, taking up most of the room. Clay's clothes were thrown about over chairs and tables so that she could hardly see the furniture. There were two cups by the coffeepot, and she knew without asking that Maggie had assumed they'd be sharing the drink. Pouring a cup of coffee, she took it to him where he sat on the edge of the bed, his shirt unbuttoned, as he pulled on his boot. She couldn't help a lingering look at his chest, deep tan and thickly muscled.

"Thank you," he said as he took the cup and watched her turn back to the coffeepot. "Still afraid of me?"

"Of course not," she said as she poured another cup of coffee, but she didn't look at him. "I've never been afraid of you."

"I was just thinking that maybe you should be. I like your hair like that. And what's that thing you have on? I like that, too."

Turning, she gave him a radiant smile. Her hair hung down her back to her waist. "It's a nightgown," she said, thinking that she was glad she hadn't covered it with a robe. The high-necked, sleeveless bodice was made of cream-colored Brussels lace, and the thin silk that fell away from the high waist was almost transparent.

"I'm late this morning. Here." He held out his cup and saucer to her in a commanding way.

She took it from him, still smiling, but she didn't move away as he pulled on the other boot. "How did you get that scar by your eye?"

He started to say something, but as he looked at her he stopped, his eyes twinkling, his mouth soft, unlike its usual grimness. "A bayonet wound during the Revolution."

"For some reason, I get the feeling you're laughing at me."

He leaned closer to her. "Never in my life would I laugh at a beautiful woman standing by my bed wearing only her nightgown," he said, running one finger across her top lip. "Now put that down," he said, nodding to the cup and saucer she held, "and get out of here."

Smiling, she obeyed him, but stopped when she had her hand on the door that connected her bedroom to his.

"Nicole."

She froze.

"I have a couple of hours of work to do, then I eat at about nine in the kitchen."

A nod was her answer as, without turning, she went into her own room and closed the door behind her, leaning against it for a moment. He had said her name and said she was beautiful. Laughing at herself for being a silly schoolgirl, after hurriedly dressing in a simple, sturdy gown of brown calico, she left the bedroom to go downstairs.

All morning, Nicole searched for the twins. She'd expected to find them still asleep, but their beds were empty. She asked people on the plantation, but everywhere she got only shrugs, and no one seemed to know where the children were.

At seven-thirty, she went to the kitchen, made crêpe batter, and set it aside to allow the flour to absorb the milk. Afterward, she spent another hour searching before, quite frustrated, she returned to the kitchen. She made crêpes while Maggie peeled and sliced peaches that were so ripe and juicy they fell apart in her hands. Nicole generously splashed the peaches with almond liqueur that was made on the plantation and wrapped the peaches in the thin, delicate crêpes, drizzled them with honey, and added a dollop of whipped cream.

When Clay appeared in the kitchen, Maggie and her three helpers left, mysteriously finding other work they had to do. Nicole set the plate of peaches and crêpes before him, and he got one bite before she asked the question she'd repeated at least twenty times that morning.

"Where are the twins?" When she saw Clayton calmly continue chewing and his shoulders begin to lift in a shrug, she got angry. Pointing the fork she held at him, her voice raised. "Clayton Armstrong! If you dare tell me you don't know where they are, I'll . . . I'll—"

Looking up at her across the corner of the table, his mouth full, he took the fork out of her hand. "They're around somewhere. They usually come in when they're hungry."

"You mean they have no supervision? They're just allowed to run free? What if they were hurt? No one would even know where to look for them."

"I know most of their hiding places. What is this? I've never had anything like this. Did you make it?"

"Yes," she said impatiently. "But what about their schooling?"

Clay was giving his full attention to the plate of food in front of him and didn't bother answering her.

Snarling and muttering something in French under her breath, Nicole grabbed the plate of crêpes from under his nose and held it aloft—over the slop bucket kept for the pigs' food. "I want your attention and some answers. I'm tired of getting no answers."

Clay bounded over the edge of the table and threw his arm around her waist, her back to his chest. When his grip had forced all the air from her lungs and she was helpless, he grabbed the plate of crêpes and set it safely on the table. "You shouldn't interfere with a man's food." He was teasing, but he didn't release her. Only when he felt her body start to go limp did he allow her any air. "Nicole!" he demanded, and turned her around in his arms. "I didn't mean to hurt you." He held her close to him, but lightly, as he listened to the return of her normal breathing.

Nicole leaned against him, hoping he would never release her.

Turning her gently, he helped her sit down. "You're probably hungry. Here, eat some of this," he said, putting a second plate of peaches and crêpes in front of her before retrieving his own.

Nicole sighed heavily, and she caught a teasing look from Clay, as if he could read her thoughts.

After breakfast, Clay told Nicole to follow him. He stopped

in the shade of a cedar tree by the servants' quarters where a very old man sat whittling slowly. "Jonathan, where are the twins?"

"In that old walnut tree by the overseer's house."

Clay nodded curtly and started to turn away, Nicole on his heels.

"That your new missus?" Jonathan asked.

"She is." There was little warmth in Clay's voice.

Jonathan grinned, showing toothless gums. "Somehow I thought you'd marry a blonde, one a little taller and plumper than that one."

Clamping his hand around Nicole's wrist, Clay turned away sharply as the old man's laugh rang in their ears. Nicole was burning with questions, but she didn't have the courage to ask them.

The twins were indeed scampering about in the old tree. Nicole smiled up at them and asked them to come down, saying she wanted to talk to them. The children giggled and climbed higher into the tree.

She turned to Clay. "Maybe if you asked them, they'd obey."

He shrugged. "It's not me who wants them. I have work to do."

With a look of disgust at him, she again asked the twins to come down. They merely looked down at her, their eyes bright and mischievous, and she knew that if she was ever to have any authority over them, she had to win this contest. She turned back to Clay. "What would you do if you wanted them down? Order them?"

"They don't mind me any better than they do you," he said, looking up at them in conspiracy. "If it were me, I'd go up after them."

The twins' giggle was a challenge, and she knew Clay's lies were, too. Not for a moment did she believe that the children didn't obey him. Lifting her dress, she kicked her shoes off. "If you would give me a boost," she said.

Clay's eyes lit up. "With pleasure," he said as he bent and cupped his hands for her.

She knew he could have lifted her to the first branch, but he was going to give her as little help as possible. What none of them knew was that Nicole was an excellent tree climber. There'd been an old apple tree on her parents' estate that she knew by heart. Pulling herself onto a low branch, she stood up and saw the ladder leaning against the other side of the tree. She looked down at Clay as he stared up at her, his hands on his hips, his legs wide apart. He was thoroughly enjoying himself.

Several minutes were spent scampering around the tree, her skirt held to her knees, showing her bare legs. She caught Alex first and lowered him to Clay, who, she was grateful to see, was willing to help her at least that much.

Mandy climbed out onto a thin little branch and grinned at Nicole. Nicole grinned back and started crawling toward her. As the branch began to crack, Mandy yelled, "You're too heavy!" Looking down, she laughed. "Catch, Uncle Clay," she called as she gleefully jumped into her uncle's waiting arms.

Too late, Nicole realized she was too heavy for the thin branch. It began to break away more. "Jump!" a voice commanded. Without thinking, Nicole let go and landed in Clay's arms.

"You saved her, Uncle Clay! You saved her!" Alex chanted.

Nicole, more frightened than she wanted to admit, looked up at Clay. He was smiling! She'd never seen such a smile before, or maybe it was that lately whatever Clay did seemed right, and she smiled back at him brilliantly.

"Let's do it again," Mandy shouted, and started for the ladder.

"No, you don't!" Clay said. "She got you, and you're hers now. You do what Miss Nicole says. And if I get one bad report—" He narrowed his eyes at them, and they backed away.

"I guess you can let me down now," Nicole said quietly.

His smile faded, and he stared at her in a puzzled way. "I'm curious. Have you always gotten into trouble like you have since I've known you, or is this new?"

The smile she gave him had one slightly curled lip. "I kidnapped myself, and I forced myself into marriage with you all for your pleasure." Her voice dripped with sarcasm, but Clay didn't take it that way.

Looking down at her bare legs slung over his arm, her dress lifted to above her knees, twisted in such a way that she couldn't pull it down, he grinned again. "I don't know which I like better—this, or you standing in front of the light in your nightgown."

As Nicole realized what he meant, she blushed furiously.

He set her on the ground. "As much as I'd like to stay and see what else happens, I have to get back to work." Still smiling, he walked toward the fields.

That night, when Nicole couldn't sleep, she told herself it was because she was uncomfortably warm. After putting on a thin silk dressing gown over her nightdress and tiptoeing down the stairs and out into the garden, she walked along the dark path, the tall hedges towering over her to the tile pool where she sat on the edge and put her feet into the water.

The night was alive with frogs and crickets and the smell of honeysuckle, making it cool and pleasant in the night air. As she started to relax, she began to think. In the years of the terror, and the year she and her grandfather had hidden with the miller, she'd never lied to herself. She'd always known that someday it would all end, and it had.

Now she faced another disaster in her life, but this time she was lying to herself that there wouldn't be an ending. She was a Frenchwoman, and Frenchwomen were noted for their practicality, but she was behaving like some silly, romantic child.

She had to face the fact that she'd fallen in love with Clayton Armstrong. She didn't know when it had happened, maybe in that first meeting when he had kissed her. All she knew now was that her thoughts and emotions, her very life, had begun to pivot around the man. She knew she wanted to provoke his anger so he'd hold her in his arms, and she wanted to parade in front of him in a thin little nightgown.

Pulling her knees up and putting her forehead on them, she felt like a woman of the streets because of the way she acted, but she knew she would do anything to have him touch her, hold her.

But what did he think of her? She was not his Bianca, as he'd called her that night on the ship. In a short time he would rid himself of her, and when she walked away she might never see him again.

She had to prepare herself for the end. These past few days had been wonderful, but they had to stop. She'd loved her parents a great deal, but they'd been taken from her, and later she'd transferred her love to her grandfather, and again she'd been left alone. Each time she'd given her whole heart, and when it had been torn out of her she'd wanted to die. She couldn't let it happen again. She couldn't let herself love Clayton so completely that she couldn't bear seeing him finally with the woman he loved.

Glancing up at the dark windows of the house, she saw a red glow that could only be the tip of Clay's cigar. He knew she was down here, knew she was thinking of him. She knew she could get herself into his bed if she wanted, but she wanted more than a night with him, as sweet as it would be. She wanted his love, she wanted him to say her name the same way he had said Bianca's.

Standing, she walked back to the house. The upstairs landing was empty, but the smell of cigar smoke was strong.

Chapter 6

NICOLE LOOKED over the top of the book she was holding to watch Clayton walk toward the house. She saw that his shirt was torn, his trousers and boots muddy. When he glanced her way, she looked back at her book, as if she hadn't seen him.

She and the twins were sitting under one of the magnolia trees at the southwest corner of the family garden. In the three weeks since the night she'd sat alone by the pool, she'd spent a great deal of time with the children—and very little with Clay. Sometimes she could have cried when he had asked her to join him for dinner or breakfast and she had pleaded fatigue or someone who needed her help. After a while, he'd stopped asking. He began to eat more meals in the kitchen, with Maggie for company, and sometimes he didn't come back to the house at night but slept in the quarters with his men—or women, for all Nicole knew.

Janie was still very busy in the loom house getting ready for winter, and Nicole spent several afternoons with her friend, who never asked questions like Maggie did.

Inside the house, Clay stood for a long time at the upstairs hall window looking out at the garden and at Nicole sitting with the children. He didn't understand her sudden coldness to him, why she'd changed from a laughing, friendly woman to one who was always tired, always working.

Striding across the floor of his bedroom to a tall chest, he removed his torn, muddy shirt and carelessly tossed it across a chair. The drawer he opened was full of clean, ironed shirts, and as he went to grab one he paused and looked around him. For the first time since his brother had died, his room was clean. His dirty clothes were taken away and returned clean and mended.

As he thrust his arms into the shirt, he went to Nicole's room. It also sparkled with cleanliness and sunshine. An enormous bowl of flowers stood on top of the bow-front chest, and a small vase of three red roses was on the little table by her bed. The embroidery frame held a half-finished piece of work. He touched the bright silk threads.

She'd been in his house less than a month, but already the changes were enormous. Last night, Alex and Mandy had shown him proudly how they could write their names. The food served on the plantation had always been good, if plain, but under Nicole's supervision new dishes had been added daily.

Clay had always thought he didn't care one way or the other what his house was like—only the fields interested him—but now he suddenly realized he liked the smell of beeswax, and seeing the twins clean and cared for. The only piece missing was Nicole's company, the way she laughed and made him laugh.

On his way down the stairs, he stopped and wondered how she'd been able to get the help to clean the house. Everyone on the plantation had a job, and as far as he knew about it, no one had neglected his or hers. It dawned on him that Nicole had done the scrubbing herself. No wonder she was always tired!

Smiling, he took an apple from a bowl on a table in the hall. She probably thought she was repaying him for those damned dresses he had bought her. First he went to the kitchen and told Maggie to find a couple of girls to help Nicole in the house, and then he went out to the garden.

"School's out," he said as he took Nicole's book away from

her, and the twins were gone before either of the adults could blink an eye.

"Why did you do that? It isn't time to stop yet."

"They need a holiday. Or at least you do."

She backed away from him. "Please, I have a lot to do."

Clay frowned at her. "What's wrong with you? Why are you acting like you're afraid of me?"

"I'm not. It's just that there's so much to do on a place this size."

"Are you trying to tell me I should get back to work?"

"No, of course not. I just—"

"Since you don't seem capable of finishing a sentence, then let me. You work too hard. You act as if you're one of the slaves, except that I don't work them as hard as you work yourself." Grabbing her hand, he pulled her forward. "Maggie's packing us a picnic lunch, and you and I are going to spend the rest of the day in idle pursuits. Can you ride a horse?"

"Yes, but—"

"You aren't allowed to say no, so it's better to be quiet."

He didn't release her hand as they walked across the plantation to the stables, where Clay put a soft leather side-saddle on a palomino mare for her, lifted her into the saddle, and headed for the kitchen. Maggie smiled broadly as she handed Clay the bulging saddlebags.

They rode for an hour, leaving the higher ground where the house and dependencies were, and went to the lower fields. The flat, rich bottomland followed the river in an arch that half encircled the higher ground of fields planted with cotton, tobacco, flax, wheat, and barley. To the east of the house were pastures where cattle and sheep grazed separately, and everywhere there seemed to be barns and tool sheds. They stopped once to feed apples to a pair of enormous draft horses. As Clay talked to her about the quality of cotton, the ways of curing tobacco, she watched him, saw the pride of ownership in his eyes, how he cared for his land and the people who worked for him.

The sun was high in the sky when Nicole looked across the river and saw something that was very familiar to her—a water wheel. Staring through the trees at the stone and brick structure, she was flooded with memories. She and her grandfather had always lived in luxury, their every need had been satisfied before they had thought to want it, but when the Revolution had sent them into hiding they'd learned to survive. They had dressed as the miller and his wife did, and they had worked as they did. Nicole had scrubbed the kitchen twice a week, and she had learned to run the mill when the men went away to deliver grain.

Smiling, she pointed across the river. "Is that a grain mill?"

"Yes," Clay answered without much interest.

"Whose is it? Why isn't it running? Could we see it?"

Clay looked at her in astonishment. "Which one should I answer first? It belongs to me, and it isn't running because I've never hired anyone to run it and because the Backes mill my grain. And, yes, we can go see it. There's a house farther up the hill. You can just see it through the trees. Would you like to go across?"

"Yes, I would."

There was a little rowboat moored at the edge of the river, and Clay threw the saddlebags in, helped Nicole inside, and rowed them across. Standing back, he watched as she tramped across the overgrown path and started walking around the mill.

"It looks to be in good condition. Could I see the stones inside?"

Clay took the key for the big lock on the double doors from its hiding place, watching as Nicole inspected the grooves in the stones and muttered things about bolting cloth and a good millstone dresser. When she finished her inspection, she started asking more questions, until Clay held up his hand in protest.

"Maybe it would be quicker if I explained," he said. "When my brother was alive, we could run a bigger place, but now, with just me, I decided the mill was too much. When the miller died last year, I didn't look for another one."

"But what about your grain? You said the Backes have a mill."

"A small one. It's just easier to send it over there than to worry about running this place."

"What about the other farmers? Surely people like Janie's father need a mill. Or do they go to the Backes' too? Isn't it far away?"

Clay took her hand and led her outside. "Let's eat lunch, and I'll answer all your questions. There's a pretty place on the top of that rise."

When the lunch of cold baked ham, pickled oysters, and apricot tarts was spread on a cloth, Clay was the one who asked questions. He wanted to know why Nicole was so interested in the mill.

Nicole was very aware of him, close to her, that they were alone together in the quiet, secluded woods. "My grandfather and I worked at a mill for a while. I learned a great deal about them then."

"Your grandfather," he said as he stretched out, his head on his hands. "We've been living in the same house for some time, yet I know so little about you. Did you always live with your grandfather?"

Looking down at her hands, she was silent. She didn't want to talk about her family. "Not long," she said quickly, and looked back at the mill. "Did you ever consider selling the mill?"

"No, never. What about your parents? Were they millers, too?"

It took Nicole a moment to understand what he meant, and the idea of her elegant mother—her hair elaborately dressed and powdered, three tiny star-shaped patches at the corner of her eye, in a gown of heavy brocaded satin—working in a mill made her want to laugh. Her mother believed bread originated in the kitchens.

"What's making you laugh?"

"The idea of my mother working in a mill. Didn't you say there was a house here? Could we see it?"

Quickly, they gathered the lunch things, and Clay showed her the house, which was completely boarded. It was a simple one-room house with an attic, old-fashioned but strong and sturdy.

"Let's go back across the river. There's something I want to talk to you about and a place I want to show you."

Clay did not row them straight across the river but went up-stream, past the planted fields, stopping at a point in the bank that looked to be impassable. The shore was thickly covered with shrubs, and willow trees dripped into the water.

Clay stepped out of the boat and tied it to a stake hidden by the bushes. He offered Nicole his hand and helped her to stand on the approximately one foot of sand at the edge of the river. He grabbed an enormous myrtle bush and pulled it aside, revealing a fairly wide path. "After you," Clay said, following her. The myrtle bush slipped back into place, once again hiding the path.

The path opened into a grassy clearing that was completely surrounded by trees and shrubs, and it was like entering a large, roofless room. Along two sides were flowers, a riot of them. Nicole recognized some of the perennials. Though heavily choked by weeds now, they were surviving and producing.

"It's lovely," she said, twirling about, the sweet grass about her ankles. "Someone made this. Surely it didn't grow naturally."

Clay sat down on the grass and leaned against a rock that looked as if it had been chosen for its comfort. "We made it as kids. It took a long time, but we spent every moment we had on it. We wanted a private place."

"It certainly is that. You could walk within a foot of it and not see it. The brush is too thick."

Clay's eyes had a faraway look. "My mother thought the dogs were carrying her seedlings away. She'd visit someone and leave with five cuttings. When she got home, there'd only be four. I often wondered if she suspected us."

"By *us* do you mean you and your brother?"

"Yes," he answered quietly.

Nicole's eyes twinkled. "Surely the two of you didn't plant the flowers. I can't imagine two boys risking punishment to steal iris bulbs. Could there have been a young girl involved?"

Clay's face hardened, and he didn't speak for a moment. "Elizabeth planted the flowers."

The way he said it made Nicole know that this Elizabeth had meant a lot to him, but she couldn't tell if he loved her or hated her. "James and Beth," she said quietly, sitting beside him. "Is their death the cause of your sadness, the reason you rarely smile?"

He turned to her with a face full of anger. "Until you are prepared to confide in me, don't ask for confidences *from* me."

Nicole was stunned. She thought she'd cleverly avoided answering his questions about her family, but he had been sensitive enough to realize that she was hiding something. Just as her past was still too painful to speak of, so must his be. "Forgive me," she whispered. "I didn't mean to pry."

They sat in silence for several minutes. "You said you wanted to talk to me about something," Nicole said.

Clay stretched out and let his mind change from his dead brother and sister-in-law to a more pleasant subject. "I've been thinking about Bianca," he said, his eyes turning dark. "When I planned the kidnapping, I also sent a letter to be delivered to her father after the packet had been out to sea for a week. I didn't want him to worry about her, but at the same time I didn't want him to think he could prevent our marriage. That's why I arranged the proxy marriage, which of course didn't go as I planned."

Nicole was only half listening to him. She wouldn't have believed his words could hurt so much, and to cover the pain she let her mind wander to the mill. She could run that mill. Maybe she could find work in America, or maybe she could live and work in the mill—and be near Clay.

"Remember the frigate that came in just before your ship?" Clay was saying. "I sent a letter to Bianca on that ship. I explained everything to her. I told her that by mistake I'd been married to someone else but that the marriage would be annulled immediately. Of course that was before I had the letter from the judge."

"Of course," Nicole said flatly.

"I also sent her passage money to America. I told her that I still wanted her and asked her to please forgive me and come to America." He stood and began to walk around the open area. "Damn! I don't know why all this had to happen. I couldn't return to England, not when I'm the only one running the plantation. I wrote her several letters and begged her to come to me, but she always had excuses. First her father was very ill then she was afraid to leave him. I could see that she was afraid to leave England. Sometimes the English have odd ideas about Americans." He looked at Nicole as if he expected her to answer but she didn't.

He went on. "It will be some time before she receives my letter, then months before I know if she accepts me or not. "That's where you come in." He looked at Nicole with hope in his eyes but still she didn't speak.

"I don't know what you feel about me. At first I thought you liked my company, but lately . . . You see how little I know about you. In the past weeks I've come to . . . respect you a great deal. My house is pleasant again, the twins love you, the servants obey you. Your manners are excellent and I believe you could manage a few social functions. It would be nice to have people visit again."

"What are you trying to say?"

He took a deep breath. "If Bianca refuses me, I'd like to remain married to you."

Her eyes turned from brown to black. "A marriage that would produce children, I assume."

Clay's eyes crinkled, and he smiled slightly. "Of course. I must admit that I find you quite attractive."

Nicole didn't think she'd ever been so angry in her life. She could feel the anger from her toes to her hairline. She stood up slowly, and it was a strain to speak. "No, I don't think that would do at all."

He grabbed her arm as she turned away. "Why not?" he demanded. "Isn't Arundel Hall big enough for you? With your looks, maybe you could get something bigger."

The hard slap she planted on his cheek echoed through the woods.

He stood there, his cheek turning red, his fingers digging into her flesh. "I would like the courtesy of an explanation," he said coldly.

She jerked away from him. "*Cochon!* You ignorant, vain man! How dare you make such a proposition to me!"

"Proposition! I just proposed marriage to you, and I think I've shown a damned lot of respect for you in the last few weeks. After all, you are legally my wife."

"Respect! You wouldn't know the meaning of the word. True, you've given me a separate bedroom, but why? Because you respect me, or so you could tell your beloved Bianca that you hadn't touched me?"

The expression on his face answered her. "Look at me," she fairly shouted, her accent thick. "I am Nicole Courtalain. I am a human being with feelings and emotions. I am more than a case of mistaken identity. I am more than the fact that I am not 'your' Bianca. You say you propose marriage to me, but look at what you offer. Now I am mistress of the plantation, called Mrs. Armstrong by everyone. But my whole future hangs by a thread. If Bianca accepts you, then I'm to be cast aside. If she refuses you, then you will make do with second choice. No! Not even second choice. I happened to be in the wrong place at the wrong time. There was no choice."

She took a deep breath. "No doubt, you thought I'd remain and be the twins' governess if Bianca did come to America."

"And what would be wrong with that?"

She was so angry she couldn't speak. She pulled back her foot and kicked him. Her toe hurt more than his shin through his heavy boots, but she didn't care. She spat several French curses at him, then turned toward the path.

He grabbed her arm again. He was angry, too. "I don't understand you. I could have any of half the women in the county if Bianca refuses me, but I've asked you. What's so horrible about that?"

"Should I be honored? Honored that you will allow poor little me to stay with you? Do you think I want to be an object of charity all my life? It may surprise you, Mr. Armstrong, that I want a little love in my life. I want a man who loves me, as you do Bianca. I don't want a marriage of convenience but one of love. Does that answer your question? I'd rather starve with a man I love than live regally in your fine house with you when I'd know every day how you were pining for your lost love."

He looked at her so strangely that she had no idea what he was thinking. It was almost as if for the first time he was thinking of her as being something besides a mistake.

"Whatever you think," he said quietly, "I didn't mean to insult you. You are an admirable woman. You have made an intolerable situation into one that is a pleasure for those around you, if not for yourself. All of us, myself most of all, have used you thoroughly. I wish you'd told me earlier of your unhappiness here."

"I'm not unhappy—" she began, but she had to stop because tears clogged her throat. Another moment and she would throw her arms around him and say she'd stay with him on any terms whatsoever.

"Let's return, shall we? Let me think about it a while, and maybe I can arrange a more suitable situation for you."

She followed him down the path numbly.

Chapter 7

CLAYTON LEFT her at the stables. Nicole couldn't understand how she managed to walk back to the house. She tried to keep her head up, and she focused on one thing—the house.

She had barely shut the door to her bedroom before the tears came. The year of hiding had taught her the art of crying without making a sound. She flung herself on the bed, and the sobs tore through her.

Everything she'd said had been wrong. He hadn't meant the marriage proposal as she took it. And now he spoke of a "suitable situation." How much longer would she have before he sent her away? If Bianca came, could she bear to see Clay touch her, kiss her? Would she cry herself to sleep every night when she saw them shut the door to the bedroom they shared?

Both Maggie and Janie tapped on her door and asked if she were all right. Nicole managed to answer that she'd caught a cold and didn't want to spread it. Her swollen sinuses did make her sound as if she were ill. Later in the day, she heard the twins whispering outside her door, but they didn't disturb her. Nicole stood up and decided she'd felt sorry for herself long enough. She washed her face and removed her dress. Clay's footsteps sounded in the hallway, and Nicole stopped, holding her breath. She could not possibly face him yet. She knew that her heart would be in her eyes. During dinner, she'd probably beg him to allow her to stay near him—as his shoe polisher if that was all that was available.

She removed her chemise and slipped into a nightgown, the lace and silk one Clay had admired. She didn't know what time it was, but she was very tired and meant to go to bed. A summer storm was gathering outside. At the first distant rumblings of thunder, she closed her eyes very tightly. She couldn't remember her grandfather now, she couldn't!

She was reliving that whole dreadful night. The rain slashed against the windows of the mill, and the lightning made the outdoors as bright as day. It was the lightning that showed her her grandfather.

She sat up screaming, her hands over her ears. She didn't hear the door open or Clay cross to her bed.

"Quiet. You're safe now. Be still. No one can harm you," he said as he pulled her into his arms.

He held her like a child, and she buried her face in his bare shoulder. He rocked her against him and stroked her hair. "Tell me about it. What was your dream about?"

She shook her head and clutched desperately at his arms. Awake, she knew that her dream had been real. She knew she would never awaken from the nightmare. A flash of lightning lit up the room, and Nicole jumped, trying to pull Clay closer.

"I think it's time we talked," he said as he lifted her in his arms, keeping a quilt twisted about her.

Nicole shook her head mutely.

He carried her into his bedroom and set her in a chair as he poured her a glassful of sweet sherry. He knew she hadn't eaten since lunch, and he knew the alcohol would go straight to her head.

It did.

When he saw her begin to relax, he took her empty glass from her, refilled it, and set it on the table by the chair. He poured another glass for himself. Then he lifted her and sat back in the chair, holding Nicole close to him, the quilt across them both. The storm outside made them seem especially isolated in the dark room.

"Why did you leave France? What happened at the miller's house?"

She hid her face in his shoulder and shook her head. "No," she whispered.

"All right, then, tell me about a good day. Did you always live with your grandfather?"

The sherry made her feel warm and languid. She smiled in a lopsided way. "It was a beautiful house. It belonged to my grandfather, but someday it was to be my father's. It didn't matter; there was room for all of us. It was pink outside. My bedroom had cherubs painted on it. They were falling off a cloud. Sometimes I'd wake up and open my arms to catch them."

"You lived there with your parents?"

"Grandfather lived in the east wing, and I lived in the main house with my parents. Of course, we kept the west wing for the king's visits."

"Of course," Clay answered. "What happened to your parents?"

Silently, tears began to run down her face. Clay held the glass and gave her another sip of sherry.

"Tell me," he whispered.

"Grandfather was home from Court. He was away so often. He came home because so many people were unsafe in Paris. My father said we should all go to England until the people calmed down, but my grandfather said that Courtalains had lived in the chateau for centuries, and he was not going to leave it. He said the rabble wouldn't dare oppose him. We all believed him. He was so big and strong. His voice alone could scare anyone." She stopped.

"What happened that day?"

"Grandfather and I went riding in the park. It was a beautiful spring day. Then we saw smoke through the trees, and my grandfather spurred his horse forward. I followed him. When we broke through the trees, we saw it. My beautiful, beautiful house was going up in flames. I just sat there and stared. I couldn't believe it. My grandfather led my horse to the stables and lifted me off it. He told me to stay there. I just stood there and stared and stared, watching the fire turn the pink bricks black."

"What about your parents?"

"They'd gone to a friend's house and didn't plan to get back until late. I didn't know my mother had torn her gown and they'd returned early." The sobs became stronger.

Clay cuddled her close to him. "Tell me. Get it out."

"Grandfather came back, running through the garden hedges to the stable. His clothes were dirty with smoke, and under his arm was a little wooden box. He grabbed my arm and pulled me into the stables. He threw all the hay out of a long box and pushed me into it. Then he climbed into it, too. We lay there for only a few minutes before we heard the people shouting. The horses were screaming from the smell of the fire. I wanted to go to them, but my grandfather held me still."

She stopped, and Clay gave her more of the sherry.

"What happened when the mob was gone?"

"Grandfather opened the hay box, and we got out. It was dark, or it should have been. Our home was blazing, and it was nearly as bright as day. Grandfather pulled me away when I looked back at it. 'Always look ahead, child, never look back,' he said. We walked all that night and most of the next day. At sundown, he stopped and opened the box he'd taken from the house. There were papers inside it and an emerald necklace that belonged to my mother." She sighed, remembering how they'd used the emeralds to help the miller. Then she'd sold the remaining two to buy a partnership in her cousin's dress shop. "I still didn't understand what was happening then," she continued. "I was such a naive, sheltered child. My grandfather said that it was time I grew up and heard the truth. He said that people wanted to kill us because we lived in a beautiful, big house. He said that from now on we must hide who we are. He took the papers and buried them. He said that I must always remember who I am, that the Courtalains are descendants and relatives of kings."

"Did you go to the miller's house then?"

"Yes," she said flatly, as if she planned to say nothing more.

Clay handed her the glass of sherry. He didn't like getting her drunk, but he knew it was the only way to get her to talk. For a long time, he'd sensed she was hiding something. This afternoon, when he'd asked her about her family, there'd been a quick look of terror across her eyes.

He stroked her hair back from her forehead, the curls damp with perspiration. She was so small, yet she carried so many things inside her. Today, when she'd gotten so angry at him, he realized how right she was. Since she had arrived, he'd never looked at her without wishing to see Bianca's blond features. Yet now, when he thought of all the things she'd accomplished since she'd been in America, he knew she wasn't second-rate to anyone.

He took the empty sherry glass away from her. "Why did you leave France and the miller's house? You must have been safe there."

"They were very kind." Her accent was growing thicker. Some of her words seemed to be pronounced more inside her throat than in her mouth. Each syllable came out as if it had been covered in cream. "My grandfather said I should learn a trade and that milling was a good one. The miller said a girl could never understand stones and grain, but Grandfather only laughed at him."

She stopped and smiled. "I could run that mill of yours. I could make it pay."

"Nicole," he said in gentle, commanding tones. "Why does the storm bother you? Why did you leave the miller's house?"

She stared at the window as the rain began to beat against the glass. Her voice was very quiet. "We had plenty of warning. The miller had come back from town before he'd even sold the grain he had in the wagon. He said there were some troublemakers down from Paris. Many people knew about my grandfather and me. He had been an aristocrat all his life, and he said he was too old to change. What no one understood was that my grandfather did treat everyone equally. He treated the king the same way he treated the stable boy. He said that after Louis XIV died, there'd been no more men born."

"The miller came back in a hurry," Clay urged.

"He told us to hide, to escape, anything so we'd be safe. He'd grown to love my grandfather. Grandfather laughed at him. A storm came and with it the townspeople. I was in the top attic of the mill, counting feed sacks. I stared out the window, and when the lightning flashed I saw them coming. They carried pitchforks and scythes. Some of them I knew. I had helped them with their grain."

Clay felt her body shudder, and he held her closer. "Did your grandfather see them?"

"He bounded up the stairs to where I was. I told him I would face the angry people with him, that I was a Courtalain also. He said he wanted more Courtalains, and I was the only one left now. He spoke as if he were already dead. He grabbed an empty feed bag and put it over my head. I think I was too stunned to speak. He tied the top of it, then whispered that if I loved him I wouldn't move. He piled full bags of grain around me. I heard him go down the stairs. Minutes later, the mob entered the mill house. They searched the attic and several times came very close to finding me."

Clay kissed her forehead, held it against his cheek. "And your grandfather?" he whispered.

"I worked myself free when they were gone. I wanted to get out and make sure he was safe. As I looked out the window—" Her body contracted violently, and he wrapped her closer to him.

"What was outside the window?"

She jerked away from him, pushing at him. "My grandfather was there. He was there, smiling at me."

Clay stared in puzzlement.

"Don't you understand? I was in the attic. They'd cut his head off and stuck it on a pike. They'd carried it high over their heads like a trophy. The lightning flashed, and I saw him!"

"Oh, God," Clay moaned, and he pulled her back to him even though she fought him. As she began to cry, he held her, rocked her, caressed her hair.

"They killed the miller, too," she said after a while. "The miller's wife said I had to get away, that she could protect me no longer. She sewed three emeralds into my dress and put me on a ship to England. The emeralds and my locket were all that was left of my childhood."

"And then you stayed with Bianca and were kidnapped by me."

She sniffed. "You make it sound as if all my life were bad. I had a very happy childhood. I lived on a great estate, and I had hundreds of cousins for playmates."

He was glad to see she was recovering. He hoped that talking of the tragedy would have some lasting effect. "And how many hearts did you steal? Were they all in love with you?"

"None of them were. One cousin kissed me but I didn't like it. I wouldn't let any of them kiss me again. You're the only one—" She stopped and smiled, then ran her finger along his lips. He kissed it, and she held the finger up to look at it. "Stupid, stupid Nicole," she whispered.

"Why do you call yourself stupid?"

"The whole story is quite comical, really. One day, I'm riding in the park. The next, I wake up on a ship bound for America. Then I'm forced to marry a man who says I'm a thief." She didn't seem to feel Clay wince. "It would all make an excellent play. Beautiful heroine Bianca is engaged to handsome hero Clayton. But their plans are disrupted by the villainous Nicole. The audience would hang on to their seats until the end of the play, when the course of true love runs straight and Bianca and Clay are reunited."

"And what of Nicole?"

"Ah! A judge gives her some papers that say she never existed, that the time she spent with the hero never was."

"Isn't that what Nicole wants?" he asked quietly.

She held the finger Clay had kissed to her lips. "Poor, ignorant Nicole has fallen in love with the hero. Isn't that funny? He's never even looked at her in their ten-minute marriage, but she's in love with him. Do you know that he said she was an admirable woman? The poor, dumb thing is standing there, begging, wanting him to offer her passion, and he talks of all the things she can do, rather like buying a mare."

"Nicole—" he began.

She giggled and stretched in his arms. "Did you know that I'm twenty years old? Half my cousins were married by the time they were eighteen. But I was always different. They said I was cold and unfeeling, that no man would ever want me."

"They were wrong. The minute you're free of me, you'll have a hundred men asking you to marry them."

"You're anxious to get rid of me, aren't you? You'd rather have your dreams of Bianca than have me, wouldn't you? I am stupid. Sexless, motherly, virginal Nicole, in love with a man who doesn't even know she's alive."

She looked up at him. Somewhere there was a sober part of her brain that was listening to what she'd said to him. He was smiling at her. Laughing! Tears came to her eyes again. "Let me go! Leave me alone! Tomorrow you can laugh at me, but not now!" She struggled to get off his lap.

He held her tightly. "I'm not laughing at you. It's just what you said about being sexless." He ran his finger across her upper lip. "You really don't know, do you? I can almost understand why your cousins shied away from you. There's an intensity about you that's almost frightening."

"Please, let me go," she whispered.

"How can any woman as beautiful as you not be sure of her beauty?" She started to speak, but he put his fingers over her lips. "Listen to me. That first night on the ship, when I kissed you—" He smiled in memory. "No woman's ever kissed me like that. You asked nothing in return, only to give. Later, when I saw you terrified of the dogs, I think I would have walked through boiling oil to get to you. Don't you understand, can't you see how your presence affects me? You say I've never even looked at you. The truth is I've never stopped. Everyone on the plantation is laughing at the weak excuses I make to come to the house every day."

"I didn't know you even knew I was here. Do you really think I'm pretty? I mean, my mouth, and to me a beautiful woman is blonde and blue-eyed."

He bent and kissed her, lingeringly, caressingly. He ran his lips along hers, then his tongue and his teeth. He touched the tip of his tongue to each corner of her mouth, then fiercely took her lower lip between his teeth, tasting the firm ripeness of it. "Does that answer your question? Several nights I've had to sleep in the fields in order to get some rest. With you in the next room, I've never been able to sleep more than a few hours."

"Maybe you should have come to my room," she said huskily. "I don't think I would have turned you away."

"That's good," he said as he kissed her ear, then her neck, "because I'm going to make love to you tonight even if it's a matter of rape."

Her arms slid around his neck. "Clay," she whispered, "I love you."

He put his arms under her and stood up, then carried her to the bed. He lit a candle beside the bed. The delicious bayberry scent floated through the room. "I want to see you," he said, and sat beside her on the bed. The lace bodice of the nightgown was fastened with seventeen tiny, satin-covered buttons. Slowly and carefully, Clay unbuttoned each one. His hands against her breasts made Nicole close her eyes.

"Did you know that I undressed you the night I took you from the dogs? Leaving you alone in that bed was the hardest thing I've ever done."

"That's how my dress got torn."

He didn't answer her as he took her arms out of the lace bodice, then lifted her to remove the rest of the gown. He ran his hand down the side of her body, pausing at the curve of her hip. She was small but perfectly proportioned. Her breasts were high and full, her waist tiny, her legs and hips slim. He bent his head and kissed her stomach, rubbed his cheek against it.

"Clay," she whispered, her hand in his hair, "I'm frightened."

He lifted his head and smiled at her. "The unknown is what's frightening. Have you ever seen a naked man?"

"One of my cousins when he was two," she answered honestly.

"There's a big difference," he said, and he stood to begin unfastening the side buttons of his pants, the only garment he wore.

She was shy when they dropped to the floor, and she kept her eyes on his face. He stood quietly, and she knew he expected more of her. His chest was tanned from the sun. It was wide and muscled. The deep curve of his muscles played with the candlelight. His waist was very slim, his stomach muscles forming separate ridges. Quickly, her eyes went to his feet, his strong calves, and his heavily muscled thighs. He was a man who spent a great deal of time on a horse, and his thighs showed the result. Her eyes went back to his face, and he still wore a look of waiting.

She looked downward. What she saw did not frighten her. He was Clayton, the man she loved, and she wasn't afraid of him. She gave a low, throaty laugh of relief and pleasure. She opened her arms to him. "Come to me," she whispered.

Clay smiled at her as he stretched out beside her on the bed.

"Such a beautiful smile," she said as she ran a finger along his lips. "Someday, maybe you'll explain to me why I see it so seldom."

"Maybe," he said impatiently as he caught her mouth under his.

To Nicole, Clay's skin was electric. The size and strength of him made her feel small and feminine. As he kissed her neck, she ran her hand over his arm, feeling the dips and curves of it. Suddenly, she realized that he was hers, that his body was hers to explore and taste. She leaned toward him and kissed that smile of his, ran her tongue across those even white teeth she so seldom saw. She placed little nipping bites along his neck, pulled at his earlobe with her teeth. She moved her thigh between his.

Clay was startled by her actions. Then he laughed inside his throat. "Come here, my little French vixen." He pulled her close to him and rolled with her across the bed.

Nicole laughed joyously, delightfully. He held her on top of him, ran his hands through her hair, then up her body to her breasts.

Suddenly, his expression changed, darkened. "I want you," he whispered.

"Yes," she answered. "Yes."

Gently, he laid her on the bed and moved on top of her. The alcohol on an empty stomach, the catharsis of telling someone about her grandfather, all conspired to relax her. All she knew was that she was with the man she loved and wanted. She wasn't afraid when she first felt Clay enter her. There was a moment of pain, but she forgot it at the thought of being closer to Clay.

A moment later, her eyes widened in surprise. Always before, when she'd imagined lovemaking, she'd imagined a rather holy pleasure, a feeling of closeness and love. The feeling that was coursing through her veins had nothing to do with love—this was fire!

"Clay," she whispered, then tilted her head backward and arched her body.

He went slowly at first, restraining himself, knowing this was her first time. But her reactions inflamed him. He'd guessed that she was a woman who understood passion instinctively, but he had never guessed the depth of her. Her throat was exposed, and he could see the blood pounding there. She clutched at his hips, ran her hands down along his body. She made him feel as if she enjoyed him as much as he did her. The women he'd had in his lifetime usually were demanding or believed they were doing him a favor.

He fell on top of her as his thrusts became harder and faster. She pulled him closer, closer, wrapping her legs around his waist. When they exploded together, they still clung, their bodies united, their sweat mingled.

For Nicole, it had been a new, wondrous experience. She'd expected something heavenly and uplifting. The animal passion she'd experienced was so much more than she knew existed. She fell asleep in Clay's arms.

Clay would not release her even the slightest distance. For all the times he'd spent in bed with women, he felt that this had been his first. For the first time in years, he fell asleep with a smile on his face.

When Nicole woke the next morning, it was some minutes before she opened her eyes. She stretched luxuriously, knowing that when she did open them she'd see Clay's dark-paneled bedroom, the pillow his head had touched. She sensed he was gone, but her happiness was too great to be spoiled.

When at last she looked about her, she was startled to see the white walls of her own room. Her first thought was that Clay had not wanted her to remain in his bed. She tossed the light quilt aside and told herself that was absurd. More than likely, he was concerned that she should have a choice about someone finding her in his bed or her own.

She went to the wardrobe and chose a lovely dress of pale blue muslin, the high waist and the skirt trimmed in deep blue satin ribbon. There was a note on top of the dresser. "Breakfast at nine. Clay." She smiled, and her fingers trembled as she buttoned the dress.

The hall clock struck seven, and she wondered how on earth she was going to wait until nine before seeing him again. A quick check of the twins' rooms showed they were dressed and gone.

She left the house by the garden door, but as she stood there under the little octagonal porch, she paused a moment. She usually went to the left, to the kitchen. Suddenly, she turned on her heel and took the right-hand stairs that led to the path to Clay's office.

She'd never been in Clay's office before, and somehow she got the impression that very few people did go there. It was shaped like a miniature of the main house, rectangular with a high-pitched roof. Only the dormers and the porches were missing.

She knocked lightly at the door, and when no answer came she lifted the latch. She was curious about the place where the man she loved spent so much time.

The wall facing the door contained two windows, which were surrounded, floor to ceiling, with bookshelves. The overhanging maple trees made the room cool and dark. The end walls contained oak files and a cabinet for rolled documents. She stepped fully into the room. The bookshelves were filled with books on Virginia law, surveying, and the raising of different crops. She smiled and ran her finger along some of the leather bindings. They were clean, and she knew from Clay's habits that the cleanliness came from use instead of a dust rag.

Still smiling, she turned toward the opposite wall where the fireplace was. Instantly, her smile faded. Over the fireplace hung an enormous portrait—of Bianca. It was Bianca at her very loveliest, a little slimmer than Nicole remembered her. Her honey-blonde hair was drawn away from her oval face, fat sausage curls hanging over one bare shoulder. Her eyes were deep blue and sparkling, her little mouth was drawn into a slight smile. It was a mischievous, impish expression, one Nicole had never seen. It was a smile meant for someone she loved very much.

Still stunned, she looked at the mantel. Slowly, she walked toward it. A little red velvet beret lay there. She'd seen Bianca wear an identical one several times. There was a gold bracelet beside it, one she'd also seen Bianca wear. The inscription read, "B, with all my love, C."

Nicole stepped back. The portrait, the pieces of clothing, all went together to form a shrine. If she didn't know better, she would have thought it was a memory set up to a dead woman.

How could she fight this? Last night he'd said no words of love to her. She remembered with horror all the things she'd said to him. Damn him! He knew how she reacted to the least little bit of alcohol. It had always been a family joke that if anyone wanted to know any of Nicole's secrets, all they had to do was give her two drops of wine.

But this morning she was different. This morning, she must try and salvage what was left of her pride. She walked across the garden to the kitchen and had breakfast. Maggie kept giving broad hints about Mr. Clay returning and that Nicole should eat with him. Nicole ignored her.

After breakfast, she went to the wash house and got cleaning supplies. Once inside the main house, she changed into a serviceable dress of midnight blue calico, then went downstairs again to start polishing the morning room. Maybe the work would help her make some decisions.

She was busy on the spinet when Clay's lips touched her neck. She jumped as if she'd been burned.

"I missed you at breakfast," he said lazily. "I would have stayed with you if it weren't so close to harvest time." His eyes were dark, hooded.

Nicole took a deep breath. If she stayed here with him, she'd spend every night with him, until he finally got the woman he loved. "I'd like to talk to you."

He reacted immediately to her cool tone. His back stiffened. The lazy, seductive look left his face. "What is it?" His tone matched hers.

"I can't stay here," she said flatly, trying not to let him see her pain. "Bianca—" It hurt her even to say the name. "Bianca will surely come to America soon. I'm sure when she receives your letter and the passage money, she will take the first ship here."

"There's nowhere for you to go. You must stay here." It was a command.

"And be your mistress?" she flared.

"You're my wife! How can you forget that when you constantly remind me that you were forced into the marriage?"

"Yes, I'm your wife. For the moment. But how long will it last? Would you still want me for your wife if your dear Bianca walked through that door right now?"

He didn't answer her.

"I want an answer! I think I deserve that much. Last night, you purposefully got me drunk. You knew what it did to me, that's why I don't remember the night you saved me from the dogs."

"Yes, I knew. But I also knew you needed to talk. I had no other purpose in mind."

She turned away for a moment. "I'm sure you didn't. But there I was, sprawled across your lap, begging you to make love to me."

"It wasn't like that. Surely, you must remember—" He stepped forward.

"I remember everything." She tried to calm herself. "Please listen to me. I have some pride, even if it doesn't seem so at times. You're asking too much of me. I can't stay here as your wife, truly your wife, knowing that any day it may all end." She covered her face with her hands. "I've had too many endings in my life!"

"Nicole—" He touched her hair.

She jumped away from him. "Don't touch me! You've played with my feelings too much. You know what I feel about you, and you've used it already. Please don't hurt me anymore. Please."

He stepped away from her. "Believe me, I never meant to hurt you. Tell me what you want. What is mine is yours."

I want your heart, Nicole wanted to scream. "The mill," she said firmly. "It's nearly harvest time, and I can have it running in a couple of weeks. The house looks sound, and I could live in it."

Clay opened his mouth to say no, then he closed it, took a step backward, picked up his hat, and turned toward the door. "It's yours. I'll see the deed is drawn up. I'll also sign over the indenture papers to two men and a woman. You'll need the help." He put his hat on and left the room.

Nicole felt like the wind had been knocked out of her. She sat down heavily in a chair. A night of love and a morning of horror.

Chapter 8

NICOLE LOST no time leaving the house. She knew that her resolve wouldn't be strong for very long. She rowed herself across the river to the mill. It sat on a hill with a long wooden trough leading from the fall of the river to the top of the water wheel. It was a tall, narrow building with a stone foundation and a brick body. The roof was of split wooden shakes. A porch ran along the entire front of the building. The water wheel itself was one and a half stories high.

Inside the building, Nicole climbed to the second story, where two doors opened onto a balcony overlooking the wheel. As far as she could tell, the buckets on the wheel were in good shape, though the ones resting at the bottom could possibly be rotten.

The enormous millstones inside the building were five feet in diameter and eight inches thick. She ran her hands along the stone and recognized the irregular network of quartz. The stones were of French burr, the finest in the world. They had been brought to America as ballast in the hold of a ship, then carried downriver to the Armstrong plantation. The stones were deeply grooved, with a series of radiating ridges. She was pleased to see that the stones were well balanced, coming very close together but not touching.

Outside in the sunlight, she walked along the hill to the little house. She could tell very little about it because of the lumber nailed over the windows and doors.

A commotion toward the river drew her attention.

"Nicole! Are you here?" Janie was yelling as she trudged up the hill.

The large, pink-cheeked woman was a joy to see, and they hugged as if they hadn't seen each other every day since they had left the ship.

"It didn't work out, huh?"

"No," Nicole said. "It didn't work out at all."

"I was hopin', what with the two of you already being married and all—"

"What are you doing here?" Nicole wanted to change the subject.

"Clay stopped by the loom house and said you were moving over here, that you were going to run the mill. He said to pick out two good men, take all the tools we needed and help you. He said that if I wanted to I could live here, and he'd pay me just the same."

Nicole looked away. Clay's generosity was almost too much.

"Come on, you two," Janie yelled. "We got work to do." Janie introduced two men to Nicole. Vernon was tall and red-haired, while Luke was shorter and dark. Under Janie's instructions, the men used crowbars to pry the boards off the front door of the house.

It was still dark inside, but Nicole could see it was a beautiful little house. The bottom floor was one large room, an eight-foot-long fireplace along one wall, a staircase with a hand-carved balustrade in the corner. Three recessed windows were in two walls, the door and a window in another. There was an old pine chest under one window, a long, wide table in the center of the floor.

As the men pried the boards off the windows, very little light came through. The noise sent hundreds of little feet scurrying.

"Phew!" Janie said, and wrinkled her nose. "It's going to take a lot to clean this place up."

"Then I guess we'd better get started."

By sundown, they'd made some progress. The upstairs was a low-ceilinged loft, the sides of the room dropping off sharply. Under the filth, they found some beautifully crafted woodwork. The interior walls were plastered, and a coat of whitewash would make them like new. The clean windows let a great deal of light through.

Vernon, who'd been nailing down loose roof shingles, suddenly called that a raft was coming across the river. They all went down to the edge of the river. One of Clay's men was poling the raft ashore. It was loaded with furniture.

"Wait, Janie, I can't accept that. He's done too much already."

"This is no time to be proud. We'll need that stuff, and besides, it's only out of Clay's attic. It's not like it was costing him anything. Now, come on and grab one end of that bench. Howard! I hope you brought some whitewash—and a couple of mattresses."

"This is only the first load. When I get through, you're gonna have all of Arundel Hall on this side of the river," Howard answered.

Janie, Nicole, and the two men worked for three days on the house. The men slept in the mill, while the women fell each night, exhausted, onto straw-filled mattresses in the attic of the house.

On the fourth day, a short, gnarled man appeared. "I hear there's a woman here who thinks she can run a mill."

Janie started to give the man a piece of her mind, but Nicole stepped forward. "I'm Nicole Armstrong, and I plan to run the mill. Can I help you?"

The man watched her closely, then held out his left hand to her, palm down.

Janie was just about to speak to the man about his manners when Nicole took the offered hand in both of hers and turned it over. Janie grimaced, for to her the palm of the man's hand was mutilated, with gray lumps all over it.

Nicole ran her hands over the man's, then smiled brilliantly at him. "You're hired," she said.

His eyes twinkled. "And you know what you're doin'. You'll run your mill just fine."

When he was gone, Nicole explained. The man was a millstone dresser. He used a chisel and sharpened the grooves in the millstones. To do this, he'd cover his right hand with leather and leave his left one bare. Over the years, his left hand would become embedded with bits of stone. The men showed their left hands with pride. It was a symbol of their experience. There was a saying, "to show one's mettle." Mettle was an old English word for crushed stone.

Janie went back to work, muttering about gloves being made for left hands, too.

When the trough to the river was cleared of debris and the water flowed over the top of the water wheel and made it turn, there was a shout that could be heard for miles.

Nicole wasn't surprised less than a day later, when their first customer arrived on a little barge loaded with grain to be ground. She knew Clay had sent a man upriver and another down with word of the reopening of the mill.

It had been nearly two weeks since she'd seen him, yet there wasn't a moment that she didn't think of him. Twice she'd caught a glimpse of him riding through his fields, but each time she'd turned away.

One morning after the mill had been running for three days, she woke very early. It wasn't light yet, and she heard Janie's deep breathing of sleep from across the room. She hurriedly dressed in the half-light, leaving her hair hanging freely down her back.

Somehow, she wasn't surprised to see Clay standing in front of the water wheel. He wore trousers of light tan and high boots with a top cuff turned down. His back was to her, his hands clasped behind him. His shirt was especially white in the dim light, as was the broad-brimmed hat he wore.

"You've done a good job," he said without turning. "I wish I could get half as much work out of the servants as you do."

"I guess it comes of necessity."

He turned and looked at her, his eyes intense. "No, not necessity. You could come back to my house at any time."

"No," she breathed. "It's better this way."

"The twins keep asking for you. They want to see you."

She smiled. "I've missed them. Maybe you'd let them come across."

"I thought you could come to them. We could have dinner tonight. A ship docked yesterday and brought some things from France. There's brie, burgundy, and champagne. They're being brought downriver today."

"It sounds tempting, but—"

He stepped forward and grabbed her shoulders. "You can't mean to avoid me forever. What do you want from me? Do you want me to tell you how much I miss you? I think everyone on the plantation is angry at me for making you leave. Maggie serves my food either burned or raw, nothing in between. The twins cried last night because I didn't know some damned French fairy tale about a lady falling in love with a monster."

" 'Beauty and the Beast.' " Nicole smiled. "So you want me to come back so you'll get a decent meal."

He lifted one eyebrow. "Don't twist my words. I never wanted you to leave. Will you come to supper?"

"Yes," she said.

He grabbed her and gave her a swift, hard kiss, then released her and left.

"I thought things weren't workin' out," Janie said from behind Nicole.

Nicole had no answer for her. She walked back to the house to start the day's work.

During the long day, Nicole could hardly contain her nervousness about having dinner with Clay. When Vernon weighed the bags of grain and called out the numbers to Nicole, she had to ask him to repeat the figures so she could record them correctly. However, she did remember to send Maggie a recipe for *Dindon à la Daube*, a boned turkey that was stuffed and served in a casserole. Maggie loved good food so much, and Nicole knew she'd probably make two of the turkeys, one for the main house and one for her and her staff.

At six o'clock, Clay's rowboat came to the shore with his estate manager, Anders. He was a tall blond man. He lived with his wife and two children in a house just south of Clay's office. His children often played with the twins. Nicole asked after his family.

"Everyone's fine except that we all miss you. Karen made some peach preserves yesterday, and she wants to send you some. Is the mill working? You seem to have quite a few customers."

"Mr. Armstrong has spread the word, and more and more people are bringing their grain."

He gave her an odd look. "Clay is a respected man."

They reached the shore, and Nicole noticed that Anders kept looking upriver. "Is something wrong?"

"The sloop should have been back by now. We heard last night that a ship was in, and Clay sent the sloop out early this morning."

"You aren't worried, are you?"

"No," he said as he helped her from the rowboat. "It could be anything. The men could be having some ale with the ship's passengers—anything. It's just Clay. Ever since James and Beth drowned, he's anxious if the sloop is an hour overdue."

They walked side by side toward the house. "Did you know James and Beth?"

"Very well."

"What were they like? Was Clay very close to his brother?"

Anders took a long time answering. "The three of them were

very close. They practically grew up in each other's pockets. I'm afraid Clay took their deaths too hard. It changed him."

Nicole wanted to ask a hundred more questions. How had it changed him? What was he like before their deaths? But it was not fair to Clay or to Anders to ask now. If Clay wanted to talk to her, he would, just as she'd confided in him.

Anders left her on the garden porch. The house was as beautiful inside as she remembered. The twins seemed to appear out of nowhere and grabbed her hands to pull her upstairs. They had a long list of stories they wanted her to tell them before they went to sleep.

Clay was waiting for her at the foot of the stairs, his hand outstretched to her. "You're even prettier than I remembered," he said quietly, and looked at her hungrily.

She looked away from him and started toward the dining room, her hand still caught firmly in his. She wore a gown of raw silk, the weave slightly nubby in places, the sheen gentle and subdued. It was a warm apricot color trimmed in satin ribbons of a darker apricot. The neckline was very low. The tiny cap sleeves and the bodice were trimmed with a row of seed pearls. The pearls gained luster from Nicole's skin. Her hair was intertwined with pearls and apricot ribbon.

Clay did not once take his eyes off her as they walked into the dining room. Nicole saw immediately that Maggie had outdone herself. The table fairly bowed under the sheer quantity of food.

"I hope she doesn't expect us to eat all that," Nicole smiled.

"I think she's trying to let me know that if you're here the food will improve. It would have to improve over what it's been."

"Did the sloop arrive yet?" She saw the frown cross his face before he shook his head.

They had just sat down at the table when one of the plantation workers burst into the room. "Mr. Clay! I didn't know what to do," he said in an explosion of words. He held his hat in his hands and threatened to destroy it any minute. He was very nervous. "She said she'd come all this way to see you and that you'd string me up if I didn't bring her."

"Calm down, Roger. What are you talking about, and who are you talking about?" He threw his napkin onto his clean plate.

"I wasn't sure I believed her. I thought she might just be some English scum tryin' to pull the wool over my eyes. But then I got a good look at her, and she looked so much like Miss Beth I thought it was her."

Neither Nicole nor Clay heard the man, for standing just behind him was Bianca. Her dark blonde hair was limp and straight about her round face. Her little mouth was pursed into a pretty little pout. Nicole felt as if she'd forgotten what Bianca was really like. Her life had changed so drastically in the last few months that the time in England seemed as if it had never happened. Now she vividly remembered the way Bianca liked to control people.

Nicole turned to Clay and was astonished by his expression. He looked as if he were seeing a ghost. There was a look of incredulousness as well as rapture on his face. Suddenly, it seemed that her whole body was turning to water. She knew then that deep within her she'd always hoped that when he saw Bianca again he would know he no longer loved her. As sharp tears stung the corners of her eyes, Nicole knew she'd lost, that he'd never looked at her as he was now staring at Bianca.

Nicole drew her breath in slowly and deeply, then stood and walked across the room to Bianca. She held out her hand. "May I bid you welcome to Arundel Hall?"

Bianca gave Nicole a look of hate and ignored the hand offered to her. "You act as if you own the place," she said under her breath, then smiled demurely at Clay. "Aren't you glad to see me?" she said teasingly, the dimple appearing in her left cheek. "I have traveled a long way to be near you."

Clay's chair nearly fell as he dashed across the room to Bianca. He grabbed her shoulders with both his hands, then stared at her face with a burning intensity. "Welcome," he whispered, and kissed her cheek. He did not notice the way she recoiled from his touch. "Take the trunk upstairs, Roger."

Roger backed away from the group. He'd just spent six hours in a sloop with the blonde woman, and a couple of times he had to restrain himself from throwing her overboard. He wouldn't have believed it was possible for one woman to find so many things to complain about in so short a time. She railed against Roger and his men's lack of subservience toward her. She seemed to expect all the men to cater to her merest wish. The closer the sloop got to the Armstrong plantation, the more Roger was sure he'd made an error in delivering her to Clay.

Now, looking at the way Clay stared at the woman, Roger was astounded. How could he look at her like that when that pretty little Miss Nicole was standing there, her heart in her eyes? Roger shrugged, jammed his hat on his head, and carried the trunk up the stairs. Boats were his business, and he was thankful women were not.

"Clayton!" Bianca said sharply, twisting out of his grip. "Aren't you going to ask me to sit down? After that long trip here, I'm afraid I'm exhausted."

Clay attempted to take her arm, but she eluded him. He held a chair for her, to the left of his at the head of the dining table. "You must be hungry," he said as he took another place setting from the chippendale cabinet.

Nicole stood in the doorway and watched them. Clay hovered over Bianca like a mother hen. Bianca swept the green gauze of her dress aside and sat down. Nicole was aware that Bianca had gained at least twenty pounds since she'd last seen her. She was tall enough to carry the weight, and as yet it hadn't distorted her face, but her hips and thighs had greatly increased in size. The high-waisted fashions concealed it to a degree, but the sleeveless style completely exposed her heavy upper arms.

"I want to know everything," Clay said, bending toward her. "How did you get here? What sort of passage did you get?"

"It was dreadful," Bianca said, lowering her pale lashes. "After your letter to my father arrived, I was desolate. I realized what an awful mistake had been made. Of course, I came on the next available ship." She smiled up at him. After her father had shown her the letter, she'd laughed heartily at the joke played on poor, stupid Nicole, but two days later she'd received another letter. Some distant cousins of hers lived in America, not too far from Clay, and they'd written Bianca to congratulate her on her catch. They seemed to think she knew of Clay's wealth and asked to borrow from her as soon as she married Clay. Bianca dismissed the cousins instantly, but she was furious to read of Clay's wealth. Why hadn't the stupid man told her he was rich? Her anger quickly turned from Clay to Nicole. Somehow, the conniving little bitch knew about Clay and had arranged to go in Bianca's place. Immediately, Bianca told her father she planned to go to America. Mr. Maleson just laughed and said that as soon as she earned the money she could go; it didn't matter to him.

Bianca turned to Nicole, still standing in the doorway. She smiled like a gracious hostess. "Won't you join us?" she asked sweetly. "A cousin of yours came by the house to ask after you," she said when Nicole was seated. "She had some wild story about your going into business with her. I told her you worked for me and that you had no money. She said the most fantastic things about your selling some emeralds and working at night. It was really quite preposterous. To make sure, I searched your room myself." Her eyes sparkled. "A passage to America is so expensive, isn't it? But, then, you wouldn't know, would you? My ticket cost about what I'd guess a partnership in a dress shop would cost."

Nicole kept her chin up. She wouldn't let Bianca see that her words hurt. But she rubbed her fingertips in memory of the pain of sewing in the dim light.

"It's so good to see you," Clay said. "It's like a dream come true, having you here again beside me."

"Again?" Bianca asked, and both women looked at him. He was staring at Bianca strangely.

Clay recovered himself. "I meant that I'd imagined you here so often that it does seem as if you've returned." He picked up a bowl of candied yams. "You must be hungry."

"Not at all!" she said, but her eyes never left the food. "I know I couldn't eat a thing. In fact, I may give up eating altogether." She laughed delightedly at this statement. "Do you know where they put me in that horrible frigate? In the lower deck! With the crew and the livestock! It was beyond belief! The porthole leaked, the roof leaked, and for days on end I lived in semidarkness."

Clay winced. "That's why I had arranged a cabin for you on board the packet."

Bianca turned to look across the table to Nicole. "But, of course, I didn't get such luxurious treatment. I imagine your food was better than mine, too."

Nicole bit her tongue to keep from commenting that whatever the quality was, the quantity seemed to have been more than sufficient.

"Then maybe Maggie's cooking will help make up for it." Clay held the bowl a little closer to her.

"Perhaps just a little, then."

Nicole watched quietly as Bianca helped herself to some of each of the twenty-some dishes on the table. Never did she pile her plate high or seem to eat very much of anything. A disinterested observer would have said she was a moderate eater. It was a way she'd learned over the years to conceal her gluttony.

"Where did you get that dress?" Bianca asked as she delicately poured honey over a bowl of spoon bread.

Nicole knew her face must be turning pink. She remembered

too well Clay's accusations that she'd stolen the fabrics from Bianca.

"There are some things we must discuss," Clay said.

His words saved Nicole from having to respond.

Before he could continue, Maggie burst into the room. "I heard you got some company off the sloop. She a friend of yours, Mrs. Armstrong?"

"Mrs. Armstrong?" Bianca said, and looked at Nicole. "Is she referring to you?"

"Yes," Nicole said quietly.

"What is going on here?" Bianca demanded.

"Maggie, would you leave us?" Clay said.

Maggie was very curious about this woman Roger had railed about for the last hour. It had taken four tankards of beer to calm him. "I just wanted to know if you were ready for dessert. There's almond cheesecake, peach and apple tarts, and a custard pie."

"Not now, Maggie! There's something more important than food to be discussed."

"Clay," Bianca said quietly. "It's been so long since I've had anything fresh. Maybe we could have the peach tarts."

"Of course," Clay said instantly. "Bring it all." He turned back to Bianca. "Forgive me. I'm too used to giving commands."

Nicole wanted to leave. More than anything else in the world, she wanted to get away from this man she loved who had suddenly turned into a stranger. She stood up quickly. "I don't believe I want any dessert. If you'll excuse me, I think I'll go home."

Clay rose with her. "Nicole, please. I didn't mean—" He looked down, for Bianca had placed her hand on his. It was the first time she'd voluntarily touched him.

Nicole's stomach turned over when she saw the look in Clay's eyes. She hurried out of the room, out of the house, and into the cool night air.

"Clay," Bianca said. She removed her hand from his arm as soon as Nicole turned away, but she'd seen the power her touch had over him. He disgusted her as much as she remembered. His shirt was open at the throat, and he didn't bother to wear a coat. She hated touching him, hated even being near him, but she'd suffer a lot to own the plantation. All the way up from the wharf, she'd looked at the houses around her, and that odious man from the boat said Clay owned it all. The dining room was richly furnished. She knew the wallpaper had been painted to order for the room. The furniture was obviously expensive, even if there was so little of it. Oh, yes, if she had to touch him to get this place, she'd do it. After they were married, she'd tell him to stay away from her.

Maggie brought in an enormous tray loaded with hot, deep-fried tarts and cool cheesecake. The custard pie was topped with an apricot glaze. "Where did Mrs. Armstrong go?"

"Back to the mill," Clay said succinctly.

Maggie gave him a suspicious look and left.

Bianca looked up from a plate heaped with three desserts. She told herself that since she'd eaten so little supper she could now be generous with herself. "I'd like an explanation."

When Clay was done, Bianca was finishing a second piece of custard pie. "So now I'm to be discarded like so much refuse, is that correct? All my love for you, all the misery I've gone through to get to you, means nothing. Clayton, if you'd only let those kidnappers tell me they were from you, I would have gone with them gladly. You know I wouldn't have stayed away from you." She blotted her lips gently, and tears came to her eyes. They were genuine. The thought of losing all Clay's wealth made her want to rage. Damn that Nicole! The opportunist!

"No, please don't say that. You belong here. You've always belonged here."

His words seemed strange, but she didn't question them. "When this witness to the marriage returns to America, you'll get the annulment? You wouldn't let me stay here and then . . . then discard me, would you?"

He raised her hand to his lips. "No, of course not."

Bianca smiled at him, then stood. "I'm very tired. Do you think I could rest now?"

"Of course." He took her arm to lead her upstairs, but she jerked away from him.

"Where are the servants? Where's your housekeeper and butler?"

Clay followed her up the stairs. "There are some women who help Nicole, or did help her before she moved across the river, but they sleep over the loom house. I never felt I needed a butler or housekeeper."

She stopped at the top of the stairs, her heart pounding from the exertion. She smiled demurely. "But now you have me. Of course, things will change."

"Whatever you wish," he said quietly, and opened the door to the room that had once been Nicole's.

"Plain," she said, "but adequate."

Clay walked to the bow-front cabinet and touched a porcelain figurine. "It was Beth's room," he said, then turned back to her. His look was that of a desperate man.

"Clay!" she said, her hand at her throat. "You almost frighten me."

"Excuse me," he said quickly. "I'll leave you alone." He left the room abruptly.

"Of all the rude, boorish—" Bianca began under her breath, then shrugged. She was glad to be rid of him. She looked around the room. It was too austere for her. She touched the white and blue bed hangings. Pink, she thought. She'd redo the bed in pink tulle with layers of ruffles. The walls would be papered in pink also, and maybe she'd have flowers painted on the paper. The walnut and maple furniture would have to go, of course. She'd replace it with some gilt furniture.

She undressed slowly and slung her dress across a chair back. The memory of Nicole's apricot silk made her angry. Who was she to wear silk, when she, Bianca, had to make do with gauze and muslin? But just wait, she thought, she'd show these ignorant Colonists what real style was. She'd purchase a wardrobe that would make Nicole's look cheap.

She slipped on a nightgown from the trunk that Roger had placed in the room and climbed into the bed. The mattress was a little too firm for her taste. She drifted asleep thinking of all the changes she would make in the plantation. The house was obviously too small. She'd add a wing, her own private wing where she wouldn't have to be too near Clay when they were married. She'd buy a carriage. A carriage that would surpass the queen's! The roof would be supported by gilded cherubs. She fell asleep smiling.

Clay quickly left the house to go to the garden. The moonlight glistened on the water in the tile pool. He lit a long cigar and stood quietly in the shadow of the hedges. Seeing Bianca had been like seeing a ghost. It was almost like having Beth back again. This time, though, nothing would take her away—not his brother, not death. She would be his for all eternity.

He dropped the cigar and crushed it under his foot. He strained his ears to hear the mill's water wheel, but it was too far away. Nicole, he thought. Even now, when Bianca was so near him, he thought of Nicole. He remembered her smile, the way she had clung to him while she cried. Most of all, he remembered her love—for everyone. There wasn't a person on the plantation to whom Nicole hadn't extended her kindness. Even lazy, mean old Jonathan had said some good things about her.

Slowly, he turned to go back to the house.

Bianca woke slowly the next morning. The comfort of the bed and the good food were a luxury after her days aboard the ship. She had no problem remembering where she was or what she planned to do; she'd spent all night dreaming about it.

She threw the covers back and made a little face at them. It was really too much to ask her, as mistress of such an estate, to sleep under linen covers. The very least she could abide would be silk. She pulled a pink cotton dress from the trunk and thought it was disgusting that Clay should leave her without a maid.

Outside the room, she gave a quick look down the hallways, but she had no curiosity about the house. It was enough that it was hers. Now her main interest was the kitchen, which had been pointed out to her last night.

She cursed the distance from the house to the kitchen. From now on, she'd see that food was brought to her so she wouldn't have to walk for it.

She stepped inside the big kitchen regally. It was all like a dream come true. All her life, she'd known she was destined to command. That idiot father of hers had laughed at her when she'd said she wanted the estate that the Malesons had once owned. Of course, the Armstrong plantation could never come close to the estates in England; how could anything in America compare to England?

"Good mornin'," Maggie said pleasantly, her arms covered in flour to her elbows as she prepared biscuit dough for the noon dinner. "Anything I can help you with?"

The big room was alive with activity. One of Maggie's helpers watched after three pots set in the coals of the fireplace. A little boy lazily turned a haunch of meat on a rotisserie. Another woman pounded dough in a large wooden bowl, while two girls chopped pounds of vegetables.

"Yes," Bianca said firmly. She knew from experience that it was best to establish superiority over servants right away. "I would like for you and the other servants to line up and get ready to receive my instructions. From now on, I expect you all to stop what you are doing when I enter a room and pay me the proper respect."

The six people in the room stopped what they were doing and stared, open-mouthed.

"You heard me!" Bianca commanded.

Slowly, awkwardly, the people moved toward the east wall. All except Maggie. "Who are you to be givin' orders?"

"I do not have to answer your questions. Servants should know their place. That is, servants who want to keep their employment," she threatened. Bianca tried to ignore Maggie's hostile stare and the fact that she didn't line up with the others. "I would like to talk about the food that comes from this kitchen. Judging by last night's supper, the food is a bit plain. It needs more sauces. For instance, the ham's glaze was quite delicious." She smiled smugly, knowing her praise would brighten their day. "But," she continued, "more of the sauce should have been served."

"Sauce?" Maggie asked. "That ham was glazed with pure sugar. Are you saying you want me to send in a bowl of melted sugar?"

Bianca gave her a withering look. "I am not asking for your comments. You are here to obey my wishes. Now, about breakfast. I expect it to be served in the dining room promptly at eleven. I want a pot of chocolate made with three parts cream and one part milk. I would also like some more of those tarts that were served last night. Dinner is to be served at twelve-thirty, and—"

"You think you can go that long on just a few dozen fried pies?" Maggie asked sarcastically as she removed her apron and slammed it down on the table. "I'm gonna talk to Clay and find out just who you are," she said as she shoved past Bianca.

"I am the mistress of this plantation," she said, her back straight. "I am your employer."

"I work for Clay and his wife, who, thank the Lord, is not you."

"You insolent woman! I'll see Clay fires you for this!"

"I may quit before he can," Maggie said, and started for the fields.

She found Clay inside a tobacco barn where the long leaves were being hung for drying. "I want to talk to you!" she demanded.

In all the years Maggie had worked for his family, she'd never given any of them any trouble. She was quite outspoken, and more than once her ideas were used when it came to improvements made in the plantation, but her complaints were always fair.

Clay made a futile attempt to wipe the black tobacco gum from his hands. "Has something upset you? The chimney blocked again?"

"It's more than the chimney this time. Who is that woman?"

Clay stopped and stared at her.

"She came into my kitchen this mornin' and started demanding we all obey her. She wants her breakfast served in the dining room. She thinks she's too good to come to the kitchen like anybody else."

Clay angrily threw the dirty cloth away. "You've lived in England. You know that the upper class doesn't eat in the kitchen. For that matter, neither do most of the other plantation owners. It doesn't seem like such an outrageous request. Maybe it would do us all some good to learn a few manners."

"Request!" Maggie sneered. "That woman wouldn't know the meaning of the word." She stopped suddenly, and her voice became quieter. "Clay, honey, I've known you since you were just a boy. What are you doin' now? You're married to one of the sweetest women ever created, but she runs off and lives across the river. Now you bring into your house some snotty girl who's the spittin' image of Beth." She put her hand on his arm. "I know you loved them both, but you can't bring them back."

Clay glared at her, his face becoming angrier by the moment. He turned away from her. "Mind your own business. And give Bianca whatever she wants." He walked away, his head high, the shadow of his broad-brimmed hat hiding the pain in his eyes.

In the late afternoon, Bianca slammed out of Arundel Hall. She'd spent hours on the plantation, talking to the workers, making suggestions, offering advice, yet nowhere had she been treated with respect. The estate manager, Anders, had laughed at her idea for a carriage. He said the roads in Virginia were so bad that half the people didn't even own carriages, and certainly not ones with gold cherubs holding up the roof. He said that nearly all the traveling done was through the river. At least he didn't laugh at Bianca's list of fabrics she wanted. He merely stared at it with his eyes wide and said, "You want monogrammed sheets of pink silk?" She informed him that all the best people in England had them. She ignored his remark that she wasn't in England.

And everywhere she heard Nicole's name. Miss Nicole had helped in the garden. Bianca sniffed. Why shouldn't she? She had once been Bianca's maid, not a lady with a baron for an ancestor, as Bianca had.

After a while, though, Bianca grew tired of hearing Nicole's name. She was also sick of hearing the little Frenchwoman referred to as the mistress of the plantation. She walked toward the wharf and the rowboat that would take her to the mill. She planned to give Nicole a piece of her mind.

Roger rowed her across the river, and Bianca was angered at his insolence. He told her right away that he didn't want to have anything more to do with her.

Bianca had to walk up wooden steps beside the dock that jutted into the water, then up a steep path to the little house. The top half of the Dutch door was open, and she saw a large woman bending over a small fire in the enormous fireplace. She let herself in. "Where's Nicole?" she asked loudly.

Janie stood and looked at the blonde woman. Nicole had come back early from dinner with Clay the night before, and all Janie could get from her was that Bianca had arrived. She said no more, but her face told a great deal. Her eyes showed her sadness. Today, she'd gone about her work as usual, but Janie felt that much of the life was gone from her.

"Won't you come in?" Janie said. "You must be Bianca. I was just making some tea. Maybe you'd like to join us."

Bianca looked about the room with disgust. She saw nothing charming in the plaster walls, the beamed ceiling, or the spinning wheel by the fire. To her it was a hovel. She dusted a chair with her fingertips before she sat in it. "I would like for you to get Nicole. Tell her I am waiting and don't have all day."

Janie set the teapot on the table. So this was the beautiful Bianca that Clay was so crazy about. She saw a woman with a colorless face and a body that was rapidly turning to fat. "Nicole has work to do," Janie said. "She'll be here when she can."

"I have had about enough insolence from Clay's servants. I'm warning you that if—"

"If what, missy? I'll have you know that my duties lie with Nicole, not Clayton," she half lied. "And furthermore—"

"Janie!" Nicole said from the doorway. She walked across the room. "We have a guest, and we must be gracious. Would you care for some refreshment, Bianca? There are some warm crullers from breakfast."

When Bianca didn't answer, Janie muttered something about her looking as if she could eat all the grain in the mill.

Bianca sipped her tea and ate the soft, warm, sugary crullers with disdain, as if she were forcing herself. "So, this is where you live. It's some comedown, isn't it? Surely Clayton would have allowed you to stay on the plantation in some capacity. Maybe as assistant cook."

Nicole put her hand on Janie's arm to keep her quiet. "It was my choice to leave Arundel Hall. I wanted to have a means of supporting myself. Since I knew about running a mill, Mr. Armstrong kindly deeded this place to me."

"Deeded!" Bianca said. "You mean he owned this, and he just gave it to you? After all you'd done to him, and to me?"

"I'd like to know what she's done to you," Janie said. "It seems to me she's the innocent party."

"Innocent!" Bianca sneered. "How did you find out Clayton was rich?"

"I don't know what you mean."

"Why else would you have volunteered so readily to go with those kidnappers? You practically leaped on that man's horse. And how did you get the captain to marry you to my fiancé? Did you use that skinny little body of yours to entice him? You lower classes always do things like that."

"No, Janie!" Nicole said sharply, then turned back to Bianca. "I think you'd better go now."

Bianca stood, smiling slightly. "I just wanted to warn you. Arundel Hall is mine. The Armstrong plantation is mine, and I don't want any interference from you. You've taken quite enough of what belongs to me, and I don't plan to give you any more. So stay away from what I own."

"What about Clay?" Nicole said quietly. "Do you own him, too?"

Bianca curled her lip, then smiled. "So that's how it is, is it? My, my, what a small world. Yes, he's mine. If I could have the money without him, I would. But that's not possible. I'll tell you one thing, though, even if I could get rid of him, I'd see you never got him. You've caused me nothing but misery ever since I met you, and I'd die before I let you have what was mine." She smiled more broadly. "Does it hurt, seeing the way he looks at me? I have him right there." She held out her plump, white hand, then slowly curled it into a tight little fist. Still smiling, she turned and left the room, leaving the door open behind her.

Janie sat down at the table beside Nicole. She felt like she'd just been run between the grinding stones. "So that's the angel Clay sent me to England to fetch?" Janie shook her head slowly. "I wonder if any man's ever been born who had any sense about women. What in the world does he see in her?"

Nicole was staring at the open doorway. She wouldn't mind losing to a woman who loved Clay, but it hurt to see him with Bianca. Sooner or later, he'd find out what she was like, and when he did he'd be miserable.

The twins burst into the room. "Who was that fat lady?" Alex asked.

"Alex!" Nicole said. Then her reprimand lost its bite as Janie started laughing. Nicole tried to keep from smiling. "Alex, you shouldn't call people fat."

"Even if they are?"

Janie's laughter was too loud for Nicole to speak. She decided not to go into Bianca's weight. "She's a guest of your Uncle Clay," she said at last.

The twins exchanged looks of silent communication, then turned quickly and sped down the path.

"Where do you think they're going?" Janie asked.

"To introduce themselves, probably. Ever since Ellen Backes taught them how, they've not lost an opportunity to bow and curtsy." Janie and Nicole looked at each other, then silently left the house. They didn't trust Bianca with the twins.

The two women got there just in time to see Alex make his bow before Bianca. They stood on the edge of the wharf. Bianca seemed to be pleased by the twins' formal manners, even if their clothes and faces were somewhat dirty. Mandy stood quietly by her brother, smiling proudly.

Suddenly, Alex lost his balance, and to keep from stumbling

and perhaps falling off the wharf, he grabbed the nearest thing to steady himself, which was Bianca's dress. The fabric tore away at the seam of the high waist, leaving a long, gaping hole.

"You nasty little beast!" Bianca said, and before anyone could speak, she slapped Alex hard across the face.

The little boy balanced on the edge of the wharf, his arms twirling for a moment before he fell backward into the river. Nicole was into the water past her ankles before Alex came up the first time. He grinned at her look of fright and swam ashore. "Uncle Clay says you shouldn't swim with your shoes on," he said as he sat on the bank and began to unbuckle his. He nodded at Nicole, still standing in the water, her shoes soaked.

Nicole smiled at him and stepped back onto the dry land. Her heart was still pounding from the fright of seeing the boy fall.

While Janie's and Nicole's attention was on Alex, Mandy looked at the big woman beside her. She didn't like anyone who'd strike her brother. She took a step closer to Bianca and dug her little heels into the dock. She gave one good, hard push at Bianca and then stepped back quickly.

Everyone turned at Bianca's little squeal of fear. She fell almost as if she were in slow motion. Her lack of strength and muscle tone made her especially helpless. Her fat little hands clawed at the air.

When she hit the water, the splash threatened to flood the wharf. Mandy was drenched. She turned, the front of her dress soaked, water dripping off her eyelashes and nose, and smiled in triumph at her brother. Janie started laughing again.

"Stop it, all of you," Nicole commanded, but her voice was shaky with suppressed laughter. Bianca had looked so funny when she fell. Nicole walked to the other side of the wharf, and the others followed her. Bianca rose slowly out of the water. It was barely knee deep, but she'd gone completely under when she fell. Her blonde hair was straggling in thin, straight bits about her face. The curls she'd so carefully created with a hot iron were gone. The water plastered the thin cotton of her dress to her, and she may as well have been nude. She'd gained more weight than Nicole had realized. Her thighs and hips were so fat they were lumpy. She had a roll of fat around her middle where her waist should have been.

"She *is* fat!" Alex said, his eyes wide in wonder.

"Don't just stand there, get me out of here!" Bianca demanded. "My feet are caught in mud."

"I think I'd better get the men," Janie said. "The two of us aren't strong enough to pull in a whale."

"Hush! All of you!" Nicole said, then went to the rowboat to pick up an oar. "She doesn't like men. Here, Bianca, grab this, and Janie and I will pull you out."

Janie dutifully grabbed one end of the oar. "If you ask me, that woman only likes herself, and she doesn't like her that much."

It took some doing on the women's part to get Bianca out of the mud. She wasn't very strong, in spite of her size. When she was standing on the shore, Roger appeared out of the trees, where he'd obviously been for some time. His eyes were twinkling in delight as he helped Bianca into the rowboat and rowed her back across the river.

Chapter 9

CLAY WAS bent over the old tree stump, fastening chains around its long, deep roots when the lone rider approached. In another hour, the sun would be down. He'd been working since long before sunup. He was tired and his body ached thoroughly, not just from today's work but from several days of work without stop.

When the chains were finally secured around the log, he hooked them onto the big percheron's collar. The massive feet of the horse dug into the ground, mud and bits of grass flying as it obeyed Clay's commands to pull. Slowly, the log began to come out of the ground.

Clay took a long axe and hacked at the thin tendons that held the large stump in the ground. When it was finally free, Clay led the horse and the dragging stump to the edge of the newly cleared field. When he had the chains detached and was rolling them on the ground, the man spoke.

"Good work! I haven't enjoyed a show so much since I saw some dancers in Philadelphia. Of course, they had better legs than you."

Clay looked up sharply, then slowly he began to grin. "Wesley! I haven't seen you in ages. Did you and Travis get your tobacco in already?"

Wes Stanford stood up and stretched. He wasn't a tall man like Clay, but he was powerfully built, with a deep, thick chest and heavily muscled thighs. He had thick brown hair and very dark eyes, which laughed often. He shrugged. "You know Travis. He knows he can run the world by himself. I just thought I'd let him manage a part of it alone."

"You two quarreling again?"

Wesley grinned. "Travis would tell the devil how to run Hell."

"And no doubt the devil would obey him."

The two men looked at each other and laughed. Their friendship had grown over the many years they'd been neighbors. They'd been drawn to each other because they were both younger brothers. Clay had always stood in the shadow of James, while Wesley had to deal with Travis. Many times, Clay had been thankful for James whenever he was around Travis. He didn't envy Wes for having such a brother.

"What are you doing out here clearing your own fields?" Wes asked. "Did all your men leave you?"

"Worse," he said, removed his handkerchief from his pocket and wiped the sweat from his face. "I've got problems with women."

"Ah," Wes smiled. "Now, that's a problem I could deal with. Anything you'd like to talk about? I brought a jug, and I've got all night."

Clay sat down on the ground, his back to a tree, and accepted the jug of corn liquor from Wes, who sat down beside him. "When I think of what's happened to my life in the last few months, I don't know how I've lived through it."

"Remember that summer that was so dry, and three of your tobacco barns burned and half your cows died?" Wes asked. "How does it compare to that?"

"That was an easy time. I got more rest then."

"Lord!" Wes said seriously. "Drink some more of this, and tell me what's been going on."

Wes loved Clay's idea about kidnapping Bianca and then having her married to him by proxy. "So what happened when she got here?"

"She didn't. Or at least she didn't come in with Janie on the packet."

"I thought you said you paid the captain for performing the service."

"I did. He married me to someone, all right, but not to Bianca. The kidnappers took the wrong woman."

Wes stared at his friend with wide eyes and an open mouth. It was a while before he could speak. "You mean you went to meet your bride only to find out you were married to some woman you'd never met before?" He took a deep drink when he saw Clay's glum nod. "What's she look like? A hag, right?"

Clay leaned his head against the tree and stared up at the sky. "She's a little thing, French. She has black hair and big brown eyes and the most desirable mouth ever created. She's got a figure that makes my hands sweat every time she walks across a room."

"Sounds to me like you should be rejoicing, unless she's stupid or mean."

"Neither. She's educated, intelligent, a hard worker, the twins love her, and everybody on the plantation adores her."

Wes took another drink. "She doesn't seem like much of a problem to me. I don't believe she's real. She must have some flaw."

"There's more to this," Clay said and reached for the jug. "As soon as I learned about the mistaken marriage, I wrote Bianca in England and explained everything."

"Bianca's the woman you originally were to marry? How did she take it? I don't guess she liked your marrying someone else."

"I didn't hear from her for a long time. Meanwhile, I spent a lot of time with Nicole, who was legally my wife."

"But not your wife in any other way?"

"No. We agreed to get an annulment, but there had to be a

witness that the marriage had been forced, and the only one who'd testify was already on his way back to England."

"So you forced yourself to keep company with a beautiful, charming woman. Poor man. Your life has been hell."

Clay ignored Wes's jibes. "After a while, I began to see what a gem Nicole was, so I decided to have a talk with her. I said that if Bianca read my letter and decided she wanted nothing more to do with me, I'd like to remain married to Nicole. After all, my first obligation was to Bianca."

"That sounds fair enough."

"I agree, but Nicole didn't. She raged at me for half an hour. She said she wasn't going to be second choice to any man, and . . . I don't know what all else. It didn't make much sense to me. All I knew was she wasn't very happy. That night—" He stopped.

"Go on! This is the best story I've heard in years."

"That night," Clay continued, "she was sleeping in Beth's room, and I have James's, so when I heard her scream I went to her right away. She was scared to death of something, so I fed her a lot of liquor and got her to talk." He put his hand over his eyes. "She's had an awful life. The French mob carried her parents away to the guillotine and burned her house, then later they killed her grandfather and carried his head around on a pole in front of her."

Wes grimaced in disgust. "What happened after that night?"

It wasn't what happened after that night but during it that was so important, Clay thought. Every night, he lay awake remembering the night he'd held her in his arms and made love to her. "The next day she left me," he said quietly. "Not really left me, but moved across the river to the old mill. She's running the place now and doing a damn good job of it."

"But you want her back, is that it?" When Clay didn't answer, Wes shook his head. "You said women problems, not woman. What else has happened?"

"After Nicole got the mill going, Bianca showed up."

"What's she like?"

Clay didn't know what to answer. She'd been living in his house for two weeks, but he didn't know any more about her than when she arrived. She was asleep when he left in the morning, asleep when he returned. Once Anders had talked to him about her spending so much money, but Clay had dismissed the complaint. Surely he could afford a few garments for the woman he was to marry. "I don't know what she's like. I think I fell in love with her the moment I saw her in England, and nothing's changed since then. She's beautiful, lovely, gracious, kind."

"It sounds to me like you know quite a lot about her. Now, let me look at the situation. You are married to one gorgeous creature and engaged to and in love with another equally gorgeous woman."

"That's about it." Clay grinned. "You make it sound like something desirable."

"I could think of worse situations. Being a lonely bachelor like me, for instance."

Clay snorted. Wes was far from needing more women in his life.

"I'll tell you what I'll do," Wes grinned, and slapped Clay on the leg. "I'll meet both women and take one of them off your hands. You can have whichever one I don't want, and that way you won't have to choose between them." He was teasing, but Clay was serious, and Wes frowned. He didn't like to see his friend so troubled. "Come on, Clay, it's bound to work out for the best."

"I don't know," Clay said. "I don't seem to be sure of anything lately."

Wes stood up, rubbing his back where the bark had bitten into his skin. "Is this Nicole still at the mill? Do you think I could meet her?" He saw a sudden flash go across Clay's eyes.

"Sure. She's there with Janie. I'm sure she'd welcome you.

She seems to keep open house for everyone." There was a trace of disgust in his voice.

Wes promised Clay he'd return to Arundel Hall later for some of Maggie's cooking. Then he mounted his horse and rode toward the wharf. He rode slowly over the familiar path so he could think. Seeing Clay again after so many months had been a shock. It was almost as if he'd been talking to a stranger. As boys, the two had spent a lot of time together. Then, suddenly, a cholera epidemic had killed Clay's parents and Wes's father. Wes's mother died a short time later. The two families of James and Clay, Travis and Wesley had been drawn closer together by their mutual tragedies. There were long periods of separation as the young men worked the two plantations, but they'd gotten together whenever possible.

Wes smiled as he remembered a party at Arundel Hall when both Clay and Wes were sixteen. The boys had bet each other they could each get one of the luscious Canton twins behind the hedges. They'd both succeeded easily, except that Travis found out about it and grabbed each boy by the scruff of the neck and pitched them into the tile pool.

What had happened to that Clayton? Wes wondered. The Clay he knew would have laughed at this absurd situation with the two women. He would have grabbed the one he wanted and carried her upstairs. He knew the man who arranged the kidnapping of an English lady, but the man who acted as if he were afraid to go home was a stranger.

He dismounted his horse under a tree by the wharf, then unsaddled him. His guess was that what was wrong with him was the Frenchwoman. He'd said she was working for Bianca—her maid, no doubt. Somehow, she'd arranged to substitute herself for Bianca and had gotten herself married to a rich American. No doubt, she was now somehow blackmailing Clay into keeping her as his wife. So far, she'd already managed to get the mill and some property out of him.

And what about Bianca? Wes felt a surge of pity for the woman. She'd come to America expecting to be married to the man she loved, only to find someone else in her place.

He tied his horse and then went to the rowboat and rowed himself across. He was quite familiar with the mill, as it had been one of his favorite places when he was a boy. He smiled as he saw the twins crouched by the bank of the river, intent upon the complete lack of movement of a bored bullfrog.

"What are you two doing?" he demanded sharply.

The twins jumped in unison, then turned and smiled up at him. "Uncle Wes!" they yelled, giving him the honorary title. They scrambled up the bank to where he waited with open arms.

Wes grabbed them both by the waists and swung them around while they giggled uproariously. "Did you miss me?"

"Oh, yes," Mandy laughed. "Uncle Clay is always gone now, but Nicole is here."

"Nicole?" Wes asked. "You like her, do you?"

"She's pretty," Alex said. "She used to be married to Uncle Clay, but I don't know if she is now."

"Of course she is," Mandy said. "She's always married to Uncle Clay."

Wes set the children down on the ground. "Is she at the house?"

"I think so. Sometimes she's at the mill."

Wes rubbed the heads of both children. "I'll see you later. Maybe you can go back across the river with me. I'm meeting your Uncle Clay for supper."

The twins backed away from him as if he were poisonous. "We stay here now," Alex said. "We don't have to go back there."

Before Wes could ask any questions, the children turned and ran into the woods. He walked up the hill to the little house. Janie was inside, alone, intent over the spinning wheel. Wes opened the door silently and tiptoed behind her. He planted a loud kiss on her neck.

Janie didn't move or act surprised in any way. "Nice to see you again, Wes," she said calmly. She turned to him with twinkling eyes. "It's a good thing you weren't born an Indian. You couldn't sneak up on a tornado. I heard you outside with the twins." She stood up and hugged him.

Wes hugged her hard, lifting her feet off the ground. "You certainly haven't been starving yourself," he laughed.

"But you have. You're getting downright skinny. Sit down, and I'll get you something to eat."

"Not much. I'm supposed to meet Clay for supper."

"Humph!" Janie said as she filled a bowl with split pea soup with chunks of ham. On a plate she put cold, cracked crab legs and beside that a little bowl of melted butter. "You'd better eat here, then. Maggie's on the warpath, and her cooking's not what it can be."

"I guess that has to do with Clay's women," he said, his mouth full of crab. He smiled at Janie's look of surprise. "I saw Clay before I came over here, and he told me the whole story."

"Clay doesn't know the whole story. He's blind to most of it."

"What's that supposed to mean? It seems to me it's simple. All he has to do is get the marriage annulled to this Nicole and he's free to marry Bianca, the woman he loves. Then he can be happy again."

Janie was so angered at Wes's statements that she couldn't speak. She had the iron ladle from the pea soup in her hand, so she just conked him on the head with it.

"Hey!" Wes yelled, and put his hand over the hot mess in his hair.

Janie was immediately contrite. She wouldn't hurt Wes for the world. She grabbed a rag and dipped it in cool water to clean his hair.

While Janie was leaning over Wes, blocking him from view, Nicole entered. Janie started to move aside so Nicole could see him but then decided not to. Wes peered curiously around Janie's substantial form.

"Janie," Nicole said. "Do you know where the twins are? I saw them a few minutes ago, but now they seem to have disappeared." She removed a straw bonnet from her head and hung it on a wooden peg by the door. "I wanted to give them a few lessons before supper."

"They'll come home, and besides, you're too tired to work with them."

Wes was aware that Janie was purposefully hiding him yet allowing him to watch Nicole. Of all his thoughts about her, he knew she'd never been anyone's maid. She walked with a quiet grace and elegance that showed she'd never been a servant to anyone. And what Clay had said about her beauty was an understatement. His first thought was to throw roses at her feet and beg her to leave Clay and take him.

"Clay sent a message over today," Janie said.

Nicole paused, her hand on the stair rail. "Clay?"

"You remember him?" Janie said, watching Wes's face. "He asked if you'd attend supper with him tonight."

"No," Nicole said quietly. "I can't, though maybe I should send something. Maggie hasn't been cooking much lately."

Janie snorted. "She's refusing to cook for that woman, and you know it."

Nicole turned and started to speak. Then she stopped. Janie seemed to have grown two new legs. She left the stairs to walk closer to Janie.

"Hello," Wes said, then brushed Janie's hands away and stood. "I'm Wesley Stanford."

"Mr. Stanford," she said politely, holding out her hand to him. She gave Janie a troubled look. Why had she hidden this man? "Won't you please sit down? Could I offer you some refreshment?"

"No, thank you. Janie's already taken care of that."

"I think I'll go look for the twins," Janie said, and was out of the house before anyone could speak.

"Are you a friend of Janie's?" Nicole asked as she poured a mug of cool cider for him.

"More a friend of Clay's." He watched her face, his eyes always going to her mouth. The upper lip intrigued him. "We grew up together, or at least we spent a lot of time together."

"Tell me about him," she said, her eyes wide and eager. "What was he like as a little boy?"

"Different," Wes said, watching her. She's in love with him, he thought. "I think this . . . situation upsets him."

She stood and walked toward the fireplace behind him. "I know it does. I assume he told you the story." She didn't wait for his nod. "I tried to make it easier for him by moving out. No, that's not true. I tried to make it easier for me. He'll be happy again when our marriage is annulled and he's free to marry Bianca."

"Bianca. You worked for her in England?"

"In a manner of speaking. Many of the English kindly took us in after we fled our own country."

"How did the kidnappers get you instead of Bianca?" he asked bluntly.

Nicole blushed, remembering the scene. "Please, Mr. Stanford, let's talk about you."

Wes knew that her blush told more than her words. What sort of a woman would be so generous as to offer to prepare food for the man she loved when she knew he'd be eating with another woman? He'd already made one wrong judgment, and he wasn't going to make any more. He'd wait until he saw Bianca before he developed another opinion.

An hour later, Wes reluctantly left the quiet orderliness of Nicole's little house to go to Arundel Hall. He hadn't wanted to leave, yet he was looking forward to meeting Bianca. If Nicole was Clay's second choice, then his first must be truly an angel.

"What did you think of her?" Clay asked as he greeted Wes at the end of the garden.

"I'm thinking of sending some kidnappers to England. If I do half as well as you, I'll die happy."

"You haven't seen Bianca yet. She's waiting inside and is anxious to meet you."

Wes's first look at Bianca was one of shock. It was like seeing James's wife Beth again. He was instantly taken back to the days when the house had been full of love and laughter. Beth had a talent for making everyone welcome. Her loud laugh could be heard throughout the house. There wasn't an itinerant peddler within miles who wasn't welcome at her table.

Beth was a large woman, tall and strong. Her energy affected everyone. She could work on the plantation all morning, ride in a hunt with James and Clay all afternoon, and Wes suspected from James's constant smile that she could make love all night. She used to gather children to her bosom and hug them exuberantly. She could bake cookies with one hand and hug three children with the other.

For a moment, Wes felt his eyes blur with tears. Beth had been so alive that it was almost possible to believe she'd come back to earth.

"Mr. Stanford," Bianca said quietly. "Won't you come in?"

Wes felt like a fool and knew he must look like one. He blinked a few times to clear his eyes, then looked at Clay. He knew and understood the turmoil inside Wes.

"We have so few visitors here," Bianca was saying as she led the men into the dining room. "Clayton promises me that quite soon we will be able to have visitors again. That is, as soon as all of this unfortunate situation is put to rights and I am truly mistress here. Won't you have a seat?"

Wes was still mesmerized by her, by the resemblance to Beth; but the voice was different, the movements were different, and there was a dimple in her left cheek that Beth didn't have. He took a chair across from hers with Clay between them. "How do you like our country? Is it a great deal different from England?"

"Oh, yes," Bianca said as she ladled a thick pile of sauce over three slices of ham. She handed the silver gravy boat to Wes. "America is so much more crude than England. There are no towns, no places to shop. And the lack of society—decent society, that is—is appalling."

Wes paused with his hand on the gravy ladle. She had just insulted his country and his countrymen, but she didn't seem at all aware of her rudeness. Her head was bent over her plate. Wes dipped some of the gravy onto his plate and then tasted it. "Good God, Clay! Since when has Maggie been serving bowls of sugar with her ham?"

Clay shrugged disinterestedly. He watched Bianca as he ate.

Wes was beginning to be suspicious of the whole relationship. "Tell me, Mrs. Armstrong," he began, then stopped. "I beg your pardon, but you're not Mrs. Armstrong—yet."

"No, I'm not!" Bianca said, casting a malevolent look at Clay. "My maid thrust herself at the men who were to take me to Clay. Then, while she was on board the ship, she persuaded the captain that she was Bianca Maleson and managed to get herself married to my fiancé."

Wes was beginning not to like the woman. It had taken a few minutes to get past her resemblance to Beth, but even now that was starting to fade. She was soft and fat where Beth had always been strong and firm with large bones. "Your maid, you say? Wasn't she an escapee from the French Revolution? I thought only the aristocracy had to flee the country."

Bianca waved her fork. "That is what Nicole tells everyone. She says her grandfather was the Duc de Levroux, or at least her cousin told me that."

"But you know better, don't you?"

"Of course. She did work for me for some months, and I should know. It is my guess that she was a cook somewhere, or a seamstress. But please, Mr. Stanford," she said and smiled, "do you really want to talk about my maid?"

"Of course not," Wes smiled back. "Let's talk about you. It's rare that I am in such charming company. Tell me about your family and more about your ideas of America."

Wes ate slowly as he listened to Bianca. It wasn't easy to keep eating and still listen. She told him of the pedigree of her own family, of the house her father once owned. Of course, everything in America was dreadfully inferior to what was in England, especially the people. She itemized the faults of all of Clay's servants, told how they mistreated her, refused to obey her. Wes made little sounds of sympathy, all the while amazed at the quantity of food she was eating.

Once in a while he stole looks at Clay. Clay remained passive, as if he didn't hear or understand Bianca's words. Once in a while, he looked at Bianca with a glazed expression as if he didn't really see her.

The dinner seemed to go on forever. Wes was amazed at Bianca's sense of security. She never seemed to doubt that she and Clay would be married quite soon and that she would own Arundel Hall. It was when she started talking of tearing the east wall out of the house and adding an ornate wing, "not so plain as this house," that Wes wanted to hear no more.

He turned to Clay. "Why are the twins staying across the river?"

Clay frowned at Wes. "Nicole could give them an education, and they wanted to go," he said flatly. "Would you care to join us in the library, my dear?"

"Heavens, no," Bianca said sweetly. "I wouldn't think of intruding on you gentlemen. If you would excuse me, I think I will retire. It's been an exhausting day."

"Of course," Clay said.

Wes muttered goodnight to her, then turned and left the room. When he was in the library, he poured himself a stiff shot of whiskey and downed it in one gulp. He was pouring a second one when Clay entered the room.

"Where's the portrait of Beth?" Wes asked through clenched teeth.

"I moved it to my office," Clay said as he poured himself a brandy.

"So you can be near her all the time? You have a copy of Beth walking around your house and a portrait of her in the office where you spend the rest of the day."

"I don't know what you're talking about," Clay said angrily.

"Like hell you don't! I mean that vain, overweight bitch you've taken in as a substitute for Beth."

Clay's eyes flashed. He was the taller of the two, a strong, hard man, but Wes was powerfully made. They'd never fought.

Suddenly, Wes calmed. "Look, Clay, I don't want to yell. I don't even want to argue with you. I think you need a friend right now. Can't you see what you're doing? That woman looks like Beth. When I first saw her, I thought she *was* Beth. But she's not!"

"I'm aware of that," Clay said flatly.

"Are you? You look at her as if she were a goddess, yet have you ever listened to her? She's about as far removed from Beth as humanly possible. She's a vain, arrogant hypocrite."

The next moment, Clay's fist came smashing into Wes's face. Wes reeled against the desk and spun backward where he landed on one of the red leather chairs. He rubbed his jaw and tasted the blood inside his mouth. For a moment he considered going after Clay. Maybe a good fight would knock some sense into his head. At least a fighting Clay was one he recognized.

"Beth is dead," Wes whispered. "She and James are dead, and no matter how much you try, nothing is going to bring them back."

Clay looked at his friend slumped on the chair, rubbing his jaw. He started to speak but couldn't. There were too many things to say and too few. He turned and walked out of the room, out of the house, and toward the tobacco fields. Maybe a few hours' work would help calm him, keep him from thinking of Beth and Nicole—no, of Bianca and Nicole.

Chapter 10

THE TREES were changing to the glory of autumn colors. The reds and golds blazed. Nicole stood on top of a hill that looked down on the mill and her house. Through the trees she could see the sunlight sparkling on clear, rushing water.

It had been ten days since Wesley Stanford had visited her and more than a month since that horrible night when Bianca had returned to her life. She had thought the hard work of the mill would block him from her mind, but it hadn't.

"Enjoying the quiet?"

Nicole jumped when she heard Clay's voice. She hadn't seen him in all the time he'd been with Bianca.

"Janie told me where you were. I hope I'm not intruding."

She turned slowly and looked up at him. The sun was behind his head, making the curling ends of his dark hair golden. He looked tired and older. There were deep circles under his eyes, as if he hadn't been sleeping well. "No," she smiled. "You weren't intruding. Are you well? Is your tobacco harvested?"

His mouth changed from a hard line to a soft smile. He sat down on the ground, stretched out on it, and stared up at the sky through a brilliant tree of red-gold leaves. He seemed to relax instantly. Just being near Nicole made him feel better. "Your mill seems to be doing well. I came over to ask a favor of you. Ellen and Horace Backes are giving a party for us. It's a real Virginia party, lasting at least three days, and you and I are the guests of honor. Ellen wants to welcome my wife to the community."

When Clay stretched out at Nicole's feet, his long legs extended, his muscles straining against the open shirt, she felt as if she were going to melt. She wanted to sink to the ground beside him and put her cheek against that brown skin. He was sweaty from the fields, and she could almost taste the salt of him as she imagined kissing his throat. But when she saw him relax near her, her impulse changed—she wanted to kick him. Her body felt like it was on fire, but he acted as if he'd just entered the peace and quiet of his mother's house.

It took a moment for her to understand his words. "I guess it would be rather embarrassing for you to have to tell Ellen that I refuse to go, wouldn't it?"

He looked up at her with one eye open. "She has met you and knows we're married."

"But she doesn't know that we won't be married very long."

Nicole turned away to start down the hill, but Clay grabbed her ankle. She stumbled and fell forward onto her hands and knees. He sat up, put his hands under her arms, and lifted her.

"Why are you getting mad at me? I haven't seen you for weeks, and when I do I invite you to a party. It seems you should be pleased instead of angry."

She couldn't very well tell him that his calmness made her angry. She sat back on the grass, away from his hands. "It just doesn't seem right that we should appear publicly as husband and wife when in a few months the marriage will be annulled. It seems you'd want to go with Bianca and tell everyone about the silly error. I'm sure it would make a wonderful story."

"Ellen's met you," he said stubbornly. He had no answer for her questions. All he knew was that the prospect of spending three days—and nights—with her made him happy for the first time in months. He took her hand from his lap and studied it for a moment. It was so small, so neat and clean, and it could give such pleasure! He raised it to his lips and kissed the soft pads of her fingertips one by one. "Please go," he said quietly. "All my friends, people I've known all my life, will be there. You've worked hard the last few months, and you need a holiday."

She could feel her bones beginning to melt at the touch of his lips on her fingers, yet a part of her cried out in anger. He was living with another woman, one he said he loved, but he kissed her, touched her, invited her to parties. It made her feel like his mistress, someone kept hidden and used only for pleasure. Yet now he wanted to take her to meet his friends.

"Clay, please," she said weakly.

He nibbled the inside of her wrist. "Will you go?"

"Yes," she said faintly, her eyes half closed.

"Good!" Clay snapped, dropping her hand and standing up. "I'll pick you and the twins up at five tomorrow morning. And Janie, too. Oh, yes, you'd better bring some food. Maybe something French. If you don't have everything you need, tell Maggie to get it from the storehouse." He turned and walked down the hill, whistling.

"Of all the insufferable—" Nicole began, then smiled. Maybe if she understood him she wouldn't love him so much.

Clay was thinking about tomorrow night. He'd be alone with Nicole, sharing a bedroom with her in Horace's big, rambling house. With that in mind, he could forego a quick tumble on the hillside where anyone could see them.

As soon as Clay was out of sight, Nicole stood up suddenly. If she was going to have to prepare food for three days, she'd better get started. She started planning as she went down the hill. There'd be chicken baked in Dijon mustard, pâté wrapped in a pastry shell, a cold vegetable mold, cassoulet. And pies! There'd be pumpkin, mincemeat, apple, pear, blackberry. She was out of breath by the time she reached the house.

* * *

"Good morning," Clay called as he tied the sloop to the wharf on Nicole's side of the river. He grinned at Nicole and Janie and the twins standing amid several enormous baskets. "I'm not sure the sloop will sail with that much on board, especially after all the food Maggie sent."

"I thought she might decide to cook something for you when you told her you were taking Nicole," Janie said.

Clayton ignored her as he began handing the baskets to Roger, who stored them in the bottom of the boat. The twins laughed as he literally threw them into Roger's arms.

"You seem cheerful this morning," Janie said. "It makes me almost think you've come to your senses."

Clay grabbed Janie by the waist and kissed her cheek heartily. "Maybe I have, but if you don't hush, I'm going to throw you into the boat, too."

"Maybe you can throw her," Roger said loudly and quickly, "but I can guarantee that I'm not going to try to catch her."

Janie snorted in indignation and held Clay's hand as she stepped down to the boat.

He held out his hand for Nicole.

"I might try to catch that one," Roger laughed.

"This one's mine!" Clay said as he lifted Nicole from the dock and held her tightly as he stepped into the boat.

Nicole stared up at him with wide eyes. He suddenly seemed to be a stranger. The Clay she knew was solemn and quiet. Whoever this was, she liked him.

"Let's go, Uncle Clay!" Alex shouted. "The horse races will be over before we get there."

Clay slowly lowered Nicole, then held her lightly with one arm for a few moments. "You look especially lovely this morning," he said, and ran his finger along her ear.

She merely stared at him, her heart pounding wildly.

He released her abruptly. "Alex! Untie us. Mandy, see if you can help Roger steer us out of here."

"Aye, aye, Captain Clay!" the twins laughed.

Nicole sat down beside Janie.

"Now, that's the man I remember!" Janie said. "Something's happened. I don't know what, but I'd like to thank the person who did it."

They heard the noise of the party a half a mile before they reached the Backes's wharf. It wasn't even six in the morning, but half the county was already spread out across the lawn. Some people were on the far side of the river shooting at ducks.

"Did you send Golden Girl over to Mrs. Backes?" Alex asked.

Clay gave the boy a look of disdain. "Wouldn't be much of a party if I couldn't empty everyone's pockets, would it?"

"Think she'll beat Mr. Backes's Irish Lass?" Roger asked. "I heard she's a fast horse."

Clay grunted. "It'll be no race at all." As he spoke, he buttoned his shirt and reached for a cravat from a basket close to the front of the boat. He quickly tied it, then slipped on a vest of creamy brown satin. A double-breasted coat of chocolate cord came next. The buttons were of brass, the front of it cut away, the back hanging to just above his knees. His buckskin trousers fit like a second skin. He wore tall, Hessian boots, taller in front of the knee than in the back. He gave them a quick buff, showing their mirror-like shine. He put on a dark brown beaver hat, the brim softly curved.

He turned to Nicole and offered her his arm.

Nicole had never seen him in anything except work clothes. Now the man who cut tobacco was transformed into a gentleman worthy of Versailles.

He seemed to understand her hesitation, and he grinned broadly. "I certainly want to seem worthy of appearing with the world's most beautiful bride, don't I?"

Nicole smiled up at him, glad she'd taken such care with her dress. Her gown was made of white lingerie silk, very fine and heavenly to touch. It had been hand-embroidered in England with tiny gold-brown jonquils. The bodice was velvet of the same rich, deep gold as the flowers. The collar and cuffs were trimmed in white piping. Her dark curls were entwined with ribbons of gold and white.

As Roger tied the sloop to one of the wharfs at the end of the Backes's property, Clay said, "I almost forgot! I have something for you." He reached inside his pocket and produced the gold locket she'd left on the ship so long ago.

Nicole clutched it tightly in her hands, then smiled up at him. "Thank you."

"You can thank me properly later," he said, and kissed her forehead. Then he turned to toss baskets to Roger who stood on the edge of the wharf. He held her close for a moment when he lifted her to the wharf.

"Here they are!" someone yelled as they walked toward the house.

"Clay! We thought maybe she was deformed, the way you keep her hidden away."

"I keep her hidden for the same reason I hide my brandy. Too much exposure isn't good for brandy or wives," Clay shouted back.

Nicole looked down at her hands. She was puzzled by this new Clay, by his announcement to the world that she was his wife. It made her feel almost as if she were.

"Hello," Ellen Backes said. "Clay, let me have her for a while. You've had her for months."

Reluctantly, Clay released her hand. "You won't forget me, will you?" he said as he winked at her. Then he followed several men toward a race track. She saw him take a long, deep drink out of a stoneware jug.

"You certainly have done wonders with him," Ellen said. "I haven't seen Clay so happy since before James and Beth died. It's almost as if he'd been away for a long time but now he's come home."

Nicole could say nothing in reply. The laughing, teasing Clay of today was a stranger to her. Ellen never gave her a chance to speak before she started introducing her to people. Nicole was bombarded with questions about her clothes, her family, how she had met Clay, where they'd been married. She didn't lie actually, but neither did she tell of being kidnapped and forced into marriage.

The front of Ellen's enormous house faced the river. She'd seen so few American houses, and this one was a surprise. Clay's house was pure Georgian, but Ellen's and Horace's house was a mixture of every architectural style imaginable. It looked as if each generation had added a wing in its favorite style. The house rambled in several directions with long wings, short wings, passageways leading to separate buildings.

Ellen saw Nicole staring at the house. "Remarkable, isn't it? I think I lived here a year before I learned my way around the inside. It's much worse inside than out. It has hallways that lead nowhere and doorways that open into other people's bedrooms. It's really frightful."

"And you obviously love it," Nicole smiled.

"I wouldn't change a brick, except I'm thinking of adding another wing."

Nicole looked at her in astonishment, then laughed. "Maybe another story? Not one wing has a fourth story."

Ellen grinned. "You are a clever child. I think you truly understand my house."

Someone called Ellen away, and two women began asking Nicole more questions as she helped set up the food. There were at least twenty trestle tables set about the lawn. Some were laden with food; some had benches set by them. Every family seemed to have brought as much food as Nicole and Janie. A pit had been dug, and hundreds of oysters were being roasted. Some slaves were turning a whole hog over a spit and coating it with a tangy sauce. Someone told Nicole it was a Haitian way of cooking called barbeque.

Suddenly, a horn sounded from far across the plantation.

"It's time!" Ellen yelled, and removed her apron. "The races are about to begin."

As a body, all the women pulled off aprons, lifted their skirts, and began to run.

"Now that the beauty is here, we can begin," a man greeted them.

Nicole stood a little aside from the other women, who were gathering at the edge of the carefully tended oval track. Her hair had fallen somewhat in the wild run. She pushed a glossy curl under a ribbon.

"Here, let me," Clay said from behind her. His hands did very little for the stray curls, but his fingertips on her neck sent little shivers down her spine. He turned her around. "Enjoying yourself?"

She nodded, staring up at him. His hands were on her shoulders, and his face was close to hers.

"My horse is about to run. Would you give me a kiss for luck?"

As always, the answer was in her eyes. His arms slid around her waist as he drew her close to him. He held her for a moment, his face buried in her neck. "I'm so glad you came with me," he whispered, then ran his lips along her cheek and finally captured her mouth. Nicole could feel herself weaken, her legs growing limp as she clung to him.

"Clay!" someone shouted. "You have all night for that. Come and tend to your horses now."

Clay lifted his head from Nicole's. "All night," he whispered, and ran his finger along her upper lip. He released her abruptly and walked toward a man who looked like a larger version of Wesley. The man slapped Clay on the back. "Can't blame you, though. You think there're any more beauties like her in England?"

"I got the last one, Travis," Clay laughed.

"Just the same, someday I think I'll go have a look for myself."

Nicole stood watching the men walk away. She'd probably been introduced to Wes's brother, but all the names and faces had run together.

"Nicole!" Ellen called. "I've saved you a place by me."

Nicole hurried forward to watch the horse races.

It was three hours later when the men and women walked together back to the food that waited for them. Nicole was flushed with laughter and sunlight. She had not enjoyed herself so much since before the French Revolution. Her French cousins used to complain that the English were so somber, that they lived only for work and church, that they had no idea how to have fun. She looked about at the Americans around her and knew her cousins would enjoy these people. All morning they'd laughed and shouted. The women had been quite raucous, loudly delivering their opinions about a horse's worth. And they weren't always for their husbands' steeds, either. Ellen had wagered against Horace several times, and now she was bragging that Horace was going to have to dig her a new flowerbed himself and order fifty new tulip bulbs from Holland.

Nicole had stood silently, an outsider, a spectator, until Travis had seen her frowning at one of Clay's horses.

"Clay, I don't think your wife likes your horse."

Clay barely glanced at Nicole. "My women wager with me," he said, with a meaningful look at Horace.

Nicole stared at Clay's back as he adjusted the light saddle on the horse, while his jockey stood by. She knew about horses. The French loved racing as much as anyone on earth, and her grandfather's horses had regularly beaten the king's. She raised one eyebrow. So! His *women* bet with him, did they?

"He won't win," she said firmly. "His proportions aren't right. His legs are too long for his chest depth. Horses like that are never good runners."

Everyone within hearing distance stopped, mugs of beer and ale halfway to their lips.

"Come on, Clay, you going to let a challenge like that stand?" Travis laughed. "Sounds to me like she knows something."

Clay barely paused in tightening the girth. "Care to put a little money on that?"

She stared at him. He knew she had no money. Ellen nudged her. "Promise him breakfast in bed for a week. A man'll kill himself trying to win that." Ellen's voice carried across half the racetrack. She, like nearly everyone except Nicole, had had too much to drink.

"That sounds fair to me," Clay grinned, and winked at Travis in thanks for starting the whole idea. Clay seemed to think the wagering was ended.

"And what do I get when the horse loses?" Nicole asked loudly.

"Maybe I'll bring *you* breakfast in bed," Clay said with a leer, and the men around him laughed in appreciation.

"I'd prefer a new winter cape," Nicole said coolly, then turned away to go back to the track. "A red wool one," she threw over her shoulder.

The women around her laughed, and Ellen asked if she was sure she wasn't an American by birth.

When Clay's horse lost by three lengths, he had to take a lot of ribbing. They asked if Nicole shouldn't take care of the tobacco as well as the horses.

Now, as the women walked toward the house, they laughed together over their wins and losses. One pretty young woman had promised to shine her husband's boots personally for a whole month. "But he didn't say which side of them," she laughed. "He'll be the only man in Virginia whose socks can see themselves."

Nicole looked at the mounds of food and realized she was ravenous. The stoneware plates stacked on one table were enormous, more platters than plates. Nicole helped herself to a little of everything.

"Think you can eat all that?" Clay teased from behind her.

"I may have to refill it," she laughed. "Where do I sit?"

"With me if you can wait long enough." He grabbed a plate and piled it much higher than Nicole's, then took her arm and led her to a large oak tree. One of the Backes's servants smiled and set large tankards of rum punch on the ground by the tree. Clay sat down on the grass, his plate in his lap, and began to eat. He looked up at Nicole, who still stood, her plate in her hand. "What's wrong?"

"I don't want to get grass stain on my dress," she said.

"Hand me your plate," Clay said as he set his on the ground beside him. When her plate was beside his, Clay grabbed her hand and pulled her into his lap.

"Clay!" she said as she started to move away. He held her where she was. "Clay, please. We're in a public place."

"They couldn't care less," he said as he nuzzled her ear. "They're more interested in food than in what we're doing."

She pulled back from him. "Are you drunk?" she asked suspiciously.

He laughed. "You do sound like a wife, and, yes, I'm a little drunk. You know what's wrong with you?" He didn't wait for her answer. "You are completely sober. Do you know that you are absolutely delightful when you're drunk?" He kissed the end of her nose, then grabbed the tankard of rum punch. "Here, drink this."

"No! I don't want to get drunk," she said stubbornly.

"I am going to hold this to your mouth, and you either swallow it or you'll ruin your dress."

She considered refusing to obey him, but he looked so endearing, like a naughty little boy, and she was so very thirsty. The rum punch was delicious. It was made from three different rums and four fruit juices. It was cold, with bits of ice floating in it. It went to her head immediately, and she took a deep breath, feeling her tensions leave her.

"Feel better now?"

She looked at him from under her thick lashes, then ran her finger across his cheek bone. "You're the most handsome man here," she said dreamily.

"Better than Steven Shaw?"

"You mean the blond man with the hole in his chin?"

Clay grimaced. "You could have said you had no idea who I was talking about. Here," he handed her plate to her. "Eat something. You'd think a Frenchwoman wouldn't get drunk as easily as you do."

She leaned her head against his shoulder and pressed her lips next to his warm skin.

"Here, sit up," he said sternly, and lifted a piece of cornbread to her mouth. "I thought you were hungry." The look she gave him made him shift his legs uncomfortably. "Eat!" he commanded.

Nicole reluctantly turned her attention to the food, but she enjoyed sitting on his lap. "I like your friends," she said through a mouthful of potato salad. "Are there more horse races this afternoon?"

"No," Clay said. "We usually give the horses and jockeys a rest. Most of the people play cards or chess or backgammon. Some of the others find their rooms in that maze Ellen calls a house and take a nap."

Nicole went on eating calmly for a while. Then she lifted her eyes to look at him. "What are *we* going to do?"

Clay smiled in such a way that only one side of his mouth moved. "I thought I'd give you some more rum and then ask you."

Nicole stared at him, then reached for her mug of punch. After she'd taken a long drink, she set it on the ground. She suddenly gave a big yawn. "I do believe I need . . . a nap."

Clay quietly removed his coat and put it on the ground beside him. Then he picked her up and set her on it. He kissed the corner of her surprised mouth lightly. "If I'm to walk you across the yard to the house, I need to be in a decent condition to do so."

Nicole's eyes went downward to the bulge in Clay's buckskin trousers. Then she giggled.

"Eat, you little imp!" he commanded in a mock fierce tone.

A few minutes later, Clay took her half-finished plate from her and pulled her to stand beside him. He slung his coat over one shoulder. "Ellen," he called when they were closer to the house. "Which room did you put us in?"

"Northeast wing, second floor, third bedroom," she answered quickly.

"Tired, Clay?" someone laughed. "Funny how tired newlyweds get."

"You jealous, Henry?" Clay called over his shoulder.

"Clay!" Nicole said when they were inside the house. "You're embarrassing me."

Clay grunted. "The looks you're giving me are making *me* blush." He pulled her along behind him as he wound his way through the corridors. Nicole had only an impression of an odd mix of furniture and paintings. The furnishings ranged from English Elizabethan to French court to American primitives. She saw paintings worthy of Versailles and some so crude they must have been done by children.

Somehow, Clay found the room. He pulled her inside and grabbed her into his arms while he slammed the door shut with his foot. He kissed her hungrily, as if he couldn't get enough of her. He held her face in his hands and tilted it to slant across his.

She gave up to his control of her. Her mind was whirling with the nearness of him. She could feel his sun-warmed skin through his cotton shirt. His mouth was hard and soft at the same time, and his tongue was sweet. His thighs pressed against her, demanding yet asking.

"I've waited a long time for that," he whispered as he pressed his lips to her earlobe. He pulled at it with his teeth.

Nicole pushed away from him. As he watched with a puzzled expression, she walked to the other side of the room, then lifted her arms and swiftly began to remove the pins from her hair. Clay stood still and watched her. He didn't even move as she struggled with the buttons down the back of the dress. The sight of her, alone in a room with him, was what he'd dreamed of for a long time.

She moved her shoulders forward and slipped out of the dress. Under it she wore a thin cotton gauze chemise. The low neckline was embroidered with tiny pink hearts. It was tied under her breasts with a thin pink satin ribbon. Her breasts swelled above the delicate, nearly transparent cloth.

Very, very slowly, she untied the bow of the ribbon and let the gauze slide to the floor.

Clayton's eyes followed the fabric, going over every inch of her from her high, firm breasts to her little waist to her delicate feet. When he looked back at her face, she raised her arms to him. He took one long step across the room, lifted her in his arms and laid her gently on the bed. He stood over her, looking at her. The sunlight through the curtained window showed her skin to be flawless.

He sat down on the bed beside her and ran his hand over her skin. It felt as good as it looked, smooth and warm.

"Clay," Nicole whispered, and he smiled at her.

He bent and kissed her neck, the pulse at the base of her throat, then moved slowly to her breasts, teasing them, savoring the rigid pink peaks.

She buried her fingers in his thick hair and arched her neck backward.

Clay stretched out on the bed beside her. He was fully clothed, and Nicole could feel the coolness of the brass buttons of his vest against her skin. The buckskin of his pants was warm and soft. The leather of his boots rubbed against her legs. The clothes against her bare skin, the leather and brass, were all male, all strong like Clay.

When he moved on top of her, she rubbed her leg against the

side of his boot. The buckskin caressed her inner thigh. He moved to one side and began to unbutton his vest.

"No," she whispered.

He looked at her for a moment and then kissed her again, deeply, passionately.

She laughed throatily when he lifted his leg and ran the smooth leather of his boot along the length of her leg. He unfastened the buttons at the sides of his trousers, and Nicole moaned at the first touch of his manhood.

He lay on top of her, holding her tightly as if he were afraid she'd try to leave him.

Slowly, very slowly, Nicole began to come alive again. She stretched and breathed deeply. "I feel like I've just gotten rid of a lot of tension."

"Is that all?" Clay laughed, his face pressed into her neck. "I'm glad that I was able to be of some service. Perhaps I should wear my spurs next time."

"Are you laughing at me?"

Clay rose on one arm. "Never! I think I'm laughing at myself. You have certainly taught me some things."

"I have? Such as?" She ran her finger along the crescent scar by his eye.

He moved away from her and sat up. "Not now. Maybe I'll tell you later. I'm hungry. You wouldn't let me eat much an hour ago."

She smiled and closed her eyes. She felt deliciously happy. Clay stood up and watched her. Her black hair fanned out beneath her, making a splendid contrast with the curves of her body. He could see that she was already half asleep. He bent and kissed the tip of her nose. "Sleep, my little love," he whispered softly, then pulled the other half of the bedspread over her. He tiptoed from the room.

When Nicole awoke, she stretched lazily before she opened her eyes.

"Come on, get up," said a husky voice from across the room.

Nicole smiled and opened her eyes. Clay looked at her in the mirror. His shirt was thrown across a chair, and he was shaving.

"You've slept most of the afternoon. Are you planning to miss the dancing?"

She smiled at him. "No." She started to get out of bed, then realized she was nude. She looked around for something to cover herself. When she saw Clay watching her with interest, she tossed the bedspread aside and walked toward the wardrobe where Janie had hung her clothes. Clay chuckled and resumed shaving.

When he finished, he went to stand behind her. She wore an apricot satin dressing gown, and she puzzled over her clothes for something to wear.

Clay suddenly grabbed a gown of cinnamon-colored velvet. "Janie said you should wear this." He held it up and eyed it critically. "There doesn't look like there's much to the top of it."

"I supply that," she said smugly, and took the dress from him.

"Then I guess you won't need these."

She turned and saw what he held. Pearls! There were four strands of them, held together by four long gold clasps. She held the necklace in her hands, felt the creamy texture of the pearls. But she didn't understand how it was to be worn. It looked more like a long belt than a necklace.

"Put the dress on and I'll show you," Clay said. "My mother designed it."

Quickly, Nicole slipped into her chemise, then the gown. The bodice was very low, the sleeves mere straps across her shoulders. Clay fastened the hooks and eyes up the back. He then pinned one of the clasps to the center back of the dress, the second one to her shoulder. The third clasp was fastened to the center of the deep décolletage, another one on the other shoulder, then making a full circle to the back. The four strands were threaded in such a way that they draped. Two strands went across the breasts, while the others hung gracefully across the velvet.

"It's beautiful," Nicole breathed as she looked in the mirror. "Thank you for allowing me to wear it."

He bent and kissed her bare shoulder. "My mother gave it to me to give to my wife. No one else has ever worn it."

She whirled to face him. "I don't understand. Our marriage isn't—"

He put a finger to her lips to stop her. "Let's just enjoy tonight. There's time to talk tomorrow."

Nicole stood back as he dressed. She could hear the musicians on the lawn below. She was quite content not to think of any time but the moment. Reality was Bianca and Clay together in his house. Reality was his love for another woman.

They left the room, and Clay led her again through the maze of a house out to the garden. The tables had been reset with more food, and the people lounged about, eating and drinking. Nicole had hardly found time for a bite of food before Clay pulled her onto the platform that had been laid for dancing. The energetic Virginia reel left her breathless.

After four dances, Nicole begged Clay to let her rest. He led her away from the group to a little octagonal pavilion set under three willow trees. It had become night while they were dancing.

"The stars are beautiful, aren't they?"

Clay put his arms around her and drew her close, her head resting on his shoulder. He didn't speak.

"I wish this moment could go on forever," she whispered. "I wish it would never end."

"Have the other moments been so horrible? Have you been so unhappy in America?"

She closed her eyes and moved her cheek against him. "I have spent my happiest moments here and my most miserable." She didn't want to speak of it. She lifted her head. "Why isn't Wesley here? Did he have to return to take care of his plantation so his brother could come? And who is that woman with Wesley's brother?"

Clay chuckled and pushed her head back down. "Wes didn't come because I guess he didn't want to. As for Travis, he's mean enough he could run his place from England if he wanted to. And the redhead is Margo Jenkins. As far as I can tell, she's determined to get Travis whether he wants her or not."

"I hope she doesn't get him," Nicole murmured. "Did you and Wesley quarrel?" She felt him stiffen against her.

"Why would you ask that?"

"I think your temper makes me ask that."

He relaxed and laughed. "We did have a scuffle."

"Serious?"

He pulled her away from him and looked into her eyes. "It may have been one of the most serious conversations of my life." He lifted his head. "I believe they're playing another reel. Are you ready?"

She smiled in answer as he grabbed her hand and led her back to the dancers.

Nicole was amazed at the stamina of the Virginians. It had been a long day, even though she'd slept in the afternoon. On her third yawn, Clay took her hand and led her upstairs. He helped her undress, but as she was climbing into bed he held a long bathrobe up for her. She looked at him in puzzlement.

"I thought you might like a bath by moonlight," he said as he undressed and slipped into a cotton banyan, a loose-sleeved robe.

Quietly, Nicole followed him through more passages in the house to the outside. To her amazement, they came out close to the edge of the woods. She could hear the river not far away.

They walked through the lush darkness of the trees to where a bend in the river made a lovely pool. Clay put the soap and towels on the bank, undressed, retrieved the soap, and walked into the river. Nicole watched as the moonlight played on the muscles of his back. He parted the water cleanly, his long legs making very little sound as he swam to the center of the pool. He turned onto his back and looked at her. "Are you going to stay there all night?"

She hastily untied her robe and dropped it to her feet, then hurried after him. She dove under the water.

"Nicole!" Clay called when she didn't resurface. His voice held fear in it.

She surfaced behind him, nipped him on the back before she went under again. He growled at her, then grabbed her about the waist. "Come here, you little imp," he said, kissing her forehead.

She put her arms around his neck and kissed him deeply. Her skin felt good against his. The water was warm and luxurious.

Clay set her away from him, then began to lather the soap in his hands. He rubbed his hands all over her, very slowly. When he finished, she took the soap and washed him. They laughed together, enjoying the water and each other. Before Nicole could rinse herself, Clay began washing her hair. She dipped under the water to rinse. Her hair flowed out behind her in a long mass of black silver.

Clay watched her, then slowly drew her close to him. He kissed her gently, pulling her body close. He pulled back from her and looked into her eyes. He seemed to be asking her a question, and whatever answer he wanted he saw there. He kissed her again, then lifted her in his arms and carried her ashore.

He laid her gently on the grass and began to kiss her body. He kissed her wherever his soapy hands had touched. Nicole smiled, her eyes closed. She bent her head and pulled his mouth to hers. She ran her hands over his body, liking the feel of it, the strength of it.

He moved on top of her, and she was ready for him. "Sweet Nicole," he whispered, but she didn't hear him. Her senses had changed from reality to the pure passion that Clay made her feel. She lifted her hips to meet him.

It was some time later when Clay lay beside her and pulled

her close to him. He kept one thigh thrown across her. His mouth was close to her ear, and his breath was sweet and warm.

"Will you marry me?" he whispered.

She wasn't sure she heard him correctly.

"Don't I get an answer?"

Nicole could feel her body tense. "I am married to you."

He bent over her, his head propped on one arm. "I want you to marry me again, in front of the whole county. This time, I want to be there when we're married."

She was silent as he ran one finger over her upper lip. "One time you told me you loved me," he said. "Of course, you were drunk at the time, but you did say it. Did you mean it?"

She could scarcely breathe. "Yes," she whispered, staring into his eyes.

"Then why won't you marry me?"

"Are you laughing at me? Are you teasing me?"

He smiled and nuzzled her neck. "Do you find it so hard to believe that I could have any sense at all? How can you love a man you think is stupid?"

"Clay, talk to me. I don't understand what you're saying. I've never thought you were stupid."

He looked at her again. "You should have. Everyone on the plantation gave their love to you except me. Even my horses are smarter than I am. Remember when I first kissed you on the ship? I was so angry because of what I'd lost—you. I never wanted to let you go, yet there you stood telling me that you weren't really mine. I was furious when I saw that note and frantic when I couldn't find you. I think Janie knew then that I'd fallen in love with you."

"But Bianca—" Nicole began, but Clay put a finger to her lips.

"She's in the past now, and I'd like for us to go on from here. Ellen knows we were married by proxy on the ship, and she will understand if we ask to be remarried here."

"Remarried? Here?"

Clay kissed her nose and smiled, his eyes twinkling brightly in the moonlight. "Is it such an impossible idea? Then we'd have about a hundred witnesses who'd swear we weren't forced into a marriage. I don't want the idea of an annulment to come up later." He grinned. "Even if I beat you."

Her tenseness left her. "You would be sorry."

"Oh?" he laughed. "What would you do?"

"Get Maggie to stop cooking, tell the twins what you'd done so they could hate you, too, and—"

"Hate me?" He was suddenly serious, and he pulled her close to him. "We're alone, you and I. We have only each other. You must promise never to hate me."

"Clay," she gasped, trying to breathe. "I didn't mean it. How could I hate you when I love you so much?"

"I love you, too," he said, then released his hold on her slightly. "It'll probably take about three days to prepare everything for the wedding, but you do agree, don't you?"

She laughed against him. "You ask me if I agree to the thing I want most in life? Yes, I'll marry you. Every day, if you want."

He began kissing her neck hungrily.

Nicole's mind soared. She'd wanted this day to last forever. Maybe she'd never have to return to a life where she lived in one house and Clay in another. If they could only be married publicly before they returned, she felt she'd be safe. There would be witnesses to the fact that Clay loved *her* and wanted *her*.

The word *Bianca* flashed across her mind, but Clay's kisses sent all thoughts far away. Three days, he'd said. What could happen in three days?

Chapter 11

WHEN NICOLE awoke the next morning, she couldn't believe the things that had happened the night before. It all seemed too good to be true. She was alone in the bedroom, and the sun was streaming through the window. She smiled as she heard the excited voices beneath the window. The horse races were about to begin. She jumped out of bed and quickly dressed in a simple gown of butterscotch muslin.

It took her several minutes to find her way out of the house to the tables set up for breakfast. She was eating a plate of scrambled eggs when she felt a hush fall over the people around her. One by one, they all seemed to grow quiet.

She stood up and looked toward the wharf. What she saw threatened to stop her heart. Wesley walked beside Bianca. Nicole had felt safe in this place, away from Bianca, but now she saw her world starting to crumble about her.

Bianca walked toward the group confidently. She wore a gown of mauve satin with large black flowers embroidered around the hem. There was a row of wide lace at the high waist and neckline. Her large breasts were only barely concealed by the brilliantly colored dress. She carried a parasol of matching satin.

Even as Nicole watched them approach, she began to wonder at the silence of the others. She knew that Bianca's presence upset her, but why did it affect the people who did not know her? She looked at them and saw the looks of surprise on their faces.

"Beth," she heard repeatedly. "Beth."

"Wesley," Ellen called across the lawn. "You gave us such a fright!" She started walking across the grass toward them. "Welcome," she said, and held out her hand.

Even when they were close to the tables, Nicole still couldn't move. Wesley broke away from Bianca, who had already taken a plate. The women surrounded her.

"Hello," Wesley said to Nicole. "How do you like our Virginia parties so far?"

When Nicole looked at him, her eyes were full of tears. Why, she wondered. Why had he brought Bianca? Did he hate her for some reason and want her away from Clay?

"Nicole," Wesley said, and put his hand on her arm. "Trust me. Please?"

She could only nod. She had no other answer for him.

Ellen walked behind Wes. "Where did you find her? Has Clay seen her?"

Wesley smiled. "He's seen her." He held his arm out to Nicole. "Would you like to walk to the racetrack with me?"

Mutely, she took his arm.

"What do you know about Beth?" Wes asked when they were away from the others.

"Only that she was killed, along with Clay's brother," Nicole answered. She stopped suddenly. "Bianca looks like Beth, doesn't she?"

"It's a shock at first. Standing very still, she does look like Beth, but once she opens her mouth all resemblance disappears."

"Then Clay—" she began.

"I don't know. I can't speak for him. All I know is that at first I thought she *was* Beth. I know Clay's . . . concern for her is based on her resemblance to Beth. There couldn't be anything else, since she's not what I'd call a pleasant woman." He grinned. "Clay and I had a few words about her." He flexed his jaw. "I just thought maybe it would do him some good to see the two of you together."

Nicole realized he meant well, but she'd seen the way Clay looked at Bianca, had seen the way he adored her. She didn't know if she could stand to see him look at another woman that way again.

"What happened in the races yesterday? Did Clay beat Travis? I hope so."

"I think they're tied," Nicole laughed, glad to change the subject. "But would you like to hear about my plans for a new red cloak?"

It was a rule of Virginia house parties that all of the guests took care of themselves. There was food constantly in view, every game imaginable, servants to help with every wish. So, when the horn sounded for the morning's races to begin, the women felt free to leave Bianca to herself when she refused their invitations to attend the races with them. But Bianca's eyes couldn't leave the food on the tables. That horrible Maggie had all but refused to cook for her after Clay had left.

"Are you the Maleson woman I been hearin' about?"

Bianca looked across the plate she was filling to the tall man. He was thin to the point of emaciation. His worn, dirty coat hung on him. His face was obscured by long, straggling black hair and a thin black beard. His nose was large, his lips almost nonexistent, but his eyes were like two black coals peering out of the brush of beard and hair. His eyes were small and so close together that the inner corners seemed to overlap.

Bianca grimaced and looked away from the man.

"I asked you a question, woman! Are you a Maleson?"

She glared at him. "I don't see that it's any concern of yours. Now let me pass."

"A glutton!" he said, eying her heaping platter. "Gluttony is a sin, and you'll pay for it."

"If you don't leave me alone, I'll call someone."

"Pa, let me talk to her. I think she's kinda pretty."

Bianca looked with interest at the man who now stepped from behind his father. He was a strong, healthy young man, no more than twenty-five years old, but unfortunately with his father's face. The little dark eyes went over Bianca's soft white body.

"Our mother's maiden name was Maleson. We heard you was gonna marry Clayton Armstrong, and we wrote you in England. I don't know if you ever got the letter or not."

Bianca remembered the letter quite well. So this was the riffraff that dared to claim to be related to her. "I received no letter."

"The wages of sin are death!" the old man said in a voice that would carry across the plantation.

"Pa, those people over there are gamblin' and bettin' on horses. You oughtta go talk to them while we get to know our cousin."

Bianca turned and walked away from the group. She had no intention of talking with any of them. She had no more than sat down when two young men came to sit by her. Across from her sat the man who'd spoken before, and beside her was another man, a shorter, younger boy, about sixteen. The boy's looks were softened by lighter-colored eyes, the shape of them rounder, farther apart.

"This here's Isaac," said the older son, "and I'm Abraham Simmons. That man was our pa." He nodded to the old man hurrying toward the racetrack with a large Bible under his arm. "Pa don't care nothin' about anythin' except preachin'. But Ike and me got other plans."

"Would you please go somewhere else? I would like to enjoy my breakfast."

"That's enough for three meals, lady," Ike said.

"You sure are uppity, ain't you?" Abe said. "You'd think you'd be glad to talk to us, bein' as we're related and all."

"I am not related to you!" Bianca said fiercely.

Abe leaned away from the table and stared at her. His little beady eyes narrowed until they were only slits of black light. "It don't look to me like you're overflowin' with friends. We heard you was to marry Armstrong and own Arundel Hall."

"I am mistress of the Armstrong plantation," she said smugly between mouthfuls.

"Then who's that pretty little woman Clay says is his wife?"

Bianca set her jaw as she chewed steadily. She was still burning over the fact that Clay had left her to take Nicole with him. He'd behaved strangely toward her after the night that nice Mr. Wesley Stanford had joined them for supper. Clay had seemed to be watching her constantly since then, and Bianca had begun to feel ill at ease. She'd broached the idea of adding a wing to the house, and he'd merely sat and stared at her. Bianca had angrily left the room. She vowed she'd repay him for his rudeness.

Then suddenly he'd left the plantation. She was glad when he was gone; his constant presence made her nervous. She'd spent hours planning menus for her meals while he was gone. She was livid when that disgusting Maggie prepared less than half the dishes she'd ordered. While she was in the kitchen telling the cook that if she valued her job she'd better get busy, Wesley reappeared. He told her of the party and that Clay had taken Nicole.

Reluctantly, Bianca had readied herself to travel to the Backes's plantation early the next morning. How dare that horrible Nicole try to take what was hers! She'd show her! All she had to do was smile at Clay, and he'd act like he did the first night he saw her. Oh, yes, she knew what charms the women of her family had.

"The woman was once my maid," Bianca said loftily.

"Your maid!" Abe laughed. "It looks like she's Clay's maid now."

"Take your filthy mind elsewhere," she said as she rose to re-fill her plate.

"Listen," Abe said, following her. He was serious now. "I thought you was gonna marry Clay and then you could help us. Pa's never cared about anything but preachin'. We've got some land not too far from Clay's, but we don't have any stock. We was hopin' you could loan us your bull and, seein' as we're family, maybe give us a couple of your heifers."

"And some chickens," Ike said. "Ma'd like some more chickens. She's your third cousin."

Bianca whirled on them. "I am not related to you! How dare you presume on me and my prospects? How dare you speak to me of . . . animals!"

It took Abe a moment to reply. "There's somethin' wrong here, Miss High-and-Mighty. You ain't gonna get none of Clay's money, are you? You come all the way from England, and then he married your maid instead of you!" Abe began to laugh. "That's the best story I've heard in years. Just wait till I tell that one around here."

"It's not true!" Bianca said, her eyes beginning to tear. "Clayton is going to marry me! I am going to own the Armstrong plantation. It will just take time, that's all. He's going to annul his marriage to my maid."

Abe and Ike exchanged looks of suppressed laughter. "Annul, huh?" Abe smirked. "Yesterday, when she was sittin' on his lap and feedin' him, it didn't look like he was thinkin' of gettin' rid of her."

"And what about when he took her upstairs in the middle of the afternoon?" Ike said. He was at an age when he'd just discovered the opposite sex. He'd spent an hour under a tree imagining what Clay was doing with his pretty little wife. "When he come down, he had a grin from one ear to the other."

The dirty little harlot, Bianca thought. The bitch thought she could take the plantation away from her by using her body to entice Clay. She looked from the plate of food to the path to the raceway. As soon as she finished her breakfast, she'd straighten Nicole out. She put her chin into the air and walked past the young men.

"You may find you'll be wantin' a friend sometime," Abe called after her. "We don't forget family as quick as you, but our price is gonna be a lot higher from now on. Come on, Ike, let's go get Pa outta trouble."

It was an hour later when Bianca finally made her way to the racetrack. She found the entire day strenuous and wearing on her nerves. She'd be glad when she would no longer have to fight to get what she wanted. Someday, the Armstrong plantation would be hers and she'd be able to rest after meals to allow her food to digest properly. Now, all because of Nicole, she had to attend these disgusting parties with these loud, lower-class people.

She saw Nicole standing beside Ellen Backes at the edge of the racetrack. The other women were loudly yelling at the horses, but Nicole was quiet, a look of worry on her face. She kept looking toward one end of the track, where Clay stood in the midst of several men.

Bianca tapped Nicole on the shoulder with the point of her parasol. "Come here," she commanded when Nicole turned around.

With resignation, Nicole followed Bianca away from the others.

"What are you doing here?" Bianca demanded. "It's not your place to be here, and you know it! If you won't think of me or of Clay, think of yourself. I've heard how you've acted like the lowest street trash around him. What are people going to say when he rids himself of you and marries me? Who will want to marry you when they know you're such used goods?"

Nicole stared at the taller woman. All she could think of was the horrible idea of being with any man except Clay.

"Shall we go together to see him?" Bianca asked smugly.

"Do you remember how he ignored you when I first arrived from England?"

Nicole knew those few minutes were branded on her heart.

"You'll learn someday that a man must respect a woman before he can love her. When you act like a street woman, you'll be treated as one."

"Nicole," Ellen said from behind her, "are you all right? You look as if you're not feeling well."

"A little too much sun, perhaps."

Ellen smiled. "It couldn't be a little one, could it?"

Nicole's hand flew to her stomach. How she wished Ellen could be right.

"Maybe it's too much food," Bianca said. "One should never overeat and then stand in the sun. I think I'll walk back to the house. I think you should come with me, Nicole."

"Yes, do," Ellen urged.

The last thing Nicole wanted was more of Bianca's company, but she saw Clay and the men walking toward them. She couldn't bear to see Clay's eyes melt at the sight of his beloved.

There were at least three great rooms in Ellen's house, and now all of them were full of people. A sudden cold shower had sent them scurrying inside. Fires had been lit all over the house, and as the massive masonry units of the fireplaces began to heat, the house grew warm.

Clay sat in a leather wing chair, sipping a mug of small beer and watching the twins pop corn over the fire. A few minutes before, he'd gone upstairs to find Nicole asleep in their bed. He was worried about her because all morning people had told him about the woman who looked just like Beth.

"Won't you sit down?" he heard a familiar voice say. He turned to see Wes standing rather close, facing him. A figure that was unmistakably Bianca's had her back to him.

Clay hadn't wanted to see her yet. First he wanted to talk to

Nicole, reassure her, prevent her from worrying. He started to rise, but Wes gave him a look of warning. Clay shrugged and sat back down. Maybe Wes wanted to be alone with her.

"This must be a great shock to you," Wes said, his voice carrying easily across to Clay.

"I don't know what you mean," Bianca said.

"You can be honest with me. Clay told me the whole story. You came all the way from England, expecting to marry Clay, only to find he'd married someone else. Now he openly lives with her."

"You *do* understand!" Bianca cried gratefully. "Everyone seems to be against me, and I don't understand why. They should be against that awful woman, Nicole. I'm the one who's been wronged."

"Tell me, Bianca, why did you want to marry Clay in the first place?"

She was silent.

"I've been thinking," Wes continued. "It seems that we could help each other. You know, of course, that Clay is a man of some means." He smiled at Bianca's eager nod. "The last few years, my own plantation hasn't been doing so well. If you were mistress of Arundel Hall, you could help me."

"How?"

"Now and then a piece of livestock could stray onto my land or maybe a few bushels of wheat could disappear. Clay wouldn't miss them."

"I don't know."

"But you'd be his wife. You'd own half the plantation."

Bianca smiled. "Of course. Could you help me get to be his wife? At first, I was sure I would be, but lately I'm not so sure."

"Of course you'll be his wife. If you'll help me, I'll help you."

"I will. But how will you get rid of that awful Nicole? She throws herself at him and, stupid man that he is, he enjoys her harlot's ways."

"I've heard enough," Clay said flatly from where he towered over Bianca.

She turned, her hand flying to her throat. "Clay! You gave me such a fright! I had no idea you were near."

Clay ignored her and turned to Wes. "There was really no need for this. It took me a while, but I finally saw what you meant. She's not Beth."

"No," Wes said quietly, "she's not." He stood up, his eyes going from Clay to Bianca. "I think you have some talking to do."

Clay nodded, then held out his hand. "I owe you a lot."

Wes grinned and shook his friend's hand. "I haven't forgotten that punch you gave me. But I'll pick my time to repay you."

Clay laughed. "It'll take you and Travis both."

Wesley snorted, then left Clay alone with Bianca.

She was beginning to understand that Clay had heard all of her conversation with Wes and that Wes had purposely planned it so he would. "How dare you eavesdrop on me?" she breathed as Clay sat opposite her.

"Your words didn't tell me anything I didn't already know. Tell me, why did you come to America?" He didn't wait for her answer. "I once thought I loved you, and I asked you to marry me. I was . . . haunted by you for a long time, but now I realize that I never loved you, that I never even knew you."

"What are you trying to say? I have letters where you say you'll marry me. It's against the law to go back on a proposal."

Clay looked at her in astonishment. "How could you consider a breach of promise when I'm already married? No court in the world would ask me to leave my wife to marry someone else."

"They would when I tell them the circumstances of the marriage."

Clay's jaw hardened. "What do you want? Money? I'll pay you for your time. You've already accumulated a sizable wardrobe."

Bianca fought back tears. How could this crude Colonial ruffian understand what she wanted? In England, she'd not been able to mingle with the crowd of people who had once been her family's peers because of her lack of wealth. Some of the people she knew in her reduced status laughed behind her back at her proposal from an American. They insinuated that she couldn't get anyone else. Bianca had hinted that she'd had several proposals, but it wasn't true.

So what did she really want? She wanted what her family had once had—security, position, freedom from bill collectors, the feeling that she was wanted and needed. "I want the Armstrong plantation," she said quietly.

Clay sat back in the chair. "You certainly don't ask for much, do you? I can't, or won't, give it to you. I've grown to love Nicole, and I mean to keep her as my wife."

"But you can't! I came all the way from England. You have to marry me!"

Clay raised one eyebrow. "You will return to England in as much comfort as can be managed. I will try to compensate you for your time and for . . . the breach of promise. It is the best I can do."

Bianca glared at him. "Who do you think you are, you insufferable, uneducated boor? Do you think I ever wanted to marry you? I only came when I heard you had some money. Do you think you're going to discard me like so much baggage? Do you think I'm going to return to England as a jilted woman?"

Clay stood up. "I don't give a good goddamn what you do. You're going back as soon as possible, even if I have to personally throw you in the hold." He turned on his heel and left her. If he stood near her another minute, he just might hit her.

Bianca was seething. Never would she allow that disgusting man to jilt her. He thought he could demand that she marry him, then he could command her to go away just as easily, just as if she were a serving girl. Nicole! That's who was the scullery maid! Yet he tossed her, Bianca, aside for that lower-class scullion.

Her hands made fists at her side. She wouldn't allow him to do it! Once an ancestor of hers had known the nephew of the king of England. She was an important person, with power and influence.

Family, she thought. Those men this morning had said they were part of her family. Yes, she smiled. They'd help her. They'd get the plantation for her. Then no one would laugh at her!

Clay stood under the roof of one of Ellen's several porches. The cold shower beat down around him, isolating him. He took a cigar from his pocket and lit it, inhaling deeply on it. He'd had time in the last few days to curse himself for a fool, but today curses weren't enough.

In spite of what he'd said to Wes, seeing Bianca in a clear light had been a revelation. His mind had always been hindered by the vision of Beth.

He sat on the porch railing, one long leg on the floor as he watched the rain begin to slacken. Through the trees, he could see a faint glimmer of sunlight. Nicole had known what Bianca was, he thought. Yet Nicole had always been gracious and kind to the woman, had never been hostile or allowed her anger to vent itself on her.

He smiled and threw the cigar stub into the wet grass. The rain was dripping off the eaves of the house, but already the sun was making the drops sparkle on the lawn. He glanced up toward the window of the room where Nicole slept. Or did she? he wondered. How had she reacted when she saw Bianca at the party?

He went inside the house, through the corridors, and up the stairs to their room. Nicole was the most giving person he'd ever met. She'd love him, his children, his servants, even his animals, yet she'd never ask anything in return.

He knew she wasn't asleep as soon as he opened the door. He went straight to the wardrobe and grabbed a dress, a plain calico one of chocolate brown. "Get dressed," he said calmly. "I want to take you somewhere."

Chapter 12

SLOWLY, SHE threw back the covers and slipped her chemise over her head. Her body felt stiff with misery. At least he hadn't forgotten her, she thought. At least this time his beloved Bianca's presence hadn't completely blinded him. Or maybe he was taking her back to the mill, as far away from Bianca as possible.

She didn't ask where they were going. Her hands shook so badly as she buttoned the dress that Clay's hands pushed hers away. He looked at her face, watched her eyes, enormous and liquid, filled with fear and longing.

He bent and kissed her softly, and her mouth clung to his. "I don't guess I've given you much reason to trust me, have I?"

She could only stare at him, her throat too swollen to speak.

He smiled at her in a fatherly way, then took her hand and led her from the room and out of the house. She lifted her long skirt to keep it off the wet grass. Clay pulled her behind him quickly, paying little attention to the fact that she had to nearly run to keep up with his long strides.

He handed her into the sloop without saying a word, then untied the boat and unfurled the sail. The elegant little boat sliced through the water cleanly and swiftly. Nicole sat calmly, watching him at the helm of the ship. The sheer width of him looked like a mountain to Nicole—impenetrable, mysterious, something she loved but didn't understand.

Her chest began to tighten when she saw they were heading back toward the Armstrong plantation. She'd been right! He was returning her to the mill. The iron band around her chest was too tight for her to cry. When they sailed past the wharf to the mill, she felt her breath release and a wave of joy flow through her.

At first, she didn't recognize the place where Clay stopped. It seemed an impenetrable mass of foliage. He stepped out of the boat, the water up to his ankles, tied the boat, and then held his arms out for her. Gratefully, she nearly fell into them. He stared at her a moment in amusement before he carried her through the hidden gate and into the beautiful clearing. The rain had made everything fresh and new. The sunlight glittered on the raindrops on the hundreds of flowers.

Clay put Nicole down, then sat down against the big rock by the flowers and pulled her into his lap. "I know how you hate to get grass stain on your dress," he teased.

She was serious as she looked up at him. Her eyes looked worried, frightened. She nibbled at her upper lip. "Why did you bring me here?" she whispered.

"I think it's time we talked."

"About Bianca?" Her voice was barely audible.

His eyes searched hers. "Why is there fear in your eyes? Do I frighten you?"

She blinked several times. "Not you, but what you have to say. That frightens me."

He pulled her against him, her head snuggled against his shoulder. "If you don't mind listening, I'd like to tell you about me, about my family, about Beth."

All she could do was nod silently. She wanted to know everything about him.

"I had one of those idyllic childhoods that was like the fairy tales you tell the twins," he began. "James and I were loved and disciplined by the two most wonderful parents ever created. My mother was a lovely, kind woman. She had a great sense of humor, which bewildered James and me when we were younger. If she'd pack a lunch for us to go fishing, sometimes we'd open a crock and find a frog inside. It used to embarrass us that she could catch more fish than any of us."

Nicole smiled against him, imagining his mother. "What about your father?"

"He adored her. Even when James and I were grown, they'd romp and play like children. It was a very happy household."

"Beth," Nicole whispered, and felt him stiffen for a moment.

"Beth was our overseer's daughter. Her mother died when Beth was born, and she had no brothers or sisters. My mother just naturally took the little girl under her wing. And James and I did, too. James was eight when Beth was born, and I was four. There was never any jealousy about the little baby my mother gave so much time to. I remember carrying her around myself. When she could walk, she followed us everywhere. James and I couldn't spend a day in the fields without little Beth right beside us. I learned to ride a horse with Beth behind me."

"And you fell in love with her."

"Not fell, exactly. Both James and I were always in love with her."

"Yet she married James."

Clay was quiet for a moment. "It wasn't like that. I don't think anyone ever mentioned it, but we always knew she would marry James. I don't guess he ever actually proposed. I remember we had a party for Beth's sixteenth birthday, and James said didn't she think it was time they set a date. The twins were born before she was seventeen."

"What was she like?"

"Happy," Clay said quietly. "She was the happiest person I ever knew. She loved so many people. She was a woman full of energy, always laughing. One year, the crops were so bad we thought we were going to have to sell Arundel Hall. Even Mother stopped smiling. But not Beth. She told us all to stop feeling sorry for ourselves and *do* something. By the end of the week, we were able to map out a plan of economy so we'd survive the winter. It wasn't an easy winter, but we were able to keep the plantation, all because of Beth."

"Yet they all died," Nicole whispered, thinking of her own family as much as his.

"Yes," he said quietly. "There was a cholera epidemic. There were many deaths throughout the county. First my father died, then my mother. I didn't think any of us would recover from the blow, but in a way I was glad they went together. They wouldn't have liked being separated."

"But you still had James and Beth and the twins."

"Yes," he smiled. "We were still a family."

"You didn't want your own home, your own wife and children?" she asked.

He shook his head. "It sounds odd now, but I was content. There were women when I wanted them. There was a pretty little weaver who—" He stopped and chuckled. "I don't guess you want to hear about that."

Nicole vigorously nodded her head in agreement.

"I don't guess I ever met anyone who fit in with the three of us. We'd spent our childhoods together, and we knew each other's thoughts and wishes as well as our own. James and I worked together, rarely speaking even, then we'd go home to Beth. She . . . I don't know how to say it, she made us welcome. I know she was James's wife, but she took care of me just as well. She was always cooking things for me, making me new shirts."

He stopped. He held Nicole close to him, buried his face in her sweet-smelling hair.

"Tell me about Bianca," she whispered.

His voice was very low when he spoke. "At one of the house parties Beth gave, a visitor, a man from England, kept staring at Beth. Finally, he told her that he'd recently met a young woman who could be Beth's twin. James and I laughed at him because we knew no one could be like our Beth. But Beth was very interested. She asked the man a hundred questions and carefully took down Bianca Maleson's address. She said that if she ever visited England, she'd see if she could find Miss Maleson."

"But you went to England first."

"Yes. We felt we weren't getting as good a price from our English markets for our cotton and tobacco as we should have gotten. At first, James and Beth planned to go and I'd stay here with the twins, but Beth discovered she was going to have another baby. She said nothing would make her risk losing the baby on an ocean voyage, so I'd have to go alone."

"And she asked you to go see Bianca."

Clay's body turned rigid as he gripped Nicole tightly. "James and Beth were drowned only days after I left, but it took months for the news to reach me in England. I had just finished my business and had traveled to Bianca's house. By then I was terribly homesick. I was tired of poorly cooked meals and having to arrange for my shirts to be washed. I only wanted to go home to my family. But I knew Beth would have my hair if I didn't make an effort to see this woman who was supposed to look like her. I'd been invited to stay with the Englishman who'd told Beth about Bianca. When Bianca walked into the room, all I did was stare. Right then, I wanted to grab her and hug her and ask her about James and the twins. It was hard for me to believe she wasn't Beth."

He stopped for a moment. "The next day, a man came to tell me about James and Beth. He'd been sent by Ellen and Horace, and it'd taken him a long time to find me."

"It was shock as much as grief, wasn't it?" Nicole said from experience.

"I was stunned. I couldn't believe it was true, but the man had seen both of them taken from the river. All I could think was that when I returned to Arundel Hall, it would be empty. My parents were gone, and now James and Beth were gone. I thought about remaining in England, having Horace sell the plantation."

"But Bianca was there."

"Yes, Bianca was there. I began to think that Beth wasn't really gone, that it was an omen that news of her death reached me while I was near a woman so like her. At least I thought Bianca was like her. All I could do was stare at her and tell myself that Beth was still alive, at least someone I loved was still with me. I asked Bianca to marry me. I wanted her to return to Virginia with me so I wouldn't have to enter an empty house, but she said she needed time. I had no time. I knew I needed to go home. Knowing that Bianca was going to join me soon, I felt I could face the plantation, and I hoped the work would help me forget."

"Nothing can make you forget."

He kissed her forehead. "I did the work of two men, three maybe, but nothing could even dull the pain. I stayed away from the house as much as possible. The emptiness of the place screamed at me. The neighbors tried to help, they even tried to find me a wife, but I only wanted things the way they were."

"You wanted Beth and James back."

"Every day, the idea of Beth once again sitting beside me grew stronger and stronger. I accepted James's death, but I was haunted by Bianca. I thought she could replace Beth."

"So you arranged for her to be kidnapped and brought to you."

"Yes. It was a desperate measure, but I felt desperate, like I was going crazy."

Nicole moved her cheek against his chest. "No wonder you were so angry when you found out I'd been married to you instead of Bianca. You were expecting a tall blonde, and you got—"

"A little dark beauty with a funny mouth," he laughed. "If you'd taken a pistol to me, I'd have deserved it. I put you through a lot then."

"But you were expecting Bianca!" she said in his defense, lifting her head to look at him.

He pushed her back to his shoulder. "Thank God I didn't get her! I was a fool to think any human could replace another."

His words sent a thrill through her. "Do you still love Bianca?"

"I never did. I know that now. All I saw was her resemblance to Beth. Even when she came here, I never listened to her or thought about her as anything except Beth. Yet even in that state of ignorance, I knew something was wrong. I thought that when Bianca was in my house everything would be all right again, that I would feel like I did when Beth was alive."

"But you didn't?" Nicole said with hope in her voice.

"I have you to thank for that. Even though I say I didn't hear Bianca, I think that some part of my small brain must have. All I knew was that I didn't want to return home at night, that I was working harder than I ever had in the last year. But when you were living in the house, I wanted to come home. When Bianca was at the house, I preferred the fields, especially the fields closest to the mill."

Nicole smiled and kissed his chest through his shirt. His words were the most wonderful she'd ever heard.

"It took Wes to knock some sense into me," he continued. "When Wes first saw Bianca, I could see how he was affected. I felt justified then for having her in my house and not you. I knew Wes would understand."

"I don't think Wesley likes Bianca."

Clay chuckled and kissed the tip of her nose. "That's a polite way of putting it. When he told me he thought she was a vain, arrogant bitch, I hit him. It made me sick, and I didn't know if I was sick from hitting my friend or from hearing the truth. I left the house and didn't return for two days. I had a lot of thinking to do. It took me a while, but I began to see what I'd done. And I made myself face the fact that Beth was dead. I'd tried to bring her back through Bianca, but that couldn't work. What I had, but had ignored for the most part, was the twins. If James and Beth still lived, it was through their children and not some stranger. If I wanted to give Beth anything, it would be a good mother for the twins she loved so much, and not one who knocked Alex in the water because he tore her dress."

"How did you know about that?"

"Roger, Janie, Maggie, Luke," he said with disgust. "Everyone seemed to think it was his duty to tell me about Bianca. They'd all known Beth, and I guess they could sense that most of my attraction to her lay in that resemblance."

"Why did you ask me to the party?" she asked, holding her breath.

He laughed and hugged her tightly. "When it comes to brains, I think we have equally small ones. When I realized that I was trying to replace Beth with Bianca, I also knew why I spent so much time staring at the mill wharf—which needs repairing, I might add. There's a sawmill on the other side of the Backes's plantation."

"Clay!"

He laughed again. "I love you. Didn't you know that? Everyone else did."

"No," she whispered. "I wasn't sure."

"You nearly tore me apart the night of the storm when you told me about your grandfather and said you loved me." He paused for a moment. "You left me the next day. Why? We spent such a night together, then the next morning you were cold to me."

She remembered clearly the portrait in Clay's office. "The portrait in your office is Beth, isn't it?" She felt him nod against her. "I thought it was Bianca, and it looked like a shrine. How could I compete with a woman you worshipped?"

"It's gone now. I put the portrait back over the fireplace in the dining room. The pieces of garment I locked in a trunk to be stored with the others. Maybe Mandy will want them someday."

"Clay, what happens now?"

"I told you. I want you to marry me again, publicly, with lots of witnesses."

"What about Bianca?"

"I've already told her that she's to return to England."

"How did she take it?"

He frowned. "She wasn't what I'd call gracious, but she'll obey me. I'll see she is paid. It's a good thing I came to my senses as soon as I did. She's already run up enormous bills." He stopped suddenly and laughed at her. "You're the only woman I've ever met who is so considerate of her enemies."

Nicole moved away from him and looked up in a startled way. "Bianca isn't my enemy. Maybe I should love her since she was the one who gave you to me."

"I don't believe *gave* is the proper word."

Nicole giggled impishly. "I don't believe it is either."

He smiled down at her and caressed her temple. "You'll forgive me for being blind and stupid?"

"Yes," she whispered before his mouth closed on hers. The knowledge that he loved her made her especially passionate. She wrapped her arms about his neck and pulled him very close to her. Her body arched against his.

Neither of them noticed the first cold drops of rain. Only when the sky split with a slash of lightning and opened with a pure sheet of icy rain did they break apart.

"Come on!" Clay yelled as he stood up and pulled her with him.

She turned toward the path to the sloop, but Clay pulled her in another direction. They ran toward the side of the clearing opposite the river. While Nicole stood in the rain, rubbing her cold upper arms, Clay withdrew his knife and slashed at some hedges.

"Damn!" he cursed loudly when he couldn't seem to find what he wanted. Suddenly, the bushes broke away and revealed what looked to be a little cave. Clay threw his arm around Nicole and nearly pushed her inside.

She shivered. Her dress was soaked from the cold rain.

"Just a minute, and I'll have a fire going," Clay said as he knelt at one corner near the opening.

"What is this place?" she asked, kneeling beside him.

"We found this little cave—James, Beth, and I—and it's what caused us to plant the hedges and trees. James had one of the bricklayers show him how to build a fireplace." He nodded toward the rather crude structure where he was now working to build a fire. He sat back on his haunches as the fire took hold. "We always thought this was the world's most secret place, but when I was older I realized the smoke was as good as a flag. No wonder our parents never objected to our 'disappearances.' All they had to do was look out a window to see where we were."

Nicole stood up and looked around her. The cave was about twelve feet long and ten feet wide. Along the walls were set a couple of crude benches and a large pine chest, its hinges rusty and broken. Something glittered from a niche in the wall. She went to it. Her hand touched something cool and smooth. She withdrew it and held it up to the light from the fire. It was a large piece of greenish glass, and embedded inside was a tiny silver unicorn.

"What is this?"

Clay turned and smiled up at her. For a moment he was serious, then he reached out and took the piece of glass as Nicole sat beside him. He studied it as he spoke, turning it in his hands. "Beth's father bought the little unicorn for her in Boston. She thought it was so pretty. One day we were here in the cave, James had just finished the fireplace, and Beth said she hoped we would always be friends. Suddenly, she took the unicorn off the chain around her neck and said we were going to see the glassblower. James and I followed her, knowing she was up to something. She got old Sam to work up a ball of clear glass. Then the three of us touched the unicorn and swore always to be friends. Then Beth dropped it into the hot glass. She said that was so no one else could ever touch it." He looked at the glass one more time, then handed it back to Nicole. "It was a silly, childish act, but it seemed to mean a lot then."

"I don't think it's silly, and it certainly seemed to work," she smiled.

Clay wiped his hands together, then looked at her, his eyes dark. "Weren't we doing something interesting before the rain started?"

Nicole looked at him in wide-eyed innocence. "I have no idea what you mean."

Clay stood, went to the dilapidated old chest, and pulled out two of the dustiest, most moth-eaten blankets that had ever been seen. "Not exactly pink silk sheets," he said, laughing at some joke Nicole didn't share. "But better than the dirt." He turned and held out his arms for her.

Nicole ran to him, hugged him close to her. "I love you, Clay," she whispered. "I love you so much that it scares me."

He began pulling the pins from her hair, dropping them to the floor. He stroked the black, silky mass of her hair. "Why should you be frightened?" he said softly, his lips playing along her neck. "You're my wife, the only one I want or will ever have. Think about us and our children."

Nicole felt her knees begin to weaken as Clay's tongue touched her earlobe. "Children," she said under her breath. "I'd like children."

He pulled away from her and smiled. "Creating children isn't easy. It takes a lot of . . . ah, hard work."

Nicole laughed, her eyes dancing in delight. "Maybe we should practice," she said solemnly. "All work becomes easier with . . . experience."

"Come here, imp," he said, and picked her up into his arms. He carefully laid her down on the blankets. Somehow, the musty smell of them fit the atmosphere. It was a place of ghosts, ghosts Nicole felt smiling on them.

Clay unfastened the buttons of her wet dress, and as he revealed a piece of skin he kissed it. He pulled the dress out from under her, then off as if she were a child. Nicole removed her chemise herself. She was hungry to bare her skin to his touch. Clay moved her across his knee, his arm behind her back as he touched and teased her body. "You're so beautiful," he said, the firelight playing on her skin.

"You're not disappointed that I'm not blonde?"

"Hush!" he commanded in a mock stern voice. "I wouldn't change one color of you."

She turned to look up at him, then began to unbutton his shirt. His chest was smooth and hard with muscle, lightly covered with hair. His stomach was strong and flat. Nicole felt her own muscles tighten at the sight of his beautiful body. His lean hardness was such a contrast to her own softness. She enjoyed his body. She enjoyed watching him walk, the way his muscles played beneath his skin as he worked to control an unruly horse. She liked to watch him throw hundred-pound bags of grain onto a wagon. She shivered as she pressed her mouth to the warm brown skin that covered the ridges of his stomach.

Clay was watching her, saw the range of emotions cross her expressive eyes. When at last they turned to the smoky brown of sheer lust, he felt chills run up his spine. The woman fired him in a way no other ever had. No longer did he care for the words of love, but he wanted her. He nearly tore his clothes from his body, pulling off the long, tight boots faster than he ever had before.

No longer were his kisses sweet and gentle, but as he took her ear in his mouth he threatened to tear it from her head. His lips, tongue, and teeth ran down her neck, across her shoulder, then back again to her breast.

Nicole arched under his touch. His tongue on her breast sent little sparks of fire through her veins. His mouth traveled down her stomach, making it contract under the sweet torment of his kisses. She buried her hands in the thick richness of his hair, dragging his mouth back to her own.

"Clay," she whispered before his mouth on hers stopped her words.

He moved his body on top of hers, and she smiled, her eyes closed, as she felt the weight of him. He was hers, thoroughly and completely hers.

When he entered her, it was, as always, a surprise to her, a shock of delight as she reexperienced his maleness. He filled her completely until she thought she would die from ecstasy.

They moved together, slowly at first, until Nicole felt she could bear the slowness no longer. Her hands caressed the round, hard smoothness of his back and buttocks, feeling the muscles work, feeling the power that lay just under his hot skin.

When they came together, Nicole could feel the contractions in her body from her waist to her toes. When Clay rolled off her and gathered her close to him, her legs throbbed. She smiled and snuggled against him, kissing his shoulder, tasting the salt of his sweat.

They fell asleep together.

Chapter 13

WHEN NICOLE first awoke, she thought she was back in the cave with Clay. But the sun across the bed, shining through Ellen's lacy curtains, soon reminded her where she was. The place beside her was empty, but the pillow still bore an indentation from Clay's head.

She stretched luxuriously, the sheet falling away from her nude body. After they'd made love in the cave last night, they'd slept for hours. When they awoke, the moon had risen, the fire was out, and they were both cold. They had quickly bundled into their damp clothes and run for the sloop. Clay sailed it slowly down the river to the Backes's house.

Once inside the house, Clay had raided the kitchen and returned to Nicole with a large basket of fruit, cheese, bread, and wine. He laughed as Nicole became amorous after only half a glass of wine. They made love again amid the food, kissing and eating, teasing and laughing, until they fell asleep again in each other's arms.

Nicole moved and pulled a piece of apple out from under her right hip. She smiled at it before setting it on the bedside table. She knew Ellen's sheets would be stained for life after their antics of last night. But how did one apologize for that? Could she say she'd poured wine into the small of Clay's back and then sipped it out, unfortunately spilling some when he grew impatient and turned over before she could drink it all? No, that wasn't something you could tell your hostess.

She threw back the covers, then rubbed her bare arms. There was the first nip of fall in the air. In the wardrobe hung a velvet dress of just the color of the wine she and Clay had shared last night. Quickly, she put it on, buttoning the tiny pearl buttons to her neck. It was long-sleeved, high-necked, fitting tightly across her breasts and then falling away in a gathered skirt to the floor. It was a simple, elegant gown, and it was warm, just what she would need for today's coolness.

She went to the mirror to arrange her hair. She wanted to look especially nice today. Clay had said that at the noon dinner he'd announce their plans for a second marriage and invite the people to his house for a Christmas wedding. Nicole had been able to persuade him to wait and prepare a party for the event. Ellen's guests would begin leaving this afternoon, and he wanted to make the announcement before they left.

Nicole got lost only once before she found the garden door that led to the lawn where the tables had been newly set up. Several people milled about the tables, talking slowly and eating quietly. Everyone seemed to be tired and ready for the long party to end. Nicole looked forward to returning to Arundel Hall—as its mistress.

She saw Bianca sitting alone at a little table under an elm tree. She felt a twinge of conscience at the sight. In a way, it didn't seem fair that the Englishwoman had come such a long way, expecting to be married, only to discover her fiancé was already married. Hesitantly, Nicole took a step forward. Then Bianca looked up, over a plate of food, at her. Bianca's eyes were filled with the fires of hatred. Her look was lethal if not fatal.

Nicole's hand flew to her throat, and she backed away. Suddenly, she felt like a hypocrite. Of course, she could afford to offer Bianca sympathy, since she—Nicole—had won. Winners can always afford to be gracious. She turned toward the tables and picked up a plate, but her appetite was gone.

"Excuse me, Mrs. Armstrong," said a man who towered over her.

Nicole looked up from the food she was pushing around on her plate. "Yes?"

She saw a tall, strong young man, but his eyes bothered her. They were little and close together, and now they glittered wildly.

"Your husband asked if you'd meet him at the sloop."

Nicole rose instantly and walked around the table toward the man.

He chuckled. "I like an obedient woman. Clay sure knows how to train his."

Nicole started to make a retort to his statement, but she stopped herself. She knew any answer she made would not give him the setdown he deserved. "I thought Mr. Armstrong was at the horse races," she said, purposely using the formal title. She followed him across the lawn toward the river.

"Not many men let their women know where they are *all* the time," he smirked, eying her up and down, his little eyes lingering on her breasts.

Nicole stopped where she was. "I think I'll return to the house. Would you please tell my husband that I'll meet him there?" She turned on her heel and started back toward the house.

She hadn't taken two steps before the man's hand clamped hard on her upper arm.

"Listen to me, you little Frenchy," he said, his lips drawn back in a snarl. "I know all about you. I been told about your lyin', foreign ways. I know what you done to my cousin."

Nicole stopped struggling and stared at him. "Cousin? Release me or I'll scream."

"You do, and that husband of yours won't live till mornin'."

"Clay! What have you done with him? Where is he? You hurt him, and I'll . . . I'll—"

"What?" he said avidly. "You sure are hot for him, ain't you? I told Pa you were little better than a bitch in heat. I seen the way you flaunt yourself around him. No good woman'd do that."

"What do you want?" Nicole said, her eyes large.

He smiled at her. "It ain't what I want so much as what I'm gonna take. Now, are you listenin'?"

She nodded silently, her stomach rolling.

"You're gonna walk with me to that wharf where my family's boat's tied. It ain't fine like you're used to, but it's good enough for a woman like you. Then you're gonna get on the boat real quiet and we're gonna take a little trip."

"To Clay?"

"Why, sure, honey. I told you he was gonna be all right if you just did what I said."

Nicole nodded, and the man's hand moved to her elbow, but the grip was just as hard as before. All she could think of was that Clay was in some kind of danger and she must help him.

He led her to the far end of the wharf where two other men waited in an old, patched sloop. One was an older man, skinny and dirty, with a Bible under his arm. "There she is!" he said loudly. "A Jezebel, a fallen, sinful woman."

Nicole glared at the man, then started to speak, but the man who'd held her arm gave her a sharp push. She landed hard against the young boy.

"I told you to keep quiet," growled the man who shoved her. "Take care of her, Isaac, and see she don't make any noise."

Nicole looked up at the boy, who put his hands on her shoulders. His touch was gentle. His features were softer, less harsh than the other two men's. She lurched forward as the sloop moved, and the boy steadied her. She turned to look back at the Backes's house. There, riding across the lawn, wearing a large white hat, was Clay. The horse he rode was crowned with a large wreath of flowers. He had obviously just won a race and was celebrating.

Nicole's mind clicked instantly. The men didn't have Clay, had never held him. She knew she was close enough to the house that a scream could be heard. She opened her mouth and filled her lungs, but she never made that scream because a large, hard fist slammed into her face. She slumped, unconscious, into Isaac's arms.

"You had no reason to do that, Abe!" Isaac said as he supported Nicole's limp body.

"Like hell I didn't. If you hadn't been staring at her with blind eyes, you'd have seen she was about to scream."

"There are other ways she could have been stopped," Isaac said. "You could have killed her!"

"No doubt you'd have used kisses to stop her," Abe sneered. "I'm sure she's used to those. Why don't you take her now? Me and Pa'll keep watch."

"You're talkin' sinful, boy!" Elijah Simmons said. "That woman is a harlot, a sinner, and we're takin' her to save her soul."

"Sure, Pa," Abe said as he winked at Isaac.

Isaac looked away from his brother and picked Nicole up in his arms. He ignored Abe's smirks. He held her as he sat on the deck, his back against the rail. He hadn't realized she was so tiny, more like a child than a full-grown woman.

He grimaced when Abe tossed him some rope and a dirty handkerchief and ordered him to tie her up. At least if he did it, he knew he wouldn't hurt her fine skin.

He'd wrestled with himself for the last day, ever since Abe had said they were going to kidnap pretty little Mrs. Armstrong. Abe had told their father that Clay was really married to their cousin Bianca, but that the harlot Nicole had bewitched Clay until he'd deserted Bianca and openly lived with the French whore. That had been enough for Elijah. He was ready to stone the girl.

Isaac had been against the kidnapping from the beginning. He wasn't sure he believed everything Bianca said, even if she was his own cousin. She hadn't been exactly overjoyed to meet them that first day. But Abe kept ranting about the injustice that had been done when Nicole substituted herself for their cousin. He said they'd kidnap Nicole only long enough to get the marriage ended and allow Bianca time to marry Clay.

Now, holding Nicole across his lap, Isaac couldn't imagine her as a liar and a woman greedy for Clay's money. She seemed really to care for Clay. But Abe said that any woman who looked at a man like Nicole looked at Clay wasn't a good woman. Wives had to be good woman, quiet and unphysical like their mother. Isaac was puzzled by Abe's words, because if he had a choice, he'd rather marry a woman like Nicole than one like his mother. Maybe he and Nicole were two of a kind, both of them bad.

"Isaac!" Abe commanded. "Stop your dreamin' and pay attention. She's comin' to, and I don't want her screamin'. Put that gag on her."

Isaac obeyed his brother, just as he'd done all his life.

Slowly, Nicole opened her eyes. Her jaw and head hurt horribly, and it took a moment for her eyes to clear. She tried to flex her jaw, but something held her, nearly strangled her.

"Be quiet," Isaac said. "You're safe with me." His voice was a whisper, meant only for her ears. "I'll take the gag off in a minute, when we get there. Close your eyes and rest."

"She awake yet, that daughter of Satan?" Elijah called back to his younger son.

Nicole looked up at the boy who held her. She didn't want to trust any of them, but she had no other choice. She watched as he slowly blinked his eyes at her. Understanding, she closed her own, blocking out the sunlight.

"No, Pa," Isaac called. "She's sleepin'."

* * *

"Wes," Clay said, a frown making a crease between his brows. "Have you seen Nicole?"

Wes looked away from the pretty redhead who fluttered her lashes at him. "You lost her already, Clay? I think I'm going to have to give you lessons in keeping your women," he teased. He stopped when he saw his friend's face. He set down his mug of ale and followed Clay away from the tables. "You're worried, aren't you? How long has it been since you've seen her?"

"This morning. I left her to sleep while I went to the races. Ellen said she saw Nicole come downstairs but hasn't seen her since. I asked some of the women, but none of them has seen her."

"Where's Bianca?"

"Eating," Clay said. "I checked her first. There's not much she could do anyway. Several women said Bianca hasn't left the tables all day."

"Could Nicole have gone for a walk, maybe just looking for some peace and quiet?"

Clay frowned harder. "At dinner we were to announce that we planned a second marriage at Christmas. We were going to invite everyone to a party."

"Dinner was over an hour ago," Wes murmured as he watched several of the guests walk toward the wharf. They were leaving to go home. "She wouldn't have missed that."

"No," Clay said flatly, "she wouldn't."

The men's eyes met. Both were remembering James's and Beth's deaths. If even an accomplished sailor like James could drown—

"Let's get Travis," Wes said.

Clay nodded once, then turned back to the remaining guests. The knot in his stomach was growing larger.

When the question of Nicole's safety was raised, the reaction of the guests was immediate. All chores were stopped and entertainment ceased. The women quickly organized a plan to comb the woods surrounding the plantation. The children ran from one dependency to another to see if Nicole could be found. The men went to the river.

"Can she swim?" Horace asked.

"Yes," Clay said, his eyes scanning the water, looking for a small, dark-haired body.

"Did you have a fight with her? Maybe she got a ride back to Arundel Hall."

Clay turned on Travis. "No! Goddamn it! We didn't have a fight. She wouldn't have left without telling me."

Travis put his hand on Clay's shoulder. "Maybe she's in the woods picking walnuts and forgot the time." His voice said he didn't believe that any more than Clay did. From what he'd seen of Clay's new wife, she was a sensible, considerate young woman. "Horace," he said quietly, "let's get the dogs."

Clay turned back toward the house. It was all he could do to keep his rage under control. He was angry at himself for leaving her alone for even a few minutes and angry at her for whatever had taken her from him. But the worst of his anger was helplessness. She could be ten feet away from him, or fifty miles, and he had no idea where to start looking.

No one noticed Bianca standing to one side, a full plate in her hand, smiling. Her work was done now, and she could go home. She was tired of hearing people ask who she was and why she lived with Clay.

The dogs were confused by so many scents from so many people. They seemed to find Nicole's scent everywhere, and they were probably right.

While Horace worked with the dogs, Clay began to question people. He talked individually to every man, woman, and child on the enormous plantation. But it was always the same—no one remembered seeing her that morning. One of the slaves said he had served her some scrambled eggs but he couldn't remember what she had done after that.

At night, the men carried torches into the woods. Four men took their sloops up and down the river, calling for Nicole. The far side of the river was searched, but there was no sign of her.

When morning came, the men began to straggle back to the house. They avoided Clay's hot look of misery.

"Clay!" a woman shouted, running toward him.

His head jerked up immediately to see Amy Evans waving her bonnet at him as she ran from the wharf.

"Is it true?" Amy asked. "Is your wife missing?"

"Do you know something?" Clay demanded. His eyes were sunken in his head, his face covered with unshaved whiskers.

Amy put her hand to her breast, her heart pounding from the run. "Last night, one of the men stopped at our house and asked if we'd seen your wife. Ben and I said we hadn't, but this morning at breakfast, Deborah, my oldest, said she'd seen Nicole with Abraham Simmons down by the wharf."

"When!" Clay said, grabbing the stout little woman by the shoulders.

"Yesterday morning. I sent Deborah back to the sloop to see if she could find our shawls because it was too cool without them. She said she saw Abe with his hand on Nicole's arm, leading her toward the river. She said she never liked Abe, she wanted to stay away from him, so she went to our sloop, got the shawls, and never looked back."

"Did she see Nicole get on the Simmons's boat?"

"No, nothing. They were blocked from sight by that big cypress tree, and Deborah wanted to get back to the races. She didn't think anything about it, didn't even remember it until this morning at breakfast when Ben and I were talking about your wife's disappearance."

Clay was staring at the woman. If Nicole had gotten onto the boat, then she was still alive. She hadn't been drowned as he'd begun to fear. And there could be a hundred reasons why she'd gone with Abe Simmons. All the man had to do was say someone needed her, and she'd never look back.

Clay's hands tightened on Amy's strong shoulders. Then he bent and gave her a resounding kiss on the mouth. "Thank you," he breathed, his eyes once again regaining color.

"Any time, Clay," Amy said, laughing.

Clay released her and turned around. His friends and neighbors were standing quietly by. None of them had had a wink of sleep all night.

"Let's go," Travis said as he slapped Clay on the shoulder. "Elijah's wife is probably having another baby, and Abe grabbed the first woman he saw."

Clay and Travis looked at each other for a long moment. Neither of them believed his words. Elijah was crazy and far from harmless. Abe was a sullen, high-tempered young man who openly resented the wealth of the planters around him.

Clay turned away when someone touched his arm. Janie stood there, a full basket of food held out to him. "Take this," she said quietly. For the first time since Clay had known her, her cheeks were no longer pink. Her whole face was gray with worry.

Clay took the basket from her and caressed her hand firmly. Then he looked back at Travis and at Wes, who stood beside his brother. He nodded once, and the three men walked quickly toward Clay's sloop. Wes ran to his sloop first, and when he joined Clay and his brother, he carried a brace of pistols. The men were grimly silent as they cast off and started downriver toward the Simmons's farm.

All day long, Nicole wavered between sleep and unconsciousness. When she was awake, the trees passing above her seemed unreal, patterns of shade and sunlight. Isaac had placed her carefully on a pile of rags and old feed bags. The slow drifting of the boat and the dull ache of her jaw made her calm, unworried about the bindings on her ankles and wrists, the gag across her mouth.

The river system of Virginia was extensive. Abe sailed the little sloop in and out of tributaries that linked one major river to another. There were some waterways that were so narrow that the two men had to use oars to propel themselves between the enclosing trees.

"Abe, where are you going?" Isaac asked.

Abe smiled secretly. He had no intention of informing his brother of his destination. He'd found the little island years ago, and it'd always stayed in the back of his mind that someday it would be useful. Soon after they'd gotten the woman on board, Abe had let his father off at their farm. He knew that soon the men would be there to search for the woman, and old Elijah would hold them off. Elijah would never lie about the fact that he'd taken the woman, but it would be hours before anyone would make any sense out of his rantings. Abe smiled at his own cleverness. Now all he had to do was control the boy. He glanced back at the woman, tied helplessly, quietly lying on the heap of rags. He smiled and wet his lips.

At sundown, Abe guided the boat toward shore.

Isaac stood up and frowned. It had been an hour since they'd seen a light from a house. For some time, the water had been little more than stagnant green slime. The air was fetid and hostile. "Let's get out of here," Isaac said, looking about him. "Nobody could live in this stench."

"Exactly what I have planned. Jump down there and get that rowboat. Do it!" Abe commanded as Isaac started to speak.

Isaac was too used to obeying his older brother. He didn't like the slimy water, and even as he watched, a long snake slithered across its surface. He jumped over one side of the sloop, felt the greenish brown mud suck at his feet up to his ankles. He waded through it, the foamy slime attaching itself to his knees, and untied the little rowboat. He hopped inside and used the oars to guide the rowboat to the side of the sloop.

Abe stood on deck holding Nicole in his arms. He handed her down to his little brother, then lowered himself into the rowboat. "Put her in the bottom and grab the oars," he commanded. "We've still got a long way to go."

Isaac did as he was told, resting Nicole against one of his legs. He didn't like the look of fear in her eyes, and he wanted to reassure her.

Abe snorted as he looked at his brother. "Don't get any ideas about her, boy. She knows who she belongs to."

Isaac looked away, remembering Nicole with Clay. He had no idea his brother meant differently.

It wasn't easy maneuvering through the thick water. Several times Isaac had to stop and free his oars from whatever piece of unseen filth held them. It was growing dark, and the overhanging trees completely blocked what little light there was. Isaac looked up, and it seemed to him that the trees were dipping toward them, trying to devour him.

"Abe, I don't like this place. We can't leave her here. Why don't we take her back to the farm?"

"Because she'd be found there, that's why. And I don't believe I mentioned leaving her here. There! Pull into shore there."

Isaac used his oars as poles to push the little rowboat to shore. Abe jumped out and searched beside a tree for a few moments before he found a lantern. He grunted in satisfaction that it was where he left it. He lit it quickly. "Come on, follow me," he said as he left Isaac to pick up Nicole.

"Just a few minutes and I'll take off the ropes," Isaac whispered as he held Nicole in his arms.

She nodded wearily, her head against his shoulder.

Abe held the lantern high and revealed a short, stout door that looked to be set in nothing but darkness. "I found this place a long time ago," he said proudly as he unfastened the latch.

It was a small, one-room, stone cabin. Inside it was bare except for the dirt and leaves on the floor.

Isaac put Nicole down, standing her on her unsteady feet, then took the gag off her mouth. She gasped as tears came to her eyes in gratefulness. He untied the ropes from her wrists. As he knelt to untie the bindings from her feet, Abe shouted at him.

"What the hell are you doing? I didn't tell you to untie her!"

Isaac glared at his brother in the darkness. "What can she do? Can't you see she's so tired now she can hardly stand up? Is there anything to eat around here? And what about some water?"

"There's an old well out back."

Isaac looked around in disgust. "What is this place? Why would anyone want to build something here?"

"It's my guess this wasn't always swamp. The river changed course and cut this part off. There's wild pigs around here, plenty of rabbits, and a couple of apple trees by the shore. Now stop askin' questions and get some water. I left a tin bucket here last time."

Reluctantly, Isaac went out into the blackness.

Nicole leaned against the stone wall. Her wrists and ankles ached, and she still didn't have enough feeling in them to move them. She was only vaguely aware when Abe came to stand beside her.

"Tired, are you?" he said quietly as his big hand caressed the side of her neck. "You're gonna be even more tired tomorrow after I get through with you. You ain't ever been loved like I'm gonna love you."

"No," she whispered, and took a step to the side, away from him. Her numb feet refused to work, and she fell forward onto her hands and knees.

"What did you do to her?" Isaac demanded from the doorway. He bent and lifted Nicole.

"My God, boy!" Abe said in a half laugh. "Somebody'd

think you were in love with her, the way you act. What is she to you anyway? You heard the story. She's little better'n a whore."

"Are you all right?" Isaac asked, his hands on Nicole's shoulders.

"Yes," she murmured.

Isaac moved away from her, then gave her a drink from a tin cup. She drank greedily. "That's enough," he said. "Let's sit down and get some rest." He put his arm around Nicole's shoulders and led her to the far wall.

"You are younger'n I thought," Abe said with distaste. He started to say more but he stopped.

Isaac sat on the floor, then pulled Nicole down beside him. "Don't be afraid," he said when she stiffened. "I won't hurt you."

She was too weary, too cold, too numb to care about propriety. When she sat beside Isaac, he pulled her head to his shoulder, and they both were instantly asleep.

"Isaac!" Abe called, pushing his little brother on the shoulder. "Wake up!" His eyes were on Nicole. It angered him that the bitch gave so much to his little brother. Isaac wasn't even a man yet, barely fifteen, and he'd never had a woman. Yet he sure acted like he knew about women, the way he handled that Nicole. Abe watched her, had watched her for the last hour as the daylight slowly entered the little cabin. Her black hair had come unpinned, and the dampness made little curls cling to her face. Her thick lashes curved across her cheek. And that mouth! It was about to drive him wild. It made him sick to see the way Isaac's arm was so possessive around the woman, his hand resting just under her velvet-clad breast.

"Isaac!" Abe called again. "You plannin' to sleep all day?"

Slowly, Isaac came awake. His arm tightened around Nicole, and he smiled down at her.

"Come on, get up," Abe said in disgust. "You got to go to the sloop and get the supplies."

Isaac nodded. He didn't question his brother about why he should make the trip instead of Abe. Isaac had always obeyed his brother. "Are you all right?" he asked Nicole.

She nodded mutely. "Why have I been brought here? Are you asking Clay for a ransom?"

"Go get the food," Abe commanded when Isaac started to speak. "I'll answer her questions. Go on!" he commanded when Isaac seemed to hesitate.

Abe stood in the doorway and watched his young brother walk down the path.

As soon as she was alone with him, Nicole knew she should be afraid of Abe. Yesterday, her mind hadn't been working clearly, but today she sensed the danger she was in. Isaac was a sweet and innocent boy, but there was nothing sweet or innocent about Abe. She stood up quietly.

Abe whirled on her. "Now we're alone," he said quietly. "You thought you were too good to have anything to do with me, didn't you? I seen the way you hung on Isaac, the way you let him touch you and hold you." He took a step toward her. "You one of those women what only likes young meat? You only like little boys?"

Nicole stood straight, her spine rigid, refusing to let this awful man see her fear. Her grandfather's voice came to her: "The Courtalains carry the blood of kings." Her eyes darted toward the door. Maybe she could get past him to the outside.

Abe chuckled deep in his throat. "There's no way to get out past me. You might as well just lay back and enjoy it. And don't expect Isaac to come rescue you either. He'll be gone for hours."

Nicole moved slowly along the wall. Whatever happened, she wouldn't give in to him easily.

Before she'd taken one good step, a long arm shot out and grabbed a handful of her hair. Slowly, very slowly, he wound the thick mass around his hand and drew her to him.

"Clean," he whispered. "I bet that's the cleanest hair I ever smelt. Some men don't like black hair, but I do." He chuckled. "I guess you're real lucky that I do."

"I don't think you'll get as much ransom if you harm me," she said, his face close to hers. His little eyes were almost black as he stared at her, and he smelled of old sweat and rotten teeth.

"You're a cool one," he said, grinning. "How come you ain't cryin' and beggin'?"

She gave him a cold look, refusing to allow her fear to show. Her grandfather had faced an angry mob. What was one dirty, evil-minded man compared to that?

He held her by the hair close to him. He ran his other hand over her shoulder, down her arm, his thumb caressing the curve of her breast. "Your value don't depend on what I do to you. As long as I keep you alive, I can have my fun with you."

"What do you mean?" Nicole thought maybe she could keep him talking.

"Never mind. I ain't interested in explainin' myself to you." His hand moved to the curve of her hip. "That's a real pretty dress, but it's gettin' in my way. Take it off!"

"No," she said quietly.

He pulled her hair until her neck threatened to break.

Her eyes teared from the pain, but still she would not undress herself. She would not play the whore for any man.

He released her abruptly, then laughed. "You are the haughtiest bitch I ever did meet." He went to the doorway and picked up the ropes Isaac had left on the floor. "Since you won't do it yourself, maybe I'll just have to help you. You know, I ain't ever seen a woman without a stitch of clothes on."

"No," Nicole whispered, and backed away, her hands vainly trying to hold on to the stone wall behind her.

Abe laughed as he lunged at her and grabbed her by one shoulder. She tried to twist away, but she couldn't as his thick fingers bit into her flesh. He forced her to her knees. Nicole moved forward and sank her teeth into the muscle just above his knee. The next moment, she was sent sprawling across the room.

"Damn you!" Abe swore. "You'll pay for that."

He grabbed her ankle and tied one end of a rope around it. The rough hemp cut into her already sore flesh. She kicked at him, but he held her easily. He grabbed her arms and tied the wrists together. There was an iron hook embedded in the stone wall where game had once been hung. Abe lifted Nicole by the rope around her wrists and tied her to it. Her feet barely touched the floor.

She gasped at the pain of her extended arms. He tied her feet together, then lashed the rope to another hook. She was helpless, tied tightly to the wall.

Abe stood back and admired his handiwork. "You don't look like such a fine lady now," he said, rubbing his leg where she'd bitten him. He took a long knife from his pocket.

Nicole's eyes widened at the sight.

"Now you look like you're gainin' the proper respect for a man. One thing my pa knows for sure is how to treat a woman. All them women at the Backes's house make me sick. Their husbands let 'em talk, give 'em money to bet on the horses. You'd think they were men, the way they acted. Some of 'em think they're better'n men. Last summer I asked one of those girls to marry me, and you know what she did? She laughed at me. I was payin' her a great honor, and she laughed at me! Just like you! You fit in right well with them. You're so pretty, married to a rich man, you couldn't even give me the time of day."

The pain in Nicole's arms was too much to allow her much room to think. Vaguely, she was aware of Abe's rantings. Maybe she had been guilty of ignoring him, of snubbing him. "Please release me," she whispered. "Clay will pay you whatever you want."

"Clay!" he sneered. "How can he give me what I want? Can

he give me a lifetime away from a crazy father? Can he make a real lady agree to marry me? No! But he can give me a few hours' pleasure with his lady."

He moved closer to her, the knife upraised. His eyes sparkled with threat. He slipped the knife under the first button of the bodice of her gown. She drew her breath in sharply as the cold steel touched her skin. The button popped off and flew across the little room.

One by one, he cut the buttons off, then he slashed the satin sash that held the dress under her breast. He put his hand to her and gently parted the wine-colored velvet. He caressed her right breast through her thin chemise.

"Nice," he whispered. "Real nice." He used the tip of the blade to cut the chemise away neatly.

Her breasts lay bare before him. Nicole closed her eyes, tears squeezing out at the corners.

Abe stepped back to admire her. "You don't look much like a lady now," he smiled. "You look just like them women in Boston. They liked me. They begged me to come back to them." Suddenly, his mouth turned hard. "Let's see the rest of you."

He inserted the knife at the top of the long skirt and very slowly slashed the velvet to the hem. It hung open, exposing the nearly transparent chemise beneath.

"Lace," Abe whispered as he lifted the hem of the chemise. "My ma always wanted a piece of real lace so she could make a collar for her Sunday dress. And here you're wearin' lace on your underclothes." With a swift, violent motion, he jerked the chemise away.

He stared at her nude body, the round hips, the small waist, and her breasts lifted high by her uplifted arms. He ran his hand up one thigh. "So this is what ladies look like under all their silks and velvets. No wonder Clay and Travis and them others let 'em backtalk."

"Abe!" Isaac called. "You inside? One of the oars broke

and—" He stopped as he entered the cabin doorway. What he saw nearly made him ill. Nicole was tied to the wall, her arms stretched far over her head. Abe's body blocked Isaac's view, but the boy could see the pieces of Nicole's dress, the shreds of her chemise hanging to the floor. Isaac's boyish face turned from confusion to anger to rage.

"You said she wouldn't be hurt," he said through clenched teeth. "I trusted you."

Abe turned on his little brother. "And I told you to go back to the sloop. I gave you an order, and I expected it to be obeyed." He still held his knife, now aimed at Isaac.

"So you could use her, is that why you wanted me out of the way? Were you planning to use her like you did the little Samuels girl? Her parents had to send her away after that. She was scared to go to sleep at night, scared you'd come for her. Only she wouldn't say who you were, but I knew."

"So what?" Abe said. "You make her sound like she was a child. She was engaged to one of the Peterson boys. She was givin' it to him, so why not to me?"

"You!" Isaac choked. "No woman would ever want you. I've seen 'em try to be nice to you, but you only wanted the ones you had to take." He grabbed the bucket at his feet and threw it at Abe's head. "I'm sick of watchin' you use women! I've had enough! You let her go!"

Abe easily dodged the flying bucket. He grinned maliciously. "Remember the last time you defied me, boy?" he said, circling, crouched over, the knife passing from one hand to the other.

Isaac glanced at Nicole when Abe moved away. He wasn't excited by the woman's helpless position. It repulsed him. He looked back at Abe. "I remember that I was twelve the last time," he said quietly.

"So the boy thinks he's become a man," Abe laughed.

"Yes, I have."

Isaac lunged so fast that Abe didn't really see his little brother move. He was used to a controllable, awkward child. He hadn't seen his brother grow up.

When Abe first felt his brother's fist in his face, he was astonished. He slammed back against the stone wall, the breath nearly leaving him. When he eased himself up, his rage matched Isaac's. No longer did he think he was fighting his own brother.

"Look out!" Nicole screamed at Isaac as Abe lunged forward. The knife blade sank into Isaac's thigh, and Abe pulled it up, making a deep, long slash.

Isaac gasped and jerked away from the knife. The cut was too deep to bleed much yet. He grabbed Abe's wrist, forcing his older brother down. The knife fell to the floor and, like a cat, Isaac grabbed it. Abe's arm swung out as he tried to take the knife, and he felt it cut into his shoulder.

He jumped back to the safety of the wall by the door, his hand over the cut in his shoulder. Blood was beginning to ooze between his fingers. "You want her for yourself, is that it?" he said through clenched teeth. "You can have her!" He turned quickly and slipped through the open doorway. He slammed the door shut, and Nicole and Isaac could hear the bolt being shot home.

Isaac stumbled toward the door and made one weak effort to throw his weight against it. His leg was beginning to bleed, and he was going into shock.

"Isaac!" Nicole called as she saw his eyes begin to close as he leaned his back against the door. "Cut me loose, and I'll help you. Isaac!" she called again when he didn't seem to hear her.

In a blur of pain, Isaac stumbled toward her and lifted his arm toward the ropes binding her hands.

"Cut it, Isaac," she encouraged when he seemed about to forget where he was and what he needed to do.

He used the last of his strength to saw at the ropes, which were, thankfully, half rotten. When the rope fell away, Isaac collapsed to the dirt floor of the cabin and Nicole fell forward onto her hands and knees. Quickly, she untied her ankles.

Abe's bloody knife was on the floor. Quickly, she cut away her chemise, tore it into strips, then cut away Isaac's trousers to expose his wound. It was deep but clean. She bound it tightly to stop the bleeding. Isaac seemed to be in shock, not saying anything, not moving. When she finished with his leg, she gave him a little water to drink, but he wouldn't take it.

Suddenly, she was so very tired. She sat down, leaned against the stone wall, and pulled Isaac's head into her lap. The contact seemed to soothe him. She stroked his dark hair away from his forehead, then put her head against the wall. They were locked inside a stout stone cabin. They had no food or other supplies. They were on a desolate island where no one could find them, yet Nicole suddenly felt safer than she had in the last twenty-four hours. She slept.

Chapter 14

THE SIMMONS farm was located on a backwater piece of land twelve miles upriver from the Armstrong plantation. It was worthless land, rocky and unfertile. The house was little more than a shack, small, filthy, the roof needing patching. The yard of hard-packed earth was filled with chickens, dogs, a litter of pigs, and several half-dressed children.

Travis tied the sloop to the rotting wharf while Clay jumped ashore and walked toward the house, the other men behind him. The children looked up from their chores to stare with sullen, uncurious eyes. Even as young as they were, they were beaten. They'd lived a life of constant hard work with a father who told them they were doomed to the fires of eternal damnation.

Clay ignored the children as he bellowed, "Elijah Simmons!"

The skinny old man appeared from inside the house. "What d'you want?" he asked, his little eyes sleepy, as if he'd just been awakened. He turned to one of the children, a little girl of no more than four. In her lap was a chicken, and she was wearily plucking the feathers from it. "You, girl!" Elijah said. "You better not leave any pinfeathers on that bird. You do, and I'll take you to the woodshed."

Clayton looked with disgust at the old man. He slept while his children labored. "I want to talk to you."

As the dirty old man began to wake up, his little eyes nar-

217

rowed to hardly more than slits. "So! The heathen has come to seek his salvation. You'll need forgiveness for your whoring ways."

Clay grabbed the man's shirt front, lifting him so that his feet barely touched the ground. "I don't need any of your preaching! Do you know where my wife is?"

"Your wife?" the man spat. "Scarlet women are not made into wives. She's a daughter of Satan and should be taken from the earth."

Clay's fist smashed into the man's long, bony face. He slammed against the doorjamb and slid downward slowly.

"Clay!" Travis said, his hand on his friend's arm. "You aren't going to get anything out of him. He's crazy." Travis turned to the children. "Where's your mother?"

The children looked up from the chickens and beans they were working with and shrugged. They were so beaten, so defeated, that not even seeing their father hit interested them.

"I'm here," said a soft voice from behind the men. Mrs. Simmons was even thinner than her husband. Her eyes were sunken, her cheeks hollow.

"We heard that my wife was seen getting into a boat with your son. She's been missing for nearly two days now."

Mrs. Simmons nodded tiredly as if the news was no shock to her. "I ain't seen her or nobody who's a stranger." She put her hand behind her lower back to ease the pain. She looked to be six months pregnant. She didn't deny the idea that her son could have had something to do with Nicole's disappearance.

"Where's Abe?" Wesley asked.

Mrs. Simmons shrugged. Her eyes darted toward her husband, who was regaining consciousness. She looked as if she wanted to escape before he was fully awake. "Abe ain't been home for days."

"You don't know where he went? Does he know?" Clay asked, nodding toward Elijah.

"Abe don't tell anybody much. He and Isaac took the sloop and went off. Sometimes they're gone for days."

"You don't know where?" Clay asked desperately.

Travis grabbed Clay's arm. "She doesn't know anything, and I doubt if the old man does either. Abe wouldn't have let them know what he planned. I think the best thing we can do is send out a search party. We can send people to the houses up and down the river and ask if they've seen anything."

Clay nodded silently. He knew that was the sensible thing to do, but it would take so much time. He tried to block out the vision of Abe and Nicole. Abe was a man warped by many years of living under Elijah's stern, insane rule. He turned away and headed back to the sloop. His rage at his sense of frustration was horrible! He wanted to destroy and maim, anything but this slow talking, talking, talking.

Wes walked behind Clay and his brother as they returned to the sloop. He stopped when a handful of pebbles hit his back.

"Psst! Over here."

Wes looked toward the shrubs by the river and could barely see the outline of a small figure. He walked toward it, and a young girl stepped out. She was a pretty little thing with big green eyes. Although she was cleaner than the other Simmons children, she was dressed in a ragged, thin cotton dress. "Did you want me?"

She stared at him in wonder. "You're one of them rich men, ain't ya? One of them what lives in a big house on the river?"

Wes knew he was rich compared to this child. He nodded once.

She looked around her to make sure no one else was near. "I know somethin' about where Abe's gone," she whispered.

Instantly, Wes bent to one knee. "What?" he demanded.

"My ma has a cousin, a lady cousin. That's hard to believe, ain't it? This cousin come to Virginia, and Abe said she was gonna give us some money. He and Pa and Isaac went to a party, a real party," she breathed. "I never been to a party."

"What did Abe say?" Wes asked impatiently.

"He came home, and I heard him tell Isaac they were gonna take some lady away and hide her. Then Mama's cousin would give them some of Mr. Armstrong's cows."

"Clay's?" Wes asked, puzzled. "Where did they take the lady? Who is your mother's cousin?"

"Abe only said he knew where he was takin' the lady, and he wouldn't even tell Isaac."

"Who is the cousin?"

"I don't remember her name. Abe said she was really Mr. Armstrong's wife, that the little one was a liar and wanted to take what should have been Abe's."

"Bianca," Wes said in wonder. He'd always felt she was at the bottom of all this; now he was sure. Wes stared at the child, then grinned at her. "Honey, if you were older, I think I'd kiss you for this. Here." He reached into his pocket and withdrew a twenty-dollar gold piece. "My mother gave it to me. It's yours now."

He pressed the gold into the child's hand.

She held onto it tightly and gaped at him. No one had ever given her anything except curses and beatings. To her, Wesley, so clean and smelling so good, was like an angel come to earth. Her voice was very quiet. "When I grow up, will you marry me?"

Wesley grinned broadly. "I just might." He stood up. Then, on impulse, he kissed her cheek heartily. "Come see me when you grow up." He turned away quickly and went toward the sloop where Clay and Travis waited impatiently. The news that Bianca was involved and had some information about Nicole's whereabouts sent all memory of the little girl from his mind.

But not so the child. She stood silently, watching the departing sloop. All her thirteen years she'd been isolated with her family. She'd never known there was anything outside her father's meanness, her mother's hardship. No one had ever been kind to her, no one had ever kissed her before. She touched her cheek where Wes had kissed her, then turned away. She had to find a hiding place for the gold piece.

Bianca saw Clay running from the wharf to the house, and she smiled to herself. She knew he would find out she was involved in Nicole's disappearance, and she was ready for him. She sipped on the last of the chocolate, finished the last apple turnover, then delicately wiped her mouth.

She was in the upstairs bedroom, and she smiled as she looked around it. It had changed greatly in the last two months. It wasn't so plain anymore. There was pink tulle everywhere, and the finials on the bed had been gilded. The mantel was covered with little porcelain figures. She sighed. It wasn't nearly complete, but she was working on it.

Clay burst into the room, his heavy boots clanging on the hardwood floors. Bianca winced at his crudeness and made a mental note to order more carpets.

"Where is she?" Clay demanded, his voice flat and hard.

"I take it I am supposed to know what that means." Bianca rubbed her plump upper arms and thought of the winter furs she'd order.

Clay took one long stride toward her, his eyes narrowed.

Bianca gave him a look of warning. "You touch me, and you'll never find her."

Clay backed away.

"How disgusting!" Bianca sneered. "The mere hint of danger to that lying little slut, and it makes you quiver."

"If you value your life, you'll tell me where she is."

"If you value *her* life, you'll keep your distance from me."

Clay gritted his teeth. "What do you want? I'll give you half of everything I own."

"Half? I thought she'd be worth more."

"All of it, then. I'll sign the entire plantation over to you."

Bianca smiled and walked to the window to straighten a curtain. She fingered the pink silk. "I don't know what I've done to make everyone think I'm stupid. I'm not unintelligent at all. If you signed this place over to me, then took your dear French whore away, what would happen to me?"

Clay clenched his fists to his sides. It was all he could do to keep from strangling her, but he would do nothing to endanger Nicole.

"I'll tell you what would happen to me," Bianca continued. "Within one year, this place would be bankrupt. You Americans are a disgusting lot. Your servants think they are as good as their masters. They would never obey me. Then, after I am bankrupt, what happens? Maybe you'd return and buy the place back for a song. You'd have everything you wanted, and I'd have nothing."

"Then what else can I give you?" Clay sneered.

"I wonder how much you really love my maid?"

Clay was silent, staring at her. He wondered how he could ever have thought she looked like Beth.

"You say you'll readily give me your property, but will you give me anything else in order to save her? Let me explain. I guess you know that I have cousins in America. Not exactly the type one would introduce in public, but useful—oh, yes, very useful. The man Abe was agreeable to anything I suggested."

"Where has he taken her?"

Bianca sneered at him. "Do you think I'm going to tell you so easily? After all you've done to me? You've humiliated me, used me. I've been here for months, waiting and waiting, while you flaunted that bitch in front of the whole world. Now it's my turn to keep *you* waiting.

"Now, where was I? My dear cousins, of course. In exchange for a few farm animals, they agreed to do whatever I wanted, including, I'm sure, murder."

Clay took a step backward. Murder had not entered his mind.

Bianca smiled at his reaction. "I believe you're beginning to understand. Now, let me tell you what I want. I want to be mistress of this plantation. I want you to run it, and I want to enjoy its benefits. When I appear in society, I want to do so as a respectable married woman, not as some unneeded appendage as I was at the Backes's party. I want the servants to obey me."

She turned away from him for a moment; then, when she looked back, her voice was quiet. "Are you familiar with the Revolution in France? Everyone reminds me of my former maid's relatives in France. They were, I believe, mostly beheaded. The mob is still angry in France, still looking for aristocrats to take to their guillotine."

She paused. "This time Abe only took her to an island buried in the Virginia waterways, but next time she'll be put on a ship back to France." She smiled. "And don't think that getting rid of Abe will rid you of the threat. He has relatives everywhere, all of whom would be glad to help me in any way I want. And if anything happens to me, including so much as a hangnail caused by you, I've left money to ensure that Nicole is returned to France."

Clay felt as if someone had kicked him in the stomach. He took a step backward and collapsed into a chair. The guillotine! The story of Nicole's grandfather, his head on a pike, was vivid. The way she had clung to him, terrified of all that had happened to her, whirled in his head. He couldn't risk the possibility of her returning to that horror.

His chin shot up. He'd keep her safe, always watch over her, never let her out of his sight. Then he knew how hopeless an idea that was. At the Backes's, she'd only been away from him for two hours. She would have to live like a prisoner. And one moment's lost vigilance, and . . . what? Death? Terror worse than what she'd already known? He couldn't do anything that would subject her to that possibility.

He tried to reason with Bianca. "I can give you enough money so that you'll have a good dowry. You can get an English husband if you have a dowry."

Bianca snorted. "You certainly don't understand women, do you? I would return to England in dishonor. All the men would say you had paid me rather than marry me. I'm sure I'd get a husband, but he'd only laugh at me, ridicule me. I want more out of life than that."

Clay stood up, knocking over the chair. "What would you get if you married me? You know I couldn't do more than hate you. Would you want that?"

"Any woman would rather be hated than laughed at. At least hate carries an amount of healthy respect with it. Actually, I think we'd make an admirable couple. I could run your house, be your hostess. I could give magnificent parties. I would be the perfect wife. And you, on the other hand, would never be troubled by a jealous wife. As long as you ran the plantation satisfactorily, you would be completely free to pursue whatever you wish, including women." She shuddered. "As long as you kept away from me."

"I assure you, you needn't fear that I'd ever touch you."

She smiled. "If that was meant as an insult, it wasn't taken as such. I have no desire to be touched by you or any other man."

"What about Nicole?"

"Of course, we now go back to her. If you marry me, she will be unharmed. She may even stay at the mill, and you can visit her for your . . . ah, more earthly pleasures. I'm sure the two of you will enjoy your rutting."

"What guarantees do I have that after we're married one of your cousins won't pop up in the middle of the night?"

Bianca looked thoughtful for a moment. "I'm not sure you do have a guarantee. Perhaps it will hold you to your bargain if you're never quite sure what will happen to her."

Clay stood still. No guarantee. His beloved's life depended on the whims of a greedy, selfish bitch. But what choice did he have? He could defy Bianca's demands and remain married to Nicole, but he'd live his life terrified that he would find her dead. Did he love her so selfishly that he'd risk her life for a few months of pleasure? After all, it wasn't his life that was in danger, but hers. Briefly, he thought of asking Nicole for her opinion, but he knew she'd risk anything to stay with him. Was his love so much weaker that he couldn't make sacrifices for her?

"Do you know where she is?"

"I have a map," Bianca smiled, as if she knew she'd won. "I want your agreement to my terms before I give it to you."

Clay swallowed over the lump in his throat. "The marriage cannot be annulled without the testimony of the doctor who witnessed the wedding. Very little can be done until he returns from England."

Bianca nodded. "I must agree to that. When he arrives, I expect the marriage to be annulled and ours to take place. If it is delayed at all, then Nicole will disappear. Is that clear?"

Clay sneered at her. "You've made yourself more than clear. I want the map."

Bianca walked across the room to one of the porcelain figures on the bow-front cabinet, picked it up, and pulled a little roll of paper from the inside. "It's crude," she said, "but I believe it's legible." She smiled. "Dear Abe has been on the island with her for two days and a night, and it'll be another night before you reach her. He said he planned to enjoy her. I'm sure he's had plenty of time by now. Of course, she was quite used before she ever went with Abe. By the way, have you asked yourself why she went so readily with him? Why didn't she scream? The wharf is only a short distance from where there were at least twenty people."

Clay took a step toward her, then stopped. If he so much as touched her, he'd kill her. He didn't think his conscience would hurt him much, but he knew she'd carry out her threats even from death. He turned on his heel, the map clutched tightly in his hand, and left the room.

Bianca stood at the window and watched him walk toward the wharf. A feeling of triumph surged through her body. She'd show them! She'd show them all! Her father had laughed at her when she'd packed to go to America. He'd said that Clay wouldn't be too upset when he found himself married to a lovely little filly like Nicole. He'd thought the story of the mistaken marriage was so good that he'd told at least twenty people before Bianca left England. No telling how many he'd told by now.

Bianca clenched her jaw hard. She knew what they were all saying. They said Bianca was just like her mother. Her mother had taken to her bed anything that was male. As a little girl, listening to the sounds from her mother's bedroom, Bianca had vowed never to allow a man to soil her, to put his rough, greedy hands on her fine white body.

When Bianca'd said she was going to America, her father accused her of being like that woman, said she was hot for the crude American, just the type of man her dead mother liked. How could Bianca return to England after having spent months in Clay's house? She'd have no wedding ring but a great deal of money, just the way her mother used to return from her many week-long trips. Even thousands of miles away, she could almost hear the snickers and see the smirks about what she'd done to earn the money.

No! She stamped her foot. She would own the Armstrong plantation no matter what she had to do. Then, she smiled, she'd invite her father to visit her. She'd show him her wealth, her husband, their separate bedrooms. She'd prove to him that she wasn't like her mother. Yes, she smiled. She'd show them!

"Did she tell you?" Wes asked as soon as Clay reached the sloop.

He held out the map. "She told me." His voice was dead.

"That bitch!" Wes said violently. "You ought to be horse-whipped for ever bringing her to America in the first place. And to think that you almost married her! When we get back and

Nicole is safe again, I hope you throw that fat slut into the hold of a ship and get rid of her as fast as possible."

Clay stood silently, his dark eyes staring out at the river. He didn't answer Wesley's tirade; there was little he could say. Could he tell his friends he probably would marry Bianca after all?

"Clay?" Travis asked quietly, his voice full of concern. "Are you all right? You don't think your wife has been harmed, do you?"

Clay turned, and Travis frowned at the bleakness of his friend's face. "How should a man feel when he's just sold his soul to the devil?" he asked quietly.

Isaac cleaned the pan of the last of the rabbit and baked apples. He put the pan down and rested against the stone wall of the cabin, his legs stretched stiffly out on the grass. His thigh, tightly bound with strips of Nicole's petticoat, throbbed. As he closed his eyes and let the sun beat down on him, he smiled into the warmth. The air around the little island smelled bad, the water was alive with poisonous snakes, they had little or no hope of rescue, but Isaac had no desire to leave the place. In the last two days, he'd eaten better than he ever had at home, even though Nicole had only one pan to cook in. He'd been able to rest, something else that was new to his life.

He smiled more broadly as he heard the familiar swish of Nicole's velvet skirt. He opened his eyes and waved at her. She'd taken the lace off her petticoat and tied little bows down the front of her dress to hold it together where Abe had slashed it. Isaac was amazed at her. All his life, he'd thought the women who lived in the big houses were useless, but Nicole had shown no hysterics after the knife fight with Abe. She'd knelt and bound Isaac's wound to stop the bleeding, then calmly gone to sleep.

In the morning, the door was revealed to have hinges of heavy leather. Nicole used Isaac's pocket knife and sawed at the leather, while Isaac leaned against the door to keep it from falling. It had taken all their strength to open the door enough to slip through. Afterward, Isaac rested while Nicole made a snare from a piece of cord trim on her petticoat and caught a rabbit. Isaac was astonished that she knew how to do something of that nature. Nicole laughed and said her grandfather had taught her how to make a snare.

"Are you feeling better?" Nicole asked, smiling down at him. Her hair hung down her back to her waist, thick and rich.

"Yes. 'Cept maybe I'm lonesome. Could you talk to me?"

Nicole smiled and sat down beside him.

"Why ain't you afraid?" Isaac asked. "I think most women would be scared to death of this place."

Nicole thought for a moment. "I think emotions are relative. There have been times when I've been very, very frightened. In comparison, this place seems almost safe. We have food and water, the weather isn't too cold yet, and when your leg is better, we'll get off the island."

"You're sure of that? Have you looked into the water lately?"

She smiled. "Snakes do not scare me. Only people can truly hurt you."

Isaac felt a strong stab of guilt. She hadn't asked a single question about why he and Abe had abducted her. She could have, and probably should have, let him bleed to death.

"You're staring at me oddly," Nicole said.

"What's going to happen when we do get back to civilization?"

Nicole felt a surge of joy shoot through her. Clay, she thought. She would leave the mill in someone else's hands and return to Clay's house. She'd be there with him and the twins, as they were once, except now Bianca would have no power to come between them.

Her thoughts returned to Isaac. "I don't guess you want to return to your home. Maybe you'd like to work for me at the mill. I'm sure we could use another man."

Isaac's face changed from one color to another. "How can you offer me a job after what I've done to you?" he whispered.

"You saved my life."

"But I brought you here! You would never have been in this situation if it hadn't been for me."

"That's not true, and you know it," she said. "If you'd refused to go with Abe, he would have taken someone else or come alone. Then what would have happened to me?" She put her hand on his arm. "I owe you a lot. The least I can do is offer you a job."

He stared at her silently for several minutes. "You're a lady, a *real* lady. I think my life is going to be better since meeting you."

She laughed, and he watched the sunlight play on her hair. "And you, kind sir, would do well in any court in the world. Your gallantry is excessive."

He grinned back at her, happier than he ever had been in his life.

Suddenly, Nicole jumped. "What was that?"

Isaac sat still and listened. "Get me the knife," he whispered. "And you hide. Slip into the scum at the edge of the water. No one will ever find you there. Whatever you do, don't come out until it's safe."

Nicole gave him her sweetest smile. She had no intention of abandoning him, wounded as he was, to the mercies of whoever approached so quietly. And she certainly had no intention of burying herself in the scum of the water. She handed Isaac the knife. Then, when she went to help him stand, he pushed her away.

"Go!" he commanded.

Nicole slipped behind the willow trees at the edge of the island, then slowly made her way toward the quiet footsteps. She saw Travis first, his broad, thick form unmistakable. Instantly, her eyes blurred with tears. Hastily, she wiped them away and watched Travis as he walked away from her.

She felt Clay's presence behind her rather than heard him. She whirled about, her hair flying. She stood as still as if she were made of stone.

Silently, he opened his arms to her.

She leaped into them, burying her face in his neck, her body pressed hard against his. She felt his face against her cheek, and she knew his eyes were also wet.

Still holding her aloft, he turned her chin so she looked at him. He studied her face, devouring it. "You're well?" he whispered.

She nodded, her eyes on his. There was something wrong, deeply wrong. She sensed it.

He clutched her close again. "I thought I was going to go crazy," he said. "I couldn't bear it again."

"You won't have to," she smiled, relaxing against his body, enjoying the warmth and strength of him. "My own naiveté got me into this. I won't be so careless again."

"Next time you won't be given a choice," he said fiercely.

"Clay, what do you mean by next time?" She tried to push away from him.

He pushed her head to one side and began to kiss her. As soon as his lips touched hers, Nicole stopped thinking. It had been so very long since they'd been together.

"Ahem!"

Clay's head came up to stare at Travis and Wesley.

"I see you found her," Wes said, grinning. "We hated to interrupt you, but this is a filthy place, and we'd like to leave."

Clay nodded, his face serious, his dark brows drawn down over his eyes.

"What about him?" Travis said, his voice heavy with disgust. He pointed to an unconscious Isaac sprawled in the mud. The bandages around his leg were reddening with blood. There was a swelling lump on his jaw where he'd obviously been hit.

"Isaac!" Nicole gasped and pushed out of Clay's arms. She was at the boy's side immediately. "How could you?" she glared up at Travis. "He saved my life. Didn't you wonder how he got such a cut on his leg? If I were his prisoner, I could have run away from him."

Travis stared down at Nicole in amusement. "I don't guess I stopped to think at all. I came around a corner of the shack, and he came at me with a knife." His eyes twinkled. "I guess I should have stepped back and considered the situation."

"I'm sorry," Nicole said. "I think my nerves are a bit raw." She quickly started to untie the bloody bandages from Isaac's leg. "Clay, give me your shirt. I need some more bandages."

When Nicole turned, her hand out to take the shirt, she looked up at three bare-chested men, each handing her a shirt. "Thank you," she whispered, blinking back tears. It was going to be good to get home again.

Chapter 15

NICOLE PAUSED, her needle in her hand, as she glanced toward the window for the hundredth time. There was no need to try to keep from crying because her tears had all been used. It had been nearly two months since she'd seen Clay. During the first month, she'd been bewildered, confused, stunned. Then, for weeks, she'd cried. Now she felt numb, as if part of her body had been removed and she was adjusting to it.

After Clay had taken her from the island, he'd returned her to the mill. All during the long journey down the river to the Armstrong plantation, Clay had held her tightly, at times preventing her from breathing properly. But she didn't care. His arms about her were what she wanted.

When they had reached the wharf, Clay told Travis to tie the sloop first to the mill wharf. Nicole had been puzzled because she assumed she would go to the house with him. After clutching her to him almost in desperation, he had released her abruptly and jumped back into the boat, not looking back as Travis sailed the boat toward Clay's wharf.

For days, Nicole had watched for Clay. When he didn't come, she'd made excuses for him. She knew Bianca still lived in his house with him. Perhaps it was taking longer for him to get her on a ship to England.

When a month had passed and there was still no word, the

tears started. Alternately, she had cursed him, forgiven him, understood him, cursed him again. Had he been lying to her when he said he loved her? Was Bianca's power over him stronger than he had thought? She was too angry at him to think rationally.

"Nicole," Janie said quietly—there were a lot of whispers in the house now. "Why don't you take the twins and go cut some evergreens? It looks like it's going to snow. Wes will be here later, and we can decorate the house for Christmas."

Slowly, Nicole rose, but she didn't feel much in the spirit for Christmas.

"You will not tear out the east wall of my house," Clay said in a deadly serious voice.

Bianca sneered at him in disgust. "This house is too small! In England, it wouldn't be better than a gatekeeper's cottage."

"Then may I suggest you return to England?"

"I won't stand for your insults, do you hear me? Have you forgotten my cousins?"

"Since there isn't a moment when you don't mention them, I don't believe I could forget them. Now, I have work to do. Get out of here!" He glared at her over the ledger, watched as she put her nose in the air and stormed out of the office.

When she was gone, Clay poured himself a drink. He'd had about all he could take of Bianca. She was probably the laziest human he'd ever encountered. She was constantly angry because the servants refused to obey her. At first, Clay had made half-hearted attempts to force them into obedience, but soon he gave up. Why should he make them as miserable as he was?

He left the office and went to the stables to get his horse. Two months he'd spent with that bitch! Every day, he tried to think of the nobility of his gesture, how he was probably saving Nicole's life by his martyrdom. But self-inflicted pain can only go so far. Now that he'd had more time to think, he saw a way out of Bianca's plans. He and Nicole could leave Virginia. They could plan a time when they wouldn't be missed for a few days and then go west. There was new land opening all the way to the Mississippi River. He'd like to see that river.

Bianca was right about one thing. She'd be bankrupt in less than a year. He could arrange for Travis to buy back the plantation after Bianca ran it into the red. Travis and Wes could force Bianca off the land. Just so long as Nicole was safely out of the fat bitch's reach.

Clay sat on his horse just at the edge of the river. There was smoke coming from Nicole's chimney. At first, he'd stayed away from her because the sight of her caused him too much pain. Quite often in the last months, he'd stood on a hill and watched the activity across the water. He had longed to go to her and talk to her, but he couldn't until he had a plan. Now he did.

Big, fat snowflakes were beginning to fall, and as Clay watched, he heard the sound of hammering. He could see one lone figure on top of the mill, hammering loose wooden shakes down more securely.

With a smile, Clay dismounted from his horse, slapping the sleek black rump of the horse and watching as it made its way toward the stables. Then, he went to the rowboat and rowed himself across the river.

He picked up a hammer from the toolbox at the base of the ladder leaning against the mill and climbed to the roof. Wesley looked up in surprise, grinned, and silently held out a handful of nails. Clay quickly arranged the heads in one direction and began hammering, feeding the nails with his left hand as quickly as a machine. The physical labor felt good after the quarrel with Bianca.

It was nearly dark when the two men climbed down the ladder, both sweaty and tired. But it was a good tired, from labor shared with a friend.

They went inside the mill, where it was warm and a tub of water waited for them. The snow was coming down more heavily.

"We certainly haven't seen you in a while," Wes said, his voice heavy with criticism.

Clay didn't answer as he removed his shirt and began to wash.

"Janie said Nicole cried herself to sleep every night for weeks," Wes continued. "Maybe that doesn't matter to you. After all, you do have that overblown copy of Beth to keep you warm."

Clay stared at him. "You're making judgments about things you know nothing of."

"Then maybe you should explain it to me."

Clay dried himself slowly. "We've known each other all our lives. Have I ever done anything to cause this much hostility?"

"Not until now! Damn it, Clay, she's a beautiful woman. She's kind, sweet—"

"You don't have to tell me!" Clay interrupted. "Do you think I *want* to stay away from her? Has it ever occurred to you that there are circumstances beyond my control?"

Wes stood quietly for a moment. He'd been wrong not to trust his friend. He put his hand on Clay's shoulder. "Why don't you come inside? Nicole promised to make doughnuts, and the twins will be glad to see you."

"You seem rather free with Nicole's hospitality," Clay said coldly.

Wes grinned. "That's the Clay I know. If you don't take care of her, someone has to."

Clay turned and left the mill, heading toward the house. He'd not been inside the house since Nicole had moved there. Even as he stood just inside the door, the warmth of the place hit him. It was more than the physical warmth from the enormous fireplace, but something intangible, felt inside rather than against the skin.

The winter sun was coming through the sparkling clear windows. There was very little furniture, and Clay recognized most of it as the castoffs he'd sent some time ago. The dishes in the cabinet next to the fireplace were chipped and mismatched. There were very few cooking utensils.

Yet, in spite of the plainness, at that moment Clay would have traded his beautiful house for this simple dwelling. Janie bent over an iron pot of bubbling oil, turning doughnuts as they rose to the surface. The twins hovered over her, oblivious to the men standing behind them.

"Mandy," Janie said, "if you try to eat them while they're so hot, you're going to get burned, and you know it."

Mandy giggled as she grabbed a fresh doughnut and bit into it. Her eyes teared when she burned her mouth, but she wouldn't show Janie that she was in pain.

"You are as stubborn as your uncle," Janie said in disgust.

Clay chuckled, and Janie whirled to face him. "You'd better be careful when you talk about someone. They just might be listening."

Before Janie could reply, the twins screeched, "Uncle Clay!" and leaped into his arms. Clay grabbed one child under each arm and swung them around. When he lifted them, they put their arms around his neck. "Why didn't you come before? Do you want to see my new puppy? You want a doughnut? They're good but very hot."

Clay laughed and hugged them to him. "Did you miss me?"

"Yes, very much. Nicole said we had to wait until you came to see us, that we couldn't go see you."

"Is that fat lady still there?"

"Alex!" Nicole said from the staircase. "You are to remember your manners." She walked slowly toward Clay, her heart pounding in her throat. She was appalled that his presence could upset her so much. Since he'd been able to abandon her so lightly, obviously she meant very little to him. She worked at keeping her anger under control. "Won't you have a seat?" she asked formally.

"Yeah, Clay," Wes grinned. "Have a seat. Janie, you think those doughnuts are cool enough now?"

"Just about." She set the plate on the big table. "Where have you been, you ungrateful, wretched—" she hissed under her breath, unable to think of a word strong enough for him. "If you mistreat her again, you'll answer to me."

Clay smiled at her, then grabbed her rough, raw hand and kissed it. "You're magnificent as a protector, Janie. If I didn't know you, I'd almost be frightened."

"Maybe you should be," she snapped, but her eyes were twinkling.

Nicole had her back to them as she calmly poured out noggins of eggnog. With shaking hands, she set a mug before Clay.

His eyes never left hers as he lifted the cup. "Eggnog," he said. "I've never had that except at Christmas."

"It *is* Christmas!" the twins laughed.

Clay looked around him and noticed for the first time the evergreens and holly across the mantelpiece. He hadn't realized it was Christmastime. The last months of hell, spent near Bianca's nagging tongue, were fading into the distance.

"Nicole is going to make a turkey tomorrow, and Mr. Wesley and Mr. Travis are going to be here," the twins said.

Clay looked at Wes. "Think there'll be room for another guest?"

The men exchanged looks. "That would be up to Nicole."

Clay looked at his wife for a long moment, waiting for her answer.

Nicole felt her anger coming to the surface. He was using her! He spent days in bed with her, told her he loved her, then suddenly he dropped her on her doorstep like so much baggage. Now he comes sauntering into her house after months of silence, and what does he want? He expects her to kiss his feet in welcome. She stiffened her back and turned away from him. "Of course, you and Bianca are welcome. I'm sure she would enjoy the festivities as much as anyone."

Wesley smothered a laugh as he watched the frown crease Clay's brow.

"Bianca can't—" Clay began.

"I insist!" Nicole said narrowly. "May I say that one isn't welcome without the other?"

Suddenly, the atmosphere of the house was more than Clay could bear. They didn't realize the picture they presented. Wes leaned back in a chair smoking on a pipe he'd taken from the mantel. The twins happily stuffed themselves with doughnuts. The mention of Bianca's name made him remember the misery of his own household.

He rose. "Nicole, could I speak to you?" he asked quietly.

"No," she said firmly. "Not yet."

He nodded and left the warmth of the house.

Bianca was waiting for him when he entered Arundel Hall. "So! You couldn't stay away from her, could you?"

He brushed past her, not answering her.

"That man who runs the stables came to me and asked where you were. He was worried that you'd been hurt since your horse came back alone. They're always worried about you—and about her! No one on this place cares anything about me."

Clay turned and sneered at her. "You care enough about yourself to make up for everyone. Did you realize that tomorrow is Christmas Day?"

"Of course! I told the servants I wanted a special meal to be prepared. They, I am sure, will ignore me and, as usual, you won't do anything about it."

"A meal! That's your main interest, isn't it?" Suddenly, he lunged at her, grabbed her dress by the neckline. "You're going to get your wish. Tomorrow we're going to go to Nicole's for dinner." Maybe if Nicole saw them together, she'd realize how miserable he was. And he wanted to spend the day with Nicole, so badly that he was willing to subject them all to Bianca's vile personality. Perhaps she'd just eat and remain quiet.

She tried to jerk away from him but couldn't. His closeness made her stomach turn. "I will not go!" she breathed.

"Then I'll give orders that no food will enter this house all day."

Her eyes widened in horror. "You wouldn't."

He pushed her away from him until she slammed into the wall, hard. "You make me sick. You will go even if I have to carry you." He looked her up and down. "If I can. God, but it's going to be good to get rid of you." He stopped, appalled at what he'd said. He turned away, went into the library, and slammed the door behind him.

Bianca stood quietly for a moment, staring at the door. What did he mean, get rid of her?

She turned away and slowly went up the stairs. Nothing was going as she had planned. Abe had visited her soon after she'd given the map to Clay. He'd been bleeding from the cut in his arm, and Bianca had nearly become ill. The dreadful man demanded money from her so he could get out of Virginia, away from Clay's revenge. Bianca had had to pry open a box in the library to get him some pieces of silver.

She'd told him he had to stay near because she might need him again. He'd just laughed at her as he tied a piece of cloth around his arm, saying Bianca'd caused him to lose his family and his inheritance. Then he'd said something very rude about what she could do with her future needs.

Now, Bianca knew there was no one else. She told Clay she had other relatives, but that was a hollow threat. If he did throw her on a ship, no one would take Nicole as she had threatened. Nothing would happen. Bianca would be thrown aside, and no one, absolutely no one, would care.

She closed the door to her bedroom and looked out the window into the dark garden. The new snow was making it beautiful. Would she have to give it up? For a while she had felt safe, but now she was beginning to worry again.

She had to do something—and quickly. She had to get rid of Nicole before the French bitch took everything. Abe was gone, so she couldn't carry out her threat to send Nicole back to France. But, of course, Clay didn't know that—yet. Bianca had no doubt that he would sooner or later find out.

She clutched at the curtain, crushing the pink silk. The way the two of them rutted, it's a wonder Nicole wasn't pregnant by now. After seeing Clay with the twins, Bianca guessed that if Nicole were going to have a baby, his baby, no power on earth would make him leave her.

Suddenly, Bianca dropped the curtain, smoothed the fabric lovingly. What if someone else were going to have Clay's baby? Wouldn't little Miss Frenchy have her nose put out of joint? And what if Clay thought Nicole were bedding someone else? She probably would, Bianca thought. She's so hot for a man, she probably slept with Isaac on the island. Or Wesley!

Bianca smiled and caressed her stomach. Thinking always made her hungry. She started toward the door. She had a lot of thinking to do, and she'd need her nourishment.

"Merry Christmas!" Travis bellowed as Clay and Bianca entered Nicole's little house. Bianca wore a sullen, hostile look. She ignored Travis and looked at the food piled high on the big table in the center of the room. She wrenched her arm free from Clay's grasp and went toward the table.

"You choosin' that over Nicole?" Travis drawled.

"Mind your own business," Clay said sharply and walked away, Travis's laugh sounding behind him.

Janie handed Clay a small cup of liquor. He drank it quickly, needing its warmth and strength. He gasped when he finished. The stuff was delicious. "What is this?"

"Bourbon," Travis answered. "It's from the new land of Kentucky. Some peddler brought some in last week."

Clay held out his cup to Janie again.

"Go easy on it. It's strong stuff."

"But it's Christmas!" Clay said with false joviality. "It's time to eat, drink, and be merry." He raised his cup in salute to Bianca, who was slowly circling the table, nibbling little bits and pieces of food from all the dishes.

Everyone quieted as Nicole entered the room. She wore a gown of sapphire blue velvet, off the shoulders, with deep décolletage and thin embroidered blue ribbons around the high waist. Her long dark hair was down, perfectly arranged in fat curls, braided and entwined with dark blue ribbons studded with hundreds of seed pearls.

Clay could only stand and gaze at her longingly as her eyes avoided him. Knowing that she had a right to be angry didn't make the pain any less.

Wes stepped forward and offered his arm to Nicole. "Just seeing a sight like you is enough of a Christmas gift for me. Don't you agree, Clay?"

Bianca spoke as Clay stared mutely. "Is that some of the fabric that was meant for me?" she asked sweetly. "Some that you and Janie took without permission?"

"Clay!" Travis said, "You'd better do something with that woman before I do it."

"Be my guest," Clay said calmly, then poured himself more bourbon.

"Please," Nicole said, still avoiding Clay's eyes. "Let's have some eggnog. I must get the twins. They're in the mill admiring the new puppies. I won't be a minute."

Clay set his empty cup down and walked to the door with her, where he took her cape from the wooden peg by the door.

"I don't want you near me," she said under her breath. "Please stay here."

Clay ignored her as he opened the door and followed her outside. Putting her chin in the air, she walked ahead of him, trying to pretend he wasn't there.

"It's a pretty little nose, but if you don't lower it you're going to stumble."

She stopped in her tracks and whirled on him. "It's a joke to you, isn't it? Something that is life and death to me is only a cause for amusement to you. This time, you're not going to talk your way out of my anger. I've been hurt and humiliated too many times."

Her eyes were enormous and blazing in the starlight as she looked up at him, her mouth drawn tightly until her lower lip nearly disappeared. All that was left was her full, sensual upper lip. He ached to kiss it. "I've never meant to hurt you," he said quietly. "And certainly not to humiliate you."

"Then, out of ignorance, you've done a fine job, a superior job! You called me a whore five minutes after I met you. You allowed me to run your home, yet discarded me as soon as your dear Bianca appeared."

"Stop it!" he commanded, grabbing her shoulders harshly. "I know our relationship hasn't been an ordinary one, but—"

"Ordinary!" she said sarcastically. "I'm not even sure it's been a relationship. I think I *am* a whore. You snap your fingers, and I come running."

"I wish that were true." His voice was heavy with amusement.

Uttering what was obviously a French oath, she snarled at him and kicked his shin very hard.

He released her as he bent to rub his shin. Limping, he hurried after her and grabbed her arm. "You're going to listen to me!"

"Like I did when you told me about Beth? Or like the time you asked me to remarry you? Am I supposed to be naive enough to believe you again? Then, when I'm vulnerable and fall into your arms, will you again tire of me and return to your dear Bianca? There's only so much a woman will do for the man she loves."

"Nicole," Clay said, holding her firmly by one arm and caressing the other one with his hand, "I know you've been hurt. I've been hurt, too."

"Poor dear," she smiled. "You have to make do with only two women in your bed."

His jaw hardened. "You know what Bianca's like. I get closer than a foot, and she turns green."

Nicole's eyes widened; her voice was high. "You want sympathy from me?"

He fastened his hands on her shoulders. "I want your trust. I want your love. Could you stop hating me for a minute and just consider that there's a reason why I haven't seen you? Is that too much to ask after what we've been through? Maybe I have done some things to make you distrust me, but I love you. Doesn't that mean anything to you?"

"Why?" she whispered, blinking back her tears. "You just left me with no word, just dropped me as if you were through with me. On the island, all I thought about was getting home, the two of us together at Arundel Hall."

He pulled her close to him, felt her tears wetting his shirt. "Didn't Isaac mention his cousin?"

The time on the island was a blur in her mind.

"I wanted to explain then and there, but I couldn't. I was so frightened that I couldn't even speak to you about it."

She tried to raise her head, but he pushed it back down. "Frightened? But I was safe. Abe was gone. You weren't afraid of Isaac, were you?"

"Bianca is Isaac's cousin. They're one of the reasons she came to America. She guaranteed Abe a bull and some heifers if he'd take you away until she could get the marriage annulled. One of old Elijah's daughters told Wes about the plan."

"And Bianca told you where I was?"

He pulled her even closer. "For a price. She told me that if I didn't marry her, she'd have one of her many relatives return you to France." He could feel Nicole shiver against him; the thought was as horrible to her as it was to him.

"Why didn't you tell me? Why did you just leave me so abruptly?"

"Because you would have marched up to the house and defied Bianca. You would have dared her to try to send you back."

"It's what should have been done."

"No, I can't risk losing you," he said as he stroked her hair.

She pulled away from him. "Why do you tell me this now? Why aren't you still cowering behind Bianca's ample skirts?"

Shaking his head, he chuckled. "I talked to Isaac since he began working for you. He said the reason you went with Abe so quietly was because you thought I was in trouble. Was I supposed to do less, knowing that your life could be in danger?"

"Let's go back inside and tell Bianca."

"No!" It was a command. "I will not risk you, do you understand? All she has to do is arrange for your capture again. No! I won't risk it."

"So, do you propose that we spend the rest of our lives meeting at Christmas just so Bianca can have what she wants?" Nicole asked angrily.

He ran his finger along her upper lip. "You have a sharp tongue. I prefer it when you use it for something besides lashing me."

"Maybe you need to be lashed. You certainly seem afraid of Bianca."

"Damn you! I've been very patient, but I've had enough of your insults. I'm not afraid of Bianca. It's taken all my control to keep from killing the bitch. But I knew that if I hurt her, I'd hurt you."

"Isaac said Abe left Virginia. Are you sure there are any more relatives? Bianca could be lying."

"Wes went back to the girl who'd helped him before. She said that Bianca was related to her mother, and her mother had hundreds of relatives."

"But surely not many of them would do what Bianca wanted."

"People would do anything for money," he said in disgust. "And Bianca has all of the Armstrong plantation at her disposal."

Nicole put her arms around his chest, clung to him. "Clay, what are we going to do? We have to risk it. Maybe she's bluffing."

"Possibly, but I can't be certain. It's taken me months, but I've come up with a plan. We'll go west. We'll change our names and leave Virginia."

"Leave Virginia?" she asked, pulling away again. "But your home is here. Who will run the plantation?"

"Bianca, I guess," he said flatly. "I offered to give her the whole place, but she said she wanted a husband to run it."

"*My* husband!" Nicole said fiercely.

"Yes, yours always. Listen, we've been out here too long. Can you meet me tomorrow by the cave? Can you find it all right?"

"Yes," she said hesitantly.

"You don't trust me, do you?"

"I don't know, Clay. Every time I believe in you, in us together, something dreadful happens. I can't stand anything else. You can't imagine how horrible the last months have been for me. Not knowing, wondering, always confused."

"I should have told you. I know that now. I just needed time to think." He paused. "At least you haven't had to spend time with Bianca. Do you know that woman wants to tear away part of my house and add a wing? If it was left to her, she'd make it into a monstrosity like that place of Horace's and Ellen's."

"If you leave her, she'll be able to do what she likes to the house."

It was a while before Clay answered. "I know. Let's get the twins and go back." He released her and took her hand in his.

All through the long, uncomfortable dinner, Nicole's thoughts whirled. It wasn't just Bianca she was fighting but Arundel Hall also. She knew how much Clay loved his home, how he talked about the place almost with reverence. Even when he'd seemingly neglected the house for the fields, he'd been aware that Nicole had given the house the attention he felt it deserved. She always felt that was what had prompted his first marriage proposal, when he'd said he'd remain married to her if Bianca didn't arrive.

Nicole picked at her food, vaguely listening to Travis's plans to visit England in the spring. Clay was right, she didn't trust him. Too many times, she'd held her heart out to him and he'd rejected it. Even remembering the time he'd gotten her drunk and made her admit she loved him made her blush. Later, he'd invited her to his house, and when Bianca arrived he was no longer aware of Nicole's presence. He'd made love to her at the Backes's house but deserted her soon afterward. Of course, he always had marvelous reasons. First, there was the story of Beth, and now Bianca's treachery. She believed him—the stories were too bizarre to be lies—but now he said he was going to leave Virginia—and Bianca—so they could be together. He said he hated Bianca, yet he'd lived with her for months.

She stabbed at a piece of turkey. She had to believe him! Of course, he hated Bianca and loved her. There were logical reasons why Bianca lived with him and she didn't. But at the moment, she couldn't remember a single one of them.

"I think the turkey's already dead," Wes said at her side.

"Oh," she said in puzzlement, then tried to smile. "I'm afraid I'm not very good company."

Travis grinned at her. "Any woman who looks like you doesn't need to do or say anything. Someday, I'm going to find a pretty little girl and keep her inside a glass jar. I'll only let her out when I want her."

"Probably about three times a night would be my guess," Wesley said as he helped himself to more candied yams.

"I will not stand for this kind of talk!" Bianca said stiffly. "You Colonials must remember that a lady is present."

"The way I been raised, ladies don't live with men they're not married to," Travis said flatly.

Bianca's face turned red with anger as she stood up quickly, knocking over her chair and upsetting the table. "I will not be insulted! I am the one who will own Arundel Hall, and when I do—" She stopped, then let out a scream as Mandy, staring up at the big woman, her plate in her hand, let slide a great wad of cranberry sauce onto Bianca's skirt.

"You did that on purpose!" Bianca screamed, and drew back her hand to strike the child.

Everyone was on their feet to stop her. But Bianca stopped herself as she gasped, her eyes tearing; then she jumped backward from the table, holding out her foot. There, resting against her thick ankle, was a large, very hot plum pudding.

"Get it off me!" she screamed, kicking her foot.

Nicole was the one who tossed her a towel, but no one bent to help her wipe away the sticky mess. Travis pulled Alex out from under the table. "I think his fingers are burned, Janie."

"Such a waste," Wes said sadly, watching Bianca trying to balance herself as she made swipes at her foot with the towel. Her stomach was so large that she could hardly reach her ankle.

"Not a waste at all," Janie said. "In fact, I don't believe I've ever enjoyed any dessert as much."

"Clayton Armstrong!" Bianca screeched. "How dare you stand there and let them insult me like this!"

Everyone turned toward Clay. No one had noticed that all through dinner he'd been drinking heavily of the bourbon. Now, his eyes were glazed and he looked with disinterest at Bianca's gyrations.

"Clay," Nicole said quietly, "I think you'd better take Bianca . . . home."

Clay rose slowly, seeming oblivious to everyone around him as he grabbed Bianca's arm and pulled her toward the door, ignoring her screams that the pudding was still burning her. He pulled her outside as she grabbed her cape, and he took a jug of the bourbon. The cold, snow-filled air threatened to freeze the wet, sticky mass to Bianca's ankle.

Bianca followed Clay reluctantly, stumbling in the dark behind him. Her dress was ruined; she could feel the cold cranberry juice against her thighs, and her ankle hurt from the burn and the cold. Tears blurred her eyes so that she could hardly see where she was going. Once again, Clay had humiliated her. He had done nothing else since she'd arrived in America.

At the wharf, Clay grunted as he lifted Bianca and set her inside the rowboat. "You put on any more weight and we'll sink," he said, his voice slightly slurred.

She'd had all the insults she was going to take, she thought as she stiffened. "You seemed to like this new drink," she said sweetly, nodding at the stoneware jug in the bottom of the rowboat.

"It makes me forget for a while. Anything that can do that, I like."

Bianca smiled into the darkness. When they landed across the river, she took the hand he offered and stepped onto shore, following him quickly back to the house. By the time they reached the garden door, she was trembling because she knew what she must do, even though the idea came close to making her sick to her stomach.

Clay set the jug on the hall table and stepped back outside.

Bianca muttered, "Peasant!" lifting her skirts and running up the stairs to her room, ignoring the pain of her ankle and her wildly beating heart as she flung open a drawer and withdrew a small bottle of laudanum. The bourbon combined with the sleeping drug would make Clay unaware of anything that happened to him. She just had time to add a few drops to the liquor she poured into a glass. The stuff smelled vile!

Clay lifted one eyebrow at her when she offered him the glass. But he was already too drunk to question her actions. He lifted the glass in a mock salute to her, then downed the fiery liquid in one gulp. Setting the glass on the table, he lifted the jug to his lips.

Bianca merely smiled at his crudeness and watched him mount the stairs. When she heard the door to his bedroom open and each of his boots fall to the floor, she knew it was time.

The hall was dark, and Bianca stood alone, listening. The idea repulsed her; she hated a man's touch as much as her mother had loved it, but as she took one last look around the hall, she knew that if she didn't climb into bed with Clay, she'd lose all of this. She grabbed the bottle of laudanum and went up the stairs.

Inside her own room, her hands were trembling as she undressed and slipped into a pale pink silk nightgown, crying a little as she drank some of the laudanum. At least, the drug would help dull her senses.

Moonlight flooded Clay's room, and Bianca saw him sprawled across the bed. He wore nothing, and the silver light on his bronze skin made him look as if he were made of gold, but Bianca saw nothing beautiful in the sight of the naked man. The laudanum made her feel as if she were in a dream.

Slowly, she slipped in beside Clay on the bed, dreading the idea of having to make advances toward him. She didn't know if she could.

Clay needed no encouragement. He'd been dreaming of Nicole, and now the touch of a woman's silk gown, the smell of perfumed hair, made him react. "Nicole," he whispered as he pulled Bianca close to him.

But even in his drunken, drugged state, Clay knew this was not the woman he loved. Reaching out to touch her, he encountered a handful of lumpy fat and, with a muffled grunt, turned away to relapse into his dream of Nicole.

Bianca, rigid, breath held, waited for his animal lust to take over. When he merely grunted and turned away, it was some moments before she realized he was not going to touch her. Cursing vilely, she told his sleeping form what she thought of his lack of masculinity. If the plantation weren't so important to her, she'd give this caricature of a man to Nicole, and she was welcome to him.

But now there had to be something done. In the morning, Clay had to believe he'd deflowered Bianca, or her plan would never work. The laudanum she'd taken was a hindrance to her as she rose and stumbled down the stairs, but she could have been even more drugged and she'd still have been able to find her destination—the kitchen.

On the big table was a roast beef marinating in herbs, and Bianca half filled an earthenware mug with beef blood. Grabbing six leftover rolls from a cabinet to reward herself for her cleverness, she started back to the house.

Upstairs again, the rolls eaten, the laudanum making her eyes too heavy to hold open, she slipped in beside Clay and doused herself with blood, hiding the mug well under the bed. Cursing him again for making her go through this ordeal, she fell asleep beside him.

Chapter 16

THE EARLY morning sun beat down on the lightly crusted snow and flashed back into Clay's red eyes. The pain in his eyes went directly to his head where everything vile that had ever been created seemed to exist. His body seemed to weigh a thousand pounds, and each movement was an ordeal, even as he picked up another handful of snow and pressed it to his dry, swollen tongue.

Worse than his raging headache and his churning stomach was the memory of this morning. He woke beside Bianca. At first, he'd been able to do nothing but stare because his body hurt too much to be able to think.

Opening her eyes quickly, Bianca'd gasped when she saw him. She sat up, pulling the sheet to her neck. "You animal!" she said through clenched teeth. "You dirty, filthy animal!"

As she told him that he'd dragged her to his bed and raped her, Clay couldn't speak.

When she'd finished, he laughed because he didn't believe he could ever have gotten that drunk.

But when Bianca'd stepped from the bed, there'd been blood on the sheets, blood on her nightgown. Before Clay could reply, Bianca had begun telling him that she was a lady, that she wouldn't be treated like his whore, that if she had a child Clay would have to marry her.

Clay hadn't bothered to reply as he'd stepped from the bed and begun to dress quickly. He'd wanted to be as far away from Bianca as possible.

Now, sitting in the clearing he had built with James and Beth, he kept remembering things. Maybe he'd been so drunk that he had made love to Bianca. This morning, he couldn't remember anything after he'd left Nicole's.

Nicole was the one who worried him. What if Bianca did become pregnant? He pushed the thought out of his mind.

"Clay?" Nicole called. "Are you here?"

Smiling, he stood up to greet her as she came into the clearing.

"You didn't say what time. Oh, Clay! You look awful! Do your eyes feel as bad as they look?"

"Worse," he said hoarsely as he held out his arms to her.

Nicole got within two feet of him, then stopped, her eyes blinking rapidly. "You smell as bad as you look."

He grimaced. "Didn't I hear that love was blind?"

"Even blind people can smell. Sit down and rest or build a fire in the cave. I brought some food with me. You didn't eat much last night."

He groaned. "Don't mention last night."

It was an hour later, when they'd eaten breakfast and the little cave was warm, that Nicole was ready to talk as she leaned against the stone wall of the cave, a blanket across her legs. She wasn't yet ready to sit easily in Clay's arms. "I didn't sleep much last night," she began. "All night, I kept thinking about what you'd told me about Bianca and her relatives. I want to believe you . . . but it's difficult. All I can see is that I am your wife, yet she lives with you. It's almost as if you want both of us."

"Do you really believe that?"

"I try not to. But I know Beth had a strong hold over you. Maybe you don't realize how close you are to your home. Last night you talked of just walking away and leaving this place. Yet at one time you were willing to kidnap a woman merely because she looked like someone who belonged here."

"You mean more to me than the plantation."

"Do I?" she asked. Her eyes were wide, dark, liquid. "I hope I do," she whispered. "I hope I mean that much to you."

"But you doubt me," he said flatly. Through his mind was going the vision of Bianca in his bed, Bianca's virgin blood on the sheets. Was Nicole right not to trust him? Turning to the little niche that held the unicorn set in glass, he stood and held it in his hands. "We made vows on this," he said. "I know we were children and had a lot to learn about life, but we never broke the vows."

"Sometimes innocent pledges are the most sincere," she smiled.

Clay held the glass in his hand. "I love you, Nicole, and I vow that I will love you until the day I die."

Nicole stood before him and put her hand over his. There was something that bothered her. Beth, James, and Clay had touched the little unicorn, then Beth had had it sealed in glass so no one else could ever touch it. It was a silly thing, really, but Nicole couldn't help remembering Beth's portrait, so very like Bianca. A swift thought ran across her mind. When would she be worthy to touch what Beth had touched?

"Yes, Clay, I love you," she whispered. "I always have, and I always will."

Carefully, he set the glass unicorn back into the wall, unaware of Nicole's frown. He turned and pulled her close to him. "We can go west in the spring. There are always wagon trains being organized. We'll leave at different times so no one will know we've gone together."

Clay went on, but Nicole wasn't listening. Spring was months away. Spring was the time when the earth came alive again, when the crops were to be planted. Would Clay be able to walk away, to leave all the people who depended on him?

"You're shivering," he said quietly. "Are you cold?"

"I think I'm frightened," she said honestly.

"There's no reason to be afraid. We've been through the worst of it now."

"Have we, Clay?"

"Hush!" he commanded, and lowered his mouth to hers.

It had been a long time since they'd been together, not since the party at the Backes's. Whatever sensible reasons Nicole had for her fears, they fled when Clay kissed her. Her arms went around his neck and pulled his face closer to hers as his hand turned her head and slanted her mouth so that her lips parted. He was hungry for her, starved for the sweet nectar of her that would wash away the filth of the night with Bianca—a night confused with visions of Beth, a pink silk gown, and flecks of blood on a white sheet.

"Clay!" Nicole gasped. "What's wrong?"

"Nothing. Just too much to drink last night. Don't go away," he whispered as he pulled her tightly against him. "I need you so much. You are warm and alive, and I am so haunted by people." He kissed her neck. "Make me forget."

"Yes," she whispered. "Yes."

Clay pulled her down with him to the floor of the cave on top of a quilt. It was warm and sweet-smelling inside the little room. Nicole wanted him urgently, but Clay wanted to take his time. Slowly, he unbuttoned the front of her soft wool dress and put his hand inside, cupping her breast, his thumb teasing the soft crest.

"How I've missed you!" he whispered, his mouth following his hand.

Nicole arched beside him, her mind a whirl of flashing colors. As she fumbled with the buttons of his vest, she was unable to remember what she was doing, since his mouth and hands seemed to make her incapable of performing even a simple task.

Smiling at her ineptitude, Clay pulled back. Her eyes were closed, her lashes a thick, lush curve against her cheek. As he caressed her cheek, ran his finger along her lips, his reverie changed from sweetness to passion. His hands quickly unfastened the buttons of his vest, his shirt, boots, and trousers following.

Nicole lay on her back, her head propped on her arm, watching the firelight in the little cave play deliciously with the skin over his muscles, dancing from one indentation to a mound of strength. She ran her finger up his back.

He turned, nude, all golden skin and bronze.

"You're beautiful," she whispered, and he smiled at her before he kissed her again, his hand easily slipping her dress from her shoulders, running over her smooth, firm body, exploring it slowly, as if it weren't very familiar to him. When he pulled her on top of him, she lifted her hips and guided him into their lovemaking.

"Clay!" she gasped as he moved her hips, slowly at first, building rapidly until she clung to him, her hands clutching at him hungrily. She collapsed on top of him, weak, throbbing, satiated.

"Let me get this straight, lady," the burly young man said, spitting a thick stream of tobacco juice near her feet. "You want me to give you a baby? Not give you one of mine what's already born but to plant one in you?"

Bianca stood rigid, her gaze level. It had taken very few questions to find Oliver Hawthorne, a man who was willing to do something for a price and keep his mouth shut. Her first thought had been to pay him to return Nicole to France, but the Hawthornes didn't have the reputation of dishonesty that the Simmons did.

After the failed attempt to get Clay to impregnate her, she realized something had to be done or all her future dreams would collapse. It wouldn't be long before Clay realized she had no power over him. She must get herself with child, no matter what she had to do!

"Yes, Mr. Hawthorne. I want to have a child. I've investigated your family, and you seem to be especially prolific."

"Investigated, huh?" He smiled at the woman, appraising her. He didn't mind her plumpness, since he liked big women with strong backs, eager, energetic women in bed, but he did mind her look of never having worked in her life. "I reckon you mean that the Hawthornes can make babies even when they can't get their tobacco to grow."

She nodded curtly. The less she had to talk to the man, the better she liked it. "This is, of course, to be kept confidential. In public, I will not acknowledge that I have ever met you, and I expect the same treatment."

Oliver's eyes twinkled. He was a short, heavyset man with a broken front tooth, and he had a feeling the whole situation was a dream and he was going to wake up very soon. Here was a woman offering to pay him for giving her a tumble, or as many as it took to impregnate her. It made him feel like a horse put out to stud, and he rather liked the idea. "Sure, lady, whatever you say. I'll act like I never saw you or the kid before, though I warn you that my six kids all look like me."

It would serve Clay right to claim a child as his when it obviously looked like another man, she thought. The child would be short and sturdy, so unlike Clay's tall, slim grace. "That's all right," she said, the dimple appearing in her left cheek. "Can you meet me tomorrow at three o'clock behind the tannery on the Armstrong plantation?"

"Armstrong, huh? Clay havin' trouble makin' his own babies?"

Bianca stiffened. "I don't plan to answer any questions, and I'd prefer you don't ask them."

"Sure," Oliver said, then looked around them cautiously. They were on a road four miles from the Armstrong plantation, a place she'd chosen in her message to him. As he reached out and touched her arm, she jumped backward as if she'd been burned.

"Don't touch me!" she said through clenched teeth.

Frowning in puzzlement, he watched her turn and angrily

walk down the road toward the driver who waited for her around a bend. She was an odd one, he thought. She didn't want him to touch her, yet she wanted him to make her pregnant. She sneered at him as if he repulsed her, but she wanted to meet him in the afternoon to make love. In broad daylight! The thought of that made Oliver's skin glow, and he reached inside his trousers to readjust himself more comfortably. He wasn't one to look a gift horse in the mouth. Maybe more of those la-de-da ladies would need him to make up for their weak men. Maybe Oliver could make a living at this, and to hell with tobacco.

He straightened his shoulders and began to walk home.

For the next month, Nicole felt she was content, if not happy. Clay and she met often in the clearing beside the river. They were joyous meetings, full of love and plans for the trek west. They were like children, talking of what they'd take, how many bedrooms their house would have, how many children they'd have, the names they'd give them. They spoke of when they'd tell the twins and Janie of their plans, for of course they would go with them.

One evening in late February, the sky darkened menacingly and lightning threatened to split the little house in half.

"Why are you so jumpy?" Janie asked. "It's just a storm comin' up."

Nicole put her knitting into the basket on the floor, since it was no use trying to continue. Every storm took her back to that night when her grandfather was taken.

"Are you upset because you can't meet Clay?"

Astonishment showed on Nicole's face.

Janie chuckled. "You don't have to tell me what's been going on. I can read your face. I always figured you'd tell me when you were ready."

Nicole sat on the floor before the fire. "You're so good and patient with me."

"You're the one who's patient," Janie sniffed. "There isn't another woman alive who'd put up with what Clayton is giving you."

"There are reasons—" Nicole began.

"Men always have reasons when it comes to women." She stopped suddenly. "I shouldn't be saying these things. There's more to this than I know, I'm sure. Maybe there's a reason Clay is meeting his wife like some city woman."

Eyes twinkling, Nicole smiled. "City woman, is it? Maybe, someday, when I'm living with him and see him every day, I'll look back fondly at this time when I was so adored."

"You don't believe that any more than I do. You should be in Arundel Hall now, supervising the place, instead of that fat—"

As a sharp slash of lightning cut off her words, Nicole gave a little scream of fright and clutched at her heart.

"Nicole!" Janie said, jumping up, her mending falling to the floor. "Something is wrong." Putting her arm around Nicole's shoulders, she led her back to her chair. "I want you to sit down and relax. I'll make us some tea, and yours is going to have some brandy in it."

Nicole sat down, but she didn't relax. The branches of a tree slapped against the roof, and the wind whistled in through the windows, blowing the curtains. The night outside was black and, to Nicole, horrible-looking.

"Here," Janie said, thrusting a steaming cup of tea into her hands. "Drink this, and then you're going to bed."

Trying to calm herself as she drank the tea, she could feel the brandy warming her, but her nerves were too on edge to relax.

At the first pounding on the door, she jumped so high that half the tea spilled down the front of her dress.

"That has to be Clay," Janie smiled, grabbing a towel. "He knows about you and storms, and he's come to sit with you. Now, dry yourself and put on a pretty smile for him."

With shaking hands, Nicole patted at the tea-stained wool and tried to smile as she anticipated Clay's appearance.

As Janie threw open the front door, a welcome and a lecture for Clay were already taking form. She was going to let him know what she thought of his neglect of his wife.

But the man standing there wasn't Clay. He was a short man, slightly built, with thin blond hair that straggled over the collar of his green velvet coat. About his throat was a white silk scarf that was tied so it covered the lower edge of his chin. He had small eyes, a knife blade of a nose, and a small, thick-lipped mouth.

"Is this the house of Nicole Courtalain?" he asked, his head tilted backward, as if he were trying to look down on Janie, which was impossible since she was several inches taller.

His voice was so thickly accented that Janie had difficulty understanding what sounded to her like, "Ees thees thee ouse of—" The name was one Janie had never heard before.

"Woman!" the small man commanded. "Have you no tongue or no brains?"

"Janie," Nicole said quietly, "I am Nicole Courtalain Armstrong."

Obviously appraising her, he spoke less angrily. "*Oui*. You are her daughter." He turned on his heel and walked back into the night.

"Who is he?" Janie demanded. "I couldn't even understand him. Is he a friend of yours?"

"I never saw him before. Janie! There's a woman with him."

The two women rushed out into the night. Nicole put her arm around one side of the woman, the man on the other side, as Janie grabbed a suitcase from the ground and followed them.

Inside the house, they led the woman to a chair before the fire, and Janie poured tea and brandy while Nicole went to a chest to get a quilt. It was when Janie had the tea ready and handed it to the exhausted woman that she had time to get a good look at her. It was like looking at an older version of Nicole. The woman's skin was unlined, clear, and perfect, her mouth exactly like Nicole's, a combination of innocence and sexuality. The eyes, though like Nicole's, were vacant, lifeless.

"There now," Nicole said, tucking the quilt around the woman's legs before she glanced up and saw the odd look on Janie's face. Nicole looked up at the woman from where she was kneeling on the floor, her hands still on the quilt. As she looked at the familiar features, her eyes filled with tears, then slowly, softly, they ran down her cheeks. "Mama," she whispered. "Mama." She bent forward and buried her face in the woman's lap.

Janie saw that the older woman made no response to Nicole's gesture or words.

"I had hoped—" the man beside her said. "I had hoped that seeing her daughter again would bring her back."

The man's words made Janie understand the woman's vacant eyes; they were the eyes of someone who wanted to see nothing more in life.

"Can we get her to bed?" the man asked.

"Yes, of course," Janie said firmly, kneeling beside her friend. "Nicole, your mother is very tired. Let's take her upstairs and put her to bed."

Silently, Nicole rose. Tears made her face damp, and her eyes never left her mother's face. Half in a daze, she helped her mother upstairs, helped Janie undress her, unaware that her mother never spoke.

Downstairs, Janie made more tea and brandy, then sliced ham and cheese for sandwiches for the young man.

"I thought both my parents were killed," Nicole said quietly.

The man ate quickly, obviously very hungry. "Your father was. I saw him guillotined." He seemed oblivious to Nicole's wince of pain. "My father and I went to see the guillotining, as almost everyone else did. It was the only sport left in Paris, and it helped to make up for the fact that we had no bread. But my father is—how do you say?—a romantic. Every day, he'd come home to his cobbler's shop and talk to my mother and me about the waste of all the beautiful women. He said it was a shame to see the lovely heads roll into the basket."

"Could you tell the story with less detail?" Janie said, her hand on Nicole's shoulder.

The man held up a ceramic pot of mustard. "Dijon. It is good to see French things in this barbarian country."

"Who are you? How did you rescue my mother?" Nicole asked softly.

He bit into a piece of cheese liberally spread with mustard, then smiled. "I am your stepfather, little daughter. Your mother and I are married." He stood and took her hand. "I am Gerard Gautier, now one of the magnificent Courtalains."

"Courtalain? I thought that was Nicole's maiden name."

"It is," Gerard said, returning to his seat at the table. "It is one of the oldest, richest, most powerful families in Europe. You should have seen the old man, my wife's father. I saw him once when I was a child. He was as big as a mountain and, it was said, as strong. I've heard he could make the king tremble from his wrath."

"The most common of people made the king tremble," Nicole said bitterly. "Please tell me how you met my mother."

Gerard gave Janie a disdainful look. "As I was saying, my father and I went to see the guillotinings. Adele, your mother, walked out behind your father. She was so beautiful, so regal. She wore a dress of pure white, and with her black hair she looked like an angel. The whole crowd stopped talking when she walked past. Everyone could see that her husband was so proud of her. Their hands were tied behind them, and they could not touch, but their eyes met, and several people sniffed because the two handsome people obviously loved each other. My father nudged me and said that he could not stand to see such a magnificent creature put to death. I tried to stop him, but—" Gerard shrugged. "My father does what he wants."

"How did he save her?" Nicole urged. "How did he get her through the mob?"

"I do not know. Every day, the crowd has a different flavor. Sometimes they cry as the heads roll; sometimes they laugh or cheer. It depends on the weather, I guess. That day, they were romantic, like my father. I watched as he pushed his way through them, then grabbed Adele's bindings about her wrists and pulled her into the crowd."

"What about the guards?"

"The crowd liked what my father was doing, and they protected him. They closed around him like water. When the guards tried to follow, the people tripped them and gave them false directions." He stopped and smiled, finishing the last of a large glass of wine. "I was standing on top of a wall where I could see everything. It was such a sight! The people yelled every direction imaginable to the guards, yet all the while my father and Adele were walking quietly back to our shop."

"You saved her," Nicole whispered, looking down at her hands in her lap. "How can I ever thank you?"

"You can take care of us," he said quickly. "We have come a long way."

"Anything," Nicole answered. "What is mine is yours. You must be tired and want to rest."

"Wait a minute!" Janie said. "There's more to this story. What happened to Nicole's mother after your father rescued her? Why did you leave France? How did you find out Nicole was here?"

"Who is this woman?" Gerard demanded. "I do not like servants who treat me like this. My wife is the Duchess de Levroux."

"The Revolution killed all titles," Nicole said. "In America, everyone is equal, and Janie is my friend."

"A pity," he said, his eyes scanning the simple room, yawning hugely before he stood. "I am quite tired. Is there a suitable bedroom in this place?"

"I don't know about suitable, but there's places to sleep," Janie said with hostility. "The attic has the twins and us three women. The mill has some spare beds."

"The twins?" Carefully noting the fine quality of the deep gray wool of her gown, he caught Nicole's eyes. "Of what age?"

"Six."

"They are not yours?"

"I care for them."

He smiled. "Good. I believe I must make do with your mill. I would not like to be awakened by children."

As Nicole started toward her cape by the door, Janie stopped her. "You go to your mother and see that she's all right. I'll take care of him."

Smiling gratefully, she bid Gerard goodnight and went upstairs to where her mother lay peacefully sleeping. The storm had subsided outside, and gentle flakes of snow were silently falling. As Nicole held her mother's warm hand in hers and watched her, she was flooded with memories—her mother lifting her and swinging her about just before she left for a court ball, her mother reading to her, pushing her in a swing. When Nicole was eight years old, Adele had had identical dresses made for them. The king said that someday the two of them would be twins, for Adele would never grow older.

"Nicole," Janie said when she returned. "You are not going to sit there all night. Your mother needs rest."

"I won't disturb her."

"And you won't help her either. If you don't sleep tonight, you'll be too tired tomorrow to be of any use to her."

Even though she knew Janie was right, Nicole sighed because she was afraid that if she closed her eyes her mother would disappear. Reluctantly, she stood and kissed her mother before turning away to get undressed.

An hour before sunrise, everyone in the little house was awakened by hideous screams—screams of absolute terror. As the twins shot out of their beds and ran to Janie, Nicole ran to her mother's side.

"Mama, it's me, Nicole. Nicole! Your daughter. Mama, be still, you're safe."

The woman's wild-eyed terror showed she obviously did not understand Nicole's words. Even though Nicole spoke in French, the words had no effect; Adele was still afraid, still screaming, screaming as if her whole body were being torn apart.

The twins put their hands over their ears and hid in the folds of Janie's flannel nightgown.

"Get Mr. Gautier," Nicole shouted, holding her mother's flailing hands as she fought her daughter.

"I am here," he said from the head of the stairs. "I thought she might wake like this. Adele!" he said sharply. Then, when she didn't respond, he slapped her hard across the cheek. The screams stopped at once, and she blinked a few times, then collapsed, sobbing, into Gerard's arms. He held her for a moment before quickly putting her down on the bed.

"She'll sleep for about three hours now," he said, rising before turning back toward the stairs.

"Mr. Gautier!" Nicole said. "Please, there must be something we can do. We can't go off and just leave her."

He turned and smiled at Nicole. "There is nothing anyone can do. Your mother is totally insane." Shrugging as if the matter meant very little to him, he went down the stairs.

Pausing only long enough to grab her bedrobe from its peg, Nicole raced down the stairs after him. "You can't just say something like that and leave," she said. "My mother has been through some horrible experiences. Surely, after she rests and is once again sure of her surroundings, she will recover."

"Perhaps."

Janie entered the room, the twins close behind her. By silent agreement, the discussion was postponed until everyone had eaten and the twins were out of the house.

As Janie cleared the dishes away, Nicole turned to Gerard. "Please tell me what happened to my mother after your father rescued her."

"She never recovered," he said simply. "Everyone thought she was so brave when she was walking to her death, but the truth was she had long ago lost touch with reality. They had kept her in prison for a long time, and she'd seen one after another of her friends taken away to be executed. After a while, I guess her mind refused to accept that the same fate awaited her."

"But when she was safe," Nicole said, "didn't that reassure her?"

Gerard looked with interest at his fingernails. "My father should not have rescued her. There was much danger in keeping one of the aristocracy in our house. The day he took her, the crowd was for him, but later someone could turn us in to the citizens' committee. It was very dangerous for all of us. My mother began to cry every night in fear. Adele's screams woke the neighbors. They kept quiet about the woman we hid, but we wondered how long it would be before they asked for the reward offered for the duchess."

Sipping on the coffee Janie had given him, he studied Nicole for a few moments. She was especially lovely in the morning light, her skin dewy from her night's sleep, her eyes luminous as she listened to the story, and he rather liked the way she looked at him, expectantly, with great interest.

He continued, "When we heard that the duke had been killed, I went to the mill where he'd hidden. I wanted to know if there was anyone else left in the family. The miller's wife was very angry because her husband had been murdered with the duke. It took me a long while to get her to tell me about Adele's daughter and that you'd gone to England. At home, when my parents heard the story of the miller, they were very frightened. We knew we had to get Adele out of our house."

Nicole rose and went to the fire. "You had little choice. You could either turn her over to the committee or get her out of the country, under another name, of course."

Gerard smiled at her quick understanding. "And what better disguise than the truth? We were quietly married, then went abroad on our honeymoon. In England, I found Mr. Maleson, who told me you had worked for his daughter and both of you had gone to America.

"Maleson was a strange man," he said. "He told me the strangest tale, which I did not half understand. He said you were married to his daughter's husband. How can that be? Is a man allowed to have two wives in this country?"

Janie gave a derisive snort before Nicole could answer. "Clayton Armstrong makes his own laws in this part of the country."

"Armstrong? Yes, that is the name Maleson said. He is your husband, then? Why is he not here? Is he away on business?"

"Business!" Janie said. "I wish he were. Clay lives across the river in a big, beautiful house with a fat, greedy snob, while his wife lives apart from him in a miller's shack."

"Janie!" Nicole snapped. "You've said quite enough."

"The problem is, you've said too little. Anything Clay tells you, you just bow down and say, 'Yes, Clay. Please, Clay. Whatever you want, Clay.'"

"Janie! I will not listen to any more of this. We have a guest, in case you've forgotten."

"I haven't forgotten anything!" she snapped as she turned toward the fire, her back to Nicole and Gerard. Every time she thought of Clay and the way he treated Nicole, she got angry. She didn't know if she was angry at Clay for the way he behaved or at Nicole for so calmly accepting the treatment. Janie felt Clay didn't deserve Nicole, that she should end the marriage and look at other men. But every time Janie said this, Nicole refused to listen, saying she trusted Clay as well as loved him.

The thoughts of everyone stopped as the screams began again, echoing through the little house, the sheer horror of them raising chills on Janie and Nicole.

Slowly, tiredly, Gerard rose. "It's the new place that frightens her. Once she gets used to it, the screams will be less frequent." He went toward the stairs.

"Do you think she will recognize me?" Nicole asked.

"Who can tell? For a while, she had lucid days, but now she is always frightened." He shrugged before disappearing into the attic, and moments later the screams quieted.

Cautiously, Nicole went into the attic. Gerard sat on the edge of the bed, one arm thrown carelessly across Adele's shoulders as she clung to him, looking about her wildly. Her eyes opened wide in alarm when she saw Nicole, but she didn't resume her screaming.

"Mother," Nicole said quietly, slowly. "I am Nicole, your daughter. Remember the time Father brought me a pet rabbit? Remember how it got out of its cage, and no one could find it? We looked through every wing of the chateau, but we couldn't find it."

Adele's eyes seemed to become calmer as she stared at Nicole.

Taking her mother's hand in her own, she continued. "Do you remember what you did, Mother? To play a joke on Father, you released three female rabbits in the chateau. Remember the nest of baby rabbits Father found with his hunting boots? You laughed so hard. But then Father laughed when more rabbits were found inside the chest with your wedding gown. And remember Grandfather? He said you were both children playing games."

"He organized a hunt," Adele whispered, her voice hoarse from a throat raw with screaming.

"Yes," Nicole whispered, tears blurring her vision. "The king was visiting that week, and he and Grandfather and fifteen of their men dressed as if they were going to war and set out to find all the rabbits. Do you remember what happened then?"

"We were soldiers," Adele said.

"Yes, you dressed me in my cousin's clothes. Then you and some of the court ladies dressed in the soldiers' costumes. Remember the queen's old aunt? She looked so funny in men's trousers."

"Yes," Adele whispered, caught up in the story. "We had fish for supper."

"Yes," Nicole smiled. "The ladies caught all the rabbits and let them loose on the grounds, and to punish the men for being such bad soldiers, you only allowed fish to be served for supper. Oh! Remember the salmon pâté?"

Beginning to return the smile, Adele answered, "The chef shaped it into rabbits, hundreds of little rabbits."

With tears on her cheeks, Nicole waited.

"Nicole!" Adele said sharply. "Whatever are you doing in that awful gown? A lady must never wear wool. It is too confining, too concealing. If a gentleman wants wool, he should be a shepherd. Now, go and find something in silk, something made by butterflies, not by those nasty old sheep."

"Yes, Mama," said the obedient daughter calmly, kissing her mother's cheek. "Are you hungry? Would you like a tray brought to you?"

Adele leaned against the wall behind the mattress set on the floor, seeming to be unaware of Gerard, who dropped his arm from around her. "Send something light. And use the blue and white Limoges china for today. After I eat, I will rest, then send the chef so we can plan menus for next week. The queen will be here, and I want to plan something very special. Oh, yes, if those Italian actors arrive, tell them I will speak to them later. And the gardener! I must talk to him about the roses. It is so much to do, and I am so tired. Nicole, do you think you could help me today?"

"Of course, Mama. You rest, and I will personally bring you something to eat. I will speak to the gardener myself."

"You calm her," Gerard said, following Nicole down the stairs. "I haven't seen her so relaxed in a long time."

Her mind reeling, Nicole went across the room calmly. Her mother still believed she lived in a time when she had fine servants who had nothing to do except help her dress. Nicole had been young enough to adjust to a harsh, cruel world where she wasn't pampered, but she doubted if her mother could do so.

Slowly, Nicole took a small skillet from the wall, then began breaking eggs for an omelet. Clay, she thought, wiping tears away with the back of her hand, how can I go away with you now? Her mother was here, and she needed her. Janie needed her, the twins needed her, Isaac was her responsibility, and now Gerard and Adele also needed her. What right did she have to feel sorry for herself? She should be grateful that she wasn't alone in the world.

A sharp sound from the attic signaled that Adele was impatient that her meal was taking so long. Suddenly, the front door burst open, the cold air rushing in.

"Excuse me, Nicole," Isaac said. "I didn't know you had company, but there's a man here with some new bolting cloth. He needs you to look at it."

"I'll be there as soon as possible."

"He said he's in a hurry, since it looks like a big snow's comin'. He wants to get to the Backes's before it hits."

The tapping from the attic became more insistent. "Nicole!" Adele called loudly. "Where is my maid? Where is my breakfast?"

Quickly, Nicole loaded the food on a tray and hurried past Isaac up the stairs to her mother.

Adele looked at the plain wicker tray, the brown-glazed earthenware, the hot omelet oozing cheese for only a second before she picked up a piece of toasted bread between her thumb and forefinger. "What is this? Bread? Peasants' bread? I must have croissant!"

Before Nicole could say a word, Adele had smashed the bread into the omelet.

"The chef has insulted me! Send this back, and tell him that if he values his job he will not serve this swill to me again." She picked up the pot of tea and poured it over the contents, the hot tea running through the wicker and onto the bedcovers.

Looking at the mess her mother was creating, Nicole began to feel very tired. The covers would have to be washed—by hand. The breakfast would have to be recooked, and she'd have to persuade her mother to eat it, somehow without making her start screaming again. And Isaac needed her at the mill.

She carried the dripping tray downstairs.

"Nicole!" Janie nearly knocked Isaac down as she ran into the room. "The twins have disappeared. They told Luke they were going to run away because a crazy lady had come to live with them."

"Well, why didn't Luke stop them?" Nicole slammed the tray on the table. Already, Adele was tapping on the floor.

"He said he thought it was a joke, that no crazy lady lived here."

Nicole raised her hands in helplessness. "Isaac, get the other men, and let's start searching. It's too cold for them to be outside alone." She turned to Gerard. "Would you prepare my mother something to eat?"

He lifted one eyebrow at her. "I'm afraid I do not do women's work."

Janie gasped. "Listen, you!"

"Janie!" Nicole snapped. "The twins are more important now. I'll take her some bread and cheese. She'll have to make do with that. I'll join the search as soon as possible. Please," she added when she saw Janie glaring at Gerard. "I need help now. Please don't add to my problems."

Janie and Isaac left the house as Nicole began tossing bread and cheese into a basket. Adele's tapping was urgent now, and Nicole was unaware of the way Gerard watched her as he leaned nonchalantly against a wall cabinet.

Nicole felt guilty about the way she had fairly tossed the food into her mother's lap, and she could see the hurt in Adele's eyes. Leaving her mother added to her guilt feelings, but the twins must be found. Even as she ran out the door and started calling the twins, she saw the two wayward children running across the yard toward her.

Chapter 17

GLANCING AT the clock on the cabinet by the door, Nicole moved slowly from the fireplace to the kitchen table. She must remember to punch down the brioche dough in ten minutes. The twins were playing quietly in the far corner of the room, Alex with several carved wooden animals and Mandy with a wax-faced doll that was supposed to be a farmer's wife.

"Nicole," Alex asked, "can we go outside after we eat?"

She sighed. "I hope so, if the snow stops falling. Maybe you can get Isaac to help you build a snowman."

The twins grinned at each other as they returned to their play.

The door opened, and the rush of cold air threatened to extinguish the fire. "This is the coldest March I have ever seen," Janie said as she held her hands out to the fire. "I don't think spring will ever come."

"Nor do I," Nicole whispered. She balled her hand into a fist and punched it viciously into the rising dough. Spring! she thought. The time when she and Clay were to go away together. Janie said that this winter had been the wettest and coldest she had ever seen in Virginia. Because of the snow, they had all been housebound—four adults and two children caught together in the small house. In the month since Gerard and Adele had arrived, Nicole had seen Clay only once. Yet even then he had looked distracted, worried about something.

"Good morning," Gerard said as he came down the stairs. Immediately after his arrival, the sleeping arrangements had changed. He and Adele now slept in the twins' bed upstairs, while the children slept on mattresses set up each night on the first floor. Janie and Nicole slept upstairs, a curtain separating them from the married couple.

"Morning!" Janie snorted. "It's nearly noon."

Gerard, as usual, ignored her. They had come to dislike each other with a great intensity. "Nicole," he said in a pleading voice, "do you think you could do something about the noise so early in the morning?"

She was too tired from cooking and cleaning and taking care of so many people to make any answer.

"And also, the cuffs on my lavender jacket are soiled. I do hope you can clean them," he continued, holding his arms out and studying the clothes he wore. His blue jacket reached to his knees, tight about the waist, fastened with heavy black braid, and flaring broadly over his slim hips that were covered in breeches buttoned at his knee, above silk hose leading to thin, flexible pumps. A vest of yellow satin, embroidered with bright blue stars, covered a white silk shirt fastened with a green cravat. He'd been appalled when he discovered that Nicole didn't know that a green cravat meant he was French nobility. "It's a small way in which we can separate ourselves from the commoners," he said.

The tapping on the ceiling made Nicole look up from her bread. Adele was awake earlier than usual.

"I'll go to her," Janie said.

Nicole smiled. "You know she's not used to you yet."

"Is she going to start screaming again?" Alex asked anxiously.

"Can we go outside?" Mandy asked.

"No and no," Nicole answered. "You can go out later." She grabbed a small tray, poured a glass of sweet apple cider, and carried it up to her mother.

"Good morning, dear," Adele said. "You aren't looking well

at all this morning. Aren't you feeling well?" Adele spoke French, as she always did. Although Nicole had tried to get her to speak English, a language she spoke quite well, Adele refused.

"I'm just a little tired is all."

Adele's eyes twinkled. "That German count kept you dancing for too long last night, didn't he?"

It was no use to try to reason or explain, so Nicole merely nodded. If her mother came back to reality for even a short time, she began to scream, and drugs had to be used to make her stop. Sometimes, she wavered between hysteria and a fanciful calmness. During a calm stage, she spoke of murder and death, of her time in prison, of her friends who walked out the door and never returned. Nicole hated those times the most, since she remembered too many of the people her mother said had been executed. She remembered sweet, frivolous women who had never known anything except luxury and comfort all their lives. Every time she thought of those women walking toward their deaths, she could hardly keep from crying.

A voice from downstairs drew her attention. Wesley! she thought with a surge of joy, grateful that her mother was leaning back against the pillows of the bed and closing her eyes. Adele rarely got out of bed, but she sometimes demanded hours of attention.

As always, feeling a little guilty, Nicole left her mother and went down to greet her guest. She hadn't seen Wes since that awful Christmas dinner more than three months ago.

He was deep in discussion with Janie, and Nicole could tell she was explaining about Gerard and Adele. "Wesley," she said, "it's so good to see you again."

There was a big smile on his face as he turned, but it faded instantly. "Good God, Nicole! You look awful! You look like you've lost twenty pounds and haven't slept in a year."

"That's about the truth," Janie said irritably.

As Wes looked from Janie to Nicole, he saw that neither

woman looked good. The roses were gone from Janie's cheeks. Behind the women was a little blond man standing over the twins, watching the children with a slight curl of distaste on his thick lips.

"Alex and Mandy, do you think you can get some boots and heavy coats on? And Nicole, I want you and Janie to dress warmly, too. We're going for a walk."

"Wes," Nicole began, "I really can't. I have bread rising and my mother—" She stopped. "Yes, I would like to go for a walk."

Nicole ran upstairs to get her new cloak, the one Clay had had made for her because she had won the bet on the horses at the Backes's party. The deep maroon camlet, a mixture of mohair and silk, shimmered from the long, lush nap as she swirled the heavy cape around before fastening it about her shoulders. The hood hanging down her back showed the deep, rich, black mink that lined the entire cape.

The outside air felt good and clean with the snow still falling, the flakes often landing on her lashes. The dark mink framed her face as she drew the hood up.

"What's been going on?" Wes asked as he drew Nicole aside once they were outside, watching Janie, the twins, and Isaac engaging in a halfhearted snowball fight. "I thought everything would be fine between you and Clay after the Backes's party and after we got you off the island."

"It will be," she said confidently. "It will just take time."

"I have no doubt Bianca is at the bottom of this."

"Please, I'd rather not talk about it. How have you and Travis been?"

"Lonely. We're getting sick of each other's company. Travis is going to England in the spring to look for a wife."

"To England? But there are several beautiful young women right around here."

Wesley shrugged. "That's what I told him, but I think you

spoiled him. Personally, I'm going to wait for you. If Clay doesn't wise up soon, I'm going to try to steal you away from him."

"Don't say that, please," she whispered. "I think maybe I'm superstitious."

"Nicole, something is wrong, isn't it?"

Tears came to her eyes. "I'm just so tired and . . . I haven't seen Clay in weeks. I don't know what he's doing. I have this awful fear that he's fallen in love with Bianca and doesn't want to tell me."

Smiling, Wes put his arms around her, pulling her close. "You have too much to do, too much responsibility. The last thing you should have to worry about is Clay's love. How can you think he's in love with a bitch like Bianca? If she's in his house and you're here, then it's for a damned good reason." He paused. "Your safety, maybe, since I can't think of anything else that would keep Clay away from you."

Sniffling, she nodded against him. "Did he tell you?"

"Some of it, but not much. Come on, let's go help them build a snowman, or better yet, let's challenge them to a snowman duel."

"Yes," she smiled, drawing away from him. She wiped her eyes with her knuckle. "You'll think I'm no older than the twins."

He kissed her forehead as he smiled. "Some child! Come on, let's go before they use up all the snow."

A voice crying from the direction of the river stopped them. "Hello! Is anyone home?"

Wesley and Nicole turned and walked toward the wharf.

An older man, heavyset, with a fresh scar across his left cheek, was walking toward them. He wore the dress of a sailor, a knapsack thrown over his shoulder. "Mrs. Armstrong?" he said as he came to stand before her. "Don't you remember me? I'm Dr. Donaldson from the *Prince Nelson*."

He did seem vaguely familiar, but she couldn't remember exactly where she'd seen him before.

Several lines showed at the corners of his eyes as he smiled. "The circumstances were, I admit, not the best when we met, but I see things have turned out well." He held out his hand to Wesley. "You must be Clayton Armstrong."

"No," Wes said as he took the man's hand. "I'm a neighbor, Wesley Stanford."

"Oh, I see. Well, then, maybe I am needed. I hoped things had changed, I mean with this young lady being so kind and pretty."

"The doctor on the ship!" Nicole gasped. "At the marriage!"

"Yes." He grinned. "As soon as I got to England, a message reached me that I was to return to Virginia at once since I was the only witness who would testify that it was a forced marriage. I came as soon as I could and got directions to the mill. It was confusing about where the Armstrong plantation was and who lived at the mill. I took my chances and came here first."

"I am so glad you did. Are you hungry? I could scramble some eggs and there's ham and bacon and a pot of beans."

"You don't have to ask me twice."

Later, when the three of them were seated at the table, the doctor told them of the captain of the *Prince Nelson* and his first mate, Frank. Both men had been drowned on their return trip to England.

"I refused to sail with them again after what they'd done to you. I guess I should have tried to stop them but I knew they'd just get another witness, and besides, I knew the annulment laws too. I knew I'd be the witness you needed if you did want that annulment."

"Then why did you go back to England so fast?" Wes asked.

The doctor grinned. "I didn't exactly have a choice. We were all in a tavern celebrating our safe arrival. The next thing I knew,

I woke aboard ship with a splitting headache. It was three days before I could even remember my name."

A loud tapping coming from the ceiling interrupted his talk and made Nicole jump. "My mother! I forgot her breakfast. Please excuse me." With deftness, Nicole poached an egg and carefully set it atop a day-old slice of brioche, next to an apple tart on a separate plate and a steaming cup of café au lait. She hurried up the stairs with it.

"Sit with me for a while," Adele said. "It's very lonely here."

"There is a guest below, but later I'll come and we can talk."

"Is he a man? Is your guest a man?"

"Yes."

Adele sighed. "I hope he's not one of those awful Russian princes."

"No, he's an American."

"An American! How extraordinary. There are so few of them who are gentlemen. Whatever you do, don't let him use strong language in front of you. And notice how he walks. You can always tell a gentleman by his posture. If your father wore rags, he'd still look like a gentleman!"

"Yes, Mama," Nicole said dutifully before going down the stairs. Her life seemed very remote from judging whether a man was a gentleman or not.

"Wesley was telling me that Mr. Armstrong lives across the river. The marriage didn't work out, then?" the doctor asked.

"It hasn't been easy, but I still have hope." She was trying to smile.

But she didn't realize how much her face told of what she thought, or that there were sunken circles of tiredness under her eyes, almost hiding the fact that they were alive with hope—and desperation.

Dr. Donaldson frowned. "Have you been eating well, young lady? Getting enough sleep?"

Wes spoke before she could answer. "Nicole adopts people

the way some people adopt stray cats. Recently, she took on two more to care for. She has Clay's niece and nephew, who shouldn't be her responsibility, and now she has her mother, who demands queenly service, and her mother's husband, who thinks he's the king of France."

Nicole laughed. "You make it sound as if my life is a great burden. The truth is, Doctor, I love the people around me. I wouldn't give up one of them."

"I never thought you should," Wes answered. "You should just be living in the house across the river, and Maggie should be doing the cooking, not you."

Taking the pipe out of his pocket, the doctor leaned back in his chair. Things hadn't gone very well for the little French lady, he thought. The young man, Wes, was right when he said she deserved better than to be worked to death. He'd planned to travel north, to Boston, right away, but now he decided he'd stay in Virginia for the next few months. He hated the way she'd been forced into a marriage she didn't want, had always felt somehow responsible. Now he knew he must stay close by in case she did need help.

Nicole threw the hood back from her head and let the breeze touch her face. She moved the oars of the little rowboat into and out of the water. The snow was still on the ground. There were no buds on the trees, but something indefinable said that spring was in the air. It was two weeks since the doctor had first visited her. She smiled when she thought of how he'd said he'd be near if she needed him. How could she ever need him? She wanted so badly to tell him, to tell them all, that she and Clay would be leaving Virginia quite soon.

She'd been planning for months. The twins and Janie would, of course, go with her and Clay. She hated leaving her mother, but Gerard would be there, and later, when they had a house, Adele could come and live with them. Isaac could run the mill, and as long as he supported Gerard and Adele, the remaining profits could be his. When Adele joined Nicole in the west, Isaac could have the mill and run it with Luke's help.

Oh, yes, it was all going to work out perfectly.

Yesterday, Clay had sent her a note asking her to meet him in the clearing this morning. Last night, she'd hardly been able to sleep. She kept dreaming of this meeting with Clay when all their plans would begin to come alive.

She took a deep breath of the clean, cold air, then caught a whiff of smoke. Clay was already at the cave. She threw the rope of the rowboat onto the bushes that led to the clearing, then stepped ashore and tied it.

She ran down the little path. As in part of her dream, Clay stood there, waiting for her, his arms outstretched. She leaped the last few steps and flung herself at him. He was so tall, so strong, and his chest was so hard. He held her very close, so close she couldn't breathe. But she had no desire to breathe. All she wanted was to melt into him, become part of him. She wanted to forget herself, to exist only with him.

He lifted her chin so that she faced him. His eyes were hungry, dark, ravenous. Nicole felt a surge of fire sear through her body. This is what she'd missed! She strained upward to clutch at his mouth with her teeth. She gave a low sound that was half growl, half laugh.

Clay's tongue touched the corner of her mouth, just in the tiny hollow.

Nicole's knees grew weak.

Clay laughed against her throat, then picked her up in his arms and carried her inside the velvet darkness of the cave.

There was a frenzy of movement. They were two people starved for each other, desperate, eager, greedy, demanding, as the fire burned along their skin and cried angrily to be released. Their clothes were discarded in seconds, flung about the cave with total disregard.

They didn't speak as they came together. They allowed their skin to do their talking. They were fierce with each other. Nicole arched against Clay, and lightning flashed in her head. As she felt the throbbing sensations run through her, she smiled and began to relax.

"Clay," she whispered, "I've missed you so much."

He held her tightly to him, his breath soft and warm against her ear. "I love you. I love you so very much." His voice sounded sad.

She pushed away from him, then snuggled against him so that her head rested in the hollow of his shoulder. "Today is the first morning I've been able to believe it's nearly spring. It seems I've waited forever for spring."

Clay leaned over her and got her cape. He spread it over them, the mink against their skin.

Nicole smiled deliciously and rubbed her thigh over Clay's. The moment was perfect—held in her lover's arms, alone, their bodies sated, caressed by the luscious mink.

"How is your mother?" Clay asked.

"She doesn't scream as much as she did. I'm glad because it frightens the twins terribly."

"Nicole, I've told you that you should send the twins back to me. There's no room for them with you."

"Please let them stay."

He hugged her closer. "You know I wouldn't take them away from you. It's just that you have too many people and too much to do."

She kissed his shoulder. "You're kind to worry, but they're really no problem. Now, if you wanted to take Janie and Gerard, I might consider your proposal."

"Is Janie giving you problems?"

"No, not really. She and Gerard hate each other, and they constantly pick at each other. I just get tired of listening, that's all."

"If Janie hates someone, it's usually for a good reason. You haven't said much about your stepfather."

"My stepfather." Nicole smiled. "It's odd to think of Gerard as being a replacement for my father."

"Tell me about your life. I feel so removed from you."

She smiled again, feeling his love all around her. "Gerard is infatuated with being part of the French aristocracy. It seems so humorous when you realize there are hundreds of people in France wanting to be part of the common people."

"From what I hear, his being in your house isn't exactly humorous. You know that if you need anything—"

She put her fingertips over his lips. "You're all I need. Sometimes, when it gets very noisy and everyone seems to be pulling at me, I stop and think about you. This morning when I woke, I was terribly excited about the warmth in the air. Do you think the weather is the same in the west as it is here? And do you really know how to build a house? When do you think we can leave? I've been wanting to pack for a long time, but I didn't feel it was time yet to tell Janie."

She stopped when he didn't make any response. She rose on one elbow to look at him. "Clay, is everything all right?"

"Perfectly," he said flatly. "At least, it will be."

"What do you mean? Something is wrong. I can tell."

"No, nothing serious anyway. Nothing is going to upset our plans to leave."

She frowned at him. "Clay, I know you, and I know you have a problem. You haven't mentioned Bianca, yet I pour out all my troubles to you."

He smiled slightly at her. "You wouldn't know how to pour out your troubles. You are so kind, so loving, so forgiving, that half the time you don't even see how people use you."

"Use me?" she laughed. "No one uses me."

"I do, the twins do, your mother, her husband, even Janie. We all impose on you."

"You make me sound like a saint. I have many things I want out of life, but I'm practical. I know that I must wait to get what I want."

"And what do you want?" he asked quietly.

"You. I want you and my own home and the twins. And maybe some other children—your children."

"You'll have it! I swear it! It's all going to be yours."

She stared at him for a long while. "I want to know what is wrong. It has to do with Bianca, doesn't it? Has she found out about our plans? If she's threatening you again, I won't stand for it this time. My patience is nearly gone."

Clay put his arm around her firmly and pulled her head to his shoulder. "I want you to listen to me, to all of the story before you say a word." He took a deep breath. "First of all, I want to tell you that it will make no difference to our plans."

"It?"

She tried to lift her head to look at him, but he stopped her.

"Just listen to me, then I'll answer questions." He paused, staring at the ceiling of the cave. It had been three weeks since Bianca had told him she was pregnant. At first, he'd laughed at her, saying that she lied. She'd merely stood there and smiled at him, so self-satisfied. She'd been the one to have the doctor come to her and examine her. Since then, Clay had lived in hell. He couldn't believe the news. It had taken a long time to decide that Nicole meant more to him than the child Bianca carried.

"Bianca is pregnant," he said quietly. When Nicole didn't react, he went on. "The doctor came and confirmed it. I've thought about it for a long time, and I've decided to go ahead with our plans to leave Virginia. We'll make our home in a new place, together."

Still, Nicole did not say a word. She lay on his shoulder as calmly as if he'd said nothing.

"Nicole? Did you hear me?"

"Yes," she said quite evenly.

He loosened his arm so that he could move back from her, see her face.

Without looking at his eyes, she sat up, then turned her back to him and slowly pulled her chemise over her head.

"Nicole, I wish you'd say something. I wouldn't have told you at all except Bianca's already told half the county. I didn't want you to hear it from someone else. I thought I should tell you."

She didn't say a word as she slipped her dress over her head, rolled one woolen stocking on, then the other.

"Nicole!" Clay demanded, then grabbed her shoulders to turn her to look at him. He gasped at what he saw there. Her brown eyes, usually so warm and loving, were cold and hard.

"I don't believe you want me to say anything."

He pulled her to him, but her body was rigid against him. "Please talk to me. Let's get this thing out in the open and discuss it. Once we clear the air, we'll be able to make plans."

She stared at him, half smiling. "Make plans? Plans to go away and leave an innocent child with no one to care for it except Bianca? Don't you know she'll make a magnificent mother?"

"What the hell do I care about her motherhood skills? You're what I want, you and you alone."

She lifted her hands and pushed his away. "Not once have you said that the child couldn't be yours."

He stared at her, his eyes never blinking. He'd expected this, and he planned to be honest. "I was drunk, and it was only the one night. She put herself in my bed."

She gave him a cold smile. "I guess I'm supposed to forgive what's done under the influence of alcohol. After all, look at all that's happened to me because of it. I was drunk the first time you made love to me."

"Nicole." He leaned toward her.

She jumped backward. "Don't touch me," she said under her breath. "Don't ever touch me again."

He grabbed her shoulder, hard. "You're my wife, and I have a right to touch you."

She pulled back her hand and slapped him as hard as she could. "Your wife! How dare you say that to me? When have I ever been anything but your whore? You use me when you need me to get rid of your physical desires. Isn't Bianca enough for you? Are you the type of man who needs more than one woman for his lust?"

Her handprint stood out vividly on his skin. "You know that isn't true. You know I've always been honest with you."

"Know? What do I know about you? I know your body, I know you have power over me, both mentally and physically. I know you can get me to do what you want; you can make me believe the most outrageous stories."

"Listen to me, believe me. I love you. We'll go away together."

She threw back her head and laughed. "You are the one who doesn't know me. I admit I haven't shown much pride while I was around you. Actually, I've done little more than flop on my back when you enter a room, or on my knees, or astride you. I don't even ask what your pleasure is; I just obey."

"Stop it! This isn't you!"

"It isn't? Who is the real Nicole? Everyone thinks she is an earth mother, nurturing everyone, taking the responsibility of everyone's problems, asking so little from others. It's not like that! Nicole Courtalain is a woman, a full-fledged woman, with all the greeds and passions of other women. Bianca's so much smarter than I am. She sees what she wants, and she goes after it. She doesn't sit at home and wait patiently for a message from some man to meet her for a morning romp. She knows that isn't the way to get what she wants."

"Nicole," Clay said, "please calm down. You're saying things you don't mean."

"No," she smiled. "I think that for once I'm saying things I do mean. I've been in America for all these months, and I've spent all of that time waiting. I waited for you to tell me you loved me, then I waited for you to make up your mind between Bianca and me. I think how utterly stupid I've been, how simple-minded and starry-eyed. Like a child, I trusted you."

She gave a snort of laughter. "Did you know that Abe tore my clothes off and tied me to a wall? I was so stupid that all I could think of was that he'd soil me for you. Can you imagine that? You were probably in bed with Bianca while stupid little me was worrying about keeping myself clean for you."

"I've had about enough. You've said too much already."

"My, my! The demanding Clayton Armstrong has had too much. Too much of which one of us? Curvy Bianca or skinny little Nicole?"

"Stop and listen to me. I told you it doesn't make any difference to me. We'll go away just as we planned."

She glared at him, her upper lip curled into a snarl. "But it makes a difference to me! Do you think I want to spend my life with a man who could so easily abandon his own child? What if we did go west and had a child? If you saw some sweet young thing, maybe you'd run off with her and leave *our* child."

Her words stung him, and he drew back. "How can you believe that?"

"How can I not? What have you ever done to make me believe any differently? I was a fool, and for some reason, maybe your broad shoulders or some such nonsense, I fell in love with you. You, being a man, used my schoolgirl lust to full advantage."

"Do you really believe that?" he asked quietly.

"What else can I believe? I have done nothing but wait. Every minute I have waited—waited to start living. Well, no more!" She jammed her shoes on, stood up, and started toward the mouth of the little cave.

Clay quickly pulled his pants on and went after her. "You can't leave like this," he said, grabbing her arm. "I have to make you understand."

"But I do understand. You've made your choice. I guess it was a test of who got pregnant first. The Courtalains have never been fertile. Too bad, perhaps I would have won the race. Would I have the big house then? The servants?" She paused. "The baby?"

"Nicole."

She looked down at his hand on her arm. "Release me," she said coldly.

"Not until you see reason."

"You mean I'm to stay until you sweet-talk me back into your arms, don't you? It's over. It is dead, flat over between us."

"You can't mean that."

Her voice was very quiet. "Two weeks ago the doctor from the ship I came to America on came to see me."

Clay's eyes widened.

"Yes, your witness that you so urgently wanted at one time. He said he'd help me to get an annulment."

"No," Clay breathed, "I don't want—"

"It's past time for what you want. You've had everything, or should I say everyone, you wanted. Now it's my turn. I'm going to stop waiting and start living."

"What are you talking about?"

"First an annulment, then I plan to enlarge my business. There's no reason why I shouldn't make use of this beautiful land of opportunity."

A log fell in the little fireplace, and the glass that held the unicorn caught Nicole's eye. She gave a dry, cold laugh. "I should have known what you were like when we made those childish vows. I wasn't pure enough to touch the unicorn itself, was I? Only your dear, dead Beth was good enough for that."

She pushed past him and went outside into the cool morning. Very calmly, she went to the rowboat and began to row herself back to the mill wharf. Her grandfather had told her never to look back. It wasn't easy to keep her mind from crying out for

Clay. She conjured a picture of Bianca, content and pregnant, her hands resting on the mound that was Clay's child. She glanced at her own flat stomach and was thankful that she had no child.

By the time she reached the wharf, she was feeling better. She stood and looked up at the little house. It was going to be her permanent home for a while, and she thought of it as such. She would need more room, a parlor downstairs, and two more bedrooms upstairs. Immediately, she realized that she had no money. There was good, flat farmland adjoining the mill, and she vaguely remembered Janie mentioning that it was for sale. She had no money for land.

Then she remembered her clothes. They were certainly worth something. Why, the sable muff alone . . . How she'd like to throw everything into Clay's face! She'd like to have the clothes delivered to him, dumped in his hallway. But that bit of show would cost her too much. At the Backes's, several women had admired her clothes. Suddenly, she thought with regret of the mink-lined cape she'd left on the floor of the cave. But she could never go back there—never!

Plans were whirling in her head as she entered the single room of the little house. Janie was bent over the fire, her face red from the heat. Gerard lounged in a chair, insolently smashing a doughnut into a plate. The twins were in a corner, giggling behind a book.

Janie looked up. "Something's happened."

"No," Nicole said. "At least nothing new." She studied Gerard. "Gerard, I've just come to the conclusion that you would make an excellent salesman."

His eyebrows came up. "People of my class—" he began.

Nicole cut him off as she grabbed the plate out from under his fork. "This is America, not France. If you eat, you work."

He gave her a sullen look. "What is there to sell? I know nothing about grain."

"The grain sells itself. I want you to persuade some lovely young women that they will be even lovelier in silks and sables."

"Sables?" Janie asked. "Nicole, what are you talking about?"

Nicole gave her a look that stopped her from speaking. "Come upstairs with me while I show you the clothes." She turned to the twins. "And you two are going to get lessons."

"But Nicole," Janie interrupted, "you don't have time. The mill dresser is already here."

"Not me," she said firmly. "Upstairs is a highly educated woman, and she will be only too happy to tutor the children."

"Adele?" Gerard scoffed. "You won't even be able to make her understand what you want, much less get her to do it."

"We don't like the screaming lady," Alex said, holding Mandy's hand and stepping back.

"Enough!" Nicole said loudly. "I've had enough of these complaints. Janie and I are not running a free hotel any longer. Gerard, you are going to help me get some money for some land. Mother is going to take care of the children, and the twins are going to get an education. From now on, we're a family, not an aristocracy with a couple of servants." She turned and went up the stairs.

Janie grinned up at her. "I don't know what's happened to her, but I like it!"

"If she thinks I'm going to—" Gerard began.

Janie waved a hot, sticky spoon in front of his face. "You either work or we ship you back to France, and you can get your head cut off or make shoes like your father. You got that?"

"You can't treat me like this!"

"I can, and I will. If you don't get up those stairs like Nicole said, I may use my fist on that ugly little face of yours."

Gerard started to speak, but he stopped as he stared at Janie's fist in his face. She was a large, strong woman. He stepped back from her. "We aren't finished yet." He muttered several curses in French as he followed Nicole up the stairs.

Janie turned to the twins, gave them a warning look, clapped her hands smartly, and sent them scurrying up the stairs.

Chapter 18

IT WAS Wesley who sailed Nicole upriver to where Dr. Donaldson was staying and then took them all to the judge's house. Wes didn't say much when Nicole told him she wanted her marriage to Clay annulled. In fact, no one said very much, and it seemed to Nicole that everyone believed it was inevitable. She was the last one to have any faith in Clay.

It was surprising how little time it took to end a marriage. Nicole worried that since so many people had seen her with Clay and since the marriage had been consummated, it would make a difference. She found out that they could even have had children and, because of the force used during the ceremony, still have had the marriage annulled.

The judge had known both Clay and Wesley all their lives. He'd met Nicole at the Backes's party. He hated to dissolve the marriage, to declare it had never existed, but he couldn't dispute the doctor's testimony. Besides, he'd heard the gossip about the woman Clay lived with. He made a mental note to visit Clay very soon and tell him what he thought of his immoral behavior. The judge looked at the pretty little French-woman with sympathy. She didn't deserve what Clay had put her through.

He declared the marriage annulled.

"Nicole?" Wes asked when they left the judge's house. "Are you all right?"

"Of course," she said flatly. "Why shouldn't I be? If you wanted to buy some land, where would you go first?"

"To the owners, I guess. Why?"

"Do you know Mr. Irwin Rogers?"

"Sure. He lives about a mile down the road."

"Could you take me there and introduce me?" she asked.

"Nicole, what's this all about?"

"I want to buy the farmland next to the mill. I thought I'd put in a crop of barley this spring."

"Barley? But Clay can give you—" He stopped at Nicole's look.

"I am no longer related to Clayton Armstrong, nor do I have anything to do with him. I will make my own way in the world."

She started walking down the road, but Wes grabbed her arm. "I can't believe it's really over between you and Clay."

"I think it's been over for a long time, but I was too blind to see it," she said quietly.

"Nicole," Wes began, staring down at her. The sunlight on her face made her eyes sparkle. He studied her mouth, the upper lip so fascinating. "Why don't you marry me? You've never even seen my house. It's enormous. You could have all the people you take care of live there, and we wouldn't even see them. Travis and I have more money than we know what to do with, and you wouldn't have to work."

She stared at him a moment, then smiled. "Wesley, you are very sweet. You don't want to marry me." She turned away from him.

"Yes, I do ! You'd make a perfect wife. You could run the whole plantation, and everyone likes you."

"Stop!" she laughed. "You're making me feel very old." She stood on tiptoe and kissed the corner of his mouth. "I thank you for your offer, but I have no desire to leave one marriage and go directly into another one." She narrowed her eyes at him. "And if you dare look relieved, I will never speak to you again."

He lifted her hand and kissed it, rubbing her fingers between his. "I may cry, but I certainly won't look relieved."

She laughed and pulled her hand away. "I need friends more than a lover right now. If you really want to help me, maybe you could get Mr. Rogers to give me a good price on the land."

Wesley watched her for a moment. His marriage proposal had been a spur-of-the-moment thing, but now he thought how pleasant it would be to be married to someone like Nicole. She would have surprised him if she'd accepted him, but he wished she had.

He grinned at her. "Old man Rogers is going to be so pleased to sell that land, he's going to practically give it to you."

"No violence," Nicole laughed.

"Maybe a broken toe or two, but that's all."

"Well . . . if it's just toes."

They laughed together and went down the road toward Mr. Rogers's house.

They did get a good price for the land. Nicole had very little cash from the clothes Gerard had sold, but Mr. Rogers allowed her to pay off the land slowly over the years. She also agreed to grind the grain from his farm for free for three years.

"He didn't exactly give us the land," Wes said when they left. "His grain ground free for three years!"

Nicole's eyes sparkled. "But wait until he gets his bill for the fourth year!"

After they left Mr. Rogers's house, they went to the printer's office, where Nicole had handbills printed advertising her mill's rates for grinding.

"Nicole!" Wes said as he heard her tell the printer the new rates. "How do you expect to make any money? That's a third less than Horace charges."

She smiled. "Competition and quantity. Would you bring your grain to me or to Horace?"

The printer laughed. "I think she's got you there, Wes. I'm

going to tell my brother-in-law about this, and you can be sure he'll come to you."

Wesley looked at Nicole with new respect. "I had no idea there was a brain behind that pretty face."

She was serious. "I don't think there has been. Or, at least, it's been clouded with childish ideas of love and romance."

Wesley frowned as she left the printer's. He had the feeling she was hurt more than she'd admit. Damn Clay! he thought. He had no right to use Nicole the way he did.

At home again, Gerard was the one who gave Nicole trouble. The little man backed away from her in disgust.

"It was disgusting enough to have to sell ladies' dresses." He stopped and smoothed his hair. It was cut in the Brutus style, fashionably shaggy and unkempt. It lay close to his head, limp, without body or curl. "Of course, the women were pleased to meet me. They were not like the people in this house. They liked the stories of my family, the magnificent Courtalains."

"Since when has Nicole's family become yours?" Janie snapped.

"See!" Gerard shouted. "I am unappreciated."

"Both of you, stop it," Nicole said. "I'm tired of hearing you bicker. Gerard, you have proved yourself a perfect salesman. The women love your accent and your charming manners."

He preened under her compliments.

"If you want, you may give the handbills to the farmers' wives. In fact, that may be a good idea."

"Handbills are not silks," he muttered.

"But food is food," Janie said. "And if you want any, you'll work like the rest of us."

Gerard took a step toward Janie, his upper lip curled into a sneer, but Nicole put her hand on his forearm and stopped him. He looked from her hand to her face, then back again. He covered her hand with his. "For you, I would do anything."

Nicole, as politely as possible, moved away from him. "Isaac will row you up and down the river to the houses."

Gerard smiled at her as if they were lovers, then quietly left the house.

"I don't trust him," Janie said.

Nicole waved her hand. "He's harmless. He just wants us to treat him royally is all. He'll soon learn."

"You're too generous. Just take my advice and stay well away from him."

Spring came quickly to the Virginia countryside, and with it came the ripening of the early crops. It wasn't long before the enormous grindstones in the mill were again turning after the long winter break. Nicole's handbills worked, and farmers came from miles around to bring their grain to the mill.

Nicole never allowed herself a minute to relax. She hired another man to help in the fields that were seeded with barley and wheat. Gerard reluctantly helped at the mill, but he made it clear that he considered the Americans beneath him. Nicole kept reminding him that her grandfather the duke had worked in a grain mill for two years.

No one seemed to consider the idea of the twins returning to Clay, and Nicole knew it was a sign of his trust in her. Once a week, Isaac rowed the children across the river to visit their uncle.

"He looks bad," Isaac said once after he returned.

Nicole didn't bother to ask whom he meant. In spite of all her work, Clay was never far from her mind.

"He drinks too much. I never knew him to drink so much before."

Nicole turned away. She should feel glad he was so miserable, since he certainly deserved it. But somehow she wasn't glad. She left Isaac and went to the vegetable garden. Maybe a few hours of hoeing would keep her mind off Clay.

An hour later, Nicole leaned against a tree and wiped her

forearm across her face. She was hot and sweaty from the vigorous hoeing.

"Here, I brought you something," Gerard said as he handed her a glass of cool lemonade.

She nodded her gratitude and gulped all of the liquid.

Gerard brushed a piece of grass from the sleeve of her cotton dress. "You shouldn't be out here in the sun. It will ruin that beautiful complexion of yours." He ran his hand down her arm.

Nicole was too tired to move away from him. They stood in a deeply shaded place, out of sight of the house and mill.

"I'm glad we have this time alone," he said, moving closer to her. "It's strange that we live in the same house, yet we rarely have a chance to be alone, to have a private conversation."

Nicole didn't want to offend him, but neither did she want to encourage him. She stepped away. "You could talk to me at any time, I hope you know that."

He moved near her again, his hand running up and down her arm, caressing it. "You're the only one here who understands me." He spoke in French, moving his face closer to hers. "We're from the same country, the same people. No one else knows what France is like now. We're drawn closer together by our common bond."

"I consider myself an American now." She answered him in English.

"How can you? You are French as I am French. We are of the great Courtalains. Think how we could continue the line."

Nicole's back straightened as she glared at him. "How dare you!" she gasped. "Do you forget my mother? You are married to her, yet you proposition me like some scullery maid."

"How can I forget her when her screams nearly drive me mad? Do you think there is a minute that I'm not aware that I am bound to her? What can she give me? Can she give me children? I am a man, a healthy man, and I deserve children." He grabbed her, pulled her close to him. "You are the only one. In all of this heathen country, you are the only one worthy to be the mother of my children. You are a Courtalain! Our children's blood would flow with the blue of kings."

It took Nicole a second to comprehend what he was saying. She felt her stomach turn over when she did understand. There were no words to express her feelings. She slapped him hard.

Gerard released her immediately and put his hand over his cheek. "You will pay for this," he whispered. "You will be sorry you ever treated me like one of these filthy Americans. I will make you know who I am."

Nicole turned away and went back to the garden. Janie had been right about Gerard after all. She vowed to stay away from the little Frenchman as much as possible.

Two weeks later, Wes brought the news that Clayton had married Bianca.

She braced herself against the impact of the news.

"I tried to reason with him," Wes said. "But you know how stubborn Clay is. He's never stopped loving you. When he heard about the annulment, he stayed drunk for four days. One of his men found him by the side of the swamp in the south pasture."

"I assume he sobered up for his wedding," she said coldly.

"He said he did it for the child. Goddamn him! I can't understand how he could stomach going to bed with that cow."

He caught Nicole's arm as she turned away. "I'm sorry I said that. I didn't mean to hurt you."

"How could you hurt me? Mr. Armstrong means nothing to me."

Wes stood quietly and watched her go. He could strangle Clay for what he'd done to that beautiful young woman.

Arundel Hall was filthy. It hadn't been cleaned in months. Bianca sat quietly at the dining table, eating ice cream and sugar cookies. Her enormous belly stuck out in front of her so far she looked as if she were about to deliver the child at any moment.

Clay came into the house, stopping at the dining room door. His clothes were muddy, his shirt torn. There were circles under his eyes, and his hair was plastered to his head from sweat. "What a lovely sight to come home to," he said loudly. "My wife. Soon to be mother of my child."

Bianca ignored him but continued slowly to eat the delicious, cold, rich ice cream.

"Eating for two, my dear?" he asked. When he got no response, he went upstairs. Dirty clothes were slung everywhere. He pulled open a drawer and saw that it was empty. No longer were there clean, mended shirts waiting for him.

He cursed and slammed the drawer, then went out of the house, walking quickly toward the river. He spent very little time at home now. His days he spent in the fields; his evenings he sat alone in the library and drank until he thought he could sleep. Even then, he rarely did.

At the river, he stripped off his clothes and dove into the water. After his bath, he stretched out on the grassy shore and fell asleep.

When he woke, it was night, and for a moment he didn't know where he was. In a dazed, half-awake, half-asleep mood, he walked back to the house.

He heard the moaning as soon as he entered the house. Quickly, he shook himself out of the sleep. Bianca lay curled at the foot of the stairs, her hand holding her stomach.

He knelt beside her. "What is it? Did you fall?"

She rolled her eyes at him. "Help me," she gasped. "The baby."

Clay didn't touch her but ran from the house to get the plantation midwife. Within minutes he was back, the woman following him. Bianca lay just as he'd left her. He lit a lantern as the woman bent over Bianca.

She ran her hands over Bianca's still form, and when she held them up to the light they were bloody. "Can you get her upstairs?"

Clay set the lantern down and lifted Bianca. The veins in his neck stood out as he strained to get her heavy form up the stairs. He laid her gently on the bed.

"Go get Maggie," the midwife said. "I'll need help for this one."

Clay sat in his library, drinking steadily while Maggie and the midwife tended to Bianca.

Maggie quietly opened the door. "She lost the baby," she said quietly.

Clay looked at her in amazement. Then he smiled. "Lost the baby, did she?"

"Clay," Maggie said. She didn't like the look in his eye. "I wish you'd stop drinking."

He poured another glass of bourbon. "Aren't you supposed to comfort me? Shouldn't you tell me there will be other children?"

"There won't be," the midwife said from the door. "She's a heavy woman, and when she went down those stairs, she went hard. There's a lot of damage inside her, especially to her female workin's. I'm not sure she's gonna live."

Clay drained the bourbon and refilled the glass. "She'll live. I have no doubt of that. People like Bianca don't die easily."

"Clayton!" Maggie commanded. "You're taking this too hard." She went to him and put her hand on his. "Please stop drinking. You won't be fit for a day's work tomorrow if you don't."

"Work," he said, and smiled. "Why should I work? What for? For my darling wife? For the son she just lost?" He drank some more bourbon, then began to laugh. It was an ugly laugh.

"Clay," Maggie said.

"Get out of here! Can't a man be alone once in a while?"

Slowly, the women left the room.

When the sun came up, Clay was still drinking, still waiting for the forgetfulness the drink would bring.

In the fields, the hands started their day's work. It was unusual not to see Clay watching them. Toward afternoon, they began to slow down. It was nice not to have the boss looking over their shoulders. By the fourth day, when Clay still did not come to the fields, some of the men didn't bother to go to work at all.

Chapter 19

IT WAS August of 1796, one year later.

Nicole stood on top of the hill and looked down at her property. Putting her hands at the small of her back, she massaged her tired muscles. It helped to ease the pain if she could see what had caused her fatigue. The hot August sun blazed down on the tall tobacco plants. The cotton would soon be bursting its pods. The golden wheat, almost ripe, waved gently in the breeze. The sound of the millstones, grinding evenly and steadily, floated up to her. One of the twins yelled, and Nicole smiled at Janie's sharp reprimand.

It had been well over a year since her marriage had been annulled. She realized that she marked all time from that hour in the judge's office. Since that fateful day, she'd done little besides work. Every morning, she was up before daylight, seeing to the mill, to the crops that were planted and harvested. The first time she'd taken her crops to market, the men had laughed, thinking they'd be able to get her produce for a low price. But Nicole wouldn't allow herself to be cheated; she drove a hard bargain. When she left the market, she was smiling, while the male buyers were frowning and shaking their heads. Wesley walked beside her and laughed.

This year, she'd enlarged her land holdings. She'd used all her crop money from last year and bought more land. She now owned one hundred twenty-five acres of land on the high side of the river. It had good drainage, fertile soil. She had a little trouble with erosion, but she and Isaac had spent some of the winter months laying stone fields. They'd also cleared the new land. It had been hard, cold work, but they'd done it. Then, early this spring, they'd set out tobacco plants, then seeded the other fields. There was a kitchen garden, a milk cow, and chickens by the house.

The house itself had not changed. Every penny had gone into improving the land. Adele and Gerard had one side of the attic, Janie and Nicole the other. The twins slept on pallets downstairs. It was a crowded existence, but they'd all learned to get along. Janie and Gerard rarely spoke to each other, each pretending the other didn't exist. Adele still lived in a dream world of prerevolutionary France. Nicole had been able to persuade her mother that the twins were her grandchildren and that Adele must personally help educate them. For days she'd be an excellent tutor. She'd spice the children's lessons with fascinating tales of her life at Court. She told about when she was a child, about the odd habits of the king and queen of France. At least, the habits sounded strange to the children. Once Adele told the story of how the queen had her clothes brought to her every day in wicker baskets lined with new green taffeta. The taffeta was never reused and was given to the servants. The twins had dressed themselves in green leaves and pretended they were Adele's servants. She was delighted.

Yet, sometimes, some little thing would set Adele off, and her fragile peacefulness would be shattered. Once, Mandy tied a red ribbon about her neck and Adele saw the child. It reminded her of her friends' executions, and she screamed for hours. The twins were no longer frightened of Adele's screams. They merely shrugged and went away or ran for Nicole to go to her mother. After a few days, in which Adele cringed in fear talking of murder and death, she'd return to her fantasy world. Never was she aware of the present, that she was in America, that France was far away. She knew only Nicole and the twins, tolerated Janie, and looked at Gerard as if he didn't exist. She was never allowed to meet strangers, who frightened her horribly.

Gerard seemed to be content that his wife had no idea who he was. Once she saw Nicole, Adele seemed to forget all the time she'd spent in jail and the time at Gerard's parents' house. To Nicole, she spoke of her husband and her father as if they were still alive, as if they would come home at any moment.

Gerard stood away from the rest of the people in Nicole's house. He made himself an outsider. He had not been the same since the day Nicole had slapped him. He would go away for days at a time and return in the middle of the night, giving no explanation of where he went. When he was at home, he often sat by the fire and watched Nicole, stared at her until she dropped stitches in her knitting or stuck a needle in her finger. He never said anything more about marrying Nicole, but sometimes she wished he would. At odd times, when she caught him staring at her, she wished he'd confront her and they could have a good argument. But she felt foolish every time she thought of it. He wasn't doing anything wrong when he watched her.

Whatever was said of Gerard, he pulled his weight at the mill. His hand-kissing manners and his thick, rich accent brought as much business as Nicole's low prices. An extraordinary number of young women came with their fathers to have their grain ground. Gerard treated them all like French aristocrats, young or old, fat or thin, ugly or pretty. The women simpered and giggled as he took their arms and led them around the mill. He never took them out of sight of their fathers.

Only once did Nicole have a glimpse of Gerard's thoughts. A particularly plain young woman was rolling her eyes in delight as Gerard kissed her palm and murmured in French over it. By a trick of the wind, Nicole happened to hear what he said. Although he was smiling, he was calling the woman a piece of pig's offal. Nicole shuddered and walked away; she didn't want to hear any more.

She straightened her back and looked across the river. She hadn't seen Clay since he'd told her Bianca was pregnant. In a way, it seemed ages ago, yet at the same time it seemed like minutes. There wasn't a night she didn't think of him, long for him. Her body betrayed her often, and many times she wanted to ask him to meet her in the clearing. She didn't care about her pride or her higher ideals. She only wanted him, strong and hot against her skin.

She shook her head to clear her vision. It was better not to dwell on the past or to remind herself of what was not. She had a good life now, with people she loved around her. She had no right to be lonely or thankless.

She stared at the Armstrong plantation. Even from this distance, she could see that it wasn't being cared for. Last year's crops had been allowed to die in the fields. It had hurt her to see it, but there was nothing she could do. Isaac had kept her informed of what was happening. Most of the paid servants had left long ago. The indentures of some servants had been sold, along with nearly all of the slaves. Only a handful of people remained.

This spring, some of the bottomland had been planted, but that was all. The upper fields lay bare, with only rotting stems in them. Isaac said Clay didn't care and Bianca was selling anything she could find to pay for her clothes and the constant redecorating of the house. Isaac said the only person on the plantation who had any work to do was the cook.

"Not much to look at, is it?"

She whirled to see Isaac standing beside her. He was looking across the river. In the months since the kidnapping, Isaac and she had become very close. There was a bond between them forged by shared tragedy. The people who worked for her she had always felt belonged to Clay, even Janie to an extent. It was only Isaac with whom she felt this special bond. And Isaac often looked at Nicole as if he'd die for her.

"He could make it if these crops are good, and so far the weather has been perfect," she said.

"I can't see Clay getting up the strength even to harvest the tobacco, much less take it to market."

"That's absurd. No one is a harder worker than Clayton Armstrong."

"Was," Isaac said. "I know he used to be, but now all he works at is lifting a bottle to his mouth. And what if he did work? That wife of his has spent more than four plantations could afford. Every time I take the twins over there, there's a bill collector hounding Clay. If he lets this crop rot in the fields, he'll lose everything. The law will put the place up for auction."

Nicole turned away. She didn't want to hear any more. "I think there's some paperwork I need to do. Did the Morrisons bring that extra barley you asked for?"

"This morning," he said, following her. He took a deep breath and wished again, for the thousandth time, that she'd relax a little, if not for her own sake, then for his. He wished Wesley would visit, but Travis had gone to England and Wes had his own plantation to run. No one else could get Nicole to stop working even for minutes.

Gerard leaned against a tree and watched Isaac follow Nicole back to the mill. He often wondered what went on between those two. They spent many hours together. In the last year, Gerard had met hundreds of people, and most of them had been willing to tell him anything he wanted to know. He knew Nicole was a passionate woman. He'd heard from a hundred people how she'd acted at the Backes's party. She'd acted like that, like a common street woman, in front of all those people, yet she'd slapped him when he touched her.

There wasn't a day when he didn't remember the way she'd slapped him, the way she'd looked at him as if he were something from under a rock. He knew why she'd refused him. She thought she was better than him. After all, she was one of the Courtalains, whose history was intertwined with French kings and queens. And who was he? A cobbler's son. He thought she'd accept him when she found out he was related to her, but she hadn't. To her, he was a cobbler's son, and no matter what he did, he'd never change in her eyes.

Gerard thought of what he'd had to do in the last year. She'd made him prostitute himself for those crude American women. They were coarse things, uneducated, and could speak only the flat American language. He loved to watch their eyes as he said hideous things to them in French. They were too stupid to know what he said.

Then, at night, Nicole teased him, played with him until he was past endurance. Only a curtain separated his room from hers. He'd lie in bed in the darkness, Adele snoring beside him, and listen to her undress. He knew the different sound of each garment. He knew when she stood nude, in that instant before she slipped her nightgown over her head. He imagined her golden body, imagined opening his arms and her sliding into them. Then he'd show her! He'd make her regret ever having slapped him.

He moved away from the tree. Someday he'd make her regret thinking she was better than him. He imagined everything he'd do to her. He'd make her crawl and beg. Yes! She was a passionate woman, but he'd never touch her unless she came to him on her knees. He'd show her that a cobbler's son was as good as any of her snobbish French relatives.

He moved through the trees and away from the mill. The place made him sick. All of them together, laughing and talking—about him, no doubt. Once he'd overheard two men talking about "the little Frenchy." He'd grabbed a rock then but had thought better of it. There were other ways to repay them, ways that wouldn't hurt either of them. Later that fall, both men had lost tobacco barns full of their crops. One of the men had gone bankrupt.

Gerard smiled in remembrance. As he walked along the ridge, a movement across the river caught his eye. It was someone, a large woman on horseback. He stopped and stared for a moment. Over the last year, he'd seen less and less activity over there. He'd never been particularly curious about Nicole's relationship with Armstrong. He knew she'd once been married to him and had acted like his whore at the Backes's party. So many times, Gerard had imagined Nicole acting that way with him. When she'd gotten the annulment so soon after he arrived, Gerard had been pleased. He knew she was telling him who she wanted. It had thrilled him, thinking she'd gotten the annulment so she could marry Gerard. He'd waited a while, then let her know that she'd be welcome in his bed.

He clamped his teeth together in memory. She was a tease, making promises one moment, then acting as if he'd insulted her the next.

As he watched, the woman across the river raised her whip and slapped the horse smartly on the rump. The horse jumped, then lowered its head and gave a violent shudder. The woman went flying through the air and landed on her backside in a storm of dust and pebbles.

Gerard hesitated for a second, then began to run toward the wharf. He had no idea of his intentions, but he knew he must get to the woman.

"Are you hurt?" he asked when he reached her.

Bianca sat quietly on the ground, her whole body aching from the fall and from being on that cursed horse. She took a piece of dirt from her mouth and looked at it in disgust. She gave a jump of surprise when she saw Gerard. It had been so long since she'd seen a gentleman, and she recognized the French fashions immediately. He wore a green cloth coat with velvet collar and cuffs. His shirt was of white silk, the cravat tied to hide the point of his chin. His slim legs were encased in tan breeches, with six pearl buttons at the knee. His silk stockings were green and yellow striped.

She sighed heavily. It was so good to see a man in something besides buckskin and leather. It was also good to see a slim, gentlemanly form instead of the build of a field hand.

"May I help you?" Gerard repeated when the woman did not answer. He understood her look. He'd seen it often in America. The women were hungry for culture and refinement.

He stared down at her as he held out his hand for her. She was a large woman, a very large woman. Her low-cut red satin dress revealed an enormous, heaving bosom. Her arms were large, stretching the sleeves of her dress. Her face had the look of something that had once been pretty but was now bloated and distorted out of shape. In spite of the dated style of the dress and the inappropriate fabric, he knew it was expensive.

"Please allow me to help you," he said in his lush accent. "I fear that you will ruin that exquisite complexion if you stay here in the sun."

Bianca blushed a rosy pink, then took the hand he offered.

Gerard braced himself as he helped pull her up. She was even larger when she was standing beside him. She was two inches taller than he and outweighed him by at least sixty pounds.

He didn't release her hand but gently pulled her with him to the shade of a tree. With a sweeping motion, he removed his coat and spread it on the grass for her. "Please," he said with a bow. "You must rest after such a fall. A delicate young lady such as yourself should be careful." He turned toward the river.

Bianca awkwardly eased herself onto the coat, then looked at Gerard as he walked away. "You aren't leaving me, are you?"

He looked at her over his shoulder, leaving her no doubt that he would not, could not, leave her now that he'd found her.

Gerard stopped at the river and withdrew his handkerchief. It was Adele's, the only one she owned, pure silk, trimmed in Brussels lace and monogrammed AC. Gerard had carefully removed the A and left the C since he was now a Courtalain.

He wet the handkerchief and took it back to Bianca. He knelt beside her. "There is a smudge on your cheek," he said quietly. When she didn't move, he said, "Allow me," took her chin in his hand, and carefully began to wipe away the dirt.

Bianca thought it was odd that she felt no revulsion at Gerard's touch. After all, he was a man. "You'll . . . get your handkerchief dirty," she stuttered.

He gave her a smile of great tolerance. "What is silk next to a beautiful woman's skin?"

"Beautiful?" She opened her eyes very wide. Their blueness was almost obscured by her fat cheeks. The dimple in her left cheek was no longer visible but lost in the doughy plumpness. "No one has called me beautiful in a long time."

"Strange," Gerard said. "I would think your husband—surely a lady of your beauty is married—would tell you that every day."

"My husband hates me," Bianca said flatly.

Gerard considered this for a moment. He could feel the woman's need for a friend, a need to talk. He shrugged. He had nothing else to do today, and besides, sometimes the things lonely women told him became useful. "And who is your husband?"

"Clayton Armstrong."

Gerard lifted one eyebrow. "The owner of this place?"

"All of it," Bianca sighed. "At least what is left of it. He refuses to work it just because he hates me. He says he refuses to kill himself just so I can buy a few trinkets."

"Trinkets?" he encouraged.

"I am certainly frugal enough. I buy nothing I don't need—a few simple clothes, a carriage, a few furnishings for the house, nothing a lady of my station doesn't need."

"It is a shame you have such a selfish husband."

Bianca stared across the river. "It's all *her* fault. If she hadn't thrown herself at my husband, none of this would have happened."

"But I thought Nicole was once married to Mr. Armstrong." Gerard made no pretense of not knowing whom she meant.

"She was, but I fixed her. She thought she could take away what was mine, what I worked so hard for, but she couldn't."

Gerard looked about him, to the tobacco fields to his left. "What exactly does Armstrong own?"

Bianca's eyes came alive. "He's rich, or could be if he'd only do some work. There's a very nice house, except it's too small."

"And Nicole gave all this up?" he asked, half to himself.

Bianca's anger made her cheeks flush. "She didn't give it up. We played a game, and I won. That's all."

She had Gerard's interest now. "I wish you'd tell me about this game. I'd certainly like to hear about it."

He sat and listened with rapt attention to Bianca's story. He was amazed at her cleverness. Here was someone he could understand. He laughed when she told how she bribed Abe to kidnap Nicole. He was almost in awe of her when she spoke of planting herself in Clay's bed.

Bianca had never had anyone in America listen to her before, and certainly no one who showed any interest. She'd always thought her manipulation of Clay and Nicole was extraordinarily clever, but no one else had shown any interest. When Gerard seemed so eager, she went on to tell him about paying Oliver Hawthorne to impregnate her. She shuddered at the memory, told how she had to drug herself to be able to stand the man's touch.

Gerard burst out laughing. "It wasn't even Armstrong's child! How marvelous! Nicole must have been insane when she found out her dear husband was sleeping with someone else, had even made a baby." On impulse, he grabbed Bianca's fat hand and kissed the taut skin. "It's too bad you lost the child. It would have served Armstrong right if the child looked like a neighbor instead of him."

"Yes," Bianca said dreamily. "I would have liked for him to look like a fool, like he's made me appear."

"You could never look like a fool. It's the people who do not appreciate you who are fools."

"Yes, oh yes," she whispered. "You do understand."

The two of them sat quietly for a moment. Bianca felt as if she'd found her first friend, someone who was interested in her. Everyone else seemed to be on Clay's or Nicole's side.

As for Gerard, he wasn't sure what to do with Bianca's revelations, but he knew that, somehow, they'd be useful. "Let me introduce myself. I am Gerard Gautier, of the Courtalain family."

"Courtalain!" Bianca gasped. "But that's Nicole's last name."

"We are . . . related, yes."

Bianca's eyes instantly filled with tears. "You've used me," she whispered desperately. "You listened to me, yet you're on *her* side!" She started to rise, but her bulk made her awkward, clumsy.

Gerard took her shoulders in his hands and forcefully pushed her back down. "Because I am related to her certainly does not make me on her side. Far from it. I am a guest in her house, and there is not a moment when she does not let me forget that I am her charity."

Bianca blinked rapidly to clear away the tears. "Then, you know she is not the pure little angel everyone seems to believe she is! She married *my* fiancé. She tried to take Arundel Hall and the plantation away from me. Yet everyone seems to think I am the one in the wrong. I only took what was mine."

"Yes," Gerard agreed. "But by everyone, I assume you mean the Americans. But, then, what can you expect from so crude a group of people?"

Bianca smiled. "They're an ignorant lot. No one could see the way Nicole was carrying on with that horrid Wesley Stanford."

"Or Isaac Simmons!" Gerard said in disgust. "She spends many, many hours a day with that piece of trash."

A bell sounded in the distance behind them. It called the plantation workers who were left to dinner.

"I must go," Bianca said. "Could we . . . meet again?"

Gerard used his frail strength to help her up, then put his jacket on. It was not an easy task. "You could not prevent me from seeing you again. May I say that, for the first time since I've been in America, I feel as if I've found a friend."

"Yes," Bianca said quietly. "I feel the same way."

He took her hand and kissed it caressingly. "Tomorrow, then?"

"At lunch, here. I'll bring a picnic."

He nodded quickly, then left her.

Chapter 20

BIANCA STARED after Gerard for a moment. He was really a fine figure of a man—his ways were delicate, refined, so far removed from the hideous Americans. She turned toward the house and sighed at the long way she had to walk. The distance was Clayton's fault. She'd wanted someone to drive her about the plantation in a carriage, but Clay laughed at the idea and said he wasn't about to put in roads because she was too lazy to walk.

During the long, hot walk to the house, she thought of Gerard. Why couldn't she have married someone like him? Why had she gotten a mean, crude man like Clayton? She could have been happy with a man like Gerard. She repeated the name several times. Yes, life with him would be sweet. He'd never sneer at her or say mean, hurtful things.

Once inside the house, her euphoria vanished. The house was filthy beyond belief. It had not had a thorough cleaning in more than a year. Cobwebs hung from the ceiling. Clothes, papers, and dead flowers littered the table tops. The floors were scuffed and dirty. The rugs were so full of dust that just walking on them raised little clouds.

Bianca had tried to keep a staff, but Clay had always interfered with her discipline. He always backed the servants against her. After a few months, he'd refused to hire anyone to work in the house. He said Bianca's temper was too vile to force anyone to endure it. Bianca'd argued with him, told him he had no idea how servants should be treated, but he'd ignored her as he always did.

"Here's my dear—dare I say little?—wife now," Clay said. He lounged against the stairwell, just in front of the dining room doorway. His shirt had once been white, but now it was dirty and torn. It was open to the waist, only halfheartedly tucked into the wide leather belt at his waist. His tall boots were caked with mud. In his hand was a glass of bourbon, just as there always was nowadays.

"I thought the dinner bell would bring you back," he said lazily. He ran his hand across his unshaven jaw. "No matter what happens, the mere mention of food brings you running."

"You disgust me," she sneered, and went into the dining room. The big table was heaped with food. Maggie was one of the few servants who'd stayed with Clay over the past year. Bianca seated herself carefully and spread a linen napkin in her lap as she studied the food.

"Such hunger!" Clay said from the doorway. "If you were able to look at a man like that, you'd own him. But men don't interest you, do they? The only interests you have are food and yourself."

Bianca put three fried crullers on her plate. "You know nothing about me. It may interest you to know that some men find me quite attractive."

Clay snorted and took a deep drink of the bourbon. "No man could be that big a fool. At least, I hope I am the only one who's that stupid."

Bianca continued to eat, slowly and steadily. "Did you know your dear, lost Nicole was sleeping with Isaac Simmons?" She smiled at the look on his face. "She always was a slut. She used to meet you, even while you lived with me. Women like that can't live without a man, no matter what kind of man he is. I bet she slept with Abe as well. Maybe I was a matchmaker when I put them on the island together."

"I don't believe you," Clay said under his breath. "Isaac's a boy."

"What were you like at sixteen? Now that she's free of you, she can do whatever she wants with whomever she wants. I bet you taught her some of your dirty little bed tricks, and now she's teaching dear, innocent Isaac."

"Shut up!" Clay yelled, and threw his glass at her head. Either he was already too drunk to aim straight or she was becoming adept at dodging, because he missed her.

He slammed out of the house, making his way past the office and toward the stables. He rarely went into his office these days; there didn't seem to be any need. In the stables, he grabbed a jug of bourbon and headed toward the river.

He sat down slowly at the edge of the water and leaned back against a tree. From here he could see Nicole's planted fields. The house and mill were out of sight, and he was glad for that. Just seeing the health and productivity of her fields was more than enough. He wondered if she ever thought of him, even remembered him. She lived with that little Frenchman Maggie said most of the women in Virginia drooled over. He dismissed the idea of Isaac. Bianca's mind was sick.

Clay drank deeply of the bourbon. It took more and more of the liquid to make him forget. Sometimes, at night, he woke from a dream where his parents, Beth, and James all accused him of forgetting them, of destroying what was theirs. In the morning, he'd wake with new convictions, new hope, plans for the future. Then he'd see Bianca, the filthy house, the fallow fields. Across the river, the sound of laughter or the shout of one of the twins would reach him. Without thinking, he'd reach for the whiskey. The whiskey dulled his senses, made him forget, kept him from hearing or thinking.

He didn't pay any attention when the clouds covered the sun. The day progressed, and the clouds grew darker. They rumbled and rolled lazily but powerfully. In the distance, a sharp flash of lightning cut across the sky. The heat of the day vanished as the wind began to rise. It blew across the fields of wheat and barley. It blew across Clay, tugging at his loose shirt. But the whiskey kept him warm. Even when the first drops fell, he didn't move. The rain began in earnest. It pelted against Clay's hat, collected on the wide brim, then ran down his face. He didn't even notice the cold wetness as his shirt stuck to his skin. He just sat and drank.

Nicole looked out the window and sighed. It had been raining for two days, not letting up even for a minute. They'd had to stop the millstones because the river had risen so much that it was difficult to control the water coming over the shoot. Isaac had assured her that her crops were safe as long as the stone walls held, and it looked as if they would. The water was draining down the terraced field into the river. They were safe from the rain if they didn't have to worry about erosion.

She jumped when a loud pounding on the door began. "Wesley!" she said, glad to see him. "You're drenched. Come in!"

He pulled the oilcloth raincoat off and shook it. Janie took it from him and hung it up to dry.

"Why in the world did you come out in this?" Janie said. "Did you have any trouble with the river?"

"Plenty! Is there any coffee? I'm as cold as I am wet."

Nicole handed him a large mug of coffee, which he drank as he stood before the fire. Gerard sat in a corner of the room, silent, staring, uninvolved. Wes could hear the twins upstairs, probably with Nicole's mother, a woman he'd seen only once.

"Well, we're waiting," Janie demanded. "What brings you here?"

"Actually, I was on my way to Clay's. There's going to be a flood if this rain keeps up."

"A flood?" Nicole asked. "Will Clay be harmed?"

Janie gave her a sharp look. "More to the point, will *we* be all right?"

Wes was watching Nicole. "Clay's land's always been susceptible to floods, at least that bottom piece is. It flooded once before when we were kids. But, of course, Mr. Armstrong had his other fields planted then."

"I don't understand."

Wes knelt and, with a piece of kindling, he began to draw a diagram of Clay's land, Nicole's, and the river. Just below the mill, the river took a sharp bend toward Clay's land, causing the land to fall away sharply, creating a flood plain. On Nicole's side, the land was high, but Clay's was bottomland with rich, fertile soil, but it was also the basin that would catch the river's overflow.

Nicole looked up from the drawing. "Then, my land is draining into Clay's, helping the river to rise."

"I guess you could look at it like that, but I hardly think it's your fault if Clay loses his crops."

"Loses! All of them?"

Wes ran a poker through the ash map. "It's his own fault. He knows about the floods. Every year, it was taking a chance to plant there, but the land is especially rich. He's always protected himself by planting more crops on the higher ground. Clay's dad used to consider it luck when he harvested those fields."

Nicole stood. "But this year, the only crops he has are the ones in the bottomland."

Wes stood beside her. "He knew better. He knew what could happen."

"Isn't there something that could be done? Does he have to lose everything?"

Wes put his arm around her shoulders. "You can't control the rain. If you could get it to stop, then he'd be saved, but that's the only thing that would do it."

"I feel so helpless. I wish I could *do* something."

"Wesley," Janie said sharply, "I bet you're hungry. Why don't you have something to eat?"

He grinned at her. "I'd love something to eat. Tell me what's been going on here. You think maybe I could see the twins?"

Janie went to the foot of the stairs. "The Duke of Wesley is here to see their royal highnesses."

Wes looked at Nicole in disbelief. She rolled her eyes, shook her head, and sighed, then held up her hands in helplessness. Wes choked on his laughter. The twins came scampering down the stairs and launched themselves into his arms. He twirled them around, tossing them into the air as they screamed with laughter.

"You ought to get married, Wes," Janie said in a deadly serious voice as she gave a meaningful look at Nicole.

"I will, as soon as you agree to marry me," he laughed. "No! I can't. I remember, I'm already promised to one of Isaac's little sisters."

"It's a good thing," Janie sniffed. "You ask me to marry you, and I will. Now put down those young 'uns and come over here and eat."

Later, as Wes ate and answered the twins' questions, he noticed Nicole's face. He knew what was upsetting her. He reached across the table and squeezed her hand. "Everything will work out, you'll see. Travis and I will see he doesn't lose the plantation."

Nicole's head shot up. "What do you mean lose the plantation? Losing one year's crops shouldn't make him lose the whole place."

Wes and Janie exchanged looks. "Ordinarily, it shouldn't, but then men rarely lose their entire crops. Clay should have planted above the flood level."

"But even if he does lose the crops, surely he has enough cash reserve to survive. I can't believe the plantation could go under in just one year."

Wes pushed his plate away. The rain thundered down on the

roof. "You might as well know the truth. Last year, Clay let his crops rot in the field, but because of his hard work in the years before and his father's and brother's work, financially, the place was solid. But Bianca—" He faltered, watching Nicole's eyes. She tried to keep them blank, but he could read them, could see how Bianca's name hurt her.

"Bianca," he continued, "has run up some extraordinary debts. I saw Clay about a month ago, and he said she'd been borrowing money, using the plantation as collateral, in order to send money to her father in England. It seems she's trying to get back what used to be her family's house."

Nicole stood, walked toward the fire, and idly twirled the poker in the ashes. She remembered the park outside Bianca's house, the one that had once been Maleson property. Bianca never ceased to talk about how she would someday get her family home back. "And Clay just let her use his land? That doesn't sound like Clay."

Wes waited a while before he answered. "I'm not sure it is Clay. He's changed, Nicole. He doesn't really care what happens to the place or to himself. He never moves without a glass of whiskey in his hand. When I tried to reason with him, he wouldn't listen. He just ignored me. In a way, that was worse than anything else. Clay's always had a temper, and he'll strike out before he thinks, but now—" He trailed off, not finishing the sentence.

"So Clay lost last year's crops and now this year's. Are you trying to tell me he's bankrupt?"

"No. Travis and I have talked to the creditors, and we're backing Clay. I told Clay he had to keep Bianca from spending any more, though."

She turned to face him. "And did you tell Clay you were going to stand behind his debts?"

"Of course. I didn't want him to worry."

"Men!" Nicole said fiercely, then said some things in French that made Gerard, who listened passively to everything, raise his eyebrows. "How would you like for Clay to tell you he knew you couldn't handle your own land, but not to worry, that he'd take care of you?"

"It wasn't like that! We're friends; we've always been friends."

"Friends *help* each other, they don't destroy each other."

"Nicole!" Wes warned, getting angry. "I've known Clay all my life, and—"

"And now you throw an anchor to a drowning man, that's what!"

Wes stood up, his face growing red, his hands clutching the table.

Janie interceded. "Stop it, you two! You're acting like children. Worse than children, since the twins never act like that."

Wes began to calm down. "I'm sorry. I didn't mean to get angry, but Nicole, you're accusing me of some awful things."

She turned back to the fire, the poker still in her hand. She'd redrawn the bend in the river that Wes had shown her. She stared at it as she spoke. "I didn't mean anything. It's just that Clay's so proud. He loves the plantation, and he'd rather give it up than lose it."

"That doesn't make any sense."

She shrugged. "I guess it doesn't. Maybe I'm having difficulty expressing myself. Wes, isn't there any way we could keep the river from flooding?"

"Pray, maybe. If the rain stopped, the water might recede."

"Why doesn't that land flood every year? Why is it such a sometime thing?"

"The course of the river is changing. Clay's grandfather told us when we were boys that, when he was a boy, there was no bottomland, but each year the river moved a little and left some more lowland."

"Here," she said, stepping back from the map in the ashes. "Show me what you mean."

He knelt over the hearth. "I guess the river's trying to bend itself. This curve used to be straighter, broader, but over the years it's changed."

She studied the map. "What you're saying is that the river is eating away my high ground and creating this low, flat land of Clay's."

Wes looked at her in surprise. "I don't think you have to worry about it. It'll take fifty years for the river to take much of your land."

She ignored his look. "What if we gave the river god what it wanted?"

"What are you talking about?" Wes snapped. He thought she was being selfish because she was worried about the river taking her land.

"Nicole—" Janie said. "I don't like that tone of voice."

Nicole took a piece of kindling. "What if my land were cut away here?" She drew a line from one curve of the river to the other. "What would happen?"

"The land is wet and steep, and it'd probably break away and fall into the river."

"And how would that affect the water level?"

His eyes widened as he began to understand what was going on in her mind. "Nicole, you can't do that. That would take days of digging, and the land that would fall away is covered with your wheat."

"You didn't answer my question. Would it lower the water level?"

"It would give the river another place to go, to expand— maybe. How can anyone know?"

"I'm asking for an opinion, not an absolute answer."

"Yes, damn it! The river would probably love to swallow your land instead of Clay's. What does the goddamn water care?"

"I would appreciate it if you would watch your language in

front of the children," Nicole said primly. "Now, we'll need shovels, and picks for the roots and rocks, and—"

Wes interrupted her. "Have you looked outside? That rain is coming down so hard it could kill, and you're talking about working in it."

"I know of no other way to dig a trench. Perhaps you could bring the ditch indoors for us where it is nice and warm."

"I can't let you do this," Wes said flatly. "Clay can make it without your sacrifice. Travis and I will lend him the money, and next year will be better."

Nicole gave him an icy stare. "Will it? Will next year be better? Look at what we've done to him. We've all abandoned him. He's a man who needs a family. He was happy when he had his parents, James, Beth, and the twins. Then, one by one, they all left him. For a while, I gave him my love, but then I took that away—along with the twins." She lifted her arm and pointed toward the direction of Arundel Hall. "Once that was a happy house, full of people he loved and who loved him. What does he have now? Even his own niece and nephew live with a stranger instead of with him. We've got to show him that we care."

"But Travis and I—"

"Money! You're like a husband who gives his wife money instead of the attention and love she needs. Clay doesn't need money; he needs to know that someone cares. He's got to feel that he isn't alone in the world."

Wes stood and stared at her, as did Janie and the twins. Gerard lowered his lashes in a lazy way, but they didn't flicker.

"Are you guessing at the way Clay feels?" Wes asked quietly. "Or are you transferring your feelings to him? Is it you who is lonely and wants to feel someone cares?"

Nicole tried to smile. "I don't know. I don't have time to think of it right now. Every minute we waste, the river is rising and getting closer to Clay's tobacco."

Wes suddenly grabbed Nicole and hugged her. "If I ever find

a woman who loves me half as much as you love Clay, I'm going to hold on to her and never let her go."

Nicole pushed away from him and wiped a tear from the corner of her eye. "I'd like to have a few secrets, please. And, besides, I have no doubt you'll be as ridiculous as Clay and I have been. Now!" she said sharply. "Let's organize this. You wouldn't happen to have some shovels, would you?"

Janie untied her apron, hung it on a peg by the door, and then grabbed Wes's slicker.

"Where are you going?" Wes asked.

"While the two of you sit there and talk, I'm going to *do* something. First of all, I'm going to borrow some clothes from Isaac. Running around in this rain in wet skirts is not my idea of getting something done. Then I'm going to get Clay."

"Clay!" Nicole and Wes said in unison.

"The two of you may think he's an invalid, but I know better. He can dig as well as anybody, and he's still got a few men left who work for him. I just wish there was time to get Travis here."

Nicole and Wes still sat staring at her.

"Are the two of you going to grow roots? Nicole, come with me to the mill. Wes, you go stake out where the trench'll have to be cut."

Wes grabbed Nicole's arm and propelled her to the door. "Let's go! There's work to be done!"

Chapter 21

JANIE WAS shocked when she saw Arundel Hall. There was a big leak in the porch roof, and the floor was flooded. The door to the house stood half open, and the Oriental runner was soaked along one edge. She stepped inside the house and tried to push the door shut. The constant humidity of the rain had made the door swell until it was impossible to close. She rolled the wet carpet away from the door, then gasped at the warped and ruined floor before the door. The oak would have to be replaced.

Angry, she looked about the wide hallway. The oppressive wetness made the dirt and refuse inside the house stink. She closed her eyes for a moment and apologized to Clay's mother. Then she stalked down the hall toward the library.

She pushed the door open without knocking. She saw at once that it was the only room that hadn't been changed, but neither had it been cleaned. She stood in the doorway for several minutes while her eyes adjusted to the dimness.

"I must have died and gone to heaven," came a low, slurred voice from a corner. "My beautiful Janie wearing men's pants. Do you think you'll set a fashion?"

Janie went to the desk and lit a lamp, then turned it up brightly. She gasped when she saw Clay. His eyes were red, his beard dirty and scraggly. She doubted if he'd washed in weeks.

"Janie, girl, would you hand me that jug from the desk? I've been meaning to get it myself, but I don't seem to have the energy."

Janie stared at him for a moment. "How long has it been since you've eaten?"

"Eaten? There is no food. Didn't you know that my darling wife eats all the food?" He tried to sit up, but it was an effort for him.

Janie went to help him. "You stink!"

"Thank you, my dear, that's the kindest thing anyone's said to me in a long time."

She helped him stand up. He was very unsteady on his feet. "I want you to come with me."

"Of course. I will follow you wherever you wish."

"We're going out into the rain first. Maybe it'll help sober you, or at least wash you. Then we're going to the kitchen."

"Oh, yes," Clay said. "The kitchen. My wife's favorite room. Poor Maggie works harder now than when she cooked for the whole plantation. Did you know they're all gone now?"

Janie supported Clay as they went to the side door. "I know I never saw a worse case of feeling sorry for yourself than yours."

The cold rain hit both of them with a driving, slashing force. Janie ducked her head to keep from being pounded, but Clay didn't seem to notice as it cut at him.

Inside the kitchen, Janie stirred the coals and stoked the fire. She quickly set a pot of coffee on the grate. The room was a shambles, so unlike the sparkling clean place it once was. It had the look of a place that was uncared for, unwanted.

Janie helped Clay to sit down, then went back into the rain to get Maggie. She knew she'd need help sobering Clay.

An hour later, Maggie and Janie had forced an extraordinary amount of black coffee into him, as well as half a dozen scrambled eggs. All the while, Maggie talked.

"It's not a happy place anymore," Maggie said. "That

woman pokes her nose into everything. She wants us all to bow down and kiss her fat feet. We all laughed at her before Clay married her." She paused and gave Clay a harsh look. "But after that, there was no pleasin' her. Everybody who could leave did. After she started cutting food rations, even some of the slaves ran away. I think they knew Clay wouldn't go after them. And they were right."

Clay was beginning to sober up. "Janie doesn't want to hear about our problems. People in heaven don't want to know about hell."

"You chose hell!" Maggie started what was obviously a much practiced speech.

Janie put her hand on Maggie's arm to stop her. "Clay," she said quietly, "are you sober enough to listen to me?"

He looked up from the plate of eggs. His brown eyes were sunk deep into his skull. His mouth was a straight line, the corners deeply etched. He looked older than Janie remembered. "What is it you have to say?" he asked flatly.

"Are you aware of what the rain's doing to your crops?"

He frowned, then pushed his plate away. Janie pushed it back toward him. He obeyed her and began to eat again. "I may be drunk, but I'm afraid I haven't been able to block out everything that's happened to me. Maybe I should say, everything that I've caused. I'm well aware of what the rain's doing. Don't you think it's a fitting end? After all my wife," he snarled the word, "has done to get this plantation, it looks like we're both going to lose it."

"And you're willing to allow that?" Janie demanded. "The Clay I've always known would fight for what he wanted. I remember you and James fighting a fire for three days."

"Oh yes, James," Clay said quietly. "I cared then."

"*You* may not care about yourself," Janie said fiercely, "but other people do. Right now, Wesley and Nicole are out in the rain trying to slice off a few acres of Nicole's land to save yours. And all you do is sit here and wallow in your own selfish pride."

"Pride? I haven't had any pride since . . . since one morning in a cave."

"Stop it!" Janie shouted. "Stop thinking of yourself and listen to me. Didn't you hear a word I said? Wes told Nicole that your land would probably be flooded, and she figured out a way to save your crops."

"Save them?" Clay's head came up. "The only way is if the rain stopped, or maybe a dam could be built upriver."

"Or, if the river had someplace else to go besides your land—"

"What are you talking about?"

Maggie sat down beside Clay. "You said Nicole is going to save Clay's crops. How?"

Janie looked from one interested pair of eyes to the next. "You know the sharp bend in the river just below the mill?" She didn't wait for an answer. "Nicole figured out that if she dug a trench through there, the river just might take that course instead of flooding your bottomland where your tobacco is."

Clay leaned back in his chair and stared. He knew exactly what Janie meant. The excess river water needed an outlet, and one place was as good as another. It was a while before he spoke. "She'd lose several acres of her land if the river did take that course," he said at last.

"That's what Wes said." Janie poured all three of them more coffee. "He tried to talk her out of it, but she said—" She paused and looked at Clay. "She said you needed someone to believe in you, that you need to feel someone cares about you."

Clay stood up abruptly and walked to the kitchen window. It was raining so hard that he had only an impression of the outside beyond the window. Nicole, he thought. He'd been drunk for nearly a year just so he couldn't think or feel, yet it hadn't come close to working. There wasn't a minute, drunk or sober, when he hadn't thought of her, what could have been, what would have been if only he'd . . . The more he thought, the more he drank.

Janie was right, he did feel sorry for himself. All his life, he'd felt he was in control, but then his parents had been taken, then Beth and James. He thought he wanted Bianca, but Nicole had confused him. When he realized how much he loved her, it was too late. By then, he'd already hurt her so much that she'd never trust him again.

The rain whipped against the glass. Somewhere, out in that cold deluge, she worked for him. She sacrificed her land, her crops, the security of all the people who depended on her, for him. What had Janie said? To show him that someone cares.

He turned to Janie. "I have about six men left on the plantation. I'll get them and some shovels." He started toward the door. "They're going to need food. Empty the larders."

"Yes, sir!" Maggie grinned.

The two women stared at the door after Clay shut it behind him.

"That sweet little lady still loves him, doesn't she?" Maggie asked.

"She's never stopped for a minute, although I've sure tried to get her to stop. In my opinion, no man's good enough for her."

"What about that Frenchman who lives with her?" Maggie said hostilely.

"Maggie, you don't know what you're talking about."

"I got a few hours to listen," she said, and began to throw food into burlap bags. They'd return to the mill to cook. It was better to get the raw food wet than to try to transport it when it was hot.

Janie smiled. "Let's get busy. I have a year's worth of gossip to tell you."

* * *

The rain was coming down so hard, Clay could hardly see to get his men across the river. The water lapped over the edges of the shallow rowboats and threatened to swallow the men along with the land. Already the river had risen enough that it had eaten several rows of Clay's tobacco.

Once ashore, the men put their shovels over their shoulders and trudged up the hill, their heads down, letting the brims of their hats protect them somewhat from the rain. Once they arrived at the site where the others were digging, they lost no time in going to work. The Clayton who'd come to give them their orders was not a man they wanted to disobey.

Clay sank the shovel into the soggy earth. Now was not the time to let himself think he was helping Nicole in her sacrifice. Suddenly, it seemed important to him to save his crops. He wanted to harvest that tobacco as much as he'd ever wanted anything in his life.

He dug with more energy than he'd ever experienced before. He acted like a demon possessed. He concentrated so hard on moving shovelfuls of earth that he didn't at first feel the hand on his arm. When he came back to the present, he turned to look into Nicole's eyes.

It was a jolt seeing her again. In spite of the hard, driving rain, they might have been alone. They both wore broad-brimmed hats, the water running down across their faces.

"Here!" she yelled over the fury of the rain. "Coffee." She held up a mug, her hand covering the open top.

He took it and drained it without a word.

She took the empty mug and walked away from him.

He stood quietly for a moment and watched her trying to walk in the sucking mud. She seemed especially small in the man's clothing, the big boots. All around him, trampled in the mud, were stalks of nearly ripe wheat—her wheat.

He looked around him for the first time. There were fifteen men digging at the trench. He recognized Isaac and Wes at one end. To his left lay the land they were trying to cut away. The wheat bent under the pelting rain, but the hill's slope assured good drainage. Not far away was a low stone wall. Clay had watched Isaac and Nicole build those walls. Every time she'd lifted a stone, he'd drunk a little bit more. Now, all that labor was being pushed into the river, discarded as if it meant nothing. And all for him.

He stabbed the shovel into the earth again and began to dig harder.

What little light there was began to fade a few hours later. Nicole came to him once again and pantomimed that he was to stop and eat. Clay shook his head and kept digging.

Night came, and the men still dug. There was no way to have lanterns, so they dug half by instinct and half by their increased night vision. Wesley tried to keep the diggers inside the lines he'd set.

Toward morning, Wes came to Clay and motioned for him to follow. The diggers were very tired, their bodies cold and aching. The shoveling was bad enough, but combined with the viciousness of the rain, it pushed them past exhaustion.

Clay followed Wes to the end point where the trench was being cut. They were very close to being through. In another hour or so, they'd know if their labor had accomplished anything. It flashed through Clay's mind that the river did not have to take Nicole's sacrifice. It could stay where it was and ignore the canal.

Wes looked in question to Clay, asking his opinion on the formation of the mouth of the trench. The rain was too loud and hard for them to speak over it. Clay pointed at a cutaway in the bend of the river, and the two friends began to dig there, together.

The sky began to lighten with the dawn. The men could see what they had done and where they must go. Only six feet were needed to complete the deep ditch.

Wes and Clay exchanged looks over Nicole's head. She dug beside the men, never looking up. The men had the same thought. In minutes, they'd know if they would succeed or not.

Suddenly, the river answered their question. It was too greedy to wait for the removal of the six feet. The water rushed into the trench from both sides at once. The wet, soft ground fell away as if it were made of pastry dough. The diggers barely had time to jump back before they were swept away. Clay grabbed Nicole about the waist and swung her to the safe, higher ground.

All the diggers stood back and watched the river consume the wheat-planted earth. The land fell in thick, dark, rich sheets, falling into the water, then disappearing forever. The turbulent water rushed across the land like volcanic lava.

"Look!" Wes yelled above the noise.

Everyone looked across the river to where he pointed. They'd been so fascinated by the sight of the earth falling that they hadn't noticed Clay's fields. As the river moved to fill the gap left by Nicole's land, which it now carried downstream, the level lowered considerably. The last rows of tobacco that had once been buried now were seen again, flattened and ruined, but the rows above them were safe.

"Hooray!" Nicole shouted, the first to do so.

Suddenly, the tiredness left everyone. They'd worked all night to accomplish one thing and they'd done it. Jubilation replaced their weariness. They began waving their shovels about in the air. Isaac grabbed Luke's hand and they did a little impromptu jig in the mud.

"We did it!" Wes shouted over the steady rain. He grabbed Nicole and tossed her in the air. Then, he turned her and threw her to Clay as if she were a sack of grain.

Clay was grinning broadly. "*You* did it," he laughed as he caught Nicole in his arms. "You did it! My beautiful, brilliant wife!" He crushed her to him and kissed her, a deep, hungry kiss.

For a moment, Nicole forgot the time, the place, all that had happened. She kissed Clay with all the passion she felt. She felt like a starving woman, and he was the only food for her.

"Time enough for that later," Wes said as he slapped Clay on the shoulder. His eyes carried a warning. The men watched them in curiosity.

Nicole stared up at Clay, and she knew that tears mingled with the rain on her face.

Reluctantly, he set her down. He moved away from her quickly, as if she were fire and he would be burned, but his eyes held hers in fascination and question.

"Let's eat," Wes shouted. "I hope the women made enough food, because I could eat at least a wagonload."

Nicole turned away from Clay. Her body felt more alive than it had in months. "Maggie's here, so you know there's bound to be more than enough."

Wes grinned, then put his arm around her shoulders, and they started toward the mill.

There was a table set up on sawhorses, and there was enough food for a hundred hungry people. There was bread, fresh from the oven, still hot and fragrant. Crocks of cool butter awaited them. There was terrapin ragout, poached sturgeon, oysters, crab, ham, turkey, beef, and duck. There were eight kinds of pie, twelve vegetables, four cakes, three wines, three kinds of beer, as well as milk and tea.

Nicole stayed away from Clay. She took her heaping plate and sat by herself in a shadow of the grinding stones. He'd called her his wife, and for a moment she felt as if she was. It seemed so long ago that she'd been his wife, yet for some reason she knew she never was his wife, really. Only those brief days at the Backes's house had she felt she belonged.

"Tired?"

She looked up at Clay. He'd removed his wet shirt, and a towel was hanging around his neck. He looked vulnerable and lonely. Nicole ached to take him in her arms, to soothe him.

"Do you mind if I sit with you?"

She shook her head silently. They were partially hidden from the others, private.

"You aren't eating much," he said quietly, nodding toward her full plate. "Maybe you need some exercise to work up an appetite." His eyes twinkled.

She tried to smile, but his nearness made her nervous.

He took a piece of ham from her plate and ate it. "Maggie and Janie outdid themselves."

"They had your food to work with. It was kind of you to be so generous."

His eyes darkened as he stared at her. "Are we really such strangers that we can't talk? I don't deserve what you've done for me today. No!" he said when she started to interrupt. "Let me finish. Janie said I've been wallowing in self-pity. I guess I have been. I think I've been feeling that I didn't deserve what had happened to me. Tonight, I've had a lot of time to think. I believe I've come to realize that life is what you make it. You said once that I couldn't make up my mind. You were right. I wanted everything and thought it would be given to me if I asked for it. I think I was too weak to take any kind of hardship."

She put her hand on his arm. "You aren't a weak man."

"I don't think you know me, any more than I know myself. I've done some terrible things to you, yet this—" He couldn't finish. His voice was weak. "You've given me back hope, something I haven't seen for a long time."

He put his hand over hers. "I promise I'm not going to let you down again. I don't just mean the tobacco, but in my life, too."

He looked down at her hand, caressed her fingers with his. "I didn't think it was possible, but I love you more than I ever did."

There was a lump in her throat, and she couldn't speak.

He looked into her eyes. "There are no words to say what I feel for you or to thank you enough for what you've done." He stopped abruptly, as if he were choking. "Goodbye," he whispered.

He was gone before she could speak.

Clay walked quickly out of the mill, leaving his shirt behind, ignoring the people who called out to him. Once outside, he was hardly aware that the rain had slowed to a drizzle. In the early morning light, he could see how the land had changed. Where once Nicole's fields had sloped away to the river, they now fell down drastically. The river itself was calmer, like a great animal that had fed well and was now digesting its feast.

The wharf was intact, and Clay rowed himself across the much wider river to his own wharf. He walked slowly to the house. It was as if he were awakening after a year's sleep. He felt James beside him, appalled at what Clay'd done to the lovely, productive plantation.

He also saw the neglect of his house. He stepped across the puddle in the hardwood floor.

Bianca stood at the foot of the stairs. She wore a voluminous, high-waisted wrapper of pale blue silk. Under it was a pink satin gown. The collar, cuffs, and down the front and hem of the wrapper were covered with a very wide border of spiky, multicolored feathers.

"So! There you are! You've been out all night again."

"Did you miss me?" Clay asked sarcastically.

She gave him a look that answered his question. "Where is everyone, and why isn't breakfast on the table?"

"I thought perhaps your concern was for me, but instead it's for Maggie's handiwork."

"I want an answer! Where is breakfast?"

"Breakfast is now being served across the river at Nicole's mill."

"Her! That slut! So that's where you've been. I should have known you couldn't live without your disgusting, primitive needs. What did she use this time to entice you? Did she tell you something about me?"

Clay looked away in disgust and started up the stairs. "Your name was never brought up, thank God."

"At least she's learned that," Bianca said smugly. "She's

smart enough to know that I see through her, see what she's really like. The rest of you are too blind to see what a greedy, conniving liar she is."

Clay turned on Bianca with a snarl. He leaped four steps at once to stand before her. He grabbed her by the neck of her gown and slammed her hard against the wall. "You piece of filth! You have no right even to speak her name. You've never done a fair or decent thing in your life for anyone, and you accuse her of being just like you. Last night, Nicole sacrificed several acres of her land to save mine. That's where I've been all night, digging right beside her and other people who know what kindness and generosity are."

He pushed Bianca against the wall again. "You've used me all you're going to. From now on, I'm going to run this place, not you."

Bianca had to work hard to breathe. His hands were cutting off her circulation. Her fat cheeks bulged with the pressure. "You can't go to her. I'm your wife," she gasped. "This place is mine."

"Wife!" he sneered. "For the things I've done, I think I almost deserve you." He released her and stepped back. "Look at yourself! You don't like yourself any more than anyone else likes you." He turned away and went up the stairs to his room, where he fell on the bed and was asleep instantly.

Bianca stood as still as a piece of marble after Clayton left. What did he mean, she didn't like herself? She came from an old and important English family. How could she not be proud of herself?

Her stomach rumbled, and she put her hand to it. Slowly, she left the house and went to the kitchen. She knew nothing about cooking, and the barrels of flour and other raw ingredients were confusing to her. She was hungry, very hungry, and she could find nothing to eat. Tears blurred her eyes as she left the kitchen and walked toward the garden.

At the end of the garden was a little pavilion, privately hidden under two enormous old magnolia trees. She sat down heavily on a cushion; then, when she realized it was soaking wet, she started to rise. But what was the use? Her beautiful gown was already ruined. The tears ran down her face as she plucked at the feathers on her gown.

"May I disturb you?" came a quiet, accented voice.

Bianca's head shot up. "Gerard!" she gasped as more tears came to her eyes.

"You've been crying," he said sympathetically. He started to sit beside her, then saw the cushions were wet. He tossed one over the railing, then used a handkerchief, not Adele's silk one, to wipe most of the water from the wooden seat. He sat down. "Please tell me what is wrong. You look as if you could use a friend."

Bianca buried her face in her hands. "A friend! I have no friends! Everyone in this horrible country hates me. This morning, he said that I didn't even like myself."

Gerard bent forward and touched Bianca's hair. It wasn't quite clean. "Don't you realize that he'd say anything to hurt you? He only wants Nicole. He'll do anything or say anything to get her. He wants to drive you away so he can have her."

Bianca looked at him, her little eyes red over her swollen cheeks. "He can't have her. He's married to me."

Gerard smiled as if she were a child. "How very innocent you are. You're so sweet and vulnerable, so unsophisticated. Did he tell you where he was last night?"

She waved her hand. "He said something about a flood and Nicole saving his land."

"Of course, she'd save his land. She plans for it to be hers someday. She made it seem that she was making a grand sacrifice, but actually she was creating more bottomland for the Armstrong plantation. And someday she plans for it to be hers again."

"But how? There were witnesses to my marriage to Clay. It can't be annulled."

Gerard patted her hand. "You are a true lady. You can't even imagine the treachery of those two. You played some tricks on them, but they were only tricks, nothing that really hurt anyone. Even the kidnapping wasn't meant to hurt. But their plans aren't so innocent—or fair."

"What . . . do you mean? Divorce?"

Gerard was silent for a moment. "I only wish it were divorce. I think they're planning . . . murder."

Bianca gaped at him for a moment. At first, she had no idea whose murder he meant. The idea of Nicole falling off a cliff appealed to her. If Nicole were gone, her life would be a lot better. But she was puzzled about why Clay would contemplate murdering Nicole.

Very slowly did she become aware of what Gerard meant. "Me?" she whispered. "They want to kill me?"

Gerard held her hand tightly. "I'm afraid I am as naive as you are. It took me a long time to understand what was going on. I couldn't understand why Nicole would voluntarily dig away part of her land unless she had a motive that no one else saw. It finally came to me this morning. Those barbarians made so much noise in the mill that I couldn't sleep. I realized that if Nicole once again became mistress of the plantation, then the new land created by the changing of the river's course would be to her advantage."

"But . . . murder!" Bianca gasped. "Surely, you must be wrong."

"Has Armstrong ever tried to hurt you? Ever struck you?"

"This morning. He pushed me against a wall. I could hardly breathe."

"That's what I mean. He's a violent man. He's starting to lose control over himself. Someday soon, you'll find a tiny cord stretched across the stairs, and when you start down them, you'll fall."

"No!" Bianca gasped, her hand to her throat.

"Of course, Armstrong will be quite some distance from the

house when it happens. Later, all he has to do is remove the string. Then, he can play the bereaved husband, while you, my dear, will lie cold in a coffin."

Bianca's eyes were wild, frightened. "I can't let that happen. I must prevent it."

"Yes, you must be very careful. For my sake as well as your own."

She sniffed. "For your sake?"

Gerard lifted her hand, held it between both of his. "You are going to think me a cad, a man too bold. No, I cannot tell you."

"Please," she begged. "You said we were friends. You can tell me what's on your mind."

He looked at the floor but saw it was too wet to kneel upon. His silk stockings would be ruined.

"I love you," he said desperately. "How can I expect you to believe me? We've only met once before, but since then I've thought of little else. You haunt me always. My every thought has contained you. Please, don't laugh at me."

Bianca stared at him in astonishment. Never had a man declared undying love for her. Clay, in England, had asked her to marry him, but he'd been reserved, removed, as if he were thinking of something else while he proposed. The way Gerard looked at her made her breath quicken. He really did love her, she could see that. Several times since that first meeting, she had thought of him, but only as someone gentle and understanding. Now she looked at him in a new light. She could love this man. Yes, she could love someone with such fine manners.

"I couldn't laugh at you," she said.

He smiled. "Then, could I hope that you could ever return even a small amount of my affection? I wouldn't ask for much, just that I could see you once in a while."

"Of course," Bianca said, still bewildered by his declarations.

He stood and straightened his cravat. "I must go now. I want you to promise me you will be very careful. If anything were to happen to you, even if one hair on your lovely head were damaged, my heart would break." He smiled at her, then saw something on the rail of the pavilion. "I nearly forgot. Would you accept this small token of my affection?" He handed her a five-pound box of French chocolates. The candy had been given to him by a farmer's daughter who'd bought one of Nicole's dresses.

Bianca nearly snatched the box from his hands. "I have not eaten," she muttered. "He would not let me eat this morning." She threw the ribbon on the floor, then pulled the lid off. She ate five pieces before Gerard could take a breath.

Bianca stopped, her mouth full, a drop of wet chocolate at the corner of her lips. "What will you think of me?"

"What could I think but to love you?" Gerard said when he'd recovered from his astonishment at the way she'd attacked the box of candy. "I don't believe you realize that I love you as you are. I do not demand or want changes. You are a woman, a full, beautiful woman. I want no thin, shapeless girl. I love you the way you are."

Bianca looked up at him with just the expression she'd had when she looked at the chocolates.

Gerard smiled. "Could we meet again? Perhaps three days from now, at noon. I will bring a picnic lunch."

"Oh, yes," she breathed. "I would love that."

He bent from the waist, took her hand, and kissed it. He noticed that her eyes kept straying to the chocolates. After he left her alone, he stood for a moment in the shadow of a tree and watched her devour the full five pounds of candy in a matter of minutes. He smiled to himself and went back to the mill.

Three days later, Gerard sat across from Bianca in a secluded area of the Armstrong plantation. Between them were the remains of a feast. It had taken Janie all morning to prepare such a meal. Gerard frowned as he remembered the way Janie had refused at first to obey his commands and pack the picnic. Nicole's interference had made her obey. He didn't like a woman over-stepping his rule.

"He's trying to starve me," Bianca said, her mouth full of caramel cream and almond cookies. "This morning for break-fast, I was only allowed two poached eggs and three biscuits. And he canceled my orders for some new dresses. I don't know what he expects me to wear. These stupid Americans can't even sew properly. The dresses constantly tear at the seams."

Gerard watched with interest the massive quantity of food that Bianca was devouring so rapidly. He'd requested enough food for six people, yet now he wasn't sure if it was enough. "Tell me," he said quietly, "have you been careful lately? Have you watched for danger?"

His statement was enough to make Bianca put down her fork. She buried her face in her hands. "He hates me. Everywhere, I see signs of his hatred. Ever since the rains, he's changed. He won't let me eat. He's hired women to clean the house, yet when I give them orders, they won't listen to me. It's almost as if I weren't the mistress of the plantation."

Gerard unwrapped a tiny chocolate-coated cheesecake. He touched her arm and held it out to her. Her eyes were brilliant, shining through her tears as she grabbed the little cake. "If you and I owned the plantation, everything would be different."

"We? How could we own it?" She'd already eaten the cake and watched as Gerard unwrapped another one.

"If Armstrong were dead, you would inherit the place."

"He is as disgustingly healthy as one of his mules. I thought maybe he'd drink himself to death, but he hasn't touched any-thing since the rains."

"How many people know that? It's common knowledge that he's been drinking heavily for a year or more. What if he had an . . . accident while he was drunk?"

Bianca leaned back and stared at the remaining food. There

wasn't much left, and she hated to leave it, but she honestly could hold no more. "I told you, he doesn't drink anymore," she said absently.

Gerard gritted his teeth at her denseness. "Don't you think we could arrange one last time?"

Slowly, Bianca lifted her head and looked at him. "What do you mean?"

"Clayton Armstrong is an evil man. He brought you here under false pretenses. Then, when he got you to this horrible country, he used you, mistreated you."

"Yes," Bianca whispered. "Yes."

"There isn't any justice in the world that allows something like that to continue. You are his wife, yet he treats you like dirt. For God's sake, he won't even allow you to eat!"

Bianca caressed her enormous stomach. "You're right, but what can I do?"

"Get rid of him." He smiled at Bianca's gasp. "Yes, you know what I mean." He leaned over the dirty dishes and took her hand. "You have every right. You're so sweet that you don't even realize that it's your life or his. Do you think a man like Clayton Armstrong would stop at murder?"

She looked at him in fright.

"What else can he do? He wants Nicole, and yet he's married to you. Has he asked you for a divorce?"

She shook her head.

"He will. And will you give it to him?"

Again, she shook her head.

"Then he'll find other ways to rid himself of an unwanted wife."

"No," Bianca whispered. "I don't believe you." She tried to get up, but her size and all the food she'd eaten made her immobile.

Gerard rose and put out his hands to her, his legs braced against her weight. "Think about it," he said when she faced him. "It's a matter of survival. It's him or you."

She turned away from him. "I must go." Her mind was whirling with the awful thoughts Gerard had placed there. She walked very slowly back to the house. Before she entered, she checked the doorways to make sure no one was hiding behind them. As she laboriously climbed the stairs, she knelt to feel for wires that were meant to trip her.

It was a week later when Clay first mentioned divorce to her. She was very weak and tired from lack of food and rest. She hadn't had a full meal since the picnic with Gerard. Clay had given orders that Bianca was to be placed on a strict diet. She hadn't had much rest either, because she kept having dreams that Clay was standing over her with a knife, screaming that it was either him or her.

When he did speak of divorce, it was like a nightmare coming to life. She sat in the morning room. Clay had it restored to the way it was before Bianca had redecorated it. It was as if he were already trying to remove all traces of her.

"What do we have to offer each other?" Clay was saying. "I'm sure you care as little for me as I do for you."

Bianca stubbornly shook her head. "You just want *her*. You want to push me out into the cold so you can have her. The two of you planned this all along."

"That is the most absurd thing I've ever heard." Clay tried to control his temper. "You were the one who forced me to marry you." He narrowed his eyes at her. "You were the one who lied about having my child."

Bianca gasped and put her hand to the folds of flesh that covered her throat.

Clay turned away and walked toward the window. He'd learned about Oliver Hawthorne only recently. The man lost most of his meager crops in the rain, and two of his sons had died from typhoid. He came to blackmail Clay for money. After Clay told him Bianca had miscarried, he threw the man off the plantation.

"You hate me," Bianca whispered.

"No," Clay said quietly. "Not anymore. All I want is for us to be free of each other. I'll send you money. I'll see that you're comfortable."

"How can you do that? You think I'm stupid, but I know that nearly everything you make goes back into this place. It looks like you're rich because you own so much, but you're not. How can you support the plantation and send me money?"

He whirled on her, his eyes black with anger. "No, you're not stupid, just unbelievably selfish. Don't you realize how much I want to get rid of you? Can't you see the way you disgust me? I'd be willing to sell the plantation just so I'd no longer have to look at that fat thing you call a face." He opened his mouth to say more. Then he stopped and walked quickly out of the room.

Bianca sat on the sofa, unmoving, for a long time. She wouldn't allow herself to think of what Clay had said to her. Instead, she was thinking of Gerard. How nice it would be to live in Arundel Hall with him. She'd be the lady of the manor, planning menus, supervising meals, while he did whatever men do outside. In the evening, he'd come home, and they'd share a lovely meal. Then, he'd kiss her hand goodnight.

She looked about the room and remembered how she'd once had it. Now it was so bare and plain. Gerard wouldn't keep her from redecorating. No, Gerard loved her. As she was.

She rose slowly from the couch. She knew she must see him, see the man she loved. There were no choices open to her now. Gerard had been right. Clay meant to get rid of her in any way he could.

Chapter 22

"WHAT ARE you doing here?" Gerard demanded as he helped Bianca from the rowboat on Nicole's side of the river. He looked around anxiously.

"I had to see you."

"Couldn't you have sent a message? I would have come to you."

Bianca's eyes filled with tears. "Please don't be angry with me. I couldn't bear any more anger."

Gerard considered her for a moment. "Come with me. We must keep out of sight of the house."

She nodded and followed him. It was difficult walking. She had to stop twice to catch her breath.

When they were on top of a rise overlooking the house, Gerard let her stop. "Now, tell me what's happened." He listened carefully to Bianca's long, emotional outburst. "So he knows the child you carried wasn't his."

"Is that bad?"

Gerard gave her a look of disgust. "The courts frown on adultery."

"Courts? What courts?"

"The courts that will grant him a divorce and will take everything away from you."

Bianca slid with her back to a tree until she sat down. "I've worked so hard for everything. He can't take it away from me. He can't!"

Gerard knelt before her. "Do you really mean that? There are ways to prevent him from stealing from you."

She stared at him. "You mean murder?"

"Isn't he trying to kill you? How would you like to return to England a divorced woman? Everyone would say you couldn't hold a man. What would your father say?"

Bianca thought of all the times her father had laughed at her. He had said Clay wouldn't want her after he'd gotten a taste of Nicole. He'd never let her forget it if she returned in disgrace. "How?" she whispered. "When?"

Gerard sat back on his heels. There was an odd light in his eyes. "Soon. It must be very soon. We mustn't let him talk to anyone about his plans."

Suddenly, a movement caught Bianca's eyes. "Nicole!" she gasped, then put her hand over her mouth.

Gerard turned instantly. Adele stood behind him, half hidden by the trees. It had taken Nicole a long time to persuade her mother that it was safe to walk in the woods behind the house. This was only her third time out alone.

He took one long stride and grabbed his wife's arm. "What did you hear?" he said, as his hand cut into her flesh.

"Murder," she said, her eyes almost whirling in fear.

Gerard struck her hard across the cheek. "Yes! Murder! Yours! Do you understand me? You say one word about this, and I'll take Nicole and the twins to the guillotine. Would you like to see their heads roll into the basket?"

Adele's expression went past terror to something that only someone who's known great horror could comprehend.

He ran his finger across her throat. "Remember," he whispered, then pushed her away.

She fell to her knees, quickly picked herself up, and scampered back toward the house.

Gerard adjusted his cravat, then turned to Bianca. She was standing with her back to the tree, her eyes frightened. "What in the world is wrong with you?" he snapped.

"I've never seen you like that," she whispered.

"What you mean is you've never seen a man protect the woman he loves." He continued when he saw her frown. "I had to ensure that she wouldn't tell what she'd heard."

"She will. Of course she will."

"No! Not after what I said. She's insane, didn't you know?"

"Who is she? She looks like Nicole."

He hesitated. "Her mother." He went on before she could ask more questions, "Meet me tomorrow at one o'clock where we had the picnic. We'll make plans there."

"You'll bring lunch?" she asked eagerly.

"Of course. Now you must go before someone sees you. I don't want us seen together . . . Yet," he added. He took her hand and directed her to the wharf.

When Nicole returned from the mill, Janie greeted her at the door with a solemn face. "Your mother's having a bad one. Nobody can calm her down."

A horrible scream threatened to shake the roof from the little house, and Nicole ran up the stairs.

"Mother!" Nicole said, and tried to put her arms around her mother. Adele's lovely face was distorted so badly it was almost unrecognizable.

"The babies!" Adele shrieked, flailing her arms about wildly. "The babies! Their heads! They'll murder them, kill them. Blood everywhere!"

"Mother, please. You are safe!" Nicole was speaking in French, as was Adele.

Janie stood at the head of the stairs. "She seemed to be upset about the twins. Is that what she's saying?"

Nicole struggled with her mother's arms. "I think so. She's talking about the babies. Maybe she means one of my cousins."

"I don't think so. She came tearing into the house a few minutes ago and tried to hide the twins in the little closet under the stairs."

"I hope the children aren't upset."

Janie shrugged. "They're used to her. They crouched in the closet, then got out when I got her upstairs."

"He'll kill them!" Adele screamed. "I didn't know him. I never knew him. The fat lady will kill them, too."

"What's she saying now?" Janie asked.

"Just nonsense. Could you get some laudanum? I think the only way she'll calm down is if she sleeps."

When Janie was gone, Nicole continued to try to soothe her mother, but Adele was wild, frantic. She kept talking of murder and the guillotine and a fat woman. When Adele mentioned Clayton, she gained Nicole's full attention.

"What about Clay?" Nicole asked.

Adele's eyes were wild, her hair flying. "Clay! They will kill him, too. And my babies, all my babies. Everyone's babies. They killed the queen. They'll kill Clay."

"Who will kill Clay?"

"Them. The baby-killers!"

Janie stood at Nicole's shoulder. "She looks like she's trying to tell you something. It almost sounded as if she said Clay's name."

Nicole took the cup of tea from Janie. "Drink this, Mother. It will make you feel much better."

It didn't take long for the laudanum to take effect. Downstairs, Gerard was just entering the house.

"Gerard," Nicole said. "Did something happen today to upset Mother?"

He turned toward her slowly. "I haven't seen her. Is she having one of her fits again?"

"As if you'd care!" Janie said, passing Nicole on the stairs and going to the fireplace. "Considering that she's your wife, you'd think you'd have some feeling for her."

"I would certainly never share my feelings with such as you," Gerard retorted.

"Stop it, both of you!" Nicole commanded. "Neither of you is helping my mother."

Gerard waved his hand. "It's just one of her fits. You should be used to them by now."

Nicole moved to the table. "Somehow, this one was different. It was almost as if she were trying to tell me something."

Gerard looked at her from under lowered lashes. "What could she say that she hasn't said a hundred times? All she ever talks about is murder and death."

"True," Nicole said thoughtfully. "Only this time she mentioned Clay."

"Clay!" Janie said. "She's never met Clay before, has she?"

"Not to my knowledge. And she kept talking about a fat woman."

"There's no guessing who that is," Janie snorted.

"Of course," Gerard inserted with uncharacteristic enthusiasm. "She must have seen Clay and Bianca together, and since they are strangers, she was frightened. You know how strangers terrify her."

"I'm sure you're right," Nicole said. "But somehow it seemed more than that. She kept saying someone was trying to kill Clay."

"She's always saying someone is trying to murder someone else," Gerard said angrily.

"Maybe, but she's never confused the past and the present quite like this before."

Before Gerard could say a word, Janie stepped forward. "There's no use worrying about it now. In the morning, you can try to talk to your mother. Maybe after a good night's sleep, she'll be able to explain herself more clearly. Now, sit down and eat your supper."

The little house was dark and silent. Outside, the river flowed slowly, gently, now that it had come closer to straightening its course. It was especially warm for September, and the four people in the attic bedroom slept without covers.

Adele was restless. Even under the heavy dose of the sleeping drug, she still tossed and turned, her dreams puzzled and confused. She knew she had something to tell, but she had no idea how to go about it. The king and queen of France seemed to mingle with a farmer named Clayton, a man whose face she could not see. But she could see death, his death, everyone's death.

Gerard stubbed out the thin cigar he'd been smoking and silently stepped out of the bed. He stood and looked down at his wife. It had been many months since he'd taken her in his arms. In France, he'd felt honored to be married to one of the Courtalains, even one as old as Adele. But when he'd seen Nicole, his feeling for his wife had died. Nicole was a younger, more beautiful version of her mother.

Quietly, without so much as a creak of a floorboard, he went to Adele's side, then sat on the edge of the bed. He leaned across her for his pillow.

She opened her eyes for just a moment before the pillow came down over her face. She started to fight but then knew it was no use. This was what she'd waited for. All those years spent in prison, she'd waited each second for death. Finally, it was coming, and she was ready for it.

Gerard removed the pillow from Adele's face. In death, she was quite pretty, younger than he'd ever seen her look before. He stood, then walked across the room to the blanket partition that concealed Janie and Nicole's room.

He stared for a long time at Nicole, her body barely hidden

under her thin nightgown. His hand ached to caress the curve of her hip.

"Soon," he whispered. "Soon."

He returned to his bed, stretched out beside the woman he'd just murdered, and slept. His only thought was that her tossings would no longer disturb him.

When Nicole discovered her mother's lifeless form the next morning, the house was empty. The twins and Janie had gone to pick apples, and Gerard, as usual, was off by himself.

She sat quietly on the edge of the bed, held her mother's cold hand in her own, and caressed the cheek so like her own. She turned and very slowly left the house.

She walked up to the ridge overlooking the mill and the house. She suddenly felt so alone, so isolated. For years, she'd thought her family was dead. Then the reappearance of her mother had given her some solidarity again. All she had left now was Clay.

She looked across the river to Arundel Hall, so perfect in the early morning sun. But she didn't have Clay, she thought. She must realize he was gone, as surely as her mother was now gone.

She sat down on the ground, her knees drawn up, and buried her face. She would never stop loving him or needing him. Now all she wanted was the comfort of his arms holding her, telling her that life would still go on after her mother's death. Even Adele's last words had been of Clay.

Her head shot up. A fat woman was going to kill Clay. Of course! Adele had somehow overheard Bianca planning Clay's death.

Nicole's mind whirled with possible explanations. Bianca could have met someone she had hired on the mill side of the river. If Clay were dead, Bianca would own the plantation.

Nicole stood and ran to the wharf. She rowed herself across

the river in record time. Once on land again, she lifted her skirts and ran to the house.

"Clay!" she called as she ran from room to room. Even as she ran, even in her urgency, she was aware of the house. It seemed to welcome her with open arms. Beth's portrait had been replaced over the mantel in the dining room. She gave a quick look and thought she saw a look of concern in Beth's eye.

She went to the library last. The feel of Clayton's presence was overpowering. The desk was cluttered but clean, a place of constant work.

She knew exactly when he came to stand behind her, but she didn't turn. The strong smell of his sweat mingled with the leather in the room. She breathed deeply, then slowly turned to face him.

She had seen very little of him in the past year, only once for any length of time. The humble, quiet Clay who'd come to help them dig the trench was a stranger to her. But this man before her now was the man she'd fallen in love with. His linen shirt was open to the waist, and he was drenched in sweat, his hands and forearms tobacco-stained. The way he stood, feet wide apart, hands on hips, reminded her of the first time she'd seen him, through a spyglass.

"You've been crying," he said flatly.

His voice sent shivers up her spine, and she had no idea why she was there. She turned away from him, took one step toward the door.

"No!" It was a command she obeyed. "Look at me," he said quietly.

She turned slowly.

"What has happened?" His voice was full of concern.

Sharp tears mounted behind Nicole's eyes. "My mother . . . died. I must go home."

His eyes held hers for a long moment. "Don't you know that you *are* home?"

The tears were threatening to spill. She had no idea he still had so much control over her. She shook her head, her lips silently forming a no.

"Come here." His voice was quiet, but it was the sound of command.

Nicole refused to obey him. Somewhere, there was a seed of reason in her brain, and she knew she should not renew what had once been between them. But her feet were not so sensible. One of them picked itself up and took a step forward.

Clay merely stared at her, the current between their eyes nearly tangible. "Come," he said once again.

The tears broke, and her feet leaped toward him. He caught her in his arms, nearly crushing her. He carried her to the couch, where he cradled her in his arms.

"If you're going to cry, you should do it where you belong, on your man's shoulder."

He held her and caressed her hair while she cried, pouring out her grief at her mother's death. After a while, he began to ask questions. He wanted her to talk about her mother, about the good times. She told of Adele's relationship with the twins, how they were like three children together.

Suddenly, she sat upright and told him what had brought her to Arundel Hall.

"You came to warn me that you thought someone would try to kill me?"

"Not someone," she said. "Bianca. I think Mother meant to tell me that Bianca planned to kill you."

He thought for a moment. "What if she'd heard Isaac or one of the other men talking about Bianca? One of my men told me the other day that if he had a wife like mine, he'd probably kill her."

"That's awful," Nicole gasped.

Clay shrugged. "Adele could have heard a similar statement. It would probably have come out in the same gibberish."

"But, Clay—"

He put a finger to her lips and stopped her. "I am pleased that you still care enough to warn me, but Bianca is not a murderess. She has neither the brains nor the courage." His eyes went to her mouth, where he ran his fingertip along her upper lip. "I've missed your funny upside-down mouth."

She drew back from him, not easy to do considering she was sitting on his lap. "Nothing's changed."

He smiled at her. "True. Nothing's changed between us since I nearly raped you in the ship's cabin. We've loved each other since our first meeting, and it will never change."

"No, please," she begged. "It's over. Bianca—"

He raised one eyebrow. "I don't want to hear her name again. I've had a lot of time to think since the flood. I realized then that you still loved me. It wasn't Bianca who caused the problems between us; it was our own stubbornness. You knew I was afraid to lose the plantation, and I wasn't strong enough alone, and you didn't believe in me enough."

"Clay—" she began. She knew in her heart how right he was, but she didn't like to hear it.

"It's all right, love. We're going to start again. But this time, we're staying together. This time, no one will be able to part us."

She stared at him. They'd been through so much, and yet their love had lasted. She knew they would make it.

She leaned back on his shoulder, and his arms held her close. "It seems like I haven't been away."

He kissed the top of her head. "You have to get off my lap, or I'm going to throw you down on this couch and have my way with you."

She wanted to laugh and tease with him, but the pain from her mother's death was inside her too thoroughly.

"Come with me, sweet," he said quietly. "Let's go back to the mill and see to your mother. We have time later to make plans." He lifted her chin in his hand. "Do you trust me?"

"Yes," she said firmly. "I do."

He stood her on the floor, then stood beside her. Nicole's eyes widened at the bulge in his trousers. The room suddenly seemed very warm.

"Come on," he said hoarsely. "And stop looking at me like that."

He took her hand and led her out of the room.

Neither of them saw Bianca standing just inside the dining room door. She'd been outside when she saw Nicole running toward the house. She'd hurried after her, planning what she'd say to her about trespassing. Inside the house she'd heard Nicole running through it, slamming bedroom doors, acting as if she owned the place. Bianca had been in the morning room—Nicole moved too quickly for the larger woman to keep pace with her—when she saw Clay. She'd stood outside the door and listened while they talked.

She had been pleased to hear Gerard's wife was dead. They'd never spoken of the fact that he was already married, but Bianca knew the woman was old and couldn't live too much longer.

She'd frozen when Nicole said Bianca was planning to murder Clay. When she heard Clay say Bianca wasn't smart enough or courageous enough, she began to thaw. She changed from ice to fire in seconds. She knew now that she'd be able to carry out Gerard's plan. Clayton Armstrong deserved to die after what he'd said about her.

She left the house and went to find a child she could send with a message to Gerard. She knew there was little time left before Clay took steps to rid himself of her.

Nicole stood outside the mill and drank deeply from a gourd dipper. The cool, fresh well water was welcome after a hard morning inside. The autumn grains were fully ripe, and there wasn't a minute when they weren't busy.

At least, the work kept her mind off the plans she and Clay had. They'd buried Adele in Clay's family plot, next to his own mother. "So she'll always be near us," he said. Then, the two of them had gone to Bianca and discussed their futures. Clay said he was tired of secrets and wanted things in the open from now on. Bianca had been quiet, listening carefully to what Clay had to say. The offer he made her for lifetime support was very fair, and both Clay and Nicole knew it would place a great burden on both of them in future years. Clay sought Nicole's hand under the table. There was a strong sense of support between them now.

After the meeting, they hadn't spoken but had walked to the hidden clearing by the river. In spite of the fact that it had been well over a year since they'd made love, there was no urgency. They took their time, looking at each other, exploring, savoring. They were rediscovering each other.

There had been no long explanations, no rehashing of what idiots they'd been. There was no sense of something going to happen, only a deep joy that they were together again. They had felt as if they were one person, not two people who mistrusted, misjudged, and misunderstood each other.

"Nicole!"

Gerard's sharp voice brought Nicole out of her reverie and into the present. "Yes?"

"We've been looking everywhere for you. One of the twins fell up on the ridge. Janie wants you to come."

She threw the dipper down, lifted her skirts, and started running, with Gerard close behind her. The ridge was empty. "Where are they?"

Gerard stepped very close to her. "You'd do anything for them, wouldn't you? You give yourself to everyone except me."

Nicole stepped backward. "Where are the twins?"

"With the devil, for all I care. I wanted to get you up here alone. I want you to take a little journey with me."

"I have work to do. I—" She stopped when she saw the pistol in Gerard's hands.

"Now I have your attention. Or does any man who points something large and hard at you get that?"

Nicole curled her lip and cursed him in French.

Gerard smiled at her. "Quite colorful! Now, I want you to go with me—quietly."

"No."

"I thought perhaps you'd say that. Remember how you thought my dear wife overheard that Bianca was planning to murder Armstrong? For once in that crazy woman's life, she was right about something."

Nicole stared at him, her eyes wide, enormous. "You killed my mother," she whispered.

"Clever girl. Too clever. Now, if you ever wish to see your lover alive again, you will obey me." He waved the pistol. "Through there, and remember that his life depends on you."

Nicole walked through the woods, away from the mill, then down to the river where Gerard had a rowboat hidden. He delighted in the fact that Nicole had to row him across while he sat in the stern and gave her orders. He talked constantly of his cleverness, of how Nicole had enticed him and teased him since he arrived.

They landed at a far corner of the Armstrong plantation. There was a vacant tool shed there, half hidden under a tree, its door hanging off a broken hinge.

They had barely reached the door when Bianca came from the trees. "Where have you been? And what is she doing here?"

"Never mind that," Gerard snapped. "Did you do it?"

Her eyes, almost hidden by her grotesquely fat cheeks, were unnaturally bright. "He wouldn't go riding. He wouldn't do what he was supposed to. I fixed the saddle with the glass like you said, but he wouldn't go."

"What happened?" Gerard demanded.

Bianca had been holding her skirt together. Now she released it. There was a great deal of blood down the front. "I shot him," she said, as if she were surprised at the fact.

Nicole screamed and would have started running toward the house, but Gerard caught her by the arm. He hit her hard across the mouth, sending her sprawling inside the tool shed.

"Is he dead?" Gerard demanded.

"Oh, yes," Bianca said. She blinked at him, and her voice sounded strangely like a child's. She pulled her other hand from behind her skirt. "I brought the other pistol."

Gerard grabbed it from her hand, then pointed it at her. "Get in here."

Bianca frowned in puzzlement, then stepped inside the shed. "Why is Nicole here? Why is my maid here?" she asked simply.

"Bianca!" Nicole screamed. "Where is Clay?"

Bianca turned slowly and looked at Nicole as she stood pressed against the wall. "You!" she whispered. "You did this!" She half fell toward Nicole, her hands like claws.

Nicole was nearly suffocated when Bianca's great weight came crashing down on her.

"Get off her, you fat whore!" Gerard yelled. He tossed one pistol onto the floor behind him, put the other into his belt, and began to pull Bianca off Nicole.

"I want to kill her!" Bianca sneered. "Let me kill her now!"

Gerard pulled his gun and pointed it at her. "It's you who'll be killed, not her," he said.

Bianca smiled. "You don't know what you're saying. It's me, remember? The woman you love."

"Love!" Gerard snorted. "What man could love you? I'd as soon mate with one of the sows!"

"Gerard!" Bianca pleaded. "You're upset."

"You stupid, vain pig! To think you believed that *I*, a Courtalain, could ever love such as you. You will be found dead, a suicide, grief-stricken over your husband's death, which was caused, no doubt, by robbers."

"No," Bianca whispered, her hands outstretched, palms upward.

"Oh, yes," he smiled, obviously enjoying himself. "The Armstrong estate will be left to those obnoxious twins, and since there are no other relatives, Nicole will be their guardian and I will be her husband."

"Hers!" Bianca gasped. "You said you hated her."

He laughed. "It was a game, remember? You and I played a game, and I won."

Nicole was beginning to think again. Maybe she could divert Gerard's attention until someone found them. "No one would believe Bianca would kill herself over Clay. It's common knowledge that she hates him."

Bianca turned to Nicole with a look of hate. Then their one and only look of understanding passed between them. "Yes, the field hands and the house servants know that we rarely even see each other."

"But, lately, people have been saying you're reconciled, that Armstrong's stopped drinking and become the perfect husband," Gerard said.

Bianca looked bewildered.

"Bianca is an English lady," Nicole said. "In England, she's one of the peerage, and there is no peerage in France anymore. She would make an admirable wife."

"She is nothing!" Gerard said. "Nothing! Everyone knows royalty will be reinstated in France. Then, I shall be married to a duke's granddaughter. The magnificent Courtalains will live again through me!"

"But—" Nicole began.

"Enough!" Gerard screamed. "You think I'm stupid, do you not? Do you think I can't see through your schemes to keep me talking?" He waved the gun toward Bianca. "I would not have her if she were the queen of England herself. She is fat, ugly, and unbelievably stupid."

Bianca flew at him, her hands going for his face. Gerard struggled for a moment under her suffocating weight.

The pistol went off, and slowly Bianca moved away from him, her hands clutching her stomach, blood beginning to seep through her fingers.

Nicole's eyes had long been on the pistol Gerard had carelessly tossed to the floor, but now Gerard and Bianca struggled between her and it. She looked around the empty shed until she saw a loose board in the wall. With superhuman strength, she wrenched it free.

Moments after the pistol went off, Nicole hit Gerard with the board. He staggered as Bianca crumbled to the floor.

"You have hurt me," he whispered in French, his fingers touching the blood at his temple. "You will pay for that with every moment of your life."

He advanced toward her as she backed against the wall.

Bianca, her blood quickly flowing from her, looked through hazy vision to see Gerard advancing on her enemy. A pistol lay at her fingertips. She used the last of her strength to raise it, aim it, and pull the trigger. She died before she saw that her aim had been true.

Nicole stood absolutely still as Gerard suddenly jerked still. He seemed to react before she heard the shot. His eyes showed surprise, puzzlement at what had happened to him. Then, very slowly, he fell to the floor, dead, his eyes still showing his wonder.

Nicole stepped away from him. Both of them lay on the floor. Gerard's outstretched hand had fallen across Bianca's, and as Nicole watched, some death reflex made Bianca's hand tighten on Gerard's. In death, she held him as she never could have in life.

Nicole turned and ran from the shed. She ran the distance to the house. She must find Clay!

There was blood on the library floor but no sign of him. Nicole knew her heart had stopped beating long ago.

Suddenly, she stopped and sat on the couch, her face buried in her hands. She needed time to think and calm herself if she was to find him. Someone could have found Clay and taken him away. No, if that were the case, the house would be alive with activity.

Where would he go?

She stood up, because she knew where he'd go—to the clearing.

There were tears in her eyes as she ran the mile or more to the cave. Her lungs hurt and her heart pounded, but she knew she wouldn't stop.

She was no sooner through the secret gate than she saw him. He looked almost comfortable, lying beside the water, one arm outstretched.

"Clay," she whispered, kneeling beside him.

He opened his eyes and smiled at her. "I was wrong about Bianca. She was courageous enough to try to kill me."

"Let me see," she said as she pulled his bloody shirt away from his shoulder. It was a clean wound, but he was weak from loss of blood. She was giddy with relief. "You should have stayed at the house," she said as she tore a strip off her chemise and began to bind his wound.

He watched her. "How did you know?"

"We've time for that later," she said brusquely. "You need a doctor right now." She started to stand, but he caught her arm.

"Tell me!"

"Bianca and Gerard are dead."

He stared at her for a long moment. There would be time later for details. "Go to the cave and get the unicorn."

"Clay, there isn't time—"

"Go!"

Reluctantly, she went to the cave and brought back the little silver unicorn sealed in glass. Clay set it on the ground and then smashed the glass with a rock.

"Clay!" she protested.

He leaned back on the grass, with the unicorn free at last. "You once said I thought you weren't worthy to touch what Beth had touched. What you didn't understand was it was I who was unclean." He lifted himself on one elbow—he had little strength after smashing the glass—and dropped the unicorn down the front of her dress. He gave her a lopsided grin. "I'll retrieve it later."

She smiled, tears rolling down her cheeks. "I must get a doctor."

He caught her skirt. "You'll return to me?"

"Always." She shifted the bodice of her dress. "There's a little silver horn poking me, and someone must remove it."

He smiled, his eyes closed. "I volunteer."

She turned away toward the gate.

Lost Lady

Chapter 1

WESTON MANOR sat serenely and quietly in the midst of two acres of garden. It was a small house, unpretentious, looking like what it was—an English gentleman's lodging in 1797. Only the keenest observer would notice that two of the gutters had fallen somewhat or that a corner of one of the chimneys was broken away or even that some of the painted trim was beginning to peel.

Inside, the only room that was fully lit was the dining room, but here, too, could be seen evidence of neglect. In the shadows, the Georgian chairs' upholstery was frayed and faded. Tiny bits of the plaster decorations on the tall ceiling had started to chip, and on one wall there was a lighter space where a painting had once hung.

But the young girl sitting on one side of the table was oblivious to any imperfections in the room, for her eyes were glued to the man across from her.

Farrell Batsford curved his wrist in such a manner that the ruffled silk at his cuff would not be stained by the juices from the roast. Taking only a bit of the meat onto his plate, he gave a thin smile to the girl across from him.

"Stop gawking and eat your dinner," Jonathan Northland commanded his niece, before looking away from her. "Now, Farrell, what were you saying about the shooting at your country place?"

Regan Weston tried to look at her food, even to eat a few bites, but she couldn't manage to swallow any of it. How anyone expected her to be calm and eat at a time like this, when the man she loved was sitting so near her, she couldn't begin to understand. She stole another glance at Farrell, looking up at him through her long, dark lashes. He was aristocratic-looking with his long, thin nose and his almond-shaped blue eyes. The velvet coat he wore with the gold brocaded vest perfectly suited his looks and his slim, elegant body. Blond hair was arranged artfully around his narrow head, waving just a bit at the edge of his pure white cravat.

As Regan uttered a deep sigh, her uncle gave her another quelling look. Farrell wiped the corners of his thin lips delicately.

"Perhaps my bride-to-be would like to take a walk in the moonlight?" Farrell asked quietly, pronouncing each word carefully.

Bride! Regan thought. This time next week she would be his wife, and she'd have him all to herself to love and cherish, to hold, to belong only to her. Overwhelmed by emotion, she could not speak; she could only nod in acceptance. As she tossed her napkin on the table, she was aware of her uncle's disapproval. Once again she wasn't acting as a lady should. From now on, she reminded herself for the thousandth time, she must remember who she was—and who she was to become: Mrs. Farrell Batsford.

As Farrell held out his arm for her, Regan tried not to clutch it. She wanted to dance with delight, laugh with her happiness, throw her arms around the man she loved. But, instead, she followed him sedately from the dining room into the cool spring garden.

"Perhaps you should have worn a shawl," Farrell said once they were a short way from the house.

"Oh no," she said breathlessly, leaning a little closer to him. "I wouldn't have wanted to take a minute away from our time together."

Farrell started to say something but seemed to change his mind as he looked away from her. "The wind is off the sea tonight, and it is cooler than last night."

"Oh Farrell," she sighed. "Only six more days and we'll be married. I'm sure I'm the happiest girl alive."

"Yes, well perhaps," Farrell said quickly as he disengaged her fingers from his arm. "Sit here, Regan." The tone of his voice was much like the one her uncle always used with her, one of impatience and exasperation.

"I would rather walk with you."

"Are you going to start being disobedient before we're even married?" he demanded, gazing down into her wide-set, trusting eyes. Everything she thought and felt showed in those eyes. She was pretty, in a childish sort of way, in her high-necked muslin dress, but she had about as much appeal to him as a puppy begging for affection.

He took a few steps away from her before beginning to talk. "Is everything ready for the wedding?"

"Uncle Jonathan planned it all."

"Of course—he would," Farrell said under his breath. "Then I'll return next week for the ceremony."

"Next week!" Regan jumped to her feet. "Not before? But Farrell . . . we . . . I. . . ."

He ignored her outburst as he held out his arm for her. "I think we should return to the house now, and perhaps you should reconsider the whole idea of marriage if everything I do displeases you."

One look from Farrell stopped her protest. She told herself again to remember her manners and be quiet, that she must never give her beloved any reason to find fault with her.

Once they were back inside the dining room, Farrell and her uncle quickly dismissed her to her upstairs bedchamber. She didn't dare protest; she was too afraid that Farrell would again suggest calling off the wedding.

Inside her bedroom, she could release her pent-up emotions. "Isn't he wonderful, Matta?" she gushed to her maid. "Did you ever see such brocade as he wore? Only a real gentleman could choose such fabric. And his manners! He does everything correctly, everything perfectly. Oh, how I wish I could be like him, to always be so sure of myself, to know even my slightest movement was correct."

Matta's coarse, ugly face frowned. "It seems to me there should be more to a man than just pretty manners," she said in her West Country accent. "Now stand still and get out of that dress. It's past time for you to be in bed."

Regan did as she was told; she always obeyed people. Someday, she thought, she'd be a person of importance. She had money from her father, and she'd have the man she loved for her husband. Together the two of them would keep an elegant house in London where they would give the most fashionable parties, and a house in the country where she could be alone with her perfect husband.

"Stop your dreamin'," Matta commanded, "and get into bed. Someday you're gonna wake up, Regan Weston, and find out the world ain't made of sugarplums and silk brocade."

"Oh Matta," Regan laughed. "I'm not as silly as you think. I had enough sense to get Farrell, didn't I? What other girl could do that?"

"Maybe any of them with her father's money," Matta muttered as she tucked the covers around her charge's slim body. "Now go to sleep and save your dreamin' for the nighttime."

Obediently, Regan closed her eyes until Matta was out of the room. Her father's money! The words echoed through her mind. Of course Matta was wrong, she reasoned. Farrell loved her for herself, because. . . .

When she couldn't remember a single reason that Farrell had given for wanting to marry her, she sat up in bed. On the moonlit night when he'd proposed, he'd kissed her forehead and talked of his home, which had been in his family for generations.

Tossing the covers aside, Regan went to the mirror, looking at herself in moonlight-silvered image. Her wide-set, blue-green eyes looked like they belonged to a child instead of to a young woman who'd been eighteen for a whole week now, and her slim figure was always hidden under loose, concealing clothes—clothes chosen by her uncle. Even now, her heavy cambric nightgown was long-sleeved and high-necked.

What could Farrell see in her? she wondered. How could he know that she could be sophisticated and graceful when she was always dressed as a child? Trying to smile in a seductive way, she pulled her nightgown off one shoulder. Ah yes, if Farrell were to see her like this, he just might do something besides kiss her forehead in a fatherly way. A very immature giggle escaped her as she thought of Farrell's reaction to the coquetry of his sedate, gentle bride-to-be.

Quickly, she looked toward where Matta slept in the little adjoining dressing room and thought it just might be worth any consequences from her uncle to see her beloved's reaction to her in a nightgown. After hastily putting on heelless slippers, she silently eased the door open and tiptoed downstairs.

The door to the drawing room was open, candles blazing. In a golden halo sat Farrell, and Regan could do little more than marvel at him. It was quite a few minutes before she began to listen to what the two men were saying.

"Look at this place!" Jonathan said vehemently. "Yesterday a piece of plaster scrollwork fell on top of my head. There I was, reading my paper, when a damned flower came flying at me."

Farrell concentrated on the brandy in his glass. "It will all be over soon—for you at least. You'll get your money and can repair your house or buy a new one if you want, but I have a lifetime of misery ahead of me."

Snorting, Jonathan refilled his glass. "You make it sound as if you were going to prison. I tell you, you should be grateful for what I've done for you."

"Grateful!" Farrell sneered. "You've saddled me with a brainless, uneducated, clumsy chit of a girl."

"Come now, some men would be happy to have her. She's pretty, and her simple-mindedness would be liked by a great many men."

"I am not like any other man," Farrell said warningly.

Unlike many people, Jonathan did not find Farrell Batsford intimidating. "True," he said evenly. "Not many men would make a bargain such as you have."

As Jonathan finished his third brandy, he turned back to Farrell. "Come now, let's not argue. We should be celebrating our good fortune, not going for each other's throat." He raised his full glass in salute. "Here's to my dear sister, with many thanks for marrying her rich young man."

"And dying and leaving it all within your reach—isn't that the rest of the toast?" After drinking deeply, Farrell turned serious. "Are you sure about your brother-in-law's will? I don't want to marry your niece and then find out it was all a big mistake."

"I've memorized the document!" Jonathan said angrily. "I've lived in barristers' offices for the last six years. The girl cannot touch the money before she's twenty-three, unless she marries before then, and even at that she couldn't be married before she was eighteen."

"If that hadn't been the case, would you have found someone to marry her when she was twelve perhaps?"

Chuckling, Jonathan set his glass down. "Perhaps. Who knows? As far as I can tell, she hasn't changed much since she was twelve."

"If you hadn't kept her prisoner in this crumbling house, perhaps she wouldn't be such an immature, uninteresting child.

Lord! When I think of the wedding night! No doubt she'll cry and pout like a two-year-old."

"Stop complaining!" snarled Jonathan. "You'll have money enough to repair that great monstrosity of a house of yours, and all I get for years of taking care of her is a measly pittance."

"Caring for her! Since when have you left your club long enough to even know what she looks like?" Sighing heavily, he continued, "I'll leave her at my house and then go to London. At least now I'll have money enough to enjoy myself. Of course, it won't be pleasant not being able to have my friends to my house. Perhaps I can hire someone to take care of a wife's duties. I cannot imagine your niece managing an estate the size of mine." Glancing up, he saw that Jonathan's face had grown pale; his hands clutching the glass were white-knuckled.

Turning quickly, Farrell saw Regan standing in the light by the doorway. Acting as if nothing had happened, he set his glass down. "Regan," he said gently, warmly. "You shouldn't be up so late."

Her big eyes were magnified by the tears sparkling in them. "Do not touch me," she whispered, her hands clenched at her side, her back rigid. She looked so small, with her thick dark hair hanging down her back, swathed in a little girl's nightgown.

"Regan, you are to obey me at once."

She whirled on him. "Don't use that tone with me! How dare you think you can tell me what to do after the things you said!" She looked at her uncle. "You will never get any of my money. Do you understand me? Neither of you will ever get a farthing of my money!"

Jonathan was beginning to recover himself. "And how do *you* expect to get any of it?" he smiled. "If you don't marry Farrell, you won't be able to touch the money for five years. Until now you've been living on my income, but I'll tell you now that if you refuse to marry him I'll throw you into the streets, since you'd no longer be of use to me."

Putting her palms to her forehead, Regan tried to think clearly.

"Be sensible, Regan," Farrell said, his hand on her shoulder.

She backed away from him. "I'm not like you said," she whispered. "I'm not simple-minded. I can do things. I don't have to take anyone's charity."

"Of course you don't," Farrell began patronizingly.

"Leave her alone!" Jonathan snapped. "It's no use trying to reason with her. She lives in a dream world just like her mother did." His fingers bit into her skin as he grabbed her arm. "Do you know what it's been like the past sixteen years since your parents died? I've watched you eat my food and wear the clothes I paid for, yet all the while you were sitting on millions, *millions*, that I would never be able to touch. Even after you were old enough to inherit, what reason did I have to think you'd give me a pound?"

"I would have. You're my uncle!"

"Ha!" He pushed her back toward the wall. "You would have fallen for some worthless, dressed-up dandy, and he'd have run through everything in five years. I just decided to give you what you wanted and at the same time make sure I got what *I* wanted."

"Now see here!" Farrell half choked. "Are you calling me—? Because if you are—."

Ignoring him, Jonathan continued, "What's it to be? Him, or you walk out right now?"

"You can't—," Farrell began.

"I damn well can, and I am going to. You're crazy if you think I'm going to support her another five years just for the pleasure of it."

Dazed, Regan looked from one man to the other. Farrell, her heart cried. How could she have been so wrong about him? He didn't love her but only wanted her money; he'd talked of the horrors of being married to her.

"What's your answer?" Jonathan demanded.

"I'll pack," Regan whispered.

"Not the clothes I paid for," Jonathan sneered.

In spite of what the two men seemed to believe about her, there was a great deal of pride in Regan Weston. Her mother had run away from her family and married a penniless clerk, yet because she'd worked with him and believed in him they'd made a fortune. Her mother had been forty when Regan was born, and two years later she'd died with her husband in a boating accident. Regan had been left in the care of her only relative, her mother's brother. Over the years she'd had no reason to show any of the spirit she'd inherited from her mother.

"I'm leaving," she said quietly.

"Regan, be reasonable," Farrell said. "Where will you go? You don't know anyone."

"Should I perhaps stay here and marry you? Won't you be embarrassed at having such an ignorant wife?"

"Let her go! She'll come back," Jonathan snapped. "Let her get a taste of the world, and she'll come back."

Regan's spirit was leaving her quickly as she saw the hate in her uncle's eyes and the contempt in Farrell's. Before she could change her mind, before she fell to her knees before Farrell, she turned and fled the house.

It was dark outside, and the wind from the sea moved the tree branches overhead. As she paused on the doorstep, she lifted her chin high. She would make it; no matter what it took from her, she'd show them that she wasn't an ineffectual person, as they seemed to believe. The stones were cold under her feet as she walked away from the house, refusing to think about the fact that she was in public—however dark—wearing only her nightgown. Someday, she thought, she'd return to this house wearing a satin gown and tall feathers in her hair, and Farrell would go down on his knees to her, saying that she was the most beautiful woman in the world. Of course, by then she'd be renowned for her brilliant house parties, a favorite of the king and queen; she'd be celebrated for her wit and intelligence as well as her beauty.

The cold was becoming so intense that it was overriding her dreams. Stopping by an iron fence, she began to rub her arms. Where was she? She remembered Farrell saying she'd been kept a prisoner, and it was true. Since she was two years old she had rarely ever left Weston Manor. A succession of maids and frightened governesses had been her only companions, the garden her only place of amusement. In spite of being alone, she rarely felt lonely. That feeling didn't come until she met Farrell.

Leaning against the cold iron, she put her face in her hands. Whom was she trying to fool? What could she do alone in the night wearing only her nightgown?

She lifted her head when she heard footsteps coming toward her. A brilliant smile lit her face; Farrell was coming after her! As she moved away from the fence, her sleeve caught in the iron and tore at the shoulder. Ignoring the tear, she began to run toward the footsteps.

"Here, girly," said a poorly dressed young man. "So, you came to greet me, all ready for bed."

Backing away from him, Regan tripped over the edge of her long gown.

"There's no need to be afraid of Charlie," the man said. "I don't want nothin' that you don't want."

Regan began to run in earnest, her heart pounding wildly, her sleeve tearing a bit more with each movement. She had no idea where she was going, whether she was running toward something or away from it. Even when she fell the first time, she hardly slowed her pace.

It seemed like hours before she slipped into an alleyway and allowed her heart to calm enough to listen for the man's footsteps. When everything seemed to be quiet, she leaned her head back against the damp brick wall and smelled the salty, fishy odor from the sea. She could hear laughter from somewhere to her right, a door slammed, there was some metal clanking, and she could hear the call of the seagulls.

As she looked down at her nightgown, she saw it was torn and muddy; there was mud in her hair and, she guessed, on her cheek. Trying not to think about how she looked, she wanted only to control her fear. She had to get away from this bad-smelling place and find shelter before morning—a place where she could rest and find safety.

Trying as best she could to smooth her hair, pulling the torn pieces of her gown together, she left the alleyway and started walking toward the place where she'd heard the laughter. Perhaps there she would find the help she needed.

Within minutes, a man tried to grab her arm. As she jerked away from him, two more clutched at her skirt; the fabric tore in three places.

"No," she whispered, backing away from them. The smell of the fish seemed to be overpowering, and the darkness was as heavy as velvet. Again she started to run, the men following her closely.

As she looked back, she saw that there were several men behind her—just following her, not really hurrying, seeming to tease her with their pursuit.

One moment she was running, and the next she felt as if she'd slammed into a stone wall. She hit the ground, landing on her seat as if she'd been dropped from a window.

"Travis," a man above her said. "I think you've knocked the wind out of her sails."

An enormous shadow bent over Regan, and a rich, deep voice asked, "Are you hurt?"

Before she could think, she was swept from the ground and held in strong, safe-feeling arms. She was too exhausted, too terrified to consider proprieties but hid her face in the deep shoulder of the man who held her.

"I think you got just what you wanted for the night," another man chuckled. "Shall we see you in the morning?"

"Perhaps," said the deep voice against Regan's cheek. "But I may not come out until the ship sails."

The men laughed again before continuing on their way.

Chapter 2

REGAN HAD no idea where she was or whom she was with; all she knew was that she felt safe, as if she'd awakened from a terrible nightmare. As she closed her eyes and let her body sink against the man who held her so easily, she felt as if everything was going to be all right. A burst of light made her close her eyes more tightly, and bury her face more deeply into the hard shoulder.

"Whatcha got there, Mr. Travis?" came a woman's voice.

Regan felt a deep chuckle run through the man. "Bring some brandy and hot water to my room—and some soap."

The man seemed to have no trouble climbing the stairs with the extra weight of Regan in his arms. By the time he lit a candle, she was nearly asleep.

Gently he set her on the bed, her back propped against pillows. "All right, let's have a look at you."

While he seemed to inspect her, Regan got her first look at her rescuer. An extraordinarily thick crop of soft, dark hair topped a handsome face with deep brown eyes and a finely shaped mouth. There were little sparks of laughter in his eyes, tiny lines at the corners.

"Satisfied?" he asked as he went to answer the knock at the door.

He had to be the largest man she'd ever seen—a totally unfashionable figure, of course, but at the same time fascinating.

The depth of his chest was probably twice the circumference of any part of her body. No doubt his arms were as big as her waist, and she could see that his snug buckskin trousers clung to massive muscles in his thighs. Tall boots reached to his knees, and she wondered at them because she'd only seen men in silk hose and little kid slippers.

"Here, I want you to drink this; it'll make you feel better."

When the brandy was too hot in her throat, the man urged her to sip it slowly.

"You're cold as ice, and the brandy will warm you."

The brandy did warm her, and the golden candlelit room, and the man's quiet power all reinforced her feeling of security. Her uncle and Farrell seemed far away. "Why do you talk so strangely?" she asked softly.

His eyes crinkled further. "I might ask you the same thing. I'm an American."

Her eyes widened in a mixture of interest and some fear. She'd heard many stories about the Americans—men who declared war on their mother country, men who were little more than savages.

As if he had read her thoughts, the man dipped a cloth into the hot water, rubbed it on the soap, and began to wash Regan's face. Somehow it seemed so natural that this man, whose palm was as big as her face, should gently and tenderly wash her. When he'd finished her face, he began on her feet and legs. She looked down at his hair, cut just above his collar, curling a bit, and she couldn't resist touching it. It was firm and clean, and she thought that even the hairs on his head were strong.

As he rose, he took her hand and kissed her fingertips. "Put this on," he said, tossing her one of his clean shirts. "I'll go downstairs and see if I can find us something to eat. You look like you could use a good meal."

The room seemed cavernous when he was gone. When Regan stood, she weaved a bit and realized the brandy had gone to her head. Her Uncle Jonathan had never allowed her to drink spirits. The thought of that name brought back all the ugly memories. As she pulled off what was left of the torn and soiled nightgown, she began to imagine how Farrell and her uncle would feel when she returned with a big, handsome American on her arm. The Colonial was big enough to enforce anything he wanted. As she climbed into bed, wrapped in his clean shirt, the tails past her knees, she imagined how she'd be reinstated in Weston Manor, this time in glory. And the American would always be her friend, would even attend her wedding to Farrell. Of course, he would have to learn some manners, but perhaps Farrell could teach him.

She drifted off to sleep, a smile on her lips.

Travis returned to the room with a tray heavily laden with food. When his efforts to wake Regan only made her snuggle deeper under the covers, he dug into the food alone. He'd been drinking with his friends from America since early afternoon, celebrating their safe voyage and the completion of Travis's business in England. In a week he'd be sailing for Virginia.

All four of the men had been saying they'd like a sweet girl in their bed when this one ran into Travis. She was pretty, young, and clean, in spite of the pound of dirt he'd washed from her. He wondered what she was doing alone at night, running through the streets in her torn nightgown. Perhaps she'd been kicked out of the house where she usually worked, or maybe she wanted to try it on her own and found that working the streets frightened her.

Having finished most of the food, Travis stood and stretched. Whatever the girl's problem, at least she was his tonight. Tomorrow he could return her to the streets.

He undressed slowly, his hands clumsy with the buttons. The way the girl had clung to him had excited him, and he wondered where she'd learned such a trick; no other whore he'd met had used that technique.

When he was naked, he slipped between the sheets and pulled

the girl to him. Her body was limp, but as he slipped his hands beneath the shirt she began to awaken.

Regan felt the warm, masculine hands on her body, and it seemed to be part of her delicious dream. No one had offered her affection before; even as a child, when she'd longed to be held by someone, there was no one there to offer her love. In the back of her mind was the memory of some recent, horrible hurt, and she wanted someone to cling to, someone to take away the pain.

In a half-daze between sleep and wakefulness, she felt her shirt being removed. When her breasts touched his chest and felt the hardness of it, the coating of hair, she gasped with delight. Lips kissed her cheek, her eyes, her hair, and finally her mouth. She'd never kissed a man before, but she knew instantly that she liked it very much. His firm-soft lips moved over hers, parting them just a bit, savoring the sweetness of them.

As he pulled her closer to him, her arms went around his neck, glorying in the size of him, and she moved closer, pushing her body next to his, wanting to touch all of him.

But as Travis's movements grew quicker, she opened her eyes in surprise. Her senses began to return rapidly, and she started to pull away from him. Yet Travis's strength was such that he didn't notice her weak efforts to push him away. His head was none too clear from the whiskey he'd consumed, and the girl's eager response had inflamed him.

Regan pushed harder, but Travis's arms only tightened as his lips swept down on hers, sealing off any negative response she might make. In spite of her growing awareness that what she was doing was wrong, she couldn't resist for long, and so she started to respond to him fully, arching against him, wanting from him she knew not what.

Travis's hand held her head, cradling it, caressing it, his thumb running along the back of her ear. His teeth nipped her earlobe. "Sweet," he whispered. "As sweet as a violet."

Smiling, Regan moved languorously as Travis's thigh came

across hers. She moved her head to one side, allowing him access to all her throat and shoulder. She felt she might dissolve into a pool of liquid when he began to make love to her collarbone. Running her hands through his hair, losing them in the thick mass, she held his head down, didn't want him to move. When his hand first touched her breast, her body went rigid with surprise. Then, as the exquisite feeling flowed through every pore and vessel of her body, she pulled his head back to hers. Eagerly, passionately, thirstily, she sought his lips.

When he moved on top of her, her first thought was that for a man so big he was extraordinarily light. The next instant she felt pain, and her eyes flew open, her body lost its feeling of pleasure, and she pushed at him with all her might.

But Travis was past hearing her. His desire for this ardent, willing bit of heaven was raging, towering, and he could not listen to her protests.

Fuzzy from drink or not, he knew what he felt when he hit the tiny membrane. Somewhere in the back of his mind a bit of sanity told him that he was making an error, but he could not stop. He thrust into her quickly, much of his original zeal gone.

When he was finished he lay still on top of her, feeling her small, delicately boned body begin to shake with sobs. Her hot tears wet his neck, mingling with the sweat on his body.

As he rolled away from her, he didn't look at her. The sun was beginning to come in through the window, and Travis had never felt so sober in his life. When he had put on his pants and boots, and then his shirt, which he didn't bother to button, he turned back to her. Only the top of her head showed above the cover.

As gently as he could, he eased himself down onto the bed to sit beside her. "Who are you?" he asked quietly. A shake of her head and a loud sob were all the answer he got. Taking a deep breath, he pulled her upright, keeping the sheet around her bare breasts.

"Don't touch me!" she hissed. "You hurt me!"

Wincing once, Travis frowned. "I know I did, and I'm sorry, but . . ." His voice got louder. "Damn it! How was I to know you were a virgin? I thought you were. . . ." He stopped because he could see the innocence in her eyes. How could he have thought she was a prostitute? Maybe it had been the mud or the poorly lit room last night, or more likely the whiskey he'd drunk, but today he could see that he should have known her for what she obviously was. Even sitting naked in his bed, her hair a tangle about her shoulders, she exuded an air of refinement and gentility that only the upperclass English could keep in times of stress. As it began to dawn on him what he'd done—taken some lord's virgin daughter to his bed—he started to realize the seriousness of his actions.

"I don't guess I can apologize for what's happened," he began, "but perhaps I can explain myself to your father. I'm sure that he'll . . ." Understand? Travis thought.

"My father is dead," Regan said.

"Then I'll take you to your guardian."

"No!" Regan blurted. How could she return to her uncle like this, with this great American confessing what they'd done together? "If you would get me something to wear, I will leave you. You needn't bother about taking me anywhere."

Travis seemed to consider this for a moment. "Why were you running around the docks in the middle of the night? Unless I miss my guess, a child like you"—he smiled at her look—"pardon me, a young lady like you has probably never even seen the docks before."

Regan tilted her chin upward. "What I have or have not seen is no concern of yours. All I ask of you is a dress, something simple if you can afford it, and I will leave immediately."

Again Travis smiled. "I can probably manage a dress. But I'll not release you into that pack of animals out there. You know what happened to you last night."

She narrowed her eyes at him. "And what worse could happen to me than what you did last night?" She buried her face in her hands. "Who would want me now? You've ruined me."

Sitting beside her, Travis pulled her hands away. "Any man would want you, sweetheart. You're the most delightful bit—." He cut himself off.

Regan wasn't sure she knew what he meant, but she had an idea. "Why, you vulgar Colonial! You are as savage as I've heard. You pull ladies off the street and drag them to your room where you do"—she sputtered—"horrible things to them."

"Now wait just a minute! If I remember correctly, you came flying at me from out of the dark last night, and when I tried to help you up, you practically leaped into my arms. That's not the action of anyone I'd consider a lady. And as for last night, you didn't think what I did was so horrible when you were pulling my hair and running your feet up and down my legs."

Dropping her jaw in sheer horror at his words, Regan could only blink at him.

"Look, I'm sorry. I didn't mean to say anything to shock you, but I want you to get your facts straight. Had I known you were a virgin and not a street girl, I wouldn't have touched you. But we can't change the facts. I did touch you, and now you're my responsibility."

"I . . . most certainly am not your responsibility. I assure you I can take care of myself."

"Like you did last night?" he asked, lifting one eyebrow. "It's a good thing you ran into me, or there's no telling what could have happened to you."

Moments passed before Regan could speak. "Is there no end to your arrogance or your insufferability? There was nothing good in meeting you, and I now know I was better off on the streets than locked away with a mad, despicable ravisher of women such as you are, sir!"

The corners of Travis's eyes crinkled as he broke into a dazzling smile. Running his hand through his dark hair, he chuckled, "My, my. I believe I've been cursed by an English lady." As his eyes roamed over her bare shoulders, he smiled at her. "You know, I rather think I like you."

"But *I* do not care for *you*," Regan said, exasperated at his ignorance and lack of understanding.

"Let me introduce myself. I am Travis Stanford from Virginia, and I am pleased to make your acquaintance." He held out his hand to her.

Crossing her arms over her chest, Regan looked away. Perhaps if she ignored him and was rude to him, he would allow her to go.

"All right," Travis said, rising. "Have it your way, but we will get something straight between us. I am not going to release you onto the Liverpool docks by yourself. Either you tell me where you live and who takes care of you, or you remain locked in this room."

"You can't do that! You have no right!"

He towered over her, his face serious. "Last night I earned the right. We Americans take our responsibilities seriously, and last night you became my charge—at least until I find out who your true guardian is."

As he finished dressing, he watched her in the mirror, trying to puzzle out her reasons for not telling him who she was. When he had his coat on, he leaned over her. "I'm trying to do what's right for you," he said softly.

"And who gave you the right to decide what was good or bad for people you don't even know?"

Chuckling deep in his throat, Travis replied, "You're beginning to sound like my little brother. How about a kiss before I go? If I find your guardian, it may be our last moment alone together."

"I hope I never see you again!" she spat. "I hope you fall into the sea and no one ever sees you again. I hope—."

He cut her off as he lifted her out of the bed, one arm behind her back, and the other pushing the sheet from between them. As his hand caressed the soft, peachy flesh of her hip and thigh, his mouth touched hers. Gently, ever so gently, he kissed her, careful not to frighten her or to be too harsh with her.

For a moment Regan pushed at him with her hands, but his big hands on her body, and the sheer power of him as he pulled her to him were overwhelmingly exciting. It surprised her that such an arrogant bully of a man could be so gentle.

Putting her arms around his neck, she turned her head to one side as her hands lost themselves in his hair.

Travis was the first to pull away. "I'm beginning to hope I don't find your guardian. You make an awful nice armful."

As her arm went back to strike him, he laughed and held it, kissing her knuckles one by one. "It was only a wish. Now, you stay here and be a good girl, and I'll bring you a pretty dress when I get back."

She heard him laugh when the pillow she threw hit the door as he closed it behind him. The key turning in the lock sounded as if chains had been clamped to her ankles.

The awesome silence was nearly deafening as Regan sat, stunned, and gazed sightlessly at the big room. For a while she couldn't believe that she wasn't at home in her own blue bedroom, that Matta wasn't going to bring her chocolate at any moment. Instead, in the last few hours her world had crumbled about her ears. She'd heard the man she loved say that he didn't want to marry her and her only relative admit that he cared nothing for her. And now, worst of all, her virtue was gone and she was held prisoner by some savage American. Prisoner, she thought. She hadn't known it, but she'd been a prisoner all her life, held in a gilded cage of a pretty garden and a rundown house.

As these thoughts went through her mind, she began to look about the room. There was a large window along one wall, and it occurred to her that perhaps she could do something about her imprisonment this time. If she could escape, then surely she could find help, perhaps someone to take her in or to employ her. At that thought, she stopped. What could she do? How in the world could she earn her keep for five years until she came into her inheritance? The only thing she was really good at was growing flowers. Perhaps. . . .

No, Regan, she cautioned herself. Now is not the time to run off on a tangent. First she must escape and show this boorish Colonial that he could not kidnap an Englishwoman and have her remain docilely in custody.

Once out of bed, she realized that her first problem was clothes. A trunk stood in one corner of the room, but a quick examination showed it to be locked.

At a knock on the door, she jumped and had only time to slip into Travis's shirt before a rosy-cheeked, plump girl entered bearing a heavy tray of food.

"Mr. Travis said I was to bring you food and a bath if you want it," the girl said nervously, her eyes searching the room, her back firmly against the closed door.

"Can you get me some clothes?" Regan asked. "Please. I could return them later, but I have to have more than that man's shirt."

"I'm sorry, miss, but Mr. Travis said I was not to give you clothes or anything else besides food and hot water and that I was to tell you he'd hired a man to stand below the window all day, in case you tried to escape that way."

Running to the window, Regan saw that what the girl had said was true. "You have to help me," she pleaded. "This man is keeping me prisoner here. Please, please, help me escape."

The girl hastily set the tray down, her eyes wide with fear. "Mr. Travis threatened me life if I let you go. I'm sorry, miss, but I've got meself to think of." Without another word, the girl was gone from the room, and the heavy lock was securely refastened.

Regan wasn't sure at first of the feeling that ran through her.

All her life had been pleasant, uneventful, almost bland, with few problems to cope with and fewer people to know, but now everything was piling on top of her, weighing her down. She hadn't wanted to leave her uncle's house, nor did she want to remain the prisoner of some horrible man.

Picking the tray up with both hands, she threw it against the wall and then stood watching as eggs and jam went sliding down the smooth plaster surface. Her outburst did not help her mood but instead made it worse. Flinging herself onto the bed, she screamed into a pillow, kicked her feet, and slammed her fists into the feather mattress.

In spite of her anger and her complete frustration at her helplessness, her exhaustion was stronger. As her muscles began to relax, she fell into a heavy, lifeless sleep. She didn't even wake up when the maid cleaned the food off the wall, nor did she awaken when Travis entered the room, his arms full of bright boxes, and leaned over her, smiling at her sweet, innocent face.

Chapter 3

"YOU'RE A sweet tidbit to come back to," Travis whispered, nibbling at her earlobe. As she began to awaken, he stepped away, wanting to watch her as she stretched, her curvy little body molding the shirt she wore into enticing hills and valleys. As she stretched, her eyes still closed, her breasts strained against the buttons, pulling the fabric apart and letting him glimpse an exquisite diamond of flesh. A little smile touched her lips before she opened her eyes and saw him.

"You!" she gasped. With an agile leap, she flew out of the bed and dove for him, fists clenched, shirttail riding up.

Travis caught both her fists in one of his. "Now that's what I call a greeting," he practically purred, pulling her into his arms. "It's not easy for me to remember I'm supposed to treat you like a lady when you fling yourself into my arms like that."

"I did not fling myself at you," she said, gritting her teeth. "Why do you always twist everything so? You couldn't possibly believe I want anything from you except to be released. You have no right—."

A quick kiss cut her off. "You know I'll release you just as soon as you tell me where to take you. Surely a young lady like you has relatives. Give me a name, and I'll take you there."

"And have you brag about what you've done to me? No, I

couldn't possibly agree to such a thing. Release me, and I'll find my own way home."

"You are not a good liar," he smiled. "Those eyes of yours are as clear as a doll's. Every thought you have is written across them. I've told you several times the conditions under which I'll release you, and that's the end of it. I'm not going to give in, so you might as well resign yourself to the fact that you will have to."

Jerking away from him, she set her jaw. "I can be as stubborn as you." She smiled wickedly. "And besides, I know you're leaving for America soon. You'll *have* to release me then."

Travis seemed to consider this idea for a moment. "I'll have to do something with you then, won't I?" he replied, rubbing his chin. "I'd certainly hate to sail for America and leave those legs of yours without a proper protector."

Gasping, Regan grabbed an edge of the bed sheet and tried to pull it off, but a far corner was caught. As Travis moved toward her and leaned across the bed to release the corner, he slipped a hand up under her shirt and gave her buttocks a firm caress.

Regan squealed once before she stood up and snatched the sheet from him, wrapping it tightly around her lower body. "How can you treat me this way? What have I ever done to you to deserve this? I've never hurt anyone in my life."

Her words were so heartfelt that Travis lowered his eyes. "I've never done anything like this before. Maybe I should just re-lease you, but somehow I can't. It would be like throwing a wild-flower into a snowstorm or, considering the life on these docks, more like a fireplace." When he looked back at her, his eyes were soft and tender. "I don't have much of a choice about what I do. I can't let you go, yet I don't want to keep you prisoner. Lord! I don't even own slaves, much less lock up innocent little girls."

When he'd finished his speech, he sank heavily into a chair in a corner of the room, and Regan had the oddest feeling that she wanted to comfort him. During the awkward silence she noticed the boxes on top of the big trunk. "Did you bring me a dress?" she asked quietly.

"Did I bring you a dress," he grinned, seemingly over his momentary distress. Pulling string from one box, he began to unfold a piece of velvet of a color that Regan had never seen before: almost brown, almost red, but with an overall gold sheen to the fabric. As he handed it to her, draping it across her arms, he said, "It's the color of your hair, not red, not brown, not blonde, but all of them."

She looked up at him in surprise. "How . . . how romantic. I didn't know you'd—."

Laughing, he took the dress from her. "You don't know anything about me and I know even less about you. You haven't even told me your name."

Hesitating, she ran her hands across the velvet in his arms. All her clothes had always been of the cheapest cloth available. The velvet was the most beautiful fabric she'd ever seen, yet as badly as she wanted to feel it next to her skin, she was cautious. "I'm Regan," she answered quietly.

"No last name? Just Regan?"

"That's all the name I'll tell you and if you think you can bribe me with a pretty new dress, you're wrong," she said haughtily.

"I don't use bribes," he said flatly. "I've told you the conditions for your release, and the dress has nothing to do with them." Tossing the velvet garment onto the bed, he went to the other packages, tearing them open one by one and dumping them on the bed. There was a dress of pale blue silk crepe trimmed with peacock blue ribbons and a nightgown of cotton lawn embroidered with hundreds of tiny pink rosebuds. Two pairs of thin leather slippers, dyed to match the velvet and the blue, tumbled from the last package.

"They are beautiful, absolutely beautiful," Regan gasped, holding the silk to her cheek.

Watching her, Travis was enchanted. She was such a mixture

of child and woman—raging one moment, looking like an angry kitten, then changing to a girl of innocence and great charm. As he watched her smile lighting her turquoise eyes, he felt as if he'd been bewitched by her, as if a spell had been put on him so that he could think of nothing but her. He'd spent hours today in dress shops, feeling damnedly out of place but wanting to make her happy.

He sat down by her on the bed. "You like them? I didn't know what kind of dresses or colors you liked, but the woman said these were the latest fashion."

As she turned her smile toward him, he felt a flash of possessiveness tear through him such as he'd felt only for his land in Virginia. Before he could think of what he was doing, he leaned across the clothes and dragged her to him. Giving her no time to protest, he kissed her hungrily, trying to make up for every moment he'd thought of her during the day.

"My clothes," Regan gasped. "You'll crush them."

With one movement, Travis swept all the clothes up and tossed them toward the chair. "All day I've thought about you," he whispered. "What have you done to me?"

She tried to sound uncaring, in spite of the fact that Travis's nearness caused her heart to race. "Nothing I *want* to do to you. Please release me."

"Do you really want me to?" he asked throatily, running his lips along her throat.

Why, she thought, does this disgusting, vile man do these horrible things to me? But even as she was thinking this, she didn't push him away—so badly did she want to be held in his arms, so much did she like the way he kissed her, the way his breath smelled, and how his hair caressed her face. The bigness of him made her feel small and safe, taken care of, protected.

Her thoughts were interrupted as Travis's lips found her bare breasts. No more thoughts were possible as she groaned and ran her hands across his shoulders.

Slowly, Travis left her, and when she opened her eyes in bewilderment she saw him standing over her, removing his jacket. Unable to take her eyes off him, she watched as he leisurely removed his clothes.

The light of the setting sun came through the window and filled the room with a red-gold glow, transforming the ordinary room into a place of magic and jewels. Speechless, Regan could not take her eyes off the sight of Travis's body as bit by large bit was exposed. She'd never seen a naked man before, and her curiosity was acute.

Nothing could have prepared her for the sight of a nude Travis. His body was heavily muscled from years of work his arms sculpted, his chest like an ancient Roman breastplate that she'd seen once in a book. Yet his waist was slim the stomach etched with rivulets of muscle. When his pants were removed, massive thighs were revealed, each muscle outstanding, separate.

"Oh my," she gasped, her voice betraying her awe. Only when her eyes reached his manhood did she blink.

Travis laughed at her and stretched out beside her. "For all your protesting, I wager you'll be a lusty wench when you've been taught properly."

"No, don't," she said in one last feeble attempt to push him away, but Travis paid no attention to her. Deftly, he removed the last bit of her clothes and began to stroke her stomach, kneading it lightly, his fingertips playing with the sensitive area, his palm exciting her skin. All the while he kissed her, using his teeth on the curve of her ear, his tongue just grazing the warm, pulsing spot beneath her earlobe.

She ran her hands over his shoulders and down his arms, her fingers tracing each long indentation where one muscle joined another. His hard body was so different from her soft one, so strong to her weakness. Moving under him, she slipped her arms down to caress his ribs, to feel the muscles in his back as they rippled under his hot, dark skin, and then to touch the sides of his tight buttocks. Wonder was mixed with the pleasure she found in touching him, and with each fondle her heart seemed to beat harder, her breath coming deeper and faster.

"Regan, sweet Regan," Travis said in a voice she felt as much as heard in the place where their chests joined.

When he seemed to pull away from her, her fingers dug into his arms painfully. "Yes, my eager kitten, yes."

Travis entered her slowly, easily, and although she would have thought it impossible, her heart rate increased. There was no pain, just something she wanted very, very much. As she arched against him clumsily, erratically, Travis held himself away from her. "Slow, kitten, slow," he murmured, his hand on her hip, his thumb making love to her navel.

Although she had no idea what he meant, she had no choice but to obey him. As new as she was to lovemaking, she could still feel that he was holding back, taking the time to be a teacher instead of a blind participant. By slow, careful tutoring, he showed her how to enjoy herself, how to lead as well as to follow.

Regan thought her body would burst, that it was getting larger and larger, and that when it did explode she would perhaps die. Suddenly Travis increased his pace, and his excitement flowed through to her. She arched against him, and it was as if fireworks exploded inside her—brilliant, hot, dazzling fireworks.

Travis collapsed on top of her, his body limp and sweaty, and Regan felt drained and weak, but oh so very good, as if a great burden had been taken from her.

She wasn't sure, but she believed she dozed for a while, and when she awoke, the intimate time with this man who was still virtually a stranger seemed like one of her dreams. As she lay there, one of Travis's arms sprawled across her; she imagined what it would be like to see Farrell again. Of course, he'd have heard about her time with this American, and he would be ashamed of her, perhaps wouldn't even speak to her. She imagined trying to explain, saying she'd resisted, but he'd know the truth. The American said that all her thoughts showed in her eyes. Would this new experience of hers show also? Would everyone in the world see her as a woman of no virtue?

Beside her, Travis stirred, lifted himself up on one elbow, and smiled down at her. "I was right," he murmured. "With a little training. . . ."

Regan pushed his hand away from a curl of her hair. "Don't touch me!" she hissed. "You have forced me to do too many things against my will."

Travis gave an exasperated little laugh. "Are we back to that again? I thought perhaps you'd see the truth this time."

"The truth! I see the truth! I know you are holding me against my will, that you are a criminal of the lowest order."

Sighing, Travis rolled from the bed and began to dress. "I've told you why I'm holding you." He turned back to her quickly. "Do you have any idea what those men on the docks want from you? They want a violent version of what we just did."

"And what's the difference between them and you?"

"Even with your innocence you should realize that I make love to you, but they'd just throw your skirts over your head and do whatever they wanted—one after another."

"I have no skirts!" Regan gasped. "All I have is one very torn nightgown."

All Travis could do was throw up his hands in despair. "You are only going to see what you want to see, aren't you? Therefore I feel it is my duty to protect you from yourself and your rosy dreams, as well as from men who'd do you harm."

"You have no right! Please, please let me out of here."

Acting as if she hadn't spoken, Travis went to the door and bellowed down the stairs for supper to be brought up. "You'll feel better once you've eaten," he said, closing the door again.

"I am not hungry," she said, her nose in the air.

Travis clasped her chin in his hand and twisted her head to look at him. "You are going to eat if I have to force it down your throat." His eyes were hard, unlike the softness she'd always seen.

All she could do was nod in answer.

"Now," he said, cheerful once again. "Why don't you put on one of the dresses I brought you? That will make you feel better."

"You'll have to leave the room," she said weakly, still somewhat frightened by his threat. She hadn't felt the least fear of him until now.

Lifting one eyebrow at her request, he picked her up out of the bed, and stood her naked on the floor. "You don't have anything I haven't seen before, and if you don't want the landlord to see you like that you'd better get dressed."

As she looked at the clothes Travis tossed to her, she realized there was no underwear. But rather than ask for it, she slipped the velvet gown over her head and had just finished the last button when the landlord knocked. The dress was high-waisted, the deeply cut bodice front filled with sheer silk gauze. Catching a glimpse of herself in the mirror opposite the bed, she was pleased that it wasn't a child's dress. Her hair hanging down her back in a mass of unruly curls, her flushed cheeks, her bright eyes, all went together to present a picture of a woman who had just been made love to—and had enjoyed it.

The landlord's appreciative looks made Travis almost push him out the door.

"Why did you do that?" Regan asked in awe, wondering if Travis was jealous.

"I don't want him to get the wrong idea," Travis answered, lifting the cover off a piece of roast beef. "I have to leave you alone again tomorrow, and if he thought I wouldn't mind, he just might send someone else up here. The last thing I want is a fight or any other trouble so close to sailing time. Nothing is going to stop me from going home. I've been in this cursed country too long."

Deflated, Regan took the seat he offered her. After one whiff of the food, she realized how long it had been since she'd eaten. Her last meal—her eyes widened when she remembered—had been with Farrell and her uncle.

"What's wrong?" he asked, filling a plate for her.

"Nothing. I just—." She put her chin up. "I don't like being held prisoner, that's all."

"You don't have to tell me if you don't want to. Eat your supper before it gets cold."

All through the meal, Travis tried to get her to talk, but she wouldn't since she was afraid she would inadvertently give him some clues about where she lived. There was no possibility now that she could go back to the life she once knew; after what had happened this evening, she probably no longer qualified as a lady.

Putting his hand over hers, Travis leaned close to her. "It's a shame Englishwomen are taught that they shouldn't like lovemaking," he said sympathetically, correctly reading her thoughts. "In America the women are earthier; they like their men and aren't afraid to show it."

She gave him her sweetest, most insincere smile. "Then why don't you go back to America and the women there?"

Travis's laugh made the dishes rattle, and he planted a hearty kiss on her cheek. "Now, little one, I have some paperwork to do, so you can snuggle up in bed and wait for me or—."

"Or leave perhaps."

"You are persistent, if nothing else."

And you are stubborn, she thought, watching him stack the dishes on the tray and put it outside the door. Later, when she was in her nightgown and in the big bed, she watched the back of him, saw how he ran his hands through his hair as his quill pen flew across the papers before him. She was curious about what he was doing but refused to ask, refused to make their relationship more personal than it was.

As she stretched out in the bed, she began a dream in which Farrell came to rescue her, beating the American in a sword fight.

Her Uncle Jonathan would be there begging her forgiveness, saying he was quite lonely without her. The thought of Travis cringing in fear made her smile. In her vision she imagined pulling away from Farrell's arms and going to Travis, giving him her hand and forgiving him, telling him to go back to America and forget her—if he could.

When Travis slipped into bed beside her, she pretended to be asleep, but he just pulled her to him, nuzzled her ear, put his hand on her stomach, and eased into sleep. It was odd, but she felt that now she too could go to sleep.

In the morning, she was alone in the big room, but no sooner had she awakened than the maid let herself in. "Oh, beg pardon, miss. I thought you were still asleep. Mr. Travis said I was to bring you a bath if you'd like one."

Regan wouldn't humiliate herself by a repeat performance of begging the maid to release her. She told the girl to bring the tub and hot water, and in spite of herself she enjoyed the bath. It was almost a comfort to be able to do something for herself. Always before, a maid had dressed her, and washed her hair, and her uncle had chosen cheap, childish clothes for her. Clean once again, she toweled her hair, ate a big breakfast, and put on the blue silk dress. A delicate scarf embroidered with flowers in several shades of blue filled the deep neckline.

The day was long, and since she had nothing to do, she was bored. It was cool in the room, yet there was no fireplace, so she walked about, rubbing her arms. The early spring sun was weak through the window, but it was still the warmest place in the room. She pulled up a chair, gazed absently out the window, and made up her dreams, ranging from a garden plan to how she would never forgive Travis and would let Farrell run him through.

When the sun was setting and she heard what could only be Travis's voice—deep, golden-toned, filled with humor—she found her heart pounding. Of course it was only because of the sheer loneliness of the long day, but still she had to force herself not to smile when he entered.

His big brown eyes raked her as he smiled in greeting. "The dress looks good on you," he said, removing his hat and then his jacket. Practically collapsing in a chair, he gave a big sigh. "Working the fields all day would have been less work," he said. "Your countrymen are a bunch of close-minded snobs. I could hardly get anyone to listen to my questions, much less answer them."

Running her finger along the edge of the table in a nonchalant way, Regan tried to hide her curiosity. "Perhaps they didn't like your questions."

Travis wasn't fooled for a moment. "All I wanted to know was if someone had lost a pretty but unreasonable young female."

Opening her mouth to retort, she closed it, realizing he was baiting her. "And had they?"

Frowning before he answered, Travis seemed to be puzzled by what he'd discovered. "Not only couldn't I find out about a missing girl of your description, but I couldn't find anyone who'd even met a girl looking like you."

There was no reply Regan could make. There had never been visitors at Weston Manor. All she knew of life was what she'd learned from the stories of her maids and governesses, with their talk of love and gallant gentlemen, of the world outside the grounds of the house. Of course there was no one who knew of her.

Watching her, Travis tried to read what was in her face. All day the question had been haunting him: What was he to do with her when he sailed for America? He didn't tell her, but he'd hired three other men to help make inquiries about her. The night he'd found her she couldn't have run from very far, so she lived in either Liverpool or the surrounding area—or she'd been traveling through. After checking every lodging house in the area, he knew she must live there, but he could find no trace of her. She seemed to have materialized on that dark night near the docks.

"You're a runaway," he said quietly, watching when her expression confirmed his thoughts. "Only I can't figure out who you're running from and why no one is moving heaven and earth to find you."

Turning away, Regan tried not to think that it was because the people she thought loved her didn't care where she was.

"The only thing I can figure," he continued slowly, "is that you did something to make your people pretty damned angry at you. I know for a fact you weren't caught in bed with the gardener's boy, so maybe you refused to do something they wanted you to do. Did you refuse to marry some rich old duffer?"

"Not even close," she said smugly.

Travis only laughed because her eyes told him he wasn't too far wrong. But his laughter covered his true feelings. It made him very angry to think that anyone could just toss out a pure young girl into the streets, wearing only her nightgown. Perhaps in the heat of passion it could have happened, but how could they have let days go by and not searched for her?

"I was thinking that, since there doesn't seem to be any reason for you to stay in England, maybe you should go with me to America."

Chapter 4

"WHAT!" REGAN gasped, almost staggered by his words. "America is full of boorish, illiterate people who live in log cabins. What is there besides wild Indians and terrible animals, not to mention great, savage people? No, I will not under any circumstances go to that backward place."

The humor quickly left Travis's eyes as he rose to come toward her. "You damned Englishwoman! I get this all day from your 'gentlemanly' countrymen. I get snubbed because they don't like the way I talk or dress, or they had a relative killed in a war that happened when I was a boy. I'm getting damned tired of being looked at like something unclean, and I'll sure as hell not take it from you."

Backing away from him, Regan lifted her hand to her throat as if to protect herself.

"I've tiptoed around you enough, and from now on you're going to do what I say. If I left a child like you alone here, when it's quite clear you haven't a friend in the world, I'd never sleep again. I won't bore you with what America is when you have such clear ideas of your own, but at least in my country we don't toss young girls out just because they're disobedient. When we get to Virginia you'll have choices of what you can do—something more suitable for an English 'lady' "—he sneered the word—"than walking the streets as would be your only alternative if I left you here."

Narrowing his eyes, he glared down at her, pressed against the wall. "Is that clear?" He didn't give her a chance to answer before he slammed from the room, locking the door after him.

"Yes, Travis," she whispered to the still echoing emptiness.

She was glad when he was gone, since it was quite impossible to think when Travis was around. At least, perhaps, if she made him angry enough, he wouldn't force her to do those horrible things in bed, and he just might possibly release her if she provoked him. Smiling, she sat down and began to imagine her escape, how good it would be to get away from this boorish American. Imagine! she thought. The very idea of her going to America!

Snuggling in the chair, a quilt around her, she fantasized about what a dreadful place America must be, remembered every tale that had been told to her by a maid whose brother had traveled there and returned with horrible, treacherous stories, all of which the maid had told Regan in gory detail. As the candle sputtered and the room grew dark, she began to glance at the door, wondering when Travis was going to return. Sometime deep in the night, she left the chair and climbed into the big, cold bed, placing the pillows so that she could snuggle against them. They weren't as good as a large, warm body, but at least they helped.

In the morning, her head ached, and she was in a foul mood. That the American would leave her alone all night, unprotected, and at the mercy of anyone who could get the key to her room made her furious. One moment he made speeches about how much he was going to care for her, and the next he abandoned her to the mercies of any outside element.

Her sulks were interrupted when the door was given a quick tap and then unlocked. Folding her arms across her chest, she tilted her chin up, preparing to let Travis know she was unaffected by his abandonment of her. But instead of Travis's deep voice came the light laughter of women. Turning, Regan gasped in astonishment at the sight of three women who entered her room carrying great books and several baskets.

"You are Mademoiselle Regan?" asked a pretty little dark woman. "I am Madame Rosa, and these are my assistants. We have come to begin your wardrobe for your journey to America."

It took Regan several minutes to piece the story together, but it seemed Travis had engaged Madame Rosa, a French emigree and former dressmaker to one of Queen Marie Antoinette's ladies, to create an entire wardrobe for his captive. Too angry at his presumption to speak at first, Regan just sat in the bed and gave a vacant stare to the women. But as she saw the puzzled looks on their faces she knew she could not let them be on the receiving end of her anger. Her quarrel was with Travis Stanford and not these women who were merely doing their jobs.

"Perhaps I will look at your wares," she said tiredly, thinking of all the other times she'd been allowed to choose clothes. Her uncle had allowed her to wear pink or blue or white, and the only trim was what she and her maids embroidered.

Smiling delightedly, the designer and her assistants began to spread fabric samples out on the bed. There seemed to be an endless array of colors and textures, most of which Regan had never seen before. There were a dozen colors of velvet, more of satin, linen, at least six types of silk, and dozens of colors in each type. Wools took up one corner of the bed, and Regan marveled at the variety: cashmere, tartans, a long-haired softness she was told was mohair. And the muslins! There seemed to be hundreds of colors, stripes, painted, printed, embroidered, pleated.

Eyes wide in wonder, Regan looked up from the beauty of the fabrics to Madame Rosa.

"Of course, there are the trims," the woman said, signaling for those samples to be brought.

Feathers joined the fabrics, then satin and velvet ribbons,

topped by hand-drawn laces mixed with strings of tiny seed pearls, silver cord, jet beads, silk flowers, gold net, and intricately knotted frog fastenings.

Bewildered, Regan didn't move but just looked at the glorious colors.

"Perhaps it is too early for Mademoiselle," Madame Rosa said gently. "Monsieur Travis said we were to get everything done in one day so the clothes can be cut before you are to sail. He has hired a woman to sail with you to do the sewing so everything will be ready when you reach America."

As her head began to clear, Regan wondered if Travis knew what he was getting himself into; she doubted if a Colonial had any idea of the cost of women's clothes. Uncle Jonathan had certainly made Regan aware of the exorbitant fees dressmakers charged. "Did Travis ask after the cost of the clothes?"

"No, miss," the dressmaker said, surprised. "He came to my house late last night, saying he'd heard I was the best in Liverpool and he wanted a complete wardrobe for a young lady. There was no mention of price, but then I got the impression Monsieur Travis didn't need to ask."

Opening her mouth and then closing it, Regan smiled. So! The big, brawling Colonial thought he was still in the forests of America! It might be fun to play with fabrics and trims for the day, to pretend to order an extensive wardrobe, and then watch Travis's face when he received a bill higher than any sum he'd ever imagined. Of course, she'd have the bill presented before the women began to cut the clothes; she wouldn't want them to lose out when Travis couldn't pay.

"Where shall we start?" Regan asked sweetly, her eyes dancing as she thought of defeating the braggart.

"Perhaps with day dresses," Madame Rosa suggested, lifting the samples of muslin.

Hours later, Regan was quite wistful about the whole plan. Too bad she wasn't going to get the clothes, because she'd planned a wardrobe a princess would love. There were muslin dresses of every color and trim, ballgowns of satin and velvet, walking dresses, a riding habit which made Regan laugh since she had no idea how to ride a horse, capes, cloaks, redingotes, spencers, as well as many nightgowns, camisoles, and lace-edged petticoats. When she finished, there wasn't a single fabric she hadn't used and very few colors.

The noon meal was brought to them, and Regan was glad the session was over because she was getting tired.

"But we have only started," Madame Rosa said. "The furrier is coming this afternoon with the milliner, the cobbler, and the glovemaker. And Mademoiselle must be measured for everything."

"Of course," Regan whispered. "How could I have forgotten?"

As the afternoon wore on, she ceased to be astonished at anything. The furrier brought pelts of sable, ermine, chinchilla, beaver, lynx, wolf, and angora goat, and she chose linings, collars, and cuffs for the coats she'd already selected. The cobbler took samples of cloth, planning to dye a pair of soft, heelless slippers to match every outfit, and he described the walking boots he would make. The milliner and Madame Rosa coordinated hats and clothes with the glovemaker.

At dark, everyone's energy began to fade, especially Regan's. She felt bad at the thought that the day's work would come to nothing because no American could possibly pay for all the clothes she'd ordered. She told Madame Rosa she was to submit everyone's bills to Travis before a pair of scissors was raised, that she should see the money in her hands before she started filling the order. The dressmaker smiled politely and said she'd have it ready first thing in the morning.

When she was finally alone, Regan slumped into a chair, weary from the long day and the constant feeling of guilt. All day she'd known she was playing a game, but the tradespeople were going to be very angry when they learned that their day's work would go unpaid.

By the time she heard Travis's heavy footsteps on the stairs, she was feeling quite low—and it was all his fault. The moment he opened the door, she threw her shoe at him, hitting him on the shoulder.

"What's this?" he grinned. "I thought tonight you'd at least be a little glad to see me. You're always complaining because you have no clothes."

"I did not ask you to do anything about my clothes! You have no rights over me whatsoever and especially not to take me to your barbaric country. I will not go, do you hear me? I am English, and I will stay in England."

"Where all your family and friends are?" he asked sarcastically. "I've just spent another day trying to find where you've spent your life, and I can find nothing. Damn them!" he said, running his hands through his hair. "What kind of people could discard a child like you?"

Perhaps it was the tiredness from not sleeping well and the exhausting day, but her eyes filled with great, crystal tears. She'd been so angry for the last few days that she'd had no time to think about her feelings at hearing Farrell's disgust at the idea of marrying her and her uncle's declaration that he detested her. For days she'd lived in a dreamworld of hoping they would rescue her, but no doubt Travis had gone to their door. Had Farrell and her uncle told him they didn't know her?

Before she could speak, Travis pulled her into his arms. Pushing him away, she tried to protest. "Leave me alone," she whispered feebly, but even as she attempted to pull away from him, he held her tightly until she buried her face in his chest, and the sobs began tearing through her body.

Travis wasted no time before he lifted her into his arms and then sat in a chair with her, cradling her like a child. "Go ahead and cry, kitten," he said softly. "I guess if anyone deserves to, it's you."

His holding of her, this stranger who made love to her and saw that she was cared for, when the people who should care for her denied her existence, made her cry harder. Worse than anything was the end of her dreams of being rescued by Farrell, of once again seeing the man she loved. Now she'd never even have a chance to prove to him that she could be a good wife; now she was going to be dragged off to America, and they'd never even know she'd gone.

As her sobs finally began to quiet, Travis stroked her damp hair. "Want to tell me what you're so unhappy about?"

She couldn't possibly tell him about Farrell. "Because I'm a prisoner!" she said as firmly as possible, pulling away from his shoulder.

Travis continued stroking her hair, and when he spoke his voice was full of patience and understanding. "I think you were a prisoner before I ever met you. If you hadn't been, you wouldn't have been discarded like so much rubbish."

"Rubbish!" she gasped. "How dare you call me that!"

Bewildered, Travis smiled at her. "I didn't say you were rubbish, only that someone had treated you as such. What I can't understand is why you seem to want to return to someone who treats you like that."

"I ... I ... no one. . . ." she sputtered, tears beginning again. He had such a crude way of stating everything.

"It's not so bad being an orphan," he continued. "I've been one a long time. Maybe we belong together."

Regan looked up at him, thinking that she couldn't imagine this man belonging to anyone. No doubt, in spite of what he had said, he often kidnapped young girls and held them prisoner.

"I don't think I like what you're thinking," he warned. "If you're getting any ideas, let me warn you that I take care of what belongs to me."

"Belongs to you!" she exclaimed. "I hardly know you!"

He smiled just before he brought his lips down on hers and kissed her with such tenderness, such longing, that Regan found her arms going about his neck. "You know me well enough," he said huskily. "And get it through your head that you are mine."

"I'm not yours! I'm. . . ." she trailed off as he began to kiss her neck with little nibbling bites, and Regan sighed as she bent her head to one side.

"You are a temptress," he laughed, "and you're playing havoc with my work schedule." Firmly, he pushed her out of his lap. "As much as I'd like to stay with you, I have business to attend to, and I'm afraid it will take me most of the night. Did you know we sail day after tomorrow?"

Head lowered, she didn't answer him. She felt like such a fool because she'd reacted to him so quickly and so totally. Day after tomorrow! she thought. If she was ever to escape his hold over her, she must do it very soon.

"No goodbye kiss?" Travis joked, standing by the door. "Nothing to keep me warm out there all alone?"

Grabbing her other shoe, she threw it at him, but this time he ducked before it hit him. He was laughing as he locked the door behind him and went down the stairs.

At least tonight she was too tired to stay awake, but the bed did seem to get larger each night.

She woke to the quiet thunder of what could only be Travis attempting to tiptoe about the room. Keeping her eyes closed, she pretended to be asleep, even when he leaned over her and kissed her cheek. When he seemed to have left the room, she drowsily listened for the now familiar turn of the lock, and when it didn't come she sat bolt upright in bed. After rubbing her eyes twice, she was sure that what she saw was real—the door was wide open.

Not another second was lost as she jumped out of bed, slid the velvet dress over her head, and grabbed her shoes. Ever so quietly, she hugged the door with her back as she left the room and went onto the stair landing. Never having seen the inn except for the inside of one room, she was startled to see how isolated the room was—alone at the head of narrow, steep stairs, and, from the smells, at the bottom seemed to be the kitchen. Craning her neck until it threatened to break, she saw what was unmistakably Travis's leg and high boot near the foot of the stairs. But even as she began to lose hope, a clatter of horses and carriages sounded outside, and a man's voice cried for help. With great happiness, she saw Travis run for the door.

Within an instant she was down the stairs, through the nearly empty kitchen, where the few employees were intent on the activity outside, and finally out into the bright sunlight of the street.

There was no time to spend on the fact that her feet were bare, because she knew Travis would discover her escape very soon. For now she had to put time and distance between them if she was ever to manage her escape.

In spite of her good intentions, her feet began to hurt too badly to ignore them much longer, and people were beginning to notice her. Slowing down for a moment, she saw a dark alleyway between two buildings, and she made her way there, crouching down between several horrible-smelling wooden fish crates. I must think! she commanded herself, because she knew that without a plan she could never gain her freedom.

Sitting on one of the crates, she slipped on her shoes, tying the laces about her ankles. As she did so, she calmed her racing heart and began to consider her alternatives. She needed somewhere to go, a place to hide until she could get a job, and especially a place to hide until that insane American left the country.

Lost in thought, she wasn't aware of the shouts in the street until she was practically looking at Travis, his legs spread wide, hands on hips, his profile to her. It was minutes before she realized that he didn't see her, that he was only shouting orders to the people in the streets. The idea that he'd give orders to strangers renewed her determination to escape this man. Making herself as small as possible, she crouched down among the boxes, praying he wouldn't see her.

Even when he turned and ran down the street, she didn't relax or move, because she felt he wasn't one to give up. No, Travis Stanford was too sure he was right to ever give a thought to anyone else's opinions. If he'd hold someone prisoner, he'd certainly not let that prisoner escape without a fight.

Remaining in her stiff, uncomfortable position, she tried to come up with a plan. First she'd have to get away from the docks, and the way to do that was always to keep the sea at her back. Smiling, she thought that shouldn't be difficult to do and was sure she had half her problem solved. The other problem was where to go when she was away from the docks. If she could find her way back to Weston Manor, maybe Matta, her old maid, would know of some place Regan could go.

Hours and hours seemed to pass, yet the sun was still bright, the noise of the docks still loud. Using all her powers of concentration, she tried to ignore the cramps in her legs, and the ache in her back. Twice she saw Travis go by, and the second time she was close to calling out to him. Perhaps it was the pain in her aching body, but she seemed to remember all too clearly the last time she'd been alone on the docks. Of course, then she'd been wearing only her nightgown, and how could she expect to be treated as a lady when she was dressed as a woman of low morals? Now, wearing the elegant velvet dress, everyone would recognize her as a lady, and they wouldn't dare touch her.

Smiling, her confidence somewhat restored, she tried to twist her hair into some semblance of order. Yesterday the French dressmaker and her assistants had worn their hair short, à la greque, and Regan wondered if possibly she should cut hers. Maybe it would give her an added air of sophistication in her new life—whatever that was to be.

Her musings made the time pass, and when she saw that the

sun was setting she felt as if she were about to embark on a great adventure. She had escaped the awful American, and she was free to go wherever she wanted.

Slowly, painfully, she left her crouch, shaking her tired legs, and letting the blood return to them as she put her weight on them. As she stood erect, she realized that her feet were cut and the sores inside her shoes were covered with dried blood, which broke apart when she took her first step.

Pulling her courage together, she stepped toward the darkening street. A lady, she reminded herself. She must carry herself like a lady and not let a little thing like lacerated, swollen feet make her limp. If she kept her shoulders back, her spine straight, her chin high, no one would bother her—no one would dare molest a lady.

Chapter 5

NEWS OF a pretty young bit of fluff walking about the docks un-escorted spread like fire through a dry forest. Men who were too drunk to walk somehow managed to drag themselves out of a stupor and stagger in the direction of the young woman. An en-tire shipload of sailors just in from a three-year voyage grabbed bottles of rum and ran toward where someone said there was a whole passel of women just waiting for them.

Bewildered, trying very hard not to let her fear show, Regan did her best to ignore the ever-increasing crowd of men gathering around her. Some of them, grinning toothlessly and stinking of fish and worse, stuck out filthy, trembling hands to touch the vel-vet of her dress.

"Ain't never felt nothin' so soft," they whispered.

"Ain't never had me no lady before."

"Think ladies do it the same way as whores?"

Faster and faster she began to walk, weaving away from the hands and the bodies placed in her way. No longer did she think of keeping the sea to her back; all she thought of was escape.

The men of the docks seemed to toy with her just as they had the night she'd been wearing her nightgown, but it was when the young, virile, hungry sailors from the ship found her that the rel-atively gentle games ceased. When the sailors realized there was only one woman and not fifty as they'd been told, they grew angry, and their anger was directed at this one frightened-looking female.

"Here, let me at her. I need more than a feel of her pretty dress," leered one vigorous young man, reaching out and grabbing the shoulder of Regan's dress.

The fabric tore all the way to the top of her breast, exposing one fat, soft mound that made the men laugh delightedly. "Please stop," Regan whispered, backing away from the sailors, only to have three pairs of hands lift her skirt and slip up the back side of her legs.

"She may be little, but there's a lot of her in the right places."

"Stop larkin' about. Let's have at her."

Before Regan was aware of what was about to happen to her, just as she seemed to hear Travis's words about men forcing her to do what they had done together, one of the sailors gave her a firm push, and she fell backward over the men behind her. With one futile effort at a scream, she tried to right herself, but the men under her, scrambling away, held her under an ocean of grabbing, exploring hands. Over her, grinning wildly, were the sailors.

"Now, let's see what's under those pretty skirts."

The man put his hand on her skirt, and Regan kicked him in the face, sending him sprawling. Her arms were pinned above her head by the men behind her, and the second after she kicked her ankles were grabbed, legs pulled wide apart.

"You won't kick me, missy," laughed another sailor, grabbing the edge of her skirt.

One second he was above her, smiling at her terror, enjoying her struggles against the hands that held her, and the next he was flying through the air, and grabbing his shoulder, which was quickly reddening. The sound of the shot seemed to come after the sailor flew away.

Two more shots rang across the tops of the men's heads before they began to react to something besides their vicious sport.

Regan, still held by the men, was first aware of their silence, and when she felt their grip loosening she kicked out, freeing one leg. The next moment an angry, violent Travis stepped over her, and before the men could comprehend what was happening, Travis grabbed arms, necks, belts, whatever was available, and sent sailors and waterfront riffraff flying through the air.

Shaking with fear, Regan lay still as, one by one, every hand was taken from her body. Travis straddled her hips, his back to her, a pistol in each hand. "Anyone else like to try for the lady?" he challenged.

Backing away, looking like the untamed, cowardly scum they were, they muttered at Travis for spoiling their fun, but no one openly opposed the dangerous-looking American.

Sticking the pistols into his belt, Travis turned and looked down at Regan, watched her panting with fear, and quickly noted that most of her clothes were intact. With one swift gesture he bent and threw her over one shoulder like a sack of flour.

The breath nearly leaving her, Regan slammed against the back of him. "Put me down!" she demanded.

Travis gave her buttocks one hard smack, which was fortunately padded by the thick velvet, before nodding to the two other men who still held pistols on the cowering crowd, and started back toward the inn.

One of the sailors, the one Regan had kicked in the eye, yelled after Travis that Yanks certainly knew how to treat women, and the others laughed, glad they'd had no fight with the angry man. The sailor Travis had shot limped away, back toward the inner structures of the waterfront.

Regan didn't say another word to Travis as she bounced along in the awkward, embarrassing position, and she was glad her long hair hid her face from passersby, especially people at the inn. By the time he'd climbed the stairs and reached the room they'd shared, she was ready to tell him what she thought of his treatment of her, that he was little better than the ruffians on the street.

But her courage left her when Travis slammed her into the bed so hard she dove through a foot of down-filled mattress, striking the rope lacing below. Gasping for air, she surfaced, pushed her hair out of her face, and looked up into Travis's livid, raging temper.

He didn't give her a chance to speak. "Do you know how I found you?" he said through clenched teeth, the muscles of his jaw working vigorously, hands on hips. "I hired men to walk the waterfront and to report to me when there was a commotion. I knew if I waited you'd show up, and when you did they'd be all over you." Leaning forward, he snarled at her, "You lasted longer than I expected. What did you do, hide somewhere?"

Watching her face, he saw that his guess had been correct. He threw up his hands in frustration while taking heavy steps across the room. "What the hell am I going to do with you? I have to keep you locked up to protect you from yourself. Don't you have any idea at all what the world's like? I told you what would happen if you left here, but you didn't believe me. No, instead you had to get yourself nearly raped and possibly killed. The first time I found you, you were being chased by men, and now, through your own fault, it's happened again. Did you think it would be different the second time?"

Holding the torn top of her dress together, she toyed with the luscious velvet of the skirt. Her mind was working hard to block out what had just happened to her, to make it seem like one of her dreams. "I thought because I was dressed like a lady, they wouldn't. . . ." she whispered.

"What!" Travis bellowed, then sank into a chair. "I cannot believe anyone could truly, actually think—." He cut himself off to look at her, so small, probably unaware that she was shivering, a long scrape down the side of her face, and once again he felt possessive about her. "There's no question about it now. Tomorrow you leave with me for America."

"No!" she gasped, her head coming up. "I can't possibly. I must stay in England. This is my home."

"You want a home where you're attacked every time you step out the door? You want a repeat of what happened to you today?"

"This isn't the real England," she pleaded. "There are beautiful people and places full of love and friendship and. . . ."

"And what?" he asked, hard. "Money? Money is the difference between the filth just outside here and the gentility you seem to adore, the gentility that seems to have kicked out an innocent little thing like you. It looks to me like the lovely people you know are about even with the ones tearing your clothes off a while ago."

Slowly, great tears began to form in Regan's eyes, and as she looked up at Travis he saw her sadness. She needed her dreams, she thought, needed to believe in love and beauty, had to have something to make up for all the emptiness in her life.

Not exactly understanding the thoughts going through Regan's mind, Travis did see her hurt, and her tears made him weak. Instantly, he was beside her on the bed, folding her into his arms, trying his best to shelter her from whatever painful memories haunted her.

"You'll like America," he said gently, stroking her hair. "The people are good and honest, and they'll like you. I'll introduce you to half of Virginia, and before you know it you'll have more friends than you know what to do with."

"Friends?" she whispered, clinging to him, only now beginning to realize how the experience on the waterfront had upset her. There still seemed to be clutching, greedy hands on her body.

"You can't imagine all the wonderful people in America. I have a little brother, Wesley, who will love you, and of course there's Clay and Nicole. Nicole is from France and can talk French as fast as lightning."

"Is she pretty?" Regan sniffed.

"Almost as pretty as you," he smiled, caressing her hair. "And when I left she was just about to have a baby. It's probably months old by now. Of course, she's already got the twins."

"Twins?"

Travis laughed and held her away from him, wiping away her tears with his fingertips. "Don't you understand yet that I'm taking you to America, not to punish you or because I like kidnapping little girls, but because I have no choice? There's nothing else I can do with you."

His words, meant to calm her and said in Travis's own special blunt way of calling a problem by its true name, had the opposite effect on Regan. Her uncle and Farrell had said similar things about having to put up with her. She was tired of being a burden to everyone. "Let me up!" she demanded, pushing against him.

"Now what the hell's the matter?"

Twisting her head, she tried to bite his hand on her shoulder.

Travis pushed her back into the mattress and rubbed his hand. "I don't understand you at all. I save your life not more than an hour ago, and now I tell you, as kindly as you please, how I have your own best interests at heart, and you get madder'n hell at me. I don't understand you at all."

"Understand me!" she gasped, eyes spitting fire. "I wouldn't have had to run away if you hadn't been holding me prisoner, and I wouldn't have needed rescuing if it hadn't been for you in the first place. In a sense, you saved me *from* yourself *for* yourself."

Bewildered, his mouth falling open, Travis could only gape at her. "Does your mind always work that way? Do you always go down ten different twisted paths before you get to where you want to go?"

"I assume that is an American colloquialism, meant to cover your lack of logic. The fact is that you are holding me prisoner, and I demand to be released," she said smugly, arms folded, chin tilted away from him.

Travis's anger faded quickly to laughter, which he tried very hard to suppress. Whatever her understanding of logic was, it was far away from the true meaning of the word. He considered explaining again what would happen if he released her, but since she'd been assaulted twice and it seemed to have made no impression on her, he had no desire to try to explain again. Nor would he try painting a glorious picture of America for her. All he could do was to let her see for herself. He also considered throwing open the door and giving her another chance to try to make it out of the docks, or he could pay for a cab to take her wherever she wanted to go.

At this last thought, something inside him tightened. If he sent her away, he might never see her again, this starry-eyed little vixen who seemed to look at the world through her own special pink haze. The thought of the long sea voyage without her to entertain and delight him made him feel very sad.

"You're going to America with me," he said firmly as he ran his hand along her bare shoulder. He'd felt so guilty about seducing her when she was so innocent that he'd forced himself to stay away from her for two nights, but now the near panic he'd felt all day when he couldn't find her, combined with the seductive image she presented now with her bare shoulder and partially exposed breast, made him forget about logic.

"Do not touch me," she said haughtily.

"We may disagree about . . . logic"—he smiled at the word—"but there's one area where we seem to be in complete agreement."

Regan really tried to keep herself aloof from Travis's touch, but the feel of his hand—that wide, warm, sensual palm running along her neck—was impossible to ignore. She wanted to appear unaffected by what had happened to her, wanted him to think she was courageous and brave, but truthfully she wanted to climb into his lap and hide, perhaps crawl into his pocket. When he had stood over her this evening, pistols drawn, she'd never in her life been so glad to see anyone.

Turning her head to one side, his fingers stroked her neck, and she closed her eyes as his other hand went to the opposite side of her neck.

"You're tired, aren't you, love?" Travis whispered, the pressure of his hands increasing. "Muscles stiff?"

Her nod was barely perceptible as she felt her body relaxing. She had no idea what he was doing, only that by some magic he seemed to be making her body melt. She closed her eyes, giving herself over to Travis, hardly aware when he slipped off her dress and laid her naked body face down on the bed. The gentle, deep sound of his voice added to this new pleasure she was experiencing.

"When I was a boy," he said, "I shipped out on a whaler for three years. Terrible experience, but at least there were some interesting stops, such as China, where I learned to do this."

Wherever he'd learned it, she was grateful. His hands dug into her and sometimes even hurt her, but she soon found that when she relaxed the pain stopped. Fingers massaged along her spine, kneading out the soreness from crouching in the alleyway for hours. Cramps in her legs and calves relaxed, and when he started on her feet new areas of her body sank deeper into the soft mattress. It amazed her that even her arms could be tense, but Travis's hands loosened knots of tight muscle and made them limp.

Since Regan was too relaxed to move, he turned her over as if she were a heap of rags and began on her front. From the feet up, he rubbed, pummeled, stroked, gouged, caressed every pore of her body. When he reached her face, his thumbs gently touching the muscles in her cheeks, and around her nose, she was near senseless.

Feeling so relaxed, she wasn't aware of the sensuality of the massage, that the feel of Travis's strong hands, his eyes on her nude body, had awakened her passion. She felt like a big cat stretching in the sun, every muscle quiet, awaiting the adventures that lay ahead.

When Travis's hands returned to her thighs, it seemed the most natural thing in the world. A sweet, knowing smile curved her lips as she kept her eyes closed, preferring only to feel, to give her mind over to her senses. The change of pressure in Travis's hands, perhaps his own lust coming through his fingertips, was subtle, but she understood it.

"Yes, love," he growled throatily, his breath extraordinarily deep.

He didn't use his lips or any other part of his body except his hands—those marvelous, big, hard hands that she'd seen used to toss grown men about as if they were weightless. Wide, callused fingers were artfully agile, deliciously provocative as they reexplored the skin they'd just touched.

Regan felt a deep hum inside her, some primitive piece of machinery beginning to work. Arching slightly, rhythmically, she gave herself over to him. "Please," she whispered, her hands rising up his arms, fingers tracing the muscles. "Please."

Travis lost no time in obeying her, as he was close to the breaking point. The sheer sensuality of their lovemaking and the beauty of her slim young body had fascinated him, and when he entered her it was slowly, very slowly, never once relinquishing the gentle, ethereal quality of their pleasure.

Regan had learned enough about lovemaking to know to prolong their movement, and she followed his lead as if they were two heavenly bodies joined in a union that would last through eternity. Yet she could not hold off long, and soon she began to breathe quicker and to dig her hands into Travis's flesh. Within seconds their gentleness turned into ferocity, their hunger equal, greedy, starving.

When at last their passion peaked, Regan cried out and felt tears coming to her eyes at the violence of her release.

For some minutes she lay still, afloat in a sea of nothingness, sated and happy, relaxed and deeply quiet.

Slowly, Travis rolled off her, propped his head on one elbow, and looked down at her. His brown eyes were dark, and she noticed the thickness of his short lashes.

Who is this man? she wondered. Who is this man who makes my body sing to some heavenly music? He didn't say a word, and she felt she was seeing him for the first time. He held her prisoner, yet he took care of her, acted as if he valued her, and even a few times seemed remorseful about enslaving her. What sort of man could be so gentle and so strong at the same time?

Studying him, she thought how little she knew of him. What thoughts went through his mind, who were the people he loved, and, yes, who loved him? She put her hand to the side of his face, running her fingertips along his cheek. Could this man, who seemed to think the world was his for the taking, ever be made to love? Could a mere woman ever make a slave of this man, hold his strong, pounding heart in her small hands?

She moved her hand to his bare chest, felt his heart under her palm, twined her fingers in the hair on his chest, and then on impulse gave it a sharp pull.

"Stop that, you little imp," he growled, then kissed her fingers. "I'd think you'd be more grateful after the way I just made you squeal."

"Grateful!" she gasped, but concealing a smile. "Since when does a slave thank her master?"

Travis refused to take the bait but merely grunted and gathered her to him. He seemed to give no thought to the fact that he twisted her body into an impossible position.

Regan started to protest that she could not possibly sleep entwined about him in such a way, but even as she formed the words they disappeared. Feeling rather like a vine twirled about the trunk of a great oak, her body relaxed, and she drifted into a deep sleep.

Chapter 6

REGAN'S LANGUOROUS, catlike mood disappeared astoundingly quickly the next morning when Travis roughly pulled her out of bed and then dashed a handful of cold water in her face. Gasping for air, she finally managed to open her sleepy eyes just in time to see a towel flying at her.

"Get dressed," Travis tossed over his shoulder as he jammed clothes, hers included, into the too-full trunk.

Seeing her torn velvet dress further mutilated as he wadded it into a tight little ball, Regan flung herself at him. "Stop that! I will not have you treat my beautiful dress like that," she said, taking it from him and smoothing it lovingly.

Pulling back, Travis eyed her with interest. "It's torn anyway. What good is it except for a dust rag?"

"It can be patched," she said, folding the dress carefully. "I'm very good at mending my own clothes, and, besides, the nap of the velvet will hide the repair work."

"Since when have rich young English ladies had to patch their own clothes?"

She whirled on him. "I never said I was rich," she smiled smugly.

"There must be money involved somewhere, or you wouldn't have been thrown out on your ear." Eyes twinkling, he caressed her bare buttock. "Or should I say thrown out on your pretty little rear?" Before she could give him the scathing reply he deserved, he smacked her smartly. "Now get dressed before we end up back in bed and the ship leaves without us."

Thoughtfully, she began to dress; then on impulse she turned back to him. "Do you think I really could tempt you to . . . to do something?"

Travis had no idea what she was talking about, but the sight of her, half-dressed, the silk making her eyes brilliantly blue, her skin still glowing from last night's lovemaking and his head still dazzled by it, he felt that she could persuade him to do anything. "Stop tempting me and get dressed. You'll have months on board ship to play the seductress, but for now there's work to do."

Blushing because he'd misunderstood her, Regan concentrated on dressing. Perhaps, she thought dreamily, perhaps this American could be. . . . Glancing at Travis, tossing boots into the trunk on top of clean white shirts, she smiled. Maybe he could never be a gentleman, but he did have possibilities. Her eyes widened as he locked the trunk, bent, grabbed the leather handle, and rose with it hanging down his back.

"Ready?" he asked, seeming not to notice his enormous burden.

She nodded and preceded him out of the door.

Downstairs, a breakfast the size of which she'd never seen before was hot and waiting for them. "You've made me miss more meals than I ever have before in my life," Travis informed her.

She coolly glanced up at his great height, then pointedly at the thickness of his chest. "Perhaps you could stand to miss a few meals."

Travis laughed, but a few minutes later she saw him glancing at a mirror as if he were inspecting himself. His reaction made her smile, feeling a touch triumphant.

The food was delicious, and Regan was ravenous. She was pleased to see that Travis's table manners were quite good, perhaps without the delicacy of Farrell or another gentleman of his quality, but he would pass in decent society.

"Have I grown horns?" Travis asked, teasing.

Ignoring him, she looked back down at her food and wondered at her own lack of spirit. Perhaps it was yesterday's terrible experience on the docks and Travis's rescuing of her, but, truthfully, she was beginning to feel some excitement about the idea of going to America. People said that, since the people of America were free, you could get rich there. Maybe she could make her fortune in the primitive country and return to England—and Farrell—in triumph.

Travis's hand under her chin brought her out of her dream. "Were you leaving me again?" he asked quietly. "Or perhaps planning to murder me in my sleep?"

"Neither. I wouldn't waste my time."

Chuckling, Travis stood, offered her his hand, and helped her up. "I think you're going to do quite well in America. We need more women with your spirit."

"I thought you considered all American women the epitome of grace and courage."

"There's always room for improvement," he laughed, taking her arm. "Now, stay close to me and you'll be all right," he said seriously, his eyes warning her.

She didn't need a second warning, and as soon as they left the inn she found herself clinging to Travis's arm. The fishy smell and the noises peculiar to the waterfront hit her hard, and for a moment she was transported back to the time when the men's hands had clawed at her.

Travis was watching her thoughtfully, aware of the fear in her eyes. He threw the heavy trunk onto the waiting wagon and told the driver which ship to take it to. When it was gone, he turned back to Regan. "There's only one way to lick a fear, and that is to face it straight on. If you fall off a horse, you have to get right back on immediately."

Regan barely listened to this confusing bit of advice but instead moved even closer to Travis, her fingers digging into his arm. "Will the carriage be here soon?" she whispered.

"We're not getting a carriage," Travis said heartily. "You and I are going to walk to the ship. By the time we get there, you won't be so afraid. I don't want you cowering every time we get near a wharf or you smell rotten fish."

It took several moments for his words to reach her brain. Pulling away from him, she looked up in astonishment. "Is this some sort of American logic? I do not want to walk through this . . . this place. I demand you get me a carriage."

"Demand, is it?" Travis smiled. "From what I've learned in life, people shouldn't make demands unless they can carry them through. Are you prepared to walk to the ship by yourself?"

"You wouldn't do that, would you?" she whispered.

"No, love," he said quietly, grasping her hand. "I won't even leave you in this country alone, much less in this slimy place. Now, come on and smile at me. We'll walk to the ship, and you'll see how safe you are with me."

In spite of her misgivings, Regan soon began to enjoy the walk. Travis pointed to buildings, warehouses, and taverns, and told her a humorous story about a fight he'd seen in one tavern. Before long, she was laughing and had stopped clutching so desperately at his arm. Several sailors lounged against a brick wall and made remarks about her that she couldn't quite hear but certainly understood the essence of. Calmly, Travis excused himself and went to say a few words to the men. Within seconds they doffed their caps and came to murmur good mornings to Regan and to wish her a pleasant trip.

Bewildered, then as pleased as a cat with cream, she looked up at Travis as she took his arm again.

His eyes bright, he bent and kissed her nose. "Keep looking at me like that, sweetheart, and we'll never make it to the ship. We'll have to stop at one of these inns."

She looked away from him, but her shoulders went back, her chin up, and she walked as if her feet could hardly touch the ground. And best of all, her fear left her. Her fingertips never left Travis's arm, but now she knew that even this slight touch was enough to keep her safe. Perhaps it wasn't so bad being with this great American and having these men, as low as they were, nodding their heads respectfully at her.

Sooner than she wanted to be, they were at the ship, and Regan was awed by the size of it. Weston Manor could have been set on the open deck.

"How do you feel?" Travis asked. "Not scared, are you?"

"No," she answered honestly, taking a deep breath of the cleansing sea air.

"I didn't think you would be," Travis said proudly as he led her up the gangplank.

She didn't have a chance to see much before he pulled her toward the pointed front end of the ship. There were tangles of rope as big around as her leg, and overhead was a spider web of cables. "Rigging," Travis murmured as he maneuvered her between sailors and boxes of supplies.

Quickly, he pulled her down narrow, steep stairs and into a little cabin that was neat and tidy. The walls were raised, arched panels, painted in two shades of blue. Against one wall was a large bed, a table was anchored to the middle of the floor, and two chests were on the opposite wall. A skylight and a window gave the room ample light.

"Nothing to say?" Travis asked quietly.

She was surprised at the almost wistful quality in his voice. "It's very pretty," she smiled, sitting down on the seat in front of the window. "Is your room as nice?"

Travis grinned. "I'd say it's exactly as pretty as this one. Now, I want you to stay here while I see to the loading of my supplies." Pausing at the door, he turned back. "And I'll go through the passengers and find that seamstress I hired and send her to you. You might want to look through those trunks and decide what you want to make first." His eyes twinkled. "And I told her to forget the nightgowns, that I had my own way of keeping you warm."

With that he was gone, and Regan was left to gape in puzzlement at the closed door. Passengers! He'd told the passengers she was to be sleeping with him? Were these passengers American friends of his, people she hoped would someday respect her?

Before she could even contemplate the horror of this new situation, the door opened, and a tall, thin woman entered.

"I knocked, but no one answered," she said, eyeing Regan with interest. "If you'd rather, I could come back later. It's just that Travis said there was so much sewing to do, it would take the whole voyage. There's another woman on the boat—oh, no, Travis said it was a ship. Anyway, I think I can get her to help out. I don't know if she can do fancy work or not, but she can probably at least do the straight seams."

The woman was quiet for a moment as she seemed to be contemplating Regan. "Are you all right, Mrs. Stanford? Are you getting seasick, or maybe you're homesick already?"

"What?" Regan asked blankly. "What did you call me?"

The woman laughed as she moved to sit by Regan. She had lovely eyes, a full, pretty mouth, but in between was a sharp, long nose. "Neither you nor Travis seems used to being married yet. When I asked him if you'd been married long, he looked at me like he didn't think I was talkin' to him. That's a man for you! It takes them ten years before they admit they've given up their freedom." Glancing about the room, she didn't stop talking. "But if you ask me, marriage was made for men; they just get another slave when they get a wife. Now!" she said abruptly. "Where are your new clothes? I reckon we'd best get started."

There were about a hundred thoughts whirling together in Regan's head, all of them confusing. In the turmoil of the last few days she'd completely forgotten about the clothes.

The woman patted Regan's hand sympathetically. "I guess with you being a new bride with a husband like Travis and all, and going to a new country, it's just too much for you. Maybe I should come back later."

New bride, Regan thought. She was a bride in a way. At least it was pleasant to imagine that she was a bride rather than facing up to the reality of the situation.

The woman was already at the door before Regan recovered herself. "Wait! Don't leave. I don't know where the clothes are. No, Travis said they were in the trunks."

Grinning broadly, the woman held out her hand. "I'm Sarah Trumbull, and I'm happy to meet you, Mrs. Stanford."

"Oh yes!" Regan sighed, liking this woman very much in spite of her extraordinary manipulation of the English language.

Sarah was on her knees in seconds as she threw open the lid to the first trunk. Perhaps the best indication of her admiration was her complete silence as she gazed down at the riot of colors and soft, silken, finely woven fabrics. "These must have set Travis back a bit of gold," she finally managed to whisper.

A sharp wave of guilt passed over Regan as she remembered how she'd purposely chosen many more clothes than she needed just to embarrass Travis when he found he could not pay the bill. Yet, obviously, he had paid the bill, and she wondered how much it had cost him—mortgages perhaps, selling what he owned?

"You're looking a little green again. Are you sure the ship's rolling isn't bothering you?"

"No, I'm all right."

"Good," Sarah said, looking back at the trunk. "Travis wasn't exaggerating when he said this was going to take months. You think that other trunk is as full as this one?"

Swallowing hard, Regan glanced at the closed lid. "I'm afraid so."

"Afraid!" Sarah laughed, pulling a leather portfolio from the trunk. "Look at this!" she said, emptying it onto her lap. Several pieces of heavy paper fell out, and on each one were four delicate watercolors of women's gowns. "These the dresses you picked out?"

Taking them, Regan smiled. They were beautiful dresses, and the sketches themselves were works of art. As Sarah and Regan began exploring, they found that each dress and coat had been carefully cut, and the trims for the particular garments were wrapped inside.

"It looks like I have my work cut out for me," Sarah said, then laughed at her own pun. Gathering drawings and fabrics, she said she'd like to get started, and as abruptly as she had appeared she left the cabin.

For a few moments, Regan sat alone on the window seat, looking at the cabin and wondering what adventures were ahead of her. She thought of Farrell and wished he knew she was on a ship bound for America and that a wardrobe fit for a princess was being sewn for her.

She had no idea how long she sat immobile on the seat, but gradually she became aware of the sounds outside her door. For all of her life she'd been forced to stay in a very small area, and the only living she could do was inside her head. Now she realized that she was free to see and do things, that the door to her cabin was not locked, and all she had to do was walk up some stairs and she'd be on the deck of an actual ship.

Taking a deep breath, feeling like a bird let out of a cage, she left the cabin, standing for a moment at the bottom of the dark stairwell. When a door next to her opened, she jumped in surprise.

"I beg your pardon," came a polite male voice. "I had no idea anyone was here." When Regan didn't answer, he continued, "Perhaps I should introduce myself since it looks as though we're to be neighbors. Or am I being too presumptuous? Maybe the captain could do the honors."

The young man's formal manners were a welcome relief after the last few days' complete suspension of anything resembling courtesy. "We will be neighbors," she smiled, "so perhaps just this once we can suspend formalities."

"Then allow me to present myself. I am David Wainwright."

"And I am Regan Alena . . . Stanford," she said as an afterthought, not wanting to reveal her true identity or let this man know the truth about her relationship with Travis.

Gently, he shook her hand, then asked if she'd accompany him up to the upper deck. "I believe they're still loading. It may afford us some amusement to see these Americans among themselves, though I confess I sometimes have difficulty understanding their dialect."

The sun was warm and bright on the deck, and Regan caught the feeling of excitement as people rushed around her everywhere. They emerged at the base of the quarterdeck, a partial additional deck at the fore end of the ship. Soon realizing they were in the way, she and David climbed the stairs to the top of the quarterdeck. Here they had a good, high view of the activities on the rest of the ship as well as on the wharf. And here, too, she had a view of David Wainwright. He was a small man with a plain face topped with straw-colored hair. His clothes were of good wool, his cravat perfectly white, and his slim feet were encased in soft kid slippers. He was the type of gentleman she'd always known—his hands made for the keys of a piano or to idly twirl a snifter of brandy. Looking at his long, slim fingers, she thought with disgust that an uncouth man such as Travis would probably hit two keys at once with his big fingers. Of course, she had to admit that those wide fingers sometimes hit the right chords.

As her lips curved in a secret smile, she looked away from David, who was explaining why he was going to such a heathen place as America, and searched for Travis.

"I can't tell you how glad I am to be traveling with an English lady," David was saying. "When my father suggested I go and see to his holdings in that wilderness, I dreaded the journey. I've heard more than my share of stories about the place, and as if that weren't enough, just meeting a single American can turn one against the country. Look at that!" he gasped. "That is just what I was speaking of."

Below them, two sailors dropped the burdens they were carrying to the center of the deck, where another man carried them downstairs, and began shoving each other. Within seconds, one swung his fist at the other's jaw and missed, but before he could strike again the second man slammed his fist into the first's nose. Blood seemed to gush forth instantly, and the hurt, angry man began to swing wildly.

Out of nowhere, Travis appeared, grabbed the much smaller men by the backs of their shirt collars, and lifted them from the deck. There was no difficulty in hearing Travis as he told the sailors what he thought of their behavior and what he promised to do if they gave him any more trouble. Shaking them like puppies, he tossed them aside, told them to get cleaned up and return to work, as he carried both their bundles to the waiting sailor.

"That is an example of what I mean," David said. "Those Americans have no discipline. This is an English ship with an English captain, yet that . . . that American lout thinks he has every right to enforce his will over the crew. And besides, the men should not have been let off so lightly. Their bad conduct should be made an example of. Every captain knows that the only way to stop insubordination is at the very outset of it."

Regan agreed with him, of course. She'd heard her uncle say the same sort of thing many times, but the way Travis had handled the angry men seemed to her efficient and sensible. Frowning, she was puzzled by her thoughts, wondering who was actually right.

Her mind on other things, she did not at first see Travis waving at her.

"I believe that man is trying to get your attention," David said, half in disgust, half in disbelief.

Trying to be sophisticated, Regan gave Travis a polite return wave before looking away from him. She had no desire to make a spectacle of herself as he had just done.

"I don't think he was satisfied," David said wonderingly. "He now seems to be coming this way. Perhaps I should get the captain."

"No!" Regan gasped, her eyes turning to Travis and smiling in spite of herself.

"Did you miss me?" Travis laughed, sweeping her into his arms and swirling her around once.

"Let me down!" she said angrily, but her voice did not agree with the pleasure on her face. "You smell like a gardener."

"And what would you know of the smell of a gardener?" he teased.

From behind her, David cleared his throat noisily.

Blushing, Regan managed to push Travis's hands away from her. "Mr. Wainwright, this is Travis Stanford." Her eyes looked up pleadingly at him. "My . . . husband," she whispered.

Travis's eyes didn't flicker. Actually, his smile seemed to grow warmer as he thrust out his hand, enveloping David's slim, smooth one. "I am glad to meet you, Mr. Wainwright. Did you know my wife in England?"

How smoothly he said the lie! she thought. Yet how kind of him to save her honor this way. She would have thought he'd laugh at her, as he did so often.

"No, we just met," David said quietly, looking from one to the other, seeing Travis's possessive arm about Regan's small shoulders, seeing a refined, elegant English lady in the grasp of a half-savage, mannerless, working-class man. He very much wanted to wipe his palm where Travis had touched him.

If Travis saw the delicate curl of the small man's upper lip, he did not show it, and Regan was too busy trying to regain some of her dignity by pushing Travis's hand away.

"I was hoping you'd known her before," Travis said, and ignored Regan's look because his words had an odd ring to them, almost as if he wasn't telling the truth. "I have to get back to work, love," he smiled. "You stay up here and away from the lower deck, you understand?" He didn't wait for her to answer but turned to appraise Wainwright. "I trust I may leave her with you?" he said politely, formally, but at the same time he gave the impression that he was laughing. Regan very much wanted to kick him.

Swiftly, he turned and bounded down the stairs, leaving Regan to wonder if he were jealous. Perhaps Travis was worried that he couldn't compete with a gentleman of Mr. Wainwright's quality.

Chapter 7

THE SHIP sailed with the tide. Regan, too excited to eat, too curious to leave the quarterdeck even for a moment, was unaware of the way David's face whitened or of his constant swallowing. When he excused himself, she smiled and stayed where she was. Noisy seagulls flew overhead as the men ran the sails up. The rolling of the ship reminded her that they were about to set out on a journey, that with the moving of the ship she was starting a new life.

"You look happy," Travis said quietly from beside her.

She hadn't been aware of him coming up the stairs. "Oh yes, I am. What are those men doing? Where do those stairs lead to? Where are the other passengers? Do their rooms look like ours, or is everyone's a different color?"

Travis gave her a grin and fell to telling her what he could about the ship. It was a twenty-four-gun brig, the guns needed to keep away pirates. The other passengers lived in the lower deck, amidships. He didn't tell her about the close airlessness of their quarters or the strict rules governing the passengers' infrequent exercise. Only the two of them and Wainwright were allowed to come and go freely.

He explained why nearly all ships were now painted a shade of ochre. Before America's revolution, all ships had been swabbed with linseed oil, which made the wood darken with each coating. The older the ship, the darker it was. During the war, the English made a point of attacking the darker ships, until someone decided to paint all the ships the color of a newly built one.

Travis pointed to several patches of red paint and said that almost all the interiors, especially around the cannons, had been painted red so that the crew would be used to the color and not panic when, during a battle, they were surrounded by the red of blood.

"Where did you learn all this?" Regan asked eagerly.

"Someday I'll have to tell you about my time on the whaler, but for now let's get something to eat. Unless, of course, you don't feel like eating."

"Why shouldn't I want to eat? It's been a long time since breakfast."

"I was afraid you might have a touch of what your little friend had—seasickness. It's my guess that half the passengers below are spilling their guts into chamber pots."

"Really? Oh, Travis, I must see if I can help."

He caught her arm before she could reach the stairs. "There'll be plenty of sick people later, but for now you're going to eat and rest. You've had a long day."

Maybe she was tired, but also she was sick to death of his orders. "I am not hungry, and I can rest later. I will go to help the other passengers."

"And I say you will obey me, so you'd better make up your mind."

She glared up at him, refusing to move.

Leaning down, his face close to hers, he said quietly, "Either you do what I say or I carry you downstairs in front of the entire crew."

A feeling of helplessness came over her. How could she reason with this man? What could she do to make him understand that it was important to her to feel useful?

As he moved his hand toward her shoulder, she pivoted on

one foot and sped down the stairs, through the door, and into the cabin. Sitting down on the window seat, she tried hard not to cry. It wasn't easy to keep to her dreams of someday being a respected lady when she was ordered about like a child.

It was some time before Travis came back to the room bearing a tray laden with food. Quietly, he set the table before going to sit by her. "Supper's ready." He tried to take her hand, but she drew it away.

"Damn it!" he exploded, jumping up. "Why do you sit there looking like I've just beaten you? All I said was I didn't think you should miss your supper and do without sleep to help a bunch of people you don't even know."

"I know Sarah!" she gasped. "And you did not say I *should* rest; you said I *had* to rest. You never suggest anything; you always demand everything. Did it ever occur to you that I have a mind of my own? You held me prisoner in England, wouldn't so much as allow me out the door, and now you hold me prisoner in this little room. Why don't you tie me to the bed or chain me to the table? Why not be honest about what I am to you?"

Several emotions flickered across Travis's handsome face, but the predominant one was confusion. "I told you why you couldn't stay in England. I even asked that boy you were with if he'd known you. The ship hadn't set sail then, and if he'd told me, I could have taken you to your family."

More tears came to Regan's eyes. To think she'd thought Travis was jealous, and all he'd actually wanted was another chance to get rid of her. "Excuse me for being such a burden to you," she said haughtily. "Perhaps you should throw me overboard and save yourself so much trouble."

Astonished, Travis could only look at her in bewilderment. "If I live to be a thousand, I don't believe I'll be able to understand your reasoning. Why don't you eat something, and then if you want I'll take you below, and you can hold sick heads over pots all night."

He looked so sweet, his big eyes so liquid, pleading with her, trying his best to please her. How could she explain to him that what she wanted was the freedom to choose, the right to make her own decisions? She wanted to prove to herself and to her uncle that she was worth something.

Accepting his hand, she let herself be led to the table, but she couldn't seem to pull herself out of her dark mood. She pushed her food around, barely tasting it. She tried to listen to what Travis was telling her but couldn't seem to keep her mind on it. She kept thinking of her whole life as someone's prisoner, never allowed to make even a single decision.

"Drink your wine," Travis said gently.

Obediently, she drained the glass and felt her body relaxing. It seemed natural when Travis swept her into his arms, held her so securely, and carried her to the bed. While he was undressing her, she was awake only in a haze. Even when she was naked and he was kissing her neck, she only smiled and fell into a deeper sleep.

Seeing that she needed sleep more than anything else, Travis snuggled her under the covers before taking a cigar and going up to the top of the quarterdeck to smoke it.

"All settled in?"

Travis turned to the captain behind him. "We'll make it, I guess."

The captain watched Travis as he leaned on the railing, a long cigar hanging out of his mouth. "What's wrong, boy?" he asked seriously.

Travis smiled. The captain and Travis's father had been friends for years, until cholera took the older man. "What do you know about women?"

"No man knows much," the captain said, trying not to smile, glad there was nothing seriously wrong. "I'm sorry I didn't get to meet your bride. I hear she's a beauty."

Studying his cigar, Travis took a moment before answering.

"My bride, yes. I'm just having some trouble understanding her."
He wasn't a man to share confidences, and this was as much as he
could say. Straightening, he changed the subject. "You think that
furniture will be safe in the hold?"

"It should be," the captain said. "But what do you need more
furniture for? You haven't added a wing to that mansion of
yours, have you?"

Travis chuckled. "No, at least not until I have about fifty kids
to fill all the rooms I already have. The furniture's for a friend. I
did buy some land, though. I'll put in more cotton this year."

"More!" the captain gasped before gesturing toward the deck
in front of them. "This is all the space I need. I couldn't keep up
with—how many acres of land do you own now?"

"About four thousand, give or take a few."

The captain gave a snort of disbelief. "I hope that little bride
of yours is a good housewife. The place took all your mother's
talents, and you've nearly doubled it in size since your father
died."

"She can handle it," Travis said confidently. "Good night, sir."

In their cabin again, he undressed thoughtfully before climbing into bed and drawing Regan to him. "The question is, can I
handle her?" he murmured just before he fell asleep.

It took Regan exactly twenty-four hours to learn that Travis
was completely correct about what an awful job it was dealing
with seasick people. From early morning until late at night she
did little more than wash vomit from people and belongings. The
passengers were too sick to hold their heads over the porcelain
basins she held toward them and too ill to care what happened to
the contents of their stomachs. Mothers lay in their narrow
bunks, their babies crying beside them, while Regan and two
other women cleaned, tried to comfort, and worked long, hard
hours.

As if the seasickness weren't enough, the condition of the
passengers' accommodations appalled Regan. There were three

dormitories, one for married couples, and two for single men and women, and the discipline enforced by the crew to keep unmarried men and women apart was strict. Sisters were not allowed to speak to brothers, or fathers to daughters, and each worried about the other in these first few days of illness and misery.

In each dormitory were many narrow rows of hard, small bunkbeds. In the close aisles were the passengers' belongings: trunks, boxes, parcels, baskets, containing not only clothes and what goods they needed for the New World but also the food for the voyage. Already some of it was beginning to decay, the smell aggravating the passengers' nausea.

Regan and the other women ran in and out of the women's cabin, trying to get over the trunks, having to walk up and down, over and around for every step they had to take.

By the time she returned to her own cabin, which by contrast looked like a room in a palace, she was more exhausted than she'd ever imagined she could be.

Travis put down his book immediately and gathered her into his arms. "Was it difficult, love?" he whispered.

She could only nod against his chest, so glad to be near someone healthy and strong, glad to be away from the squalor and poverty she'd seen today.

Relaxing against him, half-asleep, she was hardly aware when he put her in a chair and went to answer the door. Even when she heard water splashing, she didn't bother to open her eyes. After all, she'd heard little else all day when she'd washed clothes, babies' diapers, and dirty chamber pots.

Smiling deliciously, she relaxed as Travis's hands began to unbutton her dress. It was nice to be taken care of instead of the other way around. When he gathered her naked form in his arms, she was pleased to be going to bed, but when her bottom hit the hot water, her eyes flew open.

"You need a bath, my smelly little mate," he laughed at her surprise.

The hot water, even if it was sea water, felt wonderful, and she leaned back, letting Travis wash her.

"I don't understand you," she said softly, watching him, feeling his hands, soapy and strong, run over her body.

"What's to understand? I'll tell you what you want to know."

"A few weeks ago I would have said a man who kidnapped people was evil and should be put in jail, but you. . . ."

"I what? I kidnap pretty young ladies, ravish them, yet I don't beat them? Not too often anyway," he smiled.

"No," she said seriously. "You don't, but I believe you're capable of anything. I don't understand a man like you."

"And what kind of man do you understand? Your little Wainwright? Tell me, how many men have you gotten to know? How many times have you been in love?"

He wasn't prepared for her answer.

"One man," she said quietly. "I've been in love once, and I can't imagine it ever happening again."

Travis studied her expression for a moment, the way her eyes softened with a faraway look, the gentle way her mouth curved up at the corners.

One moment Regan was thinking of Farrell, how he'd asked her to marry him, and the next she was sputtering as Travis tossed the soap into the water in front of her eyes.

"Finish it yourself, or wait for your lover to come and do it," he growled before slamming from the cabin.

Smiling, feeling she'd at last made him jealous, she left the tub and began to dry herself. She thought that perhaps it was good for Travis to realize that he wasn't the only person in her life, that maybe other people existed in the world. When she got to America and they parted ways, perhaps he'd not be so sure she couldn't make it on her own, maybe even find a man like Farrell, someone who would love her and not think she was an ignorant child.

Climbing into bed, she suddenly felt very lonely. Farrel didn't love her; he'd wanted her for her money. Her uncle didn't want her either, and Travis, this strange, arrogant, kind man, made it clear he only wanted her for the moment. Alone, tired, hungry, miserable, she began to cry.

When Travis pulled her into his arms, she clutched at him, scared that he'd leave her too. "Hush, sweet, be quiet. You're safe now," he whispered, trying to soothe her, but when her lips fastened to his, he no longer thought of comfort.

She had no idea if it was being close to the illness all day or her thoughts of being alone, but she was ravenous for Travis. She didn't think about the fact that she was a prisoner or that she should at least be a reluctant lover. Her only thought was that she needed him desperately, needed for him to hold her, to love her, to make her feel as if she were part of the world and not a useless, unneeded appendage.

Boldly, she put her fingers into his shirt opening, sending a button flying across the room. The hair on his chest was so masculine, reminding her of his maleness. Her fingertips explored, not gently but firmly, roughly even, rubbing the texture of his skin, feeling it grow hot beneath her touch.

Tossing her to the bed, he pulled back to remove the rest of his clothes. His eyes were ablaze, his mouth full and hot. As he turned to sit on the edge of the bed to pull off his boots, Regan was left with his broad, muscular back to her mercies. Her teeth nipped his shoulders while the tips of her breasts lightly and electrifyingly grazed across his spine. Lips soon followed down the deep curve of the bone, kissing, caressing, tasting his flesh. Thumbs digging into his sides, fingertips on his ribs, she stroked the back of him with the front of her. The deep indentations of muscle, his strength, now so quiet under her touch, were heady, making her surge with her own sense of power.

She kissed his earlobe, nipping it sharply, then gave a low, purring laugh. In one swift movement, Travis turned, pulled her into his arms, and was on top of her. She was as eager as he was and more than ready for him.

Travis was blinded by her forwardness, for once not holding back in consideration of her delicate sensibilities. He treated her with all the fire and passion he felt, thrusting hard, massaging her buttocks with his hands, holding her closer and closer.

When at last their release came in a tempest of rapture, they slowly, slowly began to give way to a mass of exhausted, shaking, weak flesh.

"What have you done to me?" Travis gasped, holding her so close he threatened to smother her.

Regan only clutched at him, too tired to think. As she easily fell into a deep sleep, she was unaware of Travis leaning over her, watching her, touching her hair, pulling the sheet a little closer about her. But even in her sleep, she was aware of his arms around her, of his rugged body near her, of the sweetness of his warm breath on her ear. Stirring, she opened her eyes, gave him a sleepy smile, gladly accepted his soft kiss, and then smiled again as he lay his head beside hers and she felt his body relax into sleep.

The next day was a repeat of the same hard, smelly work of helping seasick passengers. In the late afternoon, Travis told her to go to their cabin and rest or she wouldn't be any good for any-one. His tone of voice, always ordering her around, caused her to tell him just what she thought of him.

"You could be helping instead of merely lounging about the deck," she snapped.

"Lounging, am I?" Travis smiled, that half-smile, half-smirk of his that infuriated her.

For the first time she noticed his dress of soiled, sweaty cot-ton shirt and loose britches reaching to his knees, tucked into soft leather boots. A wide black-leather belt circled his trim waist. Suddenly, several questions were answered for Regan, such as how Travis could afford a private room. In payment, he obviously had to work for his passage.

"How can I help?" he asked. "Although, if you expect me to wipe dirty mouths, I won't."

If Travis had to work for his passage, so did she, and the idea of rest wasn't possible. "This morning two of the upper bunks collapsed. I've talked to the crew, but they just laughed at me."

"They probably laughed because they don't know which end of a hammer is which. What else?"

"We need someone to take care of the older children. I thought maybe you could find Sarah Trumbull. I haven't seen her for days."

"Sarah's busy," he said succinctly, "but maybe I can help with the other problems."

A great burden left Regan's small shoulders because she knew that Travis would keep his word.

"Keep looking at me like that, and I'll build separate houses for each passenger right here on deck."

Giggling and feeling much better, she went back to her duties.

In a very short time, Travis appeared at the door of the women's cabin with carpentry tools in a box. Some of the women squealed in protest because they were in various states of undress, but it didn't take Travis long to make them feel comfortable. He laughed with the women and told them the men were all dying for them to come on deck and make the voyage less tedious. In spite of what he'd said to Regan, he held one woman's head over a bowl and tenderly wiped her mouth. He diapered two babies and rearranged several heavy trunks so there was more walking room, all while he repaired the broken bunks, checked the others, and reinforced several more.

When he left, most of the women were smiling, and it felt as if fresh air had just blown through the stuffy, stinking dormitory.

"Oh my," sighed one woman whose baby Travis had changed. "Who was that glorious man?"

"He's mine!" Regan said, so loudly and with such a challenge in her voice that the women laughed, making Regan blush.

"You don't have to be embarrassed, honey. Just thank the Lord every night for being so good to you."

"Maybe she has other things on her mind at night," someone else said loudly.

Regan was almost grateful when one of the women began to groan and she could run away and escape the women's teasing. But even as she held a pan for the woman, she began to feel angry. He was flirting with all the women, right in front of her! No doubt he liked having all the women drool over him, liked being the only man allowed into the single women's cabins. Allowed! Surely Travis Stanford never did anything so common as ask permission for anything he wanted to do.

Slamming down a pitcher of water, Regan seemed to grow angrier by the moment. Of course, he had no reason to treat her as a lady since all he knew of her was in bed. The big, crude American had no idea how to treat a woman except as something for his own use. To him all women were the same—whether they were sick in bed or dressed in a gown of satin, he seemed to think they were all made for his pleasure.

Near sunset, she went on deck to wash the earthenware basins. There, surrounded by children, were Travis and two sailors showing the boys and girls how to tie knots. One girl, about twelve, seemed to be knotting a piece of fabric while a two-year-old sat on Travis's lap, absorbed in the intricacies of the puzzle of rope Travis was creating. He smiled and waved at Regan before returning to the children.

Haughtily, she put her nose in the air and returned below to the stifling cabin, gritting her teeth against the fact that even the children found him irresistible. She'd told the women he was hers, but she was fully aware that she had no power over him, that she was his captive plaything, and that when they reached America he would dispose of her quickly and no doubt pick up another woman—one not so used. With suspicious eyes, she began to look at each one of the women in the big cabin, wondering if one of them would be her successor.

By the time she was ready to leave the dormitory, she was

very angry. Her uncle had said she was mealy-mouthed, an embarrassment to him, but many things had happened to her in the last few weeks, and she was changing.

The cabin she shared with Travis was empty when she reached it, but as she stood watching the stars through the big window, the door opened.

A pewter mug sailing directly toward Travis's head made him duck quickly. "What the—?" he began.

Regan grabbed another mug from a wall cabinet. "You enjoyed flirting, didn't you?" she accused. "You liked having all the women fawn over you. 'Oh what a darling man,' they all drooled." The second mug grazed his shoulder.

As she grabbed the third one, Travis crossed the room and held her hand. Again, that half-amused little smile was on his face. "Don't let your temper get the best of you. Please try to remember that you were once an English lady."

His patronizing tone, added to the fact that he was the one who'd made her fall from being a lady, sent blind rage coursing through her veins. "I am sick of you!" she gasped as she slammed her elbows back into his ribs.

She got some satisfaction from his grunt, but before he could recover she kicked him in the shins.

As he backed away from her, rubbing his shins, his expression was one of bewilderment. "Wouldn't you like to talk about this? What's got you so riled?"

"Riled?" she mocked in her crisp accent. "I am angry because of the way you assume that you have the first right of everything in the world. Did you enjoy the way the women looked at you with great adoring eyes? It was disgusting that you used the babies to get to the women. Are you planning to kidnap one of them when you're through with me?"

"I might," Travis said, his jaw set, a tiny spark of fire in his eyes. "At least one of them might be more grateful for what you have. Why don't you ask who'd like to trade places with you?"

"You are the most vain, arrogant animal ever created!" she seethed. "Did it ever occur to you that I might not want to be held prisoner or that other women might not either? Am I supposed to be grateful that you hold me against my will, drag me onto a ship that's sailing for a country I despise, and threaten to tell everyone our true relationship if I do not remain with you?"

"I told you why I couldn't release you in England." His voice was quite low. "I've shown you every kindness, given you every stitch on your back, yet you're still too much of a romantic to see the truth. Can't you remember what it was like on the docks when those men came after you?"

It was too much like the things her uncle had said. Someone was always taking care of her, always throwing it into her face. "I'm not grateful," she said quietly. "And I do not want anything more from you. You needn't worry that I'll be attacked on board ship, so I'll leave you now and begin my stay with the single women." Looking down at the simple muslin dress that Sarah had just finished for her last night, she said, "When I get to America I will try to earn enough money to repay you for this dress. Perhaps you can sell the others."

Turning, her chin up, back straight, she started for the door.

It took Travis a moment to realize that she meant to leave him, and she was just stubborn enough to do it. Without thinking what he was doing, he grabbed the back of her dress. With Regan going one way and Travis pulling the other, the thin muslin quickly split from top to bottom, landing in a small heap at Regan's feet.

Instantly, his look changed from anger to desire, his eyes raking her hungrily, feasting on her heaving breasts well exposed above the low-cut chemise.

"No," she whispered, trying with all her might to pull away from his mesmerizing gaze.

His arm, strong and powerful, went around her waist, pulling her to him, bending her backward into an arc.

Weakly, she fought against him, wanting so much to defy him, to prove to him that she was her own person, but his touch, his lips on hers, drove her senseless.

"You'll do what I say, love," Travis growled, lifting her off the floor, his lips nuzzling her neck. "You're mine for as long as I want you."

Closing her eyes, leaning her head back, giving her body completely to his touch, she had no idea of escaping this man who controlled her so easily. When she heard the sound of tearing cloth, and felt her chemise give, she began to struggle once again.

"Mine," Travis whispered. "I found you, and you're mine."

There was no time for her to think as Travis pushed her back against the wall, her small body pinned there by the strength and size of him.

His kisses became ravenous, as if he meant to devour her. Her own breath was coming faster and faster as her hands clutched at his shoulders, fingertips digging into his flesh through his shirt, trying to pull him close enough to crush her.

One of Travis's hands lustfully traveled down her bare hip, stroked her thigh, and lifted her leg so that it rested on his hip. Eagerly, Regan grasped his body with her legs, her ankles hooked behind him, her weight supported by him as he stroked and caressed her bottom.

His hands moved excitingly, teasingly, driving her to a passionate frenzy. When his clothes fell from the lower half of his body, she didn't know. Only when he lifted her, his hands about her waist, and set her down on his manhood did her eyes open, but only for an instant.

She was completely in his power, unable to move on her own, her back to the wall, her legs clutching his hips, as he began to lift her, to control her movements, guiding her. Feeling his body against her, the undulations of his hips under her thighs, the driving force of him threatened to drive her insane. Clutching his hair in her fingers, she pulled as Travis leaned harder into her, threatening to break her, to merge his flesh with hers, to consume her. With his might he easily picked her up and lowered her, again and again, faster and faster, until she screamed under the pressure of her sweet torment. Crushingly, Travis's mouth came down on hers as he collapsed against her, her legs like a steel vice about him, her body shuddering, weak and helpless, sated, exhausted.

Gradually, she began to become aware of where she was and who she was, her body pliant, boneless against Travis's proud muscularity. He was kissing her damp neck lovingly, his arms under her bottom, supporting her. Carrying her like a child, he took her to the bed and laid her down as if she were the most precious, most delicate substance ever created.

Tiredly, as if he too had no bones left, he removed his shirt and lay beside her. "No supper tonight either," he murmured, but there did not seem to be any regret in his voice. With his last bit of strength, he pulled Regan to him, their skin sticking together from their mutual sweatiness.

"How could I ever let you leave me?" he whispered before they both fell asleep.

Chapter 8

IN THE morning, Regan could hardly meet Travis's eyes. The way he looked at her—so smug, so sure of himself—made her want to toss a knife at him. He seemed to think he knew everything about her, that he had complete control over her, that he merely had to crook his finger and she belonged to him.

How very much she'd like to wipe that expression off his face; just once she'd like to see him not get what he thought was his.

As they were eating, Sarah Trumbull gave a quick knock at the door before entering. "Oh! Excuse me," she said. "Usually the two of you are gone by this time."

"Have some breakfast, Sarah," Travis said, smiling smugly, and looking at Regan as if he understood exactly why she was avoiding his eyes.

But Sarah was more interested in a torn piece of muslin that yesterday had been a dress she had just made the day before. Chuckling, giving Travis a mock look of reprimand, she said, "Travis, if you're going to treat all my handiwork like this, there's no need for me to keep on sewing."

Running his hand through his hair, glancing quickly at Regan's averted face, he laughed. "I'll try to control myself. Now I need to help on deck. The captain is a bit short-handed this trip. Although," he grinned, "I may not have much energy left." He kissed Regan's cool cheek before he left the cabin.

A sigh to rival a hurricane escaped Sarah as she gazed long-ingly at the closed door. "If there were any more men like him, I might be tempted to get married."

If Regan had known any foul words, she would have used them. "Don't you have work to do?" she snapped.

Regan's tone didn't phase Sarah. "I'd be jealous too if he were mine."

"He isn't—!" she began hostilely, then stopped. "Travis Stan-ford belongs to no one," she said at last, before beginning to clear the breakfast dishes and put them on a tray.

Sarah decided to change the subject. "Do you know that man in the cabin across from yours?"

"David Wainwright? We met, but that's all. Is he all right?"

"I don't know, but I've been in your cabin for two days now, sewing on your new clothes, and I've never heard a sound from him. I thought perhaps he was helping with the men who are ill."

Frowning, Regan decided to investigate, excused herself to Sarah, and left the cabin. Even though she worked in the stench every day, the smell that hit her when she opened David's cabin was overpowering. The heavy darkness of the room caused her to pause for quite some time on the threshold, her eyes searching for Mr. Wainwright.

Finally, in what looked like a heap of filthy rags, she found him huddled on the window seat, his body shivering. Crossing to him, she saw immediately that he had a fever, that his eyes burned dangerously bright, and, by the tone of his ramblings, that he was delirious.

A noise at the door caused her to turn to see Sarah looking at the room in horror. "How could anyone live in this?"

"Would you tell Travis to send down some hot water, please?" Regan said firmly. "Tell him to send a great deal of it—and I'll need washing rags and soap, too."

"Of course," Sarah said quietly, not envying Regan the task she had ahead of her.

* * *

Sunlight filtered through the windows in David Wainwright's cabin, touching on Regan's hair, showing the golden strands intermingled with the darkness. More sun glistened on her soft, sweet-scented muslin gown, highlighting each of the minute, embroidered golden rosebuds. A book was held lightly by her, and as she read from it her words were as soft as the picture she presented.

David lay back against freshly laundered cushions, propped on the end of the window seat, his arm in a sling, his snowy shirt open at the throat. It had been a month since that time Regan had found him alone and ill in his cabin. At the first movement of the ship, he'd become seasick and returned to his cabin. Hours later, he'd fallen from his bunkbed and landed in such a way that he'd broken his forearm. In pain, nauseated, weak, helpless, he was unable to call for help. In an attempt to return to his bunk, he fell again, and with the new pain he lost consciousness. When Regan found him he had no idea who or where he was, and for days after the bone was set no one was quite convinced he'd live through the ordeal.

And through everything, Regan had never left his side. She scoured the filthy cabin, washed David, sat by him, coaxed him into eating a broth made from salt beef, and, by sheer will-power, kept his spirits up. He was not a good patient. He was sure that he was going to die, that he'd never see England again, that America and Americans were going to be responsible for his death. He spent hours telling Regan how he'd had a premonition that these were going to be his last few days on earth.

For Regan, she was glad of an excuse to get away from Travis's overpowering presence, glad for once in her life to be needed by someone, not to feel as if she were a burden.

"Please, Regan," David said petulantly. "Don't read anymore. I do wish you'd just talk to me." He shifted his injured arm with a great show of distress.

"What would you like to talk about? We seem to have exhausted every topic."

"Every topic about my life, you mean. I still know exactly nothing about you. Who were your parents, where did you live in Liverpool, and how did you meet that American?"

Putting the book down, she rose. "Perhaps we should go for a walk on deck. It's a lovely day, and the exercise will do us both good."

Smiling slightly, David put his feet on the floor, waiting patiently for Regan to help him stand. "My mystery lady," he said, his voice betraying that he rather liked not knowing much about her.

On deck, her arm around David's waist and his about her shoulders, the first person they met was Travis. Regan couldn't help but notice the contrast, the slim blond young man in his immaculate clothes next to Travis's brawniness, and his clothes smelling of male sweat and the salty air.

"A bit of an airing today?" Travis asked politely, but lifting one eyebrow and giving a mocking grin to Regan.

David nodded curtly, almost rudely, before half jerking Regan forward. "How could you marry someone like that?" he said when they were alone. "You are the gentlest, tenderest woman, and when I think of you having to endure the attentions of that insensitive, oversized Colonial, I am nearly made ill again."

"He is not insensitive!" she said quickly. "Travis is. . . ."

"Is what?" he said with great patience.

There was no answer to that question. Moving away from David, leaning over the rail and watching the water, she asked herself what Travis did mean to her. At night he made her cry in delight, and the way he always had a tubful of hot water ready for her in the evenings convinced her of his kindness. Yet she was always aware that she was his prisoner.

"Regan," David said. "You aren't answering my questions. Don't you feel well? Perhaps you're tired. I know taking care of me isn't the easiest task in the world. Maybe you'd rather. . . ."

"No," she smiled at the familiar complaints. "You know I enjoy your company. Shall we sit here a while?"

Staying with David the rest of the afternoon, she found she couldn't keep her mind on what he was saying. Instead, she kept watching Travis as he agilely climbed the rigging tied along the mast, as he threw great heavy rope into an orderly pile. Several times he stopped and winked at her, always aware of when she was watching him.

That night, for the first time in weeks, she returned to her own cabin ahead of Travis. When he entered, his face was lit, his eyes smiling with happiness.

It seemed he'd grown more handsome in the last few weeks, his face tanned by the sun, his muscles even harder than before.

"You're a welcome sight after a hard day. You think I could have a kiss of greeting, or did you give them all to young Wainwright?"

Her happiness faded. "Am I supposed to take that insult without a word? Just because you force me into an indecent relationship doesn't mean another man can—or even attempts to, for that matter."

Turning away from her, Travis removed his shirt and began to wash. "It's nice to know the pup hasn't tried to take what's mine. Not that he could, of course, but I like to be reassured."

"You are insufferable! And I am not yours!"

Travis merely grinned confidently. "Shall I prove to you that you belong to me?"

"I do not belong to you," she said, backing away from him. "I can take care of myself."

"Mmm," Travis smiled, coming to stand near her. Sensuously, he began to run his finger down her arm, and when her steady gaze flickered he narrowed his eyes. "Can that boy make you shiver with only one finger?"

She jerked away from him. "David is a gentleman. We talk of music and books, things you know nothing of. His family is one of the oldest in England, and I enjoy his company." She straightened her shoulders. "And I will not allow your jealousy to ruin my friendship with him."

"Jealousy?" Travis laughed. "If I were going to be jealous of someone, it would certainly be someone with more than that whining boy." His face turned serious. "But I believe the boy is getting serious about you, and I think you should stop seeing so much of him."

"Stop—!" she sputtered. "Is there no part of my life you don't attempt to control?" She calmed herself. "I am a free woman, and when I get to America I plan to take advantage of my freedom. I'm sure David is the type of man who'd want to get married and not try to make a . . . a slave of a woman."

Calmly, Travis put his hand on her shoulder. "Would you really like to trade me for a boy and a gold ring?"

As he bent to kiss her, she pulled away. "Perhaps I'd like to try," she whispered. "Surely men can't be so different. If David loved me, perhaps we could be compatible in the marriage bed."

Travis's hands on her shoulders were brutal. "If that boy ever touches you, I'll break every bone in his body—and I'll make you watch while I do it." He gave her a sharp push before he slammed out of the cabin.

That night Regan spent alone. She refused to admit to herself how much she missed him, how alone she felt without his arms around her. All night she tossed and turned, trying not to cry, attempting not to be afraid.

In the morning there were circles under her eyes, and Sarah, for once, didn't ask questions. The two women sat quietly in the cabin and sewed. Near sunset, David knocked on the door and asked if Regan would walk with him.

On deck, all she seemed to see was Travis, yet Travis never looked at her.

His ignoring of her made her angry, and as a result she turned all her attentions to David, who was complaining about the length of the voyage and the food. At her look, suddenly turned from disinterest to adoration, he stopped speaking and looked at her.

"You are especially lovely today," he whispered. "The sunlight makes your hair a red-gold."

Just then Travis was passing them, a massive piece of canvas thrown across his shoulder.

"Oh thank you, David," she said, much too loudly. "You make a woman feel like a queen with your fine compliments. I don't know when I've been so flattered."

If he heard, Travis made no sign as he continued past her, his movements not even slowed.

Again that night she was alone in the cabin. She wanted so much to show Travis that it didn't matter to her that he had abandoned her. She wanted to prove to him that she could do something on her own. So, as the days progressed, she flirted more and more openly with David, always when Travis was near.

On the evening of the third night, as David escorted her to her cabin, instead of his friendly goodnight he grabbed her, fiercely pulling her into his arms. "Regan," he whispered, his lips on her ear. "You must know that I love you. I've loved you from the first, yet every night I must lie alone in my cabin while that . . . that animal has the right to touch you. Regan, my dearest, tell me that you feel the same way about me."

With surprise, she found that his kisses and his arms around her repulsed her. Pushing against him, she tried to free herself. "I'm a married woman," she gasped.

"Married to a man who isn't worthy to kiss the hem of your gown. We'll keep quiet about our love until we dock, and then we'll have your marriage dissolved. You can't think to spend all your life with that poverty-eaten sailor. Come with me, and I will build you a house like that backward country has never seen before."

"David!" she said, pushing in earnest. "Release me this moment!"

"No, my love. If you don't have the courage to leave him, I will tell him myself."

"No! Please, no!" Suddenly she knew that Travis had been right. She didn't want David, and in the last few days she'd been using him to make Travis jealous.

David's fingers turned her face to him, and he planted hot, damp kisses on her face, suffocating kisses, as she twisted her body in an attempt to get away from him.

One moment David was holding her, and the next he seemed to be flying through the air. In astonished disbelief, she watched as Travis's fist smashed into David's face, just before the small man slammed against the wall. As he slid unconscious to the floor, Travis raised his fist again.

With one leap, Regan grabbed Travis's arm, holding on to it, her feet above the ground. "No!" she shouted. "You'll kill him."

The face Travis turned to her was a distortion of his usual countenance. His eyes were hot, black with fury, his mouth grim with his anger. In fear she stepped back from him.

"Did you get what you wanted?" he growled, his heavy brows coming together in a black scowl. Without another word, he turned and left the passageway to return to the deck.

Shaking, Regan looked at David as he was beginning to rouse, blood gushing from his nose. Her first impulse was to help him, but when she saw that he was trying to stand and knew he was all right, she fled to her own cabin. Once inside, she leaned against the door, her heart pounding and tears beginning to roll down her cheeks. Travis had been right! She had used David, toyed with his affections, almost promised what she never meant to give, all in an attempt to make Travis jealous. But Travis could not be made jealous—she was merely a possession to him.

Flinging herself onto the bed, she began to cry in earnest, deeply and sincerely.

Hours later, her head feeling stuffed, her eyes raw, having cried herself to sleep, she was awakened by the violent tossing of the ship. As she lay quietly, trying to understand what was going on, a sudden lurch sent her sprawling out of the bunk and onto the hard floor, where she lay stunned. The cabin door opened, flung back against the wall as the ship plummeted in another direction.

Travis stood in the doorway, wearing a heavy oilcloth slicker, his hair wild and wet. His legs spread as he walked toward her, rolling with the tumbling of the ship. He picked her up in his arms.

"Are you hurt?" he shouted, and until then she hadn't been aware of the tremendous noise about them.

"What's wrong? Are we sinking?" She snuggled against him, so very glad to touch him once again.

"It's only a storm," he shouted down at her. "There shouldn't be much danger since we've been preparing for it for days. I want you to stay here, do you understand? I don't want you to take it into your head to go on deck or to the other passengers. Do I make myself clear?"

She nodded against his shoulder, clinging to him, thinking that perhaps the reason for his absence for the last few days was his preparation for the storm.

Bending, he lowered her to the bed, gave her a look she couldn't fathom, and then kissed her, possessively and forcibly. "Stay here," he repeated, touching the corner of one of her swollen, red eyes.

With that he was gone, and Regan was left alone in the dark cabin. She was much more aware of the rolling of the ship after Travis left. To keep from being thrown from the bunk, she grabbed the sides as best she could. Water seeped in under the door, coating the cabin floor.

Even as she struggled to keep her balance, she began to imagine what was happening on deck. If the water was coming into her cabin, it must be washing over the sides of the ship. Her imagination, always active, began to conjure a picture of horror. Once, when Regan was hardly more than a child, a scullery maid of her uncle's had received a letter saying that her young husband had been washed overboard during a storm, and later a friend of his had come to tell her the full, gruesome story. Every member of the staff, as well as Regan, had gathered around the sailor and heard every gory detail.

Now the story did not seem like a story because above her head were actual waves as tall as a house, waves of such force that they could take a dozen men with them when they returned to sea.

And Travis was up there!

The thought rang through her head. Of course, Travis would never believe he could come to harm. No doubt he was sure even the sea would obey his commands. And it wasn't as if he were a real sailor either. He was just a farmer who'd been on a whaler as a boy, and now he had to work to pay his passage.

An especially violent toss of the ship sent Regan flying out of the bunk again. Travis! she thought, struggling to stand. Perhaps that was the wave that tore him from the decks.

A massive sound of cracking wood above her head sent her eyes upward. The ship was breaking apart! With both hands on the bunk edge, she managed to stand, and she started the long passage toward her trunk, which was fortunately bolted to the floor. First she had to find a cloak, and then she had to somehow make her way on deck. Someone had to save Travis from himself, had to persuade him to return to the comparative safety of the cabin, and if he wouldn't, someone had to watch out for him. If he were washed overboard, she planned to throw him a rope.

Chapter 9

NO STORY ever told could have prepared Regan for the blast of wind and sharp salt air that tore into her body as she opened the door under the quarterdeck. It took all her strength to push the door open wide enough to allow her onto the deck, and it slammed hard behind her. A wave of salt spray soaked her immediately, making her wool cape cling heavily to her slight frame.

Bracing herself against the stair railing, using her strength to keep upright, she blinked against the cold, piercing water that seemed to want to drill holes into her and tried to see if she could find Travis. At first she couldn't distinguish men from the parts of the ship, but her interest in the safety of Travis was stronger than the pain caused by the violence around her.

Gradually, her eyes adjusted, and, blinking rapidly to clear the water away, she made out the shadowy figures of men in the midst of the long, wide deck. Before she could make a decision about how to get to that part of the ship, a sudden lurch sent her sprawling, and, like a piece of driftwood, she was knocked down and rolled across the deck. As her body slammed into the side of the ship, she grabbed what was nearest to her—the wooden support of an iron cannon.

When the wave was past, she began to pull herself upright again, and as she did she heard the cracking sound again; only this time she could tell that it was coming from overhead. One of the masts must be breaking. Starting slowly, taking each step by inches, she began to move toward the men and the breaking mast.

Every crewman and, she was happy to see, Travis also, was holding on to a part of the ship and looking up at the splintering wood.

"Get up there, I say!" the captain bellowed, his voice even louder than the fury of the sea.

Wiping her eyes with the back of her hand, Regan could see the sailors take a step backward, and it took her a moment to realize that the captain was ordering someone to climb the rigging. She had half a mind to tell him what she thought of his request, but of course she must keep quiet and not let Travis know she was there.

But one quick look at Travis, and she saw that he'd already seen her and was making his way toward her. The look of rage on his face put the sea to shame, and without thinking Regan started back toward the door under the quarterdeck; her courage had quite suddenly vanished.

Travis's big hand caught her shoulder before she'd gone two steps. He didn't say a word, and since everything was written on his face, he didn't need to.

As the ship lurched and another wave threatened to capsize them, Travis flung his body over hers, pinning her against the railing, holding her securely with his superior strength.

"I may beat you for this," he shouted into her ear when at last the ship righted itself.

But their attention was caught by another, louder, shout from the captain. "Isn't there a man among you?"

It was at that moment, with Travis holding her arm in a painful grip, that Regan saw David and knew immediately that he'd followed her onto the deck. Even in the dim light, through the pounding spray, she could see the bruises on his face where Travis had hit him. Her eyes locked and held with his for a moment, and a wave of guilt passed through her because she saw that he knew she'd used him, that he knew he'd made a fool of himself.

A smaller wave washed across them and broke their eye contact, and when it receded she saw that David had moved forward—but he wasn't looking at her. Walking as straight as he could under the circumstances, he went toward the captain.

Stopping just opposite Travis, he shouted, "I'm a man. I'll climb the rigging."

"No!" Regan screamed, clutching at Travis's arm. "Stop him!"

David held onto the fife rail at the base of the mast and turned his head to Travis. Travis, seeming to understand David's silent plea, nodded once before clasping Regan's hands in his and stilling her.

Regan struggled against Travis, wanting to go to David, to stop him, knowing that what he wanted to do, this attempt at what amounted to suicide, was her fault.

When she saw that there was nothing she could do, she became very still, like the crew. Travis braced himself between the rail and a cannon carriage, holding Regan tightly, but his eyes never wavered from David's slight form.

The captain, glad to finally find someone brave enough to climb the rigging, was shouting instructions to David while wrapping rope about his waist. From gestures and the few words that could be heard, it was clear that David was to climb the swinging rope rigging to the first and longest yardarm, crawl along its narrow width about halfway until he was suspended over the turbulent water, and bind the splitting yardarm.

Regan could only gasp in disbelief, too astonished even to make a further protest. She knew for sure that she was watching a man go to his death. With fear, she buried her face against Travis, but he pulled her head around and made her look at David, who was poised at the base of the mast, waiting only for Regan to give him a parting glance.

Lifting her hand toward him before dropping it helplessly at her side, she stood straight, her back against Travis's chest, and watched as he grimly started the climb.

His ineptitude was immediately apparent as his feet slipped, quite often losing their grip so that he held on by only one hand. The wind tore at him, pulling his hands away, knocking the rope from under his feet.

Regan put her hand to her mouth and sank her teeth into her own flesh as she watched.

Slowly, with great difficulty at every step, David finally reached the yardarm. Hanging on to it with both his arms, seeming to pause for a moment's rest or perhaps waiting until the next great wave passed, he hesitated. When the water cleared, and the people on deck saw that he was still there, they gave a united gasp of relief.

As the ship righted itself again, David inched forward on the yardarm. A foot before he reached the break, he unwound some of the rope about his waist and put one end into his mouth.

"Look out!" came a shout from near Regan.

But David could not hear the warning as another big wave separated him from the people below.

On deck, the crashing of the wave was mixed with another sound—that of splintering wood. Holding her breath, seeming to wait an eternity before the water cleared, Regan stared fearfully up at the yardarm where David hung so tenaciously. When she could see at last, she smiled because the yardarm was still intact.

But her smile quickly receded when she saw what had broken. Above David's head was the maintop, a large platform where the men kept vigil. This platform had broken away on one side, part of it just over David's head, and from the way he lay without moving, it seemed to have hit him.

Regan clutched Travis to her, her hands holding tightly as she watched David's small, motionless figure high over her head.

She had no idea that Travis was watching her, studying the

fear on her face. She was aware of nothing until Travis pushed her away from him, wedged her body onto the deck, and clasped her hands about the heavy, anchored cannon. "Stay!" he commanded, before grabbing rope tied to the fife rail and wrapping it about his waist.

Terror of a new kind surged through Regan, a terror so great that no words would come out of her mouth, and her arms clutching the cold cannon were white with strain.

Scarcely daring to breathe, she watched Travis ascend the rigging, his feet and hands much more sure than David's, agile in spite of the size of him, or perhaps his strength was needed to hold him against the raging storm.

Each time a wave came over her and cut Travis from her view, Regan felt that she died a little bit. By the time he reached the yardarm, her body was as rigid as the iron of the cannon she gripped.

Cautiously, Travis crawled along the yardarm, straddling David when he reached him, leaning over, obviously shouting to the young man, but the fierce wind took the words away.

When David lifted himself and looked up at Travis, several of the sailors shouted encouragement. But Regan felt no relief whatsoever.

Travis and David seemed to talk for quite some time before Travis began moving forward, giving everyone more to fear as he passed David on the narrow projectile. Deftly and quickly, Travis lashed the splintering yardarm together, wrapping it tightly with the rope he carried. Twice he had to stop and cling to the pole as a wave threatened to pull him into the sea.

When he finished, he backed toward David, David handed him the rope from his waist, and Travis tied one end about his own waist. Now they were joined together for whatever fate awaited them in the long descent to the deck.

More talking was done as Travis seemed to be trying to persuade David to move from the piece of wood he held in a strangling grip.

Regan's heart almost stopped beating as she saw Travis pull on the rope, encouraging David to back toward the main mast. It was as if Travis had all the time in the world as he patiently waited for David to begin to move.

Slowly, each muscle at a time, David started backing up, and Travis guided the young man's feet onto the rope rigging. As if he were a child, Travis helped David, placed his hands and feet in the proper places, and once flung his arms across David, holding them both to the unsteady and flimsy rigging. When the wave passed, they started down again.

Regan began to breathe a bit when they were about twenty feet above the deck. She saw Travis shout at David, saw the young man shake his head, and heard Travis shout again until David nodded his head in agreement. David began to descend alone, Travis holding the rope about his waist, tying one end to the rigging.

Rising from her squatting position, Regan saw that Travis was making sure David was safe, that he was securely fastened so that if the next wave carried Travis over, he would go alone.

Guessing that as Travis glanced out to sea he saw something that the people below couldn't see, she watched, tears coursing down her face. Travis wrapped the rope around his powerful forearm; then, entangling his other arm in the rigging, he kicked out at David, whose head was now even with Travis's feet. David, unsteady and terrified, immediately lost his grip on the rigging, and his slight body swung away, falling for a few precious seconds before the slack was taken up in the hold Travis had on the rope about David's waist.

A high scream of terror escaped David before Travis began to lower him, and the sailors caught him, quickly pulling him to the deck.

But Regan's eyes never left Travis, who, as soon as he saw David was safe, dropped the rope and grabbed the rigging, ducking his head as if in protection. She left the cannon with one swift step, and that was as far as she got before the biggest wave of all hit them. The deck was flooded with cold, salty water, and in protest the ship threatened to turn over.

Regan slammed into the deck, rolled across it, and hit the fife railing with a bone-jarring jolt. Yet, in spite of her pain, all she was aware of was that above her she heard another horrible sound of wood cracking.

In spite of the angle of the deck and the rushing water, she grabbed the railing and tried to pull herself upward. A man's scream and a fleeting glimpse of a body sailing over her head and going past the deck rail did not deter her from her course. It was difficult to breathe, much less see, as she struggled to look up at the rigging where Travis hung.

Had she not been looking so hard, she would not have seen the blurry image of Travis as his hands lost their grip and he began to fall. His foot was caught in the rigging, and this saved him as he appeared to struggle for his senses and find the rope he needed to hold him fast.

The aftershocks of the big wave tossed the big ship like a child's top Regan clung and prayed and watched Travis struggling to hang on. She could see that something was wrong with him, that he was fighting more than the sea.

With one arm hooked about the rail, she wrenched a piece of rope as big around as her arm from the pins and then inched toward the bottom of the rigging.

All around her, men were shouting, and the wind and water played tricks with sounds, but Regan only saw Travis as he painfully lowered himself. Still holding on as best she could, she climbed up the rigging until she was able to touch Travis's foot.

Scared but knowing there was no other way, she wrapped the rope around his ankle and the rigging. The rope was too long and too big for her to knot properly, so all she did was wrap it, hoping she'd have time before the next wave came.

She was unprepared for the slash of a wave while hanging above the deck on just a bit of rope. She tangled her body in the rope and hung on for dear life.

After this wave, she was too frightened to move, and with her hand clasping the end of the big rope attached to Travis's ankle, she was afraid to open her eyes. She'd done all she could to save him, and now she couldn't bear to look to see if he was there or not.

It seemed to her a long time that she hung there, half-sitting, half-suspended, before she heard shouts below. Still afraid to open her eyes, she kept them wrenched shut.

"Travis!" came the clear call from below her, actually seeming quite near.

"Mrs. Stanford," called a voice that could only be the captain's.

With trepidation, she opened her eyes, still afraid to look to her left where Travis might or might not be.

Later, no one could remember who was the first to start laughing. Perhaps it wasn't a laughing matter, but the sailors were so relieved to have finally left the storm behind them, the last two waves having knocked the ship out of its path, that the sight above them was hugely entertaining.

Regan, ten feet above deck, was practically sitting in the rigging, clad only in a very wet muslin dress, her bare legs through the knotted rope squares wrapped tightly, hugging her own body, as were her arms. In one hand was an enormous rope attached to the leg of Travis, a man twice her size, who now lounged in the rigging as if he were sleeping. For all the world she looked like a little girl leading some sort of strange animal.

"Stop your yammering and get them down!" the captain bellowed.

Encouraged by their laughter, Regan dared to look toward

Travis, and at this close range she could see the blood seeping at the side of his head.

When three of the sailors had climbed to her and saw Travis's condition, they no longer laughed.

"You saved his life," one of them said, awe in his voice. "He's not even aware we're here. He couldn't have hung on without you tyin' him."

"Is he all right?"

"He's breathin'," the sailor said, but would say no more.

"No," she said when he touched her. "Get Travis down first."

Now that the seriousness of what Regan had done reached them, the sailors glanced up at her in amazement for a moment before turning away and respectfully not looking openly at her fine, bare legs.

With some dignity, Regan was able to descend the rigging with the help of a sailor. She was startled at how high up she'd gone and at the difficulty she had in getting down.

Finally on a solid surface again, she followed the men carrying Travis to their cabin. As they passed David's cabin, one of the men murmured that the young gentleman was sleeping. Regan only nodded as her thoughts were completely with Travis.

The ship's doctor came to Travis quickly and examined his head wound. "The maintop must have hit him when it broke away." The doctor turned appraising eyes toward Regan. "I hear you kept him from being washed overboard."

"Will he be all right?" she asked, not caring about his praise.

"No one can tell with these head wounds. Sometimes they live, but their minds never work again. All you can do is try to get him to drink water and stay quiet. I'm sorry I can't be of more help than that."

Regan only nodded as she smoothed Travis's wet hair from his forehead. The ship was still rolling frantically but seemed calm after the last several hours. Turning, she asked one of the sailors still in the room to get her some fresh water.

When she was alone with Travis, she started to work, undressing him first, which was no easy task considering the weight of Travis's inert body. Wrapping his naked body in dry, warm blankets that she got from a trunk, she stopped to answer a knock at the door.

Sarah Trumbull stood there. "One of the sailors came to get me, told me some wild story about you tying Travis to the sail. The man said Travis was hurt and you might need help. And he sent this."

Regan took the water she offered. "I don't need help," she said, her voice tight. "Maybe you can help the other passengers." She gave a brief nod toward David's closed door.

Sarah had only to look at the fear apparent on Regan's face to know that something was dreadfully wrong. "You have the prayers of everyone on board," she whispered, giving Regan's hand a quick squeeze.

Alone again with Travis, she began to bathe his head. The cut wasn't long, but it seemed to have been a hard knock as Travis was completely unconscious. Once he was clean and warm and he still didn't move, she stretched out on the bed beside him and cradled him in her arms, hoping to bring him back to life by sheer force of will.

Hours later she awoke, having fallen asleep from exhaustion, and her teeth were chattering with cold. She'd been unaware that she still wore her wet clothes. Travis lay still, deathlike, his skin pale, his vitality gone.

Rising quietly, she peeled away her sodden, cold dress and noticed absently that somewhere she'd lost her new wool cape and that the muslin gown was torn in several places. Poor Travis, she thought with a smile. He was going to have to buy her a new wardrobe before the first one was even finished.

The thought sent her hand to her mouth and tears to her eyes. Perhaps Travis wouldn't live to see her new clothes; perhaps he'd never wake up from his death-sleep. And all because of her! If she hadn't flirted with David, the young man wouldn't have felt compelled to show Travis that he was indeed a man. If only . . . she thought again but made herself stop.

Going to the chest, she pulled out a dress of heavy maroon corded silk, piped about the waist, neck, and cuffs with pink satin. Once dressed, she went to Travis again, bathing his cool face and washing the cut on his head which still seeped blood.

At midnight he began to move and thrash about on the bed, and Regan tried hard to restrain his flailing arms to keep him from hurting himself. Her strength was no match for his, so all she could do was throw herself on top of him, using her body weight to hold him.

By morning he grew tired again and seemed to fall asleep, although for the most part he kept his eyes closed. As the sun was entering through the window, Regan sat on the edge of the bed, her head on Travis's shoulder, and fell into a deep sleep.

What woke her was Travis's hand stroking her hair gently, calmly touching her hair and her neck. Instantly, she was fully awake, her head coming up to look at him and see if there was some lucidity in his gaze.

"Why are you dressed?" he asked hoarsely, as if that were the most important thing in the world.

She had no idea how rigidly she'd been holding her body for the last several hours, but now so much tension left her all at once that she was shaking, trembling. Great fat tears rushed to her eyes and glided down her cheeks. Not only was Travis going to get well, but his mind was unharmed.

He put a finger to her cheek, touched a tear. "The last thing I heard was the maintop breaking away. Did it hit me in the head?"

All she could do was nod, and the tears came harder. "Was that yesterday or the day before?"

"Before," she mouthed, the lump in her throat so large she couldn't speak.

Travis began to smile, winced once with pain, and then the smile returned. "So those tears are for me?"

Again, all she could do was nod.

His eyes closing once again, he kept smiling. "It was worth a little bump on the head to see my girl shed tears for me," he whispered before falling asleep.

Regan put her head back down on his chest and gave herself over to tears. She cried for all her fear at seeing Travis climbing after David, at having gone after Travis herself, and for the last several hours when she hadn't known whether he was going to live or die.

Travis was a wonderful patient, so wonderful in fact that Regan was exhausted within forty-eight hours. He took to being spoiled and pampered more easily than a new colt takes to walking. He wanted every meal spoon-fed to him by Regan, constantly needed her help in dressing, and wanted a sponge bath twice a day. Every time Regan suggested he try walking in order to regain his strength, Travis suddenly developed an even more severe headache than the one that plagued him constantly and needed Regan to run cool cloths over his forehead.

On the fourth day, when Regan was about to tell Travis she wished he had been washed overboard, she answered the door to find David Wainwright standing there.

"May I come in?" His arm was still bandaged, and there was a fading greenish bruise on his jaw.

With more strength than he'd shown in days, Travis sat up in bed. "Of course you can come in. Have a seat."

"No," David said quietly, not looking directly at Regan. "I came to thank you for saving my life."

Travis studied the young man for a moment. "I only did it out of shame because you made the rest of us look like cowards."

David's eyes widened, and he was well aware of the way he'd been paralyzed atop the yardarm and how Travis, patient even in the midst of the storm, had gotten him down to safety. Yet he also saw that Travis had no intention of repeating the story to anyone. David's shoulders straightened a little, and he gave a faint smile. "Thank you," he said, his eyes telling more than his words. Quickly, he left the cabin.

"How kind of you," Regan said, bending and kissing Travis's cheek.

His arm flew out and caught her about the waist. "Your aim's off," he growled, pulling her across him and kissing her on the mouth.

Regan's arms went around his neck, responding to him fully, her body well aware of the many days since she'd touched him in any way except an impersonal one. Pulling away from him, as his teeth gently chewed on her lower lip, she gave a deep chuckle. "An hour ago you were too weak to get out of bed."

"I still don't want to get out of bed, but it has nothing to do with weakness," he said, his hand at the back of her dress.

Instantly, she jumped out of bed. "Travis Stanford, if you tear another one of my lovely dresses, I'll never speak to you again."

"I don't care if you do speak to me," he said as he threw back the covers and showed her that he was more than ready for her.

"Oh my," she breathed, her hand unbuttoning buttons faster than anyone's hands ever had before or since.

Gleefully, naked, she sprung into bed with him, running her legs up and down his body, her face buried in the soft skin of his neck. She had waited quite a long time for him to return to her bed, and she was as ready as he was. Yet, when she tried to pull him on top of her, he wouldn't budge.

"No, my little nurse," he chuckled, and put his hands about her waist, lifting her like a doll and setting her on top of his manhood.

Gasping in surprise, it took Regan a moment to recover from her first sense of shock, but as Travis pushed her forward and took her breast in his mouth, her surprise gave way to delight. His hands ran up and down her back as his mouth teased the front of her. Never had she felt so many sensual areas touched at once. His strong hands moved back to her waist and lifted her, slowly, before setting her back down.

Regan did not think twice before she caught the rhythm herself. Her strong legs, muscled from walking about the constantly moving ship, moved her body up and down. She soon learned that she liked controlling the rhythm, fast or slow, bending to rub her breasts across Travis's chest, leaning over him, watching his handsome face turn to an angelic expression.

But her interest in watching him faded quickly, and as her passion mounted she began to move faster and faster. Travis grabbed her in a hard clasp and, never leaving her, rolled her onto her back, where he thrust hard and deep until the wave of release and delight swept over both of them.

Weak, he collapsed on top of her, his body coated in sweat, every muscle relaxed. Under him, Regan smiled and hugged him close. It added to her pleasure to have control over him, to be able to take someone as strong as Travis and turn him into this pliable, calm man atop her.

Still smiling, she fell asleep.

Chapter 10

REGAN LAY back against the cushions on the narrow bunkbed, weak and trembling, while Travis pressed a cold cloth to her forehead. Looking up at him in gratitude, she smiled as best she could. "What a time to get seasick," she murmured.

Travis said nothing as he picked up the chamber pot containing the contents of Regan's stomach and went out on deck to empty it.

Regan was quiet, too weak to move as she lay there in the bed. Personally, she felt that this new sickness had something to do with what was going on in her mind. Of course she couldn't mention it to Travis, but she was quite scared of arriving in America, of being on her own in a strange country with people whose language she sometimes had to strain to understand.

It had been nearly a month since the storm, and since then she'd done little except help Sarah sew on her new clothes. There were no more flirtations with David Wainwright, no more attempts to make Travis jealous. Instead she'd spent her time with Travis, eating with him, making love with him, and talking to him. She found he was a wonderful storyteller, entertaining her with long narratives about his friends in Virginia. There were Clay and Nicole Armstrong, of whom Travis told an extraordinary story of how Clay had been married to one woman, a

French aristocrat, and engaged to another woman. The way Travis told the story made Regan laugh until she cried, especially at the antics of Clay's niece and nephew.

He told her about his little brother, Wesley, and it took Regan days to figure out that Wes was a young man and not a child. Silently, she offered a prayer of support for any person who had to live under Travis's thumb. Then there were the Backes and all the other people up and down the river.

Regan listened with interest, adding to his stories with her imagination. Picturing these people, she conjured small, crude houses; the women in their simple calico gowns, even smoking corncob pipes; the men plain farmers hard at work in the fields. Smiling confidently, she hoped the people would not treat her as royalty merely because of the beautiful, expensive clothes she wore.

All of Travis's stories, and her own fantasies added to them, had made the long journey fly past, and it wasn't until this week that she'd begun to worry. She didn't know if the worry caused her vomiting or the other way around. All she knew was that suddenly she'd become very ill and weak, lying on the bunk, idly watching the ceiling, her stomach rolling.

Travis had been wonderful since she'd become ill, watching her quietly, holding her head over the pot, washing her face, and seeing that she rested. He'd even stopped working with the crew, not leaving her alone for more than a few minutes.

And Regan knew that all his attention was a way of saying goodbye to her. The pretty clothes and the last-minute attention were his final reward for the pleasure she'd given him on the voyage to America. Now he could be free of her, go back to his family and friends, and never have to see her again. No more would he have to put up with her flirting with other men, or her uselessness.

Tears began to trickle down her face. Why couldn't he have left her in England where at least she knew the customs of the people? Why did he have to force her to come to this strange place and then abandon her like so much rubbish?

She planned to tell him what she thought of him, but as soon as Travis returned to the cabin her stomach started heaving again, and her anger was abandoned.

"We've just sighted land," Travis said, holding her in his arms, her head cradled against his warm, comforting chest. "By this time tomorrow we should be docked in Virginia Harbor."

"Good," she whispered. "Perhaps I won't be seasick once we're on land."

This statement seemed to amuse Travis, who hugged her quickly and stroked her hair. "I think your seasickness will be over very soon."

The next few hours were a frenzy of activity. Sarah put the last of Regan's new clothes in the trunk, and Travis paid her and the other women who'd helped with the sewing. There were tears shed as Sarah and Regan said goodbye. Sarah planned to stay on the ship and travel north to New York to be with her family. All of the many women whose heads Regan had held got together and presented her with a gift of a child-sized quilt done in the Rose of Sharon pattern.

"We figured you'd need it soon," one woman said, her eyes teasing and glancing up at Travis.

"Thank you so much," Regan said, pleased more than the women could know, there being no way of telling them that they were her first friends.

That night she lay awake in Travis's arms, looking at him in the moonlight. She wished he hadn't come to mean so much to her, that she could hate him as she had once done or even find him contemptible, but now all she felt was an overwhelming loneliness that she was losing so much—this big, overpowering man whom she'd come to depend on, as well as other women who considered her a friend, who didn't think she was useless.

By the next morning she was deathly quiet. Doing her best to smile, she stood on the quarterdeck and waved goodbye to her friends, all of them glad to be off the ship, excited about coming home or entering a new land.

Travis had left her alone while he ordered the unloading of goods. When she'd awakened this morning, after sleeping very late, she'd found the ship already docked and some people already disembarked. After a quick kiss, Travis said he'd be busy until afternoon, explaining that the storm had blown them closer to America, and since they were several days earlier than expected no one was there to meet them.

Them! Regan thought with disgust as she watched Travis ordering some sailors in the stacking of crates.

"Mrs. Stanford?"

Turning toward the timid voice, she saw David Wainwright behind her. He looked thinner than she remembered, and his eyes darted to gaze at a space somewhere to the left of her head.

"I want to wish you and your husband the best of everything," he said quietly.

"Thank you," she said. His face showed all of the fear she felt, and she only hoped hers didn't look the same. "I hope we both like America more than we thought we would."

He wouldn't take her hint at the conversations they'd once shared; his embarrassment was too deep. "Tell your husband. . . ." He didn't seem able to finish but grabbed her hand, placed a hard kiss on it, met her eyes for a moment, gasped "Goodbye," and then was gone, hurrying down the gangplank.

Warmed by David's sentiments, she leaned over the rail and saw Travis frowning up at her. Raising her hand, she waved gaily at him and thought for the first time that perhaps she could make it alone in this new country. After all, she'd made friends on board ship. Perhaps. . . .

Travis gave her no more time to think, because minutes later he was telling her to hurry up and eat, to wear something sturdy, to finish putting her clothes in the trunk—in general, running her life.

He couldn't wait to get rid of her, she thought, obeying him but with a slowness Travis found maddening.

"Either you finish that in two minutes or I carry you out of here," he warned. "I have a wagon waiting for us, and I'd like to get there before sundown."

Her curiosity won out over her resentment. "Where are we going? Did . . . did you find me employment?"

Pausing, the trunk across his back, Travis grinned at her. "I found you a great job! One you're especially good at. Now, come on, let's go."

Using all her strength, Regan tried not to let his words upset her but followed him down the gangplank, her head held high.

He tossed the trunk into the ugliest, most dilapidated vehicle she'd ever seen.

"Sorry," he laughed at her obvious disgust. "I told you we were early, and this was all I could get. We're driving to a friend of mine's tonight, and tomorrow I'll borrow a sloop."

Nothing Travis said made sense to Regan. She knew a sloop was some sort of ship but didn't have any idea why Travis would want to borrow one. Grabbing her waist and plunking her down on the half-rotten wagon seat with as much ceremony as he'd used with the trunk, he climbed up beside her and clucked for the two tired-looking horses to go.

The country they traveled through looked wilder, more forbidding than England, and the road was atrocious, really little more than a rutted path. As her jarring teeth attested, Travis hit all of the ruts.

Chuckling, he watched her. "Now you see why we travel mostly by water. Tomorrow we'll be in a smooth little sloop, with no holes to fall into."

She had no idea where she'd be tomorrow as Travis seemed to want to keep her employer a secret—and she wasn't about to ask him for details, not when she knew her questions would earn that infuriating look of his.

The sun was just setting when they stopped at the first house they saw—a neat, clean, whitewashed little clapboard. Early spring flowers graced the front path, a warm breeze gently bending the colorful petals. It was a plain house but certainly of a higher caliber than Regan had expected in America.

Travis's knock was answered by a plump, gray-haired woman wearing a calico apron over her muslin dress. "Travis," she said. "We thought something was wrong. The man you sent said you'd be here hours earlier."

"Hello, Martha," he said, kissing her cheek. "It just took us longer than I thought. The Judge here?"

Martha laughed. "You're as impatient as ever. I take it this is the young lady."

Possessively, Travis put his arm around Regan. "This is Regan, and this is Martha."

Gulping once at Travis's crude manners, Regan held out her hand. "I am happy to meet you, Mrs.—?"

"Just Martha," she smiled. "You're in America now. Come into the parlor. The Judge is waiting for you."

Swept forward by Travis's arm around her, Regan was propelled into a pleasant room with clean, well-worn furniture covered in a soft green, the windows draped in a fabric of the same color. Before she could say any more, she was introduced to the Judge, a tall, nearly bald man who seemed to have no name besides Judge.

One moment Regan was shaking hands, and the next she heard the words, "Dearly Beloved, we are gathered here today in the sight of our Lord. . . ." Bewildered, thinking her hearing was faulty, she looked at the people around her. Martha was smiling angelically at her husband, who had a book open in front of him and was reading a marriage ceremony. Travis, holding her hand, had an astonishingly solemn look on his face.

It took Regan several minutes to realize what was going on. Without having been asked if she agreed, she was being married to Travis Stanford! She was standing in front of these strangers, wearing a dark green traveling dress of heavy linen, her face dirty, tired, her brow creased with worry about her future—and she was going through a marriage ceremony! Glancing up at Travis's solemn profile, she thought that for once he'd gone too far. When she got married, she was going to be asked, and she was going to wear her prettiest dress.

She realized that everyone was watching her. The Judge smiled and said, "Regan, wilt thou take this man for your husband?"

Looking up at Travis with the sweetest, most lovesick smile she could muster, she whispered, "No."

It was a moment before anyone reacted. Martha gave out a giggle that showed she knew Travis's domineering ways well, while the Judge hurriedly looked at his book. His face aflame with anger, Travis grabbed Regan's upper arm and half dragged her into the entrance hall, closing the parlor door behind him.

"Just what the hell was that little display supposed to mean?" he growled, his face very near hers.

Involuntarily taking a step backward, Regan tried to keep her courage up. She was in the right, and she had that on her side. "You never even asked me if I wanted to marry you. You didn't ask if I wanted to come to America either. I'm tired of your making all my decisions for me."

"Decisions!" he gasped. "There are no decisions to be made by either one of us. Fate has made them for us."

At her look of consternation, he groaned. "I'd try to shake some sense into you, but I'm afraid it'd hurt the baby."

"Baby?" she whispered.

Closing his eyes for a moment, Travis seemed to be praying

for strength. "You can't be so damned starry-eyed that you didn't realize that what we do in bed creates babies." At her silence, he continued in a quieter tone. "You didn't really think you'd been seasick these last few weeks, did you?"

Gently, he caressed her cheek. "Sweetheart, you're carrying my baby, and I make it a rule always to marry the mother of my children."

Stunned, Regan could form no coherent thoughts. "But employment," she whispered. "And I can't get married in this dress, and I have no flowers, and . . . and . . . oh Travis! A baby!"

Gathering her in his arms, he held her tightly. "I thought you knew. I thought you were just trying to keep it from me. I wouldn't have known either, except my friend Clay's wife threw up right in front of me one day. She told me a lot of women did that the first few months. Now, love," he said, lifting her chin. "Will you marry me?"

When she hesitated, he continued. "You can do all the work you want at my place," he smiled, "so you can satisfy any need you have to earn your keep. And as for your dress, I like you better wearing nothing, so whatever dress you wear is fine, and, besides, it's only Martha and the Judge here. For flowers I could pick some from Martha's garden."

"No," she whispered, blinking back tears. His words were so logical. Of course she was going to have a baby, and of course she'd marry him; there wasn't much else she could do because she knew she couldn't escape Travis when she had something he owned. As for her clothes, what did they matter? If she could get married without love, she could certainly do so without a pretty dress.

"I'm ready," she said grimly.

"It's not an execution," he chuckled. "Maybe tonight I can make up for today."

As she walked ahead of him into the parlor, she knew he'd never understand. A wedding was supposed to be a woman's greatest moment, a time when she felt everyone loved her and wished her great happiness. For the rest of her life she'd remember this secretive, dreary little ceremony, surrounded by strangers, the marriage taking place not because of herself but because of what she carried in her stomach. Mechanically, at the proper time, she said she would take Travis for her husband and ignored the searching look he gave her. When it came time for him to place a ring on her finger, Martha offered her own, but Regan shrugged and said politely that a ring didn't matter.

By the end of the ceremony no one was smiling, and when Travis turned to kiss her, Regan offered him her cheek. She barely tasted the wine the Judge offered and made no comment when Travis said they must leave.

Trying her best to smile, Regan bid them farewell and thanked them as Travis helped her back onto the wagon seat. The tension of the day, the wedding—if it could be called such—had exhausted her, and as she slumped in the seat Travis pulled her close to him.

"It wasn't much of a wedding, was it?" he asked heavily. "Not something a girl can tell her grandchildren about."

"No," she said simply, not daring to say any more or she'd start crying. All she wanted now was to go to sleep, and perhaps tomorrow she could think happy thoughts about her baby and about being Travis's wife.

By the time the wagon stopped, she was almost asleep, barely waking when Travis lifted her down and carried her up some stairs.

"Are we home?" she murmured.

"Not yet." His voice was serious, without its usual hint of laughter. "We're at an inn. In the morning we'll start home."

She merely nodded and snuggled against him. At least this was her wedding night. If Travis didn't know how a wedding should be conducted, at least he knew how to make the night the best a woman could imagine.

Lying on the bed where he'd left her, she listened as he carried their trunks up the stairs. Perhaps it wouldn't be so bad being married to Travis; at least now she didn't have to worry about being abandoned.

Smiling, she felt his warm lips on her cheek. "I'll be back in a little while," he murmured, sending little shivers down her spine. "You rest, because you're going to need it."

As the door closed behind him, she stretched, put her hands behind her head, and looked up at the ceiling, but she didn't really see it. Tonight was her wedding night. Last year one of the kitchen maids had gotten married, and the next day everyone teased her mercilessly, but the girl had been so radiant that nothing anyone said bothered her. Now Regan understood why.

Suddenly, she sat up. She may be expecting his baby and far from being a virgin, but tonight she certainly felt like one. With one adoring look directed toward the closed door, she thought how kind it was of Travis to give her this time alone to prepare herself. Hot water waited for her on the old dresser at the corner of the small room, and she guessed he must have sent someone ahead to prepare for them. He'd even left the keys to the trunks on the dresser.

Hurriedly, because she knew Travis would be an impatient bridegroom and wouldn't stay away very long, she opened her trunk and began to rummage through the beautiful clothes she and Sarah had sewed. Toward the bottom was a gown of gossamer silk with a bit of silver sheen to the surface. It was translucent, allowing just a hint of her hand beneath it to show through, revealing yet secretive. She'd been saving this lovely bit of moonlit silk for just such a time as this.

Quickly, she unbuttoned her linen dress, not dwelling on the fact that this traveling dress had been her wedding gown. At least she'd be able to wear something elegant for her wedding night. Naked, she began to wash, laughing all the while. Then she slipped into the gown, shivering in delight as the silk touched her skin. The feel of it was heavenly, soft, caressing, clinging to her curves in just the right places. Moving to the mirror, she was a bit startled to see the way her breasts impudently lifted the lovely fabric, the rosy crests barely visible yet somehow emphasized. Oh yes, she thought. Travis would love this gown.

Out of the trunk came the silver-backed hairbrush Travis had given her, and she pulled the pins from her hair, allowing it to cascade down her back, wispy curls about her face. She was glad she'd never cut her hair short as so many women had since the revolution in France. After only a few quick strokes of the brush, she hurried to the bed, knowing she'd taken long enough, feeling just as impatient as Travis must be.

Once in bed, she arranged herself in what she hoped was a seductive pose, half-reclining against the pillows, one arm extended, the other with fingertips grazing her shoulder. With what she hoped was a sophisticated look, she gazed languidly toward the door.

It was late and the inn was quiet, yet every time a board so much as creaked, she found herself smiling, imagining the look Travis would have when he came through the door. Each time she thought of him she arched her back a little more, thrusting her chest forward. She kept remembering how Farrell had said he dreaded the wedding night with her, that she'd probably cry and pout like a two-year-old. Tonight, although of course Farrell would never know about it, she'd prove him wrong. Tonight she'd be a temptress, a seductress, a woman who knew what she wanted—and got it. Travis would be on his knees, trembling like a bit of calves'-foot jelly, and she'd be his master.

Perhaps it was the awkward position of her back arched so far forward that first caused her pain; then she realized her arms ached and one side of her hip was asleep. Moving a bit, lowering her arm to her lap, she began to return from her dream world. She was a master at being able to escape from reality for long periods of time, and now she wondered how long she'd been in this position.

Glancing about the room, she saw there was no clock, and neither was there any moon outside the window—and the candle by the bed, which had been new, was inches shorter.

Where was Travis? she wondered, throwing back the covers and going to the window. Surely he couldn't believe she needed this much time to get ready for him. A bolt of lightning flashed and for an instant illuminated the empty courtyard below. Within minutes a soft rain began to fall, and Regan shivered as cold air came in through the poorly fitting window.

Getting back into the warmth of the bed, she looked about her, idly thinking that this room was very much like the one where Travis had held her prisoner in England. Then she'd been his slave, and now she was his wife. Of course, she had no ring, and the paper the Judge had signed was with Travis, but, she thought smiling, she had Travis's child and he'd certainly come back for that.

The thought that he might not come back made her frown. Why had she even let such an absurd idea cross her mind? Travis was an honorable man, and he'd married her.

Honorable, she murmured. Did honorable men kidnap women and take them to America against their will? He'd given her reasons for his forcing her to accompany him, but maybe all he'd really wanted was someone to warm his bed on the long voyage across the sea. And she'd certainly done that! They'd nearly set the bed on fire, and now she carried the product of that fire with her.

The rain started falling more heavily, lashing against the dark window, and with it Regan's despair began.

Travis had never wanted her. He'd said so himself a hundred times. Even once they were on board the ship, he'd still been trying to find out who she was so he could rid himself of her. He was the same as Farrell and her Uncle Jonathan—they'd never wanted her either.

The tears began to fall down her cheeks on a par with the turbulent rain outside. Why did he marry her? Had Travis somehow found out about her inheritance? He'd taken her to America, married her immediately, and now that he had that piece of paper and could claim her money he wanted nothing more to do with her. He'd abandoned her in a strange country with no money, no help, and maybe a baby to care for.

She began to cry furiously, fists beating into the pillow, sobs tearing through her. When her first passion was gone, the tears became slower, flowing out of her quietly as her anger turned to hopelessness as she asked herself why she was so unworthy of love.

The rain outside turned to a hard, steady downpour, and, after hours, her grief began to be lulled by the sound as she fell into a deep, deathlike sleep. When the first heavy steps sounded on the stairs she did not hear them, and it was only the pounding on the door that was finally able to wake her.

Chapter 11

"OPEN THIS damned door!" bellowed a voice that could only belong to Travis. Obviously he was unconcerned about waking the other occupants of the inn.

Her head feeling as heavy as a piece of granite, Regan tried to sit up, staring through her swollen eyes at the door that threatened to break under Travis's pounding.

"Regan!" Another shout came that sent her flying to the door.

Turning the knob, she said dazedly, "It's locked."

"The key's on the dresser," Travis replied, his voice heavy with disgust.

The door was barely open before Travis burst into the room—but Regan could hardly see him, for he was buried behind the most flowers she'd ever seen in her life. As an amateur gardener, she recognized many of them—tulips, daffodils, hyacinths, irises, violets, three colors of lilacs, poppies, laurel, and beautiful, perfect roses. There was no order to the flowers as they trailed behind Travis, hung down in front of him, some tied together in bundles, some loose and falling, a few covered in mud, others beaten by the rain. Even as he stood there, they fell about him like a colorful riot of lovely raindrops.

Going forward, scattering more flowers, walking on some, he

tossed the whole mass on the bed and exposed himself as a man covered in mud—and his face showed his anger.

"Damned things!" he said, pulling a bunch of violets from his shirt collar and throwing them onto the bed. "I never thought I could hate flowers, but tonight I may change my mind." As he removed his hat, water poured onto the floor. Disgustedly, he pulled three dwarf irises off his hat and tossed them with the others.

So far he had barely glanced at Regan, and his anger was so great that he didn't even notice her sheer gown or the way the early sunlight made her body glow beneath the gossamer silk.

Heavily, he sat down in a chair and started to remove his boots, but first he lifted himself and with a grimace removed a thorny rose from beneath him.

"All I planned was a simple trip north," he said as he pulled a boot off, pouring water out of it. "I have a friend who has a glasshouse, and he only lives five miles north of here. And of course a bride should have flowers, so I thought I'd just get you some."

Still, he didn't look up as he began removing his soaked, filthy coat. A flood of flowers fell from inside his jacket; crushed, falling apart, they cascaded to the floor.

Travis ignored them with a determined aloofness. "I was halfway there when it started to rain," he continued his story. "But I kept on, and when I got there my friend and his wife got out of bed and personally cut the flowers for me. They cleaned out the garden and the glasshouse."

His shirt, soaked to his skin, came off next, and more flowers drifted to the already considerable pile at his bare feet.

"It was on the way back that the trouble started. The damned horse threw a shoe, and I had to walk in that strip of mud Virginia calls a road. I couldn't stop and have a new shoe fitted and miss my own wedding night."

Fascinated, Regan could only watch him, her heart beginning to heal with every word he spoke.

"Then lightning flashed, and the horse reared and knocked

me in the mud. If that animal lives two more days, it won't be because I allow it," he threatened. "I would have let it go, but the damned flowers were on the saddle, so I had to spend two hours in the storm looking for that animal, and when I found it the saddle was gone."

Angrily, he stripped off his pants. "Another hour went by before I found the saddle and all these ... these...." he said, pulling what was left of a peony from his pants and giving a crooked smile as he slowly crushed it before letting it drop. "The bags were broken, and there was no way to carry them, so I started stuffing them wherever I could." His eyes locked with hers for the first time. "There I was, a grown man, standing in the middle of one of the worst storms of the year, filling my clothes with these thorny, itchy, smelly flowers. Do you know how much a fool I felt like, and what the hell are you crying about?" he said in the same breath and tone.

Picking up a slightly damaged and very wet rose from the bed, she held it to her nose. "A bride should have flowers," she whispered. "You did this for me."

Bewilderment and exasperation showed on Travis's wet face. "Why else would I go out on a night like this, on my own wedding night, for God's sake, unless it was for my bride?"

Regan couldn't answer, just kept her head down, tears beginning to flow.

After a moment's silent thought, Travis came to her, lifted her chin in his hand, and studied her face. "You've been crying a lot," he said quietly. "You didn't think I was coming back, did you?"

Jerking away from him, she walked to the head of the bed. "No, of course not. It's just—"

A soft chuckle from Travis made her turn. He was naked, standing like some god of old in a wealth of fragrant flowers, and she began to smile too. He had returned to her, and he'd gone to a great deal of trouble to give her what she wanted.

Travis's eyes, looking at her in the sheer gown, turned hot

with desire. "Don't I get a reward for all my work?" he whispered, opening his arms to her.

With one giant leap, Regan flew at him, her arms going about his neck, her legs around his waist.

Surprised for a moment, Travis caught her. "How could you think I'd leave you after all the trouble I've gone through to get you?" he murmured before fastening his lips to hers.

The feel of his bare skin, cool and damp between her legs, made her shiver with pleasure as she tightened her legs about his middle until she threatened to sever him in half. Only the thin bit of silk between them kept their skin apart as she rubbed against him, her breasts nearly crushed by the hard mass of his chest.

Her hands went to his hair, pulling on the wet thickness of it, her fingers disappearing into it as her lips made a hot trail across his mouth. He was here; he'd come back to her, and he was her husband, hers to do with as she wanted.

In glee, feeling powerful, she bit his earlobe much too hard.

Within an instant she found herself pulled from Travis and being flung through the air, landing in an explosion of flowers of hundreds of shades and hues and a swirl of delicate silk. Brushing four daffodils off her face, she smiled up at Travis as he stood over her, hands on hips, muscles bulging, manhood towering.

"Now that's the way a bride should look."

"Stop talking and come here," she laughed, holding her arms up to him.

But instead of going to her, he knelt and kissed her toes, one by one, his tongue teasing the soft pads. His hot mouth moved to the bottoms of her feet, and as he raked his teeth along the arch she jumped as a nerve inside her tightened, jolting her entire body.

Travis laughed, a deep rumbling sound that touched her foot, traveled up her leg, and reverberated in the center of her being.

"Travis," she gasped, lifting herself and reaching for him. Flowers under her crackled and released their heady fragrance.

But he ignored her as his lips moved upward to her knees, exploring, kissing, caressing.

Regan, ready for him, actually eager for him, felt she would go insane as he toyed with her senses. His mouth tortured one leg, and as if that weren't enough, his hand, so strong yet so sensitive, caressed the muscles of the other leg until she was weak with helplessness. Yet at the same time she felt like a tigress, wanting to claw and bite, wanting to tear at this man who threatened her sanity.

When he reached the center of her with his hands and lips, she nearly screamed, rolling her head in agony at what he was doing.

"Please, Travis, please," she begged.

Within seconds he came to her, his mouth hard on hers, but no harder than hers as she attempted to devour all of him. When he entered her, she arched high, completely off the bed, supporting him, needing him, using her hips to drive him onward.

His passion was as great as hers and his need as violent. After only a few powerful, deep, filling thrusts, his body jerked, and he clutched her to him in a bone-crushing hug as spasms racked both their bodies.

It was several moments before Regan realized she couldn't breathe, that Travis seemed to be trying to pull her inside him, and that she wanted him to.

As he relaxed his grip but still held her, his face buried in her neck, she opened her eyes and saw a long line of crushed flower petals clinging to his sweaty skin. Turning her head, breathing deeply of the lovely fragrance, she began to laugh as she put out her hand, grabbed some flowers, and playfully tossed them into the air.

One eyebrow lifted, Travis moved to look at her. "And what is so amusing?" he asked.

"Flowers for the bride!" she laughed gaily. "Oh Travis, I meant a bouquet, not a whole garden."

Leaning across her, he grabbed a handful, catching the flowers upside down and sideways, and he held out the funny bouquet. "I'm sure you could find what you wanted in this."

She moved out from under him, rolling in the flowers, tossing clumps into the air, and then began pelting him with them. "She wants flowers," Regan laughed in a mock deep voice. "I'll give her flowers. Oh Travis, everything you do is so . . . so big!" she laughed, trying for the right word. "Everything is so oversized, blown out of proportion, overpowering, domineering." Sitting up, watching him, looking at that magnificent body reclining lazily on a bed of flowers, her heart seemed to turn somersaults.

"Perhaps," she said in a cat-soft voice, "not all of you is overpowering all the time."

After a sharp intake of breath, Travis grabbed her by a handful of silk, but a short, sharp scream from Regan stopped him.

"Don't you tear one more piece of my clothing," she warned, but flung the silk gown off before he could disobey her.

"Orders and taunts," he said, his eyes narrowing as he lifted himself up onto all fours and began to stalk her like some great beast of prey.

With a squeal of delight, Regan backed away from him, bombarding him with flowers as he slowly came toward her. When she was backed against the wall, she threw her hands up in surrender. "Oh, kind sir," she said in mock fear. "Do what you will with me, but do not take my virtue."

Her skin alive, anticipating Travis's delicious pounce, she was startled when he uttered a heartfelt "Damn!"

Turning her head, she saw that he'd sat up, holding his knee. "How can you crawl around on these damned things without injury? Look at that! Have you ever seen a thorn that big?"

Regan burst into laughter so hard her stomach threatened to split. Her knees drawn up, she rolled in laughter.

Pulling the thorn from his knee and angrily tossing it onto the floor, he gave her a nasty glare. "I am glad I afford you some amusement."

"Oh Travis," she cried. "You are so, so romantic."

He stiffened at her sarcasm, his mouth turning into a straight line. "Why the hell did I get you all these goddamn flowers if I wasn't the very soul of romance?" he demanded seriously.

This statement, and especially the way he said it, sent Regan into new spasms of laughter, and it took some minutes before she became aware that she was hurting his feelings. He really had tried, she admitted to herself. It wasn't his fault if he didn't understand that a bunch of violets was often more romantic than enough flowers to fill a wagon. She'd said she wanted flowers, and he had gotten them for her. And neither was it his fault that a thorn in his knee forced him to interrupt a lovely little romantic game.

As he started to leave the bed, she put her hand on his shoulder and swallowed her laughter. "Travis, the flowers are lovely. I really do like them." When he didn't respond and she saw the muscles standing rigid on his neck, she really was sorry that she'd laughed. He'd done what he did to please her, and all she did was laugh.

"I'll wager I can make you stop being angry with me," she whispered, nuzzling his ear, her teeth running along the cartilage edge, her tongue touching the lobe. "Maybe if I kiss your sore knee, it will stop hurting," she murmured, running her lips down his arm.

"It might," Travis said, his voice especially deep. "I'd sure like to try it."

Regan, aware of how he'd tried to please her, wanted to please him. Pushing him gently, she found he was putty in her hands, and the look of wonder and pleasure on his face was intriguing. The strength of him surrendering to her was a powerful feeling.

Beginning at his knee, her lips traveled upward, her hands trailing behind, massaging his leg, glorying in the great muscle there. When she reached the center of him, Travis groaned, whispering her name. With one fluid motion he pulled her up in the bed, his eyes black and hot as he roughly threw her down beside him and mounted her in moments. He was not his usual, calm self, but a man driven beyond endurance with his blinding lust.

His violent need of her was exciting, especially because she knew she'd driven him to it. Lifting her body under him as if she were a rag doll, he thrust hard and long, pulling her, pushing her—owning her.

When at last the fury died in one massive flash, Regan was limp, weak from the raw tempest of their wild, savage lovemaking. Exhausted, they fell asleep in each other's arms.

"Get up!" Travis commanded, slapping her firm, lovely buttocks. "If we don't get started, we'll never make it to Clay's house, and if you think I'm going to spend a night on that little sloop with you, you're wrong."

Having no idea what he was talking about, she didn't make a comment but pushed her hair out of her eyes and pulled a tulip petal from where it was stuck to her cheek. "Why wouldn't you spend the night on a ship with me?" she asked idly, sitting up, feeling dazed and drained—but happy.

"It's not a ship," he answered, "but a tiny little boat, and we'd probably sink it with your acrobatics."

"My—?" she began, trying to look haughty, but sitting naked in the midst of the large pile of crushed flowers, her cheeks pink, her eyes liquid and lazy, she couldn't look like more than a tempting little wood-sprite.

Travis, his cheeks covered with shaving soap, looked at her in the mirror, and his glance made her smile and start to lean back on the bed. "Oh, no you don't," he cautioned, immediately changing his look to a threatening one. "If you don't get out of that bed this minute, I'll see that we have separate bedrooms at my house."

That absurd threat made her laugh, but just the same she got up and began to wash. She felt so good that she couldn't seem to do anything in a hurry, yet Travis wouldn't help her get dressed but stood to one side impatiently waiting for her.

When at last she was ready to leave, he half-pushed her down the stairs and to a chair where an enormous American meal awaited her. Travis set to the food like a starving man, grumbling that he never got regular meals anymore and that she was wearing him out in the prime of life, but his eyes danced with merriment.

In very short order their trunks were stowed on the little boat, they were heading up the James River toward Travis's home, and Regan began bombarding him with questions. Before, she had fought so hard against going to America that she hadn't thought much about where Travis lived.

"Is your farm very large? Do you plow the fields yourself, or do you have employees? Is your house as nice as where the Judge and Martha live?"

Looking at her in bewilderment for a moment, Travis began to smile. "My . . . ah . . . farm is a good size, and I do have a few employees, but I sometimes plow my own fields. And I believe my house is rather nice, but then maybe that's because it's mine."

"And you built it with your own hands," she said dreamily, trailing her hand in the water. Perhaps in a simple country like this, her lack of experience in household management wouldn't be so devastating. Farrell had said he knew she couldn't manage his estate, and she was sure he was right. But with a little place like Travis's, maybe a one- or two-room house, she could manage.

The increasing warmth of the sun and the pleasant thoughts soon made her drop off to sleep.

Quite a while later, she woke with a start as a shot rang out over her head. Practically falling into the water, she jumped and saw Travis holding a smoking pistol pointed toward the sky.

"Did I wake you?" he asked.

From the excitement on his face, she knew something was about to happen and didn't answer his silly question. Stretching her cramped body, she looked around as Travis reloaded the pistol, but all she saw was the river and the lush greenery on each side.

"We're near Clay's place," he said as he fired into the air again.

After a glance at the dense trees around them, she wondered how anyone could build a house there, but even as she thought it she saw the trees abruptly stop just ahead on the left.

Protruding into the water was a large wooden wharf with two boats, both bigger than the one they rode in, and as they sailed closer many buildings came into view. There were large and small houses, gardens, fields neatly plowed, workers everywhere, horses, wagons, and in general a great deal of activity.

"Is your house in this town also?" she asked as Travis maneuvered them toward the wharf.

A low chuckle she didn't understand came from Travis. "This isn't a town. It's Clay's plantation."

To her knowledge, she'd never heard the word before. As she opened her mouth to start asking questions, she was interrupted as a squeal of children's laughter took Travis's attention. Quickly, he leaped from the boat and hauled Regan onto the wharf after him, just in time to catch two of the prettiest children she'd ever seen.

"Uncle Travis!" they laughed as he twirled them about. "Did you bring us anything? Uncle Clay was getting worried about you. What's England like? Mama had two babies instead of one, and we have a new litter of puppies."

"Mama, is it?" Travis laughed.

The boy gave his sister a disdainful look. "She means Nicole. Sometimes it's hard to remember that she's not our mother."

Close behind the children came a man, tall and slim, with

dark hair and eyes, sharp cheekbones, a look of great happiness on his face. "Where the hell have you been?" the man demanded, holding out his hand to Travis and then hugging him exuberantly.

"I'm weeks early, and you damn well know it!" Travis answered. "No one was there to meet me, and I had to store my goods and borrow this sorry excuse for a boat."

Gesturing offhandedly toward the boat, Travis caused Clay to notice Regan, who was standing quietly on the edge of the wharf. But before the man could ask any questions, Travis gave a long sigh.

"Here's who I wanted to see." Hurrying forward, he caught a deliciously pretty young woman in his arms, kissing her heartily on the mouth. Instantly, the other man's attention left Regan and went to the two of them. He seemed to be working at controlling some inner emotion.

Within moments Travis was leading the woman toward the wharf. "I have someone I want you to meet," he was saying.

At close range the woman was even prettier than from a distance, with a heart-shaped face, big brown eyes, and a sensual mouth. After a quick assessment, Regan saw she was wearing a dress of deep purple muslin, with tiny green ribbons under the high waist. So much for wanting to show the Americans the new fashions! This woman's gown could be worn at court.

"This is my wife Regan," Travis said gently, looking at Regan with pride. "And this is Clayton Armstrong and his wife Nicole. And these scamps," he grinned, "are Clay's niece and nephew, Alex and Mandy."

"How do you do?" Regan said quietly, still puzzled by these people. They were far from her idea of what Americans were like.

"Won't you come to the house?" Nicole said. "You must be tired, and I doubt if Travis has let you rest much."

To that, Travis snorted and Regan held her breath, hoping he wouldn't say something crude.

When Regan merely followed Nicole docilely, Nicole smiled. "It's a bit overwhelming, isn't it?"

Regan was looking about her, trying to understand just what sort of place she was in.

A big, broad, blonde woman came running toward them, her skirts lifted high above her ankles. "Was that Travis what just come in?" she shouted before she even reached them.

"Yes, and this is his wife Regan. Regan, this is Janie Langston."

"Wife?" Janie asked, surprised. "He did do it! That Travis is a wonder. He said he was going to England and bring back a wife. Honey," she said, putting her hand on Regan's arm. "You got your work cut out for you being Mrs. Travis Stanford. I hope you got courage enough to stand up to him."

With that, she started running toward the wharf.

Chapter 12

"WHO ELSE lives here?" Regan asked Nicole.

"Quite a few people, really. There are field workers, weavers, the dairy people, gardeners—all the people needed to run a plantation."

"Plantation." Regan whispered the strange word. They were entering a long row of box hedges, and her view of the buildings around them was obscured. "Travis said you were going to have a baby, and the children said something about two babies."

A lovely smile crossed Nicole's face. "Twins seem to run in Clay's family, and four months ago I had two boys. Come inside, and I'll gladly show them to you."

Looming above them was a large brick house, about the same size as Weston Manor. Regan hoped shock wasn't showing on her face. Of course there were wealthy people in America too, and of course some of them would have mansions. It was just that in England people spoke of America as being so young that there hadn't been time to really build much of anything.

Inside the house, the rooms were startlingly lovely, large, spacious, the furniture upholstered in silk, the wallpaper hand-painted, portraits on the walls. Fresh-cut flowers graced tables and desks.

"Shall we go into the drawing room? I'll bring the children down."

Left alone in this room, Regan was further amazed at the elegance of it. A Sheraton desk with delicate inlay was against one wall, a gold-framed mirror above it. Facing it was a tall cabinet of leather-bound books.

She'd only known Weston Manor, and by comparison the English house was shabby and poor. Here everything sparkled with cleanliness and care. There was no chipped woodwork, worn upholstery, or scuffed surfaces.

Her attention left the room's furnishings when Nicole returned, a baby in each arm. At first Regan was afraid to hold either one of the children, but Nicole persuaded her she could do it. Within moments Regan had the little boy smiling and cooing back at her, hardly noticing when Travis entered and sat beside her on the sofa. They were alone in the room.

"Think we could make two at a time?" he asked quietly, taking the baby's hand and letting him grip his finger.

The expression on Travis's face as he watched the baby was one of joy. "You really want a child, don't you?" she asked.

"For a long time," he said seriously, then added with his usual bluntness, "I never much wanted a wife, but I could surround myself with children."

Frowning, Regan wanted to ask him why he'd saddled himself with a wife now, but she knew the answer. He wanted the child she carried. Later she would show him that she was of more use than for breeding stock. Together they'd work and build up his farm. Perhaps it would never be as nice as the Armstrong plantation, but someday it could be very comfortable.

"What do you think, Travis?" Clay asked from the doorway, his chest expanded several inches in pride, Mandy by his side, Alex behind him, and the second baby in the crook of his arm. Regan thought he looked as happy as anyone alive.

"Clay," Travis began. "How did those new cows work out? And did you have any mold on last year's hay?"

As the two men seemed to want to talk business and both of

them were happy with the babies, Regan handed Travis the baby she held and stood up. Travis showed no qualms about taking the child, unlike Regan who'd been afraid she'd drop him. "I think I'll find Nicole," she said, and Clay gave her directions to the kitchen. Outside the room she heard Clay say, "She's prettier than I ever thought you could get," to which Travis only snorted.

Her head held high, she went through the flower-bedecked hallway and out the back door, turned left, and headed for the kitchen, which was in a separate building. Inside the big room everyone was bustling about, and Nicole, her arms covered in flour, was directing all of it. When a young girl accidentally dropped a basket of eggs, shells and all, into a bowl of batter, it didn't upset Nicole at all. Two children, dressed plainly but cleanly, ran through the building, and Nicole just caught a pail of milk before it overturned. Even as she righted it, she looked up, saw Regan, and smiled warmly.

Wiping her hands on her apron, she came forward. "I'm sorry I had to leave you, but I wanted to see that a nice supper was prepared for you."

"Is it always like this?" Regan asked, half in horror.

"Most of the time. There are an awful lot of people to feed." She started to untie her apron. "I need to cut some herbs, and maybe you'd like a little tour before supper. If you're not too tired."

"I slept most of the way here," Regan smiled. "And I'd love to see the . . . the plantation."

Later, Regan didn't believe anything could have prepared her for what Nicole showed her. A man hitched a two-wheel wagon for them, and Nicole drove them about the plantation, pointing out each of the dependencies. Regan had been right in her first estimation. The plantation was a village of sorts, but all owned by one man. Nearly everything needed for living was made, grown, or caught on the plantation. Nicole pointed out the dairy, dovecote, loom house, stables, tannery, and carpenter shop, and around the kitchen was a smokehouse, malt house, and wash house. Nicole showed her the acres and acres of fields planted with cotton, flax, wheat, and tobacco. And across the river was a mill where their grain was ground. Cattle, sheep, and horses grazed in separate areas.

"And you manage all of this?" Regan asked in wonder.

"Clay helps some, too," Nicole laughed, "but, yes, it takes a lot of work. We don't get away much, but then we don't have to since everything we could ever want is right here."

"You're very happy, aren't you?"

"I am now," Nicole answered. "But it hasn't always been easy." Her eyes went to the mill across the river. "Clay and Travis have been friends since they were boys, and I hope we'll be friends too."

"I have never had a girlfriend," Regan said, looking at this woman who was the same small size she was. They had no idea what a striking pair they made, Nicole with her black hair, and Regan's dark brown with its red-gold highlights.

"Neither have I," Nicole said. "Not a real girlfriend I could talk to and confide in." With a smile she flicked the reins, and the horse started to move. "Someday, when we have a lot of time, I'll tell you how I met Clay."

Blushing, Regan thought that she could never, never tell anyone how she met Travis. For one thing, no one would believe her story.

"I'm hungry. How about you?" Nicole asked. "And I can feel that those babies of mine are about to starve."

"And without a doubt Travis is hungry," Regan laughed.

"Is she as young as she looks?" Clay asked, jostling his son on his arm and looking through the window at Nicole and Regan pulling away from the house in the buggy.

"Would you believe I don't know how old she is? And that is one question I'm afraid to ask. It'd be my luck that she'd turn out to be sixteen."

"Travis, what on earth are you talking about? How did you meet her? Couldn't you have found out from her parents how old she was?"

Travis had no intention of telling the story to anyone. Years ago, when Clay's older brother James was alive, he might have confided in him, but now he couldn't bring himself to tell of kidnapping his wife.

Clay seemed to understand, for there were things he didn't want to tell about himself—and what had gone on between him and Nicole. "Is she always so quiet? I don't mean to pry, but the two of you seem an incongruous pair."

"She can hold her own," Travis smiled, eyes twinkling. "To tell you the truth, I don't know what she's like. She seems to change every minute. One moment she's a little girl with dreams of romance, and the next she's. . . ." His voice trailed off as he remembered early this morning, her lips moving up his inner thigh. "Whatever she is, I find her fascinating."

"And what about Margo? I don't believe she's going to be too happy to welcome your little wife."

"I can handle Margo," Travis said in dismissal.

Old memories, only half-healed, clouded Clay's eyes. "Watch her with your wife. A woman like Margo eats sweet little things like Regan for breakfast. I know," he added softly.

"Margo can't do a damned thing, and I'll let her know it. I'll be around to protect my wife, and Regan ought to know what I feel about her. I married her, didn't I?"

Clay didn't say any more. There was a time when people had given him advice, but he hadn't listened, and he knew how easily marriage vows could be made—and just as easily broken.

* * *

That night, as Regan slipped into the canopied bed beside her husband, she told him some of her impressions of the day. "I never knew anything like this existed. It's as if Clay and Nicole were the sole owners of an entire town."

He pulled her close to him. "Then you like our plantation system?" he murmured, relaxing into sleep.

"Of course, but I am glad there aren't many of them. I don't see how Nicole can run a place this size. Thank heavens you are just a poor farmer."

When she received no reply, she looked over at Travis and saw that he was asleep. Smiling, she snuggled closer to him and drifted into a quiet, gentle sleep.

The next morning parting was surprisingly difficult as they all stood on the wharf and said goodbye. Nicole promised to visit Regan very soon and to give her any help she could. Clay and Travis exchanged comments about this year's crops, and then all too soon they were climbing into the little boat and heading upriver.

Regan found she was very excited about seeing the place where Travis lived and wondered if it could possibly be as big and wild and crude as he was. She hoped she could refine his home as she wanted to refine him.

After a while of slow, easy sailing, they came to another break in the trees. An enormous wharf with more ships could be seen in the distance.

"This isn't another plantation, is it?" she asked, moving to stand beside Travis. This looked many times larger than Clay's place, so surely this was a town.

"It certainly is!" Travis said with a big smile.

"Do you know the owners of this place?" As they sailed nearer she could see that this plantation looked like a blown-up version of Clay's. By the wharf was a building as large as Clay's house. "What is that?" she pointed.

"It's the ship's store and the warehouse. The captains can replace sails and damaged gear at the store, and goods waiting transport are stored in the warehouse. The assessor's house is that smaller building."

There were three small craft tied at the wharf, two barges, and four shallops as Travis called them. To her bewilderment Travis steered the little boat to this wharf.

"I thought we were going home," she said in consternation. "Do you want to see friends here?"

Travis leaped onto the wharf and pulled her up before she could say another word. Taking her chin in his warm hand, he lifted her face to meet his. "This," he said quietly, his eyes locked on hers, "is my plantation."

For a moment she was too stunned to speak. "All . . . all of it?" she whispered.

"Every blade of grass. Now come on and let me show you your new home."

Those were the last words they were allowed each other before a mob of people descended on them. Shouts of "Travis!" and "Mr. Stanford!" echoed from one building to another. Travis never released Regan's hand as he shook hands with what seemed like hundreds of people who came running from every corner of the plantation. And he introduced her to every person, saying this man was head carpenter, this one the second assistant gardener, this woman third upstairs maid. On and on the list went, and all Regan could do was to stand and nod at them while her mind kept repeating, They are all employees. They all work for Travis—and for me.

Somewhere during all the introducing, Travis declared the day a holiday, and before long the field hands were coming to greet Travis too. Great, thick, muscle-bound men came laughing and smiling, teasing Travis that he'd probably gotten soft while he was away. A swift wave of pride shot through Regan as she saw that none of the men was any more muscular than her husband.

As they started walking away from the river, greeting people along the way, some of the employees began asking questions. It seemed that half the plantation was falling apart.

"Where's Wes?" Travis demanded, walking so fast Regan was nearly running.

"Your Uncle Thomas died in Boston, and Wes had to go to straighten out his affairs," said a man who was an overseer.

"And what about Margo?" Travis frowned. "She could have handled some of these problems."

"About twenty of her cows are down with some sort of disease," the man answered.

"Travis," said a sturdy, red-haired woman. "Three of the looms are down, and every time I tell a man to fix them he says it's not his job."

"And Travis," another woman said. "The Backes have some new chickens from the East. Could you authorize some money to buy some?"

"Travis," said a man smoking a pipe. "Something's got to be done about that smallest sloop. Either it has to be repaired or scrapped."

Suddenly, Travis stopped and held up his hands. "All of you stop right here. Tomorrow I'll answer all your questions. No!" he said, his eyes lighting and reaching for Regan's hand. "I have a wife, and tomorrow she'll take over the women's duties. Carolyn, you ask her about the looms, and Susan, you ask my wife about chickens. I'm sure she knows more about them than I do."

Regan was glad Travis was holding her hand, because otherwise she might have turned and run away. What did she know about looms and chickens?

"Now," Travis continued. "I plan to show my bride my house, and if I get asked one more question today I will call off the holiday," he said in mock fierceness.

If Regan hadn't been so depressed, she would have laughed at the speed with which the people left them, all except for one old man standing quietly in the background.

"This is Elias," Travis said with pride. "He's the best gardener in Virginia."

"I brought something for your new missus," Elias replied, and held out a flower such as Regan had never seen before. It was a shade of purple that was at once bright and soft. The center was a sort of frilled horn with large tear-shaped petals behind it.

Putting out her hand, she was almost afraid to touch it.

"It's an orchid, ma'am," said Elias. "The first Mrs. Stanford had them brought to her whenever the captains went to the South Seas. Maybe you would like to see the glasshouses when you have time."

"Yes," she answered, wondering if this place of Travis's did without anything. After thanking him, she followed Travis as he kept walking away from the river, and for the first time she noticed the tall, sprawling brick house rising before them. Even from this distance it looked as if you could put Weston Manor and Clay's Arundel Hall in one wing.

Travis was proudly bragging about the house he obviously loved, telling her how his grandfather had built it and how all the Stanfords loved it. But with each step Regan's fear grew. Nicole's responsibilities had seemed overwhelming, but now she was wishing she was going to be living in a small place like that. How was she going to manage this monstrous house, let alone the other duties Travis seemed to expect of her?

The house, when they reached it, was larger than it seemed. A massive square center section of brick, four and a half stories high, towered over her, with two L-shaped wings radiating to each side. Travis led her up wide stone stairs to the first floor and once inside began the hurried tour of his extensive house.

He took her through a blue room, a green room, a red room, and a white room and showed her the schoolroom and housekeeper's room. Storage rooms were as large as her bedroom at Weston Manor.

With each room—each exquisitely furnished, beautiful room—Regan's fear climbed higher in her throat. How could she possibly manage a place the size of this?

Just when she thought she'd seen every room a house could contain, Travis half-dragged her up the east stairs. The rooms on this second, main floor put the ones below to shame. There was a dining room with an attached parlor for ladies' teas, another parlor for the family, a library for the men, two more sitting rooms for whatever anyone wanted them for, and an enormous bedroom with an attached nursery.

"Ours," Travis said, before pulling her into the ballroom.

Here, Regan was stunned. She'd said very little since they'd entered the house, but now she felt her legs give way under her. Collapsing onto a sofa in the corner, she stared in awed silence.

If nothing else, the sheer size of the room would have been overwhelming. Seventeen-foot-high ceilings made one feel small, insignificant. The walls were paneled, painted the palest blue, and the oak floors were polished to a gleam. There seemed to be a great many pieces of furniture—six couches covered in rose-brocaded satin, innumerable chairs with seats upholstered to match, a harp, a pianoforte, and numerous tables—but they were all set about the border, leaving the floor open, covered in a long rug from the Orient.

"Of course we roll up the rug when we have parties," Travis said proudly. "Maybe you'd like to give a party. We could invite a couple of hundred people to spend the night, and you and Malvina—she's the cook—could plan all the food. You'd like that, wouldn't you?"

It was all much too much. Tears in her eyes, her stomach aching, Regan ran through the ballroom toward the opposite door. She had no idea how to even get out of the house as she ran down a long passageway, finally opened a door, and fled into a lovely, small, blue and white room. She couldn't even remember all the names of the rooms, much less where they were.

Flinging herself to the floor, her head in her arms on the seat of a blue and white couch, she began to cry. How could he do this to her? How could he not have told her?

Within seconds Travis was beside her, pulling her into his arms as he sat on the couch. "Why are you crying?" he asked in a voice of such longing and hurt that she began to cry harder.

"You're rich!" she blurted, tears closing her throat.

"You're crying because I'm rich?" he asked in astonishment.

Even as she tried to explain, she was sure he'd never, never understand. Travis was so sure he did everything right; it had never occurred to him to doubt that he could accomplish anything. He didn't know what it was like to be useless. Now he expected her to manage the house, the dependencies, servants, and, by the by, give a party for a couple of hundred friends.

"I can't help you if you don't tell me what's wrong," Travis said, handing her his handkerchief. "You surely can't be angry because I'm not some poor farmer."

"How . . . ," she sobbed. "How can I . . . ? I've never even seen a loom!"

It took Travis a moment to piece that together. "You don't have to do the weaving; just tell someone else to do it. The women will bring their problems to you, and you'll fix them," he said. "It's all very simple."

She would never make him understand! Jumping out of his arms and off his lap, she ran from the room, down the passage, back into the ballroom, through it, and into another passage, until at last she found their bedroom and collapsed on the bed in a flurry of muslin dress and petticoats.

Even over her sobs she could hear Travis's slow, heavy footsteps as he approached. Pausing at the doorway, he seemed to study her for a moment before deciding that she needed to be left alone. As his steps retreated she began to cry harder.

Hours later, a maid, softly knocking on the door, asked her what she would like for supper. When she nearly replied "Yorkshire pudding," Regan realized she didn't even know what foods were available in America. Finally, she told the girl she didn't feel like eating and to please go away. Perhaps she could stay forever in this room and never have to face the outside world.

Chapter 13

NO MATTER what Regan's first impression was of how difficult it was to run a plantation, she was far from the reality of it. Travis left their bed before the sun rose, and within minutes there were women in her room asking her questions. When she had no idea what answers to give them, she could see the way their eyes slid to one side. Once she overheard a maid mutter something about how a man like Travis could marry a nothing like her.

And everywhere she heard the name Margo.

A weaver showed her patterns Margo had given her. A gardener set bulbs from Miss Margo. In the blue room she found dresses that she was told belonged to Miss Margo, because she stayed here so often.

In the evenings at dinner, she asked Travis about this woman, but Travis only shrugged and said she was a neighbor. After having been away from his plantation so long, he was buried in work. Even during meals he went over papers with his two clerks, computing figures of goods received and goods exported. Regan didn't have the heart to add to his burdens by telling him her problems.

And then one day Regan's world came to a screeching halt. Travis had just returned to a quick dinner, talking to her with his mouth full about the arrival of a new ship from England, when the clatter of a horse's hoofs on the brick drive outside made him start. The crack of a whip was followed by the shrill scream of a horse, and Travis was at the window instantly.

"Margo!" he bellowed down. "You strike that horse again, and I'll use that whip on you."

A deep, seductive laugh seemed to fill the dining room. "Better men than you have tried, Travis, my love," a woman's voice purred, followed by another crack and another scream from a horse.

The entire house shook as Travis tore downstairs.

Regan, her eyes wide, put her napkin on the table and went to the window. Below her was a ravishingly beautiful red-haired woman wearing a tight emerald-green habit over an awesome figure. Her large, jutting breasts, small waist, and round hips made Regan glance down at her own slight curves.

But in seconds her attention was again on the woman atop her black stallion as it pranced angrily in the courtyard. The woman seemed to be easily in control of the monster of an animal, her eyes on the front of the house, and when Travis appeared she gave that low laugh again and raised her whip.

Within seconds Travis made a leap, grabbing at the whip in the woman's upraised hand. He caught it, but she dug her heels into the horse, sending it rearing, and Travis, clutching the pommel, held on. She never seemed to lose balance or confidence as the horse's front hoofs flailed at the air, and when the animal came down she started to give it another kick.

But Travis was too fast for her. He grabbed her arm with one hand and the reins with the other. For a moment there was a tug of war, the woman's laugh filling the air, sounding like moonlight during the day. She was a large, strong woman, and with the added strength of the horse beneath her she gave Travis an excellent fight.

When at last he pulled her from the horse, she slid down him liquidly, running her breasts across his face and down his chest, and when she was in range she opened her mouth and pressed it to his in a kiss that even from Regan's position, high above, looked as if it might devour him.

She wouldn't have guessed she could fly downstairs as quickly as she did, and when she reached the front stairs the kiss was only just ending.

"Still planning to use a whip on me?" Margo said huskily but loudly enough for Regan to hear. "Or could I persuade you to use something a little smaller—a very little bit smaller, if I remember correctly," she added, rubbing her hips meaningfully against his.

Travis took her arms and set her away from him. "Margo, before you make a complete fool of yourself, I think you should meet someone." He turned around, seemingly aware of Regan's exact whereabouts. "This is my wife."

Many expressions went across Margo's classically beautiful face. The arched eyebrows drew together, and the green-gold eyes caught fire. Patrician nostrils flared, and the sensual lips curled. She seemed to start to say something, but no words came out. With one look at Travis she gave him a slap that echoed against the towering house. In another second she was on her horse, jerking savagely at its mouth and already whipping it viciously as she headed east.

Travis watched her for a moment, muttered something about "No right to treat animals that way," flexed his injured jaw, and turned back to his wife. "That was Margo Jenkins, our closest neighbor." With that calm statement he seemed to dismiss the whole episode.

Regan, stock-still, her body rigid, could see the vivid print of Margo's hand on his cheek as he bent to kiss her.

"I'll see you tonight, and why don't you take a nap? You look a little pale. We want a healthy baby, remember?" With that, he nodded for his clerk, standing behind Regan, to follow him, and he went toward the west wing of the house where his office was located.

It took Regan what seemed like an hour before she recovered enough to return to the house. The vision of the haughty, splendidly lovely Margo haunted her all day. Twice she paused before a mirror and looked at her own reflection, at her wide-set eyes, her slim figure, and her overall look of sweetness. There was nothing sweet-looking about Margo Jenkins. Sucking in her cheeks, Regan tried to imagine herself more sophisticated, a superior beauty, but with a giant sigh she gave it up.

For the next few days she began to listen when Margo's name was mentioned and found out that it had been understood for years that Travis would marry her. When Travis and Wesley were both away, Margo managed their enormous plantation as well as her own.

With every word she heard, Regan became a little less sure of herself. Had she broken up this love match when she ran into Travis on the London docks? Why had Travis married her, except because she was going to have a baby? When she tried to ask Travis these questions he just laughed. He was too busy with spring planting to be able to spend much time talking, and when they were alone together his hands on her body made her forget everything else.

A week after Margo's visit, Regan was in the East Passage, dreading her journey to the kitchen. It was time to look at the menus for next week—and time to face Malvina, the cook. The old woman had taken an instant dislike to Regan, muttering under her breath constantly. One of the maids mentioned that Malvina was a cousin to the Jenkins family, and of course she had expected, as everyone had, that Travis would marry Margo. Gathering her courage, Regan went through the long passage to the kitchen.

"I ain't got time to do nothin' else now," Malvina said before Regan could speak. "A shipload of men just come in, and I have to feed 'em."

Regan refused to back down. "That's perfectly all right, I'll just have a cup of tea, and we can discuss menus some other time."

"Ain't nobody got time to make tea," the cook snapped, giving warning looks to her three young helpers.

Straightening her shoulders, Regan walked toward the smelly, smoke-emitting cast-iron stove set along one wall. "I can certainly make my own tea," she said in what she hoped was a scathing voice, and did not reveal that she had no idea how to make a cup of tea. Turning just slightly to give the cook a lofty look, a deprecating smile on her lips, Regan picked up the tea kettle.

The smile left instantly as she gave a little scream, dropped the scalding-hot kettle, and then had to jump backward as boiling water splashed to the floor. Behind her, the cook's malicious chuckle rang out, and all Regan could do was stare helplessly at her burned palm.

"Here," said one of the kitchen maids with kindness as she pressed cool butter into Regan's injured hand. "Leave this on it, and go sit down. I'll bring you your tea." This last she said with a whisper, one eye glancing toward the cook.

Silently, her head down, Regan left the kitchen, with her fingers extended and the butter melting against the throbbing surface. She wanted to go straight to her bedroom, but a young man informed her that a guest waited for her in the parlor. Regan was just wondering how she could escape when Margo appeared at the head of the stairs, looking radiant in a blue satin dress.

"Whatever have you done to yourself, child?" she asked, sweeping down the stairs. "Charles, bring bandages to the parlor, and have Malvina send us tea. With sherry! And tell her I want some of her fruitcake."

"Yes, ma'am," said the young man, who hurried away.

Margo took Regan's wrist and led her up the stairs. "What were you doing to burn your hand so badly?" she said sympathetically.

With her pride hurt as well as her hand, Regan was glad for

the sympathy. "I picked up the tea kettle," she said meekly, embarrassed.

Margo didn't blink an eye as she led Regan to a couch. Within seconds a maid Regan was sure she'd never seen before appeared with bandages and clean cloths. "And where have you been, Sally?" Margo asked sternly. "Have you been up to your old tricks and getting out of work?"

"Oh no, ma'am. I help the mistress every morning, don't I, ma'am?" she asked, boldly looking at Regan.

Regan didn't say a word. She'd met so many people in the last few weeks.

Margo grabbed the bandages. "Get out of here, you little slut! And be careful I don't have Travis turn your indenture papers over to me."

After one wild look of fear, the maid left the room.

Margo sat down beside Regan on the couch. "Now let me see your hand. This is really a bad burn. You must have held that kettle quite some time. I do hope you tell Travis about the house servants. He lets them do as they please, and as a result they think they own the place. And Wes is certainly no better. That's why Travis has been planning for so long to get a wife. He needs someone strong who can take care of the duties of a plantation this size."

All the time she was talking, she was tenderly bandaging Regan's hand. When she was finished, the man, Charles, entered the room bearing a tray large enough to hold a pony. On it was an exquisite Georgian silver tea service, a crystal decanter of sherry with two glasses, and an astonishing array of tiny cakes and sandwiches.

"Not Malvina's best," Margo said, looking down her nose at the tray. "Perhaps she doesn't consider me a guest any longer. Tell her," she said, glancing at Charles, "that I'll speak to her before I leave."

"Yes, ma'am," Charles bobbed before he left the room.

"Now," Margo said, smiling at Regan. "I shall, of course, pour since you have that dreadful hand."

With the greatest of ease, Margo poured tea, added a good dose of sherry, and chose a cake for Regan.

"I really came to apologize," Margo began as she poured herself sherry, forgetting the tea. "I can't imagine what you must have thought of my unforgivable rudeness last week. I was really too embarrassed to return and ask you to receive me after what happened."

Regan was pleased at this regal woman's humility. "I . . . you should have come," she said quietly.

Margo looked away and continued, "You see, Travis and I have been sweethearts since we were children, and everyone assumed we would someday marry. So, of course, it was a shock when he introduced someone else as his wife." She looked back at Regan, her eyes soft and pleading. "You do understand, don't you?"

"Of course," Regan whispered. How alike Margo and Travis were, so sure of themselves, so confident. They were the rulers of the world.

"My father died two years ago," Margo said, and there was such pain in her voice that Regan winced. "And since then I've run my plantation alone. Of course, it is nowhere near the size of Travis's place, but it is adequate."

Regan felt that here was a woman who could run an entire plantation alone, while she couldn't even prepare a cup of tea. At least there was one thing she could do correctly. Lowering her head and smiling, she said, "Travis hopes our children will help him work the plantation. Of course, that will take time, but this one has a good start already."

When Margo was silent, Regan looked up and saw fire in the larger woman's eyes.

"So that's why Travis married you!" she said in a voice that came from deep inside her.

A wave of shock ran through Regan.

"Forgive me again!" Margo said, putting her hand on Regan's wrist. "I never seem to say the right thing. It's just that I had wondered why, since we were practically engaged. Travis is so honorable that, of course, he'd feel he had to marry a woman who was carrying his child. You know," she laughed, "I should have thought of that. Perhaps if I'd, well, you know, and gotten myself pregnant, he would have married me.

"Oh my!" Margo said. "I seem to be doing it again. I wasn't by any means insinuating that you were *enceinte* before Travis married you. Of course you weren't."

She rose, and Regan stood beside her. "I really must go," Margo said. "I can't seem to say anything right today." She patted Regan's hand. "I'm sure Travis fell in love with you, and that's why he chose you. This isn't the Middle Ages. Men marry women of their own choosing and not because they're going to have babies. Of course, Travis always said he'd like to have children but without a bossy wife to put up with. Of course, you, dear sweet child, could never be bossy. Now I really must go. I hope we will become the closest of friends. Perhaps I can help you with learning about Travis's likes and dislikes. After all, we've been very close all our lives."

She kissed the air beside Regan's cheek before turning to leave. "I'll leave word for the tray to be removed," she smiled. "So you don't have to worry your sweet little head about it. You just go and rest and take care of that baby Travis wants so much."

With that she left the room, and Regan collapsed onto the couch, feeling as if she'd just left a storm. It was a few minutes before she began to think about Margo's words. Choice? Travis did not choose her; she ran into him. He would gladly have released her, but she wouldn't tell him her uncle's name. Honor! Travis's honor forbade him releasing her into the streets of London, and later his honor made him marry her. What had he said at their wedding? He always married the mother of his children.

Had she forced him to marry her? Obviously their marriage had nothing to do with love. How could a man like Travis love a child who couldn't even make tea without practically crippling herself?

The days began to pass, and with each one she seemed to fall farther behind in work. The household staff seemed to take delight in changing daily. When Regan spoke to them they were insolent, and at last she found herself rarely leaving her room.

Travis came home, swept her into his arms, tossed her above his head, and tickled her until the sadness left her face. Constantly, he asked her what was wrong. He invited her to tour the plantation with him, and she went, ashamed at how much she wanted his protection. She could never admit how much of a stranger she felt in this country.

Travis never complained about her lack of authority, and no one dared be insolent with him, but he did notice that certain areas of the plantation were not being supervised properly. One day she heard him shouting at the dairymen, asking why they were slack in their job.

Twice Margo visited, and each time she talked softly to Regan before setting into the house staff for their negligence of the gracious house. After she left Regan felt drained and worse than useless.

She never let Travis know of her problems with the staff or of her hundreds of thousands of tears during the day.

One afternoon, while Regan was in the library trying to concentrate on a book, Travis entered.

"There you are," he smiled. "I thought you'd disappeared."

"Is something wrong?"

Over his clothes he wore an oiled cloth, like the sailors on board ship had worn.

"A storm is brewing, lightning cut one of the fences down, and about a hundred horses are out."

"Are you going after them?"

"Just as soon as I can get Margo, I am."

"Margo?" She closed the book. "What does she have to do with horses getting out?"

Travis laughed at her expression. "Some of them belong to her, and, besides, she can outride most of the men in the county. The plain fact, my green-eyed little wife, is that I need her."

Standing, she looked up at him. "But what can I do?"

He smiled indulgently and kissed her nose. "Not worry your pretty little head for one thing, keep my baby safe for the second, and, last but definitely not least, warm my bed." With that, he left the room.

For a moment Regan stood where she was. Her first impulse was to cry, but she was sick to death of crying! She was *not* going to sit alone and keep Travis's baby safe. Surely there must be more to life than just living for the few moments alone with a man who only cared about what she carried in her stomach.

When he really wanted something, he went to the woman he'd always gone to—Margo—Margo with her pride and arrogance, Margo with her confident ability to do anything in the world.

Without another thought, she went to their bedroom and began throwing clothes into a cloth case. The idea of doing something—anything—made her hurry. In a case on the chest of drawers was a bracelet of sapphires and a pair of diamond earrings. They'd belonged to Travis's mother, and he'd given them to her. With only a moment's hesitation, she slipped them into the bag.

Putting on a heavy cloak, she went to the door, made sure no one saw her, and started toward the stairs. At the head, she paused and looked back at what had once been hers. No! It never had been hers. With a fresh burst of resolution, she ran back to the library and scribbled a note to Travis, telling him that she was leaving and he was free to have the woman he loved. Then, opening a drawer, she emptied the contents of a tin box of cash into her pocket.

It was easy to escape the house without notice. The workers were busy securing windows and doors in preparation for the storm that hung in the air like damp wool. The house faced the river, but behind it ran a rutted path that Travis said was a road. Most Virginians traveled by water, and Regan felt sure she would escape detection if she took this route.

She walked for an hour, the air heavy with the storm, before the rain began. The path turned to mud that sucked at her shoes and made walking nearly impossible.

"Want a ride, young lady?" someone called.

She turned to see a wagon behind her, an old man atop it.

"Not much protection from the wet, but it beats walkin'!"

Gratefully she put up her hand, and he pulled her onto the seat beside him.

Margo stormed into the house, her clothes dripping, her hair in a bedraggled mess down her back. Damn that Travis! she thought. He sends for me as if I were some field hand to help him round up horses, while that precious, brainless wife of his stays at home! There was hardly a day when she didn't remember that awful morning alone with him.

The day before, she had gone to greet him on his return from England, expecting him to take her to his bed as he usually did, but instead he'd introduced that colorless child as his wife. The next morning she'd confronted him, demanded to know just what the hell he thought he was doing. Travis hadn't said much until she began enumerating Regan's faults—which she'd been told in full by Malvina, her cousin.

Travis had raised his hand to hit her but recovered himself in time. In a voice she'd never heard him use before, he told her Regan was worth two of her and that he didn't give a damn if his wife couldn't control an army of servants. He also said that if Margo ever wanted to be welcome at his house she'd better ask Regan's permission.

It had taken Margo a week to swallow her pride and go to that simpering brat. And what had she found there? The child was in tears, unable even to treat her own burned fingers. But at least Margo had found out why Travis had married her. It all made such perfect sense. Her submissiveness, combined with Travis's aggression, had gotten him what he wanted and had gotten her pregnant. Now all Margo had to do was show Travis what a waste it was to spend his life—and money—on that useless bit of fluff.

Now, angry as she always was in the last weeks, she started up the stairs. Travis had asked Margo to look in on his little china-doll wife on her way home, as Travis was going to have to spend tonight and maybe tomorrow night at Clay's house. Lightning had struck Clay's dairy, and they needed help in rebuilding it. Margo could have struck Travis when she saw the look on his face. You would have thought that spending two nights away from that brat was a tragedy.

Taking a deep breath to calm herself, she opened the bedroom door, surprised to find the room empty—and a mess. Looking at open drawers and clothes strewn over the bed, she knew it was too much to hope that a thief had entered the house and carried off the little princess. Snatching at a satin dress in a delicious shade of ripe peaches, Margo snarled. If one looked closely, there were worn places on all of her own gowns.

She threw the dress down and went through the familiar house, banging doors open, thinking that all this should have been hers. In the library, a single candle guttered over a simple note on Travis's desk. The handwriting, with all its open a's and o's, disgusted Margo.

But, as she read it, her mind began to clear. So! The runt had left Travis to the "woman he loved." Perhaps now was the time to do something about Travis's infantile infatuation with the girl.

Slipping Regan's note into her pocket, she wrote one of her own.

Dear Travis,

Regan and I have decided to become better acquainted, so we're going to Richmond together for a few days. We both send our love.

M.

Smiling, Margo hoped "a few days" was enough time to cover Regan's tracks. No doubt, the girl would be as clumsy in trying to run away as she was in everything else she attempted. But Margo could change that. By slipping a little money here and there, she could persuade people they'd never seen the runt.

It was four days later when Margo finally returned, alone, to the Stanford plantation. She was disgusted when Travis ran to greet her, jumping into the carriage and turning feverish-looking eyes up to her. "Where is she?"

Later, Margo was proud of her acting. She'd shown Travis her anger at being stood up by Regan, saying the dear woman had never shown up for their journey.

Travis's anger was frightening. She'd known him all her life, and never had she seen him really lose his self-control. Within moments he had his entire plantation mobilized in a search for his wife. Friends from everywhere came, but on the second day, when a piece of one of Regan's dresses was found at the river's edge, many people gave up the search and went home.

But not Travis. He made a circle of a hundred-mile radius around his plantation and asked questions of everyone within the circle.

Margo held her breath and prayed she'd done her work well. She was rewarded when Travis returned in a month, weary, thin, aged. Smiling, Margo remembered all the money this deception had cost her. With her plantation already in debt, she couldn't afford too many errors, so she'd taken what cash she had and bribed men and women all over the countryside. Some people told Travis they'd seen Regan and then gave him incorrect directions. Some who had seen her said they hadn't. And a few who couldn't be bribed told the truth, but further along the trail there were others who swore they'd not seen the young lady.

Gradually, Travis returned to the working of his plantation, allowing his brother Wesley to take over more and more of the running of it. And Margo went about picking up the pieces of Travis's life.

Chapter 14

REGAN FOUND the first leg of the journey almost pleasant. She kept imagining Travis's face when he found her. She would, of course, bargain with him before she returned to his home. She'd insist he fire the cook and hire a housekeeper. No! Regan would choose her own housekeeper, someone loyal to her.

The man on the wagon let her off at a stage stop, and Regan mustered her courage and went into the small inn, which seemed more like someone's house than a public establishment.

"It used to be our house," the landlady said. "But after my husband died I sold the farm land and started taking in guests. It was a lot easier than cookin' for my ten children while they was growin' up."

The landlady swept Regan under her arm and gave her a friendly lecture about traveling alone. As she ate alone in a high-sided booth, she thought of how Travis would ask this woman for directions.

In the morning Regan asked the landlady four times where the next stage was heading, in order, she realized guiltily, to impress on the woman's mind her destination.

On the second day in a stage she grew quite tired and kept glancing out the window. The storm had gone, leaving the air heavy enough to cut, and her dress clung to her. Once a horse and rider came thundering down the road toward them, and at the sound Regan smiled, sure the rider was Travis. She had her head half out the window, her hand raised in recognition, when the man on the horse galloped by. Embarrassed, she sat back in the stage.

That night there was no friendly landlady but only a querulous old man serving a stringy roast and hard potatoes for supper. Sad and tired, she went upstairs to the bedroom that, as a single woman, she shared with ten other women.

Before the sun came up she awoke and began softly crying. When the stage was ready to leave, her head ached and her eyes were swollen.

The four other passengers tried to talk to her, but she could only nod at their questions. Everyone kept asking her the same question: Where was she going?

Staring out the window in an unseeing gaze, she began to ask herself the same question. Had she run away from Travis just to show him she could be independent? Had she really believed he wanted Margo?

She had no answers for her questions but just traveled on one stage after another, watching the passing scenery, not even upset by the lack of decent food, beds, or rest.

It was in a daze that she stepped down from the stage one afternoon into a barren little place that was little more than a few houses.

"This is the end of the line, lady," the stage driver said, offering his hand to her.

"I beg your pardon?"

He looked at her with patience. For the past two days she'd been half in a stupor, and he thought perhaps she wasn't completely right in the mind. "The stage line stops here. Past Scarlet Springs is nothing but Indian country. If you want to go into that, you'll have to hire a wagon."

"Could I get a room here?"

"Lady, this ain't even a town yet. It don't have hotels yet.

Look, you either go on or you go back. There ain't nowhere to stay here."

Go back! How could she go back to Travis and his mistress?

A woman's voice came from behind the stage. "I have room. She can stay with me until she makes up her mind what she wants to do."

Regan turned to see a short, voluptuous young woman with honey-blonde hair and big blue eyes.

"I'm Brandy Dutton, and I have a farmhouse just down the road. Would you like to stay with me?"

"Yes," Regan said quietly. "I can pay you. . . ."

"Don't worry about it. We'll work it out." Grabbing Regan's bag, she led the way down the street.

"I saw you standing there, and you looked so little and lost that my heart just went out to you. You know, I must have looked the same about three months ago. Both my parents died and left me alone with nothing but an old farmhouse and not much else. Here we are."

She led Regan inside an unpainted, rundown, two-story house. "Sit down, and I'll make you some coffee. What's your name anyway?"

"Regan Stanford," she said before thinking, then shrugged because what did it matter if she didn't hide? Travis obviously wasn't interested in having her back.

Regan sipped the coffee, not really liking the taste of it. But it helped revive her, although she could feel tears growing behind her eyes.

"You look like you've had your share of tragedy, too," Brandy said as she cut a piece of cake and handed it to Regan.

A man who wanted to marry her in spite of the fact that he despised her, an uncle who detested her, a man who married her because of the child she carried—she could only nod to Brandy's question.

When she only picked at the cake, Brandy looked at her sympathetically and asked if she'd like to lie down. Once alone in the little bedroom, Regan began to cry in earnest, as she'd never cried before.

She didn't hear Brandy enter the room, only felt the woman's arms around her. "You can tell me about it," she whispered.

"Men!" Regan cried. "Twice I've loved them, and both times—."

"You don't have to say any more," Brandy said. "I am an expert on men. Two years ago I fell for a man, decided he was worth more than anyone else on earth, so one night I slipped out the window of my bedroom, didn't even leave my parents a note, and ran off with him. He said he was going to marry me, but there never seemed to be the right time, and six months ago I found him in bed with another woman."

This statement started Regan's tears harder.

"I didn't know where to go," Brandy continued. "So I came home, and my wonderful parents accepted me back and never said a word about what I'd done. Two weeks later they were dead of scarlet fever."

"I . . . I'm sorry," Regan sniffed. "Then you're alone, too."

"Exactly," Brandy said. "I own one farmhouse that's about to fall down around my ears, and I have every man coming through here swearing he can make me the happiest woman in the world."

"I hope you don't believe them!" Regan snapped.

Brandy laughed. "You're beginning to sound like me, but it's either marry one of them or starve to death here."

"I have some money," Regan said, emptying her pockets onto the bed. To her chagrin, there were only four silver coins left. "Wait a minute!" she said, going to her bag and pulling out the sapphire bracelet and diamond earrings.

Brandy held them up to the light. "One of your two men must have been good to you."

"When he was with me," Regan said stiffly. Suddenly, her face changed, and she grabbed her stomach.

"Are you sick?"

"I think the baby just kicked me," she said in wonder.

Brandy's eyes opened wide just before she began laughing. "Aren't we a pair! Two rejected females who at this moment hate the whole male race"—her tone left no doubt that that opinion would change—"with a couple of pieces of jewelry, four silver coins, a falling-down house, and a baby on the way. How are we going to put food on the table this coming winter?"

It was the way she said "we" and the hint of their being together this winter that made a spark of interest shoot through Regan. Travis didn't want her, yet she had to survive. At another kick from the baby, she smiled. She hadn't thought much about her baby in the last few months. Travis was so overpowering that she could see nothing but him.

"How about more cake and let's talk?" Brandy said.

It wasn't with glee that she thought about her future, but she had to plan something for her and the baby.

"Did you make this?" Regan asked, hungrily digging into the cake.

With pride, Brandy smiled. "If there's one thing I can do, it's cook. By the time I was ten I was doing all the cooking for my parents."

"At least you have some talents," Regan said grimly. "I'm not sure I can do anything."

Brandy sat down at the old table. "I could teach you to cook. I was thinking of baking things and selling them to the people who pass through Scarlet Springs. We two could make enough to get by on."

"This is Scarlet Springs? That's the name of this place?"

Brandy gave her a look of sympathy. "I take it you just got on a stage and went to the end of the line."

Regan only nodded as she finished her cake.

"If you're willing to try and willing to work, I'd certainly like your company."

They shook hands in agreement.

It took Brandy a week before she really began to believe that Regan could not cook, but it was ten days before she gave up.

"It's no use," Brandy sighed. "You either forget the yeast or half the flour or the sugar, or something." Dumping a hard loaf on the table, she tried to stab it with a knife but couldn't.

"I'm so sorry," Regan said. "I really try, I do."

Eyeing her critically, Brandy said, "You know what you're really good at? People like you. There's such a sweetness about you and you're so damned pretty that women like you and want to take care of you, and so do the men."

Travis had once wanted to take care of her, but it hadn't lasted long. "I'm not sure you're right, but what sort of talent is that?"

"Selling. I'll cook; you sell. Look sweet on the outside, but drive a hard bargain. Don't let anyone get away with paying less than we ask."

The next day the stage brought six people to meet others who camped outside Scarlet Springs, waiting to start the journey West. On impulse, Regan raised the prices of the baked goods, and no one questioned them but bought everything.

That afternoon she spent all the money she and Brandy had. Three of the settlers traveling West had overloaded their wagons, and they meant to throw their excess lanterns, rope, and a few pieces of clothing into the river. They were angry and wanted to make sure no one could use what they'd paid for. Regan offered to buy all of it. After running all the way to the farmhouse, she grabbed all their money from the box and paid it to the settlers.

When she returned with the merchandise, Brandy was furious. They had no money, their supplies were nearly empty, and they had a room full of equipment no one wanted.

For three days they lived on apples pilfered from an orchard four miles away, and Regan was ridden with guilt.

On the fourth day, new settlers came to Scarlet Springs, and Regan sold all the goods for three times what she'd paid for them. Crying in relief that everything had worked out, Regan and Brandy hugged each other and danced around the kitchen.

It was the beginning of everything. With this first good sale they gained confidence in themselves and each other. Both women began to look ahead to what they could do.

They struck a bargain with the farmer who owned the apple trees and purchased all his fallen apples in exchange for very little money and a loaf of bread a week from Brandy for the next six months. At night Brandy and Regan peeled and sliced apples and put them out to dry in the next day's sun. When they were dry they sold them to the westward-traveling settlers.

Every penny they made, every bargain they struck, increased the size of their business. They were up before dawn, to bed very late. Yet sometimes Regan felt she'd never been happier. For the first time in her life she felt as if she were needed.

It was during the fall that they began taking in boarders and serving meals. People came to Scarlet Springs too late to go West and had no wish to return to where they'd once lived. One man explained that his hometown had given him a going-away party, and he couldn't face returning, saying he'd missed the wagons.

Regan and Brandy looked at each other, smiled contentedly, and told the man they'd take care of him. By Thanksgiving they had six boarders, and they were all jammed on top of one another.

"Next year I'm putting down pickles and kraut," Brandy said, looking in disgust at a meal of little else but wild meat. She stopped her complaints when she looked at Regan.

Regan stood unsteadily, her stomach well out in front of her. "If you will excuse me," she said in the quietest possible voice, "I believe I'll go upstairs and have a baby."

Brandy, angered, grabbed her friend's arm and helped her up

to the bedroom they now shared. "No doubt you've had pains all day. When are you going to stop feeling like you're a burden and start asking for help?"

Awkwardly, Regan sat on the bed, leaning back on the pillows Brandy shoved behind her. "Could you lecture me later?" she asked, her face contorting.

In spite of Regan's small size, it was an easy birth. Her water broke all over Brandy, and they laughed together for just a second before a large, perfect baby girl came flying into the world. She screwed up her face, clenched her fists, and started screaming. "Just like Travis," Regan murmured before reaching for her daughter. "Jennifer. Do you like that name?"

"Yes," Brandy said, cleaning Regan and the room. She was too exhausted to consider what the baby's name was. Glancing at Regan cuddling her baby, she felt she was the one who'd been through the worst ordeal.

Within a month the women had settled in to the new routine of running the boarding house and caring for the baby. When spring arrived, so did hundreds of new settlers. One man, whose wife had died on the journey to Scarlet Springs, decided to remain with his two young children in the sparse little settlement and began building a large, comfortable house.

"This town's going to grow," Regan murmured, her baby on her arm. Looking back at the drafty old farmhouse, she began to see it with a fresh coat of paint, and, as her imagination took over, she saw an addition on the front, something with long porches.

"That's a funny look," Brandy said from behind her friend. "Mind sharing what's causing it?"

Not yet, Regan thought. She'd had too many dreams in her life, and all of them had fallen through. From now on she was going to concentrate on one goal, and she was going to work hard at achieving it.

Weeks later, when Regan did finally, tentatively, talk to

Brandy about her ideas for remodeling and enlarging the farm-house into a full-size hotel, Brandy was somewhat shocked.

"It . . . sounds like a wonderful idea," Brandy hesitated. "But do you think we—I mean, us two women—can do something like that? What do we know about a hotel?"

"Nothing," Regan said in all seriousness. "And don't let me consider what I can do versus what I want to do, or I'll never even try it."

Laughing, Brandy didn't know how to address that state-ment. "I'm with you," she said. "You lead; I'll follow."

That was another statement Regan didn't want to consider. In fact, she wanted to keep so busy that she had no time to think. Two days later she had found a wet nurse for Jennifer, unearthed the jewels from their hiding place, and boarded a stage heading north. She went to three towns before she found someone willing to pay a decent price for the bracelet and earrings. And every-where she went she visited the local inns. She found that an inn was not only a place for wayfarers but a social and political gath-ering place as well. She drew sketches and asked questions, and her earnestness and youth gained her many hours of discussion and answers to her probings.

When she returned home, tired but exhilarated and more than eager to see her daughter and her friend, she had a fat leather case filled with notes, drawings, and recipes for Brandy. And sewed inside her clothes were bank drafts for the jewelry. From that moment on there was never any doubt about who was the leader in this partnership.

Chapter 15

FARRELL BATSFORD stepped off the stage in the busy little town of Scarlet Springs, Pennsylvania, on a cool March morning in 1802. Dusting himself off, smoothing the rich blue velvet of his coat, he tugged at the lace at his cuff.

"This where you stoppin', Mister?" the stage driver asked from behind the slim, tailored man.

Farrell didn't bother to look at the driver but merely gave a brief nod of acknowledgment. Seconds later, he twirled about as the first of his two large, heavy trunks were tossed to the ground from the top of the stage. With a wide smile, the driver blinked at Farrell angelically.

"You want me to take those to the inn for you?" a burly young man asked.

Again Farrell only nodded curtly, ignoring as best he could the entire American race. As the stage pulled away, Farrell got his first glimpse of the Silver Dolphin Inn. It was three and a half stories high, with double porches across the front and tall white columns reaching to the steep roof. After tossing the young man a quarter, Farrell decided to walk about the town.

There's money here somewhere, he thought as he viewed the clean, neat buildings. Across from the inn were a print-shop, a doctor's office, a lawyer, a druggist. Close by were a blacksmith shop, a large mercantile shop, a school, and at the other end of town a tall, well-kept church. Everything was prosperous, fat-looking.

Turning his attention back to the inn, it was easy to see that the manicured building was the dominant one in the town. In the back was an additional wing, a well-tended older part of the building. Every window was sparkling clean, all the shutters newly painted, and even as Farrell watched many people came and went into the obviously thriving establishment.

Once again he took a worn newspaper article from his pocket. The article stated that a Mrs. Regan Stanford and Brandy Dutton, a spinster, practically owned an entire town in Pennsylvania. At first Farrell had thought it couldn't possibly be the Regan he'd been looking for for so many years, but a man he had sent to the town came back with a description that just could be the Regan he once knew.

Again, he thought of that night nearly five years ago when Jonathan Northland had thrown his niece from her own house. Poor, simple Regan had never realized that Weston Manor was hers, and, instead of her living on her uncle's income as Jonathan said that night, it was Northland who was living on the interest off Regan's fortune. Smiling, Farrell wondered if Northland ever realized who had alerted the executors of Regan's estate to what her uncle had done. It was a small but not adequate revenge for the things Northland had said about Farrell that night when the executors tossed Jonathan out of Weston Manor without so much as a penny. Six months later, Jonathan Northland was found stabbed to death in a wharfside gin shop, and finally Farrell's revenge was complete.

As the months and years passed, Farrell began to think more and more about Regan's millions, just lying in a bank, growing daily through the careful, wise investing of her executors. He began looking for a bride, someone with money enough to support him and his estate in a gentlemanly manner, but all the young women fell short of having the money Regan Weston possessed. Any women of her wealth wanted nothing to do with a penniless, titleless gentleman of dubious habits.

After two years of fruitless searching, Farrell persuaded himself that Regan had jilted him and had ruined his reputation with women. Therefore, the honorable thing to do was to find the child, marry her, and let her money mend his damaged reputation.

It had taken a while to trace Regan's old maid, Matta, to Scotland where she was living with relatives. The old woman suffered permanently from the pain of a misaligned jaw bone, a bone Jonathan Northland had broken for her when she tried to answer an American's questions about a young girl he'd found.

Drooling, slurring her words, drinking constantly to dull the pain, Matta disgusted Farrell until he could hardly bear being near her. Her memory was cloudy, and it took hours to get what he wanted from her, but he left with some idea of where to look.

Following one answer to another, he soon realized that Regan had sailed for America. It wasn't easy to make the decision to go after her, but he was fully aware that after years in that uncivilized country she'd probably be dying to return home.

America was larger than he'd imagined, and there were a few isolated points of civilization, but the people were disgusting, never aware of their station in life, each man believing he was a member of the peerage.

He was almost ready to return to England when he saw the small article in the newspaper. When the man he had hired to go to Scarlet Springs returned, he described a woman very like Regan in looks, but she did not seem to be the simpleton he remembered.

Now he walked across the green lawn that made a lush oval between the two main streets and entered the inn.

A large reception hall lined with white-painted paneling greeted him. Several well-dressed men and women were just entering a room to his right, and he followed them to an even larger room furnished with comfortable chairs and sofas and, along one wall, a deep, wide stone fireplace. All the furniture was newly upholstered in dusty rose and pale green striped satin. A taproom—rustic, he thought, with its oak chairs and tables, but obviously doing a brisk trade—adjoined the common room.

An enormous public dining room was across from the common room, two private dining rooms next to it. Finally, returning to the front of the inn, not touring into the old part of the building, he looked into a cozy library that smelled of leather and tobacco. Across the hall was the reception room, where a clerk politely assigned him a private bedroom upstairs.

"How many bedrooms do you have?"

"An even dozen," the clerk replied. "Plus two with sitting rooms and, of course, the owners' private apartments."

"Of course. I take it you refer to the young ladies."

"Oh, yes, sir, Regan and Brandy. Regan lives downstairs at the end of the old part, and Brandy is upstairs, just over her."

"And these are the ladies who supposedly own most of the town?" Farrell asked.

The clerk chuckled. "The preacher says that the only building they don't own is the church, but everyone knows they paid for it. They do hold the mortgages on all the other buildings. If a lawyer came through, Regan would give him the money to build a place and he'd stay here, then a doctor, and pretty soon this place became a town."

"Where might I find Mrs. Stanford?" Farrell asked, not liking the man's use of Regan's first name.

"Anywhere," he said quickly as a couple came in to register. "She's everywhere at once."

Not wanting to cause a scene, Farrell allowed the insolent man's abrupt dismissal of him. Later he'd have to speak to the manager, whoever she was.

Upstairs he found his room clean and well furnished, with warm sunlight sparkling through the window. A small fireplace was along one wall. After changing his dusty clothes, he went downstairs to the dining room. It galled him to eat in the public room, but he knew he'd be more likely to see Regan there. The menu was extensive, serving seven meats, three fish, plus cold dishes, relishes, vegetables, game, and a formidable list of pastries and puddings. Arriving quickly, the food was hot, well prepared, and delicious.

While he was sampling something called Moravian sugar cake, a woman entered the room, and every eye, male and female, glanced up at her. It was not just her extraordinary beauty that made them look, but her presence, her sense of self. This woman—small, wearing an exquisite gown of forest green muslin—knew who she was. She walked with confidence, easily speaking to first one person and then another. She looked to be a gracious lady welcoming people to her home. At one table she stopped, looked at a dish, and sent it back to the kitchen. At another table two women rose and hugged her briefly, and for a few moments she sat with them, laughing happily.

Farrell could not take his eyes off her. Superficially, she resembled the awkward girl he'd once known. The eyes were the same color, the hair the same shiny brown, but this woman, with her firm curves and her ease with people, was not at all like that simpering, terrified-of-her-own-shadow child to whom he'd once been engaged.

Leaning back in his chair, he waited calmly for her to come to him. When she saw him she smiled, but there was no recognition. A full minute later, as she was speaking to a couple across from him, her eyes lifted and met his. It was an appraising look she gave him, and Farrell gave her his most charming smile in return. He was extremely pleased when she turned and rather quickly left the room. Now he was sure there was some feeling, whether good or bad, left in her concerning him. Hate or love, he didn't care which, just so she remembered him.

* * *

"Regan, are you all right?" Brandy asked from the other side of the big oak kitchen table, where she was supervising three cooks.

"Of course," Regan snapped, then drew a deep breath and smiled. "I just saw a ghost, that's all."

The two women exchanged looks as Brandy drew Regan to a corner of the big room. "Jennifer's father?"

"No," Regan said quietly. Sometimes there didn't seem to be a moment of her life when she didn't think of Travis. Every time she looked into Jennifer's big brown eyes, she saw him. Sometimes a heavy step on the stairs made her heart skip a beat.

"Remember the man I was engaged to years ago? Farrell Batsford?" There were no secrets between the two friends. "He's sitting in the dining room."

"That bastard!" Brandy said with feeling. "What's he eating? I'll douse it with poison."

Regan laughed. "I should feel the same way, I guess, but I wonder if anyone gets over their first love. Seeing him brought back such a rush of memories. I was so frightened of everything, so eager to please, and so very much in love with him. I thought he was the most handsome, elegant man I'd ever seen."

"And now how does he look?"

"He's certainly not ugly," Regan smiled. "I guess I should invite him to my office for a talk. It's the least I can do."

"Regan," Brandy warned. "Be careful. It isn't a coincidence that he's here."

"I'm sure of that, and I have a good idea what he wants. In less than a month I'll be twenty-three, and the money my parents left me is mine."

"Don't forget that for a moment," Brandy called after Regan.

Regan went to her office next to the kitchen and sat down in the leather chair behind her desk. It wasn't that Farrell had affected her so much, but the sight of him brought back so many memories. Like a wave of cold water, she remembered the awful night she'd heard the truth from her uncle and her fiancé. One memory piled on top of another—Travis holding her, Travis telling her what to do, Travis making love to her, Travis bigger than life, and Regan constantly terrified. In the past four years, a hundred times she'd started to write him, to tell him about his daughter, to let him know they were both well and prospering. But she was always a coward in the end. What if Travis wrote her that he didn't care, which was surely the case since he'd never tried to find her? Over the years she'd learned to stand on her own two feet, but could she do so with Travis around? Would he bully her back into becoming the tearful, frightened girl she once was?

A knock on the door brought her back to the present. At her answer, Farrell opened the door.

"I hope I'm not intruding," he said, smiling, his eyes showing how much he enjoyed the sight of her.

"Not at all," she answered, rising, offering him her hand. "I was just going to send you a message asking you to join me."

Lowering his head, he kissed her hand ardently. "Perhaps you couldn't bear to face me so soon," he murmured lovingly. "After all, we meant so much to each other so long ago."

It's a good thing Farrell couldn't see Regan's face at that moment. Sheer shock was the expression that immediately registered. Why, you pompous little dandy! she thought. Did he really believe she had no memory of that hideous night so long ago, that she didn't remember the reason he wanted to marry her?

By the time he'd lifted his head, Regan was smiling. She hadn't become a wealthy woman by letting her feelings show. "Yes," she said sweetly. "It has been a long while. Won't you sit down? Could I get you something to drink?"

"Whiskey if you have it."

She poured him a water-glass full of Irish whiskey and smiled innocently when he blinked at it. Settling herself in a chair across from him, she asked, "And how is my uncle?"

"Deceased, I'm afraid."

Regan didn't respond to that, unsure of her own emotions. For all he had done to her, he was still her relative. "Why have you come here, Farrell?"

He took a while before answering. "Guilt," he finally answered. "Although I had no real say in what your uncle did to you that night, I still felt somewhat responsible. In spite of what you may have thought you heard, I did care about you. I was concerned that you were so young, and I was displeased with your uncle for keeping you in such ignorance." He laughed as if they exchanged some private joke. "You must admit you were not the most inspired of dinner companions. I've never been one for robbing from the schoolroom. Perhaps other men like that sort of thing."

"And now?" Regan smiled seductively.

"You've changed. You're . . . not a child anymore."

Before she could answer him, the door burst open and Jennifer ran in, a handful of stemless flowers clutched in a dirty hand. She was a pretty three-year-old, with Regan's smallness and Travis's eyes and hair. She'd also inherited her father's sureness in life, never cringing from anything as Regan had done at her age. "I brought you some flowers, Mommie," she grinned.

"How sweet of you! Now I know spring is really on its way," Regan answered, giving her sturdy daughter a fierce hug.

Jennifer, never shy, was staring openly at Farrell. "Who's he?" she said in a stage whisper.

"Farrell, I'd like you to meet my daughter Jennifer, and this is an old friend of mine—Mr. Batsford."

Jennifer managed to get a "How do you do?" out before she left the room as quickly as she'd entered it.

Regan gave an adoring glance at the door her daughter had just shut much too loudly, before looking back at Farrell. "I'm afraid you've seen my daughter for as long as any of us see her. She has the run of the inn and the grounds and makes use of every moment."

"Who is her father?" he asked, wasting no time.

Regan gave the lie she always gave, saying quickly that she was a widow, but, perhaps because today she was thinking so hard about Travis, her eyes betrayed the lie. She caught Farrell's quick look but said nothing more because to emphasize the lie would make it weaker.

"I must let you get back to your work," he said quietly. "Perhaps you will have dinner with me tonight?"

Still flustered over Farrell's catching of her lie, she agreed readily.

"Until tonight then," he smiled, and left the room.

Farrell went immediately to the kitchen to speak to the head chef about a very special dinner. When he was introduced to Brandy and saw the hostility in her eyes, he knew she'd been told Regan's story. Instantly, he turned on his most charming manner and asked if she'd show him the town. Feeling helpless to do otherwise, Brandy agreed and set out on one of the most charming afternoons of her life. If there was one thing Farrell had learned in the last several years in his pursuit of a rich wife, it was how to charm women. By the end of the afternoon he had Brandy believing he was an innocent victim of Jonathan Northland's greed. He told a long, complicated story of what he'd gone through to find Regan, how his conscience had eaten at him over the years. When he returned to the hotel, he had Brandy singing his praises, and he had more—the name and whereabouts of Regan's husband. By the time he was ready for dinner, a man had been dispatched to Virginia to find out the truth about Travis Stanford.

Chapter 16

TRAVIS LOUNGED against the countertop of the glass case in a Richmond dress shop, waiting with little grace while Margo tried on yet another dress.

"And how is this one, darling?" she said, returning from behind the dressing-room curtains. Very little of her large breasts were left to the imagination by the rust-colored muslin. "It's not too daring, is it?" she asked in a low voice as she walked closer to him, grazing his chest.

"It's fine," he said impatiently. "Haven't you bought enough? I'd like to get home before the sun sets."

"Home!" she said in a pretty pout. "You hardly ever leave that awful ol' plantation anymore. You used to take me dancing. You . . . used to do a lot of things with me."

Removing her hands from his chest, he gave her a tired look. "That was before I was a married man."

"Married!" she gasped. "Your wife ran off and left you! She proved she didn't want you, and what other man stays faithful to his wife, whether she's with him or not?"

"Since when was I like other men?" he answered, giving her a look of warning. They'd had this argument many times before.

The jangling of the bell on the shop door stopped Margo's next words as they both turned to see Ellen Backes enter. She was a neighbor and a friend of Travis's family. "I thought I saw you,

Travis," she said cheerfully. "Margo," she added curtly, letting it be known what she thought of Margo's pursuit of a married man. She'd never met Regan, but she'd heard about her from Nicole, Clay's wife. Having known Travis for years, she felt she knew why Regan had run away.

"The oddest thing just happened," Ellen continued. "I was in the church delivering fresh flowers for Sunday, and a man—a rather shabby little man, I might add—started asking the pastor all sorts of questions about you."

"Probably wants a job," Travis said in dismissal.

"At first I thought that, too, and of course I wasn't listening very carefully, but I swear I heard the name Regan."

Instantly, Travis stood upright. "Regan?" he whispered.

"I was going to wait until the pastor had finished, but I was afraid I might miss you."

Without another word, Travis left the room and immediately jumped into a carriage, yelling at the horses to go faster.

"Damn!" Margo said vehemently. "You would have to go and spoil my day."

"Oh, I am sorry," Ellen said with a radiant smile as Margo flounced toward the dressing room. Turning back toward the window, Ellen offered a silent prayer that Travis would find out something about his wife.

The horses hadn't come to a full stop when Travis leaped from the carriage in front of the church. Just leaving was a small man who looked as if he hadn't gone without a drink for more than a few hours in his life.

Travis, never one to stand on formalities and too angry to consider consequences, grabbed the man's shirtfront and slammed him against the clapboard wall. "Who are you?"

"I didn't do nothin', Mister, and I ain't got no money."

Travis pushed him harder into the wall. "You the one's askin' questions about me?"

Wincing from pain, trying to breathe against Travis's big fist pressed against his throat, the man gasped, "He paid me. I was just supposed to find out if you was alive or not."

"You'd better start talking. Who is he?"

"Some English dandy. I don't know his name. He said you were a friend of his but heard you were dead, wanted me to find out when you died and then tell him."

Travis pushed his fist harder into the man's throat. "You mentioned Regan."

Bewilderment crossed the man's face. "I said the man was stayin' at Regan's place."

For a moment Travis let up on the pressure. "Regan who? And where's her place?"

"Scarlet Springs, Pennsylvania, and she's Regan Stanford, like your name. I asked the preacher if you were related to her."

Instantly, Travis dropped the man and had to catch himself to keep from collapsing. "Get in the carriage. We're going to Scarlet Springs, and on the way you're going to talk."

Before the man could seat himself, Travis whipped the horses forward. As he flew past the dress shop where Margo stood outside, he didn't even slow down. At the livery stable he pulled to a halt.

"Jake," he called. "Give me a decent wagon, something that'll hold up for a longer trip, and here." He tossed money on the seat. "See the owner of this rig gets it back."

Jake barely glanced up. "If you're in a hurry, you better get goin' 'cause it looks to me like a storm's about to descend on you." Nodding in the direction of a very angry Margo, he dropped the horse's hoof he'd been cleaning and went to hitch a wagon for Travis.

Turning to the little man still on the buggy seat, Travis gave him a warning. "You move, and it'll be the last move you make." He'd hardly finished the words before Margo flew at him.

"How dare you drive past me like that!" she gasped, breathless from practically running down the street, chasing him.

"I don't have time to argue right now. I'm leaving in about five minutes."

"Leaving! Well I guess I've completed my shopping, but you'll have to stop at the four shops and pick up my purchases."

"Jake!" Travis bellowed. "Is that wagon ready yet?" He turned back to Margo. "I'm not going home, and you'll have to find someone else to take you. Get Ellen to give you a ride, and stop off and tell Wes I'll be away for a while."

Turning, he saw Jake bring the heavy wagon to the front of the stable. "Get on it," he commanded the nervous little man on the borrowed buggy.

"Travis," Margo hissed. "So help me, if you don't—." She broke off as Travis leaped onto the wagon. "Where are you going?" she screamed as he started to move away.

"Scarlet Springs, Pennsylvania, to get Regan," he yelled and then was gone in a hail of gravel and dust.

Coughing and cursing, Margo looked back at the stableman, who was grinning broadly. She knew her pursuit of Travis was a joke, and the more people laughed, the angrier she grew. But even as she was fuming, a plan began to form in her mind. Scarlet Springs, was it? Poor dear Travis left without a stitch of clean clothing. Perhaps she should pack and take him a few things. Yes, the more she thought about it, the more she was sure he needed clean clothes.

Regan was at her desk in her office, going over accounts, when Brandy walked in.

"And how is everything?" Brandy asked.

"Going quite well," Regan answered, looking at the books. "Next year we should be able to put up a couple of new buildings. I was thinking of a cabinet shop. Don't you think Scarlet Springs needs its own furniture maker?"

"You know I'm not talking about finances. How is it going between you and Farrell? You had dinner with him last night again, didn't you?"

"You know very well that I did. But to answer you, Farrell is always a delightful companion. His conversation is excellent, his manners are impeccable, and he knows how to make a woman feel like a crown princess."

"You're bored to tears by him, aren't you?" Brandy said with a sigh, sitting down.

"In a word, yes. There are no surprises with Farrell. He's so . . . I don't know, he's too perfect, I guess."

"Jennifer likes him."

Regan gave a little laugh. "Jennifer likes his gifts. Can you imagine giving a child as active as Jen a French porcelain fashion doll? She wanted to use it for target practice with the bow and arrow set you gave her."

Brandy smothered a giggle. "Perhaps Farrell expects little girls as well as big ones to be ladies."

Regan stood behind her desk. "Have we any new guests? I haven't looked this morning."

"There was some man getting out of a wagon a few minutes ago. Good-looking guy. Big."

"Brandy, you are incorrigible," Regan laughed. "But I'll go and welcome him."

Outside her office, she met Farrell. "Good morning," he said, raising her hand to his lips. "You are sweeter than the early sunshine on the drops of dew on a rose petal."

She didn't know whether to laugh or groan. "Thank you for such a lovely compliment, but I really must go now."

"Regan, dearest, you work too much. Come spend the day with me. We'll take Jennifer and go on a picnic, just as if we were a family."

"It's a tempting offer, but I really must go now."

"You can't escape me that easily," he smiled, and took her arm as they walked toward the reception area.

Regan felt Travis's presence before she saw him. He stood in the doorway, blocking the light with his big body. Her body went rigid as her eyes locked with his.

Neither of them moved; they just stood looking at each other. Wave after wave of emotion went through Regan until a loud crashing sounded in her ears. After minutes, hours it seemed, she turned on her heel and, skirts flying, fled back toward her office.

Farrell wasn't sure what was going on between Regan and this man, but he had a good idea. He didn't like this kind of reaction from her. Losing no time in following her, he was inches behind her.

"Regan, love," Farrell said as he put his hands on her shoulders. She was shaking so badly she could hardly stand.

But Regan was barely aware of him. All she heard was the pounding of her heart and the slow, heavy steps moving deliberately toward her door. Trembling, the blood gone from her head and hands, she clutched at the edge of her desk and leaned toward Farrell's strength.

The door to her office was pushed open with brutal force, slamming back against the wall.

"Why did you leave me?" Travis demanded in a low whisper, his eyes drilling into hers.

As he came closer she could not speak, could only look at him wildly.

"I asked you a question," Travis said.

Farrell stepped between them. "Now see here. I don't know who you are, but you have no right to anything from Regan."

He didn't finish what he had to say because Travis idly grabbed the smaller man's shoulders and tossed him to the far side of the room.

Regan barely noticed, only aware of Travis coming ever closer to her.

When he was inches from her, he gently touched her temple with his fingertips, and Regan felt her knees go weak. Before she could collapse, he caught her, lifted her in his arms, and buried his face in her neck. Without a word exchanged, he carried her toward the door, turned right, and went toward her apartment at the end of the hall. After two days of talking to the man Farrell had hired, Travis knew the entire floor plan of the Silver Dolphin Inn.

Her mind too full to think at all, she never considered what she was doing or committing herself to. All she knew was that Travis held her, and, more than life itself, she wanted him to make love to her.

Gently, as if she might break, he laid her on the bed and then sat beside her, his hands holding her face, fingertips caressing her cheeks and temples. "I had almost forgotten how beautiful you are," he whispered, "how delicately lovely you are."

Her hands went up his arms. How magnificent it felt to feel his strength once again, to feel the nearness of him! Her trembling began again as desire flooded her, coursing through her blood hotly.

"Travis," she managed to whisper before his mouth covered hers.

Desperate, frantic, turbulent, they began to tear at each other. There was no desire for sweetness, only a violent need that had to be fulfilled. Clothes tore away, buttons flew across the room, a handful of laces burst, and delicate stockings shredded. As they came together like a clap of thunder following a burst of brilliant lightning, they clawed and clung, drove each other deeper and deeper, trying to satisfy their overpowering, uncontrollable need of each other.

Violently, in a blinding flash, they arched together as spasms twisted their bodies. Clinging in a breathless crush for full minutes before their muscles relaxed, they finally surfaced and looked at each other, their eyes seeming to try to devour each other.

It was Regan who broke the spell—by laughing—for Travis, his chest and one arm bare, wore one shirt sleeve alone.

Glancing down at what she was laughing at, he grinned delightedly.

"The pot shouldn't call the kettle black," he said as he nodded pointedly toward the remnants of her attire.

A petticoat was bunched about her waist, while a torn one lay under them. Her stays, half on, half torn off, were crumbled under one arm, while her dress was about twelve feet across the room, dangling by a button from the corner of a picture frame. Rising on her elbows, she glanced down at her feet and saw that one stocking and its pretty lacy garter was intact while the other, with holes in it, was tangled in her toes.

Travis wore the one sleeve of his shirt and his boots and nothing in between.

With one look at Travis—his eyes dancing, his delicious body so near—she started laughing, her arms going out to him, pulling him to her as they began to roll about the bed, laughing gleefully, while Travis quite expertly tore away the remnants of her clothes. Never seeming to leave her, he took his boots off, and a loud crash of breaking china as one of the boots landed somewhere in the room caused new hilarity.

Sharp, teasing, nipping little bites on her shoulders and arms made her stop laughing and turn serious as she gave herself over to his lovemaking. Their first passion was gone, and they could spend more time reexploring, rediscovering each other. As Travis's mouth traveled down her body, she closed her eyes, gave herself over to her senses. Running her hand down his arm, she caught his hand, raised it to her lips, and began to taste those broad fingertips that gave her so much pleasure. Scraping them against her teeth, gently chewing on the soft pads, running her tongue across his knuckles, she was so aware that this was the hand of a man—scarred, hard, callused, broad, yet delicate and sensitive. She bit hard in the palm, wanting to devour him.

Travis pulled his hand away to run it over her legs, to massage, to kiss and caress, until she kicked her legs in impatience, wanting him again. When he brought his head up again, she pulled his mouth down to hers and threatened to swallow him whole.

Travis gave a low, seductive laugh and pulled her to him, both of them on their sides, facing, as he manipulated her legs around him and groaned when he entered her softness. Holding him tightly, staying with him as he moved her body, he prolonged her ecstasy for minutes, days, weeks, years, a century, as her head lolled backward, rolling, unaware of who or where she was.

When she thought she would go insane, he abruptly pushed her to her back and thrust into her long and hard until their bodies at last found release.

Without a word, exhausted, sweaty, sated, they fell asleep in each other's arms.

Regan was the first to awaken, surprised to see the sun setting outside her window. Stretching, moving away to look at Travis sprawled across the bed, she wondered if she'd ever have any sense when it came to him. For the first time in years she'd completely forgotten her responsibilities to her daughter, her friend, and her business. Quietly, so as not to disturb him, she left the bed and dressed, grabbing what was left of her mutilated garments from the furniture. Before she left the room she planted a kiss on Travis's hair and covered the lower half of him with a light quilt.

Silently, she left the room and headed toward the kitchen. Brandy must be wondering what had happened to her.

Travis awoke slowly, feeling as if he'd slept well for the first time in years. With a smile on his lips, he turned his head to look at his wife, but, instead of Regan, he encountered a pair of solemn brown eyes watching him intently.

"Hello," Travis said quietly to the little girl. "What's your name?"

"Jennifer Stanford. Who are you?"

Even before she spoke, Travis had an idea of who she was. There was a look about her of his younger brother, and the arch of her eyebrows was very like their mother's. "Is your mother's name Regan?"

Seriously, the child nodded.

Sitting up on the bed, pulling the quilt across his lower half, Travis was also serious. "What would you say if I were your father?"

Jennifer traced a pattern on the bedspread. "I might like it. Are you my father?"

"I think it would be safe to say I am."

"Are you going to live with us?"

"I was planning for you to live with me. If you were to come sit by me I could tell you all about where I live. Last year I bought four ponies just the right size for my daughter."

"You'd let me ride a pony?"

"It would be yours to care for, to ride, and to do whatever you wanted with it."

After just a moment's hesitation, Jennifer climbed onto the bed beside her father, far away at first, but as Travis's storytelling increased, soon she was sitting in his lap.

And that is how Regan found them, cuddled together, fascinated by each other. It was a charming picture.

As soon as Jennifer saw her mother, she started bouncing on the bed with glee. "This is my daddy, and we're going to go live with him, and he has a pony for me and pigs and chickens and a treehouse and a swimming pond, and we can go fishing and everything!"

After one quick look at Travis, Regan held out her arms for her daughter. "Brandy has supper ready for you in the kitchen."

"Can Daddy come too?"

"We need to talk," Regan said sternly. "He'll see you later— that is, if you eat what Brandy gives you."

"I will," Jennifer promised, waving to her father before scampering out the door.

"She's a beauty," Travis said. "I couldn't be prouder. . . ."

He stopped when Regan turned to look at him in fury. "Did I do something?"

"Did you do something?" she mocked, trying to control her temper. "How dare you tell *my* daughter we're going to live with you!"

"But of course you'll return now that I've found you. It just took me a while, that's all."

"Did it ever occur to you that I've always known where you were?" she fumed. "At any time that I wanted, I could have returned to you and that monstrosity of a plantation of yours."

"Regan," Travis said, his voice low. "I don't understand why you left, but I can tell you that you and my daughter are returning home with me."

"Right there is why I left," she said. "From the moment I met you you've told me what to do and how to do it. I wanted to stay in England, but you wanted me to come to America, so I came to America. You initiated a wedding ceremony without even asking me if I wanted to marry you. And then at that plantation of yours! I was left in charge of a hundred people who did everything they could to defy my authority. And all the while you were . . . out chasing horses with your dear Margo."

At the last, Travis smiled. "Jealousy, was that why you left me?"

Regan threw up her hands in despair. "Haven't you heard anything I've said? I don't want you to run my life, or Jennifer's. I don't want her growing up and being told when to do something and how to do it. I want her to learn to make her own decisions."

"When have I ever stopped you from making decisions? I gave you half a plantation of decisions to make, and I never interfered."

"But I didn't know how to make them. Can't you understand? I was so afraid, in a new country around strangers who constantly told me I didn't know how to do anything. I was *afraid!*"

Travis's eyes were twinkling. "From what I've heard, you've

done very well here. You didn't seem to be afraid of Americans here, so why were you there? I admit I have a fairly harsh group of judges working for me, but if you did it here, why couldn't you have done it then?"

"I don't know," she answered honestly. "Here I had to do something or starve. At your place I could have stayed in my room and never come out."

"Which you did most of the time, if I remember correctly."

She gave him a sharp look because she'd had no idea he'd known what she did during the day. Had he any idea how terrified she'd been during those months?

He continued, "After starting from scratch and buying and building a whole town, my place should be easy to run. I have a wagon here. We could pack Jennifer's clothes and yours and leave tomorrow. Or, better yet, let's leave now. You have clothes at home, and I'll buy my daughter everything new."

"Stop it!" she shouted. "Right this moment! Do you hear me? You are *not* going to start running my life for me again. I like having some power of my own. I like deciding what I want to do rather than having you or my uncle or even Farrell making my decisions for me."

His head came up. "Who's Farrell?"

With a look of disgust, she answered, "The man you so blithely tossed across the room this morning."

"So what's between you two?" he asked, his eyes in a hawk-like gaze.

"I knew Farrell in England. In fact, I was engaged to him once, and he came to America to find me."

For a moment, Travis was quiet. "You said you'd been in love with a man once. Was he this Farrell?"

She was startled at his memory. "I believe so. I was lonely, and he paid attention to me for a while, and I thought I loved him. It was so long ago, and I was a different person then."

"And how do you feel about him now?"

She walked about the room. "I don't know how I feel about anything right now. For years I was scared of everything, and then I suddenly was totally alone, and I had to sink or swim. For the last four years all I've done is balance ledger sheets and buy and sell property. Men have not been part of my life. Now all at once Farrell turns up, and I'm reminded of that unloved little girl I once was, and here you are, just like always, making me ache to touch you yet terrified you may make me into a crying child as I once was. Can't you understand, Travis? I can't return to your plantation and be smothered by you. The only way I can be myself is to stay away from you."

In spite of her best intentions, she began to cry. "Damn you!" she said. "Why did you have to come back and upset me like this? Go away, Travis Stanford! Go away and never, never come near me again." With that, she slammed out of the room.

Leaning back against the headboard, Travis smiled. When he'd first met her, he'd seen just a hint of the woman she could be, but he wasn't sure how to help her become that woman. Maybe she was right and the plantation was too much to handle. When he'd heard how the staff was treating her, it was all he could do to keep from throttling the lot of them, but he knew she needed to find her own strength.

Now, closing his eyes, thinking about her, he was overwhelmed at the woman she'd become—sure of herself, sensible, her dreams put into action, made into reality. She'd taken what was little more than a wide spot in the road and built a thriving town, and she'd raised an intelligent, sensible little daughter. No one need worry that Jennifer was going to retreat to her room and cry.

With a loud laugh of pure happiness, he tossed aside the quilt and began to dress; at least his pants and boots were in one piece. Although Regan thought she'd matured enough to resist him, he knew she hadn't. What was that old saying? Age and treachery will win out over youth and talent every time. He planned to use every means, every aid ever learned to win her back. With resolve, he left the room, wearing only the snug dark pants and tall boots.

Chapter 17

TRAVIS STOPPED at the open kitchen door, drawn to the smells coming from within. Chuckling, he remembered how Regan had always made him miss meals. With one glance about the room, he knew the luscious bit of curves and blonde hair in the corner was Brandy Dutton. He'd heard a lot about her from the weasel he'd met in Richmond.

"Excuse me," he said loudly. "I wonder if I might get something to eat in here. I'm not exactly dressed for dining in public."

"Oh my," Brandy said in such a way, smiling openly at Travis's wide chest and brawny arms, that Travis knew what he'd heard about her was true; Brandy was far from celibate.

She recovered herself. "So, you're the man who put roses in Regan's cheeks," she said heartily, coming forward.

"I put roses somewhere," he said quietly, for Brandy alone and not her staff, who were gaping unabashedly.

With a throaty laugh, Brandy took his arm. "I think we're going to get along quite well. Now sit down, and I'll get you something to eat. Elsie," she called over her shoulder. "Run down to the mercantile store and get Mr. Stanford a couple of new shirts, the biggest Will has. And take your time getting back. We have a lot to talk about."

Brandy fed Travis a meal such as he'd never had before. The more he ate of her food, the more she liked him, and between his shirtless state, the food, and his answers to her questions, she was practically in love by the end of the meal.

"Yes, she's lonely," Brandy said in answer to Travis's question. "All she does is work. It's like she's been driven to prove something to herself. For years I've tried to get her to slow down, but she'll never hear of it. She goes and goes all the time, buying more and more. She could have retired a year ago."

"No men?" he asked, his mouth full of mince pie.

"A few hundred have tried, but no one has succeeded. Of course, when you've had the best. . . ."

He smiled at her, took the new shirt from the chair back, and rose. "Regan and Jennifer are going to leave Scarlet Springs to return with me. How is that going to affect your partnership?"

"There's a new lawyer here from back East, and he could handle selling the properties and investing the money. With my half, I might like to travel, maybe see Europe. Tell me, have you told Regan she's leaving here?"

Travis only smiled in such a way that Brandy laughed. "Good luck," she called as he left the kitchen.

For two days Regan managed to avoid Travis, or at least she was able to avoid another out-and-out argument. But no one could miss him physically. Jennifer seemed to think her father was her personal playmate, and the two of them never left each other's sight. Travis even took over the task of washing his daughter's long, snarled hair, and Regan was disgusted not to hear one screech of pain or protest from Jennifer. He took her riding and tree climbing, and she was impressed at her father's agility. Jennifer showed him the whole town, announcing that he was her daddy and that she was going to go live with him and his horses.

Regan did her best to ignore Travis and his seduction of her daughter, as well as the countless questions from the townspeople.

Regan had not seen Farrell since the day Travis had arrived, and she was startled to realize, when he reappeared, that she had not thought of him in his two-day absence.

"May I speak to you privately?" he asked.

He looked tired and very dirty, as if he'd been traveling for days without sleep.

"Of course. Come to my office." When they were inside the office, door closed, she turned to him. "You look as if you have something important to tell me."

Collapsing into a chair, he looked up at her. "I have been all the way to Boston and back in two days."

"It must have been urgent business," she said, pouring him a drink. "I take it I and my father's money are involved."

"Yes, or at least your father's will. There was a copy filed in an attorney's office in Boston. I had it made and sent to America some time ago, just in case I did find you. I thought I was sure of one point in it, but I went to Boston to have it confirmed. I have here a letter," he said, removing an envelope from his inside coat pocket.

Regan took it, held it for a moment. "Perhaps you could tell me what it says."

"Your parents died when you were very young, and perhaps you don't remember, but at that time your father's brother was still alive. He was to be your guardian, and you did stay with him for a few months, but he died soon after your parents."

"I remember only Uncle Jonathan."

"Yes, he was the only other relation you had, so the executors of the will, your parents' bank, put you into his care. They, of course, had no idea what sort of a man he was. At the time the will was written, your parents thought you would be safe with your father's brother."

"Farrell, please get to the point."

"The point, my dear, is that you could not get married without your guardian's permission. Perhaps they didn't want you marrying a fortune hunter, or perhaps they didn't want to see you go through the hell they did when they were cut off by her family without a penny."

"Is that all? Surely there's more to this," she said.

"Regan, you don't understand. You were married to Travis Stanford without your guardian's written permission, and you were only seventeen."

"Seventeen! No, I'd been eighteen for months."

"In the letter is your actual date of birth. Your uncle tried to forge the date ahead so he could marry you off and get his money."

Feeling a bit stunned, Regan leaned back against the desk. "You're saying that my marriage to Travis isn't valid, aren't you?"

"Worthless. You were underage, a minor without your guardian's consent. You are not, nor have you ever been, married to anyone, Miss Weston."

"And Jennifer?"

"I'm sorry to say that she is illegitimate. Of course, if you were to marry again, the husband could adopt her."

"I don't think Travis would like someone else adopting his daughter," she said quietly.

"To hell with Travis," Farrell said, jumping up to stand before her. "I've waited for you for years. I've loved you for years. You can't blame me for shying away from a seventeen-year-old child. Instinctively I must have sensed your tender years, and you can't blame me for not wanting a child for a wife. At least I didn't force you to my bed as that man who is Jennifer's father did."

He paused, taking her hand in his. "Marry me, Regan. I'll make a good, faithful husband to you. Haven't I loved you for many years already? And I'll be a good father to Jennifer."

"Please, Farrell," she said, pulling away from him. "I must think about this. It's come as a shock finding out I've lived in sin with a man for so many years. And this could hurt Jennifer badly."

"That's why—," he began, but she put up her hand and cut him off.

"I need to be alone to think about this, and you," she smiled, "need a bath and some rest."

It was several more minutes before he left and Regan was finally alone to read what was inside the packet Farrell had brought her. A half-hour later, when she put it down, she smiled. It was true she'd never been married to Travis. How he was going to rage at this news! For the first time in years she lapsed into one of her daydreams, imagining how he'd react when she told him he had no power over her, that, legally, Jennifer was no man's daughter. For just once in her life she was going to win over Travis Stanford, and it was going to be a wonderful experience.

As for Farrell's proposal, she dismissed it. The silly man thought Regan really believed his protestations of love. He wanted her married to him before her twenty-third birthday when she would come into her parents' fortune. He'd learn soon enough that she was going to live her own life.

With a smile, she began to write Travis a note, asking him to join her for a private dinner that night.

The private dining room was set with tall, fragrant candles, cut crystal glassware from Vienna, porcelain dinnerware from France, silver from England. The wine was a delicacy from Germany, and the food was American.

"I'm glad to see that you've come to your senses," Travis said, buttering a biscuit. "Jennifer will be much better off around friends instead of all these strangers. Has she always been given the run of this place? I can't see that it's good for a child playing in the corridors of a public inn."

"And you have such a vast experience with children that you, of course, know exactly what is right for them," Regan retorted.

He shrugged, enjoying his food. "I certainly know enough to be certain there is a better place for a child than this. At my place you can spend more time with Jennifer and"—he smiled—"our other children."

"Travis—," she began, but he interrupted her.

"I can't begin to tell you how relieved I was when you finally came to your senses. But really, I was expecting more of a fight. You've grown up more than I thought."

"What!" she sputtered on her wine. "Finally came to my senses? Grown up? What are you talking about?"

He caught her hand in his, caressed her fingers, and when he spoke his voice was deep and low. "This dinner was such a surprise to me because I knew what you wanted to say." He kissed her fingertips. "I want you to know that I realize how difficult a decision it's been for you, and I'll never use it against you. You've done a brave and generous thing in agreeing to return with me. Perhaps you'd like to stay here in your little town for a while longer, but Jennifer needs more than a houseful of strangers—she needs a home, which I can, of course, give her." Again, he kissed her fingers. "You've made a wise decision."

Taking deep breaths to calm herself, as well as a deep drink of wine, Regan gave him a radiant smile. "You vain, pompous farmer," she said conversationally. "I do not plan to return to your house, and my 'little town,' as you call it, is home for my daughter."

In spite of her good intentions, her voice was rising. "I invited you here, not to tell you I was returning with you as you so arrogantly assumed, but to tell you that I am not and never have been married to you."

It was Travis's turn to sputter. Regan, for the first time during the meal, began to eat. It felt good to win over Travis!

Grabbing her wrist, he started to pull her from her seat.

"What are you doing?" she demanded.

"I assume you have a preacher in this town. He can marry us now."

"He will not!" she hissed. "And if you don't sit down I just may take Jennifer away again."

Hesitating, but not wanting to risk such a punishment, he sat down. "Tell me the whole story," he said bleakly.

Regan lost some of her cheerfulness when she saw Travis's look, and when she told him his daughter was not legally his, she almost said she'd marry him then and there. But it was at the mention of Farrell's name that his look changed.

"That two-bit piece of scum told you this?" he demanded. "He's certainly gone to a lot of trouble. What's in it for him?"

Regan was well aware that Travis knew nothing of the money she was due to inherit, money that would mean nothing to Travis but meant everything to Farrell. But, truthfully, she didn't like Travis's insinuation that Farrell had a motive besides love.

"Farrell wants to marry me," she said haughtily. "He says he loves me as well as Jennifer and wants to adopt my daughter."

"You wouldn't be such a fool," Travis said smugly. "Why would any woman want a weakling like that?"

The implied second part of that statement was, "When you could have someone like me?"

Glaring at him, Regan almost snarled. "Farrell is a gentleman. He knows how to make a woman feel like a lady. His courting is . . . exquisite," she said with feeling. "All you Americans know is how to make demands."

Travis snorted. "Any American can outcourt any weakling Englishman."

"Oh Travis," Regan smiled serenely. "You know nothing of courting. Your idea of seducing a woman is to drag her about by her hair."

"There've been a few times when you've liked being dragged about," he answered.

She lost her serenity. "That is an example of your Colonial crudity."

"And you, my dear, are an English snob. You said your birthday is in three weeks. You'll marry me on that day, and you'll do it willingly."

With that, he left the room before he heard Regan gasp, "Never!"

Early the next morning, Regan, in her office, was bombarded with news from Brandy. First there were accusations because Travis had left the inn last night, and this morning he still hadn't returned. Brandy's looks showing her opinion that Regan was in the wrong were followed by a word of warning, for a tall, red-haired woman had just registered at the inn and was asking for her fiancé, Mr. Travis Stanford.

"Looks to me like you've got some trouble," Brandy sighed.

"Oh good," Regan answered in a tired voice. "Just what I need. Doesn't anyone realize that it's not easy to run an inn this size? I have days of work piled on my desk, and, by the way, Farrell has already informed me that Travis has left, and, before him, my daughter told me. Farrell, I'm sure, has much more to say to me, but Jennifer may never say another word in my presence. Now, the redhead has got to be my dear friend Margo Jenkins. Just let me have a few minutes to collect myself and I'll be able to deal with her."

Brandy nodded and left the room.

For several moments, Regan stood quietly in her bedroom, letting her mind take her back to that time of Margo's visits to Travis's plantation. Then, Regan had been so grateful to Margo for not being angry with her, for helping with the household staff, that Regan had not seen Margo's insults for what they were. That Malvina! Regan thought. How she'd like to get her hands on that foul-tempered, lazy cook now. And Margo! Dear Margo lording it over the poor, insecure little wife, pretending to help but actually destroying what little confidence she did have.

Smiling, Regan left her office, stopped by the kitchen, and

asked Brandy to prepare midmorning tea for two women. She ignored Brandy's remarks about looking ready to do battle and then sent an invitation to Margo, asking her to tea in the library.

Margo appeared in an astonishingly short time, and Regan saw things she hadn't seen before; years of dissipation were showing on Margo's face and body. Late nights, rich food, overindulgence of every sort showed in lines and dark places, a thickening of the waist in spite of the tight lacing of her stays.

"My, my, it's the little English flower," Margo said as she entered. "I hear you own this place now. Who bought it for you?"

"Won't you have a seat?" Regan said politely. "I've ordered some refreshments. Yes, I do own the inn." Smiling innocently, she continued, "As well as the printer's building, the lawyer's, the doctor's, the mercantile store, the blacksmith's, the schoolhouse, the druggist's, plus four farms outside the town and three hundred acres."

Margo's eyes blinked once, but otherwise she showed no change of expression. "And how many men have you slept with to get all that? Travis, I'm sure, would like to know."

"How kind you are to say you think I'm worth so much," Regan said enthusiastically. "But alas, I'm afraid I don't have your skills of selling myself to get what I want. I had to use old-fashioned intelligence and hard work to get what I own. Whenever I had a spare bit of change, I didn't spend it on a new gown but used it to bargain with to buy more land and more building materials."

She stopped to answer the door to a very curious Brandy who was holding a large tray.

"How's it going?" Brandy whispered.

Regan smiled smugly, making Brandy laugh as she handed her friend the tray.

When they were alone again, with the tray on a low table between them, Regan poured tea.

"Shall we begin again?" Regan asked. "It's no use pretending that we're friends. I take it you are here because you want my husband."

Margo collected herself. This was not a battle she wanted to lose. "I see you have learned to pour tea," she said.

"I have learned a great many things in the last few years. You'll find I'm not so trusting as I once was. Now tell me what you want."

"I want Travis. He was mine until you jumped into his bed, got yourself pregnant, and forced him to marry you."

"That is one way of looking at the situation. Tell me, has Travis said he'd marry you if he were free of me?"

"He doesn't have to tell me," Margo said. "We were almost engaged when he met you, and the only problem is that he's infatuated with you. He's never had a woman leave him before, and it's driving him wild."

"If that is the case, if Travis likes women who leave him, why did you follow him here? Wouldn't it have been better to stay away and let him return to you?"

"Damn you, you little bitch!" Margo snarled. "Travis Stanford is mine! He was mine long before you were out of short dresses. You left him! You stole his mother's jewels and just walked off and left him. If I hadn't found that note—." She stopped abruptly.

Regan caught Margo's eyes for a moment, her mind concentrating. All these years she'd wondered why Travis had never found her. She'd left a trail a child could have followed, but Travis had never even bothered. But if Margo had found the note first. . . .

"Did he look for me for very long?" Regan asked quietly.

Standing, Margo glared down at her. "You don't really expect me to tell you anything, do you? Just be warned. Travis is mine. I don't believe you're woman enough to fight me. I get what I want."

"Do you, Margo?" Regan asked calmly. "Do you have a man

who holds you at night while you cry or one you can tell your deepest secrets to? Do you know what it's like to share, to love and be loved by someone?" Turning her head, she looked up at Margo. "Or do you think of people in terms of dollars and cents? Tell me, if you owned Scarlet Springs, would you be so interested in my husband?"

Margo started to speak but seemed to change her mind as, silently, she left the room.

When Regan put the teacup to her lips, she was surprised to find she was trembling. The questions she'd asked Margo were what she'd been asking herself and had not been aware of them. What did owning a town mean, anyway? She had friends here, people she'd come to love, but were they any substitute for one special person, someone who loved you even when you weren't in the best of moods, someone to hold your head when you were sick, a special person who knew all your ugly parts and still loved you anyway?

Remembering Travis's plantation and Stanford Hall, she knew that Jennifer should grow up there. Travis's hundreds of relatives' portraits were on the walls, and they were Jennifer's ancestors, too. She deserved that sort of continuity, a place that was filled with security and peace, not the ever-changing interior of an inn.

Smiling, she leaned back against the chair. Of course, it wouldn't be easy to tell Travis he'd won. No doubt he'd gloat and tell her he knew he'd win. But who cared? It meant more to spend her life with the man she loved than to give it all up because of her silly pride. Besides, there'd be ways to repay him. Oh yes, she thought. She'd make him sorry he had ever bragged about anything.

"You certainly look pleased with yourself," Brandy said.

Regan hadn't heard her friend enter the room. "I was just thinking about Travis."

"That would make me smile, too. So when are you leaving with him?"

"And what makes you assume—?" Regan began, then stopped at Brandy's laugh. "I know what you're thinking, and it's all true. You know, for years I was afraid of Travis, afraid his personality would devour me and I wouldn't exist any longer."

"But now you know you can hold your own," Brandy said.

"Yes, and I realize he's right, that his plantation is a better place for Jennifer. And what about you? How is it going to affect you if I leave Scarlet Springs? Should I get someone else to help run the inn?"

"No, don't worry about it," Brandy said, holding up her hand. "Travis and I have arranged it all. There'll be no problem."

"Travis and you! You mean you . . . and my husband . . . ? Behind my back?"

"The last I heard, he wasn't your husband any longer. And of course I knew you'd leave here. Travis is not a man a woman can resist very long. Did you know what hell he went through trying to find you after you left? And that he's been celibate since you left him?"

"What?" Regan asked as warmth spread over her. "How do you know any of this?"

"While you've been working, I've spent some time with Travis and Jennifer, and if you weren't curious, I certainly have been. Would you like to hear some of what that dear man's been through in the last few years?"

Brandy didn't wait for Regan's answer before she started on the long, detailed story of Travis's ordeal. Most of his friends believed Regan had drowned, but Travis kept searching for her in spite of everyone telling him to give it up. At one point a preacher was urging him to conduct a funeral for his dear departed wife, thinking perhaps that would rid Travis of his obsession with her.

An hour later, Regan left the library, her head in the clouds. Ignoring Farrell, who called after her, she kept looking for Travis, eager to tell him she loved him, wanted to marry him, and would return to his home with him.

By the end of the day, when he still hadn't appeared, some of her enthusiasm left her. Distractedly, she refused Farrell's dinner invitation and spent the evening with her daughter. When the second night passed and she still hadn't seen Travis, her euphoric state broke. Jennifer was sulking and shooting angry looks at her mother, Farrell was becoming quite persistent in his invitations, and Margo constantly asked Regan where Travis was.

By the third day, she wished she'd never heard of Travis Stanford. He couldn't have left her after all he'd done to find her! Could he? Oh, please God, she prayed, flinging herself onto the bed that night. Please don't let him have left me. For the first time in years, she began to cry. Damn you, Travis! she gasped. How many tears had that man made her shed?

Chapter 18

AT FIVE o'clock the next morning, Regan was awakened by someone knocking on her door. Sleepily, she rolled out of bed and pulled on her dressing gown.

Standing in the hallway was Timmie Watts, the son of one of her farm tenants. Before she could say a word, the little boy handed her a long-stemmed red rose and vanished down the hall.

Yawning, not awake, Regan looked down at the exquisite, fragrant flower. Attached to its stem was a bit of paper which she unfurled to read, "Regan, will you marry me? Travis."

It was a full minute before her mind understood what her eyes saw, and then she gave a squeal of delight, hugged the rose to her breast, and jumped into the air three times. He hadn't forgotten her after all!

"Mommie," Jennifer said, rubbing the sleep from her eyes. "Is Daddy home?"

"Almost," Regan laughed, grabbing her daughter and waltzing her about the room. "This rose, this lovely, perfect rose, is from your daddy. He wants us to go live with him."

"We are," Jennifer laughed, clutching her mother as she began to get dizzy. "We can ride my pony."

"Every single day from now on and forever!" Regan laughed. "Now let's get dressed, because I'm sure Daddy will be here very soon."

Before Regan settled on a gown of gold velvet, she threw everything she owned onto the bed. It was while she was in the midst of this mess that someone again knocked on her door. Flying to it, hoping to see Travis, she flung the door open.

Standing there was Sarah Watts, Timmie's sister, and she was clutching two pink roses. Puzzled, taking the roses, Regan watched as Sarah fled down the hall.

"Was that Daddy?" Jennifer asked.

"No, but Daddy sent us two more roses." Attached to each one was a curl of paper in Travis's handwriting, saying, "Regan, will you marry me? Travis."

"Is something wrong, Mommie? Why doesn't Daddy come see us?"

Heedless of the clothes on the bed, Regan sat down. It was just a tiny, lurking suspicion, but the extra roses made her wonder what Travis was planning. With one glance at the clock, she saw that it was just after five-thirty. One rose had been delivered at five, two at five-thirty. No, she thought. It couldn't be.

"Nothing's wrong, sweet," Regan said. "Would you like these roses for your room?"

"They're from Daddy?"

"They certainly are."

Jennifer took the flowers, holding them as if they were priceless, and carried them to her room.

At six, when Jennifer and Regan were dressed and going down to breakfast, three more roses were delivered to Regan.

"How lovely," Brandy said, already up and cooking. Before Regan could protest, Brandy took the flowers, read the attached notes, and put the flowers in a vase. "You don't look so happy. I thought from the way you've been moping for the last three days you'd be pleased to get some sign from him. Three roses with those notes attached would certainly perk me up."

"There are five roses," she said seriously. "One delivered at five, two at five-thirty, three at six."

"You aren't thinking—," Brandy began.

"I had forgotten about it, but Travis and I did have words over courting. I made some derogatory remarks about the inability of Americans to court a woman."

"Not a nice thing to have said," Brandy said, feeling very American. "Five roses before breakfast shows you what we Americans can do." With that she went back to cooking.

Feeling she'd offended her best friend, Regan went to the dining room to check that everything was ready. As she was leaving the room, the printer's boy delivered four yellow roses to her, each with Travis's note attached.

With an enormous sigh, Regan smiled at the roses, shaking her head. Did Travis never do anything on a small scale? She slipped the notes into her pocket and went to look for a vase.

By ten o'clock, her smile was gone. Every half-hour more roses were delivered, until by now she had a total of sixty-six. The quantity itself wouldn't be daunting except for the interest the deliveries were exciting within the town. The druggist and his wife came to eat breakfast at the inn, something they'd never done before, and as they were leaving, they stopped to ask Regan questions, namely, who is this Travis who'd hired their three children to deliver roses every half-hour? They were very mysterious about where the children picked up the flowers or who had contacted them, and they were discreet about the notes they'd read— but curiosity was eating them alive.

At noon, a bouquet of fifteen roses, each with a note on its stem, was handed to Regan, and that's when she began to try hiding. But the whole town seemed to be in conspiracy against her. At five minutes before the hour or half-hour, someone always found something important to say to her, something that would keep her in plain view of everyone when the next bouquet was delivered.

At four o'clock, she was presented with twenty-three roses.

"That makes two hundred and seventy-six," the owner of the mercantile store said, chalking the number on the wall beside the bar in the taproom.

"Don't you have any customers today?" Regan asked pointedly.

"Nary a one," he smiled. "They're all in here." He looked back at the jammed taproom. "Who'll give me money on when they're going to stop?"

Turning away, Regan left the room, thrusting the bundle of roses into Brandy's arms.

"Roses?" Brandy gasped. "What a wonderful surprise. Whoever sent them?"

Regan curled her lip and hissed before continuing down the hall. She wouldn't put it past Travis to have instigated all the interest in the roses. Surely the townspeople had something better to do than sit around all day and watch her collect roses. Of course, the reason he'd hired every child in town for the deliveries was to create interest with the parents.

At seven o'clock, she received twenty-nine roses, and at eight, she got thirty-one. By nine she had received five hundred sixty-one roses, of every color a rose could create. Travis's notes, the same thing over and over, were in her pockets, in her desk drawers, in a box on her dressing table, in a copper pan in the kitchen. For all her complaining, she couldn't bring herself to discard even one of the notes.

By ten she was beginning to wonder if the flowers were ever going to stop. She was tired and wanted nothing more than to climb into bed and be still.

Just as she reached her door, a child thrust a bundle of thirty-five roses into her arms. Once inside, she carefully removed each note, read it, and then stored all of them in a drawer beside her underwear. "Travis," she whispered, no longer tired. At least alone in her room she could enjoy the roses.

Someone, Brandy no doubt, had put several water-filled vases in a corner, and Regan filled one now. As she did so, she remembered the last time he'd given her flowers, on their wedding night.

She was still chuckling when thirty-six roses were delivered at ten-thirty. Roses were also delivered at eleven and eleven-thirty. At midnight, yawning, Regan answered the knock at her door to admit Reverend Wentworth from the Scarlet Springs church.

"Won't you come in?" she asked politely.

"No, I must get home. It's far past my bedtime. I just came to bring you this."

He held out a long, narrow white box, and when Regan opened it, inside was a delicate rose of fine, thin, fragile, pink-tinted crystal. The stem and leaves were also glass, tinted a soft green. An engraved silver band hung gracefully down the side, reading, "Regan, will you marry me? Travis."

Regan was speechless, afraid to touch the elusive beauty of the glass rose.

"Travis was so hoping you'd like it," Reverend Wentworth said.

"Where did he find it? And how did he get it to Scarlet Springs?"

"That, my dear, is known only to Mr. Stanford. He merely asked if I'd deliver a gift to you at midnight tonight. Of course, when the box came and it was open, my wife and I, well . . . we couldn't resist a peek. Now I really must go. Goodnight."

She barely heard him, absently closing the door, leaning against it for a second, her eyes locked on the elegant, splendid crystal rose. Holding her breath, afraid she might break it, she put it in the little vase on her bedside table, next to the first live rose Travis had sent her. As she undressed, her eyes never left either rose, and when she went to bed the moonlight seemed to highlight each rose and she fell asleep smiling.

It was late when she awoke the next morning, already eight o'clock. After one quick look at her roses and sending all of them a radiant smile, she jumped out of bed and grabbed her dressing gown. One sleeve was twisted, and as she straightened it a blue piece of paper fell out. As it fell right-side up on the floor, she saw that it read, "Regan, will you marry me? Travis."

Hastily, she stuck it in her pocket, thinking that she hadn't noticed that any of the notes from yesterday were written on blue paper. She found Jennifer's room empty. The child was often up early and in the kitchen before her mother was even awake.

Still smiling, Regan returned to her room to dress. Today she was sure Travis would show up, would come to her on bended knee and beg her to marry him. She might, just might consent. She laughed out loud.

Her laugh stopped when she found another blue note inside the bodice of her dress. Hesitating for just a moment, looking suspiciously at the note, she whirled about and began to search her wardrobe.

The blue notes were everywhere—in her shoes, in her dresses, inside her drawers, wrapped in her petticoats and camisoles, even under her pillow!

How dare he! she thought, getting angrier with each note she found. How dare he invade her privacy in such a way! If not Travis personally, then he'd hired someone to go through all her things and place the notes there. And when? Surely some of them had been put there during the night, because even the dress she'd worn yesterday had three notes in it.

Angrily, she left her apartment and went straight to her office. As far as she could tell, nothing had been disturbed in this room. Thank heavens she locked it each night.

Sitting down at her desk, she didn't at first notice the thin bit of thread stretched across the leather blotter. Suspicious, her lips set firmly, she followed it down the front of her desk to the bottom, where it disappeared underneath. On her hands and knees, she slid down until she was flat on her back. Pinned to the bottom of her desk was a sign done in three-inch letters, "Regan, will you marry me? Travis."

Teeth gritted, she tore it away and was tearing it into tiny pieces when Brandy entered the room with a few dozen pieces of blue paper in her hands.

"I see he's been in here too," Brandy said cheerfully.

"He's really gone too far this time. This is my private office, and he has no right to come in here uninvited."

"I don't want to add to your anger, but have you checked your safe?"

"My—!" she began, but stopped. Only Regan had a set of the three keys it took to open the safe. The other set was locked in a bank vault a hundred miles to the south. Even Brandy never opened the inn's safe or knew how or in what order the keys must be used; she left all that up to Regan.

Quickly, Regan went to the big safe and started the long process of opening it. As she pulled the last door, a piece of wide blue ribbon fell out. Slowly pulling it, her jaw set, her eyes angry, she saw immediately what was written on it. She didn't bother to read it but reached in and grabbed a handful of ribbon and angrily threw it toward the trashcan.

"How did you guess?" she asked Brandy as she stood.

Brandy seemed a bit nervous and gave Regan a weak smile. "I hope you're ready for this. It seems that while everyone in town was here yesterday and their stores were closed, somebody, or maybe it was an army of somebodies, put these little blue proposals all over town. The doctor found one in his bag and four in his office. Will, at the mercantile store, found six in his place, and"—she paused to stifle a laugh—"the blacksmith picked up a horse's hoof and found one on blue ribbon wadded inside the horse's shoe."

Regan sat down. "Go on," she whispered.

"Some of the people are taking it well, but some are fairly angry. The lawyer found one in his safe, and he's talking about suing. But, in general, everyone is laughing, saying they want to meet this Travis."

"I never want to see him again in my life," Regan said with feeling.

"You don't mean that," Brandy smiled. "Maybe your notes are all alike, but most of the others are quite creative. There are bits of poetry, some things from Shakespeare, and Mrs. Ellison, who plays the piano, received an entire song which she says is very pretty. She's dying to play it for you."

Regan's head came up. "Is she out there?"

Brandy grimaced. "Everyone feels as if they're involved now, and . . . most of them are out there."

"Who is *not* there?" Regan asked bleakly.

"Mrs. Ellison's grandmother, who had the stroke last year, and Mr. Watts still had milking to do, and . . . ," she trailed off apologetically because she could think of no other missing townspeople.

"Mrs. Brown's sister is visiting, came in yesterday, and she's dying to meet you. Brought all six kids over, too."

Regan put her arms on the desk and buried her face. "Can a person die by will, just by wishing it? How can I face all those people?" She looked up at Brandy, her face horribly distressed. "How could Travis do this to me?"

Brandy knelt beside her friend and touched her hair. "Regan, can't you see that he just wants you so badly that he'll do *anything* to get you back? You don't know the hell he's been through since you left. Did you know that he lost forty-five pounds when you first left him? It was a friend of his named Clay who talked him out of giving up on life."

"Travis told you all of this?"

"In a roundabout way. I did some prying, and it took a while to piece together all the facts, but I did. Right now the man is past any sense of pride. He doesn't care what he has to do to get you back. If he can enlist the whole town to help him, then he will.

Maybe his tactics are a little . . . well, maybe he's not exactly subtle, but would you rather have one rose and a man like Farrell or, what was the final count, seven hundred and forty-two roses and Travis Stanford?"

"But does he have to do all this?" Regan pleaded, flipping the thread leading to the note that had been under her desk.

"You've told me repeatedly how Travis never asked you anything, but only told you what to do and how to do it. If I remember correctly, at the ceremony you said no to him just because he hadn't *asked* you to marry him. I don't believe you can accuse him of not having asked you now. And, too, you said you wanted to be courted." Brandy stood, smiling. "This courtship may go down in history."

Regan, in spite of herself, began to smile. "All I wanted was a little champagne and a few roses."

Eyes wide, Brandy put her fingers to her lips. "Please don't mention champagne. You may start a flood."

A giggle escaped Regan. "Will he ever do anything on a normal scale?"

"Don't you hope not?" Brandy said seriously. "I'd give a lot to be in your shoes."

"My shoes are all packed full of notes," Regan said, deadpan.

Laughing, Brandy started toward the door. "You'd better prepare yourself. They are waiting eagerly for you."

Brandy laughed at Regan's heartfelt groan before leaving the room.

Taking a moment to calm herself, Regan thought about Brandy's words. Everything about Travis was overscale, from his body to his house to his land, so why did she expect his courting to be any different?

Carefully, she retrieved the ribbon from the trash and tenderly folded it. Someday she'd show this to her grandchildren. With resolve, shoulders straight, she left her office and went toward the public rooms.

Nothing could have prepared her for what was awaiting her. The first person she saw was Mrs. Ellison's grandmother enthroned in a chair, smiling at her with one side of her face, the other side paralyzed by her stroke.

"I'm so glad you could make it," Regan said graciously, as if she'd issued invitations to this party.

"Seven hundred and forty-two!" a man was saying. "And the last one was made of glass, all the way from Europe."

"Wonder how he got it here and didn't break it?"

"And wonder how he got up to my loft? The ladder broke two days ago, and I ain't had time to fix it. But there it was, just as pretty as you please, a ribbon around a bale of hay and asking Regan to marry him."

There was a man painting a vine of roses on the wall behind the bar in her taproom, and beside it were numbers—5:00 A.M., 1 rose; 5:30 A.M., 2 roses, all the way down to 38 roses at 11:30 P.M. and one rose at midnight and the total at the bottom. She didn't bother to ask who the painter was or who had given him permission to paint on her wall. She was too busy fending off questions.

"Regan, is it true this man is Jennifer's father yet you're not married to him?"

"We were married at the time Jennifer was born," Regan tried to explain. "But I was underage and—."

Someone else's question interrupted her.

"I hear this man Travis owns half of Virginia."

"Not quite, only about a third." Sarcasm didn't dull their interest.

"Regan, I don't like this man leaving notes in my private safe. I have private documents in there, and a lawyer's word to his clients is sacred."

On and on they went, hour after hour, until Regan's smile was plastered on. Only a small voice at her side made her respond. "Mommie." She looked down to see her daughter's small face, obviously worried about something.

"Come on," she said, lifting her daughter and carrying her to the kitchen. "Let's see if Brandy can fix us lunch, and we'll go on a picnic."

An hour later, Regan and her daughter were alone together by a little stream north of Scarlet Springs. They'd demolished a basketful of fried chicken and little cherry tarts.

"Why doesn't Daddy come back home?" Jennifer asked. "And why doesn't he write me letters like everybody else?"

For the first time, Regan realized that her daughter had been excluded from the notes and roses. Thinking back, she knew Jennifer's room had been free of any marriage proposals.

She pulled her daughter to her lap. "I guess because Daddy is trying to get me to marry him, and he knows that wherever I go, you go too."

"Daddy doesn't want to marry me too?"

"He wants you to live with him; in fact, I think at least half of the roses are for you, to get you to come live with him too."

"I wish he'd send me roses. Timmie Watts says Daddy only wants you, and I'll have to stay here with Brandy when you go away."

"That was a dreadful thing for him to say! And totally untrue! Your Daddy loves you very much. Didn't he tell you of the pony he bought for you and the treehouse he built? And this was before he'd even met you. Just think what he's going to do now that he knows who you are."

"You think he'll ask me to marry him too?"

Regan had no idea how to reply to that. "When he asks me, it means he wants you too."

Sighing, Jennifer leaned against her mother. "I wish Daddy'd come home. I wish he'd never go away again, and I wish he'd send me roses and write me letters."

Rocking her daughter, stroking her hair, Regan felt Jennifer's sadness. How Travis would hate knowing he had hurt his daughter by excluding her. Perhaps tomorrow she could make up for

Travis's oversight. Maybe she could find some roses, if there were any left within the state after Travis's harvesting of them, and give them to her daughter—from her father.

Tomorrow, she thought, and almost shuddered. What could he be planning for tomorrow?

Chapter 19

JENNIFER WOKE her mother the next morning, a little bundle of roses clutched in her hand. "Do you think they're from Daddy?" she asked her mother.

"Could be," Regan said, not really lying but giving the child hope. She'd placed the little bouquet on her daughter's pillow early this morning.

"They're not from Daddy," Jennifer said with great despair. "You put them there." With a fling, she tossed them across the bed and ran to her own room.

It was some time before Regan could comfort her daughter, and she was close to tears herself before Jennifer quietened. If only there was some way she could get a message to Travis and tell him of Jennifer's distress.

When they were finally dressed, both of them far from cheerful, they held hands and together prepared for what the day—and Travis—had planned for them.

The reception rooms were full of townspeople, but since there was no new excitement, often only one family member was present. Stiffly, Regan fended off their questions and kept Jennifer near her as she checked the rooms of the inn and tried to keep up a normal routine. She was quite tired of being a spectacle for everyone to stare and gawk at.

By noon nothing new had happened, and the townspeople,

deflated, began to go home. The dining room was filled but not packed, and Regan noticed Margo and Farrell dining together, their heads bent, almost touching as they talked. Frowning, she wondered what the two of them could have to say to each other.

But she had no more time to think about anything else, because the noise coming from the hall was rising in tone and pitch.

Eyes skyward, she felt like crying in despair. "Now what has he done?" she muttered.

Jennifer clutched her mother's hand. "Do you think Daddy's come home?"

"I'm sure he's done something," she said, and started for the front door.

Music began to fill the front of the inn as soon as they left the dining room. The sound of horses and wagons and other sounds she'd never heard before became louder and louder.

"What is it?" Jennifer asked, eyes widening by the second.

"I have no idea," Regan replied.

The front of the hotel was plastered with people, all frozen in their places at the six windows in front and the open door.

"Jennifer!" someone yelled, and all the people suddenly came alive.

"It's a circus!"

"And a menagerie! I saw one in Philadelphia once."

Jennifer's name was repeated several times before Regan could make a place for herself and her daughter on the front porch.

Just rounding the corner by the schoolhouse were three men, their faces painted, wearing satin clothes sewn with spots and stripes of outrageous colors, and they were doing flips, tumbling, jumping over each other.

Something on their chests seemed to be letters. It took Regan a while to make out the word because of the clowns' acrobatics.

"Jennifer," she said. "It says Jennifer."

Laughing, grabbing her daughter in her arms, she pointed excitedly. "It's for you! They're clowns, and they have Jennifer, your name, written on their suits."

"They're for me?"

"Yes, yes, yes! Your Daddy has sent you a whole circus, and if I know Travis, it's no little circus. Look! Here come some men doing tricks on horses."

More than a little stunned, Jennifer watched as three horses, beautiful, golden, long-maned horses, came galloping toward them, a man in each saddle, one standing up, another jumping in and out of the saddle, his feet barely touching the ground, and the last man's horse seemed to be dancing. As a body, they stopped in the midst of a storm of dust and saluted Jennifer. Grinning almost enough to tear her skin, she looked at her mother.

"The circus is for me," she said proudly, turning away to look at the other people beside her. "My Daddy sent a circus for me."

A stilt-walker followed the clowns and equestrians, and then came a man pulling a small black bear on a chain. Everything had Jennifer's name written on it. The music was growing louder as the band came closer to the inn.

Suddenly a hush fell over all the townspeople as around the corner came the biggest, most bizarre creature anyone had ever seen. Lumbering slowly, its massive feet making the ground quake, the animal with its trainer leading it stopped before the inn. The man unfurled a sign down the animal's side: "Capt. John Crowinshield presents the first elephant to appear in these United States of America. And at a special request of Mr. Travis Stanford, this great beast will perform for—."

Regan read the sign to her daughter, who was clinging tightly to her mother.

"For Jennifer!" a second sign heralded.

"What do you think of that?" Regan asked. "Daddy sent the elephant to perform just for you."

For a moment Jennifer didn't answer, but after a long pause

she leaned toward her mother's ear. "I don't have to keep him, do I?" she whispered.

Regan wanted to laugh, but the more she thought of her daughter's question and Travis's sense of humor. . . . "I sincerely, truly hope not," she said.

Thoughts of the elephant vanished as soon as it moved away, because behind the animal was a pretty little white pony covered with a blanket of white roses with "Jennifer" spelled out in red roses.

"What does it say, Mommie?" Jennifer asked with hope in her voice. "Is the pony for me?"

"It certainly is," said a pretty blonde woman in a revealing— scandalous actually—costume of stretchy cotton. "Your Daddy found you the sweetest, gentlest horse in this state, and if you like you can ride him in the parade."

"Could I? Please?"

"I'll take care of her," the woman said. "And Travis is on the grounds."

Reluctantly, Regan relinquished her daughter and watched as the woman lifted the child into the saddle. From the side of the pony, the woman took a vest completely covered in pink roses and slipped Jennifer's arms through it.

"Roses for me!" Jennifer yelled. "Daddy sent roses for me too."

Regan noticed she seemed to be looking for someone, and a quick glance showed Timmie Watts hiding behind his mother's skirts. Feeling rotten as she did it, Regan pulled the boy into Jennifer's sight, where the child promptly stuck her tongue out at him and pelted him with a rose. To clear her guilty conscience, Regan asked if Timmie would like to walk beside Jennifer's pony in the parade, which he accepted gladly.

Waving gaily and somewhat regally, Jennifer rode down the street toward the south end of Scarlet Springs. More men and women followed her, some walking, some on horses, all dressed outlandishly and garishly, followed by a seven-piece brass band. At the end of the parade, more clowns came, bearing signs announcing that a free performance of the circus, courtesy of Miss Jennifer Stanford, would be given in two hours.

As the last person disappeared around the curve of the road past the church, the townspeople stood silently for a few moments.

"I guess I better get on with my chores," said one man finally.

"I wonder what a person wears to a circus?" asked a woman.

"Regan," someone else began. "I'm sure this town's gonna lay down and die from boredom when you leave."

A hastily stifled giggle that could only be Brandy's made Regan turn.

"What do you think Travis is planning now?"

"To get to me through Jennifer," Regan replied. "At least I hope that's all he plans. Come in, we've got to get busy. We'll close the inn, put signs on the door, 'Gone to the circus,' and everyone can go."

"Great idea. I'll pack food for us and half the town, and we'll be ready in as little time as Travis has given us."

The two hours passed too quickly, and it seemed minutes before Regan was driving a wagon loaded with food to the circus grounds. A large enclosure had been made by stretching canvas walls around trees and posts. Long wooden benches had been set up, the ones in back taller than those in front, and already most of them were filled with townspeople. In one center section was a large space set apart by pink and orange ribbons blowing in the breeze.

"Wonder where you're to sit?" Brandy laughed at Regan's look of embarrassment. "Come on, it can't be as bad as you imagine."

The young woman in the pink tights directed both Regan and Brandy to the ribboned section and left them. Within minutes two horses, at full gallop, came tearing through the enclosure with one man on top, one leg on one horse, the other on the other horse. As he reached the end of the field, he jumped to one horse, turned both of them around, and, again at a gallop, leaped from one horse to the next.

"Oh my!" Brandy breathed.

After that, they had no time to think as the field filled with more and more horses. The horses did tricks; the men did tricks atop the horses. Two men stood on two horses, and a third man stood on the men's shoulders as the horses ran round and round the ring.

After the equestrians left, Jennifer rode into the ring, her pony led by the lady in pink, and Jennifer was wearing an identical costume of pink bits of gold glitter here and there. As Regan watched, her stomach in her throat, the woman took the little girl's hand and Jennifer stood in the saddle and slowly rode the pony once around the circle.

"Sit down!" Brandy commanded as Regan started after her daughter. "She can't fall very far, and the woman's holding her."

At that the circus woman let go of Jennifer's hand, and she cried, "Look at me, Mommie!" to which Regan nearly fainted, especially when Jennifer gave a jump and the lady caught her.

Jennifer took several bows as she'd obviously been taught, and all of Scarlet Springs applauded explosively. She ran to her mother, and Regan caught the child tightly.

"Was I good? Did I do it right?"

"You were splendid. You nearly scared me to death."

Jennifer seemed pleased at that. "Wait till you see Daddy."

It took Regan a while to calm her racing heart, and when she could speak again there was no time to ask after Travis as the elephant was once again paraded before them. The clowns did more tricks, making everyone laugh, and the little bear danced. But all the while Regan was looking for Travis.

The band had been playing constantly, and now it struck up some eerie music that made everyone quieten.

"And now, ladies and gentlemen," bellowed a good-looking man in a red coat and shiny black boots, "we bring you a death-defying act. Our next performer will walk a tightrope—without a net. If he falls . . . well, you can use your own imaginations."

"I don't think I like this part," Regan said, looking upward at the rope strung between two poles high above the ground. "Perhaps I should take Jennifer and leave."

The look on Brandy's face changed. "Maybe you should stay, Regan," she said in a funny voice.

Following Brandy's stare, Regan wasn't sure of what she saw.

Travis walked into the ring, one arm raised, as if he'd always worked in a circus. The costume he wore, of black cotton, fit him like a second skin, showing the big muscles in his thighs, his small tight buttocks, and his broad, hard chest. A black cape lined in scarlet satin hung from his shoulders. With a flourish, he tossed it to a beautiful woman wearing a tiny bit of green satin. "No wonder the man drives you crazy," Brandy said.

"What in the world is he doing out there?" Regan gasped. "Surely even Travis wouldn't do anything so foolish as. . . ."

She couldn't continue as the horns blared and Travis calmly began to climb the swaying rope ladder to the tiny platform high over their heads.

"That's my Daddy! That's my Daddy!" Jennifer yelled, bouncing up and down on the hard wooden seat.

Regan couldn't move. Her eyes didn't blink, her lungs didn't function, even her heart stopped beating as she stared at Travis on the platform above them.

At the top he again raised his arm to the crowd below, and everyone clapped loudly. There was complete silence as Travis began his slow, careful journey across the taut rope, a long pole in his hand, and it seemed an eternity before he made it to the other side.

The applause made the benches rattle, and Regan buried her

face in her hands, tears of relief coming quickly. "Tell me when he's on the ground again," she said to Brandy.

Brandy was unusually quiet.

"Brandy?" Regan said, peeking out through her fingers. Her friend's expression made her head swivel to look up at Travis again. He was standing on the platform, calmly looking down at her, seeming to be waiting for something. When she looked up at him, he hooked something onto the platform pole and another thing onto the wide black leather belt he wore.

"He's going to walk it again," Brandy whispered. "But at least he's using a safety cable this time."

Travis was several feet across the rope before everyone began to realize just what his "safety cable" really was. Slowly the banner began to unfold. "Regan" was the first word they saw, and after having seen the sentence hundreds of times in the last two days, they needed no one to read it for them.

"Regan!" they read as one. "Will" came next, then "You." Each word got louder and louder, and finally, when Travis stood at the opposite platform, they reread all of it together. If they'd worked for weeks they couldn't have orchestrated it better. "Regan, will you marry me?"

Regan's body turned red from her toes to her hair roots and possibly spread to the tips of her hair; it certainly felt as if it did.

"What does it say, Mommie?" Jennifer demanded as everyone around her began to laugh.

Regan was afraid to speak for fear of what she might say. She absolutely refused to look at Travis, who was climbing down the rope ladder amidst great cheering, clapping, and general hilarity.

"I'm going home," Regan finally whispered. "Please see to Jennifer," she said, and, her head held high, she left the ribboned seat and walked in front of the crowd and out of the canvas-wrapped enclosure. People were calling things to her, but she ignored them as she started the long walk back to the inn.

Using her key, she went inside her own apartment and thought perhaps she'd never leave it again, except maybe to sneak away one night so that she would never again look at a person from Scarlet Springs.

It came as no surprise to her that propped against her pillow was a note on heavy ivory paper. It was an engraved invitation, exquisite, costly, for her to join Travis Stanford for supper that night at nine o'clock. A handwritten message was at the bottom, saying he'd pick her up at the door to her apartment at eight-forty-five.

Feeling completely defeated, she knew there was nothing else she could do but meet him. If she refused, would he perhaps have his elephant knock her door down, or maybe he'd arrive riding it? She was ready for anything even Travis could imagine.

No one bothered her all the rest of the evening, and she was grateful to whoever had arranged such a phenomenon. She'd had more than enough of everyone's attentions.

At exactly eight-forty-five, a knock sounded on her door, and Travis stood there, dressed elegantly in a dark green coat and lighter green pants. He smiled at her and glanced at the pretty apricot silk dress she wore.

"You are prettier than ever," he said, offering her his arm.

The moment she touched him she forgave him. She wished she could have kicked herself for doing it, but all her anger and frustration, all her desire to shoot him, left her instantly.

Swaying, she leaned against him for just a second, and as she did so he took her chin in his hand and looked into her eyes. Searching her face, his eyes holding hers, he bent and kissed her gently, sweetly. "I've missed you," he whispered, before smiling and leading her toward a handsome two-seater buggy.

"Oh Travis," was all she could manage as he settled beside her, to which he laughed in a seductive way and clicked for the horse to move.

It was a clear, warm, moonlit night, heavenly fragrant and still. It was almost as if Travis ordered just such a night. After the last few days she had no idea what she'd been expecting from him, but what she saw when he halted the buggy was not it.

A quilt of patches of velvet tied with gold threads was spread on the grass beside the stream, and set on it were many cushions of midnight blue and gold. Crystal glassware, porcelain, and delicious-smelling food were laid out, all of it surrounded by candles whose sharp glare was shrouded by globes of pink frosted glass. It was a heavenly, unreal scene.

"Travis," she began as he lifted her from the wagon. "It's lovely."

He led her to the cushions and helped her into a comfortable reclining position before he opened a cold bottle of champagne. When she held a glass, he gingerly lowered himself to cushions opposite her.

"Travis, are you hurt?" she asked.

"Every damn bone in my body is hurt," he said with half a groan. "I've never worked so hard in my life as I have in the last few days. I hope you don't need any more courting."

She gasped as she started to speak but instead filled her mouth with champagne, working at not choking. "No, I think I've been courted enough," she said in all seriousness. "In fact, no one in town may ever need any more courting," she added.

"Don't press the issue," he said in warning, easing his back to a better position, grimacing at the ache. "Fix me something to eat, would you?"

Orders, Regan thought, but smiled as she heaped a plate full of hot chicken, cold roast beef, chutney, and a mixture of rice and carrots. "Was it difficult to learn to walk that rope?"

"In three days it was. Another couple of days, and I could have done it without the pole."

"You could have taken another day," she said sweetly.

"And give you time with that snob of an Englishman, Batsford? What's he been doing lately, anyway?"

"I'm afraid I've been a little too busy to notice, actually."

At that Travis smiled smugly and leaned back against the cushions, giving his attention to his food. "I'll be glad when you get home with me and I can get regular meals. Lately I've been eating with one hand, writing with the other."

"Writing? Oh yes, I wondered if the notes had been written by you. Personally, I mean."

"Who the hell else would ask you to marry him? Oh well," he smiled at her look. "I didn't mean that, and you know it. You think Jennifer liked the circus?"

"She adored it. Between the pony and the roses, I think you made her the happiest little girl alive."

The look on Travis's face was angelic. "I wasn't sure I was going to be able to get that damn elephant here on time or not. That's some animal! I'll wager it left enough manure behind for six acres of corn. I was thinking about taking a wagonload home with me to see how good it is. Chicken manure is, of course, the best, but you can't get much of that. Maybe this elephant—."

He stopped because of an explosion of laughter from Regan. Narrowing his eyes at her once, he looked away, ignoring her totally.

"Oh Travis, has there ever been anyone else like you on earth?"

With a wink, he grinned at her. "I did do well on that little rope, didn't I? Now give me some of that pie. You think Brandy'd like to come back and cook for us?"

Regan paused for a moment as she cut the pie. He'd asked her to marry him a few thousand times in the last few days, but never once face to face, and he'd never bothered to wait for an answer. And never had he said he loved her.

Handing him the pie, she spoke. "I think Brandy has other things she wants to do, but I am sure I can find a better cook than your Malvina."

Chuckling, Travis took a bite of the pie. "She gave you a hard time, didn't she? Our old family cook died six years ago, and Margo found Malvina for us. She never gave me any trouble, but she and Wes have had a few spats. You could have gotten rid of her, you know."

"I shall," she said, eyes glittering. "I look forward to doing it."

Travis was so quiet for so long that she glanced at him. In the moonlight, surely it was a trick, but his soft eyes looked almost wet. It couldn't be, because in essence she'd just said she was returning with him, could it?

"I am glad to hear that," he said quietly, then smiled to himself and returned to his pie. "Wes can help you with whatever you need while I'm in the fields."

"I think I'll be able to manage. What's Wes like? Does he spend most of his time in the house?"

"He's a good sort, sometimes a little headstrong, and I have to take him down a peg or two, but in general he helps me."

Regan tried not to smile. "You mean he voices his opinion and dares to differ with you, and you . . . do you come to fisticuffs?"

"See that?" Travis said defensively, pointing to a tiny scar on his chin. "My little brother gave me that, so there's no need for you to act like he's the injured party."

"And will you raise your fist to me when I dare to disagree with you?" she taunted.

"You've disagreed with me on every word I've ever said, and I've not hit you yet. You keep giving me children like Jennifer, and you'll always please me. Now let's go back. I need some sleep."

"Are you only interested in the children I give you?" she asked seriously.

Travis's groan, from her question or his sore muscles, was his only answer. "Leave it," he said as she started to clear away the food. "Someone will come later and pack it all." He propelled her toward the buggy.

"How many people have you hired in the last few days? And how did you get into my safe?"

Unceremoniously, he lifted and dropped her onto the buggy seat. "A man should always have some secrets. I'll tell you on our fiftieth wedding anniversary. We'll gather all twelve of our children and tell them the story of the world's most enterprising, creative, most romantic courtship ever."

Shall we mention the elephant manure? she thought, but didn't say anything as they drove back to town.

Chapter 20

AT HER door, Travis gave a bone-popping yawn, kissed her hand as though it were an afterthought, walked through her bedroom and out the door leading into the interior of the inn, and started up the back stairs to, she assumed, his own room. Stunned, surprised, bewildered, Regan stood by her bed and stared at the closed door.

After all he'd put her through, after all the proposals of marriage, he takes her out to a moonlight picnic, never once mentions marriage but instead talks mostly about elephant manure, and afterward leaves her in her bedroom without so much as a goodnight kiss. All evening he hadn't touched her, hadn't even seemed to be aware that she was near him and so very hungry for him. Of course, she'd concealed her feelings quite well, she knew that, but surely he must have been feeling some passion or at least a longing himself. Maybe making love once in four years was enough for him. After all, Travis was getting on in years; he was about thirty-eight years old now. Perhaps at that age a man. . . .

Her thoughts trailed off as she began to undress. When she'd put the dress on she'd unconsciously imagined Travis taking it off her. Maybe he didn't want a wanton for a wife, she thought. Yes! That must be it. He'd always thought they were married, and now that they weren't. . . . No, they weren't married all that time they were on board ship.

Sitting down on the bed, she pulled off her slippers and stockings. It could just be that Travis was tired, just as he'd said, and didn't have the energy for rolling around with her tonight.

She slipped into a plain white cotton nightgown, checked on her sleeping daughter, and climbed into her big, cold, empty bed. An hour later she was still wide awake and knew she'd never sleep tonight, not as long as she was in one bed and Travis in another.

"Damn his tiredness!" she said aloud, throwing back the light cover.

In her wardrobe was something she'd never worn, a gift from Brandy. It was a white silk negligee, soft, almost transparent, and so low-cut it left little to the imagination. There were only inches of bodice above a white satin ribbon, and those two inches were very tight, pushing Regan's breasts high above the fabric.

"He may be tired, but I doubt if he's dead," she smiled as she looked into a mirror. Flinging a cloak about herself, she went up the stairs toward Travis's room.

Travis was standing in the center of his room, smiling to himself, a glass of port in his hand, when Margo slammed into his room. His smile vanished immediately. "Get out," he said flatly. "I'm expecting Regan any minute."

"That trollop!" Margo hissed. "Travis, you make me sick! Do you know how you've looked the last few days? Everyone, this entire town, is laughing at you. They've never seen any man make such a complete ass of himself."

"You've had your say. Now get out," he said coldly.

"I haven't said half of what should be said. I've been asking a lot of questions in the last few days, and from what I gather you don't even know who this woman is. Why should she marry you, a big, dumb, crude American? You're so proud of that plantation of yours, but did you know your little Regan could buy it and not even miss the money?" She waited, watching to see how Travis was taking this news. He didn't pause or blink an eye, just looked at her with faint distaste.

"She's worth millions," Margo breathed. "And next week it comes to her. She can have any man she wants, so why would she want an American farmer?"

Still Travis didn't speak.

"Maybe you did know," Margo said. "Maybe you've known all along and that's why you're willing to make such a complete fool of yourself to get her. A man'll do a lot to possess that kind of money."

She didn't say another word as Travis's hand grabbed her hair, pulling her head backward. "Get out," he said, his voice low. "And may you hope I never see you again." With that he gave her a push that sent her slamming against the door.

She recovered almost instantly. "Travis," she said, throwing herself at him, her arms around his chest. "Don't you know how much I love you? I have always loved you, ever since we were children. You've always been mine. Every day I've died a little more since you brought her home and said she was your wife, and now this—all this idiocy over her, and I don't understand why. She's never loved you. She left you, but I've always been near, always close when you need me. I can't compete with her money, but I can give you love if you'll just let me. Open your eyes, Travis, and look at me. See how much I love you."

Peeling her arms away from him, Travis held her at arm's length. "You have never loved me. All you ever wanted was my plantation. I've known for years that you're in debt. I helped you often, but I'll not help you to the extent of marrying you." His voice was quiet, even gentle, and it was obvious he didn't like seeing her disintegrate like this.

When Regan quietly opened Travis's door, expecting him to be asleep and to slip into bed with him, she saw him holding Margo, his eyes looking down at her with gentleness, tenderness. Regan pivoted on one heel and began to run.

Travis discarded Margo onto the floor and took off after Regan.

Regan, knowing she'd never outdistance Travis to her own room, tried the door three down from Travis's, Farrell's room. Travis grabbed her cape just as she disappeared into the room, leaving him holding it as he heard the lock click in the door.

"Regan?" Farrell said, his eyes wide as he lit a candle, quickly pulled on his pants, and left the bed all in one motion. "You look terrified."

Eyes wide, Regan leaned against the door, her breasts heaving above the low gown. "Margo and Travis," she choked.

The next moment she sprang away from the door as something heavy hit it. At the next blow Travis's booted foot came through the wood, followed by his hand as he unlocked the door. Flinging it wide, he crossed the room in two long strides and grabbed Regan's arm.

"I've had enough games," he said. "This time you're going to obey me whether you want to or not."

"Now see here!" Farrell said, reaching for Travis's arm.

Travis looked him up and down, dismissed him, and turned to Regan. "You have twenty-four hours to pack, and then we're leaving. We'll be remarried at my house."

With a quick twist, Regan moved away from him. "And will Margo be at our wedding, or maybe you'd rather she spent our wedding night with you?"

"You can have all the jealous fits you want when we get home, but right now I am sick of walking ropes and trying to find all those goddamn roses you seem to need, and I am not going to put up with this anymore. If I have to I'll chain you to my bed, but you might as well know that you and my daughter are going to live with me."

He softened a bit. "Regan, I've done everything I know to prove to you that you love me. Haven't you realized it yet?"

"Me?" she gasped. "That I love you? I've never had any

doubts. You're the one who's been unsure of himself. You've never loved me. You had to marry me the first time. You had to—." She stopped as she looked at Travis in amazement.

He staggered backward, his hands falling to his sides limply. Blindly, his face drained of color, he began to grope for some support. He seemed to age ten years in a few seconds as he fell heavily into a chair.

"Had to marry you?" he choked, his voice weak, hoarse. "Unsure of myself? Never loved you?"

For a moment he dropped his head in his hands, and when he looked back at her his eyes were red. "I've loved you since I first met you," he said quietly. "Why else would I have cared what happened to you? You were so young and frightened, and I was so scared of losing you."

His voice grew stronger. "Why the hell else would I have risked my life on board ship to save that puppy Wainwright you liked so much? Do you know how much I wanted to throw him overboard? But I didn't because you wanted him. And you say I never loved you."

He stood, his voice beginning to get angry. "And I'll have you know you aren't the first to have my baby. I did not *have* to marry you."

"But you said you always marry the mother of your children. I thought—," she said tearfully.

He tossed his hands in the air. "You were scared and angry, didn't even know you were going to have a baby. What was I supposed to say, that I have an illegitimate child at home, that his mother tried to sue me because I wouldn't marry her?"

"You . . . you could have said you loved me."

He quietened. "I swore before witnesses to love you for the rest of my life. What more could I have done?"

She looked down at her hands. "You've never asked me to marry you, not personally."

"Never asked you to marry me?" Travis bellowed. "Goddamn you, Regan, what more do you want from me? I've made a fool of myself in front of an entire state, and you say—."

He broke off as he fell to his knees before her, his hands clasped. "Regan, will you marry me? Please. I love you more than I love my own life. Please marry me."

She put her hand on his shoulder, their faces level. "What about Margo?" she whispered.

Travis gritted his teeth, but answered, "I could have married her years ago but never wanted to."

"Why didn't you tell me that?"

"Why didn't you know without having to be told?" he shot back. "I love you," he whispered. "Marry me?"

"Yes!" she cried, and threw her arms around his neck. "I'll marry you forever."

Neither of them was aware of anyone or anything else on the earth, and they were shocked when the applause started.

Regan buried her face in Travis's neck. "Are there a lot of people out there?" she asked fearfully.

" 'Fraid so," he said. "I guess they heard the noise when you locked the door against me."

She didn't even bother to correct him, that the noise came from his foot smashing the door and not from her locking of it. "Will you take me away from here?" she whispered. "I don't think I can face them."

Triumphantly, Travis stood with Regan in his arms and started for the door. The townspeople and even the guests at the inn, several of whom had prolonged their stay from the first rose Travis sent, felt involved in this courtship and came running at the first sound of splintering wood.

The women, in heavy robes, curling rags in their hair, sighed heavily as Travis carried Regan away. "I knew it'd end happily," one woman said. "How could she have turned him down?"

"My wife's never gonna believe this story," a man said. "Maybe she'll forgive me for coming back three days late."

"You're a fool if you tell your wife this," snorted another man. "We ought to make a pact to keep it secret, or every woman in the country will expect the same kind of courting, and I for one am not walking any tightrope for any damn woman in the world. I'm telling my wife I spent these three days with another woman; it'll cause me less grief." With that he turned toward the male dormitory.

Eventually the people decided to go back to bed, jumping once as Farrell slammed what was left of his door in their faces.

For several minutes Farrell's cursing of America, Americans, and women in general did not stop. The two of them had ignored him, giving each other lovesick lies as if he weren't even in the same room. As he began to think of all the money he'd spent searching for Regan, courting her, he grew more and more angry. Yet she fell for an animal that kicked down doors, a bumbling idiot who was considered a fool by everyone who met him. The woman was insane!

And she belonged to him, to Farrell Batsford. He'd been through hell to get her money, and he wasn't going to give it up now.

Quickly, he tossed a dressing gown on and went to find Margo. He knew she wasn't a woman to take this public humiliation easily; perhaps they could work out something.

"Mmm, Travis," Regan murmured, running her leg up Travis's. The early-morning sun made her skin golden.

"Don't start on me again," he said. "You nearly wore me out last night."

"You certainly don't feel as if *all* of you is exhausted," she laughed, kissing his neck, wiggling against him.

"Unless you want to put on a show for your daughter, you'd better behave. Good morning, sweetheart," he called.

Regan turned away just in time to see her daughter, who took a flying leap at them and landed on Travis's stomach.

"You're home, Daddy!" she yelled. "Can I ride my pony today? Can we go to the circus again? Will you teach me to walk on a rope?"

"Instead of a circus, how about going home with me? I don't own an elephant, but I have lots of other animals and a little brother."

"Does Wesley know you talk about him like this?" Regan asked, but Travis ignored her.

"When can we go?" Jennifer asked her mother.

"Two days?" she asked, looking at Travis. "I have a lot to do before then."

"Now, sweet," Travis said. "Go to the kitchen and get some breakfast. We'll be along in a while. I want to talk to your mother."

"Talk?" Regan said when they were alone, rubbing against him. "I certainly like our 'conversations.'"

He held her at arm's length, and his eyes were serious. "I meant it when I said I wanted to talk. I want to know who you are and what you were doing in your nightgown on that Liverpool dock the night I found you."

"I'd really rather go into it some other time," she said, as lightly as she could manage. "I have an awful lot of work to do."

He pulled her close to him. "Listen to me. I know that what you've been through is painful. I've not pressed you since we left England, but I'm here now, and you're safe. I won't let anything harm you, and I want to know everything about you."

It was some minutes before she could speak. Against her will, she began to remember that night when she'd met Travis and her life before that. For years she'd been free, had come to know other people, to see how they lived, and she could see how much of a prison her childhood had been.

"I grew up totally without freedom," she began, at first without emotion, but as she thought of the way she'd been treated in her early life, she began to grow angry.

Travis never rushed her, only held her close to him, his arms and body keeping her safe, as she poured out her whole story. It was a long time before she got to that night when she'd overheard Farrell and her uncle conspiring together. He never said a word, but his arms tightened.

She continued her story, telling Travis how she felt about him, how he frightened her, but how she clung to him, wavering between her need to prove her own worth and wanting to hide behind his strength. She poured out all the terror she'd felt at his plantation, laughing somewhat at that scared little girl, afraid to give orders to her own servants.

She finished with the story of her leaving him, of the trail she'd left behind, of her tears when he didn't come after her.

"I could have helped you at home," he said when she'd stopped talking. "But I knew you would have resented me. The day Margo came, the day you burned your hand, I could have killed Malvina."

Twisting around, she looked at him. "I had no idea you knew about that."

"I know most of what happens on my own plantation," he said. "I just honestly didn't know how to help you. I knew you had to learn how to help yourself."

"Are you always right, my dear lovely husband?" she asked, caressing his face.

"Always. And I hope you remember it and obey me in all things from now on."

She gave him her sweetest smile. "I plan to fight you every inch of the way. Every time you give me an order I'll—."

She broke off when he kissed her soundly, just before he pushed her from the bed.

"Get up, get dressed, and go see that Brandy has enough food for my breakfast." A pillow landed on his face.

"Here I tell you I am massively wealthy and you don't even comment. Some men would like to get their hands on my money."

Eyeing her naked form, he smiled slowly. "I'm looking at what I like my hands on. As for your money, you can pay for that circus you wanted, and what's left you can give to our children."

"The circus *I* wanted," she sputtered. "All that was your idea."

"You wanted the courting."

"Courting! That was the most heavy-handed, awkward, gaudy, inept courting I've ever seen! Any Englishman could do better."

Lazily, Travis leaned back on a pillow. "I'm the one who had you coming to his room wearing a bit of transparent nothing, just begging me to make love to you, so maybe my courting wasn't so bad after all."

Regan sputtered for a few more minutes before beginning to laugh as she dressed. "You are insufferable. Shall I serve your breakfast in bed, or would you prefer a private dining room?"

"Now there's a good wench. Try and keep that attitude. I think I'll eat in the kitchen; just be sure there's lots of it."

Regan left, still laughing, and Travis wondered how he was going to have to pay for his last remarks. But whatever she did, life with her was going to be a joy. She was certainly worth all the pain he'd been through in the last few years.

Slowly, contentedly, he began to dress.

Most of the townspeople stopped by that day to congratulate Regan on her forthcoming marriage and to say goodbye to her, as they knew she'd be leaving very soon. Contrary to what Margo seemed to think, no one thought Travis was a fool. The women thought he was wonderfully romantic, and the men liked the way he went after what he wanted.

At midmorning, Regan was up to her ears in work. A maid was complaining about some odd-colored ink on a set of sheets, and everyone else seemed to be complaining also. Or maybe it was Regan's imagination caused by her sadness at leaving the big inn she and Brandy had built.

"You're sad, aren't you?" Travis asked, coming up behind her.

She still wasn't used to the keen perception of this man. She'd had no idea he was so aware of her needs and problems when she'd known him before, and now his sensitivity was startling.

"You'll feel better once you're at my house. What you need is a new challenge."

"And what happens when I learn all there is to know about running a plantation?" she asked, turning toward him.

"Couldn't happen, because I come with the plantation and you'll never learn enough about me. Now, where's my daughter?"

"She's usually with Brandy at this time of day. I didn't check because I thought you were with her." After a moment's thought, she smiled. "Where is the pony you bought her? Wherever it is, that's where she is."

"I looked in the carriage house, but she isn't there, and Brandy hasn't seen her all morning."

"Not even for breakfast?" she asked, frowning. "Travis!" she said in alarm.

"Wait a minute," he soothed. "Don't get upset. She could have gone to a friend's house."

"But she always tells me where she's going—always! It's the only way I can keep up with her while I'm working."

"All right," Travis said quietly. "You look through the inn, and I'll walk around town. We'll find her in minutes. Now go!" he said laughingly.

Regan's immediate thought was that perhaps Jennifer had a stomachache from yesterday's excitement and she had gone back to her bed, forgetting to tell anyone where she was going. Quietly, Regan walked through her bedroom and slowly opened her daughter's door. Expecting to see her daughter asleep in her bed, she did not at first understand the turmoil of the room. Clothes were strewn everywhere, drawers open, the bedclothes half on and half off, shoes scattered on the bed and floor.

"She's been packing!" Regan said aloud, relieved at the sight.

It was as she knelt to pick up a shoe that she saw the note on the pillow. Jennifer would not be returned unless the sum of fifty thousand dollars was placed at the foot of the old well south of town two days from now.

Regan's scream of anguish could be heard throughout the inn.

Brandy, her hands and apron covered with flour, was the first to reach Jennifer's room. With an arm around Regan's heaving shoulders, she led her to sit on the bed, taking the note from her.

Brandy looked up at the people standing in the doorway. "Someone find Travis," she commanded. "And tell him to get here immediately."

As Regan stood, Brandy caught her arm. "Where are you going?"

"I have to see how much money I have in the safe," she said, dazed. "I know it's not enough. Do you think I can sell something in two days?"

"Regan, sit down and wait for Travis. He'll know how to get the money. Maybe he even has some with him."

Regan didn't seem to be aware of what she was doing as she sat back down, clutching the ransom note and one of Jennifer's shoes.

Travis burst into the room moments later, and at the sight of him she jumped up and ran to him.

"Someone has taken my daughter!" she cried. "Do you have some money? Can you get fifty thousand dollars? Surely you can get that much."

"Here, let me see the note," he said, one arm firmly around her. He read it and reread it several times before looking up at the room.

"Travis," Regan said. "What do we have to do to get the money?"

"I don't like this," he said under his breath and turned to Brandy. "Have you been in the kitchen all morning?"

Brandy nodded.

"And you heard nothing? Did you see any strangers in the hall?" he asked, nodding toward the corridor that led to the kitchen and Regan's office.

"No one. Nothing unusual."

"Go find everyone on the staff and bring them here instantly," he commanded Brandy.

"Travis, please, we need to start getting the money."

Travis sat down on the bed and drew Regan between his knees. "Listen to me. There's something wrong here. There are only two ways to enter your apartment, past Brandy in the kitchen or through the back door. Brandy and her cooks are always in that hall going from the kitchen to the pantry, and no one could have walked out with Jennifer without being seen. So that leaves the back door, which I know you always keep locked. It hasn't been broken, so Jennifer must have opened it from the inside."

"But she wouldn't! She knows not to do that."

"That's my point. She'd only open it to someone she knew and trusted, someone she knew was a friend. And now my second point, who knows you can get fifty thousand dollars? No one in town knows me, and until yesterday I didn't know you had any money. Fifty thousand means someone knows a great deal more than the average Scarlet Springs resident."

"Farrell!" Regan gasped. "He knows better than I do how much money I have."

At that moment Brandy returned with the staff members, all of them quiet, wide-eyed—and behind them was Farrell Batsford.

"Regan," he said. "I just heard the awful news. Is there anything I can do?"

Travis brushed past him as he began to question the staff, asking if they'd seen anything at all unusual this morning, if they had seen Jennifer with anyone.

While they were thinking, remembering nothing, Travis grabbed a maid's hand.

"What is this on your fingers? Where did it come from?"

Stepping back, the girl looked frightened. "It's ink. It came off the sheets in number twelve."

Expectantly, he turned to Regan.

"Margo's room," she said heavily.

Without another word, he left the apartment through the back door and headed for the stables, Regan running after him. He was tossing a saddle onto a horse when she caught him.

"Where are you going?" she demanded. "Travis! We have to get the money!"

He paused long enough to touch her cheek. "Margo has Jennifer," he said as he continued saddling the horse. "She knew we'd find the ink, and she knows I'll come after her. That's what she really wants. I don't believe she'll harm Jennifer."

"Don't believe! Your whore has taken my daughter and—."

He put his finger to her lips. "She is my daughter too, and if I have to give every acre I own to Margo, I'll get Jennifer back safely. Now I want you to stay here because I can handle this better alone." He swung onto the horse.

"I'm just supposed to stay here and wait? And how do you know for sure where Margo is?"

"She always goes home," he said grimly. "She always goes to where she can be near the memory of that damned father of hers."

With that he reined away, applied a kick to the horse's side, and disappeared in a cloud of dust.

Chapter 21

IT WAS night, almost dawn three days later, when Travis jerked his horse to a halt before Margo's door. It had taken several horses to carry him all the way at the pace he'd demanded of them.

Jumping down, he slammed into her house, knowing exactly where she'd be—in the library, sitting under the portrait of her father.

"It took you a little longer than I expected," she said cheerfully as she greeted Travis. Her red hair was a mass of tangles about her shoulders, and there was a dark stain on her dressing gown.

"Where is she?"

"Oh, she's safe," Margo laughed, holding up an empty whiskey glass. "Go and see for yourself. I rarely harm children. Then come back and join me for a drink."

Travis took the stairs two at a time. At one point in his life he'd been a frequent visitor to the Jenkins house, and he knew his way around well. Now, searching for his daughter, he took no notice of the bare places on the walls where once a portrait had hung or an empty table where an ornament no longer stood.

He found Jennifer asleep in the bed he'd used when he was a boy. When he picked her up she opened her eyes, smiled, said "Daddy," and went back to sleep. She and Margo must have traveled all night, as the dust on her face and clothes showed.

Carefully, he put her back down in the bed, kissed her, and went downstairs. It was time he and Margo talked.

Margo didn't even look up as he crossed the room and poured himself a glass of port. "Why?" she whispered. "Why didn't you marry me? After all those years we spent together. We rode together, swam naked together, made love. I always thought, and Daddy always thought—."

Travis's explosion cut her off. "That's why!" he shouted. "That goddamned father of yours. There are only two people you ever loved: yourself and Ezra Jenkins."

He paused to raise his glass in salute to the portrait over the fireplace. "You never saw it, but your father was the meanest, cheapest liar ever created. He'd steal pennies from a slave child. I never cared much what he did, but every day I could see you becoming more like him. Remember when you started charging the weavers for their broken shuttles?"

Margo looked up, a desperate expression on her face. "He wasn't like that. He was good and kind. . . ."

Travis's snort stopped her. "He was good to you and no one else."

"And I would have been good to you," Margo said, pleading.

"No!" Travis snapped. "You would have hated me because I didn't cheat and steal from everybody around me. You would have seen that as weakness on my part."

Margo kept her eyes on her drink. "But why her? Why a skinny little, washed-out English gutter rat? She couldn't even make a cup of tea."

"You know she's no gutter rat, not when you demand fifty thousand dollars ransom of her." Travis's eyes began to glaze over as he thought back to that time in England. "You should have seen her when I first saw her—dirty, scared, wearing a torn and ragged nightgown. But talking like the highest-born English lady. Every word, every syllable was so precise. Even crying, she talks like that."

"You married her because of her damned uppity accent?" Margo spat angrily.

Travis smiled in a distant way. "I married her because of the way she looks at me. She makes me feel ten, no, twenty feet tall. I can do anything when she's around. And watching her grow has been a joy. She's changed herself from a frightened little girl into a woman." His smile broadened. "And she's all mine."

Margo's empty glass flew across the room, shattering on the wall behind Travis's head. "Do you think I'm going to sit here and listen to your ravings about another woman?"

Travis's face turned hard. "You don't have to listen to me at all. I'm going upstairs to get my daughter and take her home." At the foot of the stairs he turned back toward her. "I know you well. I know it's because of what your father taught you that you tried this treacherous way of getting what you wanted. Because Jennifer is unharmed, I'm not pressing charges this time. But if you ever again. . . ."

He stopped, his words trailing, and rubbed his eyes. Suddenly he was very sleepy, and as he mounted the stairs he looked like a drunken man.

Shortly after Travis left the inn, a bewildered Regan returned to her apartment. Farrell was waiting for her.

"Regan, please, you've got to tell me what's going on. Has someone harmed your daughter?"

"No," she whispered. "I don't know. I can't tell."

"Sit down," he said, his arm around her, "and tell me everything."

It didn't take but minutes before the story was out.

"And Travis left you here to suffer alone?" Farrell asked in astonishment. "You have no idea what is happening about your own daughter but trust him to get her from his ex-mistress?"

"Yes," she said helplessly. "Travis said—."

"And since when have you ever let another person run your

life? Wouldn't you rather be with your daughter than here, knowing nothing?"

"Yes!" she said firmly, rising. "Of course I would."

"Then let's go. We'll leave immediately."

"We?"

"Yes," Farrell said, taking her hand. "We're friends, and friends help each other in time of need."

Only later, as they were in the buggy and headed south toward Travis's plantation, did Regan realize that she'd told no one where she was going. The thought left her quickly as she was too concerned for her daughter's safety.

They traveled for hours, the carriage much too slow for Regan's taste, and once she dozed, her head hitting the side of the buggy. She came awake abruptly when Farrell touched her arm. He was standing on the ground beside her; the carriage had stopped.

"Why are you stopping?" she demanded.

He pulled her from the seat to stand before him. "You need rest, and we need to talk."

"Talk!" she gasped. "We can talk later, and I don't need any rest." She tried to pull away from him, but he held her firmly.

"Regan, do you know how much I love you? Did you know that I was in love with you long ago in England? Your uncle offered me money and I took it, but I would have married you without the incentive of money. You were so sweet and innocent, so very lovely."

In her distress Regan lost sight of the fact that she was alone with this man in a remote piece of woods.

Astonished, she pulled back from him. "Oh, for heaven's sake, Farrell! What have I ever done to make you think I'm stupid? You never loved me, never have, never will. All you want is my money, which you're not going to get, so why don't you be a good sport, go home to your pretty, poor house in England, and leave me alone?"

One minute she was standing, the next she was slammed against the carriage, sliding down, as Farrell's hand knocked her backward.

"How dare you speak to me like that?" he seethed. "My family comes from kings, while yours are mere merchants. That I have to lower myself to marry a woman like you, who knows more of ledgers than laces, is—."

While he was speaking, Regan was regaining her wits. Much more important than her own problems with Farrell was her anxiety about her daughter. Still on her knees from the blow, she charged at him, using her head as a battering ram, and caught him directly between the legs.

Farrell doubled over in pain and gave Regan her chance to escape.

One glance at the buggy showed he'd unhitched the horses enough that it would take a long time to be able to use that means of escape. Pulling up her skirts, she started to run back toward the road, just in time to see a dilapidated old wagon disappearing around a curve. It took all her energy to catch the wagon.

An old man, his face bristled with gray whiskers, sat on the seat.

"There's a man chasing me," she called up, running with the wagon.

"Should he catch you?" the old man said, obviously amused by the situation.

"He's trying to force me to marry him—for my money—but I want to marry an American."

Patriotism won the man over. Without even slowing, he grabbed Regan's arm and hauled her into the wagon as if she weighed nothing. With another swift motion he pushed her to the back and covered her completely with grain sacks.

Seconds later Farrell appeared on horseback, and Regan held her breath as he shouted at the old man. After pretending he was deaf for some minutes, the old man refused to allow Farrell to search his wagon; he pulled a pistol when Farrell kept insisting. At last the old man reluctantly admitted having seen three men riding by, one with a pretty woman in the saddle in front of him. Farrell took off in a flurry of hoofs and dust.

"You can come out now," the old man said, grabbing Regan's arm and pulling her to the seat.

Rubbing her arm, she refrained from asking the man to stop tossing her about like one of his feed sacks. After several ferocious sneezes, she asked if he knew where the Stanford plantation in Virginia was.

"That's a long way. It'll take days."

"Not if we change horses and travel all night. I'll pay for the horses and any other expenses."

He seemed to study her for several minutes. "Maybe we could work something out. I'll get you there in record time if you'll tell me why that Englishman was chasing you and what you want with Travis, or is it Wesley you're after?"

"I'll tell you everything, and Travis is mine."

"Lady, you got your hands full," he said, chuckling as he yelled for the horses to start moving. Within seconds they were tearing down the road, and Regan was holding on with both hands, her teeth jarring together constantly. She couldn't speak or tell any story.

An hour later the man stopped the wagon, got down, and pulled her out after him.

"What are you doing?" she asked.

"We're going by boat," he said. "I'll sail you to Travis's front door." After a mile hike they came to a little cabin and a dock reaching into a narrow stream of water. The man disappeared into the cabin for a moment and soon returned with a canvas bag. "Let's go," he said, shoving her into a boat as worn-out as his wagon had been.

"Now talk," he said once they were under way.

Days later the man dropped Regan off at the dock of Travis's plantation, bidding her goodbye and good luck. It was early morning, and the plantation was silent as she ran all the way from the dock to the house.

The door was open, and as she tore up the stairs she prayed Travis and Jennifer would be asleep in one of the rooms. She started throwing open door after door, cursing the house for being so large and causing her to take so much time.

She found him, just his hair showing above the sheet, in the fourth bedroom. "Travis!" she cried, flinging herself at him. "Where's Jennifer? Is she all right? How could you have left me not knowing and be here sleeping so calmly?" she asked, giving him a good cuff on the ear.

The man who sat up was not Travis. He was very much like him but a smaller version.

"Now what has my brother done?" he asked wearily, rubbing his ear, but as he looked at her he smiled. "You've got to be Regan. Let me introduce—."

"Where are Travis and my daughter?"

Wesley was instantly alert. "Tell me what's happened."

"Margo Jenkins kidnapped our daughter, and Travis went after her."

Before she could answer, Wes threw back the covers, not caring that he was nude, and began to dress.

"I always told Travis that Margo was no good, but he felt he owed her something so he always indulged her. She thinks she can have anything in the world, that it's hers by right. Come with me," he said, grabbing her hand and pulling her with him.

"You're very much like Travis," she said, gasping at the pain he was causing her wrist and trying to keep up with his long strides.

"There's no time for insults now," he said, leaving her at the library door while he loaded two pistols and stuck them in his belt. "Can you ride? No, Travis said you couldn't. Come on, you can ride in front of me. The two of us together aren't as heavy as Travis."

If Regan had time or the inclination, she would have been disgusted with Travis's little brother. How could there be two men like Travis? And in another year or two Wes was going to be as large as Travis.

"I'm Wesley," he said as he dropped her into the saddle before mounting behind her.

"Somehow I assumed that," she said before they took off at a breathless gallop.

At the door to Margo's house, Wes let her down. "We'll go in separately. Remember, I'll be close by you."

With that he left her, and Regan walked through the front door. It took only moments to find Margo as she sat in the library.

"Just in time," Margo smiled graciously, but her eyes were red. "You're the third visitor I've had this morning."

"Where's my daughter, and where is Travis?" Regan demanded.

"Dear little rich Jennifer is asleep, and so is her beloved father. Of course, Jennifer will wake; Travis will not."

"What!" Regan yelled. "What have you done to my family?"

"No more than you've done to my life. Travis drank enough opium to kill two men. He's upstairs sleeping until death."

Regan had reached the doorway when a shot from outside made her stop. Paralyzed, she looked down the hall toward the door. Margo rushed past her and jerked the door open, and Farrell entered, half carrying, half dragging Wesley's bleeding body.

"I found him lurking around outside," Farrell said, pushing Wes into a chair, a pistol in his hand.

"What are you doing here?" Regan gasped, going toward Wesley.

"Leave him!" Farrell said, grabbing her shoulder. "Did you think I was going to give up so easily, after all the years I'd been searching for you? No, Margo and I planned all this long ago, while the rest of you were playing with that stupid circus. Wesley here will die of his wounds received in an unfortunate hunting accident. Travis's body will never be found, and his dear little daughter will inherit everything. I will, of course, marry the little heiress's mother, who will be so distraught over her husband's death that she'll commit suicide. I will then return to England, the sole beneficiary of your estate, and Margo will generously agree to be Jennifer's guardian and care for the Stanford plantation until she comes of age—if she lives that long. Now do you see why I'm here?"

"You are both mad," Regan said, backing away from him. "No one will believe so many deaths are accidental." She turned and started for the stairs at the end of the hall, but Farrell caught her.

"You're mine now," he said, advancing toward her, his body stained with Wesley's blood.

Regan's hand went out, and she turned over the candelabra on a low table. Immediately, the curtains over a nearby doorway went up in flames. Margo's scream filled the air as she grabbed a small rug and began beating at the flames.

"Release her," said a voice from the end of the hall.

"Travis!" Regan cried, fighting to free herself from Farrell. Travis looked horrible, as if he'd just been violently ill.

"I thought you put him out of the way," Farrell yelled at Margo as she fought the fire.

"It took me a while to get all the opium out of my system," he said, holding on to the stair banister.

"Stop talking," Margo screamed, "and help me put out the fire. It's spreading!"

Farrell tightened his grip on Regan and put the pistol to her head.

Wesley, nearly forgotten and slumped in a chair behind Farrell, used his draining strength to pull a knife from his boot, and with one lunge he plunged it between Farrell's shoulder blades. The pistol flew upward, fired into the ceiling, and Farrell fell forward.

Regan reacted instantly as she ran toward Travis and the stairs. "Get Wesley," she commanded. "I'll get Jennifer."

Regan found her sleeping daughter quickly, pulled her from the bed, and ran down the stairs in time to meet Travis working hard to get his brother out of the house. Neither man had much strength, and it seemed forever before they were in the fresh, sunlit morning air and out of the smoke-filled house.

Travis gently put Wesley on the grass. "I'll get horses and a wagon," he said.

"Travis!" Regan said, touching his arm, her eyes going to the house. A flame leaped out of the first-floor window. "We can't leave Margo in there to die. She has to come out."

Travis gave her cheek a quick caress and then ran back to the house. Minutes later he came out, Margo thrown over his shoulder as she kicked and clawed, cursing him vilely.

He dumped her on the ground. "That goddamn house isn't worth anyone's life, not even yours," he said as she glared up at him.

Regan was bent over Wes, binding the gunshot wound in his side.

Travis had barely glanced away from Margo before she leaped up and ran toward the house. "My daddy is in there!" she was screaming.

Travis saw the first flames touch her skirt and knew he could not save her. Quickly, he grabbed his daughter, who was watching everything wide-eyed, and buried her little face in his shoulder.

Within seconds, Margo's whiskey-soaked dress burst into flame, and Regan turned away as Wes's arm went around her, pulling her to sob onto his shoulder.

It was a while before any of them could recover. Travis, touching his brother's forehead in affection, smiled at the man holding his wife. "Take care of my women while I go get a wagon," he said.

By the time he returned, they were surrounded by plantation workers who stood helplessly by as the house burned. It was too far gone to try to save it. Men were getting the horses out of the nearby stables, and two more men helped Travis put Wes in the back of the wagon. Jennifer sat by her uncle, too tired and dazed to speak.

When Travis and Regan were on the seat, he turned to her. "Shall we go home?"

"Home," she whispered. "Home is where you are, Travis, and that's where I want to be."

He kissed her. "I love you," he said, "and—."

"I'm bleeding to death, and you two are courting," Wesley bellowed from the back.

"Courting!" Travis snorted, clicking to the horses. "Little brother, you don't even know what courting is. As soon as you're up to the excitement, I'm going to tell you about the world's best courtship. Maybe someday you can be half as creative—." He stopped and narrowed his eyes at Regan, who'd started laughing, and his look of injury made her laugh harder.

"I think I'd rather hear Regan's side of any of your stories, Travis," Wesley said, smiling, his eyes closed.

"Home," Regan said, wiping her eyes. "It's going to be very good to get home."

Travis began to smile also as he turned the horses toward the Stanford plantation.

River Lady

Chapter 1

Virginia Riverfront
September, 1803

THE RAIN enclosed the little tavern, darkening it so that the lantern's golden light made eerie shadows on the wall. The late fall sunshine that had warmed the morning was gone now and the tavern was almost cold. Behind the tall oak counter washing pewter mugs was a woman, pretty, plump, clean, her soft brown hair caught in a white muslin cap. She hummed as she worked, smiling now and then and showing a dimple in one cheek.

The side door, not the door for patrons, opened and in a gust of cold, wet wind a girl slipped into the room, pausing for a moment until her eyes adjusted to the light. The barmaid looked up and, with a frown and a little click of disgust, hurried forward.

"Leah, you look worse every time I see you. Sit down here while I heat a toddy for you," the plump woman said as she pushed the shivering girl into a chair and went to set the poker in the fire, all the while surreptitiously studying her younger sister. If possible, Leah had lost weight. Her unfleshed bones seemed to poke through her dirty, mended dress; her eyes were sunken, the skin under them blue, her nose sunburned and peeling. There were three bloody scratches running the length of one side of her face, and a long bluish-green bruise on the other side.

"He give you that?" the barmaid asked in disgust as she jabbed the hot poker into the mug of flip.

Leah merely shrugged and eagerly put her hands out toward the hot beer and molasses drink.

"He give any reason for hittin' you?"

"No more 'n usual," Leah said after drinking half the contents of the mug and leaning back in the chair.

"Leah, why don't you—?"

Leah opened her eyes and gave her sister a hard look. "Don't start on me again, Bess," she warned. "We've been through this before. You do what you must and I'll take care of me and the kids."

Bess stiffened for just a moment before turning away. "Layin' on my back for a few clean gentlemen is a lot easier 'n what you have to do."

Leah didn't even wince at Bess's crudity. They'd had this argument too many times before for her to be shocked. Two years ago, Bess had had her fill of their crazy father who beat them constantly because "women were born in sin." The older girl had left their poor backwater farm to find herself a job, and, on the side, she was "friendly" to a few men. Leah, of course, had been beaten for Bess's sins. Now, Bess was always trying to get Leah to leave their father's shack of a house. But Leah remained to care for her six younger brothers and sisters. She plowed, planted, harvested, cooked, repaired the house, and, most of all, she protected the little ones from their father's wrath.

"Look at you!" Bess said. "You look forty-five years old and you're what? Twenty-two now?"

"I think so," Leah said tiredly. It was the first time she'd sat down all day and the warm drink was relaxing her. "Do you have any clothes for me?" she whispered lazily.

Bess started to complain again, but instead she went behind the counter and reached for cold ham, bread, and mustard. As she set a plate on the table beside Leah, she took a seat across from her. Out of the corner of her eye she saw Leah hesitate before touching the food. "You even consider not eatin' that and takin' it back to them kids and I'll cram it down your throat myself."

Leah gave a little quirk of a smile and tore into the food with both hands. Her mouth full, her eyes downcast, she said, as if the answer meant nothing to her, "Have you seen him lately?"

Bess gave the top of her sister's dirty head a sharp look. "You're not still thinkin' . . . ," she began but stopped and looked back at the fire. A flash of lightning lit the tavern.

Poor Leah, Bess thought. In many ways Leah was like their father, as stubborn and hardheaded as a piece of stone. Bess could walk away and leave the little ones, but to Leah family was everything, even if a lunatic, rampaging old man was part of her family. After their mother died, Leah had decided that she was going to take care of the kids until the last one was old enough to leave. No matter what happened, or what was done to her, she refused to leave.

And just as Leah remained with her father, she stubbornly clung to a dream. The dream wasn't the one Bess had always wanted: food, shelter, and warmth. Leah's dream was one she could never attain.

Leah fantasized about one Mr. Wesley Stanford.

When Leah was a girl. Mr. Stanford had come to their hovel, asked her a few questions, and, in gratitude for her answers, he'd kissed her cheek and given her a twenty-dollar gold piece. When Leah had told Bess of the incident, there'd been stars in the young girl's eyes. Bess had immediately wanted to spend the gold on new dresses, but Leah had gone into a rage, screaming that the coin was from *her* Wesley and that she loved him and he loved her and when she grew up she was going to marry him.

At the time, Bess's only thought had been of that shiny gold coin hidden somewhere, unspent, all its glory wasted. She began to wish this Wesley had given Leah a bunch of flowers. She tried to forget about that coin, but sometimes she'd see Leah, plow harness about her shoulders, stop and stare into space. "What you thinkin' about?" Bess would ask, and Leah would say, "Him." Bess would groan and turn away. There was no need for Leah to say who *him* was.

Years later, Bess decided she could take no more of her father's hideous temper and the constant work, so she left the farm and took a job across the river as a barmaid. Elijah Simmons had disowned his eldest daughter and had forbidden her to visit the farm or see her siblings. But during the last two years, Leah had managed to slip away a few times to visit her sister and get the clothes Bess collected for her. The townspeople wanted to help the desperately poor Simmons family, but Elijah refused to allow his family to accept charity.

On her first visit to the tavern, Leah had asked after Wesley Stanford. At the time, Bess had been enthralled with having met all the rich plantation owners, and Wesley and his brother Travis were the wealthiest. Bess had talked for thirty minutes about how handsome Wes was, what a considerate man he was, how often he visited the tavern—and how happy Leah would be when they were married. To Bess, it'd been like the creating of a fairy tale, something to pass the cold winter evenings, and she thought Leah had seen it that way too. But a few months ago, with a laugh, Bess had told Leah that Wes had become engaged to a beautiful young lady named Kimberly Shaw. "Now who are you going to love?" Bess laughed before she saw Leah's white face. Under the bruises and dirt Leah looked as if her blood were draining away.

"Leah! You can't be serious about a man like Wesley. He's rich, *very* rich and he wouldn't let a couple of . . . of, well a 'lady' like me and a scrawny, filthy thing like you in his second-best parlor. This Miss Shaw is from his own class."

Quietly, Leah slipped out of her chair and headed for the door.

Bess grabbed her arm. "It was just a dream, didn't you realize that?" She paused. "But Wesley has a third gardener that just might be interested in a woman from . . . from our side of the river."

Leah didn't answer, but, still pale, she left the tavern, and the next time she visited, she acted as if she'd never heard that Wesley Stanford was engaged. She asked Bess for more stories about Wesley. This time Bess was reluctant, so she again tried to tell her of the engagement. Leah gave her sister such a chilling look that Bess turned away. For all Leah's look of frailty, there were times when she could be imposing.

Since then Bess hadn't tried to argue with her, and every visit she lifelessly recounted Wes's last time in the tavern. She didn't mention that he was in there more often now because the tavern was on the road between his house and the Shaws'.

Now Leah leaned back in the chair, slipped her hand into her much-mended pocket, and clutched the gold piece Wesley had given her years ago. Over the years she'd rubbed it so often it was completely smooth. There'd been many nights when the pain from one of her father's beatings had kept her awake and she'd sat on the straw tick rubbing the coin and remembering every second of the time she'd spent with Wesley Stanford. He'd kissed her cheek, and to her knowledge that was the one and only kiss she'd ever received. Sometimes Bess talked about him as if he thought of himself as a god, better than everyone else, but Leah knew how kind he could be, how he could kiss a skinny, dirty little girl he'd never seen before and reward her lavishly. Vain, arrogant men didn't do such things. Bess didn't know him as Leah did. Someday, she thought, she'd see Wesley again and he'd see the love in her eyes and—.

"Leah!" Bess half shouted. "Don't fall asleep. The old man will miss you before long. You have to get back."

"I know. It's just so nice and warm here."

"You could stay all the time if—."

Leah stood, cutting off Bess's words. "Thanks for everything, Bess, and I'll see you again next month. We wouldn't be able to make it if it wasn't for you and your—."

The heavy front door flew open and a man entered, his body filling the opening, pushing the door shut behind him.

"Oh Lord," Bess gasped, paralyzed for a moment before grinning and moving toward the man. "Awful wet for anybody to be out, Mr. Stanford. Here, let me help you with that," she said, taking his coat from his shoulders and glancing toward Leah, who stood stock-still, gaping.

He hasn't changed much, Leah thought. He was taller, even more muscular than she remembered, and more handsome. His thick dark hair curled damply about his neck and there were drops of water on his lashes, making his eyes look even darker, even more intense. Bess was standing on her toes and using her hand to brush water from his dark green wool jacket. Buckskin pants hugged his big, hard thighs while tall boots encased his feet and calves.

"I wasn't sure you'd be open. Doesn't Ben ever give you the night off?" he asked Bess, referring to her boss.

"Only when he's sure I'll put the night to good use. Ain't nobody around to spend this evenin' with so I might as well tend bar," she teased. "Now you sit down and let me get you somethin' hot to drink."

Bess began ushering Wesley Stanford toward a tall, sided booth, trying to keep his back to Leah, who still stood in the middle of the room, her eyes wide.

With a chuckle, Wes disengaged himself from her pushing hands. "What are you trying to do to me, Bess?" It was then he saw Leah, and Bess saw the brief flicker in his eyes. He was judging her as a man looks at a woman and as to where she belonged on the social ladder. He obviously found her wanting in both aspects. "Who's your . . . pretty friend, Bess?"

Manners, Bess thought. Those people must be taught manners from the cradle. "This is my sister, Leah," Bess said tightly. "Leah, you best be gettin' home."

"It's early yet," Leah said, stepping forward into the light;

Bess looked at her sister as a stranger would and saw poverty and hardship hanging over Leah like a black cloud. But Leah seemed oblivious to her appearance. Her eyes were fixed glassily on Wesley, who was beginning to look at her in speculation.

"Perhaps you two ladies will join me in a glass of ale."

Bess put herself between Leah and Wes. Leah, in her innocence, was giving Wes looks that usually only a seasoned prostitute could produce. "I got work to do and Leah here has to go home." She said the last while glaring at her sister.

"Ain't nothin' waitin' for me at home," Leah said, deftly sidestepping her sister. "I'd love to drink with you, Wesley." She said the name as if she said it hundreds of times a day—which she did—and didn't notice the movement of Wes's eyebrows as she slid into a seat in the booth, looking up at him expectantly.

"The flip is good," she said.

Wes looked down at her dirty, scratched, bruised face for a second before taking the bench across from her. "A couple of flips," he said quietly to Bess.

Angrily, Bess flounced away toward the bar.

"You work for Ben now?" Wes asked Leah.

"I still live with my family." Her eyes were eating him, remembering every angle of his face, memorizing every curve. "Did you ever find your friend's wife?" she asked, referring to the first time she'd seen Wes.

For a moment he didn't understand. "Clay's wife?" he asked, then smiled, astonished. "You couldn't be that little girl who helped us?"

Silently, reverently, Leah pulled the worn gold coin from her skirt pocket and laid it on the table.

Wonderingly, Wes picked it up and held it toward the light to look at the rough hole drilled in the top of the coin. "How—?" he asked.

"A nail," she said, smiling. "It took me a while to make that hole but I was afraid I'd lose it if I didn't tie it to me."

Frowning, Wes put the coin back on the table. It was odd that the girl would keep the gold when she obviously needed so many things. Her hair, greasy beyond belief, was pulled back from her head and, idly, he wondered what color it would be if it were clean.

As Leah reached for the coin, she touched his fingertips and, her breath held, she touched them with her two fingers, marveling at the cleanliness of his nails, the shape of his big square-tipped fingers.

Bess set two mugs of flip on the table with a splash, while glaring at Leah. "Mr. Stanford, why don't you tell my sister here about that beautiful young lady you're about to marry? Leah'd just love to hear all about her. Tell her how pretty she is, how she can dance, what pretty clothes she has."

Wes moved his hand away from Leah's and chuckled. "Perhaps you should tell her, Bess, since you seem to know so much about my wife-to-be."

"I think I'll do that," Bess said, grabbing a chair from a nearby table and moving it to the end of their booth. But a look from Leah stopped her from sitting down.

"I'd rather hear what Wesley has to say," Leah said quietly, but her eyes bored into Bess's.

Bess's eyes held her sister's for a moment. Why was she trying to protect her sister? Isn't this what she'd wanted her to do? If only Leah weren't so *serious* about the man. With a sigh, Bess left them alone.

Wes drank deeply of his steaming drink while he looked at the emaciated girl across from him, and wondered how long she'd been a prostitute. She certainly was good at getting a man's attention in spite of her unappetizing appearance. The way she looked at him made him feel as if she'd been waiting all her life just for him. It was flattering, but at the same time it was disconcerting. It was almost as if she felt he owed her something.

"You were saying, Wesley . . . ?" Leah prompted, leaning forward so that he got a whiff of her body odor.

"Kimberly," he said, only half-aloud. It might be better to think of Kim or, heaven help him, he might be tempted by this fragrant witch. "You're sure you want to hear? I mean, usually one woman doesn't want to hear about another woman."

"I wanta know all there is to know about you," she said with heartfelt sincerity.

"There's really not much to tell. We met about two years ago when she came to visit her brother, Steven Shaw. Their parents died when they were young and Kimberly was sent East to live with an aunt and uncle, while Steve stayed here with relatives."

Wesley's "not much to tell" turned into an hour of extended rapture. Wes had fallen for the beautiful Kimberly instantly, but so had twenty or so other young men, and he'd had a two-year courtship battle to win her. He talked about how pretty Kim was, how gentle, delicate, how sweet-tempered, how she loved beauty, books, and music.

Leah's hands gripped the pewter mug so hard her knuckles turned white. "And you're soon to be married?" she whispered.

"Early spring. April. Then the three of us, Steven included, are traveling to the new state of Kentucky. I've bought land there."

"You'll leave Virginia?" She gasped. "What about your plantation here?"

"I don't think Virginia is big enough for my brother *and* me. For all my thirty-four years, I've been called Travis's little brother. It's made me want a place of my own. Besides, starting all over in a new land with a beautiful woman appeals to me."

"You won't return?" she whispered.

"Probably not," he answered, frowning at her intensity. In spite of her looks and her smell, he found himself drawn to her. "The rain's stopped and I better get home." He stood. "It was a pleasure meeting you." He tossed coins on the table for the drinks. "See you next week, Bess," he called as he started out the door.

Leah was after him in a second, but Bess caught her arm. "Are you sure you know what you're doing?"

Leah jerked away from her sister. "I always thought you wanted me to enjoy men."

"Enjoy them yes, but I'm afraid you're obsessed with Wesley Stanford. You're going to get hurt and hurt worse than from Pa's blows. You know nothing about men! All you know is how to plow and scrounge wild plants for food. You don't know—."

"Maybe I can learn!" Leah hissed. "I love him and he's leaving soon and I have this one chance and I'm going to take it."

"Please, Leah, please don't go after him. Something awful will happen, I know it will."

"Nothing *awful* will happen," Leah said softly and was out the door.

Wesley was just mounting his horse.

"Will you give me a ride?" Leah called, stumbling along the path in the dark.

Wes stood still, watching her in the moonlight and wishing with all his might that the girl would go away. There was something about her that was almost frightening, as if it were fate that had brought them together, as if what was going to happen were inevitable. And damn! He'd been so good, faithful to Kimberly since they'd become engaged, and he'd planned to remain celibate until they were married. But it wasn't worry of tumbling the girl that bothered him but her intensity, her seriousness. Why in the world had she kept that coin all these years?

"Let's walk," he said, holding the horse's reins, not wanting Leah's thin little body near his on the horse.

Leah had never felt so alive in her life. She was with the man she loved. Here and now was what she'd dreamed of since she was a child. With one hand on the coin in her pocket, she slid her other arm through Wesley's.

He looked down at her and, whether it was a trick of the moonlight or the concealing darkness, she looked downright pretty. The bruise and scratches, now hidden, had kept him from noticing her full lips and that her eyes were large, seductive. He gave the groan of a man lost and started walking with her.

Leah's heart was pounding rapidly by the time they left sight of the tavern. Her conscience, dulled by three mugs of beer, was telling her that Bess was right and she had no business here. Yet a part of her was saying that here was her one and only chance for love and she was going to take it. Later, when Wesley was in a faraway place and she was still toiling for her family, she could remember tonight. Perhaps he'd kiss her again.

With her thoughts in her eyes she looked up at him, and Wesley, with no thoughts at all, bent his head and kissed her.

She melted against him, her body feeling delicate and breakable in his work-hardened arms, but she kept her lips closed in a childish way. He drew back, his eyes twinkling. The girl was a mixture of accomplished whore and virginal innocence. With her eyes still closed, she moved her lips against his, put her mouth on his again, and Wesley nudged her lips open. He had a thought that she was a quick learner but soon no more thoughts crossed his mind.

The girl gave herself to him as if she'd been hungering for him, and Wesley responded with months of pent-up desire, his head pushing hers back, his hand burying in the gummy mass of her hair and turning her to better reach her lips. He withdrew, his eyes glazed, his breath coming hard. Her hair had come untied and hung to her waist; her lips were reddened.

"You're beautiful," he whispered and went for her mouth again as his hands tore at her dress top.

"No!" Leah said, suddenly frightened. A kiss was what she'd

dreamed of, a kiss and no more, but as his hands sought her bare flesh, and even as she told him no, she knew she'd never actually deny him. "Wesley," she whispered as her hands ceased to fight him. "My own Wesley."

"Yes, love," he said distractedly, his mouth traveling down her throat.

The fabric of the coarse dress was old and tore away easily. Within seconds Leah was standing nude in the moonlight. Her thin body showed every bone, every muscle. The only sign of her womanliness was her full breasts, proud and perfect.

With great care Wesley lifted her in his arms, then lay her on his cloak, which had fallen from his shoulders.

Leah, not knowing what to do, how to return the pleasure she was feeling, lay still as he ran his hands over her and unfastened his clothes at the same time.

When he entered her, she screamed in pain. Wesley lay still a moment, touched her hair, kissed her cheek.

Leah opened tear-filled eyes to look up at him, and a wave of great love came over her. This was her Wesley, the man she had always loved, would die loving. "Yes," she whispered, "yes."

Wesley continued quickly and only at the end did Leah feel even a tinge of pleasure. And when he finished with a hard thrust, he grabbed her shoulders and whispered "Kimberly" in her ear.

It was several moments before Leah understood exactly what had happened to her. *Kimberly*, he'd said.

He rolled off her, tired for the moment, his eyes half-closed, while Leah stood and pulled on the shreds of her old dress.

"Good girl," Wes said drowsily as he reached into the pocket of the pants he hadn't fully removed. "For your trouble." He flipped a gold coin toward her and it landed at her feet. "We keep meeting, you'll have a trunk full of those things."

Stunned, Leah watched him stand, fasten his pants, and pick up his cloak and hat. Reaching out, he touched her chin. "You, little girl, are going to get me in trouble." He drew back. "I hope *some* of you was clean." With that, he mounted his horse and rode away.

It was some time before Leah could move. What an absolute, total fool she'd made of herself, she thought more in amazement than anything else. She felt as if she were a child who'd just learned there were no fairy godmothers. All these years she'd been able to resist the horror of her life because at the end of the rainbow was the great god Wesley. But in the end he was just a man who'd taken what was freely offered to him.

"Free!" she exclaimed, stooping to grab the coin at her feet. Holding it for a moment, feeling how cold it was, she thought of all the food and clothes she could buy with the money and what it had cost her to obtain the coin. With a laugh at her years of childish dreams, she did what may have been the first totally impractical act of her life: she drew her arm back and threw the coin as far as she could, down toward the blackness that was the river, and when she heard a splash, she smiled.

"Not all the Simmons are whores!" she shouted at the top of her lungs.

Feeling better, willing herself not to cry, since she'd learned long ago that tears were useless, she started toward the place she called home. Her body ached and she moved slowly, knowing she'd never make it back before daylight and that there'd be a beating waiting for her. The loss of her dream made her feet heavy and she dreaded more than ever the life ahead of her.

Chapter 2

❧

March, 1804

THE TALL, steepled building of Whitefield Church was beautiful inside, with whitewashed plaster walls and sun streaming in through round-topped windows. The pastor's box was high above the people's heads, a carved walnut staircase leading to it. Below, on hard benches inside short paneled walls, sat the congregation.

Wesley Stanford sat next to his bride-to-be, holding her fingertips under the concealing folds of her pink silk dress. Kimberly Shaw reverently kept her head up and her eyes on the pastor. She was a very pretty woman with plump cheeks, big blue eyes, and a soft, desirable mouth. Now and then she'd glance at Wesley and smile, her cheek dimpling.

Next to her was her brother, Steven Shaw, a tall, big male version of Kimberly, blond, handsome, with a cleft chin.

Beside Steven were two couples, Clay and Nicole Armstrong next to Travis and Regan Stanford. Travis was moving his big form about in the seat, obviously impatient to get home, and his pretty wife was just as obviously giving him deathly looks—looks that Travis was ignoring. Clay, on the other hand, was sitting quite still, only occasionally glancing at his dark little wife, as if he weren't sure she was really there.

Wesley, his grip tightening on Kim's hand, thought of all the things he had to do before he and she left for Kentucky in two weeks. They'd be married on Sunday, spend the night—oh lovely night—at Stanford Plantation, then set out early Monday morning. Awaiting them in the new state was Wes's land with a new house and barn on it, livestock tended now by a neighbor. For the first time in his life he'd be in a place where he wouldn't be judged by what his brother did or said.

It was while Wesley was contemplating this idyllic scene that the side door of the church flew open with a bang. Reverend Smyth paused in his monotonous intonation to glance toward the disturbance, but what he saw made him cease speaking.

Crazy old Elijah Simmons, his face red with fury, was pulling behind him, her hands bound with rope, what must have been one of his daughters, but the swollen, distorted face made identification impossible.

"Sinners!" old Elijah bellowed. "You sit here in the Lord's house yet all of you are fornicating sinners!"

He pushed the girl forward so hard that she stumbled to her knees. And when Elijah pulled her up by her hair, it was clear that she was pregnant. Her hard, round belly protruded from her gaunt frame.

"Travis!" Regan said with a plea, but Travis was already on his feet ready to stop the old man.

Elijah pulled a pistol from the pocket of his coat and held it to the girl's head. "The fornicating whore doesn't deserve to live."

"In God's house!" the reverend said with a gasp.

Elijah held the girl and backed up the stairs leading to the preacher's box. "Look at her!" he yelled, forcing the girl's body back to make her stomach more prominent. "What sinner did this?"

The preacher started down the stairs, but Elijah pressed the pistol deeper into the girl's temple. She appeared to be only half-alive, one eye swollen shut, the other drooping tiredly.

Travis slowly began walking around the walled bench.

"Now, Elijah," he said soothingly, "we'll find out who did this and he'll marry her."

"The devil did it!" Elijah screamed, his head bent back, and the congregation, eyes on him, gasped in unison.

"No," Travis said calmly, inching forward. "A man did it and the man will be made to marry her. Now, let me have the pistol."

"There are no men!" Elijah said. "I kept her under my eye; I watched her day and night; I tried to beat some goodness into her, yet the slut—." He broke off as he bent the girl's arm backward. "The twelfth of September she stayed out all night. On the thirteenth of September I tried to beat some shame into her but she was born in sin and she will die in sin."

Wesley, his face turning whiter with each moment, saw his world collapsing about him. He knew the girl was Leah, the one with whom he'd spent an hour and whose virgin's blood he'd seen on his cloak the next morning. He knew, without a doubt, that the child she carried was his. If he went forward now, perhaps he wouldn't have to marry her, but he wondered if Kimberly would be able to forgive him his one lapse. But if he didn't step forward, the girl Leah might lose her life.

He stood.

"Stay out of this, Wes," Travis said from the corner of his mouth.

Wesley looked at old Elijah. "I'm the father of the girl's child," he said clearly.

For a moment all sound in the church ceased. The first sound was a half-gasp, half-sob from Kimberly.

"Take the sinner!" Elijah screeched, and he pushed Leah down the stairs.

Wesley and Travis worked together, Wes grabbing Leah and sweeping her into his arms before she hit the floor, Travis wrestling the pistol from Elijah's hand.

Everyone began to move at once, the congregation excitedly leaving the church, Steven holding Kim, who kept her head high and her eyes dry while Clay, Nicole, Reverend Smyth, Travis, and Elijah followed Wesley into the vestry.

Regan lifted her skirts and ran out the side door to the parsonage, where she demanded that hot water and clean cloths be brought immediately to the vestry. When she returned, everything was chaos. The girl lay lifelessly on a sofa, her bonds cut away, Nicole kneeling beside her. Clay stood beside Elijah, who was sitting, reluctantly, in a chair. Reverend Smyth cowered in a corner. And in the middle of the room were Travis and Wesley, bellowing at each other like two enraged bulls.

"You'd think you'd have enough sense to stay away from virginal young girls. What with all the—," Travis shouted.

"The bitch flung herself on me," Wesley answered. "How was I to know it wasn't her profession? I even paid her."

"You fool! Why did you have to pretend to be a saint and say in front of everyone that it was your kid? I could have handled it."

"Like you handle everything else in my life, Travis?" Wesley yelled, fists clenched.

The water came, the housekeeper left, her eyes wide with terror, and Regan knelt beside Nicole. Ignoring the two men in the center of the room, they began tenderly to wash the girl.

"You think Kimberly will still take Wes after this?" Regan asked Nicole, hope in her voice.

"Probably," Nicole answered, and Regan's shoulders fell.

"I wonder why she went to bed with Wesley if she was a virgin. And why she went back to that old man afterward. You know, don't you, about her sister?"

"I've heard," Nicole answered. Then, with eyebrows raised, she looked at Regan. "You're up to something."

Regan gave Nicole a look of pure innocence. "Look!" She nodded toward the frightened preacher. "They're scaring the reverend. Tell Clay to take Wes outside, and I'll get Travis out of here. I'd like to talk to this girl."

Regan had to put her small body between her husband and

his brother and beat on Travis's chest with her fists to get his attention. "I want quiet in here!" she yelled up at him. "Go somewhere else and scream at each other."

"If you're telling me what to do—," Travis began, but Clay caught his arm. "Let's go outside. The girl is sick." He nodded toward Leah on the couch.

"Sinners! All women are sinners!" Elijah screeched, and Clay grabbed the old man's arm and hauled him out the door behind Travis and Wesley, who'd already resumed their argument in full gale. The reverend tiptoed out behind them.

"That's better," Nicole sighed when the room was quiet. "How do you stand both of them under the same roof?"

"It's a big roof," Regan answered, "but they're getting worse as they get older. No!" she said quickly to Leah, who was trying to sit up. "Just lie still."

"Please," Leah whispered through swollen, cracked lips. "I must leave now while he's gone."

"You can't leave. I doubt if you can walk. Now lie still," Nicole said.

"I think we ought to take her home and feed her," Regan said, and the unsaid words *and wash her* hung on the air.

"No," Leah said. "Don't want to cause Wesley problems. Marry his Kimberly. So sorry about baby."

Nicole and Regan exchanged looks. "How long have you known Wesley?" Regan asked.

"Always," Leah whispered, leaning back on the cushions. Through her one unclosed eye she saw two women who looked like angels, exquisitely pretty, with soft clouds of dark hair, dresses of fabric woven by gods. "I must go."

Regan gently pushed her down again and applied a cloth to her swollen face. "You've known Wesley always yet you only climbed into bed with him once?"

Leah's mouth gave what could have been a smile. "Only saw

him twice." With that she fell asleep or into a state of half-sleep, half-consciousness.

Regan sat back on her heels. "I'd like to hear the rest of this story. What was Wesley doing with a girl such as this when he was supposed to be faithful to her royal highness Kimberly?"

"Her royal—," Nicole said with a smile. "Oh Regan, you haven't called her that to Wesley, have you?"

"No, but I did once to Travis. Stupid men! Both of them think she's the epitome of womanhood. You know, I'd almost rather see Wes married to . . . to that—," she pointed at the bruised mess that was Leah—, "than to the dear, delectable Miss Shaw."

Before Nicole could answer, the door burst open and in ran Bess Simmons, Leah's sister.

"I'll kill him!" she cried, falling to her knees and taking Leah's lifeless hand. "Is she alive? I'll kill him!"

"She's alive and which one do you plan to kill? Her father or Wesley?" Regan asked, standing over Bess.

Bess wiped away a tear. "The old man. Leah asked for what she got from Mr. Stanford."

"Oh?" Regan asked with interest, extending her arm to Bess to help her stand. "Then Leah did throw herself at Wesley."

"Oh yes. Stupid girl." She glanced fondly at the sleeping Leah. "She'd have done anything for Mr. Stanford."

Together Nicole and Regan ushered Bess to a chair. "Tell us," they chorused.

Within a few minutes Bess had told the whole story.

"It was through Leah that Clay found me on that island," Nicole said thoughtfully.

"And she's loved Wesley all these years?" Regan said.

"It ain't been *real* love," Bess said, "since she ain't seen him in all these years, but Leah's always had the notion that she was in love with him."

"Better than Kimberly," Regan said under her breath.

"Regan . . ." Nicole warned. "I don't think I like your thoughts."

"Bess," Regan said brightly, taking Bess's arm, "it was so good of you to come by and I swear to you that Leah will be well taken care of." Expertly, Regan escorted the woman out the door.

Leaning on the closed door, Regan's eyes were bright. "The girl saved your life and she's been in love with Wesley for years."

"Regan, are you going to interfere in this? This is between Wesley and Kimberly. We should take the girl home, nurse her back to health, deliver the child, and perhaps find them a place of employment."

"And what about Wesley's child?" Regan said righteously. "Are we going to let it be raised by strangers?"

"Perhaps Wes and Kim could adopt—?" Nicole began but stopped. "Perhaps that is a bit farfetched."

"With dear, sweet Kimberly it is. I doubt if she'll be able to put up with the nuisance of her own children much less someone else's." Regan sat down. "Look at her, Nicole, and tell me how you think she'll look when she's healed and clean."

Nicole hesitated, but she did as Regan bid. Nicole had an idea what Regan was hinting at and she was sure she should stop her, but at the same time she agreed with Regan. For months now she'd been hoping something would happen to prevent Wesley from marrying Kim.

As dispassionately as she could, Nicole studied Leah's battered face. "She has good features, good bones. I can't tell about the eyes in this condition. She may never be pretty, exactly, but neither do I think she'll be ugly."

"Oh well, we couldn't hope to beat Kimberly's loveliness. Nicole!" she said, rising. "I think we should insist that Wes marry the mother of his child, that he do the honorable thing by her."

"Regan . . ." Nicole gave a sigh of exasperation. "It just

won't work. You know Travis could fix it so the girl would never want for anything and Wes does *not* have to marry her."

"He'd more likely be happy with this stranger than he would with Kimberly. This girl *loves* Wes and I know Kim cannot love anyone except herself."

"But Wesley loves Kim," Nicole said stubbornly, trying to reason with her friend. "He does *not* love this girl. And besides, what do we know of her? Maybe she's worse than Kim ever thought of being."

Regan gave a snort of disbelief. "You heard the sister. This girl could have had an easy life in the tavern but instead, she chose to stay and support her brothers and sisters even though she had to bear beatings from that crazy old father. How many people do you know who would do that? Miss Shaw?"

"Maybe not Kimberly but—."

"We have a choice between Kimberly or this battered, unloved, unappreciated girl."

That made Nicole laugh. "Oh Regan, really, you do exaggerate so. None of what you're saying means anything. Wesley will make up his own mind."

Regan looked thoughtful for a moment. "If you and Clay agreed with me and we got Travis on Kim's side—Wesley *always* does the opposite of what Travis wants—we might be able to get what we want."

"Clay can't stand Kimberly," Nicole said, half under her breath.

"And what about you, Nicole, what do you think of Kimberly?"

Nicole looked down at Leah for a long moment. "I hate to see anyone I love unhappy. Wesley has borne Travis's criticism for so long."

"And wouldn't it be nice for him to have a chance with a new wife in a new land—a *real* chance for happiness, not one doomed to failure?" Regan whispered.

"Clay *thought* he wanted to marry Bianca but fate stepped in and we were married instead," Nicole said under her breath.

"We're going to help fate a little, aren't we, Nicole?" Regan urged.

Nicole looked up, eyes laughing. "I'm afraid so—and *afraid* is exactly the right word."

In spite of Nicole's original reticence, she was the one most enthusiastic in bringing about Wesley and Leah's marriage. Clay looked into his wife's eyes and remembered too well how he'd wanted to marry one woman and had ended with another. Besides, he'd had too many run-ins with Kimberly to ever take her side.

Rubbing his jaw in some private memory, Clay said, "I owe Wes one. He helped me get away from Bianca. I just hope this Leah proves to be a better woman."

"That's my worry too," Nicole answered.

But when Clay, Regan, and Nicole reached the strangely quiet Wesley and Travis, there was no need to persuade anyone.

"You talk to him!" Travis seethed at Regan. "He thinks he has to marry the little two-bit whore. He's willing to give up his whole future because the cunning slut arranged it so he was her first customer. If he'd had any sense and waited a few minutes in the church, probably twenty men would have admitted to tumbling her. I wonder if she faked virgin's blood on *their* cloaks?"

Regan, her hand on her husband's arm, seemed reluctant to speak.

Nicole went to stand near Wesley, to look up into his bleak eyes. "You don't believe that, do you?"

Wes shook his head. "I don't want to marry her but it's my duty. She carries my child."

"And what about Kimberly?" Nicole asked softly.

"She—," Wes turned away for a moment. "That was killed when I stepped forward in the church."

"Wesley," Nicole said, her hand on his arm, "I don't know the girl, but I think she has qualities that could make her a good wife."

Wesley snorted. "She's fertile. Now, shall we get this over?"

"For God's sake, think about it for a few days at least," Travis exploded. "Maybe you'll come to your senses. We can find the girl a husband. The cobbler's boy is looking for a wife. He could—."

"Travis, you can take your cobbler and—."

"Wesley!" Regan interrupted. "Are you going to hate Leah when she's your wife?"

"I shall give her and the child the best of everything. Now, shall we go inside to my—," he smiled in an ugly way—"bride?"

Leah became Mrs. Wesley Stanford before the sun went down on that fateful Sunday. Through some inner strength, she held herself upright and answered the nervous preacher's questions firmly. She didn't quite understand how it had all come about, but it was so much like one of her dreams, standing in a marriage ceremony with the man she'd always loved, that the pain in her body seemed to slip away.

The solemn group didn't say a word when the service was complete. Leah was helped to make her mark beside Wesley's signature in the church registry, then Clay's strong arms carried her to a waiting wagon. She was too ill to notice where she was or that her new husband and his brother refused to look at her.

She was placed in a boat, rowed upstream, and put into another wagon. At long last she was gently laid on a soft, clean bed.

"*My* room," Wesley snorted at Regan as Clay put the girl on the bed. "It's fitting then that I should leave."

"Leave!" Regan gasped. "With a new wife and—."

Wesley's look stopped her. "If you think I can look at that every day and stay sane you don't know me very well. I have to go away for awhile and get used to the idea." He pulled a carpetbag from a wardrobe bottom and shoved clothes into it.

"Where are you going?" Regan whispered. "You won't leave her and the baby?"

"No, I know my duty. I'll take care of both of them but I need some time to resign myself to . . . *that!*" He sneered at the sleeping Leah on his bed. "I'll go to my farm in Kentucky, do some work, and should be back in the spring. The kid'll be old enough to travel then."

"You can't stick us with your leavings," Travis said from the doorway. "You were the noble one who felt he had to make an honest woman of her. *Woman!* I can't even tell if she's human. Take her with you. I don't want to be reminded of your stupidity."

"Take the expense of her keep from my half of this place," Wesley shouted.

"Don't part like this," Regan pleaded, but Wesley was already gone. "Go after him," she told Travis. "Nicole and I will take care of the girl. Don't part with your brother like this."

After hesitating, Travis touched his little wife's cheek, then tore down the stairs. From the bedroom window Regan watched the brothers embrace before Wesley started toward the dock and the boat that would take him west.

Chapter 3

TWO DAYS after Wesley left, Leah was delivered of a stillborn child. She cried over the tiny coffin then was ushered back to bed where she slept for days, waking only briefly to eat lightly.

When Leah finally woke and looked about her, she was sure she was in heaven. She lay in the middle of a big four-poster bed hung with cream-colored cloth. The walls were painted white and hung with pictures of sailing ships and men hunting, and there were chairs, tables, and cabinets such as she'd never seen before.

She allowed herself only a moment to enjoy the view before she swung her legs out of bed. She was wearing a cap on her head and a brilliantly white gown; wonderingly, she touched the garment while her head stopped spinning.

"What do you think you're doing?" asked a woman from the doorway. "Miss Regan!" she shouted over her shoulder.

When Regan arrived, Leah was struggling with the woman to be allowed out of bed. "Sally, that will be all."

"You don't know what her kind's like," the maid said, sniffing, pushing at Leah's shoulders.

Regan drew herself up. "Sally!" she commanded. "Out of this room and I'll speak to you later." When she was gone, Regan turned to Leah, who was again trying to sit up. "You must rest."

"I have to see about the little ones. The old man'll let them starve."

Gently, but with force, Regan pushed Leah back into bed. "That's all been taken care of. Travis and Clay went to your farm and got all your brothers and sisters and they're being placed in people's homes. As for your father, no one's seen him in weeks, not since he . . . came to church. Right now all you have to do is rest, eat, and get well. When you're better, you can see your family. Ah, here's the food."

Leah was bewildered when a prettily painted wooden tray laden with food was placed over her legs.

"I didn't know what you'd like so I ordered a variety," Regan said, lifting domed silver lids to show fragrant, hot food.

"I . . ." Leah stammered.

Regan patted her hand. "Eat as much as you can and enjoy it, then I want you to sleep. We're going to fatten you up before we set to work. The chamber pot's under the bed." With that Regan left the room.

Leah tore into the food with both hands, eating as she always did—as fast as she could. She was unaware of the flecks of food she splashed on the bed hangings. When she finished, she used the chamber pot and emptied it out the window, just as she had at home. Scratching, she went back to bed and slept, missing Travis's furor when he heard what Leah had done with the contents of the chamber pot.

For ten days Leah did nothing but rest and eat and, as her scratches and bruises finished healing, Regan looked at her in speculation. Regan had told Leah about Wesley's leaving for Kentucky, pretending that it was something he'd intended to do all along.

Leah learned to leave the chamber pot for a maid, but she never had the courage to leave the bedroom. She sat at the window and looked out at the acres of buildings that went with

Travis's plantation, saw the hundreds of people moving about their jobs, and she began to feel restless.

"When am I gonna start that work you mentioned?" she asked Regan.

Regan took Leah's chin in her hand and studied her face in the sunlight. The bruises were almost completely healed. "How about tomorrow morning?"

"Good." Leah smiled. "You got anything I can wear? Somethin' old," she said, nodding toward Regan's blue silk dress.

"I don't think we'll worry about your wardrobe yet," she said thoughtfully. "Yes, I think we'll start tomorrow if Nicole is available." She gave Leah no time to ask questions. "I must go. There are so, so many preparations to make," she said distractedly as she left the room.

When Leah woke the next morning, both Nicole and Regan were standing over her wearing worn, coarse dresses of muslin, their hair covered, and stern expressions on their faces.

"It's not going to be easy," Regan murmured. "Where do we start?"

"Body first, hair tomorrow."

Before Leah could say a word, each woman grabbed an arm, pulled her from the bed, and led her out of the bedroom. Leah, while being half dragged, gazed about her in wonder at carpets, pictures, furniture of magnificence. They led her downstairs to a relatively plain room that was still beautiful compared to where she'd lived. "Is this gonna be my room? Wait a minute!" she gasped as Regan and Nicole practically tore the nightgown from her. She bent, struggling to cover her nude body. "You can't—."

"Get used to it, Leah," Regan ordered, "because you won't be wearing any clothes for a couple of days."

"You have no right—," she began, grabbing her gown from the floor.

"Get in!" Regan commanded, pointing to an enormous tub standing in the middle of the room.

Leah stood perfectly still where she was, holding her discarded gown before her.

Nicole took over. "Leah," she said firmly. "You're a Stanford now and with the name and the beautiful house go certain responsibilities. For one thing, you cannot sit at a dining table smelling worse than a mule, which you do right now. Therefore, Regan and I are going to devote the next few weeks—or months if need be—to making you into a Stanford. We're going to clean you, cream you, mask you, and when that's finished we're going to tackle your grammar, your walk, your manners, and anything else that needs work."

Leah looked from one woman to the other. "When you get through with me will I smell like you do? When Wesley comes back will he see me wearin' a pretty dress?"

Regan and Nicole exchanged smiles. "A beautiful dress. Wesley will be proud to have you as his wife."

Days later she wondered whether she would have gotten into that first tub of water if she'd had any idea what those two fiendish women had planned. She'd assumed they'd be happy with her clean skin, but Nicole clucked over her.

"This won't do at all. Too many years of neglect."

Leah, wrapped in a cotton robe, was led to another room and in this one sat a tub of . . . "What *is* that?" she said with a gasp.

"Mud," Regan answered, laughing.

So Leah was immersed in mud, made to stand in her birthday suit until it dried, and given three more baths. Then she lay on a table while Nicole and Regan tried to scrub her skin off with coarse leather gloves. She was put into another tub of water, this one greasy with vegetable oil, and when she was removed they rubbed her with cucumber cream.

"Not bad," Regan said at the end of the day, hair straggling in her eyes, her dress filthy. "I think we accomplished a lot." She smacked Leah on her bare bottom, handed her a robe, and escorted her upstairs.

Exhausted, but her skin feeling tingly and alive, Leah fell into the bed.

The next morning Nicole and Regan were there again. Leah groaned and pulled the covers over her head.

"Oh no, Leah," Regan said, laughing, "greet the day with a smile." She pulled the covers off, but Leah did her own walking downstairs to the torture chambers.

"I've been itching to do this," Nicole said, pulling the cap from Leah's dirty hair. "I wonder what color it is?"

Leah sat in a hard chair while Nicole took a stiff-bristled brush to her scalp, scrubbing so hard it brought tears to her eyes.

"Dandruff," Nicole murmured, but Leah didn't even know what that was.

While Nicole scrubbed, Regan applied a cornmeal mixture to Leah's face. When the mask was dry, they began washing her entire head. It took four shampooings to remove years of grease and dirt.

"I won't swear to it but I think there're touches of red in here," Nicole said.

Even wet, Leah's head felt lighter than it ever had, but before she could speak, Nicole began dumping handfuls of mayonnaise on her newly clean hair. Her head was wrapped in a very hot towel and she was left alone in the darkened room, her head leaning backwards, grated raw potato under her eyes.

Wesley, she kept thinking. I'm really, truly his wife, and he's worth all of this.

In the evening her hair was washed again and rinsed with rainwater mixed with lemon juice, vinegar, and rosemary. Nicole had covered all the mirrors on their path from Wesley's bedroom to the storage areas where they were working, so Leah had no idea how she looked, but as she sank into the bed she knew she smelled better.

Leah was appalled to learn that Nicole and Regan expected her to change her underclothes and bathe every single day. She felt that if it'd been done once it was done forever, but on the third day they pushed her into a tub again. They were determined to soften Leah's skin since it bore calluses from years of work. Her elbows and knees were scrubbed raw, then bleached with lemon juice and massaged with strawberry cream.

And always there were lectures. Nicole taught her how to care for her skin and hair even if she spent all day in a field behind a team of horses. Since Leah couldn't read, they made her memorize recipes for creams, facial masks, hair conditioners, and shampoos; on and on they went, making Leah recite them until she could repeat them even asleep.

After two weeks of treatments, Nicole, her hands in Leah's clean, soft, shining hair, stood back. "Do you think we can show her now?" she asked with a smile.

"Wait." Regan laughed. "Put this on, Leah." She held out a deep green silk taffeta dressing gown, embroidered with tiny, colorful birds.

"I couldn't." Leah hesitated, but Nicole's look stopped her. Leah dropped the plain muslin gown she wore and slid her arms into the silk, her eyes rolling slightly at the feel of it. "It's lovely."

"All right, now stand right here," Regan ordered, posing Leah before a full-length mirror that was draped with a bed sheet.

When Regan, with a flourish, pulled the sheet away, Leah made no reaction—because she had no idea who the person in the mirror was. She turned to see who was behind her, but when the reflection moved also, she stood still.

The woman in the mirror was not just pretty; she was beautiful. Long, thick auburn hair cascaded about her shoulders, down her back, and big green, intense eyes looked out of a square-jawed face marked with a full, sensuous mouth. Tentatively, Leah lifted her hand to touch her own cheek—and the next minute she collapsed in a heap on the bed while Regan and Nicole laughed.

"I think we've succeeded," Regan said in triumph, then her head came up. "I want to show her off. Just a bit, right now."

"It's early," Nicole warned.

"Come along, Leah," Regan said, taking Leah's hand.

Regan led Leah through a part of the house she'd never seen before, through long hallways, past a vast dining room. "Does this place have an end?"

"You'll learn your way around. Now we're going to Travis's office."

"Wesley's brother?"

Regan gave a short laugh. "Wesley is usually thought of as Travis's little brother."

"Not to me," Leah said with confidence.

Travis was sitting behind an enormous desk, ledgers open before him, one of his clerks beside him. Regan stood Leah before the desk and when the clerk looked up, his mouth dropped open in amazement. Travis glanced up, saw the man's expression, and turned to look at Leah.

"Good God!" he said, sucking air through his teeth. "She's not—."

"She is," Regan said proudly.

"Fetch us some tea," Travis commanded his clerk. "And stop gawking! Here, sit down. Leah, is it?"

As if she'd always been treated as a lady, Leah demurely sat on the upholstered chair Travis held for her. The robe had parted somewhat and was exposing a great deal of cleavage, which Travis was enjoying. He looked up to see Regan glaring at him.

"Filled out some, hasn't she?" he said with a grin.

The tea arrived almost instantly with two maids and a butler carrying a big silver tray, all three of them and Travis's clerk gaping at Leah.

"Out! All of you!" Travis commanded.

Leah sat still, returning all their looks with curiosity, wondering who they were and what their jobs were.

When the room was clear, Travis poured tea for Leah into a fragile porcelain cup and held it out to her with great politeness.

"I *am* hungry," Leah said and noisily moved her chair closer to the desk where the tray of cakes and sandwiches had been set. She blew loudly on the tea, slurped it so it bubbled through her teeth, set the wet cup down on the wooden desktop, then picked up three small pastries, mashed them in her saucer, poured cream from the silver pitcher over them, and began eating the concoction with her teaspoon. Halfway through she looked up to see Travis, Regan, and Nicole gaping at her.

Nicole was the first to recover. "We have a bit more work to do yet," she said softly before sipping delicately from her teacup.

"That you do," Travis said with a grunt.

Leah resumed eating.

Three days later Leah swore she hated those little cups and saucers that looked so pretty but seemed to always be falling apart in her hands. Regan threatened Leah's life if she broke one more piece of expensive imported porcelain, so Leah again tried to learn how to handle them.

"What does it matter *how* you eat as long as you get it inside?" Leah half cried as Nicole again corrected her use of a fork.

"Think of Wesley," Nicole said, using the phrase as a slogan to urge Leah on—and it always worked. The women used Wesley to entice Leah, to force her to be patient and learn the manners she needed to know. And they got the whole story from Leah about how she'd met Wes, how she'd loved him forever.

After Leah had been at the Stanford Plantation for two months, her father, Elijah, was found dead in the river. Travis paid for a funeral that was beautiful. For the first time since she'd married Wesley, Leah saw her brothers and sisters. Each of them had gained weight, were unbruised and clinging to the hands of the people who'd taken them in. They looked at Leah with wide eyes, not even sure who she was, and left with their new families; Leah shed tears of joy because they seemed so happy now.

Once, Leah looked across her father's coffin and into the gaze of a beautiful young woman. But before Leah could even look her fill at this vision, Regan nudged her and Leah turned away. When she looked back, the woman was gone.

"Who was she?" Leah asked later.

"Kimberly Shaw," Regan answered tightly.

The woman who was supposed to marry Wesley, Leah thought, feeling very smug. She may have wanted him but I got him.

Seeing the woman, Leah resolved to work harder so she'd please Wesley when he returned in the spring.

Leah set her cup down easily, quietly, as if she'd always known how to eat and drink properly, leaned toward Travis, and smiled prettily. "And do you think this new cotton gin will help speed production? You don't think the cotton market will collapse like the tobacco market did?"

Regan and Nicole leaned back in their chairs and watched their protégé with pleasure. It had taken months of work, but Leah was passing the test. They'd never attempted to instruct Leah in *what* to talk about, merely *how* to say the words, so they were surprised when her main interest was farming. But of course she'd never been able to read—and they'd not yet tried to teach her how—so Leah talked of what she knew: farming.

And Travis was eating it up, Regan thought with disgust. Sometimes, when Regan was talking about household problems, she'd see Travis's eyes glaze over, but with Leah asking about his beloved fields, horses, and blacksmith shop, Travis was practically on the edge of his seat.

"In the morning," Travis was saying, "you can ride out with me and have a look at the tobacco."

"No," Nicole said softly. "Tomorrow Leah goes home with me. I have been away too long and it's time we dressed her."

"She looks dressed to me," Travis said appreciatively, looking at the low-cut muslin gown Leah wore.

"Travis," Regan warned, ready to tell him what she thought of his ogling of Leah.

Nicole laughed and prevented the impending quarrel. "No, Leah must go with me. The fabrics I ordered have come at last and my seamstress is there. Also, I'll start teaching her how to manage a plantation. She can start on someplace small before tackling this monster of yours, Travis."

After a frown, Travis smiled, then took Leah's hand and kissed it. "I'm going to miss your pretty face around here but Clay'll take care of you."

Later Regan walked with Leah to Wes's bedroom. "Nicole has an army of French craftsmen at her place. She and Clay went back to France last summer and returned with people Nicole had known when she lived there. Her dressmaker used to work for the queen. Now sleep well because you'll leave early in the morning. Good night."

Leah removed her dress, an altered one of Nicole's, put on a clean nightgown, and slipped into bed. It was July now, she thought. There was all the winter to go and then spring before Wesley would return to her. Touching her clean, soft hair, she knew she looked very different, and she prayed that she'd please him when he returned. More than anything, she wanted to please him. "I will be the best wife in the world to you," she whispered and fell asleep smiling.

In the morning before it was even light, Nicole and Leah were escorted by Travis to the dock. In the five months that she'd been there, Leah had barely seen the plantation except from her window, because she'd always been inside with Regan and Nicole, practicing her walk, her grammar, her table manners, how to sit, how to stand, whatever ordeal could be imagined for her.

At the dock, Travis bent and kissed her cheek, and touching the place, Leah looked up at him in wonder. "We'll miss you," he called as a man helped Leah into the waiting sloop.

Smiling, she waved to them until they sailed out of sight. How heavenly, she thought, how warm and kind and loving everything was. For moments she could almost forget what it was like to be angry twenty-four hours a day.

She turned to Nicole, who was watching her. "If Wesley were here it'd be perfect," Leah said laughing, hugging herself.

"I hope you're right," Nicole murmured, mostly to herself, before looking away.

Chapter 4

AT THE dock of Arundel Plantation waiting to greet Nicole were identical twin boys, six years old, and two beautiful seventeen-year-old twins who were introduced as Alex and Amanda. Clay waited impatiently while everyone else hugged his wife, then he swept her into his arms for an embarrassingly passionate kiss, after which they walked away, each holding one of the boys' hands and looking into each other's eyes.

"They're always like that," Alex said half in disgust.

"They're in love, you idiot," Amanda snapped before turning to Leah. "Would you like to see the cloth that came in? Uncle Clay says it's for you."

"I have better things to do, so if you ladies will excuse me," Alex said as he mounted a beautiful roan horse and rode away.

"We don't need him anyway," Amanda said. "Come on, we have to hurry. Madame Gisele is awful when she's kept waiting. If she bullies you too much, just threaten to send her back to France. It makes her keep quiet for a few minutes at least," Amanda confided.

As Leah and Amanda walked together, Amanda chattering away, Leah was watching the early morning bustle going on about her as people went in and out of what seemed to be hundreds of buildings. Leah asked questions.

"The overseer's cottage, workers' quarters, ice house, the stables through there, the kitchen," were Amanda's answers. "She's upstairs waiting for us." Amanda led Leah through an octagonal porch at the back of a big brick house, up some beautiful stairs, past tables covered with freshly cut flowers. "Mom—I mean Nicole—likes lots of flowers. Here we are, Madame," Amanda said politely to a tiny little woman with a big nose and fierce black eyes.

"You have taken your time," Madame Gisele said in such an odd way that Leah didn't quite understand her.

"It's her accent," Amanda whispered. "Took me awhile too."

"Out!" Madame commanded. "We have work to do and you are in the way."

"Yes, of course," Amanda said, laughing as she curtsied before leaving the room.

"Insolent girl!" Madame snapped, but there was affection in her voice. Then her eyes were on Leah, walking around her, examining her.

"Yes, yes, a good figure, a bit large in the bosom but your husband likes that, no?"

Leah smiled, turned red, and began to study the wallpaper of the attic room.

"Come, come, don't stand there. There's work to be done. Show me what you like so we can begin." She motioned toward shelves along one wall that were loaded with bolts and rolls of fabric.

Leah stuck out her finger to touch a piece of deep blue velvet. "I . . . I don't know," Leah said. "I like everything. Nicole and Regan usually—."

"Ah!" Madame Gisele cut her off. "Madame Regan is not here and Nicole is no doubt in the throes of passion with that magnificent man of hers and she will be of no use for days. So! Now you must learn to rely on yourself. Stand up straight! No dress will ever hang properly if your shoulders droop so. Have some pride in yourself. You are a beautiful woman, you have a rich, handsome husband who will return to you soon and now we will dress you splendidly. You have much to be proud of so *show* it!"

Yes, Leah thought, she is perfectly correct. I *do* have a lot to be proud of. She turned toward the fabric. "I like this," she said, touching a rust-colored velvet.

"Good! And what else?"

"This and this and . . . this one."

Madame Gisele stood back for a moment, looked up at Leah, then gave a short laugh. "You may look frightened but you're afraid of no one. True, no?"

Leah considered the question seriously. "Nicole and Regan are so sure of themselves. Everything they do is perfect."

"They were born to wealth but people like you and me . . . we have to learn. I will help you, that is, if you aren't afraid of hard work."

Leah smiled at that, remembering the feel of the plow harness about her shoulders. "People who live in houses like this don't even know what work is."

"You will do," Madame Gisele said, laughing. "You will do."

What followed for Leah were days of measurements, pinnings, and being bullied by Madame.

"Lingerie!" the little woman said repeatedly. "You may have to forego silk for everyday wear on that nasty farm you're going to, but underneath you'll be a lady."

At first Leah was shocked by the semitransparent garments of Indian cotton, but she soon grew to like them. Madame and her workers created a stunning wardrobe for Leah with many plain, everyday dresses of printed muslin and several silk and velvet creations for whatever society existed in the new state of Kentucky.

And always, Madame helped build Leah's confidence. "You are a Stanford now and entitled to the privileges that go with the name."

Unconsciously, Leah began to stand straighter, and within

another month, she acted as if she'd always eaten her meals at a table and worn satin dresses.

When the fall harvest was in and Clay could relax, he began to spend time with Leah. Each morning they went out together and he taught her to ride.

"I like her," Clay told Nicole one night. "She's very serious, always wanting to please, trying to learn everything at once."

"It's for Wesley," Nicole said softly, looking up from the needlework in her lap. "Even after the way he's treated her, leaving her after their one night together and again leaving her after their marriage, she still believes the sun rises and sets on that man. I just hope . . ."

"You hope what?" Clay asked.

"Wesley is so much like Travis and when either one of them gets something in his head it's not easy to change."

"And what do you want to change?"

"Kimberly," Nicole answered.

Clay gave a snort of disgust. "Wes was saved when he didn't marry that bitch. Kimberly believes the world should be laid at her feet, and, unfortunately, it generally is."

"And most often it's put there by Wesley. I don't think he's going to easily forget Kimberly."

"He will," Clay said with a chuckle. "Wes isn't stupid, and after he spends a few weeks alone with a beauty like Leah, he'll never even remember that Kimberly exists."

Nicole had her own ideas of the stupidity of men when it came to pretty women, but she said nothing as she turned back to her sewing.

It was that winter, as work on the plantation began to slow down, that Leah discovered weaving. When Nicole showed Leah the loom house, Leah was reluctant to leave. The beautiful cloth, the coverlets taking shape under the women's hands, shuttles flying, treadles working smoothly, fascinated Leah.

"Would you like to try your hand on a loom?" asked a big blonde woman who Nicole introduced as Janie Langston.

"I'm not sure I could do that," Leah said hesitantly. There seemed to be thousands of threads on the loom going in and out of looped strings, with a metal comb tied to a wooden bar.

"Would you like to try?" Janie urged as Leah reverently touched a piece of woven cloth.

"Very much," Leah said positively.

Nicole led Leah around more of the plantation, but Leah didn't see much of it because her mind was still on the fabrics she'd seen. "Do you *really* think I could make something like that?" Leah asked while she was supposed to be looking at the dairy cows. She'd milked cows since she could walk and they didn't interest her, but the idea of being able to create such beauty did.

"Yes, Leah, I believe you could. Would you like it if we went back to the loom house now?"

Leah's eyes sparkled in answer.

Leah spent the next months seldom more than a few feet away from Janie, who taught her everything from caring for sheep, shearing, and dyeing to spinning, dressing a loom, and weaving. And Leah took to it all as if she'd been born with a shuttle in her hand.

In the evenings she sat behind a spinning wheel and the threads she produced were even and very fine. During the days she put her stool near the loom heddles and pulled threads through according to Janie's intricate pattern without a single error and without losing her patience. When she wove she threw the shuttle straight through and brought the beater back with a great deal of strength.

In January, Janie said it was time to learn to draft her own patterns.

"But I can't read," Leah said.

"Neither can my other weavers. Now, first you learn to draw your pattern."

In the next few weeks Nicole twice found Leah asleep over a table covered with pattern drafts, intricate graphs of blocks of numbers and treadling charts, as well as tie-ups. She'd extended the numbers to draw the six harness patterns on paper to check herself for errors. There were names such as double chariot wheel, double bow knot, velvet rose, snail trail, and wheel and star.

Nicole helped Leah to bed, and in the morning Clay asked that she come to his office.

"I thought you might like to have this," he said, handing her a large book bound in blue leather.

"But I can't—," she began.

"Open it."

She saw that the pages were blank and she looked at him, puzzled.

Clay stood beside her. "On the cover it says, Arundel Hall, and every year I have several of the books bound to use for permanent records. Nicole told me of your loom patterns so I thought you might like to record them in this. You could take it to Kentucky with you."

To Clay's complete bewilderment, Leah collapsed in a chair, the book held close to her, and she began to cry. "Did I do something wrong?" he asked. "Don't you like the book?"

"Everyone is so kind," Leah cried. "I know it's because of Wesley but still—."

Clay knelt before her, put his fingers under her chin, and lifted her face. "I want you to listen to me and believe what I'm saying. At first we *did* take you in because you'd married Wes, but we forgot about him months ago. Nicole and I and our children have come to love you. Remember how the boys came down with the measles at Christmas and you stayed up with them? Your kindness, the love you've given us, have more than repaid us for what little we've done for you."

"But all of you are so easy to love," she answered through tears, "and you've given me the world. I've done so little for you."

Standing, Clay laughed. "All right, we're equal then. I just don't want to hear any more about what we've done for you. Now I need to go back to work."

Leah stood and on impulse threw her arms around Clay. "Thank you so much for everything."

He hugged her back. "If I'd known I'd get this kind of reward I would have deeded you the plantation. Now go on back to your looms."

Smiling, she left the office.

In February, Regan and Travis came to fetch her.

"You've had her long enough," Travis said to Clay while grinning at Leah. Regan had said, with some disgust, that Travis had quickly *forgiven* Leah for trapping his little brother after Travis saw how pretty Leah'd turned out to be.

With tears in her eyes, Leah hugged all the Armstrong family good-bye.

"Oh yes," Clay said, eyes dancing, "I thought you might like to have this." He nodded toward a wooden crate standing with several others on the wharf.

Puzzled, Leah walked toward the box. Behind it was a loom, a beautiful piece of work in cherry with brass fittings.

As Leah gaped soundlessly, Clay put his arm around her. "It breaks down for packing and you can take it to Kentucky with you. If you start crying again I'll keep it," he warned.

Again Leah hugged him as Travis said he'd send someone to get the loom. Leah, hating to part with the loom for even a few days, grabbed the long comblike reed and clutched it. As Travis lifted her into the little sloop, she held the reed and waved as long as she could see the Armstrongs on the dock.

On the sail back to Stanford Plantation, Regan asked Leah hundreds of questions and at the same time noticed the many changes in Leah. She held herself erectly, looked people in the eye, and her movements were unconsciously graceful.

As they walked from the dock to the house, Regan was thinking that Leah was ready for anything—until she looked up at the house. Standing on the porch, one hand delicately poised on the iron railing, was Kimberly Shaw, her blonde hair drawn back from her lovely face, rings of curls down her neck. Her fragile prettiness was set off by a silk gown and matching cloak of deep pink.

"Is she Wesley's Kimberly?" Leah asked in a whisper.

"*You* are Wesley's wife, remember that, Leah," Regan said under her breath as Kimberly walked down the stairs and toward them.

"Kimberly!" Travis said, pleased. "It's been so long since we've seen you." He caught her shoulders and kissed her cheek. "Have you met Leah, my sister-in-law?"

"Only briefly," Kimberly said in a pretty, soft voice as she held out her hand. "I am Kimberly Shaw."

To Regan's disgust, she could see Leah weakening before Kim. Kim had a way about her of apparent sweetness that made people want to do her bidding.

"I am very happy to meet you," Leah said softly.

"If you ladies will excuse me," Travis said, "I have to get back to work."

When he was gone, Regan invited Kim in for tea.

"If it's not too much trouble," Kim said. "I do have some news I want to tell."

"About Wesley?" Leah asked eagerly, following Kim up the stairs.

"You haven't heard from him?" Kim asked, eyebrows raised in speculation.

"Have you?" Regan interrupted, leading the way into the small parlor as she ordered tea from a servant.

"Not often," Kim said modestly. When they were seated, she spoke again. "I want to be honest about everything and I was, to say the least, very upset at what happened last year. I couldn't bring myself to even hear Wesley's name for months afterward."

Leah toyed with her fingers in her lap. She had given so little thought to how this woman must have felt at losing the man she loved.

"As you know," Kim continued, "it was planned that Wesley and I, with my brother Steven, would travel to Kentucky together and I'd looked forward to going to a new state with . . . with . . ." She stopped as the tea was brought in.

When the servant was gone, Regan spoke. "You didn't come here to tell us about last year's plans, so why are you here?"

Big fat tears clouded Kim's pretty eyes. "Since that day in church my life has been awful, just dreadful. Regan, you really can't imagine what it's been like. I'm laughed at constantly. Every time I go to church someone makes a remark about how I was . . . jilted." She glanced at Leah, who was still looking at her hands. "Even the children are making up rhymes about what happened."

She buried her face in her hands. "It's too awful. I can't bear it any longer."

In spite of herself, Regan felt her heart go out to the woman. "Kim, what can we do? Maybe Travis could talk to the people or—."

"No," Kim said. "The only way is to leave. Leah," she said, pleadingly, and Leah met her eyes. "You don't know me, but I want to ask you to do something for me, something that will save my life."

"What can I do?" Leah asked seriously.

"In Wes's last letter to me, he said he was returning at the end of March, then the two of you and my brother would start the journey to Kentucky."

A month! Leah thought. In just a month Wesley would be home and she would really be his wife.

"Let me go with you," Kimberly was saying. "I could travel with Steven and the four of us could go somewhere where no one knows what's been done to me. Please, Leah, I have no right to ask anything of you, I know, but it was because of you that—."

Regan stood and cut off Kim's words. "I think you're asking too much of Leah and I don't think she should—."

"Please, Leah," Kim asked. "Maybe I can find a husband in Kentucky. Here everyone laughs at me. It's miserable, really miserable and you already have Wesley, the one man I've ever loved and—."

"Yes," Leah said firmly. "Of course you may go with us."

"Leah," Regan said, "I think we should discuss this."

"No," Leah said, looking at Kim. "It's my fault that this has happened to you and I'll do what I can to give you back some of what you've lost."

"That's not your responsibility," Regan began, but Leah gave her a look she'd never seen before.

"Would you pour?" Leah said to Regan, and Regan sat down and obeyed her.

Chapter 5

LEAH PUT the last stitches in the border of the coverlet, a blue and white Irish chain pattern, and smoothed it in her lap. She looked up at Janie's laugh.

"Is it my imagination or are your hands shaking?"

Leah returned her smile. "I think they are a bit." She paused. "Was that the bell?"

Janie laughed harder. "I'm afraid not."

"You don't think they'd forget to ring it, do you? I mean, they wouldn't let Wesley arrive and not tell me."

"Leah," Janie said, her hand on her shoulder, "Travis and Regan are waiting to see him too. The minute he's sighted, they'll ring the bell."

At that moment came the loud, excited clang of the bell by the wharf.

Leah didn't move but her face drained of color.

"Don't look so scared," Janie said with a laugh. "Come on, let's greet him."

Slowly, Leah rose, looking down in doubt at her dress. She wore a deep rust-colored silk twill that brought out the auburn in her hair, and the high waist was trimmed with black silk ribbons, with more ribbons entwined in her hair, which was piled on her head in a mass of glossy curls.

"You look beautiful," Janie was saying as Regan rushed into the room.

"Are you going to stay here all day?" Regan demanded. "Don't you want to see him?"

"Yes!" Leah gasped. "Oh yes!" And together the three of them left the loom house at a run.

Two weeks before, Travis had received news from Wesley saying that he and Steven were returning around the second of April; today was the third. Travis had sent someone upriver to watch for the men, and the moment they were seen the big wharf bell was to be rung so everyone could come to greet the returning men.

Now, as Leah was running, she touched the gold coin pinned to the inside of her pocket, the coin Wesley had given her so long ago. Would he be pleased with the way she'd changed? As they drew near the wharf and she could see Travis talking to someone, she stopped running. I will make you the best wife in all the world, my Wesley, she vowed. You'll never regret having lost your Kimberly.

Leah was behind the gathering crowd as everyone pushed to greet the returning men, but as people moved about, Leah had her first glimpse of him. He'd put on some size while he'd been gone and now stood as big as Travis; covering his broad shoulders was an outrageous costume of pale leather, fringed about the shoulders and down the sides of his pants legs. Crisscrossing his shoulders were straps to a couple of pouches, one decorated with an intricate design of tiny beads. On his head was a broad-brimmed hat that looked as if it'd made the journey back and forth to Kentucky tied to the bottom of a wagon wheel.

Leah looked at him and felt her heart begin to beat faster, her throat closing in anticipation. She'd waited for this moment for years and years.

"Here she is," Travis was saying, slapping his brother's shoulder.

As he said the words, Leah saw Wesley's face turn from the joy of greeting to one of coldness, and she hesitated.

Regan came forward and took Leah's arm. "Come on. He doesn't even recognize you."

Hesitantly, shyly, Leah stepped toward her husband.

"She's changed some, hasn't she?" Travis was saying with pride. "Could have knocked me over with a feather when she cleaned up so pretty."

Blushing, but very pleased, Leah looked up through her lashes at Wesley. He was looking toward the fields over her head.

"You have to tell me how last year's crops were," Wes was saying. "And I'll need some seed to take back with me. Ah!" He smiled. "Is that Jennifer?" he called to Travis and Regan's five-year-old daughter who was running toward her uncle. "Excuse me," Wesley said and made his way through the crowd to greet the child.

For a moment everyone was too embarrassed to speak, but as they cast looks of sympathy toward Leah, the crowd began to break apart.

Leah, stunned at Wes's lack of greeting, watched as he and Jennifer walked toward the house.

"That bastard—!" Travis began, but Regan put her hand on his shoulder and shook her head. "I think I'll talk to him," Travis said and left Leah and Regan alone on the wharf.

"Leah—," Regan began.

"Leave me alone," Leah snapped. "I don't need sympathy from anyone. I was stupid to think there could ever be anything between us. I'm just a poor girl from the swamp of the river with a whore for a sister, so why should he even bother to look at me?"

"Stop it!" Regan commanded. "Wesley isn't like that. Maybe he was shocked when you were so pretty. After all, he's never seen you looking as you do now."

Leah gave her a look of contempt. "I am not quite that stupid."

"Let's go to the house," Regan urged. "Travis will talk to him and find out what's wrong." She took Leah's arm. "Please," she pleaded.

Leah allowed herself to be pulled along by Regan, but she held her head high as everyone they passed gave her a look of pity.

They were barely inside the house when the sound of shouting came to them, and both women stood paralyzed at what they heard.

"You expect me to stop hating her merely because she cleaned up pretty?" Wesley was shouting. "I've hated her from the moment I married her, ever since she made it impossible for me to have the woman I loved. All winter I worked long, long days trying to sweat out my hatred of her, but I couldn't. I wouldn't even sleep in the house knowing that the slut was going to be living in it. She's ruined my life and now you expect me to fall all over myself merely because she's washed her face?"

Regan didn't allow Leah to hear any more, except for a few crashes as a fight between the brothers seemed to break out, before she shoved Leah up the stairs to the room Leah was to have shared with her husband. Regan leaned against the door, so shocked and hurt that she couldn't move.

Not so Leah, who went to the wardrobe where her new dresses mixed with Wesley's suits. "I won't take much," Leah was saying. "But I'll need a few clothes. Perhaps you can sell what's left and the money will help repay what you've given me."

Regan took a moment to react to Leah's words. "What are you talking about?"

Leah folded two dresses, her hands and body shaking. "I'll go back to the farm. I worked it before and I can certainly work it enough to support myself. Maybe I can still have the loom Clay gave me and sell some weaving."

"You're running away?" Regan gasped.

The face Leah turned to her was filled with fury. "All of you may think I'm nothing, that because I grew up without the finer things of life that I'm not worth much, but I have my pride and I'll not stay here where I'm hated."

"How dare you!" Regan seethed, her teeth clenched. "No one before today has treated you with anything but respect and how dare you insinuate that we have!"

The women were practically nose to nose before Leah turned away. "I'm sorry," she whispered. "Please forgive me."

"Leah," Regan said softly. "Don't do anything you'll regret. I wish you hadn't heard what Wes said, but I'm sure something can be worked out."

"Such as?" Leah whirled. "Should I go to live in that house with him? My father always hated me, but he hated everyone else too. There was nothing personal in it. But now my . . . my husband hates *me* and only me. I never wanted to impose myself on him. I wish my father'd shot me rather than come to this." She went back to the wardrobe to take out a straw bonnet.

"Leah, you can't go back to that farm. That place is nothing but a breeding ground for mosquitoes and Travis said the roof fell in on the house this winter. You can't—."

"What are the alternatives? And don't say that I should stay here with you. I've never been an object of charity before and I won't be now."

"Damn that Wesley!" Regan said. "I thought that in a year he'd come to his senses. If he'd just open his eyes he'd see that Kimberly is—." She broke off, her eyes wide as she stared at Leah. "Leah," she said quietly. "If you go back to the farm and Wes returns to Kentucky with Steven and Kimberly, what are people going to say?"

Leah gave an exasperated sigh. "People from my class have never had the luxury of wondering what people will say. When your own father drags you, pregnant, into a church with a gun held to your head, there isn't much worse that can happen to you in your lifetime. People will just say I'm another Simmons whore and that they knew so all along."

"Is that what you want? Do you like the idea of walking into a store or the church and having people whisper about you?"

"As a Simmons, I've never had any choice in the matter."

"You *aren't* a Simmons. You're a Stanford. Did you forget that?"

"No one need worry. I'll give Wesley a divorce or an annulment or whatever he wants. There's no child, so he has no further obligation to me."

"Leah," Regan said and took her hands. "Sit down here and talk to me. You can't go running away from every adversity. Once I tried to run away from my problems rather than staying and trying to work them out. I put myself through a great deal of needless pain. You have to think of yourself and not sacrifice yourself because of one stupid man."

For the first time Leah realized Regan was angry at Wesley.

"Oh yes, I'm angry at him," Regan answered the unasked question. "Wesley has no idea what he's been saved from. I knew for a long time what his precious Kimberly was like and I took a chance that you weren't like her. You've lived with us for nearly a year and we've all, Clay and Nicole included, come to love you, and damn Wesley! I'm so angry at him I think he almost deserves Kimberly."

Suddenly Regan stopped. "That's it!" She gasped. "That's it!" She stood and walked a few feet away. "I know how to solve everything. We—," she broke off to laugh. "We are going to give Wes just what he *thinks* he wants—Kimberly."

"Good," Leah said tiredly, gathering her clothes in her arms. "I'm sure they'll be very happy together. Now, if you don't mind, I think I'll go."

"Leah, no," Regan said, halting her. "Listen to me."

* * *

Leah dressed carefully for dinner that night, wearing a low-cut gown of deep forest green that matched her eyes. In spite of her efforts, no one seemed to notice anything throughout the stilted dinner. Wesley was sporting a bruise on his jaw and Travis kept moving his left arm gingerly, as if it hurt him. Regan, after a few choice words about some of her furniture being broken, said nothing. The men ate in silence while the women remained quiet, picking at their food.

When Leah could stand no more, she rose. "I would like to talk to you in the library," she said to the top of Wesley's head, and when he looked up at her with cold eyes, she returned his look with matching ice.

He gave her no answer, but when she turned, she heard him move to follow her.

When they were alone in the library, she offered a silent prayer that she'd be able to say what she wanted to. Regan's plan was a good one and would ultimately save Leah's pride, but for the moment the idea repulsed her. She wanted no part of this man who so obviously hated her.

"I have a proposition to make you, Mr. Stanford," she began.

"Oh come now, you can call me Wesley. You've certainly worked for that right," he said with a hint of a sneer in his voice.

Leah, her back to him, made her fingers into claws as she took several deep breaths to calm herself. She faced him. "I want to get this over as quickly as possible because I don't want to be near you any more than you want to be near me."

"That's probably true," he said with a snort. "No doubt you wanted this house and that pretty dress more than you wanted a man cluttering up your life."

"Why I did spend that one night with you is beyond my reasoning now, but the fact is that we are married and I'd like to do something about that."

"Ah, blackmail," he said in a self-satisfied way.

"Perhaps," she said as calmly as she could. "I have a plan."

She went on before he could interrupt her again. "I believe I know how to get what we both want. You want your Kimberly and I want a decent place to live."

"Stanford Plantation isn't enough for you?"

She ignored him. "I apologize for our marriage, for my father having forced it. I even apologize for having . . . given myself to you that night, but I can't change that now. If I gave you an annulment now I would still have to live here in Virginia and face down all the gossip over what has happened. But I have an alternate plan."

She drew a deep breath. "A few weeks ago your Kimberly came here and asked to accompany us to Kentucky in the hopes that she could escape the talk about how she was jilted and, perhaps, in a new state, she could find herself a husband."

It gave Leah no pleasure to see Wesley wince at the idea of someone else marrying the woman he loved.

"It seems that now," Leah continued, "our roles are reversed. I have heard how you hate me, that you cannot bear sleeping in a house I may some day live in and, whether you believe it or not, I have enough pride that I don't want to force myself on someone who detests me. Now! What I propose is this: that the four of us leave Virginia as planned, but once we're out of sight of people you know, I will cease pretending to be your wife—our marriage is no more than pretense—and will become your . . . cousin, I guess is good enough. Or perhaps I should be Miss Shaw's cousin if you can't bear any relationship with me. Kimberly can travel as your fiancée and when we arrive in Kentucky our marriage can be annulled or whatever, making both of us free."

"And how much am I to pay you for this generous offer?"

She sneered at him. "I will work on the journey to Kentucky in exchange for my bed and board, but once in Kentucky I'll set up my own weaving business and support myself. Regan has provided for me and we have an arrangement whereby I can repay her. You'll have no further obligations to me once we reach the new state."

He looked at her in disbelief. "You're willing to let me out of this marriage you worked so hard to get?"

Red rage filled her. "I never even suggested marriage! I did *not* come to you when I knew I was carrying your child. I tried to conceal the fact, but when my father found out he beat me senseless. Half the time in the church I wasn't sure what was going on. If you hadn't been so 'noble' and had waited, I would have asked you *not* to marry me. Now I'm attempting to get us both out of this situation. If you can't stand the idea of my going to Kentucky with you, let me know and I'll return to my father's land. In fact, on second thought, I think I should do that anyway, because I'm not sure I can bear your company on the journey. Excuse me and I'll go now and talk to Travis about the legalities of ending this marriage."

She shut the door behind her and for a moment leaned against it. Never had she been so angry before. Nothing her father had ever done had affected her as this did. Perhaps it was because it was the end of a dream. Regan's plan had seemed good when she first heard it and she would have liked to earn her living as a weaver and to get away from people who'd always call her "one of those Simmonses," but it had been an unattainable dream. With a caressing hand, she touched the velvet of her dress. On the farm there'd be no need of velvet dresses. With her shoulders straight, she went in search of Travis.

For a moment Wesley sat in stunned silence, then, with force, he threw his hat against the closed door. He didn't know which made him angrier, that the girl had overheard him or that she was taking everything so calmly. She was so cool, maybe a little angry, but certainly she didn't act as a *woman* should.

"Damnation!" he cursed under his breath as he went to retrieve his hat. The last thing in the world he wanted was a woman who told him what to do and how to do it. All his life he'd lived under Travis's rule. Even when their parents were alive, Travis had been in control of his younger brother. When Wes was a toddler Travis had always been there, shouting orders, giving directions. It seemed to Wes that Travis had always been an adult, had never been a child, had never had a child's doubts as mortals did.

And Travis had never needed anyone. He was running most of the plantation by the time he was fourteen. Travis never read a book, never did anything that was just for pleasure. He was born knowing Stanford Plantation was his, and he had no qualms about treating everyone, including his parents, as employees.

When Travis met his wife he'd treated her as though she were someone who worked for him, and, because of this, she'd run away. Away from Travis, she'd managed to become someone in her own right, but she couldn't have done so while standing in Travis's overpowering shadow.

Wesley had always worked for Travis, but to escape he'd taken long trips all over the world. He'd drunk champagne from a beautiful woman's slipper in Paris. He'd made love to a duchess in England, and in Italy he'd nearly fallen in love with a black-haired singer.

In the end he'd known he was deluding himself. He was a farmer and he'd never be happy away from the land. But, as soon as he had returned home, Travis had begun giving Wesley orders about five minutes after his arrival. And it was then Wes decided he had to get away permanently. The new state of Kentucky was said to have rich, fertile land and he went to see it. He loved the state and the people, people who had a feeling that things were moving and changing. He bought several hundred acres of land near a little town called Sweetbriar, repaired the house that someone had built years before, and returned to Virginia one last time.

But he'd no more than returned when his life was forever changed: he met Miss Kimberly Shaw. For the first time, Wes had felt he was looking at a *real* woman, a woman who was proud of being a lady. Kimberly couldn't read a ledger of accounts, couldn't even really ride a horse. What Kim knew about were sewing, pressing flowers, what colors to paint a house—and most of all, how to look up at a man and make him feel like a *man*.

Wesley began to imagine returning home from the fields to the pretty little house Kimberly would decorate for them, putting his head in her lap and letting her soothe away all the tensions of the day. No doubt she'd have a dozen domestic crises a day, all of which Wesley would have to solve. Kimberly *needed* him. For the first time in his life Wesley felt wanted, felt as if he weren't just another strong back that would do as well as any other. When Kim looked up at him Wes felt twenty feet tall.

Everyone kept warning him that Kim was helpless, but no one understood that that was just what he wanted. He didn't want some woman who was as perfect as Travis, some woman who could run a plantation with one hand and raise children with the other. Kimberly was soft, sweet, clinging, and needed protection from all of life's hardships.

And now he'd lost her! This winter when he'd worked so hard on his new farm he'd had time to regret his rashness in marrying the Simmons girl. He knew the story of how she'd remained on her father's farm when she could have run away. But instead she'd stayed with her younger siblings and done the work of a couple of men.

Wes was sure she was a paragon of all the virtues; if he died tomorrow and willed her the Kentucky farm, she could no doubt run it single-handedly; in fact she could probably run it better than he could. But what no one seemed to realize when they were telling him "for his own good" that Kim was a helpless butterfly was that she was exactly what he'd always wanted.

Crumpling his hat, he put his hand on the doorknob. Whatever the girl Leah was, she was his wife and he had an obligation to her. Maybe she had planted herself in his arms, maybe she had planned to get some money from him, but since he had been dumb enough to fall for her tricks he deserved what he got.

"Lord, protect me from competent women," he prayed as he went in search of Leah.

Chapter 6

TWO MINUTES after she left Wesley in the library, Leah began shaking. At first she thought it was from anger, but she soon recognized it as fear. For the past year she'd tried not to think about what would happen when Wesley returned. She'd tried her best to hope that he'd hold out his arms to her and love her, but instead, he'd rejected her publicly.

Leah was accustomed to anger. Anger was what had fed her while she worked her father's farm. Anger had kept her from giving in and being beaten down. Her father had taken away everything except her anger and her pride—and both of these had come to the forefront with Wesley.

But now that she'd vented her anger she was frightened. She didn't want to go back, alone, to her father's farm. For a year she'd lived within the heart of two loving families and she'd had hopes of having her own family. If she returned to the swamp she'd no doubt remain there the rest of her life. Perhaps with her weaving . . .

"Leah."

Wesley's voice interrupted her thoughts. Immediately she straightened her shoulders. She was standing in the hallway and had no idea how long she'd been there feeling sorry for herself. "Yes," she said coolly, and braced herself against another of his attacks. This was the man she'd dreamed of so long and she'd thought that when she got him all her problems would be solved, but actually they were just beginning.

"I came to apologize," he began, watching her. She was pretty, he thought, in a haughty sort of way. Her eyebrows peaked in the middle, making her look arrogant, willful. "I haven't really had time to think over your plan but it sounds as if it could work. I don't imagine you want to stay here in Virginia any more than I do and I do have a duty toward you."

"No," she said quietly, her eyes smoky dark. "You have no obligation toward me. I have always taken care of myself and I will continue to do so. Our marriage will be dissolved and you'll be free of me."

The corner of Wesley's mouth quirked, but not in amusement. "I'm sure you're able to take care of any number of people, but would you rather farm that bit of filthy swampland you own or come to Kentucky and—what is it you want to do—weave?"

It flashed through Leah's mind to wonder what she'd ever seen in this autocratic man to ever think she cared about him. He offered her this choice as if he were amused because he knew how it wasn't really any choice at all. How she'd like to toss his offer back into his face! But for all her pride, she wasn't going to do something stupid.

"I would rather go to Kentucky," she snapped angrily. "But I want it known that for all I am a Simmons and not of your class, I pay my own way. I will never be a burden to you."

"There was never a question of whether you would be a burden to me. I'm sure you can handle anything," he said with a hint of disgust.

He would have said more but a whisper of "Wesley" behind him made him turn. Kimberly stood there, her soft body encased in swirls of light pink silk, her big eyes already filling with tears.

Before Wes could move, Kim pressed the back of her hand to her parted lips and in the next second she started a slow sink toward the floor, her lashes fluttering prettily.

Wesley caught her in his arms long before she hit the floor. Sweeping her up, the pink silk floating about him, he looked down at her with concern. "Water!" he commanded to Leah, who was standing motionless. "And brandy!" Wes added as Leah turned away.

"My darling," Wes whispered as he sat down with her on a long bench against the wall.

Leah had never seen anyone faint before and she was sure Kimberly was dying. Lifting her skirts, she took off for the kitchens at a run.

"Leah!" Regan called, starting to run after her. "What's wrong? Did Wesley—?"

"Brandy and water," Leah demanded from the head cook. "And quick." She turned to Regan even as she grabbed the tray handed her. "Miss Shaw just fell to the floor. I think she's dying." With that she started running again.

"Kimberly faints regularly," Regan called. "And don't let her have too much of that brandy. She likes it too much."

"Regularly?" Leah gasped in disbelief. "The woman must be ill." When she reached the hall, Kim was lying on the bench, Wesley kneeling beside her, holding and kissing her fingers.

"I'm such a burden to you, my darling Wesley," she said softly. "You are so good to put up with me, and especially since we'll never . . . I can never be . . ."

"Hush, love," Wesley whispered. "It's all going to work, you'll see." He turned, saw Leah, and his voice changed. "You took long enough. Here, love," he said, lifting Kim and holding a snifter of brandy to her lips.

Kimberly drained it all in a gulp.

"Not so fast! You'll choke!" Wes cautioned.

"Oh my. I'm just so upset I don't know what I'm doing. What did you mean when you said we'd work things out?" She glanced up at Leah, who was silently watching the scene.

Gently, Wes smoothed back a curl from Kim's temple. "The

four of us, you, me, Steven and . . . Leah will leave for Kentucky and once we're there my marriage, such that it is, will be dissolved, then we can be married."

For a moment, Kim didn't say a word. "How will we travel?"

"Leah will be my cousin and you my intended."

Kim gave another glance to Leah. "Couldn't the marriage be dissolved just as well here in Virginia?"

A very slight frown crossed Wesley's brow. "I'm sure it could, but legally Leah is my wife and I have a responsibility toward her. If I left her here the gossips would kill her."

"Of course, Wesley dear," Kim said tiredly, fluttering her lashes. "Can you ever forgive me for being so insensitive? Oh dear! I seem to be suddenly quite chilled. Would you please get me a shawl? I do hate to be a bother."

"You could never be a bother," Wes said before leaving them.

When they heard his footsteps on the stairs, Kim opened her eyes, sat up, and gave Leah a wide-eyed look. "Are you really, truly going to give up Wesley?"

"Are you all right?" Leah asked, still shocked at Kim's fainting.

"Oh yes, perfectly. I would love some more brandy though. Brandy makes me feel so good. I always feel brandy is my reward for pleasing Wesley. He so loves for me to faint. Leah, I just knew you were going to be a kind person. I knew it when you agreed to let me travel with you to Kentucky. I've heard how you used to run that dreadful farm of yours and I know you'll be so handy on this trip. I can't cook or lift heavy things and horses terrify me. I just know you'll be wonderful to have around and we'll become great friends. Uh-oh, here comes Wes." She hurriedly put the empty glass on the tray, slid down on the bench, and resumed her helpless look.

"Here you are, dear," Wes said tenderly, wrapping the shawl about Kim.

Bewildered, Leah stepped back and watched as Kim allowed

Wes to treat her as a helpless invalid. No one noticed when Leah left to return the tray to the kitchen. Leah wasn't sure whether to laugh or cry at the situation. Kim's "Wesley so loves for me to faint" made her want to laugh, but the idea of any woman play-acting to attract a man disgusted her, and Leah vowed she'd never allow herself to faint, no matter how much it pleased a man.

Leah managed to avoid Wesley for the next few days, although she caught glimpses of him now and then through a window or from around a building. She dressed carefully each morning until she realized that she wanted him to notice her. The night of his arrival she put on her prettiest nightgown—just in case—but her husband stayed away from her. He was distantly polite when he saw her but nothing more. And as Leah went about her work of preparing for the journey ahead, her pride began to take over. She refused to allow Wesley's rejection to hurt her.

The day they were to leave dawned clear. The wagon was loaded high and Travis had tied a piece of canvas across the top. Wesley already sat on the seat, reins in hand. A cage of chickens was fastened to the back; a milk cow on a lead rope trailed behind.

"We'll miss you," Regan said, hugging Leah. "Tell Wesley what you want to say and he'll write it for you, but don't lose contact with us." She leaned forward to whisper. "I'm going to have a baby in the fall."

"Congratulations!" Leah laughed, hugging her again. "I hope it's a little boy just like Travis. Goodbye, Jennifer," she called, hugged Travis once again, and then was lifted onto the seat beside Wesley.

As Leah turned and waved, Wesley clucked to the horses and they started the journey.

As soon as she was alone with Wesley, Leah felt uncomfortable. She began studying her fingernails, but quit, tucked her hands under her, and sat on them. "We're to meet the Shaws at their place?" she asked, but when Wesley merely nodded she said no more.

They drove past the tavern where Bess worked and Leah wished she could stop and say good-bye to her sister, but one glance at the tautness in Wesley's profile and she knew she wouldn't ask him for a thing. She straightened her back and looked ahead.

The sun was barely up when they reached the plantation where Steven and Kimberly were staying. It was a tiny place compared to Clay's, and some of the outbuildings looked as if they needed repair. But what caught and held Leah's attention was the utter chaos surrounding a half-packed wagon. From out of the jumble of voices, boxes and animals, Kim came running toward Wes.

"Oh, Wesley, dearest," she called, "you have to help us. Steven is refusing to take all of my clothes and all of the beautiful things I have for our house. Please, you must talk to him."

Wesley jumped from the wagon, gave Kim a quick, reassuring caress with the back of his hand, then went toward the wagon. Leah was left to help herself down. When she reached the wagon it was easy to see what was wrong, yet even as she circled the mess she couldn't believe her eyes. None of the goods loaded on the wagon had been packed with any sense of order. A small, fragile hatbox was crushed under two fifty-pound bags of seed. A steel-bound trunk teetered atop the arms of a gilded chair.

"You can see there's no more room," came a man's voice from the opposite side.

Leah bent her knees and peeked through the arms of the chair to get her first glimpse of Steven Shaw. He was as lovely as Kimberly—blond, blue-eyed, cleft chin—perfect.

"Wesley, dear," Kim was saying, "you must find a way. I can't possibly leave anything behind. You wouldn't want me to be unhappy, would you?"

Heaven forbid that catastrophe, Leah thought as she began

untying the ropes across the goods in the wagon. If it was repacked from the floor up, they'd probably be able to get everything on.

When Wesley walked to the side where Leah was untying the ropes he gave her a look of surprise; then there was just a hint of disgust. He looked away. "Can you climb to the top of this mess and hand me that trunk?"

"Of course," Leah said, smiling to herself. Maybe he *did* realize his precious Kimberly was little more than an ornament.

"Somehow I was sure you could," Wesley said under his breath in a way that puzzled Leah.

Leah and Wesley worked well together, unloading then repacking the wagon, while Steven and Kim squabbled. Kim cried over her crushed hat while Steven complained about Kim's lack of help.

A couple of times Leah felt Steven watching her, but he looked away just as she turned.

When they finished Leah looked to Wesley, in truth expecting some sort of thanks, but all he did was grunt. "You can ride with Steven," he said as he tied the last rope.

Stunned, Leah watched him walk away. "With pleasure," she called after him and fought down the urge to throw a rock at the back of his head. Maybe she should set fire to the fringe on his buckskins.

A hand touched her arm and she looked up into Steven Shaw's dancing blue eyes. "May I?" he asked, nodding toward the wagon seat.

Instantly, Leah didn't trust him. When she was a girl her two older brothers used to bring men home and sometimes they had looks in their eyes such as the one Steven now had. Of course, she told herself, she was wrong.

Wesley and Kim pulled out onto the road first. No one came from the house to say good-bye and suddenly Leah felt very alone—among strangers, traveling to more strangers.

"Will you miss your friends?" she asked Steven, but all she got was a sidelong look from him that made her stop talking.

They traveled west for hours, and Leah didn't try again to talk to Steven. They stopped for an hour to eat sandwiches Regan had sent, and Wesley hovered over Kim, who cooled herself with a sequined fan and unbuttoned the top buttons of her pale blue silk dress. Wesley was appreciative and Kim rolled her eyes in modesty.

"That Wesley's a lover," Steven said to Leah. "Only he can't have both of you." He gave Leah a look from head to toe.

Frowning, she moved away from him.

In the afternoon as they neared a cluster of houses four men rode toward them. Wesley shouted and Steven halted the wagon.

"Send Leah up here!" Wesley bellowed back.

Leah froze in place. She had no intention of obeying this man who ignored her all day yet ordered her about when it was convenient for him.

Steven gave one look at her face and chuckled. "She wants none of you, Stanford," Steven shouted. "Better leave her here with me."

With a curse Wesley bounded from the wagon. "They're coming to greet the newlyweds," he said tightly, looking up at her. "Unless you want all of Virginia to find out about us, you'd better come to the wagon with me."

"What do *I* care about Virginia? It's your name that needs saving."

"Damn you!" Wesley gasped as he grabbed her arm and pulled.

Leah wasn't expecting violence and so was unprepared for his strength. With a gasp she went flying into Wesley's arms just as the four riders reached them.

"Can't keep your hands off of her, can you, Wes?" said one man, laughing.

"Just lookin' at you, ma'am, I can see why Wes grabbed you off the church steps."

"Put me down!" Leah hissed at Wes, who was holding her as if she weighed nothing at all.

"We planned a little goin' away party and you're the guest of honor. We'd be pleased if you'd honor us with some of your time."

The fourth man was gawking at Leah. "Who'd think that one of those Simmonses would clean up to look like that?"

One of the men glared at him. "Excuse him, ma'am. Vern never did have no manners. We got everythin' waitin' at the inn. Bess Simmons is there."

"Sure, of course we'll be there," Wesley said.

"See you then!" they called as they turned to ride away.

"*Now* will you put me down?" Leah demanded.

Wesley turned back to his wife in his arms and for the first time he seemed to look at her—but the glance was broken after only seconds.

"Oh Wesley," Kim began to cry. "That was so humiliating to me. *I* should have been in your arms. They should be giving *us* this party."

Wes nearly dropped Leah as he ran to comfort Kim. As Leah steadied herself against the wagon Steven, above her on the seat, laughed nastily. "Haven't you learned how to fight with tears? My sister's an expert at it."

Leah ignored him as she walked to the back of the wagon to check on the animals. It was there that Wes found her.

"I think you better ride with me," he said tightly.

She glared at him. "If you're trying to save my reputation, you needn't bother. I'm sure your friends will be prepared for anything when a Simmons is involved."

She turned away toward the cow, but Wesley grabbed her arm and pulled her to face him. "I don't give a damn if you don't care for your own reputation but I'll not have it said that Kimberly has broken us up. She's innocent in all this and I'll not have her name dirtied further."

She jerked away from his grasp. "I should have known that you were concerned only for your dearest Kimberly. So for your Kimberly I'm to play your wife for the night? The idea repulses me!"

He gave her a hard look as his voice lowered. "I will tell you this only once: Don't you ever again say anything against Kimberly. She has suffered a great deal because of you and if our spending one evening together will help keep her name clean you'll do it if I have to break some of your little bones. Tonight we'll be a loving couple, do you understand that?"

"Perfectly," she said through clenched teeth.

Wesley turned on his heel and left her, and as Leah looked up, in the distance stood Kimberly, smiling prettily and confidently before she swept away in a swirl of silk, Wesley trotting along after her.

"Damn, damn, damn!" Leah cursed under her breath as she angrily adjusted the cow's harness.

"My little sister does have a way of getting men," Steven said from behind her.

Leah ignored his ingratiating tone and blinked back tears. She would not cry!

"But then you have your own way of interesting a man," Steven said as he touched her arm. "Those friends of Wesley's were surprised to see a Simmons looking like you. Ol' Wes was lucky that night when you climbed in bed with him. Of course he wasn't so lucky when he had to marry you. Men marry women like my sister but women like you were made for only one thing—love. Now I could give you—."

He didn't finish his sentence because Leah grabbed the cow's feed bag and slammed it into the side of Steven Shaw's smirking face.

"Bitch!" he yelled, rubbing his face, but Leah was already running to the front wagon where Wesley sat waiting for her. Without a word, she climbed into the seat.

Damn them, she thought. Damn each and every one of them. Steven thought she was a whore, Wesley threatened her with violence if she didn't obey him, and Kimberly smiled and drank brandy like a sailor. I'll do what Wesley wants, she seethed to herself. Tonight I'll be the most loving wife this side of the mountains. We'll leave Virginia with everyone thinking we're so in love that Kimberly *couldn't* come between us. I'll save Miss Shaw's reputation, but I wonder if she's going to like the process.

Chapter 7

LEAH DIDN'T speak to Wesley for the rest of the ride to the inn. Even though she knew what she wanted to do, she wondered how in the world she was going to stand him long enough to pretend to be his wife. And, too, Leah began to wonder just how Wesley's friends were going to treat her. Already one of them had made a comment about her being a Simmons. Would they treat her as Steven Shaw did?

As they neared the inn, Leah steeled herself because ten men were waiting for them. The wagon hadn't rolled to a stop when all ten of them rushed forward each pushing the other for the privilege of helping Leah from the wagon.

"Welcome, Mrs. Stanford."

"Wesley doesn't deserve someone as pretty as you."

"Clay says you like to weave. My sister sent some drafts for me to give you."

"And my mother sent you some flower seeds."

Bewildered, Leah looked from one smiling face to another. "Th . . . thank you," she stammered. "I had no idea . . ."

One of the men gave a hard look to Wesley. "The women were pretty upset that Stanford Plantation didn't give a party to celebrate your marriage. We wanted them to come today, but they thought since they hadn't been invited maybe they weren't wanted."

691

It was Wesley's turn to stammer. "No, it was just that we . . . I mean no one . . ."

One man laughed. "Take a look at her, men. If you had a wife that looked like her, would you want to share her?"

Leah was so pleased by their compliments that she blushed.

"Come on inside. You all must be tired. May I?" The man held out his arm to Leah.

"Since when have you earned such a privilege?" another man asked, extending his arm.

"I believe I saw her first," said a third man.

"Here!" Wesley interrupted. "Before any of you start a fight, I'll escort my own wife."

Trying to hide her surprise, Leah took Wesley's arm and walked with him into the tavern.

Bess waited inside for her. "I'd never have known you," was all Bess could gasp, standing apart from her sister.

Leah left her husband's side and opened her arms to Bess. Hugging her sister, Bess laughed. "It *is* you, isn't it?"

"Every dirty inch," Leah returned.

"They're fillin' a tub for you now. Miss Regan said you'd be wantin' a bath, just like all the other ladies do." She looked up at Wes. "Now you behave yourself while she's gone and I'll return her to you soon enough."

Bess quickly ushered Leah upstairs where two men were filling a large tub. As soon as they were alone, Bess began undressing Leah.

"Bess, I can do that myself. There's no need for you to act as if you were my maid."

"Someone should!" Bess snapped. "Someone needs to be good to you after that story Miss Regan told me. Are you really going to give up your own husband willingly, without even a fight?"

"I have no intention of fighting to keep a man who doesn't want me," Leah said stiffly.

"Listen to you. You sound just like our old man. When you get somethin' in your craw there's no stoppin' you. Just for once, Leah, don't be so stubborn. Don't just *give* Wesley away."

"Bess, you're being silly. Wesley was never mine. He wants Miss Shaw and he shall have her. After tonight I'll not even be his wife in name. I'm going to be his cousin."

"Cousin, schmusin. You are his *wife!* Nothing will change that."

"It will when we get to Kentucky." Leah, nude, put one foot into the water. "It's amazing how easily one can get used to being clean. I think I'll stay in this water all night. If I did I wouldn't have to pretend to be my husband's dear devoted wife."

"That's a good idea," Bess said quickly. "You stay there and I'll get you some clean clothes."

Leah sat back in the tub, closed her eyes, but in minutes Bess returned, a huge grin on her face.

"There's trouble in paradise," Bess said gleefully. "Wesley and that Miss Shaw were having an argument."

"She'll forgive him," Leah said tiredly.

"Miss Shaw didn't like the idea of Wesley taking your arm and Wesley said he had to pretend to be your husband. Miss Shaw wanted to know just how far he planned to carry the pretense. Wesley tried to calm her but Miss Shaw said that two could play the game and if he so much as touchced you he'd be sorry."

"And?" Leah asked, trying to conceal her interest.

"Wesley said he didn't like being threatened and he was doing all this for her and he'd do his duty and do what he had to do."

"Duty!" Leah gasped, sitting up.

Bess smiled. "I guess he means his duty is to touch you."

Leah sat back in the tub. "Bess, there's a black trunk in the back of the wagon, on the left. Inside is a dress of gold velvet. Would you bring it to me?"

"A special dress, is it?" Bess asked.

"What little there is of it is special," Leah said, closing her eyes as Bess left the room.

Leah thought of the dress and knew that if Wesley didn't care for her, at least some of the men would notice her. Perhaps she wouldn't get as much attention as Kimberly, but it would be better than she got while riding on the wagons.

The door opened.

"That didn't take long," Leah said, opening her eyes to see Wesley standing there.

He didn't move as he looked at her, her beautiful body clearly visible in the water, her breasts just breaking the surface, her legs stretched out, parted.

"If you've seen enough, you can leave now."

Reluctantly, Wes looked back at her face. Steamy little curls touched her neck. "Bess said—." He didn't finish but turned and left the room.

With shaking hands Leah began washing herself, and she wasn't sure if she was shaking with anger or because she had suddenly and inexplicably remembered every detail of the time Wesley had held her in his arms.

When Bess returned with the dress, she had such a smug, knowing look on her face that Leah refused to say a word about Wesley's return to the room. Even when Bess gave broad hints, Leah still didn't comment.

The gold velvet of the gown made Leah's skin look even creamier, and the neckline was cut so low that only imagination was left.

"I can't do it," Leah said, looking at herself in the mirror. "There's too much of me and too little cloth. I told Regan I'd never wear this dress."

Bess adjusted the last curl on top of Leah's head. Her long, perfect neck eased down into the beautiful sculpture of her collarbone and breasts. "You will too wear it! I've seen ladies with even less on."

Leah gave her a look of disbelief.

"They just had a lot less to show than you so less looked like more."

"Oh Bess." Leah laughed. "I'm going to miss you."

"Not if I have my way and you get your husband back," Bess said with a sniff.

"I never had him to begin with."

Bess didn't answer but shoved her young sister out the door.

Standing at the top of the stairs Leah had a chance to survey the scene below. Kimberly sat in a chair wearing a sedate turquoise silk dress; she looked absolutely lovely and six men surrounded her. Wesley leaned against the cold fireplace, talking in a tight-jawed way to two men, his eyes constantly shifting to Kim, and there were sparks of anger in the looks. Leah wasn't sure whether she should laugh or be disgusted, but somewhere in her was a bit of jealousy.

As she began to descend the staircase, she was pleased to see first one pair of male eyes, then another, travel upward toward her. At Stanford Plantation she'd always been treated with respect, but she often wondered if it was only because she was married to Wesley.

"May I?" asked one man at the foot of the stairs, his arm extended. The other nine men stood still, gaping in such a way that Leah felt her confidence return.

"Thank you," she said graciously, taking his arm.

Kim stood suddenly and said in an expert half-plea, half-command, "Am I to be left all alone? Do only *married* women get any attention?"

Quickly two men ran to her side—but eight stayed by Leah.

"Supper is waiting. Shall we go in?" a man asked.

Leah looked up to see Wesley, still near the fireplace, his eyes fastened to Kim's retreating back. He didn't seem aware that anyone else was in the room.

Leah, feeling a quick surge of anger, excused herself from the men near her. "Perhaps you should go ahead. My husband and I will follow you."

Leah planted herself in front of Wesley. "You're making a fool of yourself!" she hissed up at him.

He didn't hear her at first.

With disgust Leah used her thumb to poke him sharply in the ribs.

"What are you doing?" he asked angrily, then as his eyes focused on Leah, they turned smoky for just a second. He recovered himself. "Trying to show the men what they missed?" he asked, one eyebrow raised as he looked at the low, low cut of her gown.

She willed herself not to blush. "You're looking after Kimberly as if she were a bitch in heat. If you plan to save her name I think you should exercise a little control."

He looked at her in speculation. "Are you always sensible?"

"I try to be," she answered, puzzled.

"I thought so. Come on, let's be the loving couple." He took her upper arm in his hand and led her into the dining room.

They were greeted with uplifted tankards and one toast after another.

"To Wesley, who had the sense to look for a jewel where no one knew there was even a mine."

"To Leah, who agreed to put up with a cantankerous, stubborn mule who is only a little better than Travis."

The word *Travis* made them groan as Wesley pulled the chair of honor out for his wife.

Kimberly sat directly opposite Leah and gave her a hurt look that said Leah had betrayed her. Leah felt a pang of guilt as Kim turned away to talk to the man next to her.

For all the warning he'd been given, Wesley still watched Kim with hot eyes.

Telling herself she was doing this to save Wesley and his beloved Kim, Leah leaned across Wesley's arm to reach the pepper and pressed her breasts against him. Wes reacted instantly, turning surprised—and interested—eyes toward his wife. Leah smiled up at him sweetly.

"If you would pass me the pepper I wouldn't have to reach," she said softly.

His eyes flickered downward. "Reach, by all means. Reach for whatever you want."

"Wesley!" Kimberly said sharply, and he looked away from Leah. "I was just trying to remember when we last saw the Ellingtons. Wasn't it at the harvest ball?"

It was obvious to Leah that Kim was reminding Wes of some private, probably risqué, meeting.

Didn't Kim realize it was her reputation being saved? Leah clutched Wesley's arm, leaned into it, and looked up at him through her lashes. "The harvest ball and moonlit nights," she murmured. "Sometimes the moon causes people to do memorable things."

Wesley narrowed his eyes at Leah, then bent to put his lips near her ear. "You'd better stop this little game or you'll get more than you bargained for."

Quickly Leah moved away from him. What did she care if Wes made a fool of himself in front of his friends? Except that she had some pride, too. She didn't want to leave Virginia with people saying that maybe a Simmons could get a man but couldn't hold one. They'd probably never hear of her divorce unless Regan or Travis told, so there was some advantage in leaving the people with an impression that she was good enough to remain with one of the high and mighty Stanfords.

Chastised and no longer so sure of herself, Leah gave her attention to the food, pushing it around on her plate, her head down, speaking only when she was asked a direct question. She no longer felt like competing with Kimberly. Disinterestedly, Leah watched Kim flirt with one man after another.

As the meal progressed things began to change. The man

next to Leah started talking about the new cotton gin and within minutes Leah forgot about Kimberly. From cotton the conversation went to sheep and the prevention of diseases in one's livestock. More men joined the talk.

Within twenty minutes, as Bess and two other women cleared the table, Leah, the ten friends of Wesley, and Wes himself were deep into a discussion of crops and animals. Steven ate, not interested in anything else, and Kimberly looked ready to cry, but Leah was oblivious to the looks directed toward her.

"My father lost nearly everything when the tobacco market collapsed and I'll not put everything into cotton now," one man said.

"I agree," Leah answered. "We're going to raise some sheep and I believe that someday American wool will be in demand."

"You'll not compete with the English markets."

"I'll hire spinners who can do as well as any English-woman!" Leah said vehemently.

"*Can* she spin, Wes?" a man asked, laughing.

Leah suddenly became aware of who she was and where she was and she looked down at the uneaten apple tart on her plate. "I'm afraid I've overstepped myself," she said softly.

To her surprise, Wesley put his arm around her. "To tell you the truth, I haven't been married long enough to know whether she can spin or not."

Astonished, Leah looked up at her husband. His eyes were bright and he seemed almost proud of her.

"Go ahead and kiss her, Mr. Wesley," Bess said from across the table. "You look like you're dyin' to, and we'd all like a little proof that you love her. Isn't that right, men?"

To Leah's anger, Wesley gave a glance to Kim.

He was *not* going to humiliate her. "I don't need much encouragement to kiss my own husband," she said seductively as she slid her arms around Wes's neck.

The moment her lips touched his, she began to regret her actions. She wanted to prove something to the strangers around her, show them she really was good enough to be loved by a man of Wesley's stature, but she forgot any sensible reasons for kissing him. For a year she'd lived with couples who loved each other passionately, and until she began to kiss Wesley she was unaware how this had affected her. She very much wanted to be touched, wanted a release for her passion.

At first Wesley was cool, but he felt Leah's excitement, felt the commitment in her kiss, and he responded. He forgot the people around them as he kissed her deeply, hotly, searingly. His hand covered her head, his fingers demolishing the ordered curls there.

"Wesley," someone said with some embarrassment, "maybe you should wait until later."

Leah was helpless in Wesley's arms, as helpless as she'd been on the one other occasion when he'd touched her.

A hand touched Wesley's shoulder just as he was beginning to seek the soft curve of Leah's breast. The man's hand tightened. "Wes!"

Gradually Wes began to surface, and when he broke away from Leah his eyes took a moment to focus.

For seconds, Leah lay back on Wesley's arm, her eyes closed, her dark hair streaming over his buckskins. When she opened her eyes and became aware of where she was, she sat up abruptly and her face turned several shades of red. Her one glance at Wes showed him to be looking at her with puzzlement, and a vein in his throat pulsed rapidly.

"I . . ." she began, pulling away from him. A hand on her head showed her hair to have fallen. "Excuse me, I must . . ." she didn't finish as she turned and fled through the room and up the stairs to her bedchamber.

She was barely inside when Bess burst in. "I have *never* seen a kiss like that. Not in all my born days have I seen somebody get kissed like that. That Wesley is some man! Not only is he the best-lookin' thing this side of the mountains, he's also the best lover."

"Will you *please* stop talking?" Leah half cried. "How can I face any of them again? They'll never believe I'm a lady now. I wanted to leave Virginia with the people saying I'd become a lady, but what do I do but act like a Simmons whore." She paused, then gasped. "Oh Bess, I am sorry."

"You haven't hurt my feelings, and those men down there are going to dream about you tonight."

"Just what I wanted," Leah said as she sat down heavily on the bed. "Do you think I could slip out the back door and never see anyone again?"

Bess chuckled. "Let me fix your hair and then you will go downstairs again. You should have seen that Kimberly's face. She was spittin' nails."

"I was under the impression you thought Miss Shaw was the perfect example of a lady."

"Hold still!" Bess commanded, her hands in Leah's hair. "I thought that before my own sister was transformed into the most beautiful, elegant lady that Virginia has ever seen."

"Bess," Leah said, turning, "go with us. I need a friend. I'll teach you how to weave and you can go into business with me."

"And leave my nice warm tavern and my nice warm men for a clackety ol' loom? Those Stanfords didn't teach you any sense, did they? You take your Wesley and live on your farm and milk hundreds of cows every day, but not me. I want a life of ease. There, you're all prim and proper again. Now go down and smile. You've got Kimberly on the run."

Leah laughed. "I will miss you so much. Kim will run straight into Wesley's arms as soon as this night is over and he'll kiss her so well it'll make our kiss—." She paused, remembering. "Our kiss will mean nothing," she finished quietly. "All right, I'm as ready as I can be. If my husband can playact a kiss I can at least recognize it as such."

"That was no playacting," Bess called behind her sister, but Leah either didn't hear or ignored her.

Chapter 8

IT TOOK all Leah's courage to face the people downstairs once again. She was so sure they'd treat her as if she were a whore that she wasn't prepared for the warm welcome. Three men had arrived while she was upstairs, two with fiddles, one with a banjo, and they were already beginning to play.

Before Leah had a thought she was shoved into Wesley's arms and he led her in the first minuet.

"You seem to have regained your composure," Wes said before Leah was taken away from him to dance with another.

For hours Leah was whirled from one man to another. Once, she saw Kim dancing with Wesley, and he was looking at the blonde woman with concern. Leah pretended she didn't see them.

Twice during the night she heard the name Justin Stark mentioned, but she never had enough breath to ask who he was.

At midnight Wesley announced that the party was over, that they needed an early start the next morning. He took Leah's arm and half pushed, half pulled her toward the stairs.

Leah felt wonderful. She'd had much too much of the delicious punch Bess had given her and she was humming as she entered their room. On the bed was her most beautiful nightgown, a translucent concoction of silk and ruffles. Leah picked it up, held it close to her, and began dancing about the room.

"Are you drunk?" Wesley asked calmly as he slipped his buckskin shirt over his head.

"How lovely!" Leah said under her breath as she looked at Wesley, bare from the waist up.

There was a spark of interest in Wes's eyes—perhaps more than a spark.

Leah stopped dancing, although her head didn't stop. "Are you going to make love to me?" she whispered.

Wesley's face changed as he looked at her in the golden light of the single lamp in the room. He took a step toward her. "Maybe I could be persuaded."

Leah dropped the gown from the front of her and stood waiting for him, her breath held, her heart pounding. She wanted more than anything for him to hold her, to kiss her again. When he was close to her she touched his bare chest, her fingertips wrapping in the abundant hair on his chest. "Wesley," she whispered as his head moved down toward hers.

A loud, quick knock on the door wasn't even heard until the door opened and Steven Shaw entered. "It looks like my little sister was right."

"What the hell are you doing in here?" Wesley asked angrily.

"Unlike you, Stanford, I don't have two women in two rooms. My little sister is bawling her eyes out because she believes you're doing just what you are." He gave Leah a hooded look. "I told her what a man of honor you were and that you could be trusted. Somehow, after seein' this little filly after you all night, I knew I was lyin'."

"Get out of here," Wesley said tiredly, moving away from Leah. "Tell Kimberly I'll be there in a few minutes."

"As soon as you finish here?" Steven chuckled but left the room before Wes could say a word.

"Leah, I'm sorry," Wes began.

Leah glared at him. Her mood, loosened by the liquor, easily changed from love to hate. "Sorry you didn't get to finish what you started? Sorry you didn't get to take advantage of the weakness of one of the Simmons whores?"

"I don't know what you're talking about," he said, reaching for his shirt. "You're my wife and—."

"*I* am your wife? Do you mean me who has begged you all evening to stop drooling over the divine Miss Shaw?"

"I'd advise you to watch your tongue," he warned.

"My tongue!" She gasped. "Don't you know that we Simmonses have better uses for our tongues than to talk with them? Isn't it in our bloodstream?"

Calmly, Wesley pulled his shirt on over his head. "Look, I really don't know what you're so upset about. You were the one who wanted to travel as my cousin and you've always known how I've felt about Kim. I've always tried to be honest and fair."

"Fair! You nearly attack me in this room and you call that fair?"

Wesley almost smiled. "You've done everything possible to entice me this evening, and that dress isn't exactly made to calm a man down."

"I didn't wear it for you," she said softly as she turned away to hide her humiliation.

Wesley smiled at the back of her. "Leah, really, I *am* flattered that you'd go to so much trouble to get me into your bed. It made me feel good to have you flirting with me even while you were dancing with other men, and I'm sure you could have seduced me if Steven hadn't interrupted, but the truth is, I really should keep to our bargain. For Kim's sake I'm going to try to resist your considerable charms."

"You what?" she said breathlessly, turning to face him.

"I owe something to the woman I love and she needs me, all of me, to stand by her, and in the future I'm going to try to resist you."

"Is that what happened before?" she whispered. "That in spite of all you could do, you gave in to my enticement of you?"

"I really need to go, so maybe we could discuss this another time. But, yes, you did throw yourself at me once before."

"Throw myself at you? As I did tonight?"

"Leah," he began, taking a step toward her, "I think I've hurt your feelings."

"Feelings!" She gasped. "Women like me don't have feelings. Didn't you know that? Women from my class of people, women who didn't grow up wearing silk, are capable only of seductions and enticements. When we get to Kentucky, I won't open a weaving shop, I'll . . . I'll merely open my legs."

Wesley's face hardened. "You've misunderstood everything I've said. All I wanted was to thank you for the compliment of offering me your body."

"I won't do it again," she said coldly. "Next time I offer it, it will be to someone else."

"Not while you're my wife!" he snapped.

She gave him a nasty little smile. "Shouldn't you go to your Kimberly? If you make her cry too long her pretty eyes will be red. How does *she* seduce you? Do her tears pull you into her bed?"

"Kimberly is a virgin," Wes said tightly, his eyes narrowed.

Leah threw up her hands. "A whore and a virgin fighting over you. Poor Wesley, you must spend some sleepless nights. Go to her."

"Leah, I never said you were a whore," he began.

"Get out of here!" she screamed.

"If you need me . . ."

"Need you!" she yelled at him. "You're the last person I'd ever need. I wish I could go to Kentucky by myself and I'd never have to even see you again. Now go to your dear Kimberly. She *needs* you."

Wesley seemed to want to speak, but instead he turned and left the room.

Immediately Leah fell to her knees, the sobs tearing through her. Need him, he'd said. No, she didn't need him, but she *wanted* him, or wanted someone, a man who cared enough to jump when a tear ran down her cheek. A man who had never known her family, who didn't believe she was a whore before he even saw her.

Sometime during the night Leah removed her dress and slipped on her nightgown. She'd cried all she could cry and all that was left was an empty hollowness, a feeling that life was never going to change. She'd been born in a swamp and she'd always be a part of the swamp. Pretty clothes would never cover the vileness with which she'd been born.

In the morning as Leah lay awake, Wesley slipped into the room; Leah knew he didn't want anyone thinking he hadn't spent the night with his wife.

"You're awake," he said as the early light illuminated the room. "Leah, about last night—."

She rolled to the side of the bed, got out, and walked across the room to the small trunk that held her clothes. She felt as if her spirit were dead and she didn't care about anything. Without a thought she slipped the gown off, careless of her nude form presented to Wesley as she began dressing.

"You never give up, do you?" he exploded angrily.

But Leah didn't even bother to turn around. When she was dressed, she turned to face him. "I'm ready whenever you are. Your friends won't know where you slept."

Frowning, he put his hand on her arm. "Leah, I've never meant to hurt you."

She looked from his hand to his face. "Never touch me again. Do you understand me? Never, ever again do I want you to touch me." With that she opened the door, waited outside the room for him, and together they walked down the stairs, looking for all the world like a couple who'd just spent the night together.

Leah parted from her sister quietly, and just as quietly she mounted the wagon beside Wes. He reached out his hand to help her, but one look from Leah made him withdraw.

At noon she gathered wood, built a fire, and cooked a hasty meal while Kimberly bathed some of the dirt from her face. Steven conveniently disappeared and Wes was busy with the animals. During the meal Kimberly chatted about the last party they'd attended in Virginia and repeatedly told Leah she should have been there. Leah silenced Kim by saying she had been too pregnant at the time to attend a party.

While Leah cleaned up from the meal, Kim announced that it was time for Leah to ride with Steven and from now on she'd be Wesley's fiancée and Leah his cousin. She seemed to think there'd be some protest, but there was none.

Leah climbed onto the wagon beside Steven. He made one comment about how he'd be glad to replace Wes if she felt any urges, but when he got no response from Leah, he took the reins and shut up.

At night, while Leah prepared supper, Wes rode to the nearest inn, and when he returned he reported that the place was too filthy to inhabit and they'd camp with the wagons. Kim sniffed about how she needed a bath, so Wes hauled buckets of water, heated them, hung a blanket screen, and prepared a bath for Kim. She conveniently lit a lamp behind the blanket so everyone around was treated to a silhouette of Kim's languorous bath.

"No screams of jealousy?" Steven said to Leah under his breath as Wes watched Kim in obvious rapture.

Leah didn't bother to answer as she cleared the supper dishes.

The next morning dawned hot, and Leah unbuttoned the top of her dress.

"Is that for me or him?" Steven asked. "If it's for Stanford you may as well close it. All he's interested in is my sister and she's an expert at keeping a man tailing after her. You ought to learn something from her. Never be too honest, at least not with gentlemen like Stanford. He'd rather look at a woman from behind a blanket. But you and me," he said with a chuckle, "we like skin."

He clucked to the horses and they were off.

Leah tried to still her trembling. She prayed she was not like Steven Shaw.

Toward noon they had to ford a river. The water, heavy with spring melts, was over the hub of the wheels.

"If we take it slowly we'll be able to make it," Wes informed Steven as they all stood on the bank.

"I'm frightened, Wesley," Kim said, clutching his arm.

"Don't be." He smiled. "We'll come through this. What about you, Leah, scared?"

"No," she said flatly. "I think we'll make it. Others have before us."

"I knew you'd feel that way," Wes said before turning away.

"Hallo!" came a man's voice from across the water. A tall, slim man in buckskins similar to Wesley's waved at them.

"It's Justin Stark," Wes said, smiling. "He'll be traveling with us."

Leah paid no attention to the man waiting on the far side but turned back to the wagons.

Wesley eased his wagon and horses into the water with utmost care. The horses shied, but Wes controlled them.

"He's afraid!" Steven said contemptuously. "He's scared to risk his hide. Hiyah!" he called to the horses, cracking his whip over their heads.

"No!" Leah said. "Wait until they're across."

"I'm not spendin' all day here and I'll not let that Stark fellow think I'm a coward."

Steven whipped the horses forward into the deep water.

"What the hell are you doing?" Wesley bellowed back at them.

"Not eatin' your mud," Steven called as he pulled alongside Wes's wagon.

"Keep to the right! Keep to the right!" the man on the land shouted at them.

Leah, hanging onto the seat with both hands, repeated the man's instructions to Steven, but Steven ignored her as he cracked the whip again.

The right front horse stepped into an underwater nothingness, screamed, and pulled the other horses after him. The heavy wagon tipped to one side and Steven went flying into the water. Leah released her hold on the seat and grabbed two flying reins as Steven released them. The others fell to the side.

"Keep a tight rein!" the man on land shouted. "Control that horse!"

Leah tried to obey him, wrapping the reins around her arm while trying to ease down far enough in the seat to get the dangling reins.

"Help her, Wes!" the man shouted. "Let that woman drive and help the redhead!"

Leah barely heard the man's shouts as her fingers inched toward the reins. She screamed once, when the frightened horses pulled until her arm nearly came off.

"Leah!" she heard Wesley shout but couldn't understand what he was saying because Kimberly had started to scream hysterically.

Quick tears of relief blinded Leah for just a second when her fingers tightened over the loose reins. Using every ounce of her strength she managed to control the frightened horses, pull the wagon to the right past the deepest part of the hole, and inch them toward the far bank.

The stranger from the shore swam toward her. "Good girl. Now hold them steady."

"Steven!" Leah yelled down at him as the horses touched land. Even while the back of the wagon was still in the water, Leah was pulling off her shoes. She'd always been a strong swimmer and now she wondered if the others realized Steven had fallen into the river.

"Here!" Leah gasped, tossing the man the reins just before she jumped down from the wagon and into the water.

"What the hell—!" the man began and then gave his attention to the horses.

"Where's Leah going?" Wesley demanded of the man.

"She yelled something about Steven."

"He's not here?" Wes said, but was in the water after Leah in seconds.

Leah dived for what seemed to her like hours, but there was no sign of Steven. Wesley and the stranger joined her after a few minutes, and when she surfaced she told them where she'd already looked.

Near dusk they found him, lying at the bottom at the edge of the river, the side of his head dented from his fall. Wesley pulled him onto land.

Leah stood over him, panting, exhausted from the afternoon's search. After the first hour she'd discarded her dress, since the long skirt hampered her. Now, in her dripping underwear, she was too cold, too tired to care about proprieties.

Wesley, seeing Justin looking at Leah, removed his shirt and slipped it over her, concealing her almost to her knees.

"No! No! No!" screamed Kimberly as she came toward them, her eyes on her brother's body.

Wesley moved away from Leah to comfort Kim in her grief and, if possible, Leah's shoulders drooped even more. Kim and Wes walked away into the growing darkness, Kim's sobs breaking the nighttime stillness.

For a moment neither the stranger nor Leah spoke.

"You ought to get into some dry clothes," the man said softly, watching her.

Leah merely nodded once and stood there, shivering.

The man moved closer to her. "I'm Justin Stark and you're—?"

Leah couldn't even answer him as she stared down at Steven's cold, lifeless body. Tears began to roll down her cheeks.

Without another word, Justin swept Leah into his arms.

She tried to pull away, but she was too weak, or perhaps she needed comfort, even from a stranger.

"Go ahead and cry, little girl," Justin whispered. "Anybody as brave as you deserves to cry."

Leah wasn't sure where all the tears came from—or why they came—but she began to cry as she'd never cried before. It was so good to be close to someone, to be held in a man's strong arms.

When the man unbuckled a blanket from his horse, Leah was hardly aware of it. Even when he gently removed her wet clothing she didn't protest. He wrapped her nude, wet body in the blanket, snuggled her against him, and sat with her on a fallen log. At some time he began to rock her and Leah gradually stopped crying, but she clung to him. Even when she fell into a deep sleep, she still clung to him.

"Is she asleep?" Wesley whispered to Justin.

Justin nodded. "You have a bed made up for her?"

Wes glanced at his boot toe. "I only made one for Kim. Leah usually makes her own bed." Justin didn't say another word and Wes disappeared for several minutes. "It's ready," he said when he returned.

Very carefully Justin stood while holding the sleeping Leah, and as if she were a fragile piece of glass, he laid her on the pallet of blankets Wesley had prepared.

For a moment Justin knelt over her. Then he stood and motioned Wes away into the silence of the forest. "Who is she?" Justin demanded.

"My . . . cousin," Wes answered. "What difference does it make who she is?"

Justin looked at Wes as if he were crazy. "Difference? I guess it matters to me because she's the most magnificent woman I've ever seen. Did you see the way she handled that team? And the way she risked her own life looking for that guy that drowned? I could see you had your hands full with that screaming bit of uselessness. Lord deliver me from women like that! Who is she anyway?"

"The woman I'm going to marry," Wesley said rigidly.

"Oh well . . . ah . . . I didn't mean anything," Justin stammered. "It's just that when you see the two women together, it makes that blonde *seem* worthless. No, I didn't mean that exactly."

"I think you've said more than enough."

"Right," Justin said sheepishly, but quickly raised his head. "Who is she?"

"Kimberly Shaw. The man who drowned was her brother."

"Oh I see. That's why she worked so hard to save him. I wonder if any of my sisters would risk their lives for my dead body. He was a lucky man to have a sister like her."

"No," Wes said softly. "Kimberly is the blonde. Leah is the woman who did the diving."

"And what is her relationship to the dead man?"

"None," Wes answered.

Justin turned away toward the trees. "Your cousin, is she? You were born under a lucky star. She attached to somebody? No, don't tell me. I don't care if she's plannin' to marry somebody. I think I'd go after her no matter how many men stood in my way. How'd you like me for a cousin by marriage?"

"Wait a minute, Justin. You're going too fast. You know nothing about Leah. She's pretty, I grant you, but she's the kind of woman that makes a man feel useless. You spend an hour around her and you'll begin to wonder if men are needed on this earth. There isn't *anything* she can't do all by herself and she always lets you know she needs nobody else. You marry her and in a year she'll be running your farm and your life and you won't be worth your weight in horse manure to her."

After an astonished moment, Justin began to laugh. He slapped Wesley's shoulder. "You can have all your pretty little blondes who sit on a wagon and scream while their brothers drown, but for me, I want a *woman*."

"You don't know what you're asking for," Wes warned. "Two weeks with Leah and you'll be looking for someone to make you feel like a man."

Justin smiled. "All she has to do is be a woman and that makes me feel like a man. Now I think I'll bed down. Tomorrow I'm going to start courting."

"Courting? But—," Wes began.

"Do you have any reason to object?" Justin asked coolly.

Wesley could only shake his head.

"All right then. Let's go to bed. In the morning we'll have a funeral."

Wesley watched Justin lay out a pallet where he could watch Leah in her sleep, then Wes went to where his own bed was. "Poor man," he muttered. He wished there was some way to save Justin from himself.

Chapter 9

LEAH WOKE early to the sounds of Kimberly's sobbing. Wesley was holding her and trying to comfort her, but Kim seemed inconsolable. With a groan for her aching head, Leah threw back the blanket covering her, then gasped because she was stark naked. With a blush that covered her entire body, she remembered what had happened the night before. A quick glance around the campsite showed that the stranger was not there.

"Wesley," Leah said through a hoarse throat.

Wesley, intent on Kim's problems, didn't hear her.

Leah cleared her throat. "Wesley!" she said urgently.

He looked around, obviously annoyed. "Yes?"

"Could you get me some clothes?" She hated to ask him, but she wasn't going to parade before him wrapped in a skimpy blanket.

With one eyebrow raised, Wes left Kim to go to the wagon and extract a brown cotton dress for Leah, not bothering with her underwear. "You certainly do make an impression on a man when he first meets you," he said, eyeing her bare shoulders.

Leah snatched the dress from him. "Go back to your Kimberly," she said angrily, just as Kim let out a loud wail.

With resignation Leah dressed under the covers, rose, and gathered the water buckets. On her way to the river she saw

Justin, the man who had recently joined them, stripped to the waist, digging a grave.

"Good morning," he called to her, his eyes alight.

Leah could barely murmur a reply because she ducked her head in embarrassment at the memory of being undressed by this man.

Immediately Justin was beside her, taking the buckets away from her. "Sleep well?" He laughed when she merely nodded, still not looking at him. "You're not going to let a little thing like a lack of clothes come between friends, are you? Why I've undressed hundreds of women."

She looked up at him, eyes wide.

"Maybe not hundreds." He smiled, his eyes almost eating her. "And certainly none as pretty as you. Don't turn away. Are you always so shy?"

She lifted her chin and looked at him. "I don't think I'm ever shy, but now I am . . ." She wanted to change the subject. "You'll be traveling with us?"

"All the way into Kaintuck." They were at the river and he took the buckets from her to fill them. "I grew up in the town where Wes bought his farm. All winter he worked like a demon on that place. I guess he was trying to get it ready for Miss Shaw."

"I guess so. Do you also farm?"

"Sure, and a little huntin' on the side. No, I'll carry them," he said when Leah reached for the full buckets.

"I can take care of my own jobs, thank you," she said stiffly.

Justin smiled at her, and his already handsome face looked even better. "I have no doubt you could carry a hundred buckets, but would you be so cruel as to deny me the pleasure of carrying them for you?"

For a moment, Leah didn't answer, but then she smiled. "I would hate to be called cruel. By all means, Mr. Stark, carry the water."

"Justin," he said with a laugh. "All my ladies call me Justin."

"*All* of them?" She laughed in return and felt better than she had in weeks.

"You two certainly seem to have forgotten what happened yesterday," Wesley said, glowering down at them. "I'd think you'd at least have a little respect for Kimberly's grief."

Justin's face lost its smile. He was a smaller man than Wes, but he didn't back down. "I think Leah showed a great deal of respect when she nearly drowned searching for a man who isn't even related to her. Just because that woman of yours cries loud doesn't mean she's willing to risk anything except tears."

Leah glanced up at the two furious men and excused herself because she was afraid of letting them see her smile. Justin's words made her want to smile all over. With a lightened heart she set about her chores of tending the animals, cooking breakfast, and readying the wagon for the day's journey. She didn't know if Wes and Justin continued to argue, but when they all gathered at the grave site, the two men seemed to have come to terms. Kim leaned heavily on Wesley's arm while he talked about what a good man Steven Shaw had been.

After the service, such as it was, Kim allowed Wes to help her inside the wagon where she lay down.

Justin tossed his pack and saddle in the second wagon, tied his horse behind, and climbed on the seat beside Leah, taking the reins from her. "I don't know if that woman and I are going to get along at all."

In spite of Leah's denial that she was shy, she really didn't know what to say to Justin. But she needn't have worried. Justin told her about his hometown of Sweetbriar, about his three sisters and four brothers, about his nieces and nephews. He told stories about who was in love with whom in the town and about how pretty Miranda Macalister was driving all the single men crazy.

"You included?" she asked timidly.

"I've looked at her a few times, but I've always had an idea of what the woman I wanted was like."

"And?" Leah encouraged.

"She's like you, Leah," he said softly, looking away only when the lead horse stepped into a rut.

Leah felt a wave of fear go through her. This man knew nothing about her, that she was a Simmons from the Virginia swamps, that she had a whore for a sister and her father had been crazy. It was a while before she talked, and then it was only in monosyllables about her weaving.

They stopped briefly to eat cold meat and potatoes, and Kim didn't leave the wagon. At night Leah made dinner over a fire she'd built. She watered and fed the animals. Justin cut firewood while Wes tended to Kim, who was distraught and incapacitated by her grief over her brother.

For days they traveled west with Justin beside Leah, talking to her, asking her questions, and each day Leah's sense of guilt grew. Regan and Nicole had been kind to her in spite of the fact that she came from the swamps. But they'd always known about her. She felt she was leading Justin on, lying to this man who was so nice to her. If he knew what she was really like, where she was from, he would probably treat her as Wesley did.

A week passed and Kimberly's grief did not subside. Leah began taking Kim's meals to her in the wagon, where Kim clung to Leah and cried.

"Don't," Justin said one evening, putting his hand on Leah's arm as she filled a plate for Kim. He turned to Wes. "Isn't it about time she stopped being a princess? Leah isn't her waiting woman."

"Kim's still grieving for her brother," Wes said stubbornly.

"Then you wait on her. Not Leah!" He grabbed the plate from Leah and thrust it at Wes.

They ate in silence and Kim came out of the wagon to sit, leaning against a tree while Wes hovered over her.

With seeming disgust, Justin threw the last of his coffee into the fire. "We all need a rest. There's a waterfall a few miles from here and I thought maybe tomorrow Leah and I could ride over there." He smiled at her across the fire. "Maybe do some washing."

Leah looked down at her cup. "I do need to do some washing," she murmured.

Before the morning was fully awake, Justin was standing over Leah, wanting her to hurry up so they could go.

"But what about breakfast?" she asked, gathering dirty clothes into a bundle.

"Let the duchess fend for herself for a day."

Leah suppressed a giggle. "I'm ready."

"Leah!" Kim called and came running to them. She was very pretty in the early light. She held out a couple of dresses and some underwear to Leah, "Would you mind? It looks like I have all the camp work to do today since you're going off to have fun, so could you do this little thing for me?"

"Of course," Leah answered, but Justin grabbed the clothes.

"You can do your own laundry," he began.

Leah put her hand on his arm and took Kim's clothes. "Of course I'll wash them."

"Come on," Justin said in disgust, half-pulling Leah to his saddled horse. "Why do you let her take so much from you? You're worth fifty of her." He mounted the horse then pulled her up behind him.

"No I'm not," Leah whispered, but she didn't think Justin heard her.

They traveled north for over an hour, away from the houses that dotted the countryside, away from sight of other wagons that traveled westward. After another hour, Justin dismounted and lifted his arms up for Leah. When he held her aloft, hands on her waist, he lowered her slowly and kissed her gently.

Leah felt no sparks, but it was a pleasant kiss. She looked away when he set her on the ground.

He looked at her, a puzzled frown on his brow. "Who's hurt you, Leah?" he asked softly. "I've never met a woman as pretty as you who hung her head all the time and thought she was another woman's slave."

"There are things about me you don't know," she said, pulling away from him, but she kept her chin up. "And I'm no one's slave."

"Then why are you so frightened of Wes?"

"Frightened?" She gasped. "I'm not afraid of him—or any man!" She lowered her voice. "But there are things between Wes and me, things you know nothing about." She could feel the anger in her growing. "I'd better get started with the washing."

"Forget the washing!" Justin said fiercely, grabbing the bundle from her. "What's between you and Stanford?"

"Not what you mean," she flashed at him, eyes bright with anger. "Wesley Stanford hates me, just as I hate him and all his kind who let my family starve while they spent money on fine clothes and horses. Wesley's horse cost more than what all nine of us lived on for over a year."

She moved away from him, knowing she'd disgusted him. He wouldn't care about her now that he knew who she was—and she wasn't going to let him see how his change hurt her. "You and your fine manners," she said, seething. "All of you men are alike. You think because we're poor you can get what you want from us. But let me tell you that only *one* of us Simmonses is a whore."

"Is that what you think of me?" Justin gasped. "That I think you're a . . . a . . ."

"Go on and say it!" she shouted at him. "I've certainly heard the word enough times from men and women like you. Pretty clothes on the outside and filth inside."

Justin stood still for a moment, looking as if he were in shock. "Is that what you think I am? Some rich dandy that grew up in a big house with servants to wait on me?" Quickly he turned around, and when he looked back he was grinning. "I wish the people of Sweetbriar could hear this. One of the Stark boys accused of having manners and riches. Oh Leah," he said, beginning to laugh. "I don't know how poor you grew up but you'll have to go some to beat me. Sit down here and let me tell you the *true* story of my family."

Bewildered, Leah sat beside him on the ground and listened to the true version of Justin's life. It wasn't that he'd lied when he'd told her of his family earlier, but he'd left out all the bad—because he thought Leah was a lady born and raised, and he didn't want to shock her with the tales of his life.

Justin told about his father, Doll Stark, who, it was rumored, was the laziest man east of the Mississippi. It might have been a joke to others, but to the rest of the family it was a constant battle to survive. Doll would spend his days in the Macalister trading post, laughing, enjoying himself, while his wife and children tried to feed themselves from a few acres of overworked land. Justin, the oldest boy, grew up hating his father. Doll would eat a massive breakfast, for which the family had worked, disappear until nightfall, come home, eat more, then spend hours trying to impregnate his wife. Justin would lie awake and hear the quiet sounds and hate his father even more. As for Doll, he never asked how his family fared or how Justin worked long, long hours to keep meat on the table.

And the town merely joked about Doll's laziness. The only time they interfered was when Justin's oldest sister, Corinne, told some lies and caused some trouble with the town's precious Macalisters.

"Is this the Macalister with the pretty daughter?" Leah was beginning to understand that Justin was one of her kind, not Wesley's. Maybe Justin wouldn't hate her, as Wes did, because of where she came from.

"The same one," Justin said. "Now tell me of your family."

Leah hesitated. At least Justin's lazy father was liked by the townspeople. What good could she say about her own family? A glance at Justin showed her that he was prepared to wait until doomsday for her to speak.

She began slowly, watching for signs of revulsion from him, but when she saw only interest and concern on his face, she launched into her story rapidly. She told of her eldest brother kidnapping a woman, of her sister's prostitution, of her father's insanity, the way he beat his wife and children. And last of all, she told of the constant, backbreaking work she'd always had to do.

The forest seemed especially quiet when she finished and she held her breath for Justin's reaction, afraid to look at him.

"And even though you were Stanford's cousin, he let you suffer through that? He's never said, but isn't he rich?"

"Massively," Leah murmured, still not looking at him.

"What made him finally rescue you? Or did he hire you to wait on his princess Kimberly?"

Leah took a deep breath. "My father died and the children were adopted by other planters. I . . . wanted to come west, to go where no one knew me, so Wesley's sister-in-law gave me money to start a weaving shop and Wesley allowed me to travel with him."

Justin was silent for a while and Leah wondered if he believed the last part of her story. "Where did you learn your pretty manners?" she asked tentatively.

"Macalister's wife. An English lady. And you?"

Leah began to smile as she briefly told of Regan and Nicole's transformation of her. It was beginning to sink in that this man didn't mind that she was a Simmons. Perhaps not all men were like Wesley. Perhaps in this new state she wouldn't be judged by who her father had been.

"They sure did a good job." Justin laughed as he stood. "Now that's enough seriousness for today. Come on and see the waterfall." He grabbed her hand and led her up the steep, rocky hillside. There at the top was a pool and a short, hidden waterfall.

"Not the biggest I've ever seen but one of the most private. How about a bath?"

Instantly Leah's eyes narrowed at him.

He ignored her obvious suspicion. "You go first while I wait down the hill for you and when you're finished, give me a call." With that, he turned and left her alone.

Leah hesitated only seconds before removing her clothes and climbing into the pool. Using soap she'd brought for the laundry, she shampooed her hair and used the waterfall for rinsing. The pressure of the water nearly pushed her under. When she emerged, a long time later, she felt better than she had in months. She was no longer burdened by a secret past; a handsome man waited for her; she was on her way to a new land, new people; she had her weaving—and now she had clean hair. What more could a woman want in life?

She was laughing when she reached the bottom of the hill and Justin.

"I won't be but a minute," he said, racing up the hill to the pool for his own bath.

With energy Leah knelt on a rock and began the laundry, and a very short time later Justin joined her. With a grimace he started to help her rinse the clothes.

"And does this little frilly nothing belong to princess Kimberly?" Justin asked, holding up a nearly sheer chemise trimmed with tiny silk ruffles.

Her face red, Leah snatched it from him. "That one happens to be mine."

"Oh?" he asked, one eyebrow raised. "Then this is her ladyship's." He lifted a pair of drawers that were faded yellow and torn at the waistband. "She may be a lady on the outside but not where it counts. We ought to do her a favor and lose these."

Before Leah could blink, Justin tossed the worn-out drawers into the river.

"No!" Leah gasped, laughing as she hitched her skirt to her knees and walked into the river, following the underwear, which was rapidly heading downstream.

Justin came wading in behind her, grabbed the drawers, and caught Leah's arm at the same time, purposefully nearly causing her to fall. "Watch yourself." He smiled as Leah clung to him. In an instant his arms were around her and he was kissing her, and Leah liked this so much better than the first time he'd kissed her.

Neither of them heard Wesley plowing through the brook until he'd grabbed Justin's shoulder and shoved him into the water. "Is this how you're to be trusted?" Wesley bellowed. "Do you always attack the women you're supposed to be caring for?"

Justin came out of the water in a rage and Leah knew this was the beginning of a brawl. She put herself between the two men. "You have no right to interfere in my life," she yelled up at Wesley.

"Interfere?" he spat back at her. "You're my . . . You're in my care," he finished. "Damn you, Justin, what if you caught a man behaving like this with your sister?"

"I'd demand he marry her," Justin said calmly. "I'm leaving, Wes, because I don't want this to become a fight. I don't want there to be hatred between a woman's husband and her relatives." With that he walked out of the water toward his waiting horse.

Wesley didn't speak until he heard Justin's horse moving away. "Who does he mean by 'husband'?" he asked accusingly.

Leah snatched Kim's underwear from the driftwood where it had caught and started out of the river. There was no need to lift her skirt since it was soaked.

"I asked you a question," Wes demanded once they were on the bank.

"I didn't tell him about us if that's what you mean," she snapped. "You can relax. Your pure Stanford name wasn't sullied by me. Now if you'll excuse me I need to rewash a garment of your fiancée's."

Wesley's mouth hardened. "Is that what you two were talking about so long? Kim?"

She threw Kim's wet drawers on his boots. "It may surprise you to know that we lower class people have things to talk about other than our betters."

"It didn't look to me like you were doing much talking when I arrived. Both of you were wet. Did you go swimming together? Did you let him take your clothes off *again?*" He took her shoulders and pulled her to him. "When he kissed you," he whispered, "did he make you feel like you do when I kiss you?"

Leah would have given a great deal not to react when Wesley touched her, but she was utterly powerless. It wasn't the same as kissing Justin; this was surrender. His body crushed next to hers, his lips touched hers, and she felt or saw nothing else. She remembered no hate, had no thoughts at all.

When he released her, she was dazed, barely able to stand upright.

"It didn't look as if you were feeling like that in Justin's arms," Wes said so smugly that Leah's eyes flew open.

She knew with every fiber of her body that she *had* to wipe that look off his face. Without thought, she used a trick her brother had taught her. She brought her knee up between Wesley's legs.

Immediately he crumpled, and Leah ran to his horse, mounted quickly, and started back to camp. As she rode, knowing he'd have to walk back, she laughed with pleasure, but after a few minutes she halted the horse. Maybe she'd injured Wesley. She had a right to be angry, but she didn't feel right in hurting him.

She was still hesitating when Wesley dropped from a tree above her, catching the horse's reins.

"How—?" she began.

He didn't answer her but began to lead the horse back to the waterfall. She didn't like the look of blind anger in his eyes and she dared not speak to him. Would he beat her?

At the river he stopped. "Get down and get the clothes," he said in a steely voice.

Leah obeyed him.

He mounted his horse, took the wet laundry from her, and offered his hand to help her behind him. She was afraid of the look on his face, scared to refuse him, and when seated she tried to keep from touching him, not wanting him to remember she was there.

Once, the horse stepped sideways and Leah nearly fell off.

"If you can't bear to touch me at least hold onto the damn saddle," he said with a growl, and again Leah obeyed.

They were silent the rest of the way to the camp and Leah might have thought Wes hated her before, but now his anger was like a hot red cape encircling him—a cape that would burn one's fingers if one dared touch it. She was careful to avoid him.

Chapter 10

TWO DAYS later they met the Greenwoods: Hank and Sadie and their three little boys. Leah was the one who suggested they travel together. For the last two days it had been very unpleasant traveling with Kim, Wes, and Justin. Wesley kept watching, staring at her with dark eyes, while Justin treated her as if she might break at any moment, and Leah was beginning to find his hovering an annoyance. Kim seemed oblivious to the tension and just kept demanding more and more from Wes.

The Greenwoods and their noisy, active children were exactly what was needed to take away some of the tension within the group. There were many travelers on the road heading for Kentucky and even farther west. They were drawn by the enticement of riches beyond belief, of fertile, virgin land that was theirs for the asking. There was no longer an Indian problem and Kentucky was a state, so they felt safe, protected from hardship. Some of the travelers were well prepared, their wagons loaded with goods. They'd sold their farms and had money to buy new land in the west. But too many others had merely walked away from where they'd lived, their families trailing behind them with no more than the clothes on their backs and a sackful of food.

All along the way were inns, and although the majority of them were too filthy to consider, they charged much for their services and received whatever they asked.

Leah was reminded of her own childhood when she'd see a family of children dressed in rags, looking gaunt and worn-out but trudging westward, dutifully following their parents. At first secretly, she began to feed some of these children, not letting Wesley see her because it was, after all, his food. The evening of the day they met the Greenwoods, while everyone was sitting around the campfire she'd tentatively suggested that they offer food to some people with several children who were camped not too far away.

It was one of the few times Kim expressed a strong opinion. "Aren't you being awfully free with someone else's goods?" Kim asked. "People should learn to take care of themselves. If we start giving them things they'll never learn to depend on themselves. They'll always expect us to take care of them."

For a while no one said a word and when someone did speak, it was about something else.

That night Leah stayed awake for a long time, and when she thought everyone else was asleep she threw back her blankets, crept silently to the wagon to get the bag of food she'd secretly prepared earlier, and made her way through the darkness toward the people camped nearby. They had four young children and nothing but a handcart of goods. Silently she set the bundle of food near the cart and started back toward her own wagon.

She'd gone only a few yards when a voice made her jump in surprise.

"Quiet or you'll wake them," Wes whispered, motioning for her to follow him further into the trees.

Leah swallowed hard, knowing he'd caught her stealing from his supplies. She prayed he wouldn't return her to Virginia. She stopped when he did, but she couldn't meet his eyes.

"What did you give them?" he asked.

"Bacon, flour, p . . . potatoes," she stammered, then looked up at him beseechingly. "I'll pay you back. I didn't mean to steal the food. It's just that the people looked so hungry and—."

"Ssh," he said, and she could see in the moonlight that he was smiling. "Look there." He pointed.

Through the trees she could see the people's banked fire. By the cart was her bundle and near it was another bundle just like hers. She looked up at him quickly. "Yours?" she asked, astonished.

He grinned. "Mine. I couldn't stand to see them hungry either."

They were silent a moment, sharing their secret. "How long have you been . . . ?" Wes began.

Leah looked at her bare feet. "Since we started. That's why I haven't minded being in charge of the food. No one else looks at it but me so I know how much I can afford to give away and not be discovered. I didn't mean to steal," she began again, looking up at him.

"I can afford a few potatoes," Wes said. "I'll bet we're pretty low on supplies."

Leah looked guilty. "Very low. I was planning to tell you soon but . . ."

He chuckled. "As soon as you absolutely had to, no doubt. In the morning make me a list and I'll get everything. Maybe you ought to double whatever you think we'll need. Now let's get back before we're missed."

Leah hesitated. "Wesley," she whispered. "I don't know how to write. How can I make a list?"

He turned and looked at her, and his look made her blush. Once she would have run into his arms. She wished she could forget how she'd once loved him.

"I guess you'll have to go with me," he said, so softly she barely heard him.

Together they went back to their own camp. Wesley walked Leah to where her bedroll lay and when they stopped, he smiled at her in conspiracy, gave her a wink, then turned toward his own bed on the far side of the camp.

Leah fell asleep with a smile on her face.

In the morning Leah didn't want to look at Wesley because she was afraid she'd see hatred in his eyes and that the night before would turn out to be a dream.

"You're sure you don't mind us traveling with you?" Mrs. Greenwood asked for the hundredth time.

Turning, Leah smiled at her. "Of course not. I'm looking forward to spending time with your children. Until this trip, I've always been surrounded by children, and I miss them."

Sadie Greenwood laughed. "You may get more of them than you want. My three are a handful."

At that moment the baby began to cry. "Let me," Leah said, running toward the toddler, Asa, who'd just fallen. The boy was used to strangers; he clung to Leah, and as she held him hot tears came to her eyes.

"Are you all right?" Wesley asked from behind her; it was as if he'd been watching her and came when she needed him.

"My child would have been nearly his age," Leah choked out, hugging the boy who was no longer crying. She turned back to the wagons.

"*Our* child," Wes murmured, but she didn't hear him.

The next few days were very pleasant. Leah rode with Mrs. Greenwood and they swapped recipes, Sadie's of food, Leah's of how to concoct beauty creams, and talked endlessly about children.

"And which one of those men are you going to choose?" Sadie asked.

Leah kept her eyes on the horses. "I don't know what you mean."

Sadie chuckled. "At first I thought it was Justin, since he's always hovering over you, but then that good-looking Wesley could never take his eyes off you, so I asked him how closely you were related."

"You *asked* him?" Leah said with a gasp.

"Years ago I quit trying to cure myself of nosiness—and so

did Hank. Or maybe he just gave up on me. It's an absolute curse on me. I always want to know everybody's business."

"What did Wesley say about our relationship?" Leah asked softly.

Sadie gave her a quick look from the corner of her eye. "He said you were cousins by marriage and not blood relatives at all."

Leah laughed at that. "That's certainly true," she said, and to change the subject she asked Sadie something about the children.

That night Sadie had her first run-in with Kimberly. It had started quite innocently. Sadie was used to taking charge, used to organizing people to get things done. Leah, Wes, Justin, and Hank were seeing to the livestock while Sadie was starting supper and managing the children, who were restless after riding all day. She began giving Kimberly things to do. At first cooperative, Kim obeyed Sadie, but after being given five tasks in a row Kim set the pan down, murmured, "I have to go into the woods," and didn't return until everyone was sitting down to eat.

Sadie was silent all through the meal, but twice, when Kim asked Wes to fetch something for her, Sadie gave Kim hard looks. After dinner, Leah began clearing the dishes when Sadie stood.

"I think Miss Kimberly should clean up since she didn't bother to help make camp or cook the meal," Sadie said loudly.

Her husband looked as if he wanted to crawl under a rock. "Now Sadie," he began, "I'll help clear."

Kimberly was already on the outskirts of the camp, obviously preparing to escape.

Leah looked at Wes, but he was studying his empty plate. Justin was watching Sadie with interest.

Sadie stood firm. "She didn't help this morning or at noon. She didn't help with the animals or tonight's meal. She won't drive a team nor does she help load or unload. I'll not be anybody's servant, Hank Greenwood. I'm a free American."

Kimberly was obviously too astonished to speak, but now she looked pleadingly at Wes.

Slowly, Wes stood. "Come on, Kim," he said softly. "I'll help you clear the dishes."

The group broke apart immediately. Hank grabbed Sadie's arm. "Are you happy now that you've made a scene? It's their business who does what around the camp." He led her away into the shadows.

Kim started crying. "How could you let her say those things about me?" she wailed, falling into Wesley's arms. "You know I'm not strong like the rest of you. I wish I could be like Leah but I just can't. And no one seems to care about how much Steven's death upset me. It's so difficult for me to adjust to his being gone. Oh Wesley, please don't leave me. I need you so much. I just couldn't live without you."

Leah stood rooted to where she was, watching Wes comfort Kimberly.

"Walk with me?" Justin said, pulling Leah by the arm, leading her into the darkness. "Sadie said what I've wanted to for a long time. What amazes me is how Wes can put up with her."

Leah jerked away from him. "I'm getting tired of hearing about how bad everyone thinks Kim is. Maybe she senses how much you dislike her and that's why she refuses to help." She stopped. "I'm sorry. Maybe I'm just tired in general. I think I'll go back." Quickly she turned and ran back to the camp.

Wesley was just pouring hot water into a pan to wash dishes while Kim, looking sulky, was prepared to dry them.

"Go away," Leah told Wes gently. "Kim and I'll do the dishes." She barely glanced at him but he left the women alone.

"I didn't mean—," Kim began. "That woman is so awful. Does she know my brother just died?"

Leah started washing dishes. "I think she believes that even grief is no excuse to get out of work. Tomorrow morning why don't you stay by me and I'll help you stay busy?"

"But, Leah, I do stay busy. I always have so much to do. I

have to look nice for Wesley and my hair takes so much time. Sometimes I wish I were like you and didn't worry when I get grease stains on my clothes or soot smudges on my nose. Justin likes you as you are, but Wesley wants me to be beautiful and I have to be. Doesn't anyone understand that?"

Leah rubbed her cheek on her shoulder and glanced down at her dress. It was indeed stained.

Kim moved closer to Leah and began to whisper. "I'm beginning to worry about Wesley. He doesn't kiss me as often anymore. He used to always be clutching at me, but now he just looks at me."

"Kim," Leah said in exasperation. "Why are you telling me this? How can I help you?"

"I just thought you might know some enticements because you're a . . . well, because you're not a virgin and I thought maybe your sister might have given you some hints." She stopped at Leah's look. "I didn't mean to offend you," she said as if wounded. "I just thought you might know some things."

"Kimberly," Leah said evenly. "*You* wash the dishes." With that she turned away.

That night Leah was awakened by a touch on her shoulder and looked up to see Wesley leaning over her.

He put his finger to his lips and motioned her to follow him. She slipped her dress over her head and went into the woods behind him. When they were far enough away, he turned to her.

"About a mile down the road is a family that needs help. I made up a package of goods and thought maybe you'd like to go with me to deliver it. Unless you're too tired."

He sounded like a little boy, afraid she'd turn him down. "I'd love to," she answered.

They walked for a while, not speaking.

"Pretty night, isn't it?" Wes asked.

"Very."

"You and Justin have a fight?" he asked bluntly.

She shot him a look of challenge. "You and Kimberly have a fight?"

He grinned at her, and she grinned back.

"You like him, don't you?" Wes persisted.

"He's one of my kind. We both grew up poor."

"Oh," Wes said. "I always had money but I also always had Travis. I'm not sure if I wouldn't give up the money if I could have grown up without Travis."

"Only a rich man would say such a thing. *No* brother is worse than poverty."

"At least you were free to think your own thoughts. Travis always told me what to think and how to think it. That's why Kim—." He stopped.

"Why Kim what?" Leah asked quietly.

"Kim needs me," he said, stubbornness in his voice.

"Kim needs something," Leah answered. "But I wonder if anyone knows what it is. Is that the camp?"

"No, it's farther away. For some reason they camped in a little canyon. If a rain came they'd never get out fast enough. You don't mind a bit of a climb in the dark, do you?"

Leah shook her head, but later she wished she'd questioned his idea of a "bit of a climb." They seemed almost to scale a rock wall in order to reach the bottom of the canyon. Wesley went first, then as Leah came down above, he took her ankles, moved his hands—quite unnecessarily, Leah thought—up her legs to her hips, then plucked her off the wall and set her on the ground. She meant to speak to him about his conduct, but he was grinning so winningly she laughed with him. He grabbed her hand and started down the canyon.

"There it is." He pointed. "You stay here while I deliver the package, then we're off again."

Leah crouched down behind a rock and watched as Wes made his way toward the sleeping travelers. She almost felt like a thief, as if they were doing something wrong, skulking about in the middle of the night, intruding on sleeping people.

Wesley was just entering the camp when Leah saw a man coming from the opposite direction, a long-barreled fowling gun slung across his arm, a big dog at his feet. Instantly she knew there was going to be trouble.

She stood just as Wes saw the man and dog. Wes raised his hand to give greeting, but the dog set up a howl and ran toward Wes in attack and the man raised his gun. Wesley sensibly dropped his bundle, turned, and started running back toward Leah.

"Go!" he shouted over the growing din of voices and barking dogs.

"Come back here, you thievin' varmint!" someone shouted, close behind Wes.

Leah grabbed her skirts and took off at a dead run, inches in front of Wesley.

The gun went off and the air exploded with bits of shot. Behind her Wes grunted, but when Leah looked back he shoved her shoulder. "Up the damned wall!" he said with a growl, and the next thing Leah knew she was grabbed by a big hand on her seat and shoved upwards, her cheek grazing rock.

She scrambled up the side of that rock like a fly, heaving herself over the top and crawling on her hands and knees before running with all her might.

Wesley tackled her, slamming her into the ground just as more of the fiery shot whizzed over them.

"What *is* that?" She gasped from under him.

"Quiet!" he hissed, covering her head with his hands, protecting her slight body with his own.

Leah couldn't breathe, but she was much too frightened to need to breathe.

"They got away!" came a voice from below them. "Leastways I ain't goin' up that rock to look for 'em. I reckon they'll think twice before they try stealin' again."

For a long while they lay quietly.

"Wesley," Leah managed to say. "I can't breathe."

He rolled off her, stood, and grabbed her hand. "Let's get out of here."

He pulled her along behind him at a galloping pace until he stopped and leaned against a tree, his chest heaving. Leah did the same.

When they'd caught their breath, they looked at each other.

Wesley was the first to grin. "So much for our Good Samaritan acts."

Leah gave a little laugh. "We could have been killed."

Wes grinned wider. "Wonder what he'll think when he finds the bag of food?"

Leah couldn't refrain from laughing any longer. "I hope his dog doesn't get it sooner. Oh Wesley, I never went up a rock faster in my whole life! I thought you were going to throw me over the top."

"I tried to. That dog was so close I could smell its breath." He laughed. "You weren't hurt, were you?"

"A few scrapes and bruises, that's all. I'll be sore tomorrow. What about you?"

He was still laughing. "A bloody side, but not bad."

That sobered her. "Where?" she demanded, moving in front of him and grabbing the buttons of his shirt.

"You sure are eager to get my clothes off, woman." He grinned down at her.

"Shut up, Wesley," she said conversationally, unbuttoning his shirt. In the moonlight she could see two long, deep scratches. "They don't look bad, but they ought to be washed. Let's get to the water."

"Yes ma'am," he said happily, following her as she walked through the woods to the nearby stream.

Wesley removed his shirt while Leah tore part of her petticoat away to wash the cuts. "What would men do without women's petticoats?" Wes murmured. "You are a very pretty young woman, Leah," he whispered, then touched her chin so she looked at him.

The air was filled with the charges between them, dancing lights of the moon on the water drawing them together.

Leah's fingers moved from the cuts on Wes's side to his dark, warm skin, upward to the dark mass of curling hair on his chest. She couldn't move away when his lips came near hers.

"We are still married, you know," he murmured.

Leah awoke from her trance. "If you're trying to seduce me, Wesley Stanford, you have just failed. Here! Clean your own wounds." She jumped up and started back to the camp.

Wes grabbed his shirt and ran after her. "I didn't mean anything, Leah, honest," he pleaded. "I just thought—."

She whirled on him. "You thought that I was an easy woman and available so you'd take what you could get, didn't you? Why didn't you ask your virginal Kimberly out tonight and try to seduce her? Because she's good and I'm bad, right? It's all right to try what you can with a Simmons but not with a lady like Miss Shaw. Well, you were wrong! I gave myself once to you because I *wanted* to, and the next time I'll choose the man and he won't be one who tricks me."

"You mean Justin," Wes said angrily, then changed his tone. "Leah, I didn't mean to trick you. Everything just sort of happened. I wasn't trying to seduce you because you're experienced, but you're a pretty girl and—."

"And any pretty, experienced girl will do, is that it?"

His face changed, his pride took over. "I'm not Justin and you're not Kimberly, so we're even." He brushed past her to return to the camp.

Instantly Leah's anger drained away and she knew she'd been wrong. Wesley was right. What had happened had not been planned and she'd been wrong to ruin the moment.

She started to call out to him but stopped herself. It was better this way. Lately they'd been becoming too friendly. When it came time for their separation and his marriage to Kimberly, she didn't want to be in love with him. Yes, it was better to stay away from Wesley and concentrate on Justin. Perhaps Justin could make her forget all the feelings she'd ever had for Wes.

Chapter 11

LEAH FOUND it quite easy to concentrate on Justin. He always seemed to be just a few feet away from her, always ready to help with any chore. He smiled at her a great deal and gave her flowers.

One evening as Leah was standing by the wagon holding a handful of wildflowers Justin had given her, Sadie approached. "So you're thinkin' of choosin' the little one," Sadie said.

"I'd hardly call Justin small," Leah answered, not pretending to misunderstand. "Besides, there's never been any choice in the matter. Wesley Stanford is engaged to Kimberly and he's very much in love with her."

Sadie snorted. "He may have been at one time, but that was before he had to spend twenty-four hours a day in her company."

"What do you mean?"

"Don't act innocent with me, young lady," Sadie chided. "I know very well that you can sense what's going on between them."

"I haven't seen anything," Leah said. "And besides, it doesn't matter to me what Wesley does. I think I may be falling in love with Justin."

Sadie only grunted as she went into the woods to empty a pan of dirty water.

Two nights later they camped near three families, one of

which played fiddles, and they invited everyone to an impromptu dance.

Leah spent a long time choosing her dress and in washing and brushing her hair until it shone and sparkled like melted rubies. Her low-cut dress was deep rose-colored silk that caught the light when she moved. Darker rose ribbons were entangled in her hair and tied under her breasts.

"You look like a princess," Sadie's oldest son said with a gasp when he saw her.

At the dance were five women and fifteen men. Four of the men were the big, good-looking, energetic sons of one of the women, and they caught the hands of Leah and Kimberly instantly, leading them into romping dances near the cooking fire.

"I don't like this," Kimberly said as she tried to catch her breath between dances.

Leah didn't have time to reply as another man pulled her away to dance with him.

"You seem to be enjoying yourself," Wesley said later as he pulled her into his arms.

"I don't want to fight you," she said, enjoying the music and the moonlight.

"You look beautiful, Leah," Wesley whispered. "You've changed since—."

He stopped at the sound of Kimberly's insistent voice from across the camp. "Wesley!" she demanded.

"You'd better go," Leah said, starting to pull away from him.

Wesley wouldn't relinquish her hands. "Not yet," he said, his jaw set. "I'll go when *I'm* ready."

She gave him a cold look. "You'll leave when Miss Shaw pulls your chain," she said hotly. "Now if you'll excuse me I'd rather dance with someone else."

She was shaking as she walked away, and when she saw Justin she clung to his arm. "I need to get away from this crowd," she murmured, and Justin led her into the dark forest.

Once out of sight of the people, Leah nearly flung herself into Justin's arms and planted her lips on his. She needed to feel she was a woman. She was sick of rejection, sick of feeling as if she'd been discarded. She'd thrown her body and her love at Wesley and he'd used what he wanted and told her he wanted no more. Kimberly sat on her throne and Wesley knelt before her, offering gifts.

"Marry me," Justin whispered, kissing her face and neck. "Marry me tonight."

She drew away from him. "You don't have to marry me," she said. "Just because I tend to . . . throw myself at men doesn't mean one of them has to marry me. Or marry me forever," she added.

"Leah," Justin said, grabbing her shoulders. "I don't know what you're talking about. I love you. I've loved you from the beginning and I want to marry you. I want you to be my wife and live with me."

"For how long?" she snapped. "Don't you have a girl back home?" She pulled away from him. "I can't marry anyone." Turning, she ran back to their own wagons, only to nearly run into Wesley and Kim.

"I can't go back there," Kim was saying, tears in her voice. "I'm so tired and all those men kept touching me. I don't like it."

"You don't seem to like for any man to touch you," Wesley said. "Even me."

"That's not true. I don't mind when you touch me except when you hurt me. Please, Wesley, let's not argue. I really must sleep."

Leah didn't want to overhear any more of the conversation. She stepped forward. "I'll take care of Kim," she said softly, putting her arms around the blonde woman who was beginning to cry.

For some reason Leah's action angered Wesley. "You can take care of her, can't you?" he said under his breath, teeth clenched.

"You can take care of anything and anyone. Is that it? Leah the mighty can rescue a man with one hand, raise half a dozen children with the other. Nothing is too much for Leah, is it? She can look beautiful even in dirty dresses." He paused. "Go take care of someone else. I'll see to Kim."

With that he half jerked Kim away from Leah and led her toward the wagons.

Leah stared after them in stunned silence, sure that Wesley's outburst was one of the oddest things she'd ever heard. Did he expect all women to be like Kim? No work would ever get done if they all sat around and tended their hair. Surely Wesley must realize that. No doubt he was angry again because he somehow thought she wasn't being good to his darling Kimberly.

Angrily, Leah turned away. Why was she spending more time thinking about what Wes wanted when she'd just received a proposal of marriage? And why would Justin want to marry her?

Her head was aching when she went to bed and before long she was crying—and she didn't know why she was crying.

For the next three days it rained. The skies opened up and let loose a deluge that threatened to never end.

Justin drove the wagon, Leah beside him, through deep, sucking mud puddles. Rain poured over them and no hats or rain clothes could keep them dry.

Wesley had made a place for Kim inside the wagon and brought all her food to her. Twice Leah caught Justin smirking at Wesley, and Leah thought perhaps Wes was going to remove a few of Justin's teeth.

On the fourth day the sun shone weakly and flashed off the muddy land. In the evening it wasn't easy to get ready for the night's camp while walking around mud puddles as big as fish ponds.

Leah made her way between two deep mud holes to reach the

wagon. They'd had to set up camp some distance away and now she was carrying heavy bundles and trying to balance on the little ridge between the mud holes.

Wesley stood by the wagon, watching her from under the brim of his hat. His buckskins were still wet in places.

Leah pulled a large bundle of food from the wagon and started toward the camp.

"Here," Wes said, holding out a bag she knew contained a skillet. "You'll need this."

Leah glanced down at her bundle, then returned to take the skillet.

"And this," Wesley said as he looped a horse's bridle over her shoulder.

"Maybe I should come back for some of these things," Leah said, looking at her shoulder and then at the narrow bridge of land she must walk across.

"You mean you can't carry everything at once?" Wes asked, one eyebrow arched.

"I guess so," she began, as Wes draped another bridle on her other shoulder.

"And this, of course," he said, putting a bag's drawstring over her neck so the heavy sack hung down her back.

"Is that all?" she asked in exasperation, her legs beginning to bow under the weight.

"That should do it. Oh, here's one last thing. Justin's hat." He settled the too-big hat on her head, nearly covering her eyes.

"I can't see very well," she mumbled, head back.

"That shouldn't bother you, should it? Nothing bothers Leah. Leah can do anything. Now, you'd better get going because people need those things." He turned her about, pointed her toward the narrow strip of land, and gave her a little push.

Leah was too busy concentrating on where she had to walk to think about what Wesley was trying to do to her. At the first step she took, the hat fell forward and more of her vision was blocked. To compensate she tilted her head back further and the sack dragging on her neck hurt.

She did quite well for about ten steps, then halfway across, her left foot sank into a soggy bit of ground, and when she tugged at her foot she began to lose balance. One of the bridles slipped down her arm, further upsetting her. She tried to shrug it upward, but just then her foot came loose.

For a moment she teetered on the brink, then suddenly she fell backward into the soft, oozing mud.

Blinking, she sat there, still clutching all her bundles. A fat drop of mud slid down her forehead, her nose, and as it came near her lip, Leah blew at it.

It was then that Wesley's laughter made her look up. He was standing on the dry piece of land and bending over her, his face a study in amusement. "It looks like somebody found something the ever-competent Leah can't do. You thought you could carry half the wagon and maneuver through the mud. It looks like you *can't*," he said with great glee.

Leah raised one arm, mud all the way up to her armpit, and tried to push her dripping hair out of her eyes. Justin's hat was half floating, half sinking down beside her. She had no idea what Wesley was talking about. Slowly she began to remove her bundles and put them on dry land.

"You couldn't even ask for help when you were falling," Wes said as he took the food bag from her. "If I hadn't been here you wouldn't have anyone to help you out of this mess."

"I wouldn't be here if you hadn't given me so much to carry," she said, removing the bag from around her neck.

"Did it ever occur to you, Leah, to say no?" He wasn't laughing now. "Why do you have to do everything yourself? Why don't you ever ask anyone for help?"

Leah looked at him and suddenly realized that she was sitting practically up to her nose in mud because he was trying to teach her some kind of lesson. Of course she needed help at times! But lately all she'd done was try to do her work and Kim's. She was trying to care for and protect the woman *he* loved.

Wes didn't see the look in her eyes change. Nor did he see her hands sink into the mud at her side. As he reached for the last bundle, Leah's arm flung out and threw a great gob of mud smack into Wesley's smiling face.

As he sputtered, spitting out mud, she started bombarding him with great handfuls of the nasty stuff. Moments later she stopped and he looked down at himself, covered with big splotches of mud. Leah, still sitting, looked up at him. "You think your Kim will greet you with open arms?" she said with a smile.

"Why you little—," he began, then took a flying leap at her.

Leah rolled away just as Wes hit, and he landed face-down in the mess. When he looked up, only his eyes white, Leah started laughing.

"Wesley." She gasped as she started to stand. "Here, let me help you up."

With a little grin, Wes lifted his muddy arm to Leah's extended hand, but when she took it, he pulled.

"No!" She gasped again before sliding back down, this time getting mud on the few clean parts of her body.

"You insufferable—," she began. "How could you do this? Look at me!"

"I am," he said with a chuckle. "I am." His eyes were on her dress front, which was plastered to her.

It was difficult, if not impossible, to retain one's pride while completely covered in mud. Leah was angry that Wes had caused her to fall, and now he was giving her lustful looks. She was sick of his leering at her. She was more than just a body.

With fists clenched, Leah pulled herself up and launched herself at Wes.

With laughter Wes opened his arms to her, and as she tried to hit him, he enclosed her in his embrace and began rolling with her.

"Stop it!" she screamed, beginning to try to kick free of him. "Wesley!"

"You can't do everything, can you, Leah?" He laughed, tossing one of his muscular legs over both of hers. "Can you?"

She struggled against him, under him. "Of course I can't. I never said I could."

He was grinning down at her, his eyes and teeth white. "You sure are dirty."

"No thanks to you," she snapped, then her face changed. She couldn't help laughing; they must be an awful sight. "You're not exactly clean yourself." She stopped struggling as she looked up at him.

"Tell me something you can't do by yourself."

"What? Oh Wesley, can't you ask your idiot questions later? Let me up so I can take a bath."

His mud mask didn't move and when she pushed at him and he still remained immobile, she sighed.

"There are a lot of things I can't do."

"Such as?"

Leah had to think for a moment. "You've just seen me doing household chores. I've always done farm work so I'm good at it."

"I'm waiting," Wes said stubbornly.

"Hunting!" she said, pleased with herself. "I went hunting with my brother once and I got so scared he brought me home. We heard a bear at night and it frightened me. Now there! That's something I can't do."

"Anything else?"

"You are impossible. There's mud in my ears even! Please let me up. Oh, all right. I can't read, I can't write, guns frighten me, being away from people scares me. I hate men who care only that I'm a Simmons." She said the last with a great deal of venom.

"Guns, huh?" Wes said, seeming to ignore her last statement. Tightening his grip on her, he began to roll again.

"Wesley!" she exclaimed.

"Guns and hunting!" He laughed, turning over and over in the mud.

Leah could only cling to him and try to keep from drowning.

"Well lookee here!" came Sadie's voice over them. "If it ain't a couple of pigs wallowin' in the mud!"

Leah was sure her face was red under its coating of mud, but Wesley was grinning.

"I heard you ladies think mud is a beauty cream. I just thought I'd try it and Leah consented to show me how it's done. That's right, isn't it, Leah?"

"Release me, you oaf!" she hissed at him.

"Wesley!" came Kim's voice. "Whatever are you and Leah doing in the mud together? Did you fall?"

"I think I have," Wes said softly, to Leah alone, looking at her in wonder. He rolled off her to look up at Kim. "Leah fell and I jumped in after her." There was a tone to his voice that was almost a challenge.

"Oh," Kim said, blinking. "I don't guess a person can swim in mud."

Leah did not laugh. That was to her credit.

Wes slowly began to stand. "I guess we better get cleaned up." He held out his hand to Leah.

She wasn't sure whether to trust him again, but this time there was no laughter in his eyes, and she accepted his offered hand. He swept her into his arms and Leah didn't protest.

"Wesley—," Kim began.

"I have to take Leah to the river," he said blandly, walking past her.

There was something in Wesley's look that made Leah keep quiet. Behind them Sadie said, "Come with me, Kimberly, and I'll make you something nice to drink."

At the river Wesley left her alone, and when he walked back to camp he was frowning.

Kimberly brought Leah a towel and clean clothes.

"Leah," she said, puzzled, "I don't think a lady should get into a mud puddle with a man. I really don't think it's the proper thing to do."

"Kim," Leah said, "I certainly didn't do it on purpose. I fell."

"And Wesley was saving you?" Kim seemed to want reassurance.

Leah merely nodded.

"Wesley isn't as nice to me as he used to be," Kim continued. "Last night he was very rude to me and today he hardly spoke to me at all."

Leah paused in dressing. "What did you say just before he was rude to you?"

"I was talking about when we get married and I said I was looking forward to it and that I was glad I could wear white. I mean, with his first marriage, you couldn't—." She stopped at Leah's look. "I didn't mean anything about you, Leah. You can wear white when you marry Justin. No one in Kentucky will know the truth and I'm sure neither Wesley nor I will tell anyone."

Leah kept her back straight as she started back to the wagons. She completely forgot to ask what rude thing Wesley had replied to Kim's declarations of her virginity.

Chapter 12

WITHIN THE next few weeks they began to approach the new land of Kentucky. Instead of feeling excitement, Leah began to worry about how these new people would react to a divorced woman. When she was in Virginia, she'd wanted to leave behind a decent memory of at least one of the Simmonses. She didn't want people saying that a gentleman had married her but he'd had sense enough to get rid of her. The new land had seemed far away then.

But now she wished she'd gotten the divorce in Virginia. If she had, she could enter Kentucky as a free woman. Now she'd have to start her life here with an ugliness that would stain her as badly as her family had in Virginia.

As she rode beside Justin, she was silent. He still wanted to marry her even though he knew about her family. But would any man want her after they knew she'd been married and miscarried a child? Kim knew how important her virginity was and she hung onto it at all costs.

Regan and Nicole had said Leah was a lady, but Leah couldn't believe them. Kim was a lady. Everyone was polite to her. The man who loved her waited on her hand and foot. He treated her with respect, and even after this long trip she still retained her virginity. But with Leah, men were always lusting after her. Kim was right: no lady would roll in the mud with a man. Or throw herself at him and end up pregnant.

"What are you thinking, Leah?" Justin asked from beside her.

"Not thoughts one can share," she answered.

"I'd hoped you were thinking about your answer to my proposal."

"I was, in a way. There are some things you need to know about me."

"I'm not easily shocked. Leah, something is troubling you. Even if you don't return the love I have for you, I'm still your friend. You can tell me anything."

She was silent for a moment, wishing she could believe him. But if she told him now he'd never want to see or speak to her again. And she wanted these last few days of pretending that a handsome man wanted to marry her before he learned the truth and came to hate her.

"It isn't Wesley, is it?" he asked with some hostility in his voice.

She laughed at that. "Wesley Stanford is the last man on earth who might be interested in me. He's in love with Lady Kimberly and doesn't know anyone else exists."

"I wish I were as sure of that as you are."

Leah didn't answer him. She felt only her dread of meeting new people and being branded as a brazen woman. She'd seen the way men in Virginia, who knew of her family, treated her. She wondered if she could bear it in Kentucky. Perhaps she should get the divorce from Wesley in his town of Sweetbriar, then leave there as soon as she was free. She just prayed that her reputation wouldn't follow her.

That night in camp everyone seemed to be subdued. Wesley kept his eyes on his plate of food, and Kim's eyes were red and swollen. Justin watched Leah while she mechanically went about her chores.

"I'd think you'd all be glad to be near home," Sadie said with a sigh, "but I've been to more cheerful funerals."

The next day Wesley paid a young man to ride ahead to his

farm in Sweetbriar and tell the people that they would be arriving soon. Leah wanted to cry in frustration. Soon he'd have to tell people of their marriage and start divorce proceedings. Leah wondered if Kim would invite her to the wedding so Leah could see Kim's pure, white, flawless gown.

The wagons rolled closer to the border of Kentucky each day and everyone's mood seemed to grow more glum. Once, Justin angrily accused Leah of not accepting his proposal because she wanted all the men in the state pursuing her. Leah put her face in her hands and began to cry. Justin didn't make any more accusations after that.

Twice, Leah heard Wesley tell Kim he was too busy to get her whatever she wanted. Kim retreated to the wagon to sleep. By the time they reached Kentucky she was sleeping twelve hours a night and taking a three-hour nap every afternoon.

And Wesley didn't speak to anyone. He did his chores, but retreated into himself, seemingly unaware that anyone else was near him.

"That young man is considerin' somethin' powerful hard," Sadie said as she and Hank took their leave. "I'm hopin' he's decidin' which woman he wants."

Leah just looked at her. "You're too much of a romantic, Sadie. Wesley has been in love with Kim for years. He's probably trying to force himself to wait until the wedding." She couldn't add that it'd be a long time before their wedding because of the inconvenience of Leah and Wes's marriage.

Leah hugged all the family good-bye and she was very glad that they'd never know the truth about her. They'd never learn of how she'd flaunted herself at Wes and he'd discarded her.

It was a silent group that trudged ahead toward Sweetbriar, Kentucky.

On the fourth day after Sadie, Hank, and their children had left, two men came galloping toward them. One was Oliver Stark, Justin's nineteen-year-old brother who worked for Wesley. The other was John Hammond, a tall, handsome man in his thirties with prematurely gray hair.

"The farm's doin' just fine," Oliver said, grinning at Wesley and his brother. "It sure took you a long time gettin' here."

"I didn't expect to see you here, John," Wesley said, extending his hand.

"The man you sent ahead said you had two of the prettiest women he'd ever seen with you. It looks like he was right," he said, looking Leah and Kim over.

Kim looked down at the ground. As usual, her eyes were red from crying.

"I'd like to introduce the ladies," Wes said, but Kim put her hand on his arm, her eyes pleading.

"Let me speak to Leah, please," Kim half whispered.

Wesley's jaw flexed, but he nodded and looked back at the men and began to ask questions about his farm.

Puzzled, Leah followed Kim to the back of the wagon. Something was upsetting her greatly. "Are you all right, Kim?" she asked, concerned.

"Wesley is being beastly," she spat out. "Once he makes up his mind to something, nothing will change it."

Leah couldn't believe she was being asked to comfort the woman who was to marry her husband. "I would think you'd be glad of that. He decided to marry you and *nothing* will change his mind, not even his marriage to someone else."

Kim gave her a hard look. "Sometimes he changes his mind. It takes him awhile to decide to do it but when he does, nothing will make him change."

"What in the world are you talking about? Oh!" Leah gasped as she slipped and nearly fell. The wagons were stopped on a narrow road on the side of a steep hill. Below them ran a stream with no trees in between.

"Watch out!" Kim said. "You nearly fell!"

Leah smiled. "It's not steep enough to be a danger. Unless the wagon fell on top of me, I guess."

Kim didn't reply to this. "Leah," she said slowly. "I need my pink hat. It's in that little brown trunk on the far side of the wagon. I'd get it but you're so much more agile than I am. Would you get it for me? Please?"

When Leah hesitated, Kim persisted. "You'll get rid of me soon and you won't have to help me out anymore."

Sighing, Leah agreed. Kim had been so upset lately that Leah couldn't refuse her request. Besides, anything that would postpone their arrival into Kentucky was good for her. She climbed into the back of the wagon and began looking for Kim's trunk.

When Kim returned to the men at the front of the wagon she was frowning. They were deep in conversation, not even aware of Kim as she stood by the horses on the side away from the steep drop. With one glance upward to be sure the men were busy, she slowly removed her bonnet, pulled out a four-inch-long hat-pin, and with great deliberation stuck it into the horse's rump.

"Hey!" John Hammond shouted.

Kim turned frightened eyes toward the man, knowing he'd seen what she'd done.

But no one reacted to John's shout because instantly the horse reared, frightened the other horses, and the wagon began tumbling down the side of the hill.

"Oh damn!" Wes cursed, watching the wagon. Then he stiffened. "Leah! Where's Leah?"

Kim's eyes were locked onto John Hammond's and she couldn't speak.

Wesley didn't bother to wait for an answer as he ran down the hill after the wagon, Justin on his heels. Oliver and John followed quickly. Kim stood where she was in the road, not moving.

When the wagon stopped, leaving a trail of goods behind it, the horses screaming in pain, Leah was nowhere to be found.

Wesley was throwing trunks and bags of food everywhere while Oliver cut the horses loose.

"Where is she?" Wesley demanded while Justin scanned the hillside, looking for her body.

"Kim is up there," came a voice beside Wesley.

Wesley turned to see Leah standing calmly behind him.

"What happened? How badly are the horses hurt? How much can be saved?" Leah asked all at once as she started to help Oliver with the horses.

"Damn you!" Wesley hissed, then the next second he caught her in his arms and kissed her so hard he hurt her.

"Wesley!" She gasped, pushing at him. "People are watching." She looked at Justin, who was scowling furiously, and John, who was watching them with great interest.

Wesley set her down and, for the first time in weeks, his face showed happiness. "Gentlemen, allow me to introduce my wife, Leah Stanford."

Only John saw Kim faint, and he was quickly up the hill after her.

Leah's knees gave way and Wes swept her off the ground. "Don't you have anything to say, honey?" Wes asked her.

Chapter 13

IT TOOK hours to clean up the mess of the wagon. One horse had to be destroyed and the other three were badly scraped and cut, but they'd heal in time. Some sacks of seed had burst open and most of the contents were lost, but few other goods were really hurt.

At the top of the hill, Kimberly was crying loudly while John Hammond tried his best to comfort her. Justin was very angry and threw goods about with force, never once looking at Leah or Wes. Oliver kept looking from one person to another while Leah, with shaking hands, tried to help sort the misplaced wagon contents.

But Wesley acted as if nothing at all was unusual. He was smiling, even humming at times, and telling everyone what to do.

"Leah, honey," Wes said, "hand me that little hat-box."

Obediently Leah picked it up, but as she looked at him smiling at her she threw it at his face, turned, and ran toward the stream, tears in her eyes.

Wesley caught up with her, took her shoulders and turned her to face him. "What's wrong, honey? I thought you'd be happy when I told everyone the truth about us. It's what you wanted, isn't it?"

She moved away from him and tried to calm herself. "I knew it had to happen sometime, but when I heard you say it . . . You ought to tell your friends about the divorce and for heaven's sake, stop calling me 'honey.' "

"Divorce?" He looked puzzled. "Oh no, you don't understand. I've decided we should *stay* married. There won't be any divorce."

"I think I'll sit down," Leah said quietly before she almost collapsed onto the damp ground. "Could you explain all this to me?"

He grinned down at her confidently. "It's just that I've come to like you, Leah. I was pretty mad at first. Well, all right, more than a little mad and maybe I didn't give you much of a chance, but you'd ruined all my plans and all I could think of was losing Kim."

He hunkered down in front of her. "But on this trip I've come to know you. I thought I wanted a woman like Kim who needed me, but Kim needs a maid more than she needs a man. And besides, you need me, too. You're always trying to take on too much, always trying to do everything for everyone else."

"So you decided I needed you, too," Leah said softly.

"Yes. And besides, you're more fun than Kim. It took me a long time to make the decision but I decided we'll stay married. It just makes sense anyway and it'll cause a lot less trouble."

"And Kim?" Leah asked.

Wes looked down at his feet. "I used to think I loved her but I'm not sure I ever did. I'm not sure I've ever loved any woman. And I think Kim may be more interested in my money than in me," he said, his jaw clenched. "I've worked things out with her. She'll receive a handsome sum from me every month until she marries. She's pretty so I'm sure she'll have no trouble finding a husband."

He was quiet for a moment. "Aren't you going to say anything? I thought you wanted to marry me. That's why you seduced me that first time, isn't it?"

Leah stood and walked away from him. "I want to make sure I've heard you correctly. You don't love me and you've never loved

Kim, but between the two of us you've chosen me because it's easier than a divorce and remarriage, and besides, I'm more fun and I need you to protect me from myself. Is that about it?"

He frowned up at her. "I guess so, but you make it sound awfully cold. I think we'll make a good team, Leah. Between the two of us we'll build a place bigger than my brother's and I know you're fertile so we'll have lots of children."

"And would you like to check my teeth also?"

He stood. "I think you're getting mad. Here I am giving you what you wanted and you're getting mad. Do you expect me to go down on one knee and declare undying love for you? I'm not sure I know what love is. I thought I loved Kim but now all I know is I've had enough of her tears and helplessness and I want something different."

She was breathing deeply to try to calm her fury. "And what happens to me when you decide you want more than just fun and my needing you? Will you go back to Kim or perhaps choose another woman?"

"Are you accusing me of . . . of being fickle?" he said.

She smiled at him. "As much as any woman trying to choose the right color of dress."

He took a step toward her and Leah backed away. "I don't want to stay married to you," she said. "I don't want your big farm and I especially don't want your children. You may have decided you like me but I do *not* like you. I will not build my future with a man who may run out on me at any moment. I don't want a husband who bases everything on a fun wallow in the mud. What if you and some other woman fall in a river? No! I cannot live with someone as fickle as you. Now I'm going to announce to everyone our intention to obtain a divorce." She turned on her heel, but Wes clamped a hand down on her shoulder.

"You will *not* make any such announcement," he said under his breath. "I've made my decision and I didn't do it lightly. I thought about this for a long time."

"And I don't make my decision lightly. I've known about our divorce always and I've come to accept it. We'll do the procedure in your town of Sweetbriar and after it's over I'll leave, maybe even leave Kentucky altogether."

His hand tightened on her shoulder. "You'd rather go through that than stay married to me?" he asked, astonished.

"I don't really have much choice. Maybe I can get away from my reputation as a loose woman but I'd never be able to live with a man who was so . . . so dishonest and changeable. I'd spend my whole life wondering from day to day if the kids and I would have a man to provide for us."

Wesley looked shocked. "No one," he said, "no one, man or woman, has ever hinted that I might not be trustworthy. I've never taken my responsibilities lightly."

"Tell that to Kim," she said, turning away again.

"Damn you!" he half yelled, grabbing both her shoulders and making her face him. "If you were a man I'd call you out for what you've said to me. But for you . . . you *will* remain married to me. You understand that? And furthermore, tomorrow we're going on a hunting trip, just the two of us, and we're going to act married. We're going to travel together, eat together—and sleep together."

She tried to twist away from him. "Get your hands off of me!"

"I'm going to put my hands all over that pretty little body of yours and you can damn well get used to it. You're my wife and you're going to start acting like a wife."

"I hate you," she said, seething.

"I don't bear you any great love at the moment either."

"I will *not* submit to you. I will *never* be your wife."

He dropped his hands from her shoulders and his eyes were steely hard. "I don't believe you have any choice in the matter. As my wife you're my property. Tomorrow morning at dawn you'll leave with me even if I have to tie you to the saddle. Is that clear, you stubborn little cat?"

"I'll do what you say because you have the legal right and the muscle to force me, but I'll fight you every step of the way. What you get from me you'll have to take and I guarantee you'll find no pleasure in the taking. Is *that* clear, you stubborn oaf?"

He tipped his head back and gave her a nasty little smile. "You'll give to me, Leah," he said seductively. "By the time we leave the forest you'll be begging for me to touch you."

She returned his smile. "You think more highly of yourself than anyone else does. I don't beg."

He narrowed his eyes at her. "Let's put it this way: We'll stay in the cold, wet, scary forest until you *do* slip into my arms—and my bed—with a smile on your lips and an eager, warm, little body. So if you ever want to see a house or a soft bed again you'll give in to me."

She looked up at him in astonishment. "Do you forget how I grew up? Only recently have I even seen the comforts you've known all your life. I can hold out much longer than you can."

Wesley took her chin in his hand, forced her to keep facing him, then slowly he brought his mouth down on hers and kissed her sweetly. His lips were warm and moist and in spite of herself Leah leaned into him. He pulled away abruptly. "Can you hold out against me, Leah? Can you resist me while camped on some lonely mountainside when the cats howl and the bears come close to the fire? Just remember that I'll always welcome you to my bed."

She met his eyes with hostility, but his hand on her face felt good. She jerked away.

"Go and get ready for tomorrow's journey, wife," he commanded as he turned and left her.

"Of all the most ridiculous . . ." Leah muttered when she was alone. Virginal Kim wouldn't give him what he wanted, but he was sure a Simmons would. Maybe he'd begun to realize that Kim was never going to be a great bed partner, and since his upbringing as a gentleman wouldn't allow him to divorce merely because he wanted to try other women, he had decided to stay with Leah. She was a swamp rat and there was no need to treat her with any respect, no need to consider what she wanted as he would have with a lady like Kim.

"Men!" she said aloud. Wesley thought he could change women as he did clothes. Well, this woman was going to change his mind. He thought she'd seduced him the first time so he'd have to marry her. Even after all she'd told him, he still believed that. But maybe that was better than his knowing the real reason she'd walked into his arms. How could she have ever thought she loved him?

She straightened her shoulders because now she faced the ordeal of confronting the others. Both Justin and Kim were going to be very angry with her.

Slowly, reluctantly, she walked back toward the wagons.

The first sight that greeted her was Justin's fist plowing into Wesley's jaw. Quickly John Hammond and Oliver grabbed Wesley's arms.

"You could have told me from the beginning," Justin said loudly. "And putting Leah through hell! She doesn't deserve that. She was your wife, but she had to watch you paw Kimberly for months."

Pausing just below them on the hillside, Leah smiled to herself. It was good to hear someone defend her.

"Leah," Justin shouted, as he ran down the hill toward her. He held her at arms' length and looked into her eyes. "It's true, isn't it?" he whispered. "This is what's been hanging over your head all this time, isn't it? You could have told me."

As he started to pull her into his arms, Wesley's hand clamped on his shoulder. "That's my wife you're handling, Stark, and if you want to keep your face on that side of your head, you'll release her."

Leah stepped between the men before another battle started. "Justin," she said loudly, "legally, he is my husband and he has the right to change his mind as often as he pleases. Today he wants me, tomorrow I may be free again."

"Leah," Wes warned.

"I'm sorry, Justin. I wish I'd had enough courage to tell you before this happened. But I was afraid . . ." She looked down at the ground, unable to continue.

"I understand, Leah," Justin said. "It's him I blame for this. You don't deserve a woman like her, Stanford."

Wesley put his hand possessively on Leah's shoulder. "Deserve her or not, she's mine and I plan to keep her."

Chapter 14

LEAH TRUDGED along behind Wesley through the silent, roaringly loud forest. Her eyes kept darting this way and that, trying to see behind trees and bushes. A sound in the distance made her jump. Ahead of her, Wesley didn't even turn at Leah's sound.

In the morning he'd turned every time she'd given a little squeal of fright, then smiled smugly and turned back around. Leah swore she'd be quiet from now on, but she broke her vow constantly. Never had she been so far away from people. She'd grown up surrounded by brothers and sisters and the only time she'd left was to live at Wesley's plantation, where there'd been even more people near her. On the trip toward Kentucky, they'd never been out of sight and sound of many people.

Now for the first time in her life she was alone—or at least very close to it. The way she felt now, Wesley didn't count as a human being. Very early that morning they'd loaded goods into packs.

"Which horses do you plan to take?" John Hammond asked.

"We're going where a horse can't go," Wesley answered, slinging the pack on his back.

Refusing to comment or even look at Wesley, she put on her much smaller pack. She was swearing to herself that she'd show no fear.

Kimberly stayed close to John and it was unusual to see her

up so early in the morning. Usually she stayed in bed until break-fast was cooked. Leah wasn't sure if Kim wanted to be near John or if he was insisting she stay there. But Leah was too caught up in her own problems to worry about Kim.

"Ready, Mrs. Stanford?" Wes asked.

Leah wouldn't look at him, but when he started walking, she was behind him.

Now they'd been walking for hours. Leah was tired, and long ago they'd left all sights and sounds of other people. Only she and the buckskin-clad man in front of her seemed to be left on the earth.

"Can you climb up there?" Wes asked, stopping and pointing.

Leah looked up at the steep climb to what seemed to be a cave opening. Curtly she nodded, but she wouldn't look at Wes.

"Give me your pack."

"I can carry it," she said, starting forward.

Wesley caught her pack and half pulled it from her back. "I told you to give me your pack and that's what I meant. You give me any more trouble and I'll throw you over my shoulder and carry you."

Still without looking at him, she slipped out of the pack and handed it to him. It wasn't an easy climb, especially in her long skirt, but every time she had difficulty, Wes was there with a hand freeing her skirt edge, steadying her at her waist, and once giving her a boost on her seat.

When she reached the top, she didn't thank him but stood on the ledge, flattened against the stone wall and peering into the blackness that was the cave. "Do you think there are any bears in there?" she whispered.

"Maybe," Wes answered unconcerned as he put their packs on the ground. "I'll have a look."

"Be . . . be careful," she murmured.

"Worried about me, are you?"

She met his eyes. "I don't want to be left here alone."

"I guess I deserved that," he half grunted, removing a heavy knife from the sheath at his side and a candle from his pack.

"Shouldn't you take the rifle?" she asked, aghast.

"Rifles are useless in close combat. How about a kiss before I enter?"

"I'm to reward you for putting us in the middle of nowhere in front of a bear's den? Maybe there's a whole family of bears in there and we'll both die."

His eyes twinkled. "If I could but die with your kiss on my lips . . ."

"Go on! Get it over with."

Wesley's face turned serious as he disappeared into the cave. "It's bigger than I thought," he said, his voice sounding hollow. "There're some Indian paintings on the walls and some signs of camp fires."

She could hear him moving in the cave and when he spoke again his voice sounded farther away.

"Doesn't look like there are any signs of bears. A few bones. Looks like lots of people have camped here."

For a few minutes he said nothing else and Leah began to relax from her rigid stance and took a step closer to the cave opening. She could hear Wesley walking about and now and then see the flicker of his candle flame.

"Is it safe?" she called.

"Sure," he yelled back. "Clean as a whistle."

In the next few seconds everything happened at once.

Wesley said, "Uh oh," then bellowed, "run, Leah! Hide!"

Instantly, Leah froze right where she was, smack in the middle of the wide cave opening.

In a lightning flash of buckskin fringe, Wesley came tearing out of the cave, and inches behind him was a big old black bear, its fat rippling as it lumbered after Wesley.

The bear brushed past Leah so closely that her nostrils flared at the smell of it. But she could no more move than the rock behind her could.

The bear didn't seem to notice her at all in its pursuit of Wes.

Only her eyes able to move, Leah watched Wes tear down the hillside.

"Climb a tree, Leah," he yelled back at her.

Tree, Leah thought. What is a tree? What does it look like?

She was still wondering this when she heard a loud splash to her left.

"Move, Leah," she commanded herself. But nothing happened. "Move!"

When she did move, it was quickly. She ignored Wes's order to climb a tree and took off, running toward the sound of the splash. She stopped, chest heaving, by a little pool of water that was surrounded by rock. Everything was perfectly quiet. There was no sign of Wesley or the bear. Just the birds singing, the late afternoon sunshine, the smell of grasses.

The next thing she knew her ankle had been grabbed and she was being dragged downward. Instinctively she began to struggle.

"Stop kicking!" Wes's voice hissed—his voice alone, because Leah still saw no one.

When she paused in her struggles, Wes jerked her into the water.

"What—?" She gasped just as Wes put his hand on the top of her head and pushed her underwater.

Her breath held, furious, she saw him submerge and she glared at him through the clear water.

He pointed and she looked. There above them, sniffing the air, was the bear. Wes motioned for her to follow him underwater and she did.

He swam to the opposite side of the little pool and stuck his head up behind some hanging greenery. Leah came up struggling for breath and instantly Wes put his fingers to her lips.

With a sideways glance Leah saw the bear in the same place and she moved away from the animal, which happened to be nearer Wesley. His arms opened and he pulled her to him, her back against his front. She couldn't struggle because the sound might carry to the bear.

Wesley caught her earlobe between his teeth and began to nibble on it.

She tried to move away.

He released her ear and nodded meaningfully toward the bear.

She tried to tell him with her eyes that she almost preferred the bear's mauling, but Wes's grip wouldn't let her move.

He began to nuzzle her neck, his kisses trailing upward to her hairline.

The water was warm, heated all day by the sun, and it was relaxing Leah's tired muscles. As Wes continued to explore her neck and the side of her face, Leah leaned back into him, turning her head to give him freer access.

"The bear's gone," he murmured.

"Mmm?" Leah said, her eyes closed.

Wesley ran his teeth down the sensitive cord in her neck and Leah turned a bit in his arms. Her body felt as soft and liquid as the water surrounding her.

"The bear's gone," Wes repeated as the tip of his tongue touched her earlobe. "Shall we finish this on land? Of course maybe we could continue in the water. I'm certainly willing."

She whirled about, treading water. "How dare you—."

"How dare I!" He laughed. "Why do you keep lying to yourself, Leah? All I have to do is touch you and you're mine. Don't leave. Let's stay in the water. I've never—."

Leah, who was trying her best to make a dignified exit to the shore, turned to face him, her eyes flashing fire. "If you are planning to inform me of your previous conquests, please restrain yourself. I have *no* interest in what you have or have not done.

And for your information, I react to *all* men who touch me just as I react to you. It's something all of us Simmons women are born with. I thought you knew that. After all, isn't your interest in me due to my whorelike nature?"

"Damn you, Leah!" Wes seethed, moving near her. "Why do you keep saying those things about yourself? I saw you with Justin. I'll wager he never touched you."

"Then you'd lose your money." Grabbing her skirt she left the pool to stand on the bank, wringing out the wetness.

Wesley stood beside her, his big body outlined by his wet buckskins. "You'll give me what I want, Leah."

When she didn't look at him, he moved away. "We'll camp over there," he said, nodding.

As soon as Wesley was gone, Leah's shoulders drooped. With her wet skirt dragging behind her, she sat on a rock. She couldn't give in to him. She could not allow herself to do that. How many times had she already lost him? They'd made love and he'd tossed a coin at her and walked away. They'd been married and he'd left her alone, bruised and pregnant. And when he'd returned from Kentucky he'd refused to look at her, he'd said he wanted Kimberly and had again rejected Leah.

Three times, Leah thought. He'd deft her three times and now she was supposed to trust him? Did he find pleasure in toying with her, watching her fall for him, then leaving her? Did he need that to make him feel like a man? To him it meant nothing more than a night's pleasure, but Wesley was something special to Leah. She'd loved him so deeply for so many years. When her father had beaten her she'd lain in pain and thought how someday Wesley Stanford would come to save her. When she'd lost their baby she'd cried, but she'd known there'd be other children—Wesley's children. But now that she knew what he was like she feared that he'd discard her as soon as she was pregnant. After all, her usefulness would be past.

And what about when they left the forest to go to Wesley's

town of Sweetbriar? Wesley was willing to admit to a few close friends that Leah was his wife, but what if he wasn't willing to announce the fact before a whole town? No, a Simmons must be hidden in the woods, kept secret, not allowed into polite society.

Of course Wesley was a man and, as he pointed out every few minutes, Leah was a lusty woman. So he'd take her to the woods, play a nasty little game with her where she had the choice of his bed or months in the forest, and when she gave in to him, then what? Why of course, he'd return to his clean little farm and all he had to do was announce that she'd tricked him into marriage and that she was a loose woman and any judge in the land would grant a decree of divorce. Wes would be free and Leah would be . . .

Leah stood, taking a deep breath. Leah would once again be left with a broken heart. And there were just so many times a woman's heart could be torn apart and still heal. If she fell for Wesley again and he left her, she wondered if she'd be able to pull herself together for the fourth time. For her own sake, she had to resist him. She couldn't let him discard her again.

Through the trees she saw the flicker of firelight and knew Wesley had set up camp. With a shiver she started toward the fire.

"Coffee?" Wes asked, extending a steaming mug to her.

She shook her head and reached for the skillet Wes held.

"No." He pulled back. "You rest. I'll cook supper."

"Don't be ridiculous," she snapped. "Men can't cook."

"They can't? Well, my pretty little wife, you just sit there and I'll prove you wrong."

Leah sat, her eyes on her hands.

Wesley was frying bacon, moving it about in the skillet and watching her. "Did I ever tell you about Paris?"

"Paris?" She looked up. "I've never heard of Paris, Virginia."

Wesley smiled at her. That wet dress of hers clung to her, but he knew that when it was dry it'd be loose and concealing. With a grin he remembered the low-cut dress she'd worn that night at the inn. She'd look good in Paris, wearing a pretty bonnet that set off her dark hair.

"Paris is across the ocean in a country called France."

"I'm sorry I haven't had the benefit of your education. My father didn't see the need to send his slave-children to school."

He ignored her. "One night about five of us had dinner in a private room." He stopped. "Perhaps I shouldn't tell you that story." He looked up at her. "Maybe you'd like to hear how my brother Travis courted Regan."

"Oh yes," Leah said. She'd love to hear about her friend.

"Well then, go and put on some dry clothes and while we eat I'll tell you the story."

Later they ate beans, bacon, biscuits, and coffee while Wes told, with much exaggeration, Leah was sure, an outrageous story of what Travis had done to win the return of his wife. There'd been hundreds of roses involved, an uncountable number of proposals on paper, and at last a circus in which, according to Travis, he had risked his life and had been the star of the show.

"*How* many roses?" Leah asked.

"Travis said thousands, but Regan always rolls her eyes, so who knows?"

"I've never seen an elephant."

"Travis brought back a wagon load of manure, said it'd make the tobacco plants grow twice as tall."

"Did it?" Leah asked, her eyes wide.

"Didn't do anything different that I could tell. Now that you've had your bedtime story, it's time for bed."

Leah braced herself and the flicker in Wes's eyes showed her that he saw her movement.

"I've made your bed over there," he said coolly. "I'm on the other side. If you get frightened, let me know. I'm a light sleeper." With that he tossed out the dregs of his coffee and went to his own pile of blankets.

Quietly Leah went to her own bed, grateful that he wasn't going to try to entice her to his bed.

For a long time Wesley lay awake, looking up at the stars.

He hated the way she jumped whenever he came near her. And her reaction was puzzling to him. She'd wanted to marry him. According to Travis she'd first gone to bed with him because she thought she loved him. So now she had him, he'd decided to stay with her, and she acted as if he were a disease she might catch. He didn't understand it at all.

Of course maybe he had been a little hard on her at first. It was just that he'd been so damned mad because he'd lost Kim, and Leah seemed to be one of those women he'd always detested, the kind of woman who needed no one and nothing. But as they'd traveled together he'd come to see that Leah needed a great deal. She needed someone to protect her from everyone who took advantage of her. Kim made Leah wait on her. Justin expected Leah to fall for him. And even Wesley had started relying on her. It was so easy to give a task to Leah because the word *no* wasn't in her vocabulary. She seemed to think she was the world's slave.

At first Wes had spoken to Kim about how much work she piled on Leah. Kim had been bewildered. She said Leah *wanted* to do all the work. Wes realized right away it was no use trying to talk to Kim. In fact, he began to realize he couldn't talk to Kim about anything. In the evenings he'd sit with Kim and want to tell her something about himself and he'd see her eyes dart around and more than once she'd jump up in the middle of a sentence. At those times, Wesley's eyes would dart to where Leah was leaning forward, listening intently to every word Justin was saying. And Wesley would think, she's *my* wife!

Wes wasn't sure when he began to be bored by Kim. Perhaps it was the time she screamed so loudly that everyone came running, thinking she'd been bitten by a snake. A honeybee had stung the back of her hand. Very calmly Leah had put baking soda on the sting and Wesley had led a shaking, crying Kim away to the wagon where she'd immediately gone to bed. Later Wesley had seen Leah trying to put something on the back of her own neck. It'd taken awhile to get her to show him what she was doing, but she'd leaned against some wild honeysuckle and had three bee stings on her neck.

"And you didn't say anything?" Wesley asked.

"They're only bee stings," she said, shrugging.

She wouldn't let him help her with the baking soda paste and so he left her, but after that he was much more aware of her.

And he began to ask himself questions.

Life on a farm was never easy, and contrary to what many people thought, he didn't have a great deal of cash. Half of Stanford Plantation was his, but the wealth of it was tied up in land. Only if it were sold would Wes get his money. Travis had agreed to pay Wes what he could, and whatever complaints he had about his brother, Wes never doubted Travis's honesty. So if Wes wasn't rich, couldn't afford an army of servants, what was he going to do with a wife who went hysterical at the sting of a little honeybee? Would Wes have to plow all day, then come home and take care of the house too? Would he have to bring Kim breakfast in bed each morning?

At one time, actually while he was living under the domineering rule of his brother, he looked forward to someone leaning on him. Kim didn't lean, she lay down most of the time.

And when he kissed her! Kim would say, "You may have two kisses tonight, Wesley." She'd purse her lips tightly and go *smack, smack,* then give a coy little laugh, as if she'd done something improper and highly suggestive, and move away from him.

For a while those prim little kisses and that suggestive little laugh had enticed him. He'd believed what she wanted him to believe—that when she let herself go she was going to be uncontrollably passionate. But somewhere along the way he'd stopped believing her. He began to imagine that even after they were married she'd still be saying, "You may have two kisses tonight, Wesley." Or maybe as her husband he would be allowed three.

Once, he'd tried to force her to some passion, but she'd pulled away from him, frightened, and when she recovered herself she chastised him as if he were a little boy she planned to spank.

He didn't try again after that—and he stopped taking his nightly dose of kisses, if they could be called that.

And the more he pulled away from Kim, the more aware he became of Leah. He became aware of her quiet efficiency, how she handled what could have become crises. And her generosity was unbelievable. Nothing was too much for her to do. She asked little of anyone but gave very much.

The longer they traveled together, the more Wes grew to like her. He wasn't sure exactly when he made his decision to keep her—perhaps it was a gradual one—but he knew he'd rather marry Leah than adopt Kim.

He'd wanted to tell Leah right away but somehow he sensed she might be a little reluctant to embrace him with open arms. He couldn't figure out why she might be, because he was, after all, giving her what she wanted, but who could understand women's minds?

So he'd thought about it a long time and decided he needed to get her into a situation where she had to depend on him—if there was such a situation. Leah was so infuriatingly competent that he wondered if he could make her need him.

Then when they'd had the mud wrestle—he smiled at the memory—he'd found out about her fear of the lonely forest. And so of course that was where he arranged to take her.

And just as he'd predicted, basing his guess on the odd workings of women's minds, Leah had turned stubborn when he'd told her she could stay with him. Give women what they wanted and damned if they didn't decide they wanted something else!

Now here they were, all alone, and Leah acted as if she

couldn't stand him. If he lived a hundred years he'd never understand women.

But she'd come around. If need be they'd spend months alone in this forest; he planned to court her, woo her, win her. Maybe he could even get her pregnant again. Now that wasn't a bad idea at all. If she were swelled up with his child, surely she'd give him less trouble. They'd get back to Sweetbriar and his farm and there'd already be a child on the way.

Oh Leah, he thought, looking across the dying fire toward her, no woman could ever resist a Stanford man when he set his mind to winning her.

With that decision made, he turned on his side and went to sleep.

Chapter 15

LEAH WOKE with a sense of dread. The forest was still and by the look of the moon it wasn't very late—but something was deeply wrong. Quickly she turned her head to look at Wesley. His eyes were open and there was warning in them. She obeyed his silent command and lay still while she watched him inch his rifle a little closer to his body.

"No need for that, mister," came a voice from behind Leah that made her go rigid. She'd never thought to hear that voice again; she had prayed never to hear it again.

"We're just travelers like you and the lady," the voice continued.

Leah lay still as out of the darkness came a tall, skinny body. In the moonlight she could see a bearded face.

Slowly, making every move count, Wesley sat up, the rifle never out of his hands. "Who's with you?" Wes asked in such a sleepy voice that Leah looked sharply at him, then noticed the alert look in his eyes.

"Jus' me and one of the boys. Mind if I have some of your coffee?"

The thin man didn't wait for an answer but knelt by the luke-warm pot. He didn't bother looking in Leah's direction.

He wouldn't, Leah thought with anger. Her brother Abe had never had much use for women unless there was ransom money involved. Years ago, after Abe had kidnapped Nicole Armstrong, he'd disappeared off the face of the earth, and none of the Simmonses had heard from him again. Now he was a great deal thinner, years older, but Leah had no doubt he was her brother, probably up to no good, and Wesley was right in staying near his weapon. But perhaps if Leah let her brother know who she was he'd leave them alone.

"I'll get you a cup," she said loudly, eyes on Abe's narrow back in its worn black coat. She wasn't sure, but she believed he tightened at the sound of her voice.

Moving quickly, she threw a handful of branches on the dying fire and urged it into a light-giving blaze. With slow deliberation, she poured him a cup of coffee and handed it to him across the flames.

He looked at her for only an instant and Leah wasn't sure he recognized her. After all, when Abe left she'd been only fourteen, and since then she'd grown into a woman and her manners and speech had changed greatly. But Abe's face hadn't changed much. It was still narrow, with close-set black eyes and a big nose that looked like some bird ready to attack from its perch on top of a dirty, scraggly beard.

"I'd like to see your friend," Wes said.

Abe turned to Wes, again ignoring Leah. "He's just a boy, no harm in him, but if you want to see him . . . Bud, come on out here."

Leah was pouring another cup of coffee and nearly dropped it at the sight of the man stepping from the shadows. Or perhaps he *was* the shadows because he was by far the biggest man she'd ever seen. Both Wesley and Travis were big, powerfully built men, but this young man nearly dwarfed them. He was at least six feet eight inches, maybe taller, well over two hundred pounds. He wore baggy, coarse linen trousers tucked into tall black boots molded over giant calves. His upper body was bare except for a sheepskin slung over one shoulder, and his arms could only be described as massive. They more resembled sculptured tree trunks than arms. The man, truthfully not more than a boy, had a handsome, unsmiling face set on a neck that looked to be about the size of Leah's waist.

"Jus' one of the boys," Abe repeated, a chuckle in his voice.

"Coffee?" Leah managed to ask, her neck craning to look up at the big man.

"Bud likes to keep his hands free," Abe said, not allowing the *boy* to answer. "You folks just passin' through?"

"Hunting," Wes answered, still not moving from where he'd slept and not turning his back on the giant near him.

Abe creakily lifted his spindly little body, tossing the dregs of coffee on the ground. "We got to be goin' now. Thank you kindly, missus." He handed the empty cup to Leah and it was then she was sure he recognized her. His close little eyes bored into hers and swept down her dress, which was far better than anything he'd ever seen her wear before. "Come on, Bud," Abe said and started into the darkness, the silent giant moving noiselessly behind him.

Leah's head spun with thoughts, the first of which was that she was sure Abe was up to no good. Of course he'd never done anything honest in his life as far as Leah knew, so she wasn't surprised by this thought.

"What do you think they wanted?" Wes asked, watching her.

Leah jumped guiltily at the sound of his voice. She couldn't very well tell someone of Wes's class that the nasty creature was her brother and had probably meant to knock them over the head and rob them. Maybe he'd refrained because he had some family feeling. More likely he'd not harmed them because they were awake. Abe was a backstabber.

"I guess they were just traveling, like us," she said, then stretched exaggeratedly. "I certainly am tired. I'll be asleep again in minutes."

With great show, Leah rearranged her pallet, smiled merrily

at Wes, yawned, and looked for all the world as if she went right
to sleep.

Never in her life had she been more awake. Somewhere near
them in the forest was her sly, devious, cowardly, thieving, treacherous older brother—and she knew he'd want payment from her
for not causing them misery.

Every pore of her body seemed to be listening. She held her
breath as Wesley, seeming to believe her words, settled down to
sleep.

An hour went by and Leah's body began to ache. When was
Abe going to make his move? She planned how she'd roll toward
Wes and grab the rifle.

Another hour passed. She began to wonder if she really could
shoot her own brother.

A noise from Wesley startled her, but it was only a soft snore
followed by his turning over.

When Abe's signal came, a high-pitched whistle, Leah was
past ready. Slowly, making no noise, she pushed herself out of the
blankets and left the campsite. She didn't allow herself to consider the forest at night or remember that great, enormous man
who trailed her brother, but she made her way over fallen logs,
past frightening shadows toward the whistle that would repeat itself when she lost her way.

She traveled at least a mile before Abe oozed himself from behind a willow tree.

Leah jumped back, her hand to her throat.

"Scare you, baby sister?"

"Only as any other criminal would."

Abe looked almost hurt. "I thought maybe you'd be glad to
see me. I sure was glad to see you."

"Where's that creature of yours?"

Abe merely nodded upward to a space above her head.

Leah glanced to the side to see the shadow of a huge arm.
Again she gasped as she turned to see the young man not ten

inches from her. She moved away from the towering mass of him while he remained impassive.

Abe took her upper arm. "Don't mind Bud," he said, pulling her away. "He ain't too, you know." He tapped his head with his finger.

"I don't guess he has to be," Leah snapped as she jerked out of Abe's grasp. "When did you last have a bath?" She wrinkled her nose.

"Ain't you the fancy one! Last time I seen you you was dirtier 'n I ever been. I guess that was before you took up with the likes of the Stanfords."

Leah drew herself up rigidly. "I happen to be Mrs. Wesley Stanford."

"You!" Abe gasped, stepping away from her. "You, a Simmons, *married* to a Stanford?" He began to smile. "Hear that, Bud? My very own little sister thinks someone like a Stanford *married* her."

Bud gave no indication he heard Abe.

"I never knowed you was such a liar." Abe began to laugh. "All the Simmons women are whores but they're usually honest whores. Even Ma—Hey!"

He didn't finish his sentence because Leah administered a ringing slap to his laughing face.

"You little—," he began. "You want me to set Bud on you? He can tear bits like you apart with one hand. Bud!"

Bud didn't move and neither did Leah as she stared straight up at him, hoping he wouldn't see her trembling. Bud looked at her for a moment, then lifted his eyes to look into the forest's darkness.

"Well," Abe said, "maybe Bud's not in the mood tonight."

Leah released her pent-up breath. "Maybe he has a mother too and believes people *should* be slapped for saying bad things about their mothers."

"Hell, Bud and Cal ain't got mothers. Somebody carved 'em

out of a mountain. Look, Leah, forget the pea brains. I got some business to talk to you about."

"Who is Cal?"

"I told you to forget 'em! Now listen, I didn't mean none of them things about you bein' a whore. I mean, even if you are it don't matter to me because all I want is your . . . your brain," he said brightly. "You allus was the smartest one in the family. Ma used to say it was too bad you was born a Simmons. You followin' me?"

"Only too well. I'm beginning to realize you want something from me."

"See?" He grinned. One of his incisors was rotting away. "I knew you was smart. And look at you too. Pretty as a lady and you talk all refined."

"You don't need to waste your flattery. What do you want from me?"

"I want you to join us."

"Us? Join you?" she asked in dread.

"You don't have to act like you're better 'n me. I got somethin' good goin' for me. I'm gonna *be* somebody."

Leah stood still and waited for him to continue. It wouldn't do to antagonize him further, especially not with the hulking man hovering over them.

"I want you to join Revis and me and the boys. We got a little deal goin' whereas we help ourselves to the people travelin' over the Wilderness Trail. I reckon you been travelin' with 'em and you know their ways better 'n us and since you're so smart you can plan things for us."

"Plan?" Leah whispered, beginning to understand. She'd heard, of course, of a gang of robbers preying on the westward travelers, but they'd never molested the Stanford party. "*You* are one of the robbers? Thievery is how you're planning to make something of yourself?"

"I ain't always plannin' to steal," Abe said righteously. "I'm puttin' the money away to buy me a little store—or I will put it away as soon as I pay off a few debts."

"Gambling, no doubt," she said. "And you think *I* would even consider becoming a part of your hideous den of thieves?"

"Don't you go callin' me names, you little whore. Ma and Pa know you're hidin' out with a Stanford?"

"For your information, both Ma and Pa are dead, and I told you before that I am married to Wesley Stanford."

"Oh, yeah, and Bud here flies. Hey! How come if you're married to Stanford you two was sleepin' apart?"

Leah looked at her shoe. "It's a long story," she mumbled.

"Only one way a Stanford'd marry a Simmons. He got you pregnant, didn't he? And only them Stanfords would think they'd have to marry a slut—" He broke off. "Look Leah, married or not, the man don't want you. Anybody with any sense—even Bud here—would be able to see that. Why's he keepin' you in a woods, hidin' away with you?"

Abe's words were too close to how Leah actually felt. "I have to go. It'll be daylight soon," she whispered. "Wesley will miss me."

"He ain't gonna miss you. He'll be glad to get rid of a Simmons whether she's his wife or not. Come on with me now, Leah. Join us. We'll make you rich."

"Rich!" She spat. "Rich from stealing other people's goods? Those people on that trail have *worked* all their lives for what they have and you think I'm going to help you take it away from them? You make me ill! Worse than ill! I wonder if scum like you has a right to live!"

"Why you—," he said, before lunging at her.

But one silent step forward from Bud made Abe stop.

Leah blinked her eyes in astonishment and, with her heart pounding from anger and fear, she dared greatly and put her hand on Bud's bare forearm. "Bud," she said through a closed throat, "will you lead me back to my husband? I don't know the way."

Without a sound Bud slipped away into the trees.

"Don't try to bother me again or Wesley'll make you sorry," Leah said to Abe before following the shadow of Bud.

She slipped into her sleeping pad seemingly only minutes before Wesley woke. She did her best to conceal her nervousness from him, but every sound made her jump. Wesley mentioned her dislike for the forest and told her she had nothing to be afraid of.

"Men are the real danger," he said, eyeing her. "Take those two last night."

"What about them?" she asked nervously, then calmed herself. "They weren't dangerous, were they?"

"Maybe you should answer that."

"Me? Why me? How could I know anything about them?"

He was silent for a moment. "I just thought women were supposed to know these things, that's all. Women sometimes say they sense when people are good or bad."

Leah cursed herself for jumping at him. He didn't know the man from last night was her brother. He didn't know she'd sneaked away to talk with him. But she was acting so guilty he was going to guess something was wrong.

"Only rich women have time to guess people's motives. A Simmons like me has to take people as they are," she snapped at him.

Wesley seemed about to speak but changed his mind. "True to form," he muttered. "All right Simmons-Stanford, stay close to me." With that he began to plow through the trees quickly, leaving Leah standing.

"Damn, damn, damn!" she cursed as she followed him.

For most of the day he stayed very far ahead of her. Only now and again did she glimpse his buckskins. Mostly she kept her head down and trudged along behind him, trying her best not to think of her brother Abe. Would he do something in revenge because she'd refused his request?

By twilight she was beginning to convince herself that Abe did have some family feeling and he wasn't going to retaliate. Still she kept a lookout behind every tree. She half expected to be kidnapped. That would be Abe's style.

A shot rang out, echoing off the trees and hills, reverberating all around her.

"Wesley!" she cried and knew with every fiber of her body that it was Abe who'd fired that shot. "Wesley!" she screamed and began to run.

Wesley's big body lay on the forest floor, silent, still, half sitting against the pack on his back. A great, gaping hole was in his chest.

"Wesley," Leah said with a gasp, dropping to her knees before him. "Wesley."

He didn't answer her but lay there completely still.

"He's still breathin'," came a voice over her head. "I didn't aim to kill him."

"You!" Leah hissed and launched at her brother.

Abe put his hands up to protect himself. "I told you I needed you and since you ain't got no family feelin's I had to do somethin'."

Leah stopped hitting her brother when she realized the stupidity of his words and turned back to Wesley. Bud was kneeling beside Wes, his big fingers probing at the wound.

"He *is* alive, isn't he?" she asked again going to her knees.

Bud nodded once as he removed a knife from his side.

"No!" Leah screamed, grabbing the big forearm with both her hands. "Please don't kill him. I'll do whatever you want."

Bud gave her a quick, hard look before using the knife to cut away the torn part of Wesley's shirt.

"Them boys won't kill nothin'," Abe said in disgust, rubbing his arms where Leah had struck him. "Let Bud take care of Stanford and you come with me."

"I won't leave him," Leah said stubbornly. "I'll get you for this, Abe Simmons. If my husband dies I'll—"

"He ain't gonna die. I'm a good shot and it took me all day to come up with this plan. I figured you'd do most anythin' to keep from losin' all that Stanford money so I thought if maybe I laid him low you'd be willin' to do somethin' for me while he was healin'.' "

"You stupid—," she began. "How could you shoot someone just to get help with your criminal ways? Wesley, can you hear me?"

Leah was vaguely aware of the big man, Bud, as he began to feel Wesley's ribs. Leah was glad for the help as her eyes were full of tears of rage and frustration.

"Here," Abe said, grabbing Leah's arm and pulling her upright. "Let the boys see to him. They're good at doctorin'. You and me got some talkin' to do."

"I wouldn't talk to you if—."

"You want me to finish him off? It seems to me you ain't in a position to do much bargainin'. You already showed me you ain't got no real family feelin's so I don't know why I should care about you."

"You've never cared about anybody but yourself."

Abe stood still, glaring at her. "You tell me when you're ready to listen."

"Never, I—," A groan from Wesley made her turn back to him.

"Leah," he whispered, his eyes barely open. "Get out of here. Save yourself." With that, his head fell to one side.

"No!" she cried. "He isn't—?" She looked up at Bud who shook his head once.

"You got a choice, missy," Abe said. "You help me and I'll let you take care of your rich boy, but you keep refusin' me and callin' me names and I'll let him rot right here. And you better make up your mind fast 'cause he looks like he's about to bleed to death."

Leah didn't take more than a few seconds to make up her mind. "I'll help you," she whispered, her hand on Wesley's cool forehead. "What do I have to do?"

Chapter 16

LEAH LOOKED down at Wesley's sleeping form. His wound was clean now and she realized it wasn't as bad as she'd thought, although he'd lost a lot of blood. He lay on a fairly clean bed in an old cabin that was hidden on the side of a mountain.

Slowly she moved from her seat on the side of the bed and took the pan of dirty water outside to empty it. Standing outside the door, silhouetted in the early dawn light like mountain guardians, were the young men, Bud and Cal. She'd been too upset about Wesley to know exactly when the brother had made his appearance, but now there were two of them, both massive, both silent, almost indistinguishable from each other. The brothers had carried the unconscious Wesley to the cabin, and without speaking a word they'd helped her wash and bandage him.

"He's sleeping," she said tiredly to the silent men, one on either side of the door. "In time I think he'll be all right."

"Told you he would be," Abe said loudly, making her jump as he slipped around the side of the cabin.

"Do you always have to sneak up on people?" She seethed at him, her eyes blazing.

"You've got to be the unfriendliest sister a man ever had. You gonna listen to me or we gonna fight over that rich man of yours?"

Everything in her hated having to cooperate with him. She'd

do what he wanted in order to save Wes, but as soon as he was well, she'd get away from Abe. "What is it you want from me?" she asked belligerently.

Abe grunted but otherwise ignored her tone. "You don't have to do much to help out a member of your very own family. All I need you for is to do a little brain work. And maybe a little cookin'," he said under his breath.

Her head came up sharply. "So that's it, is it? You don't need me to help plan your robberies, all you want is someone to fetch and tote for you."

"Now Leah," he began, then stopped and gave her his rotten-toothed grin. "Sure, that's all we want. You come along and cook for us, do a little cleanin' and them other things women do. Ain't nothin' wrong in that, is there? There ain't nearly as many of us as all them kids Pa had."

Leah felt almost relieved. She'd hated the idea of having to plan robberies and although the running of the camp would be hard work, she'd rather do that than something directly bad.

Abe was watching her. "That makes you feel better, don't it?" he said as if talking to a kitten. "You just have to do a little cleanin', a little cookin', although these here boys eat a powerful lot."

"And what do I get in return?"

"You get to look after your rich husband." He looked down at his shoe. "Although maybe you better not tell Revis about him. Maybe it oughta be our secret," he said, ignoring the presence of the two young giants.

Leah glanced from Bud to Cal, but their faces were impassive. She wondered how intelligent the men were and wondered too if they realized how degrading Abe's treatment of them was. "Who is this Revis?"

"My partner!" Abe blurted with pride. "Him and me are in this together. We run the whole show."

"What happens when Wesley recovers?"

Abe grinned at her. "I'll tell Revis you run away, couldn't stand all the work. It's happened lots of times before. We sorta wear women out."

"You shot my husband to get a replacement cook?" She spat at him. "If cooks are so easy to come by and you have to rehire them so often, why did you have to *shoot* someone?"

Abe looked puzzled for a moment then smiled happily. "I wanted my sister near me. I ain't seen you in a long time."

Leah grabbed a long piece of wood from the woodpile and started toward him.

"You hurt me, Leah, and you'll never find your way out of this forest," he half warned, half pleaded, covering his face with his arms.

She lowered the wood inches away from his head. "You dirty rotten blackmailer," she hissed before turning back toward the cabin and Wesley.

"You boys ain't no use at all," Abe said from behind her. "Wait till I tell Revis how you let somebody threaten me, nearly killed me she did. Revis'll have a few words to say to you two."

Leah took her time repacking her few belongings before leaving with her brother. She wished Wesley would wake up so she could tell him some story about where she was going, although she hadn't had a chance to come up with anything good yet. But he slept hard, his breathing deep and slow. There was a furrow of pain across his brow.

She sat beside him and touched his cheek. At this moment she couldn't seem to remember why she'd been so angry with him for the last few months. All she could remember was being a young girl and falling in love with him. Maybe it was Abe's presence that was reminding her of the nasty farm she'd grown up on. Thoughts of Wesley had kept her sane.

"You get through moonin' over him, you better come on. Revis'll want breakfast. He don't like the boys out of his sight for very long."

Quietly Leah leaned forward and kissed Wesley's sleep-softened lips. "I'll return as soon as I can," she promised him, then left the cabin.

Abe gave a squint toward the rising sun and said, "Let's get goin'." He was obviously beginning to get nervous.

The trail down the mountain was a maze through brambles and rocks. While they were fighting their way down, Leah tried to think. It would be to her advantage to find out all she could about this gang she was reluctantly joining.

"Where are Bud and Cal?" she asked, pushing a briar away from her face.

"They don't like walkin' with other people. They're too dumb to know people ought to stick together. Even Revis can't make 'em understand."

"Is this Revis ever able to control them?"

Abe stopped and turned to face her. "If you're thinkin' of gettin' the boys on your side against me, you can stop it right now."

Leah tried not to let him see that this was just what she'd been planning.

"Revis and the boys is brothers," Abe said smugly before turning around. "Some families stick together," he added.

"You mean there's another one of these 'boys'? There are *three* of these giants?"

"Naw, Revis is just regular size and not stupid or nothin' like the boys. They ain't real, blood-related, but Revis's ma got Bud and Cal from somewheres when they was babies. They was raised right alongside of Revis and that means somethin' to 'em."

Leah made a face behind his back, sick of his hints that she was disloyal.

They walked in silence for a while.

"Do Bud and Cal talk?"

Abe snorted. "Only when you pester 'em. I figure they got such little brains they don't have much to say."

"You think the more people have to say the bigger brains they have?"

"Sometimes you're too clever, Leah. I ain't so good with words, but Revis is. You try your words on him. And you be careful you don't start attackin' him with logs 'cause the boys protect Revis. I'd sure hate to see my own sister hurt."

"I'm sure you would," she said sarcastically.

"Ain't me got no family feelin's, it's you."

Leah didn't bother to make a reply.

In another few minutes they came into view of a little clearing with a ramshackle cabin, a woodpile, and a stream nearby. Leah stopped and looked down on the scene as an emaciated woman emerged from the back of the cabin and began loading her thin arms with logs.

"Who's that?" she asked.

"Verity," Abe answered. "She's our last, er, a . . . cook. She didn't hold up very long at all. It's them boys, always eatin' and eatin'," he added, his eyes slipping to the side.

Leah didn't question his story but kept her eyes on the woman as they went down the hillside. The woman didn't even look up. In fact, she looked too tired to care who walked into the clearing.

"Fix up some grub," Abe commanded the woman, his voice deepening.

The woman Verity didn't move any faster as she trudged into the cabin.

Bud and Cal appeared in the clearing as if they'd never left.

After only a moment's hesitation, Leah followed Verity into the cabin, went straight to the woman, and took the wood from her. "You sit down," she ordered gently. "I'll cook."

A flicker of surprise was Verity's only reaction before she went to a corner of the cabin and crouched on the floor.

"Not there!" Leah said, shocked. "Sit at the table."

Verity turned frightened eyes toward Leah and shook her head.

"Are you afraid of Abe?"

Verity shook her head.

"Bud or Cal?"

Again she shook her head.

"Revis," Leah whispered and saw the woman try to make herself smaller at the mention of the name. "I guess that answers that," Leah said, beginning to look into bags of supplies. "That *would* be the type of man Abe got himself into partners with," she murmured.

If there was one place Leah felt comfortable, it was in front of a cooking fire. All her life until she'd married Wes, she'd been involved with food—growing it, storing it, and cooking it. Now as she began to work, it was in the back of her mind that maybe a good meal would help get Bud and Cal on her side. She'd probably need any help she could get if this Revis was as brutal as Verity had indicated.

The supplies in the cabin were abundant, and after Leah found a woman's dress inside one of the sacks, she realized they were stolen. She refused to let her spirits fall. Bud and Cal had helped her with Wesley and she was going to repay them with a good meal, a very good meal.

"Can't you hurry up?" Abe demanded. "Revis might come back at any time."

"If you'd stay out of my way I could get done faster." She handed Verity a hard-boiled egg.

"She don't deserve nothin' to eat. In this group if you don't work you don't eat."

"Someone has worked her nearly to death. Now get out of here or I'll tell Bud and Cal you're interfering with my cooking."

To her surprise and delight, Abe's face lost some color and he immediately left the cabin. "Well, well, it looks like Abe is a little afraid of the boys." She looked toward Verity for confirmation, but the woman was greedily stuffing the egg into her mouth.

From start to finish it took an hour and a half to prepare a meal, the size of which astonished even Leah. "Bud, Cal," she called out the back door.

"You weren't gonna call me, were ya?" Abe whined as he pushed past her into the cabin.

The little interior consisted of a fireplace, a big table, five chairs, and some blankets in the corners. Scattered everywhere were bags of heaven-knew-what, Leah thought.

When Leah stepped back into the cabin she saw that Bud and Cal were already seated at the table, already beginning to eat. Leah sat across from them, Abe at the head. When she tried to get Verity to join them the woman cringed deeper into her corner.

"Don't bother her," Abe snapped. "She's scared of Revis. Don't know why, though," he added quickly. "Revis is a real nice man, ain't he, boys?"

Neither Bud nor Cal bothered to acknowledge Abe's question, but ate the food Leah had prepared. Their manners were good, much better than Abe's as he shoveled food into his mouth.

As Leah ate, she worried about Wesley. Would he rest? Would he try to get up and find her? Was he hungry? How was she going to find her way back to him?

"Eat up!" Abe commanded. "Revis don't like skinny women."

A little alarm went off in Leah's head. "Of what concern is my weight to your partner in crime?"

"Oh nothin'," Abe said hurriedly. "Just that Revis is a real gentleman and he likes pretty women."

She leaned forward. "No *gentleman* robs people for a living."

"Well said," came a voice from behind Leah.

Leah whirled about as Abe jumped up, knocking his chair over. "Mr. Revis," Abe said with a gasp, awe, respect, and some fear in his voice.

Leah wasn't sure what she'd expected, but the man standing in the doorway wasn't it. He was tall, broad-shouldered, slim-hipped, with black, curling hair. His dark, dark brown eyes were riveting. Set in a handsome, square-jawed face, his eyes bored into hers as his lips curved into a sardonic smile.

Chills started to form on Leah's spine.

"This is her, Mr. Revis," Abe said. "This is my sister. Ain't she pretty? And she's real strong too. You ain't gonna wear her out in no month or two."

Leah couldn't look away from the man. There was something frightening about him, yet fascinating. She wet her lips.

Slowly, like a cat, the man approached her. He wore a black silk shirt, black wool trousers, and black leather boots. Gracefully he extended his hand to her.

Leah accepted and for a moment she thought she was back in the Stanford drawing room. She rose to stand before him as if he were bidding her to dance with him.

"She is indeed lovely," Revis said in his deep voice.

"I knew you'd like her, Mr. Revis. I just knew it. She's real willin' too. And she's got fire in her. She'll make you real happy."

Leah stood there holding Revis's hand while standing in the midst of the squalid cabin. Behind her were the quiet sounds of Bud and Cal continuing to eat. Slowly she began to hear her brother's words.

For a moment she looked from Abe to Revis and quickly it all became clear to her. Revis was no one's partner, least of all Abe Simmons's partner. And Leah wasn't there to cook, but she was there as some sort of human gift to this good-looking, charming villain.

She snatched her hand away. "I think there's been a misunderstanding," she began. "I came here to cook."

"Ain't she a caution!" Abe gave a nervous laugh. "My little sister knows lots about men, just loves men, and I can see she likes you a lot, Mr. Revis. Go on, Leah, give him a kiss."

Leah whirled on her brother, a snarl on her lips. "You said you wanted a cook but you expected me to whore for you, didn't you? Well listen, you piece of slime, I don't whore for anybody, especially not for criminals like this one."

Abe turned white. "Mr. Revis," he began, "she don't mean that. You know how all the ladies like you. She just thinks you'll like her better if she's a little hard to get."

"You—!" Leah gasped and lunged at her brother.

Revis's strong arm lashed out and caught Leah by the waist, pulling her to him. "Whatever the reason, I'm glad you're here," he said softly. "I like my women to have a little spirit." His free hand began to run up and down her arm. "I'll enjoy taming the tigress."

"Enjoy this then!" she exclaimed as she kicked him in the shins.

Whatever happened as a result of her action, she knew it'd be worth it for the look on Revis's face. Why did handsome men always assume women were going to fall for them? "No dirty thief is going to touch me," she said with bravado, but the next moment she was backing away from Revis.

"Get her, Mr. Revis. She's an ungrateful sister and she deserves whatever you give her," Abe shouted.

Revis's eyes were cold, hard, frightening as he advanced on Leah.

She backed around the side of the table, putting a chair between them. "Leave me alone," she warned. "I don't want you touching me."

"You're much too pretty for me to care what you want." Revis tossed the chair across the room.

Leah kept backing, her hands going across the shoulders of Bud and Cal who kept on eating. "Help me," she pleaded, but the young men ignored her.

"The boys obey only me," Revis said, advancing. "Now why don't we stop these games and you come to me? I rule this little empire and everyone here gives me what I want. Or they wish they had," he added.

Verity began whimpering in the corner.

"Is that what you did to Verity? Force her?"

Revis gave a secret little smile. "When my women disobey me, I punish them."

In spite of herself, Leah shivered. If she ever got out of this she'd take a whip to her brother. Her eyes flickered toward Abe and in those few seconds, Revis was upon her.

He caught her arm and wrenched it behind her back forcing her close to him. "You have fire in you, my pretty," he whispered, "a fire that I plan to share."

"Stop it!" she cried, and there was more pleading in her voice than she intended.

Revis's lips went to her neck. "You'll learn to enjoy what I offer," he said silkily.

Leah could hardly think. It wasn't that she was responding to his hot mouth on her neck, but somehow she knew that if he got what he wanted from her, her life, and probably Wesley's, would be over. The only way she could save herself was to stop him.

She wasn't any match for his strength, but Bud and Cal were. If only she could get them involved.

"I don't like this public lovemaking," Revis whispered. "Come outside where we can be totally alone. I'll show you the man inside this thief you're so frightened of."

"I'm not—," she began.

Revis's hand tightened on her throat, the thumb pressing into a pulse spot. "Perhaps you should be frightened. I like a woman's resistance."

"Because you can't find a woman willing to have you?" she spat up at him.

Revis raised one dark eyebrow. "Perhaps you should be taught a few manners. A little pain might make you less unwilling."

"She deserves it," Abe injected.

"Shut up," Revis said with a growl, his eyes never leaving Leah's face. "Did your stupid brother tell you about me? I take what I want and I use it until it's all gone. You can't resist me, can't fight me, because I always win."

With that his mouth took hers in a rough, fierce kiss.

When he was done, the light in his eyes told Leah he was sure she'd want him now. He was certain his kiss would make her fall down at his feet.

With a snarl, Leah spat in his face then turned her head away as he raised his hand to strike her.

"Bud and Cal," she said, "if you don't protect me, I'll never cook for you again."

The statement made Revis halt his hand in midair. Abruptly he released her, pushing her back against the cabin wall. His handsome face twisted into an ugly smile. "You think you can turn my brothers against me? Do you think that perhaps you can control what is mine?"

"No, I . . . I don't want you touching me, that's all. I don't want control." Something about him frightened her more than ever. Her hands clutched at the wall behind her as if she might be able to claw her way to freedom.

"You need to learn that I am the master here and no damn woman—." Again, he raised his hand to strike her.

But the blow never landed.

Bud's big hand lightly gripped Revis's wrist. "The woman will cook," Bud said in a soft, gentle voice, but there was no mistaking the command it held.

Revis's face was a study in astonishment. He started to speak, but as he looked from the men flanking him, making him seem small by contrast, his eyes went back to Leah and what she saw made her shiver. He hated her now and for a moment she almost wished she'd given in to him.

Revis twisted his arm from Bud's grasp, turned on his heel, and left the cabin.

For a moment all was silent. Then Verity began to cry loudly. Abe sat down heavily in a chair. "Oh Lord, but you've done it now, Leah. Revis ain't one you oughta make mad."

Bud and Cal looked at one another then quietly left the cabin. With shaking hands, Leah began to clear the table.

Chapter 17

IT WAS late at night when Leah finally was able to sneak away from the robbers' cabin. Revis hadn't returned, but his attack on Leah had frightened Verity so much that it had taken Leah hours to calm her. In her hysteria, the woman had started saying that Revis would come back and kill them all. Leah washed the frail woman and finally got her to sleep.

Abe started to tell Leah what he thought of her turning Revis down, but a few choice words from Leah made him leave the cabin. Most of the long day Leah spent cooking and at the noon meal she tried her best to thank Bud and Cal for helping her. The young men acted as if they didn't hear her. On impulse Leah kissed each one on the cheek.

"You ain't thinkin' about beddin' them dummies, are you?" Abe wailed. "You cain't turn down Revis for these goons."

"Abe," Leah said evenly, "I've just about heard enough from you. If you—."

Abe cut her off. "You make me or Revis too mad and I'll let him know about that rich boy you got hidden away. So think twice about threatenin' me."

Leah had not said much after that and Abe snickered in self-satisfaction and kept reminding her of little chores that needed doing.

It was night when she got everything cleared away and began

the long walk to the cabin where Wesley was hidden. All the way up she invented a story to give him as to why she hadn't been with him.

She was very tired when she entered the cabin, but her heart was pounding. Would Wesley be all right?

She lit a lantern by the bed and breathed a sigh of relief when she saw Wesley sleeping peacefully. He opened his eyes immediately.

"Leah?" he whispered.

"I'm here now. I brought you some food. Can you eat?"

He was silent as he watched her. "Where have you been, Leah?" he asked softly as he eased himself into a sitting position.

"Don't sit up! Lie still and I'll feed you." She tried to stop him, but he brushed her hands away.

"I want an answer."

There was a command in his voice and suddenly it was all too much for Leah. She collapsed onto the edge of the bed, buried her face in her hands, and began to cry.

"Leah, honey," he began, reaching out to her. "I didn't mean to make you cry."

"I . . . I'm sorry," she said, sobbing. "I'm just tired and so many things are happening."

"What sort of things?" he asked, his jaw clenched. "Who shot me and why were you gone all day?"

Leah wiped her eyes with the back of her hand. Tired or not she was now going to have to give the performance of her life. "Oh Wesley," she said. "It was such an awful accident. The men were hunting and they shot you by mistake. They helped me carry you here then left. I guess they were afraid you'd come after them when you recovered so they wanted to get away."

She took a deep breath. Now was the hard part. "After I got you here, a little girl appeared at the door. She begged me to come to her house. Her father was dead but her ma and six brothers and sisters were all down with the measles and there was only the girl to look after them. I felt that you'd be all right here alone since what you really needed was rest so I went with her. All day I've been cooking, cleaning, and nursing sick people."

She stopped abruptly and looked at him, her eyes begging him to believe her. She wasn't sure she could handle a fight with him on top of everything else.

Wesley's eyes bored into hers. Never in his life had he heard such a string of lies, yet she was begging him to believe her. There were circles under her eyes, her dress was food-stained. He knew no one lived in these woods, which was why he'd originally brought her to them. He also knew there was a nest of robbers here and if anyone tried to settle, they usually forfeited their lives.

Yet Leah was making up a story about a woman and seven kids living here. Right now he was too weak to get up and find out the truth about where she'd spent the day, and from Leah's look of fear she wasn't about to tell him what was really going on.

"That's just like you to take on other people's problems," he said, forcing a little smile.

"You . . . you don't mind?" Leah asked, holding her breath. Was he really going to believe her and not tear his wound open when he went searching for her?

"Leah," he said softly, "have I been such a tyrant that you'd believe I'd force you to stay with me and leave a widow and some children to die? Is that what you think?"

"No . . . I'm not sure I knew what to expect. You don't seem as badly injured as I thought. I was worried about you here alone."

And too scared of something to stay with me, he thought, but he took her hand and kissed the palm. "Can you stay or must you return?"

She dreaded the trip through the night down the mountainside, but she was afraid of remaining with Wes. Revis might start to look for her. "I have to return. Will you be all right?" She stood.

"I'll miss you but I'll survive. You go on and get as much sleep as you can. I'll just eat and sleep some more. My side hurts too much to do anything else." His voice was a study in tiredness.

"Yes," Leah murmured, and while she still had some energy she left the cabin.

"Goddamn her," Wesley muttered as soon as the door closed. What in the world had she gotten herself into? First she'd slipped off into the night to meet that good-for-nothing who'd visited their camp and all the next day she was jumpy as a rattlesnake. The next thing he knew he'd been shot, and while he was bleeding to death, she was fighting with that scoundrel.

Today Wesley had stayed in bed, eating food someone had left for him and waiting for his wife to return. And when he had seen her again, she'd looked ten years older and scared to death.

What the hell was going on?

Carefully, his hand on his bandaged ribs, he swung out of the bed. For all the blood he'd lost, the wound really wasn't that bad and he'd purposefully tried to get rid of Leah before she started wanting to inspect it. If she could lie, so could he, and his lie would be to tell her he was sicker than he was.

Outside he cocked his head and listened. It was easy to hear Leah thrashing her way down the mountainside. If she meant to do anything in secret, she was making a poor job of it.

As he started following her, he heard the sound of another person off to his left. It was a heavy person and Wesley guessed it was the big man he'd first seen in his camp. He was trailing Leah, staying just out of sight of her.

Soundlessly Wes slipped to the left, and as he traveled he picked up a large tree branch. With the size of the man, it'd take something heavy to get his attention.

Following the man and Leah, Wes traveled quite awhile before he halted above the cabin in the clearing. Silently he watched as Leah walked to the back, and in the moonlight he could see the thin man run to meet her.

The words of "Where the hell have you been?" floated up to him.

Wesley crouched on the ground, watching the scene, puzzled for a moment, wondering just exactly what Leah was involved in.

But the next moment he came upright because the stick he'd been carrying had someone's foot planted on it. He looked up into the eyes of the young giant he'd first seen yesterday. Instinctively Wesley drew his fist back, but someone behind him caught it. He swiveled about and saw a second giant.

Wes pulled his arm out of the man's grasp. "Either one of you touch my wife and I'll kill you!" he said, seething. He wasn't exactly in a position to threaten, but that didn't stop him.

"She is safe for now," one of the men said.

"Come back to your cabin now before you start to bleed."

Wes looked from one man to the other in the moonlight and suddenly he knew that what was going on involved great danger—and Leah was somehow caught up in it.

"My wife needs help, doesn't she?" he said, praying he could trust these two.

"Come to the cabin and we will talk," said one of the men.

Four hours later, Wesley was again alone in the little cabin. The lantern was out and it was dark in the room, but Wes was sure his anger was enough to provide half the world with light.

The two young men, Bud and Cal, had difficulty at first in talking, almost as if their voices had never been used very much. But, after some persuading and when they saw Wes's intense interest, they started talking as if they couldn't stop.

They didn't remember their parents but had been adopted by Revis's mother when they were three years old and already so big that people stared at them. Even as a boy, Revis had been a thief, yet he'd been charming too. While other people treated Bud and Cal as if they were freaks because of their size and their silence, Revis had been good to them. Revis's mother used the boys as an extra team of oxen, so when Revis suggested they travel westward, Bud and Cal had agreed.

Now they'd been living in the Kentucky forest for four years and even as good as Revis was to them and as much as they owed him, they didn't like the way he treated the women he brought to the cabin. A few times Bud and Cal had tried to help the women, but the women had screamed in terror, especially after Abe made up stories about the young men.

But Leah was different. She hadn't taken Abe's word that they were stupid and she'd been kind to them.

"Leah takes on everyone's problems," Wesley muttered. "Will you help her escape?"

Bud and Cal looked at each other. "She will not go without you. Abe says that if she leaves he will tell Revis where you are."

"Revis would kill you," Cal said flatly. "He does not like other men touching his women."

"Neither do I!" Wesley snapped before beginning to question the men about all of Revis's operation. Wes knew that thieves had been robbing the westward travelers for years, before Revis came west. All Bud and Cal knew was that Revis reported to someone called the Dancer and they knew nothing about him.

"I'd like to find out who this Dancer is," Wesley said thoughtfully.

The men rose. "We have to return now. Revis will be back. You just get well and we will watch out for your pretty lady."

"She is a lady, isn't she?" Wes said as they left.

Now he sat alone, thinking over what he'd just heard. He was impressed, very impressed, that Leah was risking so much to protect him. Thinking back over their marriage, he hadn't done much to make her love him. For just a moment he thought of Kimberly and wondered how she'd have reacted in the same situation. He was certain Kim would never risk her pretty neck or her cherished virginity to help anyone.

"I'll make it up to you, Leah," he whispered into the darkness. Right now he must leave Leah's protection to the boys, but when he was well and didn't think he might bleed to death at the least movement, he was going to protect her himself. And further, he was going to see if he could do a little more for her than just be a burden.

Chapter 18

LEAH DIDN'T sleep much that night. She kept having terrible dreams about all that could happen to Wesley alone in that cabin. Who knew what these woods held? That bear they'd seen could tear down the door and get him. Or even worse, Revis could find him and put a bullet through his heart.

When she woke, her head hurt and her eyes were swollen.

"You better stop lookin' like that," Abe said as she started breakfast. "Revis likes pretty women."

"I don't care what your Revis likes. I'll do what I please."

Abe leaned closer to her. "It better please you to please him or it just might please me to tell him the whereabouts of your rich lover."

With shaking hands, Leah returned to the skillet full of frying bacon.

It wasn't until after breakfast, when she'd cleared everything away and was starting the noon meal, that she saw Revis. He was leaning against the side of the cabin, trimming his nails with a long, thin-bladed knife.

Leah jumped, then put her chin up and walked past him.

He caught her hair and wrapped it about his wrist, pulling her toward him. "So, the lady's too good to speak to the thief."

"Leave me alone! I don't want your attentions and I have work to do. Bud and Cal—."

He jerked her head back. "You'll regret turning them against me," he said, putting his lips near hers.

Leah saw him smile then felt a tug at her head. The next moment he pushed her away and held up a long strand of her hair in triumph. Leah's hand flew to the back of her head, feeling the ragged edge where he'd cut it. As she ran into the house, Revis's laugh followed her.

All day Leah worked herself nearly to the breaking point, cooking, cleaning, ignoring Abe's jibes, protecting Verity, who cried when any man came too near her.

And everywhere she looked, Revis seemed to be there watching her. He'd suddenly appear out of the forest or from behind the woodpile or he'd be standing silently in a corner of the cabin. He never got close enough to touch her, since after he'd cut away her hair either Bud or Cal was always close to her. Twice Leah caught Revis looking at the boys as if in speculation.

At sundown Revis disappeared and not long afterward Leah told Bud she was going to visit her husband. The big man nodded once and Leah wasn't really sure if he understood her or not. If she ever got time, she was going to find out if the young men were as stupid as Abe said they were.

"You better be back here afore Revis comes back," Abe warned, but Leah ignored him.

The lying was what was destroying her, Leah decided as she trudged up the mountainside. She seemed to be telling everyone a different story. Wesley was lying alone in a cabin, no doubt cursing his luck at being stuck with a Simmons. He'd decided to stay married to Leah because she was more "fun," but where was the pleasure now?

When Leah opened the cabin door, Wesley knew he'd never seen a more forlorn-looking person. She looked so miserable he almost wanted to laugh. Ever since he'd known her no matter what was dished out to her, she fought back. He never felt guilty about telling her what he thought because if she disagreed, she did so loudly.

But the woman entering the cabin now looked as if she'd given up, as if she didn't want to bother with life's hardships any longer.

Immediately Wes knew there was only one cure for her misery: he was going to make love to her.

He held out his hand to her.

With a frown Leah ignored his hand. "I brought you some food."

"I'm not hungry. Come sit by me."

That's all I need, Leah thought, Revis after me during the day, Wesley pestering me at night. "I need to get back."

"Leah," Wes said with surprising firmness for one so ill. "Sit down."

She didn't really feel much like having a fight and besides, what could he do?

When she sat on the edge of the bed, Wes put an arm around her and drew her back so she was leaning against the wall. He nestled his big, warm body next to her small, rigid one.

"Chicken, potatoes, beans, cornbread," he said softly, looking inside the basket she'd brought.

With his free hand, he took the basket, leaned across her, and set it on the floor. That done, he didn't quite straighten up but kept lying half across her.

"I . . . I must go." She halfheartedly pushed at him.

"Leah," he murmured, trailing a finger down her cheek, "you aren't afraid of me, are you?"

"Of course not," she snapped. "I've got to go, that's all. I'm not afraid of any—"

She stopped because he kissed her, not just a simple kiss but a long, lingering, soft kiss that began to take the tiredness out of her.

"You were saying?" he said, caressing her cheek and neck with his big hand.

"Any man," she said, trying not to look at him. "I'm not afraid of any man, any . . ."

Wesley began kissing her neck in hot little kisses that were oh, so very nice.

"It occurred to me today, Leah, that even though you've been married for years and even had a baby, you've never been made love to."

She pulled away from him. "That's absurd. How can I have a baby if . . . I mean you . . . the night of the storm we . . ."

"My beautiful wife, I thought you were a prostitute and used you as such. Had I known that was our early wedding night I assure you I'd have acted differently."

"Differently?" she asked, curious. It was rather nice to be held by someone, to be touched and caressed.

"Wait a minute!" she said with a gasp. "You can't touch me. I swore you'd have to take whatever you wanted from me, that I'd never give in to you. Just because I'm a Simmons doesn't mean—"

"Shut up, Leah," he murmured, "and consider yourself forced." His lips took hers and held them—and held them until Leah's arms slipped around his neck and pulled him closer. With one arm he pulled her down into the bed, one thigh going over both of hers.

When he pulled away from her, he saw wonder in her eyes and Wes felt a wave of guilt that this woman was his wife yet he'd taught her nothing. Slowly, with great patience, he began to caress her body.

The dress she wore was dirty, stained, and very loose on her. With a practiced hand, he began to undo the buttons down her front.

"Wesley, I don't think . . ." Leah began. "Maybe we shouldn't . . . oh dear!"

His hand slipped inside her dress, his warmth going through

her layers of underclothes. He kissed her again as he lifted her off the bed and slipped the dress from her shoulders.

As the dress lay about her waist, it was Wesley's turn to look at her in wonder. Never had he seen women's underwear like this. Nearly transparent fabric showed the rosy pink crests of her nipples, floated downward, and barely concealed her creamy skin.

Leah immediately turned a pretty shade of pink. "Nicole's dressmaker thought that since my outerwear had to be coarse, my underwear should be . . . should be . . ."

"Let's see the rest of you," Wes said eagerly, and before Leah could say a word he lifted her and removed four cotton petticoats to reveal lacy drawers that showed her long, firm legs to advantage.

"Leah," Wes said in a slightly shaky voice as he grabbed her to him and began to kiss her passionately.

Leah responded instantly. She'd never been taught that she shouldn't enjoy sex, and as a result she acted with as few inhibitions as a child. She began kissing him back with enthusiasm.

Wesley, surprised for a moment, perhaps remembering Kimberly's rationing of kisses, smiled with pleasure at his wife's response. His hands began a journey down her body, and her warm skin, barely covered by the silken fabric, excited him more.

While kissing her neck he began to unfasten the buttons to her underwear.

Leah was losing herself to his touch. Her sexual experience consisted of one quick fumble more than a year and a half ago. This caressing was different and it was sending the oddest feelings through her body. Her fingers clutched at Wesley's head, entwining in his soft hair.

She protested when he pulled his mouth from hers and groaned with pleasure when his lips touched her throat. When his lips encircled her nipple, she lay still as one shock wave after another went through her.

"Wesley?" she asked in such a surprised way, her head coming up.

He paid no attention to her but continued to make love to her breasts.

Leah swallowed hard, her head rolled back, and she arched her body upwards in an instinctive reaction. Wesley's hard hands gripped her waist tightly as his hot mouth moved down her body.

She grabbed handfuls of his shirt, caught buckskin fringe in her mouth. "Skin," she murmured. "Let me touch you."

Wesley came out of his clothes instantly and soon knelt over her wearing nothing but a bandage across his ribs.

Some part of Leah's mind told her she should be concerned about his wound, but truthfully she didn't care if it tore apart—at least right now she didn't care. Her eyes trailed down to his swollen manhood and with no shyness she clasped it in both hands.

Wesley gave a deathlike groan and fell on her, kissing every part of her he could reach before climbing on top of her. He'd been worried she'd be afraid of him, but her eagerness was more than he could bear.

She arched to meet his first thrusts, threw her legs about his hips and pushed. Wes grabbed her and rolled to his back so she was on top. His hands on her waist, he guided her up and down, sometimes watching her, glorying in the look on her face, her expression of pure, undiluted pleasure.

When Wes could stand no more, he flung her to her back and with two blinding thrusts, brought both of them to a height of pleasure neither had experienced before.

Both lay together, locked in each other's arms, until Wes raised himself on one elbow and looked down at her. Her eyes were glazed, her mouth soft, her hair in sweaty curls about her face. There was wonder in Wesley's eyes: to think this hot little beauty was his very own wife, to have forever! Anytime he wanted her, she was his.

Leah opened her eyes and the look she saw on Wesley's face made her come back to reality.

"I have to go," she said abruptly.

He frowned because he didn't want her to go, but he knew she must. Right now the only way he could protect her was by letting her go, entrusting her care to the two large strangers. "Go then," he said with more harshness than he meant. It was difficult for his pride to allow what his common sense was forcing him to do.

Leah heard only the coolness in his voice and quickly she began to dress. She didn't say a word as she slipped from the cabin into the darkness. But halfway down the mountain she sat down on the ground and began to cry.

She was never, never going to be a lady! Not all the cosmetics, pretty clothes, and hair rinses in the world were going to change her into a lady. She made vows of chastity, then at the first opportunity, she frolicked in the bed with a man who had done all manner of rotten things to her.

At each thought she cried harder. What would Regan or Nicole do now? No doubt Revis would see that they were ladies and he wouldn't even try to molest them. It was only because she was a Simmons that Revis wanted her. And now that she'd shown Wes she wasn't anything like a lady, he'd probably be glad to turn her over to someone like Revis who was her own type.

After a while she tried to collect herself and started down the mountain. Wesley Stanford might think she was of the same class as Revis, but Leah knew she wasn't.

The cabin was silent when she entered, except for Abe's snoring in a corner. There were no beds, so Leah took a place on the floor beside Verity, who often whimpered in her sleep.

The next morning Leah woke to the loud sound of Revis's boots on the floor.

"Get up all of you!" he said with a growl. "You," he said, addressing Leah, "where are the boys?"

Leah refused to be frightened of him. "Behind you," she shot at him.

Revis gave her an angry look before turning. "I got a wagon sunk in the mud about two miles down the road. You two go get it out and Abe, you lazy nothin', go help them."

"Yes, Mr. Revis," Abe said cheerfully. "Come on, you big louts, let's get to work. We'll have it out in no time."

Leah held her breath for a moment, afraid Revis would stay with her, but he left with the others. Breathing a sigh of relief, she started cooking breakfast. No doubt the boys would be even hungrier after a morning's exercise.

It was while she was reaching for a slab of bacon that hands caught her about the waist.

"They're gone now," Revis said into her ear.

She twisted away from him. "Don't touch me or—"

"Or what?" he half purred, advancing on her. "You can't get away from me."

Leah kept backing. "Why do you even want me?" she asked. "You're a good-looking man and you could have your choice of women. There must be women prettier than I am who are quite willing to have you." She backed into a wall.

He grabbed her arm. "Ladies like you always think they're too good for somebody like me. You think you're better than highwaymen."

"Ladies!" she exclaimed. "Abe is my brother. Do you think any *lady* could be related to that piece of filth?" Keep him talking, she thought. Maybe the boys will get back before he touches me.

"I'm not convinced he's your brother." Revis drew her to him. "What makes you stay here? Each night you leave here and go up the mountain. But you come back."

He smiled at her gasp.

"Did you know the boys follow you? And when I try to follow, one of those stupid brothers of mine stops me. What do the three of you do on top of that mountain?"

"You're disgusting. Now release me before they return."

"We have hours. I sunk that wagon in two feet of mud. They'll never get it out. And while they're wallowing, I'm going to have myself a lady."

"No." She twisted in his grasp.

"What's up the mountain, little sister? Shall we go have a look? Would you like to go with me and see what we can find?"

"No! I mean, why not? There's nothing up there except a little privacy. I need to get away from the stench of you and this hideous place."

"So why don't you leave? Why do you stay and cook and take care of that nothing that used to be a woman?"

Leah couldn't think of a quick answer to his question.

"Come on, lady, tell me."

"I promised to help my brother. He did something for me once and I owe him," she said in one breath.

"Abe never did anything for anybody. What are you hiding?"

Before Leah could answer, Bud appeared in the doorway, the lower half of his body covered in mud. Silently he walked across the room and put his hand on Revis's shoulder.

With a flash of hatred, Revis whirled on the young man. "You got it out already?" he snapped.

Bud nodded once.

Leah clutched at the wall behind her as Revis shot her a malevolent look before leaving the cabin. "Thank you," she whispered to Bud.

For the rest of the day Revis seemed always to be near her and that night she was afraid he would be able to follow her and find Wesley. She didn't dare make the trek up the mountain and risk discovery.

"Will you take this to him?" she whispered to Bud, holding out a food-laden basket, her eyes pleading.

He nodded briefly but said nothing. Leah wasn't sure how much she could trust the boys, but now she had to depend on them. "Don't let Wesley see you," she said. "He doesn't know that I'm . . . where I am."

Later Leah lay alone on the coarse blankets on the cabin floor and remembered the night before in Wesley's arms. Her husband wanted her because she wasn't a lady and Revis wanted her because he thought she was a lady.

"Men!" she hissed into the darkness and Verity, waking, crawled nearer to Leah.

"Ssh," Leah soothed as Verity began to whimper. "No one will hurt you."

But even as she said it, Leah knew she was lying. Revis obviously didn't like being thwarted and Leah knew he was going to do his best to hurt her.

Chapter 19

LEAH WOKE to even louder whimpers from Verity and when she opened her eyes she saw Revis kneeling over the woman, caressing her arm. Verity began to inch away, her head sliding up the cabin wall.

"Leave her alone!" Leah said.

"Will you take her place?"

"No, but——."

"She's not like you, Leah," Revis said, using both hands to caress Verity's arms. "This one is easily terrorized. She doesn't have much of a mind now, but I could make her lose what she has. All I have to do is . . ."

He broke off as his hands went to Verity's throat.

"Stop it!" Leah commanded, grabbing his forearm. "I'll call Bud and Cal. They won't let you harm her."

"I won't harm her. All I'll do is let her see me. Wherever she looks that's where I'll be."

Leah knew instantly that what he was talking about would work. Verity had a very tenuous grasp on sanity as it was with Revis intimidating her she'd not last long. "Why?" Leah whispered. "Why would you hurt her? She's nothing to you."

"Because I want something from you," Revis said. "I want you to take a ride with me."

This took Leah aback. "A ride? Where? And when you get me away from the cabin do you attack me?"

Abruptly, Revis moved his hands away from Verity and sat back on his haunches. "Maybe I've been a little too rough on you. Your brother'd spent an hour an' a half telling me how pretty you were and how willing you'd be to jump into my bed. So when you resisted me I thought it was an act, but when you used my own brothers against me . . ." He gave her a reproachful look. "I'm only human, Leah, and I guess I got a little angry."

Leah sat quite still, looking at him, her mouth half-open in astonishment.

"And I don't want to terrorize this young lady either, but I want to show you that I'm not such a bad person and I know the only way you'll come riding with me is if I blackmail you."

Leah looked at his handsome dark face, his eyes begging her to believe him.

Revis caught both her hands in his. "I know I'm a thief, but maybe you could help me find a way out. Just get to know me a little, Leah. Let me show you that I'm human. I swear by everything I cherish that I won't hurt you. I won't touch you at all. We'll just ride down the mountain a little way, talk some, look at the flowers. That's all. I swear to you."

"I . . . I don't know," she stumbled. "The boys wouldn't—."

"The boys can't know!" Revis snapped. "Now that you've turned my own brothers against me even they don't trust me. If you and I go off together and come back and you've not been harmed maybe I can win their trust again. Do you know what it's like to lose the people you love most?"

Leah thought she just might cry at that question. She'd lost everyone she'd ever loved. Even the man she'd spent her childhood loving had turned against her. "Yes," she whispered, "I know what it feels like to lose people."

"Then help me," he begged. "Give me a chance to prove to

my brothers that I still deserve their respect. And let me show you the man behind the villain."

He grinned at her then and his smile, which she'd never seen before, was charming. What could it hurt if she rode with him? And if she didn't he'd no doubt keep his threats about terrifying Verity.

"Please, Leah," he said softly, squeezing her hands.

"All right," she agreed. "How do we get away?"

"Right after breakfast slip into the trees. Tell one of the boys you need privacy. They'll obey you. I'll wait for you at the bottom of the ridge." He smiled again. "Thank you, Leah. This means a lot to me."

With that he stood and left the cabin.

While she was cooking breakfast, Leah thought about Revis's words. Who was she to judge a person when her own brother and father were criminals? Perhaps Revis wasn't all bad. Maybe some of him was good. He did take care of Abe and his young brothers who were possibly too stupid to be able to take care of themselves. Maybe there were extenuating circumstances. Maybe there were reasons why he thieved. Maybe she *could* help him, show him there were other ways.

By the time she'd cleared away breakfast, she was actually looking forward to her ride. As she picked up the empty dishpan, Verity caught her arm.

"Don't go," Verity said in a hoarse whisper. "Revis is evil."

In spite of herself, Leah pulled away from Verity. She couldn't very well say what she thought, that Verity was frightened of her own shadow. Verity was afraid of Bud and Cal. No doubt she'd warn Leah not to be alone with one of those harmless giants.

"I'll be fine," Leah said patronizingly. "You just rest and when I return I'll bring you some flowers."

"Leah," Verity pleaded.

"Go rest," Leah half ordered and the light went out of Verity's eyes. Slowly the scared little woman turned back toward her corner.

Leah clucked her tongue for a moment over the woman's lack of courage, but she didn't waste time thinking about Verity. As soon as she started getting along with Revis, she could get Wesley out of the forest.

A half hour later she was running down the mountainside. It'd been quite easy to escape the boys and now she was looking forward to a morning away from work. When she saw Revis, she smiled tentatively.

"Come on." He half laughed. "Your horse awaits you, my lady."

At first Leah was so pleased to be away from her worries for a few minutes that she barely noticed Revis. It was hot and the air was hazy with mist—and it all looked beautiful.

"There's fire in you, Leah," Revis said beside her. "You'd be a good partner for a man."

"I'm a married woman," she said, patting the horse's neck.

"And where is your husband?"

"In Sweetbriar, Kentucky," she said quickly. "Are we going anyplace in particular?"

"Just down the mountain. Any man who'd let you out of his sight would be a fool. I could give you a silk dress."

She smiled at him. "I have several silk dresses, thank you. And I don't think my husband would want me to remain here." How she wished that were true!

"Is there nothing I can do to persuade you to stay with me?"

In spite of telling herself it didn't matter, it was very nice to be desired by this good-looking man. He thought she was a lady even though he knew she was a Simmons.

The woods began to thin as stumps showed where travelers had cut down trees.

"Isn't that the Wilderness Trail down there?" she asked,

looking at the deep, permanent wagon ruts. "We'd better go back."

"No," he said. "There's a stream across the trail. I want to show you something."

"But if someone sees you . . . I mean . . ."

"I know what you mean, Leah," he said heavily. "Could I show you something now?"

"Of course." They were sitting on their horses in the middle of the well-worn trail and just a little way away was the smoke from a camp fire.

Out of his pocket Revis pulled a black silk handkerchief, and while Leah watched he tied it about his face.

She didn't like what she saw. She'd almost forgotten that he was a thief. "I think we'd better return."

"Not yet, my lofty princess," he said as he grabbed the reins of her horse.

The next minute they were thundering down the trail toward the camp fire smoke, Leah barely able to hang onto the saddle. Once she screamed "No," but Revis paid no attention.

They burst like storm clouds into the clearing where two wagons sat. The settlers, each involved in some task about the campsite, looked up and froze.

Revis shot one man through the forehead.

Aghast, for a moment Leah couldn't move. Then, in one motion, she was off her horse and onto the ground, running toward the dead man. A woman near her screamed.

Revis rode his horse near to where Leah hovered over the man. "Get their goods, Leah," he said coolly.

"You animal!" she screamed and began to beat Revis with her fists.

Revis leveled his pistol and shot the woman beside Leah in the shoulder.

By now there were five settlers and two children standing by the wagons, looking in horror at the masked man and the people near him.

"If you don't obey me you'll have to choose who'll die next," Revis said as he pulled another pistol from his saddle.

The bleeding woman at Leah's feet began to cry.

"You have about ten seconds to obey me, Leah," Revis said.

"What . . . what do I do?" She knew that now only action counted and words were useless.

"Get that man's hat and fill it with whatever they have." He pointed with the pistol. "Any of you give my partner any trouble and I'll put a bullet through your head."

"I'm not—," Leah began but stopped. When she stood before the settler, he looked at her with hate.

"The Lord will see you burn for this," the man hissed at her as he handed her his hat.

"No, please, I—."

"Listen to him, Leah," Revis said. "All of you, I want to introduce Mrs. Leah Simmons Stanford of Virginia and soon to be of Sweetbriar, Kentucky."

With shaking hands, Leah walked in front of the settlers as they put their watches and rings into the hat. One woman spit a great glob into Leah's face. Leah only halfheartedly wiped it away.

"Come on, Leah, honey," Revis said coaxingly. "We need to get back and these good people need to bury their dead."

At her horse she hesitated.

"If you stayed here they'd tear you to bits and if you don't go with me I'll kill two more. I think I'd like doing that," he said so that only she heard.

As if she were in a daze, Leah mounted her horse. Revis again took the reins and pulled her with him into the forest.

Just after crossing the Wilderness Trail, he stopped and pulled off his mask. "I told you I'd make you pay for using my brothers against me," he said. "In a few days everyone for miles will know about the lovely Mrs. Stanford who is a thief as well as a murderess."

"No," Leah whispered.

"And now, my pretty Leah, you have a real reason to stay with me. You leave my protection and the secrecy of our cabin and you'll be arrested and hanged by the neck until dead." With that he began to laugh. "You'll get used to it," he laughed. "On the next raid you'll know just what to do. And since you'll already be well-known, we won't have to cover that pretty face of yours

"Let's go," he said, laughing. "Blood always makes me hungry."

He led her horse up the intricate, secret path to the cabin while Leah sat on the horse and knew her life was over.

Chapter 20

BY THE time Revis and Leah reached the cabin, Revis was cursing her because she looked as if she were living death. He didn't want any more women like Verity, who'd never recovered from seeing Revis shoot her husband. He wanted a woman who wasn't afraid.

At the cabin he dismounted, leaving her still on top of her horse. He stalked inside, threw some food into a sack, and returned to his horse. Still cursing his luck with women, he angrily pulled Leah from her horse and stood her on the ground. Immediately she collapsed in a heap, drawing her knees into her chest. She didn't cry or make a sound; she just lay there.

With a sneer at her, Revis rode away.

Hours later, Abe found her there.

"Damn you, Leah, you're supposed to feed us! It's time to eat and ain't nothin' cooked. And what're you doin' layin' in the sun? You'll get burnt and then Revis won't like you anymore."

Leah didn't move. Her eyes were open but she didn't seem to see anything.

"Leah?" He knelt beside her. "You been hurt?" There was concern in his voice. "You gonna talk to me or you rather just lay around?"

Tentatively he touched her forehead. Her skin was hot, but she didn't move at his touch. Frowning, he stood upright and gave a high-pitched whistle.

Quickly both Bud and Cal appeared from the forest.

"Look here at my sister," Abe said indignantly. "Either of you know what's wrong with her?"

Cal knelt by Leah, his big body shading her. Slowly he reached out a hand and touched her cheek. He looked up at his brother, seemed to get an answer to his silent question, and the next moment he lifted Leah into his arms.

"Hey!" Abe protested. "You can't do that. You leave her here. I'll take care of her."

Cal started toward the forest with Leah.

"You hear me, you overgrown piece of dog crap?"

Bud planted himself in front of Abe.

"Here! Get out of the way," Abe commanded. "You can't take my sister off to who-knows-where. And that rich husband of hers ain't gonna want her if she's sick. She ain't got nobody but me."

For all Abe's protesting, he stayed where he was when both brothers disappeared into the woods.

Wesley was outside the cabin, shirtless, walking around, flexing and unflexing his arms, trying to get strength back into his side. He halted when he heard the footsteps coming up the path. Usually Bud and Cal didn't use the briar-covered path but came their own way through the underbrush.

Wesley slipped out of sight until he was sure his visitors were indeed the boys. When he saw Cal carrying Leah, he ran forward.

"Is she hurt?" he asked as he took her from the young men. "What happened to her? Did that Revis—? I thought you two were watching her."

Leah lay limp in his arms, her eyes closed as if she were unconscious. He took her into the cabin and put her on the bed. He kept a bucket of water in the cabin and now he dipped a cloth in it, a cloth that had once been part of his bandages, and put the cool fabric on her forehead.

Leah groaned, turned to her side, drew her knees into her chest, and lay still.

"You two better start talking," Wes said, his eyes narrowed. "And fast."

Cal spoke first. "She told me she wanted privacy this morning and we gave it but after an hour we began to look for her."

"We followed horse tracks down the mountain and at the bottom we heard shots," Bud said.

"By the time we got there Revis had killed a man and shot a woman. He and Leah were riding fast back up the mountain. When we got to the cabin she was like that and Revis was gone."

Wesley walked away from the cot. "I thought all this Revis did was rob people."

"He kills people when he feels like it," Bud said with a stiff jaw.

Wesley banged his fist against the wall. "What a fool I was! How could I have left her there? I should have taken her away immediately."

"You would have bled to death," Cal said flatly.

Wes was quiet for a moment as he turned to stare at Leah. "No doubt she witnessed the shootings and that's what's wrong with her."

Suddenly he crossed the cabin in two strides, grabbed her shoulders hard, and lifted her to a sitting position. "Damn you, Leah!" he yelled in her face. "Why do you think you have to save the world? Why couldn't you have told me the truth? Why did I have to be so stupid as to believe you? I thought you'd be all right and now look at you. Damn you! Damn you!"

Wesley began shaking her and kept it up until Cal put his hand on Wes's shoulder. Abruptly, Wes stopped and saw there were tears in Leah's eyes. He pulled her to him fiercely. "That's it, sweetheart, cry all you want. You're safe now."

Bud and Cal silently left the cabin.

Once Leah's tears started, she couldn't seem to stop them.

She clung to Wesley with all her strength and cried against his bare shoulder. When her body started convulsing, he made her drink water.

"Now tell me about it," he said patiently.

"No," she whispered. "No."

"Leah." He took her chin in his hand and tipped her swollen, red face upwards. "I never believed that cock-and-bull story of yours about the sick kids and I've always known about Revis and your brother Abe. Right now I want you to tell me everything that's happened."

"I have to stay here forever," she said, hiccupping. "They'll hang me."

"You're making no sense whatever. You saw Revis kill someone today, didn't you?"

She pulled away from him. "I *helped!* I held a man's hat and collected goods. I *stole!*"

She waited to see the shock on his face, but there was none.

"What did this Revis do to force you to steal? What did he threaten you with?"

Again Leah's eyes filled with tears. She had thought Wesley would believe she stole because it was her nature to do so. "He said he'd kill more people if I hesitated."

"Bastard," Wes said under his breath. "Anything else?"

She didn't want to tell him the rest. Never again could she live amid decent people. "Revis wore a mask," she whispered, "but I . . . I didn't."

"Oh," Wes said, glad it wasn't worse. "I'm sure they saw you were forced into it and that actually you were saving their lives."

"No!" she screamed and jumped off the bed. "You don't understand. Revis told the people I was his partner. He told them my name, that I was Mrs. Leah Simmons Stanford of Virginia, soon to live in Sweetbriar, Kentucky. He made me a criminal. He made me a thief. I can never leave here! If I do they'll hang me."

"Leah," he said in sympathy as he walked toward her and tried to pull her into his arms.

"Get away from me! Don't ever touch me again! You're the clean Mr. Stanford. Nothing like this would ever happen to you. They'd take one look at the Stanford name and know you're innocent but me, a Simmons, I'd—."

He grabbed her shoulders. "Stop feeling sorry for yourself. According to our marriage papers you're a Stanford too. Look, Leah," he said, calming himself. "All this isn't as bad as you think. There are courts of law and we'll hire the best lawyers. Bud and Cal can testify about how Abe forced you into Revis's camp and I'll bet someone today heard Revis order you to participate. There are ways to get out of this, even if you are accused. So stop saying you have to stay here."

Leah was sure she'd never wanted to believe anything as much as she wanted to believe this. "Do you think so?" she whispered. "Is there a chance?"

"More than a chance. Now let me see a smile because I'm sending you out of here right now."

"Here? You mean back to Revis's cabin?"

Wes's jaw hardened. "You're not going back to that place ever again. I'm going to send you down the mountain with Bud and Cal. They'll take you to Sweetbriar. I have friends there and if need be they'll hide you until I can get there and straighten everything out."

"But where will you be?"

"I have a little unfinished business yet. I owe somebody something. Now come on." He grabbed her hand and pulled her outside. "Bud and Cal'll take care of you and Revis won't be able to harm you again."

She pulled out of his grasp and squinted up at him in the sunlight. "Why aren't you going to Sweetbriar with me?"

"I told you, I have work to do."

Leah thought for a moment and then sat down on the ground, her arms folded.

"Just what is that supposed to mean?" He glared down at her.

"I'm not leaving here. You're up to something and I don't like it."

Anger surged through Wesley's entire body as he grabbed her shoulders and lifted her off the ground. "*You* think *I* am up to something?" He seethed into her face. "I have lain here helpless for days while you got yourself into one mess after another and you tell me you don't trust *me?* Leah, for two cents I'd turn you over my knee. When are you going to realize that you can't run the world singlehandedly? I could have gotten us out of this days ago if you'd only asked for my help. But no, Mrs. Stanford has to do everything her own way. I've tried, Leah, I've tried really hard to be nice to you. You wanted to handle all this on your own so I let you. It was my own stupidity that kept me from realizing how much real danger you were in."

He dropped her to her own feet. "Damn you again and again! I don't know any man in the world who'd stand for what I've stood from you. You insult me, tell me I'm fickle then act as if I'm some helpless idiot you have to protect. You know what your problem is, Leah?"

She looked up at his furious, handsome face with wide eyes. "No. What's my problem?"

"You've always had control, that's what. From what I gather, you commanded that whole family of yours like you were some general, and on the trip here you took on everybody else's work and actually ran the whole trip."

Leah just stood there, blinking.

"My patience is all used up now and I've had enough of lying back and letting you have your way. Starting today you're going to be my wife and you're going to honor that part in the wedding vows that says *obey*. You understand me?"

"Maybe," she said, but at his look she changed her mind. "I understand you thoroughly."

"Good! Your first order is that you are leaving these woods right now. I'm staying here because I plan to find out more about who this Revis's boss is. And when I get ready I'll return to you and our farm but not before then. Is that clear?"

"Yes," she said thoughtfully. "Revis doesn't do all the robberies on his own?"

"Somebody else organizes them. Revis is nothing but a two-bit thief, not smart enough to run the business. But he knows the identity of his boss and I want that information. Are you ready to go?"

"I'd like to know who'd do this awful thing, too."

"Good," he said impatiently. "I'll tell you when I get home." He gave a whistle. "Bud and Cal will take you home."

"Won't Revis miss them?"

"I have some plans." He glared at her. "None of which I plan to tell you. All I want for the next few months is to know you're safe. I don't need or want your interference in any of this. I'll clean out this band of thieves once and for all."

"All by yourself?" she asked aghast.

"You were planning to take care of Revis and me all by yourself. Did you think that Revis was going to shake your hand good-bye when you decided to leave?" His voice softened. "Here're the boys. Now give me a kiss good-bye."

"I don't like this," she murmured as he pulled her into his arms. "Won't you need some help?"

"Shut up, Leah."

She didn't say another word as his mouth closed on hers.

"I wish we had more time," he said against her lips.

Leah gave herself over to his kiss, losing all thoughts of Revis and his boss.

When Wesley pulled away from her she stared up at him because she knew she loved him. Actually, she'd never really stopped. He'd done some awful things to her and maybe she should hate him, but she didn't.

"And what's that look for?" He smiled down at her. "If I weren't so concerned about getting you out of here I'd take you back into the cabin."

She leaned into him, causing him to frown in puzzlement.

He smoothed a strand of hair back from her eyes. "I don't think I've ever noticed how pretty you are. Even after days of sleeplessness you're the prettiest girl I ever saw. Leah." He paused. "Thank you for what you did, for putting yourself in Revis's clutches in order to save me. It was . . . kind of you."

Pulling away from him, she thought she might just start crying again. "I'll see you in Sweetbriar?" she whispered.

Grinning, he kissed her lustily again. "I'm not about to tarry when I have you waiting for me. Now scoot." He turned her about and smacked her firmly on the seat.

An hour later, Leah was halfway down the mountainside with Bud in front of her, Cal behind—and already Leah was making plans.

Once out of Wesley's arms, she'd been able to think more clearly. If she went ahead to Sweetbriar as he'd told her to do, she just might face legal charges. Her only hope was to get someone to hide her and who was she going to ask? Kimberly? Justin?

And thinking of Kimberly, would Wesley return to pining for her if Leah wasn't around to remind him that she was alive? At night when he was alone, would he remember Kim's pretty blonde face rather than Leah's tearstained one? He just now had noticed that Leah was pretty, but would he *remember* it?

Tramping down the mountain, Leah kept thinking. Maybe if she had more time with Wes he might grow to love her. Didn't he already say he liked her? And wouldn't he need help with Revis? How was he going to find out all the information he wanted? And too, Wesley said he had a debt to pay, but didn't Leah owe Revis something for making her a part of his murders?

The more she thought about it the more she was sure she should return to help Wesley.

But first she'd have to escape Bud and Cal. As they walked, she began to look for a hiding place, a place to spend the night all alone in the big, lonely forest. She shivered.

"You would like to rest?" Bud asked from behind her.

"Oh no," she said sweetly, smiling up at the big man. "I'm just fine." Wesley, she thought, was worth the trial of being alone in the forest.

Chapter 21

ESCAPING THE boys was harder than Leah had imagined, and hiding from them was even more difficult. She practically buried herself under leaves and shrubs, then held her breath as Bud and Cal walked all around her. After a nearly silent conversation, they separated and went north and south. Leah didn't move but stayed in her crouched position until her legs ached.

At sundown the young men returned and inspected the ground carefully. They seemed to know she was near them and wanted to give her time to emerge from hiding. But Leah waited until nightfall before she crept out of her hole. Bud and Cal were nowhere to be seen as she started up the mountain.

Every sound made her jump and after only a few yards, her spine was rigid with fear. It wasn't until after hours of struggling that she felt someone was near her. "Revis!" she exclaimed, then stood still.

"Bud and Cal," she said with a sigh. "I know you're there so come out."

As if they were part of the forest themselves, the young men emerged to stand beside her.

Perhaps she should have felt that she'd been caught, but she suddenly felt safer and was actually glad to see them. With a grin she looked up at them. "Now what happens? Do you take me screaming down the mountain? I warn you, I *will* scream. And kick, too," she added as an afterthought.

The men seemed puzzled by her. "Why do you want to return to Revis? Your husband wants you safe."

"And who will keep Wesley safe with both of you gone? And Revis will hurt Verity because there's no one to protect her and he'll probably beat Abe because I've escaped."

"You care for your brother?" Cal asked.

"Perhaps. I'm not sure. I do know I can't run away and let Wesley take on Revis by himself. Will you help me?"

Bud looked at Cal.

As Leah watched, the two young giants seemed to engage in silent communication. Abe had said they were brothers to Revis, but right now she wondered how close they really were.

"Do either of you ever ride with Revis on his robberies?"

"No," Bud said.

"Then why . . . ? Why do you stay with him?"

"He pays us for firewood and game and for watching his cabin to see that no one comes near."

Leah's curiosity was piqued. "Does he pay you well?"

"We have bought land in the town at the foot of the mountain. We are going to be farmers."

"The town . . . ? You mean Wesley's Sweetbriar? How much land do you have?"

They looked at each other. "It is now eight thousand five hundred sixty-two acres."

"Thousand?" Leah whispered. "The two of you own thousands of acres of land?"

"Wesley knows our land and says it is good. He said he will help us build a house and help us buy seed and tools."

Leah couldn't help laughing. According to Abe the boys were stupid, but in truth they were smart enough to make themselves rich. "When are you planning to leave Revis?"

"We owe him something. He helped us when we were children," Cal said. "But our debt is close to being paid. We will leave soon."

"And now you have a new protector. Wesley will help you as much as you need. And if you'll help me now I'll . . ." She couldn't think of what she had to bargain with. "I'll cook for you. While you're building your house and barn I'll give you meals."

For the first time ever, in the moonlight, she saw the men smile, and they looked even younger. Their size made them frightening and she guessed they were used to stares and odd remarks, but she was rapidly growing fond of them.

"On the way down here," she said slowly, "I saw a patch of wild strawberries. Have either of you had strawberry cobbler with a thick crust on the top, little holes cut in it with hot strawberry juice oozing over the crust? Or maybe you'd like something called chicken in a coffin. It's a chicken baked with—."

Bud cut her off. "What do you want done?"

"We do not murder people," Cal injected.

"No! I didn't mean—." She saw they were teasing her. "Does Revis know what the two of you are really like?"

Cal's face hardened. "Revis thinks we are his, as his mother did, but Revis does not treat us like slaves. We make him pay us well for what we do. You should not return to him."

She wanted to explain things to him. "Cal," she said quietly, "if Bud were in trouble would you risk your own safety to help him or go somewhere safe? Wesley is the man I love and I believe I can help him."

"I would die for my brother," Cal said, "and he for me. We will help you."

"We will take you back to Revis and when your man returns—."

"Returns! Where did he go? What's he up to?"

"He did not tell us. He said only that he would be back in two days. You can stay at Revis's cabin until then or we will hide you in the woods."

"I'll go back to Revis. At least there I can help Verity and see that everyone is fed. Shall we start walking?"

Bud looked down at his foot. "Perhaps we should wait until morning, when there is light."

"But I'd like to get back in case Wesley . . ." She stopped. "I guess we can't pick strawberries at night, can we?"

"No," Bud said with a smile.

"What did you boys eat when you were growing up?"

"Gray things," Cal said grimly. "Big bowls of gray."

Leah tried not to laugh at his bleakness. Someday perhaps they could visit Stanford Plantation and see the vast quantity and variety of food there. And too, they might like to meet Clay Armstrong's pretty young niece.

She sat down. "I guess we could get some sleep." Without another thought she curled into a ball on the damp ground and went to sleep. One thing about having guardians half the size of a mountain, it made one feel safe.

Leah had just finished putting another meal on the table in the little cabin, but she hesitated calling the men in to eat. Wesley had just arrived, sunlight flashing off his buckskins, his face serious as he talked to Revis. Leah could see the tension in the cruel smaller man; Revis's shoulders were hunched together as if he expected a blow any minute.

Over the past few days Leah had stayed close to Bud and Cal. She was amazed at how deep her hatred of Revis went now. Again and again she saw him kill the settler and shoot the woman. Once he tried to sweettalk her into believing he'd done it out of his growing love for her, but Leah knew he'd murdered the travelers because he couldn't abide being turned down.

The closer Leah stayed to the boys the more she liked them.

They were silent while Abe spoke to them and of them as if they had the intelligence of the floorboards. A few times she caught Bud's eyes twinkling.

Revis brought a load of fresh eggs and cream to the camp and Leah made a big custard covered in burnt sugar. But before she'd allow Bud or Cal to have a morsel, she made them tell her what they knew about Wes. They knew only that Wes was pretending that he was from the Dancer and would work with Revis.

"I'm sure Revis will welcome him with open arms. He'll just love sharing his command," Leah had said with disgust.

Now Wesley was outside explaining something to Revis, and Leah's throat was dry in anticipation of how angry he was going to be with her. Maybe she should have obeyed him and gone to Sweetbriar, but then she'd had another look at him. Neither Kimberly Shaw nor any other woman was going to get him if she could help it!

"Abe," Leah said as she saw her brother walking toward Wesley. Abe would tell Revis who Wesley was. She was almost to the door when she heard Abe say, "Who's this, Mr. Revis?"

Leaning against the door, Leah breathed a sigh of relief and smiled. Somehow Wesley had taken care of Abe. What in the world had Wes promised Abe to make him go against his precious Mr. Revis?

Now the only unaccounted problem was Leah. She smoothed her hair, her dress, and tried to brace herself. She hoped he wouldn't be too surprised to see her.

She was bending over the fire when he entered the cabin.

"And who is this pretty bit, Revis?" Wesley drawled. "I heard you had all the comforts up here but I didn't know about this one."

Slowly Leah turned to face him. There was no surprise on his face, but his eyes were shooting fire.

"Leah's mine," Revis said in a hard voice. "I don't share her and there's no question of who she belongs to."

Wesley, with a slow smile, stepped nearer Leah. Only she could see his face and what she saw there made her step backward. His anger made her afraid.

"Wesl—," she began.

He grabbed her about the waist, pulling her to him. "Watch out, pretty lady, you're about to step into the fire. My name's Wesley Armstrong, what's yours?" His eyes were warning her and threatening her all at the same time.

Over his shoulder she could see Revis as his dark face turned darker. Here was something she hadn't considered. If she showed Revis she preferred Wesley, would Revis slip a knife into her husband's ribs?

"Unhand me, you filthy thief," she said loudly and watched the confusion in Wesley's eyes. "None of your kind will ever touch me." Taking advantage of Wes's astonishment, she pushed away from him.

Wes began to recover himself. "I think I'd like to have this little filly, Revis," he said smugly. "Maybe we can work out a deal."

"Leah is mine," Revis repeated, teeth clenched.

"Maybe the lady should choose." Wes smiled as he confidently advanced toward her. "Maybe you have trouble with women, but I don't. Come here, wench."

"Wench!" Leah said with a gasp. Perhaps she did love him, but this wench business was a little too much. To her right was a bowl of cornbread batter she had just mixed. With a little cat smile forming on her lips she lazily lifted the bowl, then with a quick motion tossed the contents into Wesley's smiling face. While he stood there flinging globs of batter off his face, Leah turned to Bud and Cal. "This overdressed peacock is the same as the other one. If he gets too near me I'll serve you raw bacon for breakfast."

Out of the corner of her eye she saw Revis give a satisfied grunt, turn on his heel, and leave the cabin. Now all she had to deal with was Wesley's rage. "Wench indeed," she snapped before moving out of Wesley's reach.

Before he left the cabin to wash, he didn't say anything to Leah, but the look on his face made her swallow hard.

"Do you think he will beat you?" Bud whispered.

"Would you let him?" she asked, aghast.

"You were mean to him," Cal answered.

"Be quiet and eat," she said, and only then realized they were laughing at her. "I hope you realize it was *your* cornbread I dumped on him. Maybe next time it'll be the apple tart I'm baking for supper."

"We will not let him beat you!" Bud and Cal said, eyes wide, then they grinned at her. "You sure are an exciting woman, Leah."

"I hope Wesley agrees with you," she said heavily before turning back to the fire.

As the sun began to set and Leah was once again loading the table down with food, Wesley entered the cabin. If he looked at her, Leah didn't see because she was afraid to turn in his direction. She knew he didn't understand why she'd turned him down. No doubt he thought he could protect her better if she were *his* wench.

Still playing her role, she stepped completely out of his reach when she put food on the table. She could feel the eyes of both Revis and Wesley on her.

"So you know of this rich wagon?" Revis was saying to Wes. "The Dancer sent you to lead for this one job?"

Wes looked around the room at Bud, Cal, Abe, Verity, and Leah. "Perhaps we should talk later."

Revis gave a slow grin. "Bud and Cal are my brothers. Abe wouldn't talk, would you, Abe?"

"No sir, Mr. Revis," Abe said with his mouth full. "Secrets are safe with me."

"And Verity is too frightened to tell anything," Revis continued.

"And the pretty one?" Wesley asked.

"She's mine and she can't leave," Revis said in a hard voice. "Now tell me what you were sent here to tell me."

As Leah served food, Wesley mapped out a plan to attack a pair of wagons that looked as if they belonged to settlers but were in truth carrying gold.

"The Dancer always knows of these things," Revis said as he leaned back in his chair and lit a thin cigar. "And tell me, how's he doing? He looked fit the last time I saw him."

"You know the Dancer," Wes said. "He's healthy as always. He mentioned the last time you met, at his house."

"At the party, yes."

"He seemed to be angry about you and a young woman."

Revis smiled. "His daughter, actually. Didn't he mention that the young lady who was so taken with me was his beautiful daughter?"

Wesley grinned, too. "The Dancer failed to mention that little detail. Now if you'll all excuse me I think I'll tramp up the mountain to that pond I saw and take a bath."

He stopped in front of Leah and ran a finger down her cheek. "Perhaps you, pretty lady, will join me."

She gave him her sweetest smile. "I will indeed have to bathe now that you've touched me, but I'll not bathe with you. That would defeat the purpose, wouldn't it?"

She felt a little guilty at the look on Wesley's face and at the way his hand dropped as if she were something he no longer wanted to touch. The cabin was silent as he left, except for a soft chuckle from Revis.

Later only Bud and Cal were still in the cabin, still eating at the table.

Leah removed her apron. "I'm going to Wesley. Will you see that Revis doesn't come near us?"

Bud looked at his plate. "What is for supper tomorrow night?"

"Are you blackmailing me?" She smiled at them. "Do a good job tonight and I'll show you what I can do with that brace of doves you brought in." With only a bit of hesitation she kissed each one of them on the forehead. "Good night, my lovely princes."

With that she was out the door and running through the dark forest, up the trail to the cabin where Wesley had stayed. Above that was the pond. The whole time she traveled, she tried to come up with a way to cool his anger. The more she thought about it the more she was sure that she should let her body do the talking.

She stood on a little rise for a moment, looking down at the pond, at Wesley's long body swimming lazily about. The moonlight gleamed on his dark skin.

This wasn't going to be nearly as difficult as she'd thought. Coughing a few times to get his attention, and when she was sure he was looking at her, slowly, she began to unbutton her dress. Easily, the stained, sturdy garment fell to the ground and what was left was a semitransparent chemise.

She walked toward him; he was treading water, watching her, the fabric clinging to her thighs with each step, and when she reached the foot of a tall tree she paused. Eyes locked with his, she unfastened the chemise and let it fall.

The last layer of clothing was a pair of drawstring pantalets, so sheer they left nothing to the imagination, and short, soft silk stays.

When Leah was a child, to escape her father's wrath she'd learned to be very good at climbing trees and now, with agility, she pulled herself onto a long, heavy branch that overhung the pond. Balancing herself, she walked about halfway out. Then, looking down at Wesley, she removed her stays and dropped them to the ground, freeing her full breasts to the moonlight. Next she removed the clinging pantalets and tossed them down.

Nude, she didn't look at her husband, but very calmly walked to the end of the branch, balanced for a moment, then made a perfect dive into the cool water, not two feet from him. When she came up, he caught her arm.

"Lord, woman," he more breathed than said, "you do know how to get a man's attention."

Without another word he pulled her out of the water, half dragging her so that her legs floated out behind her, and led her to the shore. "Leah," he whispered as he pulled her into his arms, their wet bodies sticking together as if they were one.

With hands on both sides of her face, he kissed her hungrily and Leah put her arms about his neck, knowing that this moment was worth all his anger.

His hands moved down her wet back, playing with the damp tendrils of her hair as his lips caressed her face, kissing her eyelids, her cheeks.

Suddenly he pushed her away. "Here, let me look at you."

Color rose to Leah's face. Perhaps he wouldn't find her pleasing.

He held her hands, pulled her arms out to the side and let his eyes travel down her body. "When we get home I want to keep you in my house just as you are now. I'll never let you wear any clothes."

"Oh Wesley," she said in a girlish giggle. "I'd freeze in the winter."

"Not with me to keep you warm," he said as he pulled her to him and began to nibble her neck.

Leah shivered, chills running up and down her spine and down the backs of her legs. The movement caused Wes to pull her closer, and when he kissed her again she felt fire run through her and attempted to move closer to him.

With a soft, seductive smile, Wesley pulled her down to the ground, but when Leah started to touch the grass, Wes moved her to the top of him. "That skin of yours shouldn't touch the hard ground. Just touch me, my pretty wife." With that he lifted her and set her down on his maleness.

With a gasp Leah began to move atop him, undulating to the delicious rhythm that began coursing through her body. Wesley caught her hips in his powerful hands and helped her move. And when she felt her body reach a crescendo, she fell forward, wrapping her arms about his neck, pulling him ever closer while his hard thrusts made her feel as if she were drowning.

"Wesley," she cried as her body convulsed against his.

He held her so close she felt as if she might break.

Then suddenly he pushed her off him. "You certainly changed your tune. Are you sure you wouldn't rather be with your lover instead of your husband?"

With a deep sigh, Leah rolled away. "Why is it that men are so agreeable when their male member is standing upright and so disagreeable at other times?"

Wesley made a noise that was half laughter, half shock. "Where are you off to? Back to Revis? What's he like when his male member—?" He stopped because Leah swung around to glare at him, and since her beautiful nude body was still a highly unusual sight to him, all he could do was gape.

"Just because I'm a Simmons and you're a lordly Stanford doesn't mean I jump into bed with every man who asks me, and if you ever again insinuate that I've been to bed with Revis, of all people, I'll never speak to you again. *Or* let you make love to me. Is that clear?"

He stood, catching her shoulder just as she reached her clothes on the bank. "I'm sorry, Leah. I guess I was just mad about today. The boys told me how you've kept away from Revis. But why the hell did you turn me down this morning? If Revis knew you were mine he'd think twice about touching you. Now I can't protect you, at least not openly. Your little stunt of dumping cornmeal on me cost us a lot."

"I knew you wouldn't understand," she said heavily. "I refused Revis because he's a thief and I'm a married woman, so how would it look if you, another thief, walked in and I fell into your arms? Wouldn't he be suspicious?"

"Well, I am . . ." Wesley said.

"You're what?" she demanded. "My husband? We don't want Revis to know that, do we?"

"No, I meant I'm . . . I'm a lot better looking than Revis and it would make sense that you'd want me and not him."

"Oh Wesley," she exclaimed, beginning to laugh.

"You don't think so?" He was indignant.

Still laughing, she put her arms around him. "Yes, I do think so. I honestly believe you're the best-looking man I've ever seen."

He held back from her. "Better than Revis?"

"Much."

"And my brother Travis?"

"By far."

He grinned at her for a moment before beginning to kiss her.

As difficult as it was, she pulled away from him. "We can't stay. Revis will want to know where I am. If we're both gone he'll suspect something."

"I can handle Revis. I'll tell him the better man won the lady."

"No," she said as her fingers played along the muscles on his chest. "Please don't do that. You don't know him. He's evil. One night you'll be sleeping and he'll slip a knife into you. Please," she begged.

With a little frown, he caressed her cheek. "What happened to the little cat who was spitting at me on the way up this mountain? Where's the woman vowing to never give me anything but what I took?"

She pushed away from him. The last thing she wanted to do was tell him she loved him. When and if they ever got off this mountaintop and he abandoned her, she wanted to have some of her pride left. And when he walked out she wanted to be able to tell him she didn't care, that he'd given her a few hours of bed pleasure and that was all she'd wanted.

She twisted away from him. "Of the two of you, you're safer. If I stayed with Revis I might end up like Verity, and besides, you said you and your money could get me off from the murder charges."

"Is that all I mean to you, Leah?" he asked quietly. "I'm someone whose money you can use?"

She tried to keep her voice from shaking. What was she supposed to say, that she thought she might lie down and die if anything happened to him? "We were married because you thought we had to be. *I* was nearly unconscious. I wanted to end the marriage but you refused to oblige me, so legally we're still attached and because of that and because it was my brother who shot you, I joined Revis's gang in order to protect you. After all this is over I think my duty to you is finished."

"Duty?" he said. "And what about this?" His eyes roamed down her nude body.

She gave him a lusty grin. "We Simmons women enjoy a tussle with a handsome man. I wouldn't bed Revis because I think he may be a man who likes pain."

He moved away from her. "God, but you're a cold-blooded woman, Leah. I guess I should feel privileged that you didn't leave me to bleed to death after your brother shot me."

She wouldn't answer him because all her concentration was on not crying. How much she wanted to tell him she loved him and have him tell her the same thing. But if she told him, he'd probably only laugh at her and say that of course someone of her class would love someone of his high station in life. No, it was better to keep her pride, if not her heart.

"I have to go now," she said, turning and beginning to pull on her clothes.

"Yes, do go," he said as he walked away from her.

Leah gave way to silent tears then. The fragile bond between them had been broken.

Chapter 22

LEAH DIDN'T sleep much that night, but she cried some, hugged Verity some, and was generally miserable. She wished with all her might that she'd never even met Wesley Stanford. If she'd only listened to her sister and not walked out after him that night at the tavern and leaped on him like a starved animal, she wouldn't now be in the midst of a den of thieves. Or be walking off the end of tree branches without any clothes on and making a fool of herself. Or spending hours in the strong arms of the man she loved.

"Damn!" she said aloud as she tossed the blanket off and rolled away from Verity.

"It's time to get up," she said. "And today you're going to help me cook," she said on impulse. Perhaps work could give Verity a little of her self-respect back.

While she was cooking breakfast Wesley entered the cabin, but he didn't speak to her. In fact he was so cool there was a definite chill in the air.

"Would you like some breakfast, Mr. Armstrong?" she asked.

"Not from you," Wesley snapped just as Revis entered the cabin.

Leah saw the scowl on Revis's dark face and knew he was considering Wes's attitude. "This one's not as smart as you, Revis," Leah said smoothly, setting a platter of bacon on the table.

"He thought he could have me for the asking and he doesn't take kindly to being told no. Breakfast is ready."

Twice during the meal Leah saw Revis watching Wesley, and to distract him she leaned over his shoulder as she set dishes on the table. Revis must hate someone else coming into his territory and he would hate Wes more if he thought the newcomer was succeeding where he'd failed.

"When is this job of yours, Armstrong?" Revis asked.

"Tomorrow morning. They'll be four miles down the mountain by then."

"And what makes you so sure about how fast they're traveling?"

"I have my ways," was all Wesley would answer.

It was later, as Leah and Verity were clearing the table, that Abe came to his sister.

"You two have a lovers' quarrel?" he hissed into her ear.

"Revis and me?" she asked, pretending not to understand.

"You and that Stanford fella. You two was lookin' sparks at each other all mornin'."

"I never looked at him," she protested.

"Not when he was lookin' at you. And he watched you ever' minute. Leah, you two lovebirds is gonna ruin ever'thin'. I ain't never gonna be respectable if you two get killed. And Revis'll kill you both when he finds out you're playin' him for a fool."

"What did Wesley promise you if you helped him?"

"None of your business. Me and him got a business deal goin'. As soon as he finds out about the Dancer we're leavin'. All of us. That is, if he'll still have you. You oughta watch yourself, Leah. You ain't never gonna get a husband like that again."

"I thought you hated all the Stanfords."

He gave her his rotten-toothed grin. "I don't hate anybody what promises to share his money with me." He leaned closer to her. "You don't think he's lyin', do you? He'll do what he says, won't he?"

"Yes, I'm sure he will."

Later at the noon meal Wesley didn't appear, and when Leah could, she asked Cal where he was. After telling Cal where she was going, she again asked him to keep Revis away. With a sackful of food she trudged up the hill to where Wesley was chopping wood.

For a moment she stood watching him, looking at the sweat gleaming on his muscular back, and found that her own palms were sweaty. But all lust within her died when Wes turned and saw her, his face angry.

"I brought you something to eat," she said with a dry throat.

Slowly he put down the ax and came toward her.

Instinctively she backed away.

"I'm not going to attack you if that's what you're afraid of."

"I'm not. I came to tell you something. Abe said that you and I . . . this morning . . . I mean, he was afraid that Revis might begin to suspect something about us."

"Such as that you and I were rolling about in the bushes and then we had a quarrel?"

She looked up at him for a moment, watching as he took a seat on a tree stump. "Did you *want* Revis to believe that?"

"Of course. Why else would I have been acting sulky and angry?"

"Acting?" She sat down on the ground, not far from his feet. "I don't understand anything."

"Something I learned from my brother was that it's best not to let women in on your plans. I was hoping, after I learned you had stupidly returned to Revis's camp"—he gave her a look of reproach—"that you'd do the sensible thing and pretend to fall madly in love with me at first sight, but I knew that'd be too much to ask from a woman. Especially you, Leah. You have the most contrary mind I ever saw. Every time I give you what you want, you change your mind. You wanted to marry me and when I did, you changed your mind."

She started to defend herself, but he waved her words aside.

"That's neither here nor there except that I wanted you safe in Sweetbriar and when you wouldn't go there I hoped to be able to protect you here. But you always seem to know exactly how to do the opposite of what I want."

"I couldn't go with you when I'd turned Revis down. He would have—"

"If you tell me again that Revis would kill me, I may strangle you. Leah," he said, calming himself, "do you think I am so little of a man that you have to use your own sweet little body to protect me? I've told you I wasn't going to let you control things and damned if you don't just keep on trying to control everything and everybody. If I tell you to walk left, you walk right. Not only do I have to concern myself with Revis and the Dancer, but I have to worry about what you're going to do next because you think you're the only smart one in the world. Except for Revis," he added with a hurt look in his eyes. "For some reason you think this Revis is so smart he could kill me without me even knowing about it."

"It's not that he's so smart, but he's so evil. You're not. You're good and kind and—"

He was looking at her with his head to one side, a hunk of cornbread halfway to his mouth. "Last night you said I was the best-looking man you'd ever seen and today I'm good and kind. Are you falling in love with me, Leah?"

"Never!" she exclaimed, but her face turned pink.

"Too bad," he muttered.

"What kind of plans do you have?" she asked quickly, to cover her confusion.

"To be honest, Leah, I'm afraid to tell you the truth. If I told you what I want to do you might decide it was too dangerous for me and do something that would be the opposite. Of course I could tell you the opposite of my plans and then by sheer accident you might end up helping me."

"Why you—!" she spat at him as she rose.

He caught her thigh in his hand and pulled her to him, her mouth near his. "How come you said all those mean things to me last night when you really think I'm good and kind?"

"How come you only believe the good I say about you and not the bad? Have you *ever* listened to me?"

Releasing her, he looked back into the bag of food. "Not much I don't, because to tell the truth, Leah, you don't make much sense to me. You're always leaping—or diving—into my arms and then saying the damnedest mean things to me. It just seems to me that if you *really* didn't like me you wouldn't be taking off your clothes in front of me as often as you do."

Leah had absolutely no reply to his words. Quietly she sat down again. "What plans do you have for Revis?" she whispered.

"I want to make him mad," Wesley replied simply.

"And you're using me to make him mad?"

"I was planning to, but now it's so hard because you fight me all the time. I have this fear of coming to a showdown with Revis, telling you to get behind me and you throwing yourself between us saying something real dumb like, 'You'll have to shoot me first.' That gives me nightmares, Leah. I wonder if maybe if I said, 'Get between us, Leah,' you'd stand behind me. But I'm not sure that'd work either. Lord, but you are a problem."

"So how have you changed your plans?" she asked meekly.

"I've just had to be calm. I'm afraid to provoke Revis and get him to talking because I'm afraid of what you'll do. Bud and Cal have tried to get you away a couple of times but you stick beside either Revis or me, like you've got to protect both of us. Or maybe it's just to protect me from Revis since you seem to think he's perfectly able to protect himself and I'm not."

"I didn't mean . . ." she began. "Have I really been awful?"

"Worse. Have you ever even heard the word *obey*? Did you maybe learn that it meant do-the-opposite?"

When she looked up at him she saw he was smiling at her. "Maybe I could learn."

"That's what Bud and Cal said, but I think you've got a head made of iron and the last thing I want to do is risk that pretty little head."

"So I've fouled up your plans and made it impossible for you to find out who the Dancer is, and also maybe put your life in jeopardy because I might interfere with your protecting yourself."

"That's about it." He was now eating a piece of peach pie. "But you sure have made the last few days interesting. You pour cornbread batter in my face, you dive stark naked into my baths, you yell at me so furiously all the best parts of your body start bouncing. I just wish I had time to enjoy all this properly without worrying about Revis."

She turned away to hide her pink face. "So now what do you plan to do?"

"I'm trying to figure it out. I tried to talk the boys into carrying you away, but they agreed that all you had to do was mention something like strawberry pie to them and they'd do whatever you asked."

She started to laugh. "What if I swear to obey you? Would that help?"

"You swore before a preacher to obey me, but it went in one ear and out the other."

"But this is important!"

"And being married to me isn't?" he snapped.

She wasn't going to answer that. Obviously if she told him it was he who hadn't wanted their marriage, he'd never listen to her. Or probably he'd twist it around and hear her saying something good—or maybe he'd only watch the "best" parts of her bounce. "I promise that I'll listen and obey. If it's a good plan," she added.

"Not good enough," he said, licking his fingers. "I want total obedience and I'll take nothing less. I don't care if you think my plan is stupid, dangerous, or what. Either you agree to obey or I'll leave you in the woods tied to a tree."

"You wouldn't," she half laughed.

His eyes were deadly serious. "Try me."

"I don't think I shall," she said with some nervousness. "I swear to you that I'll obey your orders. Now will you tell me?"

Wesley was still reluctant to tell her and she found that what he really wanted were kisses of persuasion. Leah, for all her seeming abandonment of the night before, was shy with him. He was and he wasn't her husband. He was hers only as long as they stayed hidden in the woods.

He told her his plan and she was astonished by it. Wesley had contacted Justin and Oliver Stark and John Hammond to ask for their help. They were to load two of Wesley's wagons with valuable goods and Revis was to steal from them.

"You'll be stealing what you already own," Leah said.

"Better that than some innocent victim. I hope that once Revis knows I'm an actual thief, he'll trust me more."

"Wesley," she said, pushing out of his arms, "how did you know the Dancer has a daughter and how did you know about his house?"

"I didn't. I just guessed. Revis likes to think women want him so I played on his vanity."

"Wasn't that a little dangerous? Suppose he was testing you too?"

"He has no reason to suspect me and he's never been out from under the watch of Bud or Cal so he couldn't have contacted the Dancer. Now stop worrying and give me another kiss."

Later, as Leah was rolling out pie crust, she thought over her conversation with Wes. For all his bragging, Wes still might need help tomorrow. But how in the world was she going to persuade him to let her go with him?

Revis solved her problem. At supper he said either Leah went too or there would be no raid.

"What the hell do we want with a damn woman?" Wesley exploded.

"I don't trust her. I won't leave her here unguarded. She sneaks around these woods too much as it is."

"So what? Let her go. Maybe these wagons will have more women. You can pick one of them. Surely one of them will like you more than this one does."

"That's why I want her," Revis said, watching Leah's stiff back. "She goes or there's no raid."

Before Wesley could say a word, Leah stepped between them. "I've already been publicly branded a thief, I might as well go again. Besides, maybe I can find a new dress."

Abe looked at her with his mouth hanging open, Bud and Cal continued eating, and Wes refused to look at her while Revis studied her through a haze of cigarette smoke.

That night, as Leah was emptying dirty dishwater, Wes caught her by the waist and pulled her into the shadows.

"Tomorrow, watch me. I'll give you signals as to where you're to stand. Don't even get off your horse. There shouldn't be any shooting but if there is, even if it's only someone dropping his gun, you head your horse due east and go as fast as you can. Are you listening to me, Leah?"

Suddenly he grabbed her head and pulled her close to his shoulder. "I just wish you were more sensible than you are. Please don't do anything heroic. Under no circumstances do I want you to do anything noble. Don't try to save anyone's life or lead the robbery or anything else dumb like you usually do. Stay on your horse, stay calm, and run if there's any danger. Do you understand me? Will you obey me?"

"To the letter. I'll not put anyone in jeopardy."

"Now, I have another plan. As we ride away, just as we get into the trees, I want you to quickly turn your horse around and go back. Sssh," he said, putting his fingers to her lips. "It's all arranged. I saved it 'til now to tell you because I wasn't sure if Revis would demand that you go with us or not. Justin will take care of you and see that you get to Sweetbriar."

"But Revis will know that you're in on this if you don't come after me."

"That's my worry, not yours," he snapped. "I just want you to obey. Now what are you going to do?"

Quietly she repeated his instructions. "You'll protect Verity? Please don't let Revis hurt her."

"If you obey me, I'll take care of Verity, even if I have to drag her into my own bed."

Leah stiffened. "Perhaps such a drastic measure won't be necessary."

"I guess that's as close to a jealous fit as I'm going to get. Kiss me, then go in and sleep. We'll leave early in the morning."

"Yes," she whispered. "Yes."

Chapter 23

MORNING CAME much sooner than Leah wanted. All night long as she tossed and turned she had the feeling something was going to go wrong. Deep inside her she knew that something awful was going to happen today.

With heavy eyes, she prepared sacks of bread and cheese to take with them as they began the trek down the mountain. Only Verity was to remain behind.

Wesley emerged from the woods riding a huge roan stallion, followed by Bud and Cal on equally large black stallions. The horses pranced and snorted as if in anger, while their masters easily controlled them.

"We ride," Wesley said as Leah mounted a sedate chestnut mare.

All down the long trail Leah's heart beat faster and faster. Twice she caught Revis looking at her and again she knew that something was about to happen. Any man who could kill merely to insure that a female he wanted couldn't run away would not follow another man's lead so easily. And Revis had been very quiet about Wesley's entering the group.

By the time they reached the bottom and sighted the wagons, Leah could barely sit in the saddle. Once Wesley gave her a sharp look of warning to which she nodded curtly in acknowledgement, but otherwise he paid no attention to her.

Revis, Wesley, and Abe, flanked by Bud and Cal, approached the wagons as Leah held back. She watched them pull masks over their faces and saw them level guns at the drivers. She saw Justin get down from the seat, and from the second wagon came John Hammond, walking slowly, both with their hands up. On the wind she could hear Wesley giving orders to Oliver Stark to remove goods from the wagon.

In many ways it was like a play. She knew all the actors, yet some of them were pretending not to know each other. They were doing unreal things such as wearing masks and threatening each other. Perhaps she should be enjoying the charade, but each minute her heart increased its pace.

What was wrong? What was wrong?

Revis gave a low whistle in Leah's direction and when she looked at him, he silently motioned her to come nearer. Purposefully she didn't look at Wes. He might signal her to disobey Revis and she didn't want Revis to turn on Wesley.

As she nudged her horse forward something in the trees caught her eye. It was just a flash of a shiny glint. At first she ignored it, but as she stood beside Revis, looking down at Justin, she realized she had just seen the sun flashing off a gun barrel.

"You'll never get away with this," Justin was saying in a convincing manner.

Leah hardly heard any of what was going on around her. She wondered if there was more than one gunman hidden in the trees. Were they Wesley's men and he just hadn't told her about them or were they Revis's men?

Wesley was giving orders, John was obeying, and Justin was arguing while Leah was trying to think. Secretly she jammed the stirrup into her horse's side, making it jump. While she looked as if she were trying to gain control, her eyes searched the tree line. There was concern on Wesley and Justin's faces, but Revis watched her with the unblinking gaze of an eagle. He watched her eyes.

They're his men, Leah thought. Those men belong to Revis.

"Whoa girl," Leah said, patting her horse's neck and leaning forward to adjust her stirrup. One of the glints in the trees moved.

"Cover me," Wesley said to Revis as he dismounted.

Revis nodded once and leveled his pistol at Justin while Wesley and Bud began to load goods onto the horses. Abe sat on his horse, his eyes darting around.

He's as nervous as I am, Leah thought.

When all the goods were loaded, Leah knew that what was going to happen would start soon.

Revis dismounted.

"Let's get out of here," Wesley said.

"I want to see inside those wagons for myself."

"Are you saying you don't trust me?" Wesley threatened.

"I don't trust anybody."

It seemed to Leah, that Revis made what was a strange move in the way he stepped between Wesley and the wagon. As he moved, Leah's head instinctively came up and again she saw a glint in the trees.

Without another thought she raised both legs and slammed her heels into her horse's side and went charging straight for Wesley. Complete confusion erupted.

Wesley jumped out of the way, was knocked down by the rump of Leah's horse, and as he went sprawling in the dirt three shots were fired.

All of them hit Revis in the chest.

Bud grabbed the reins of Leah's horse as Leah half jumped from the animal. "Wesley, are you hurt?"

He gave her a very odd look, his mask about his neck. "No." He looked up at Justin, who was bending over Revis.

Justin shook his head.

With a frown Wesley went to Revis and held the dying man's head in his lap.

"You thought you were so smart," Revis whispered. "You

thought I'd believe you. I knew you were the one she visited. She turned everyone against me, even my own brothers."

He stopped to cough. His chest was soaked in blood seeping from the three wounds.

"Who is the Dancer?" Wesley asked. "Do something good in your life and tell me who he is."

Revis gave a bit of a smile. "I thought that's what you wanted to know." He closed his eyes for a moment, then opened them to look from one face above him to another.

"Macalister," he whispered. "Ever hear of Devon Macalister?"

"You're lying," Wesley said.

Revis started to speak but coughed again and fell dead in Wesley's arms.

Gently Wesley lay the dead man on the ground and rising, his eyes caught Justin's. "He was lying."

"Yes," was all Justin said before turning away.

Wes's eyes caught Leah's and he took her hand, leading her toward the trees.

"But what about the gunmen?"

"I'm sure they're long gone." He stopped, facing her. "You saved my life. Those shots were aimed for me. Thank you."

She turned pink under his praise. "You aren't angry that I disobeyed you?"

"Just this once I'm not. We're both free now. We can go home."

Pulling away from him, Leah walked farther into the woods. *Home* meant Sweetbriar, Kentucky, a place where she might or might not be wanted as a criminal. A farm waited for her there with a magnificent barn and a run-down house that Wesley had told his brother he couldn't bear to repair because he hated the idea of working on it for someone like Leah. Kimberly with all her charms and her prettiness waited for them at *home*.

"What's bothering you?" Wes asked, his hand on her shoulder.

"Do we have to go right now? I mean couldn't we have a little time here?"

"Just the two of us? No Bud and Cal? No Revis or Abe? No Verity?"

"Yes, just a day or two. I know you want to get back but—."

"But I'd much rather frolic in the woods for a few days with my pretty little wife. Right now I owe you a great deal. Don't you want something from me that's a little more difficult?"

She wanted so many things from him that she couldn't say a word. She couldn't very well just ask for his love, but she knew she had to earn it. In the woods she could be herself, but as soon as they reached Sweetbriar she'd have to try to live up to the Stanford name.

"No," she answered. "All I want is to stay here for a while."

With a soft kiss Wesley told her he was glad to give her what she wanted.

It took hours to sort out everything in the cabin on the mountainside. When Verity heard of Revis's death, she stood fully upright, not slumping as she had. She walked out of the cabin with Leah, who escorted her to Justin's wagon. She didn't seem afraid of the other men as Leah feared she would be. Softly Verity asked to see Revis's body, and when the sheet was pulled back she smiled and stood even straighter. She then proceeded to tell Justin about some of her relatives in the East.

Revis's cabin was ransacked and all the goods, except for a sack of food, were removed.

"Find the owners of the jewelry if you can and distribute the food to whoever needs it," Wesley told Justin.

As they were stacking goods, Justin caught Leah's arm. "Is he good to you? You look different."

"He *is* good to me," Leah said with some surprise. "I don't know what will happen in Sweetbriar when he sees Kim again, but—."

"Kim?" Justin said, his head coming up. "Didn't Wes tell you that she and John Hammond were married a few days ago?"

"No," Leah said, trying to catch her breath. "No one told me."

It was dark when the overloaded wagons were ready to leave. Leah stood by Wesley and waved good-bye, giving John an especially hearty send-off. She was very happy when they were gone at last.

"Something certainly put a sparkle in your eye. It wasn't Justin, was it?" Wesley asked, one eyebrow raised.

"You didn't tell me Kimberly was married."

"I guess it slipped my mind." He shrugged. "Let's go up the mountain and see who can get out of their clothes the fastest."

"And what do I get if I win?" she said with a laugh.

"Me and my male m——."

"I understand," she interrupted. "What are we waiting for?"

For three days they did little else but make love. They didn't talk about themselves or anyone else, and Leah refused to think of what awaited her in Sweetbriar.

The cabin that had been so full of hate and fear was now full of laughter and teasing. They chased each other about the table, made love on the table, under the table, and once half on a chair, half on the table.

On the morning of the fourth day she knew it was over. As she curled against Wesley's nude body she felt the tension in his muscles.

"I'll start packing," she said, but he caught her to him before she could move away.

"I've never enjoyed myself more in my life, Leah," he whispered, hovering over her lips. "Even the time with Revis was almost enjoyable because you were here."

She held her breath, praying he would say he loved her, but he rolled away and sat up.

"But the honeymoon's over because we need to get back. I've got crops to put in, animals to feed, people to set to work and—."

"And a wife who's known as a thief," Leah said flatly.

"We'll fix that," he said, brushing her words aside. "The Dancer is more important."

"Why did you say Revis lied when he told you who the Dancer was?"

Wesley stood, his big body beautiful in the hazy early morning light in the cabin. "Devon Macalister is my friend, a very good friend of mine, and it's going to go against everything I believe to prove he's the leader of thieves. And yet"—he paused—"he does have access to knowledge and he does know the woods.

"Goddamn it!" Wes suddenly bellowed, and his mood changed from that of a lover to one of brooding silence.

Leah had her own grim thoughts. It was easy for Wesley to dismiss her fears, but Leah couldn't. She kept seeing the hatred in the eyes of the woman Revis had wounded. Would that hatred be in other people's eyes?

As they went down the mountain, they were quietly occupied with their own dark thoughts.

Chapter 24

LEAH STOOD on the hill, reins trailing behind her, and looked down at what her husband said was her new home. It wasn't Stanford Plantation, but it was large and sprawling, with two barns, three sheds, acres of cultivated fields, and an L-shaped log cabin.

"There's a spring not far from the house," Wesley was saying, "and I'll put in a kitchen garden for you this week." He paused. "Do you like it, Leah?" he asked quietly. "It's not the house Travis gave his bride, but I'll add onto it soon, I promise."

Turning, she smiled at him. "It's better than I'd ever hoped for. I like it very much."

"I had Justin and Oliver make some repairs on the house."

She looked away because she didn't want him to know she remembered that he'd said he couldn't bear even sleeping in the house because she was to live in it and not Kim.

They mounted their horses and as they rode onto Wes's land three dogs came out to greet him. Oliver Stark, his sleeves rolled up, came from the barn.

"Am I glad to see you! I've got a horse foaling and it's breech. Know anything about horses?"

Wes was on the ground and following Oliver in seconds. "The house is yours, Leah," he called behind him.

For a moment Leah sat there studying the house with its

deep, columned porch. Hers. Her very own house, her very own husband. Months ago in Virginia she'd imagined this time. She'd hoped Wes would be in love with her and she'd thought of how he'd carry her over the threshold and they'd be the picture of wedded bliss.

But the actuality was that she was to enter alone, her husband might or might not be in love with Kimberly, Leah was publicly known as a thief, and Wes was not by any means in love with his wife.

"Good morning."

"Good morning."

Leah looked to each side of her horse to see identical twin boys, big, strong, sturdy boys of about seventeen, with handsome faces, dark skin, and brilliant blue eyes.

"I'm Slade," said one, eyes twinkling.

"And I'm Cord Macalister. Welcome."

"We work for Wes. Actually we keep the place going better when he's not around," said Slade.

"Wes has an awful habit of interfering with us. Would you like to see the house?"

"Or the fields? Or the town? Sweetbriar's not much, but it's what we have to offer."

"Can I help you down?"

"I'll help too."

"Wait a minute!" Leah laughed. "You're going too fast for me. Yes, I'd like to get down, and yes, I'd like to see the house, but no thank you, on the town. At least not today."

Cord walked around the horse to stand beside his brother and they were indistinguishable from each other.

"Allow me," Slade said, arms extended.

"And me," Cord added.

Their humor was infectious and Leah allowed herself to be helped down by both young men and they did it with ease and grace, as if they often, together, lifted women from horses.

"It's not much," Cord said. Or was it Slade?

"But we did the best we could. Justin told us so much about you that we wanted to make the house nice."

"Bud and Cal had a few things to say about you too."

"You met them then? They're safe?" Leah asked.

"Safe!" Slade snorted. "Except that at first we thought they were breeding bulls and almost put them out to pasture, I reckon they're safe enough."

Again laughing, she started toward the open cabin door.

"Wait a minute, aren't new brides supposed to be carried over the threshold?" Slade asked.

"By their husbands they are," came a deep voice from behind them.

They all turned to see Wesley.

"You two weren't planning to volunteer to carry *my* wife, were you?"

"No sir," both boys echoed with wide eyes. "Never even crossed our minds."

With a laugh and a shake of his head, Wes came forward. "Get out of here and get back to work—and stop flirting with my wife," he shouted as they scurried off, after they'd given big winks to Leah.

"Nice boys," Leah said.

"Huh!" Wes said with a snort. "They're the bane of this town. Every woman they see falls in love with them, and then spoils them. Their father and I are the only people who give them any discipline. Now, about that carrying." Bending, he swept her into his arms.

"You know how this custom started, don't you? The Romans captured their brides and had to forcefully carry them into their houses. Are you a reluctant bride, Leah? Am I going to have to drag you into my bed tonight?"

She took him seriously. "I'm afraid not. When it comes to . . . *that*, I don't seem to have much resistance."

With a chuckle he kissed her long and lingeringly as he carried her inside the house. Still holding her, he seemed to be wanting some reaction from her.

To Leah, the cabin was very nice. It was large with simple, plain furniture, glass windows, a big stone fireplace, a hallway to the left, and her beautiful loom set not far from the fireplace.

"Bedroom?" she asked, nodding toward the hallway.

"With a great big featherbed. No expense has been spared when it comes to that room."

She smiled up at him. "It's a very nice house. I like it very much."

"You're not disappointed that it isn't like Travis's house?"

"No," she said honestly. "I was born in a swamp and this house suits me better than that mansion of Regan's."

"Mmm," he said, frowning. "I'm not sure I like my house being compared to a swamp."

Before she could answer he kissed her again, then set her down. "I'll have to go see about my foal. Anything you need, tell Oliver or, if you must, go to the twins. I'll have to double their work load to keep them away from you. Trouble is, they pretend to be each other and I never know who's working and who's not. See you later."

With that he was out the door.

As she looked about the place realizing it was hers, Leah told herself everything was going to be all right. Wesley would grow to love her because she was going to be a good wife to him, Kimberly would have no power over him, and everyone everywhere was going to live happily ever after.

With a smile she set about making the cabin more completely hers. It was larger and far cleaner than the shack in which she'd grown up with her enormous family.

In the bedroom were her trunks of clothes that Nicole had given her. Pulling a gown of lavender silk from the trunk, her rough hands caught on the fine fabric.

"First things first," she said aloud. Before a clean house and food on the table, Wesley would come home to a sweet-smelling wife with creamed, perfumed skin. In the kitchen she began searching for the ingredients for the creams and lotions Regan and Nicole had taught her to make.

It was hours later when her skin and hair seemed to be somewhat restored after the time in the forest. The roughness and redness of her hands were gone and her hair was gleaming in soft waves as she sat on a stool before the fireplace to dry it. It was nearly sundown, there was no meal prepared, and she hoped Wesley wouldn't be angry. To encourage his good humor, she wore a semitransparent dressing gown without a stitch on under it.

When Wesley walked in the door he paused, hat in hand, and stared at her. The firelight showing through her gown made her look as if she had a delicate layer of fairy cloth over her beautiful body.

Unnoticed, his hat fell to the floor as he advanced toward her and pulled her into his arms, her thick hair tangling around his forearms.

"I didn't cook anything," she whispered as his lips descended.

"And I don't plan to wash," he replied. "If you can overlook me, I'll forgive you."

He kissed her then, pulling her to him as if he were starving.

Leah clung to him. He'd been working in the fields and his clothes were damp with sweat, his hair curling about his neck. Her fingers went up his neck to intertwine in the curls.

Wesley began to kiss her throat as his hands ran over her arms. Her body was hot from being near the fire and with his sweat and her heat, they nearly sizzled upon touching.

Wesley swept her into his arms, carried her into the bedroom, and carefully laid her on the featherbed.

"Take that off," he commanded in a low, husky whisper as he stood back from her.

The fading sunlight streamed through the single window,

making a golden haze of light in which Leah knelt on the bed, the deep mattress fluffing about her. Slowly she undid the little silk ties that held the gossamer garment together. Then, raising her head to meet his eyes, she languidly slid the silk off her shoulders but managed to keep most of her body hidden. For a moment she held it in front of her, concealing herself from him.

"And now you," she murmured, toying with the silk.

With a crooked grin, Wesley stripped himself of every stitch of his work clothes, flung them to a corner, and made a leap for her.

Leah, not expecting this sort of exuberance, squealed and rolled out of his way. The silk gown stayed on the bed, caught underneath Wesley.

"Pretty little thing," he said as he pulled it from under him, then tossed it to the floor. "Come here," he commanded.

Leah stayed against the wall, her arms held demurely so most of her was covered.

"No," she said easily. "I worked all day on smelling good and now you expect me to roll around with some sweaty, unclean man. Ladies don't—."

He caught her ankle, pulled her down into the bed, and dragged her toward him. "I guess we'll just have to make you smell a little less sweet." With that he pushed her down into the feather mattress and covered her clean body with his dirty one, rubbing against her, smearing her with his sweat.

"Wesley!" Leah gasped, and she knew nothing had ever felt as good as this man. "Wesley," she said again, her eyes shut.

He smiled at her then and began to kiss her body, starting at her neck, his lips grazing her breasts, moving down to her stomach, his big hands toying with the muscles by her hipbones, his tongue licking around her navel. His hands parted her thighs, rubbing the inner recesses as his lips followed his hands.

Working his way downward, he reached her feet and with his tongue caressed the little pads of her toes.

Leah was almost crying with desire by the time he made his way up her body again. He hovered over her lips for just a moment.

"Is the answer still no?"

"No," she murmured, then her eyes flew open. "I mean yes. Oh Wesley." She sighed and pulled him closer as her legs began to rub up and down his.

He made love to her with tenderness, so slowly she was frantic for him when he finally pulled her to him and with hard thrusts brought them both to a peak of ecstasy.

They lay together, wrapped about each other, their skin sticky and wet.

"You planning to feed me?" Wesley murmured against her shoulder.

With a laugh, Leah pushed at him. "I guess the honeymoon is over. But first we wash."

As he rolled off her, Wesley sniffed. "You should wash. You smell like you've been out in the fields all day."

"You!" she exclaimed, starting to pummel his chest.

"I sure do love the way you bounce, Leah. Now stop trying to entice me and go fix me something to eat."

"And if I don't?" she challenged.

"I'll do something else with that bare little bottom of yours, such as smack it." His threat lost meaning as he began to kiss her, and she snuggled against him.

A loud knock on the door made her pull away. "Who do you think that is?"

"Probably Bud and Cal. Seems you promised to cook for them."

"When? Oh yes, when they were going to take me back to Revis's cabin. But tonight I haven't cooked anything."

Wesley moved to the side of the bed. "I'm sure that if you just explain to them that you spent the day making yourself pretty in order to seduce me, they'll understand."

"I could tell them I dumped dinner over your head. They'd understand that even more."

The knock sounded again.

"Come on, get dressed," Wes said as he pulled on his pants. "You can fry up half a hog and that'll do fine. You know, I think I like making love to you in a bed." With that he left the room and moments later Leah heard him talking to Bud and Cal.

Hurriedly she dressed, pulled her hair back from her face, and went to join them. It was obvious that the big men were so glad to see her that they weren't going to mind too much about food.

While Leah fried ham and potatoes, boiled water for corn on the cob, and mixed cornbread batter, they all talked. Bud and Cal slowly told about their farm, about the animals they planned to buy, and what kind of house they'd build.

"Perhaps you should build two houses," Leah suggested, "in case you get married."

Bud and Cal looked at one another. "No women would marry us. Women are afraid of us."

"I'm not," she said, a hand on each big shoulder, "and I'll bet Sweetbriar is full of women who'll fall in love with you."

"If Abe can do it, so can you," Wesley said, his mouth full of corn.

Bud and Cal slowly broke into big grins.

"What about my brother?" Leah asked, filling their plates with food.

"I forgot you were here 'working' all day," Wesley said, his eyes smiling at her. "You haven't heard about Abe."

"Will *someone* please tell me?"

"You do the honors, Bud," Wes said. From the sound of his voice he seemed about to burst into laughter.

"Abe fell in love," Bud said softly, his attention on his food.

Leah sat down. "Is that true?" she asked Wes.

"As far as anyone can tell," Wes answered. "He took one

look at Miss Caroline Tucker and fell in love. Two days later he asked her to marry him."

"Marry him? This is my brother Abe you're talking about? No mistake? Abe never loved anyone but himself in his whole life."

"He does now. Pass me the potatoes, Cal," Wes said. "You boys don't know how lucky you were to get anything to eat."

"What's the rest of it?" Leah asked. "There's something you're not telling me about my brother. What's Caroline Tucker like?"

Wes nearly choked on a piece of ham. "Describe her, will you, Bud?"

" 'Bout my size," was all Bud answered.

Leah digested this. "My brother fell in love with a woman the size of one of you?" she asked in disbelief.

"Shorter than us," Cal said.

"Wesley!" Leah threatened.

"I wasn't there but Oliver said that your brother arrived in town, took one look at the . . . ah, very large Miss Tucker, and fell in love. He said something to Oliver about she'd never been hungry and I guess he liked that idea. He followed her around town until she asked him to dinner with her parents and sometime during the meal he stood up and asked for Caroline's hand in marriage. He told them he had been a thief and had done some bad things in his life but with Caroline's help, he was going to become a new man."

"Gracious!" was all Leah could answer, completely astonished by this news.

They finished their meal, Wesley removed pipes from a wall cabinet, took one, and handed the other two to Bud and Cal.

As Leah cleaned up, she thought of how pleasant this moment was. She still glowed from Wesley's lovemaking and behind her were people she cared about. After Bud and Cal left, Leah and Wes gave each other baths out of basins of hot water, and ended up making love in a leisurely manner on the floor before the fireplace.

When they went to bed, it was to snuggle comfortably in each other's arms.

Hours before daylight the next morning, Wesley was up and out of bed while Leah started the day's chores and had her first real look at the outside of her new home.

The number of animals on the farm was impressive. About a dozen geese lived under the porch and set up a racket whenever anyone walked past them. Thirty ducks waddled around the yard. Behind the house was a well-built, completely fenced chicken house, and Leah went inside, her apron full of crushed corn. To her left she could hear hogs grunting and behind her was the bleating of sheep.

"Wool," she said, smiling. Wool to be spun for weaving on her precious loom.

Still smiling, she left the chicken yard but her smile disappeared instantly. Wesley was coming toward her and in his arms was the unmistakable form of Mrs. John Hammond—Kimberly.

Chapter 25

"I think she's fainted," Wesley said with concern.

"Did you ask her to?"

"Leah," Wes warned. "I'm taking her into the house. She may need help."

"I'm sure she does," Leah said under her breath, but she followed him.

"Just put her on the bed," Leah directed, "and you can go back to work. I'll take care of her."

"She scares me to death when she does that," Wes said with a frown. "You think I should get a doctor?"

"She'll be fine, now please go."

Reluctantly Wesley obeyed her.

"He's gone," Leah said. "You can open your eyes now."

With a bouncy little smile Kim sat up on the bed. "How nice! A featherbed. You look so pretty, Leah." Her face changed. "I don't have time anymore to look pretty. Just look at my hair. Dull as mud."

"What do you want, Kimberly?" Leah asked flatly. "What did you think your fainting was going to get you from Wesley?"

She looked up at Leah with sad eyes. "I never intended to faint, but Wesley always did love it so. John just hates for me to faint. He says such awful things to me that I've just about stopped."

"Chalk one up for John," Leah murmured.

"But Wesley just loves fainting women. Have you fainted for him?"

"No, Kimberly," Leah said patiently. "I really need to get to work. I have breakfast to cook and other chores to do and—."

Kim suddenly buried her face in her hands and began to cry. "Oh Leah," she wailed, "you aren't even glad to see me. After the way you ruined my whole life I'd think you could spare a little sympathy for me. I got married and you haven't even asked me about it and you're really the best girlfriend I ever had."

Waves of guilt spread over Leah as she sat on the bed and took Kim into her arms.

"How was your wedding, Kim?"

Kim began to sniff. "Just awful! Just dreadful, awful, terrible, that's how it was. The only people there were an old skinny man named Lester and his wife and John and me. No one else came to see my pretty dress, no one even wished us happiness."

She looked up at Leah. "It was the dress I would have worn to marry Wesley if you hadn't taken him away from me. Oh Leah, I still don't understand why you did that. Wesley was all I had except Steven, and he never liked me."

"Kimberly," Leah began, not knowing what to say.

Kim moved off the bed to stand before Leah. "Look at this awful dress. It's *brown!* Did you ever see me wearing brown before? John says it's better for all the chores he makes me do. And look at my hands! They're red and raw. Oh how I wish you'd never taken Wesley away from me."

"If you had Wesley, you'd still have to work. I don't have any servants and right now I have to cook." Sweeping past Kim, she left the bedroom to go to the fireplace.

Kim followed her. "But at least Wesley wouldn't make me do the things at night that John does."

Leah gave a quick glance skyward. "All men expect 'night things' and Wesley is no exception."

"But is Wesley so . . . forceful?"

"Yes! Here, sit down and peel this potato."

"I can do that," Kim said brightly, taking the potato and a chair. "Are you mad at me, Leah?" she asked after a moment.

"What do you care?" she snapped, then calmed. "Kim, I'm trying to be patient. I'm sorry Wes felt he had to marry me. I certainly never set out to harm anyone and if you'll remember, Wesley is the one who decided we should stay together so maybe you should be angry with him."

"Oh well, men," Kim said blandly, peeling the potato. "Wesley liked you better because you're so exciting. All sorts of things happen around you. I'm sure Steven was drowned because he was showing off for you, and Justin fell in love with you, then Wesley decided you are more interesting than I am. And you are, Leah. The only interesting thing I do is faint and my husband doesn't even like for me to do that. So, see, it really was all your fault. Do you plan to keep Wesley or can I have him back someday?"

"Kimberly," Leah said slowly, "you're talking about dissolving two marriages. You can't do that very easily."

"I don't know. Wesley's friend, Clay, was married to Nicole, then married to someone else, then married to Nicole again. I really truly don't like John much."

"Then why did you marry him?"

She paused in her peeling. "It was the oddest thing, but after Wesley chose you over me, I felt as if I weren't pretty anymore. I know that's silly, but I almost felt ugly and then John asked me to marry him and that made me feel pretty again so I said yes. I just didn't realize men could be so different. Wesley was always so nice to me."

"But John is mean because he makes you work and do things in bed?" Leah had almost cooked a whole meal while Kim was peeling one potato.

"More or less," Kim said, but before she could say more, the geese outside set up a racket, the door opened, and in came Wesley, followed by Oliver and the Macalister twins.

"I think I forgot to tell you that the hands eat breakfast with us since they've already put in a few hours' work."

Leah only had time to shake her head at him before she began throwing more eggs and ham into skillets.

Kimberly acted as if all the men had come to see her; she preened under the twins' flirting with her and prettily complained to Oliver that his brother Justin was quite unpleasant to her.

"Oh, that was nice," Kim purred when she and Leah were alone again. "It's never nice like that at my house. Leah, John's going to be gone all day. Could I stay with you? I'll help you do what you need to do and later maybe you can put something on my hair to make it nice and shiny like yours."

Leah knew Kim would be a nuisance all day, but she didn't have the heart to refuse her request.

"You may stay," Leah said and was rewarded with Kim's arms about her neck.

"Thank you so much, Leah. It's so good to have a friend."

They spent the day together, Kim chattering constantly about her former life of dances and handsome young men while slowly doing the chores Leah gave her. She didn't complain anymore about Leah's "taking" Wesley from her, nor did she again mention her husband John.

Surprisingly for Leah, Kim turned out to be good company. She was slow at doing things, but once she understood what was to be done she was willing enough, and in the afternoon they laughed a lot together while Leah washed Kim's thick blonde hair.

Toward evening when Kim had to leave there were tears in her eyes. "No other woman has ever been nice to me," she cried softly. "They were all like Regan, so unkind, always mean to me."

Leah was silent, accepting the compliment but not trying to explain exactly why women disliked Kim so much. Perhaps it was the way she treated women, as if they didn't or shouldn't exist. "Please come again," she said sincerely when Kim left. "I enjoyed myself."

At supper Wesley calmly announced that in the morning Leah, Bud, and Cal were going into Sweetbriar with him.

Three faces suddenly showed fear.

"It's just a quiet little town," Wes said with some disgust. "Nothing's going to hurt you. Except for what Abe's told people, no one knows what happened in the mountains. Neither Justin nor Oliver nor John has said a word so you're all safe."

"What about the woman who Revis shot?" Leah asked quietly. "He told all those people who I was and where I lived. I've had one safe day here, but it won't last if I go into town."

"That's absurd, Leah!" Wes said explosively, then clenched his jaw. "And what about you two?"

Bud looked at Cal. "We will stay here with Leah," Cal said softly.

"Damn all of you!" Wes shouted, jumping up and knocking over his chair. "I'll not live with a bunch of cowards. You're going with me in the morning even if I have to drag you."

No one laughed at the idea of Wes or any man trying to drag Bud or Cal someplace, but the three of them looked into their coffee cups and nodded.

"That's better," Wes said. "I have to see to the cows." He left the cabin, obviously still angry.

"We did not like Revis," Cal said, "but we liked staying away from people. People are afraid of us."

Leah didn't want to think of all the things that could happen tomorrow. Wesley could cause trouble with this man who Revis had said was the Dancer—Devon Macalister; Bud and Cal could be laughed at and get their feelings hurt, and she . . . she didn't want to think of that.

Her head came up and she really looked at Bud and Cal. She was used to seeing them bare-chested, wearing sheepskin and leather, but perhaps if they wore shirts people wouldn't be as likely to laugh at them.

"Do you own any shirts?"

"Shirts do not fit us," Bud answered.

"Of course," Leah said, rising and looking at the kitchen yet to be cleaned. "If you'll help me tonight, I'll make both of you shirts. I think I can have them ready by tomorrow morning."

Slowly it began to seep into the young men what Leah planned to do, and their eyes started to shine.

"Do you think you can wash dishes without breaking them?"

Bud gave her an indignant look. "We have repaired robins' broken legs; we can do your dishes."

Wesley returned to see Bud and Cal doing women's chores and Leah cutting huge pieces from yards of heavy blue cotton. With a smile, because he knew something had happened, he asked if he could help.

Leah didn't get to bed until three in the morning. The shirts were done except for the buttonholes, but she figured the boys could wear them unsewn for one day. Tired, she crawled into bed beside Wesley and he sleepily pulled her to him.

"All done?"

Yawning, she nodded.

"Next time you adopt somebody I hope they're smaller than those two. I have to work three hours longer every day just to feed them. Couldn't you adopt stray cats instead of stray people?"

Leah wasn't listening to him because she was already asleep.

With a smile he pulled her closer and went back to sleep.

For Leah, daylight came much too early. She was so nervous she cracked an egg directly into the fire, completely forgetting to use a skillet, and Bud and Cal, who'd come for breakfast, were so jittery they each ate only four pork chops, six eggs, half a loaf of bread, three fried apples, and a partridge. A pittance.

"Hope neither of you faints from hunger today," Wesley said

as Leah cleared the table, but no one responded. Oliver, Cord, and Slade went to work while Wesley packed the wagon with food for the noon meal. He was determined to spend the whole day in Sweetbriar and show the three of them that things weren't as bad as they thought.

Leah and Wes sat on the wagon seat on the ride into town while Bud and Cal sat stiffly in the back, their eyes glum.

Sweetbriar wasn't very large; a few houses, a livery stable, a general store, a ladies' clothing store, a blacksmith shop, a few more shops here and there. Nothing that looked especially frightening, but the eyes of the people milling about were all on the newcomers.

"They're watching us," Leah whispered.

"Of course they are," Wes snapped. "They've never seen you before."

As they stepped down from the wagon a woman in her fifties came toward them and Leah drew back, but Wesley pushed her forward.

"You must be Leah Stanford," the woman said, smiling. "I've heard so much about you from Abe."

"Abe?" Leah said stupidly.

"I'm Wilma Tucker and maybe you haven't heard, but my daughter Caroline is engaged to your brother. We're all going to be family. My son Jessie—he's a senator now," she said proudly, "he's coming back for the wedding. Floyd and me are real proud of your brother and you don't look a thing like him."

Leah began to smile and at the same time she started to relax. "I haven't seen my brother for a while but Wesley told me about the wedding. May I introduce some friends of mine?"

Bud and Cal were still sitting on the edge of the wagon. With a glare Leah motioned for them to rise.

"My goodness," Wilma said, looking up at them. "How nice and big you are."

"This is Bud and Cal . . ." Leah had no idea what their last names were, but as she looked at them they were smiling down at Wilma. Obviously they liked the woman because she wasn't afraid of them.

"Haran, ma'am," Cal said softly.

Wilma smiled. "Oh yes, you bought the land near Wesley's. Abe was saying—. Oh, here's my daughter now."

Leah was glad she was prepared for the sight of Caroline Tucker. Caroline seemed at least as wide as she was tall, with a pretty, freckled face. Perhaps she appeared outrageous, but Leah found herself liking Caroline right away.

"You're Leah," Caroline said, holding out a fat little hand. "Abe said you were the prettiest woman in the world."

"Did he?" Leah was genuinely pleased.

"I was supposed to meet him today, but I haven't seen him anywhere."

With a jolt, Leah realized she was imagining Caroline and skinny, angular Abe in bed together. She really hoped Caroline didn't get on top. Leah straightened herself. "I haven't seen him since we arrived."

"I just saw him," Wes said as he was looking over the leather harness. "He was going into that white house at the end of town."

"That's where Lincoln Stark is living!" Caroline said angrily, stamping her surprisingly small foot. "Abe is gambling again. He promised he wouldn't. Oh Ma!"

Before Wilma could say a word of caution, Caroline was hurrying down the street toward the white house.

Obviously Wilma was embarrassed. "Abe really did promise," she said meekly. "And Caroline does have a mind of her own, and I think she really does love Abe and—."

She stopped because the loud slamming of a door was like a shot fired, and seconds later came the muffled sounds of shouts from the little house. The five of them were silent as they heard what sounded like furniture being tossed about, and then a stool came flying through the window.

"I guess I'd better go see what's happening," Wesley said, looking at Wilma, who was beginning to look frightened.

"I hope Caroline isn't hurt," Wilma whispered, and all of them began to follow Wesley as he advanced on the house.

Just as they reached it the door flew open and a deck of cards came flying out, catching the wind and fluttering like big snowflakes.

"Ain't no woman gonna tell me—," came Abe's voice. "Here! You watch out! Don't you hurt Lincoln again! Caroline, I'm warnin' you!"

Wesley tore up the two porch steps to the open door, looked inside for a moment, his mouth open in astonishment, then began backing down as his face split into a grin.

"She all right?" Wilma asked.

With the beginnings of some deeply felt laughs, Wesley just nodded toward the door.

Within seconds, Caroline Tucker emerged with Abe's thin body slung across her left shoulder.

"Put me down, you goddamn, overgrown horse!" Abe bellowed into her back.

"Hush up, Abe, my ma's lookin'."

Immediately Abe quieted, and as Caroline walked down the stairs she paused before her mother. "He'll never gamble again, Ma," she said solemnly.

"That's true, Miz Tucker," Abe said. "Caroline done showed me the light. Leah! That you just standin' there?" he hissed from his upside-down position. "You fergit I'm your brother? You oughta help me."

Leah was trying very hard not to laugh. "Hello, Abe. Fine day, isn't it?"

After giving his sister a dirty look, he began caressing Caroline's backside. "Caroline, honey," he said sweetly, "you oughta have more respect for me than this."

"I think I'll take Abe home now, Ma," Caroline said. "And I'm going to have a word with Doll Stark about that boy of his leading my man into sin."

"Me?" came a voice from behind them. Standing on the porch leaning heavily against the rail, was a pleasant-looking young man—or had been. Now one eye was about to turn black, and blood was pouring from his nose. Holding an already soaked handkerchief to his nose, he glared at Caroline. "That precious Abe of yours started this game. It weren't *my* fault."

"Hah!" Caroline snorted, her nose in the air as she walked away regally, bearing Abe across her shoulder.

Abe's words floated to them on the wind. "You sure were pretty in there, Caroline. I sure liked the way you punched Lincoln all them times. You sure we gotta wait for the weddin' 'fore we—?"

"Hush, Abe," Caroline commanded. "Don't talk dirty."

"Yes, sweetheart," Abe said, his hands moving up and down the backside of her.

Wesley was the first to erupt as he removed his hat, slapped it across his knee, and broke down with laughter.

Leah wanted to stop him for fear of offending Wilma, but Wilma put her arms out and fell against Wesley, the two of them barely able to stand for laughing so hard.

"They been like that ever since they met," Wilma said between gasps. "Abe seems thrilled she wants him."

"And Caroline's wild happy 'cause somebody wants her," Wesley finished. "They are a pair."

"I'm bleedin' to death and you two are fallin' apart laughin'," Lincoln Stark accused.

Leah, still so shocked by the whole scene she couldn't yet laugh, looked at Bud and Cal and saw they were grinning from ear to ear, so she went to Lincoln. "Let's go in the house and I'll see if I can get the bleeding stopped."

It was sometime later when Wesley came into the house, still smiling. "There are some people out here I want you to meet. They're the twins' parents, Linnet and Devon Macalister."

The Dancer, Leah thought, washing out the bloody cloth she'd been holding to Lincoln's nose. Now was when she'd be exposed as a thief.

Chapter 26

AS LEAH left the little house she prayed that Wesley wouldn't let his temper show, that he'd be cautious and not blurt out what he felt about a man who'd planned robberies for years. But what greeted Leah was not what she expected.

Wesley was talking to the man as if they were the best of friends, smiling at him, his eyes alive. Macalister was tall, lean, dark-skinned, and very handsome. His black hair had bits of gray in it and his eyes crinkled against the sun, all of which added to his sharp good looks. Beside him was a pretty little woman with a delicate-featured face, big eyes, dark blonde hair and a curvy little body. She didn't look a day over twenty-five, but she had to be quite a bit older if she was the mother of Slade and Cord.

"You must be Mrs. Stanford," said the woman in a pretty, crisp accent. "I'm Linnet Macalister. And this—," she pulled a little girl from behind her skirts, "this is my youngest daughter, Georgina. I believe you've met my sons."

Instantly Leah liked this lovely woman and she wondered how much Linnet knew about her husband's illegal activities.

The little girl gave Leah a shy smile, then ran to her father, tugging on his pants leg until he picked her up.

"Leah, honey," Wesley said, "come here. I want you to meet Mac."

Right away Leah knew it was going to be difficult to dislike Devon Macalister. "How do you do, Mr. Macalister."

The man looked at his wife as if sharing some private joke. "Mac will do," he said in a deep, pleasant voice. "Wes says you like to weave. Lynna has some patterns for weavin', and Miranda spins wool."

"Miranda's our eldest daughter," Linnet explained. "This morning she was visiting Corinne Tucker's eldest daughter and she should be back fairly soon. Perhaps you and I could leave the men to their talk and I could show you Sweetbriar."

"That's very kind of you, but I'd hate to take so much of your time." Truthfully Leah wanted to sit in the back of the wagon with a blanket over her head. That way she'd be sure no one recognized her.

"Go ahead," Wesley said. "Linnet knows everybody a lot better than I do." He gave her a hard look of warning that only she could see.

"What about Bud and Cal?" she asked quietly. She felt much safer with the men near her, as if they could protect each other.

With a sigh Wes looked down at her. "The boys will go with us, and Mac and I will protect them with our lives. If any children hurt your boys we'll string the kids up right there. No trial or nothin'. And if any—."

"Stop it!" she hissed, but she was smiling. "They're just . . . you know."

"Delicate," Wesley said seriously. He leaned back toward Mac. "She's talking about those two bulls over there. Leah's afraid somebody will laugh at them and hurt their feelings."

Mac gave a snort of disbelief.

"You just go with Linnet," Wesley said, "and I'll meet you at Mac's store about noon." Bending, he gave her a quick peck on the cheek. "And we'll take care of your boys."

Leah felt a little lost when Wesley and Mac, followed by the towering Bud and Cal, walked away, but Linnet soon put her at ease.

"Everyone in town is dying to meet Wesley's new wife. We've known Wes for years and seen him work hard on his farm, so of course everyone is curious about who he was doing all the work for," Linnet said. "I wouldn't be surprised if nearly everyone in Sweetbriar came to town today just to see you."

With a laugh at Leah's grimace, Linnet continued. "You'll have to get used to this town. There's no such thing as a secret to them. It's not that they're nosy, just that they're . . . concerned, I guess. When I first came here twenty years ago—."

"Twenty years!" Leah said in disbelief. "You don't look much over twenty now."

"How kind you are. My eldest daughter is nineteen. Here comes Agnes Emerson. Her husband died a few years ago and now her son Doyle runs their farm."

What followed for Leah was a confusing array of names and faces. There were people who'd only been in Sweetbriar for a year or two, but that special light in Linnet's eyes was reserved for the parents and children of people who, Linnet said, had been in the town for years. Leah found it impossible to keep all the people straight. She met Nettie and Maxwell Rowe and was told their youngest daughter, Vaida, was the town schoolteacher and their eldest, Rebekah, was married to Jessie Tucker who was now a state senator.

"Everyone seems to be very proud of this Jessie Tucker," Leah said.

Linnet smiled. "Jessie would inspire pride in the people around him no matter what he did. How many of the Starks have you met?"

"Quite a few," Leah said with a laugh. "How many are there?"

"New ones every year. Gaylon Jr. went to Boston last year to attend school. He's a very intelligent young man and we all hope he'll become governor or even president."

As they walked through the town, stopping in stores and meeting people, Leah became aware of the strong sense of community. In Virginia, no matter how many times she reminded herself that she had become a Stanford, she still thought of herself as a Simmons. The swamp seemed to pull her toward it, and Regan and Nicole, for all their kindness, always seemed as if they'd been created in another world that was far removed from Leah's.

But here in this little town with all the people wearing clothes of homespun cotton or wool, often patched garments, she began to feel as if she belonged. In spite of what Wesley had accused her of, of wanting Stanford Plantation, Leah had never wanted to be rich. Her dreams had been about safety, a place where she was sure she wasn't going to be beaten. Stanford Plantation had been safe, but the delicate dishes, the silk clothes that made her constantly worry about tearing them, the manners she had to memorize, all the things that came naturally to Regan and Nicole, all made Leah nervous.

This town was safe and it wasn't formal. Most of the people she met slurred their words and made no pretense at talking in the way Nicole had taught Leah, a way that was sometimes difficult for Leah to remember. Linnet, for all her plain cotton dress, seemed to exude a ladylike air that reminded Leah of Nicole.

Linnet's daughter Georgina soon lost her shyness when she saw an older woman walking beside twin girls, and Georgina ran ahead to meet them.

"That's Justin and Oliver's mother, Esther," Linnet said with some sadness in her voice as they approached the woman. "Doll's nearly worn her out with having so many children. The twins are her granddaughters. Their mother, Lissie, died in childbirth."

Leah was introduced to Esther Stark and the six-year-old twins, and afterward Linnet led Leah to the Macalister store. "It's grown some in the last few years," Linnet explained, "and now I do the bookkeeping so Devon has more time off. It's all worked out quite well," she said in a dreamy way that seemed private to Leah.

Before the empty fireplace sat an old, thin man, idly whittling on a stick.

"This here the new one?" the man asked.

"Allow me to introduce Doll Stark," Linnet said. "This is Mrs. Leah Stanford."

Leah nodded to the man, all the while remembering everything Justin had said about his father.

Doll looked at Leah for a long moment and seemed to sense her dislike of him. "I think I'll go see to some things," he said, rising.

When they were alone in the store, surrounded by shelves of merchandise, Linnet spoke, a small frown on her face. "He's a very lonely man now since Phetna and old Gaylon died." At the puzzled look on Leah's face, she explained. "After Devon and I were married, Doll used to sit in here with his friends, Gaylon and Phetna, but when they died, most of the life went out of Doll. Devon has been trying to find someone to sit in here with Doll but no one nowadays seems to have quite such a capacity for inactivity. Perhaps it's all the travelers passing through here. Everything seems so much faster now."

Leah could hear all the love in Linnet's voice and it was the same as hearing another side to the story. Justin despised his father for his laziness while others loved Doll for it.

It was while they were inside the store that they heard a woman's screams outside.

"That's Miranda," Linnet said with a gasp and started running.

Outside, tearing down the main street, was a runaway team

of horses pulling a wagon that lurched drunkenly from one side to the other. On the seat, trying her best to hold on, was a pretty young girl with wild, frightened eyes, hair flying about her face.

"Devon!" Linnet screamed as the wild wagon ran past Leah and her. The next moment the two women started running after the wagon, Linnet's face a mask of terror.

Neither Mac nor Wesley was in the street to see the wagon, but Bud and Cal were. It was amazing that men so big could act so quickly. As if they'd planned their actions together, Bud ran to the back of the wagon while Cal spurted ahead to the front.

Bud jumped on the back of the wagon and agilely made his way to the seat and the frightened girl. With one hand he caught her about the waist while steadying himself with his powerful legs wide apart.

Miranda, with a little scream when Bud first touched her, turned and clung to him, instinctively trusting him with her life.

Meanwhile Cal ran in front of the horses, grabbed the harness, and used his big body to create resistance. For a few seconds he was pulled under, his heels tearing into the dirt, then the horses began to slow and Cal gained control.

Mac and Wesley walked out of the feed store to see Bud standing in the back of the wagon, Miranda clinging to him with all her might, while Cal gathered the loose reins and secured the horses.

"Miranda," Mac said breathlessly, and in one step was at the foot of the wagon. "Come here, princess." He held up his arms to her.

Miranda, obviously shaken and still frightened, looked from her father to Bud, who still held her; she closed her eyes and remained where she was.

"What—?" Mac began, but Linnet put her hand on her husband's arm as Bud walked to the edge of the wagon.

Cal put up his arms for Miranda.

"Two," was all Miranda whispered before sliding into Cal's massive arms and snuggling against him.

Everyone around this trio could do little more than stare. Leah wondered if young Miranda was always so forward, and she also wondered why the boys had said people, especially women, were afraid of them. This young lady certainly didn't seem afraid of them.

"Miranda!" Mac said sharply as she gazed up into Cal's big brown eyes.

With seeming reluctance Miranda turned to her father.

"Are you all right? You're not hurt anywhere?" Mac asked, stiff-jawed.

"No," she said slowly, making no attempt whatsoever to leave Cal's arms. "I'm quite all right." When Bud stood beside them she reached out her hand to his.

They were a striking trio, Miranda so small, Bud and Cal so large, the three of them wrapped together, unaware of anyone outside their tight circle.

"Miranda," Wesley said, laughter in his voice, "may I introduce Bud and Cal Haran."

"You're Cal and you're Bud," she said softly and was rewarded with a nod from both of them. "Thank you for saving my life."

Before a word could be said Miranda astonished them all by climbing onto the wagon underpinnings, slipping her arms about Cal's neck, and kissing him thoroughly. Again Linnet put her hand on her husband's arm while Miranda moved to Bud and kissed him too.

Moving back, Miranda put her hand on each big shoulder. "Come with me and I'll fix you something to eat."

Together they walked away, leaving an astonished group behind them.

"Well, that should kill the romance." Wesley broke the silence. "As soon as she finds out how much those two eat she'll run from them."

"I don't like it, Linnet!" Mac said explosively. "I don't like it at all. She's never acted like that before. How come you raised a daughter that'd act like that about two strangers?"

Quite calmly, Leah thought, Linnet ignored her husband's temper. "I'm afraid it must run in my family. I believe your daughter has just fallen in love."

"In love!" Mac snapped at her. "She doesn't even know them. Sometimes, Linnet, you say the—."

"Devon," Linnet said sweetly, "may I remind you that I fell in love with you when I first saw you? Why should your daughter do any differently?"

Mac stiffened. "There's a lot of difference between me and those two! I was rescuing you and—." The anger suddenly went out of him. "Which one do you think she's in love with?" he asked heavily.

With a sigh Linnet looked toward their store. "I hope I'm wrong but it looks as if she wants *both* of them."

Before Mac could speak, Wesley slapped him hard on the shoulder. "Congratulations, Mac. Two sons-in-law at once. And believe me, you'll need all the supplies in your stores to feed them."

Mac cast Wes a black look. "No daughter of mine—," he began but stopped with a look of disgust. "Women!" he said between clenched teeth. "Come on, Lynna, let's see what she's up to now."

Glumly Mac escorted his wife toward their store.

Turning, Leah smiled up at Wesley. "I don't know if that solves something or starts new problems. Bud and Cal certainly did seem to take to Miranda, didn't they?"

"Are you jealous?" he asked, half-serious, half in jest. "From now on you may not be the only woman in their lives."

The sunlight on his face, his eyes shadowed by his broad-brimmed hat, made him look especially enticing. Her eyes went to his lips.

"Leah," Wesley said huskily. "You're singeing my eyebrows."

Embarrassed, she looked away.

A crowd of people had gathered when Miranda's wagon had torn down the street and many people had stayed, chuckling, to watch Miranda reward her saviors, but now they were moving away.

"That's her!" gasped a heavyset woman, looking straight at Leah.

Leah froze where she was. Never would she forget that woman's face. When Revis had shot her husband, the woman's hatred had gone to Leah's heart.

"She killed my husband," the woman said loudly, and the next moment she was advancing on Leah with hands made into claws.

"Murderer!" the woman screamed. "Murderer!"

Leah didn't move but waited for the woman, almost as if she deserved what she got.

Wesley put himself between Leah and the enraged woman. "Don't," he said kindly.

"She killed him!" the woman screeched. "He was all I had in the world. We were gonna build a farm together. Now everythin's gone because of her." Still screaming, she began to kick Wesley, hitting him with her fists.

"Get in the wagon, Leah," Wesley said calmly. "Go! Now!" he commanded when she didn't move.

Leah tried to keep her chin high, but it wasn't easy because she could feel the eyes of everyone in town on her. Stiffly she climbed into the wagon, her eyes straight ahead.

After a few moments Wesley sat beside her and without a word to her clucked to the horses to go.

Leah didn't blame him for not speaking to her. And imagine, she'd just started to think that Sweetbriar might be safe. What little safety there had been was now gone—as were her chances for gaining her husband's love. No Stanford could love a woman accused of murder.

Chapter 27

WITH HIS shoulders hunched and his hands in his pockets, Wesley stood in the Macalister store, listlessly ordering supplies. It was raining hard outside.

"Think it'll flood?" Doll asked.

"I don't know," Wes replied glumly.

"Sure ain't no sunshine in here," Doll complained. "What happened to that wife of yours?" Doll looked at Mac. "I ain't seen her in weeks."

Mac's head rose above the counter. "She's cookin' for them two bears," he said with anger. "That is when my daughter ain't cookin' for 'em. Wes, I ought to wring your neck for bringin' them two here. Miranda cried all night last night sayin' she wanted *both* of 'em and damned if her mother didn't act like she thought it was a goddamn fine idea."

He went to the back of the store for a moment and returned with more goods. "Anythin' else?"

"You know anything about women?" Wesley blurted.

Doll gave a derisive snort.

After a glare in Doll's direction, Mac said, "Before I met Lynna I knew lots about women but ever' year now I know less. You got problems?"

"He's married, ain't he?" Doll said. "Then he's got problems."

Wesley leaned against the counter, looking at his boot toe. "I used to think I understood women too, but I don't. I thought that if you had a wife and you were kind to her, didn't beat her, gave her a good home and pretty dresses, she'd be happy."

"But yours isn't happy," Mac said. "They want love too."

Wesley stiffened. "She couldn't have any complaints there. I keep her pretty busy."

Doll gave a chuckle.

"No," Mac said, "that ain't enough for a woman. She wants you to love her. I don't know how to explain it. You just know when you love her."

"Oh that." Wes waved his hand. "I fell in love with Leah a long time ago. She's got more courage than anybody I ever met."

"So what's your problem?" Mac asked.

"You remember a month ago when that woman accused Leah of murdering her husband?"

Mac grimaced. "That's the day Miranda met those two boys of yours. I ain't likely to forget it. But I thought you got all that straightened out."

"I thought so too. I found two people who'd been there when Revis killed the woman's husband and they heard Revis threatening Leah. So I took the two to the woman but she wouldn't listen, just kept screaming about Leah. There wasn't anything I could do about her so I took the two men around town and let them tell everyone in Sweetbriar the truth about Leah."

With a nod, Mac agreed. "Sounds sensible to me. So what's wrong with your wife?"

Wesley sat on top of a cracker barrel. "Leah has more courage than anyone," he repeated. "In Virginia she used to tell me off about every two days and later I was shot and she put her own life in jeopardy to save me, who she kept saying she didn't like very much. Of course she didn't mean that. Leah's crazy about me," he added quickly. "Nothing ever seemed too much for her, but this woman screaming at her has changed Leah. All she does now is chores and sit at that blasted loom of hers. And the least little thing makes her cry."

"Is she breedin'?" Mac asked. "Women get funny at that time."

"I don't think so. I've asked her twenty times what's wrong and she just cries and says she'll never be respectable now."

"I guess you told her about the two men, didn't you?"

"Sure," Wes answered. "I even brought them to the house, but Leah said their word didn't matter because the woman thought Leah'd killed her husband. Everybody in Sweetbriar knew about Revis's robberies and I told a few women about how Leah joined the gang because I was wounded and they believed me. Nobody in town is against Leah except that one crazy old woman, but Leah just plain won't believe me. She won't come to town, won't see anybody but Kimberly and Bud and Cal."

There was quiet in the store for a few minutes, only the rain beating down on the roof.

"I never did like those Hayneses," Doll said quietly.

For a moment Mac looked startled, and it was awhile before he spoke. "You ever think maybe somebody's payin' this woman to keep to her story about Leah?"

"Paying her? To lie about Leah? Why?" Wesley was bewildered. "What could anyone gain by making the town think Leah's a murderess?"

Mac walked out from behind the counter. "I know what you've told the townspeople about this Revis and I know you only told 'em because of Leah, but I think you left out a lot."

Wesley set his jaw. "Maybe you ought to tell me what I didn't say."

"Maybe you didn't hear," Mac continued, "but about four years ago several of us men went into the woods and cleared out the whole nest of robbers. It was . . . successful, but Lyttle Tucker and Ottis Waters were killed. It wasn't long before the nest was filled again, only this time all the women of Sweetbriar marched on us and said they'd leave us if we went after the robbers." There was anger in Mac's eyes. "Sometimes the women of this town don't rightly act like women should."

"I liked it better when my woman disobeyed me," Wesley said sullenly. "If I'd wanted somebody who obeyed me I'd have married Kimberly."

"Linnet don't even know how to obey," Mac snapped. "Sometimes I think she stays up nights thinkin' up ways to do what I don't want her to do."

"Leah used to do that but—."

" 'Fore you two get so hot for your women you have to run home to 'em for a little lovin', why don't we get back to the Haynes woman and her callin' Mrs. Wesley a murderer?"

Mac ignored Doll's first remark. "The Hayneses ain't been here long and we've had some trouble with 'em, with stealin' and the like. This woman that accused Leah was a Haynes before she married and now that she's a widow she's livin' with 'em."

He paused. "A few of us men speculated some on how come that den of robbers is always filled and they always seem to have new leaders ever' few years. Even if you kill the leader, a new one comes back real soon. There ain't been no robberies since this Revis was killed, but I'm expectin' any day to hear of one."

Wesley was cautious. "How do you explain the leaders being replaced?"

"There's somebody behind all the robberies, somebody that don't live in the woods that's plannin' them all."

"And who is he?" Wes asked quietly.

"How the hell would I know?" Mac snapped. "You think he'd be free if I knew who he was?"

Doll turned around in his chair to look at Wesley. "Mac," he said slowly, "that boy knows more'n he's tellin'." With that he turned back around.

Mac gave Wesley a hard look. "That true? You in here fishin' to see what we know?"

Wesley began to get angry. "I'd never heard that the men of Sweetbriar had ever cleared out the robbers."

"You think we hear about other people's misery and just sit on our asses doin' nothin' about it? Is that the kind of people you think we are? I lost Lyttle Tucker in that fight and he was one of the best friends I ever had."

Doll came out of his chair. "Goddamn you, Macalister! I thought that once you got some gray hairs you'd calm down. But you ain't. You're just as hotheaded now as you always was. I don't know how that sweet little Lynna puts up with you."

"She puts up with me just fine!" Mac yelled. "Better'n anybody can put up with you, old man."

"Stop it!" shouted Linnet from the doorway, rain dripping off her. "I could hear you two shouting outside even in this downpour. Hello, Wesley. I haven't seen you for weeks."

Mac, rigid with anger, went behind the counter.

"Hello, Linnet," Wesley said softly.

"Wesley," Linnet said pleasantly, "would you please tell me what's been going on in here?"

"I don't know if I should . . ." Wes began.

"Tell her," Mac snapped. "Cain't nobody keep a secret from her."

Briefly Wesley told her about Leah's refusing to leave the farm, about her unhappiness, and then about what he'd done to clear her name. Then he told of what had led up to the argument.

Linnet thought for a moment. "*Do* you know something about the robbers?"

Wesley wasn't going to tell Mac that Bud, Cal, and Abe had been part of the robbers, not when Miranda might marry Bud or Cal. "There is a leader," he said quietly. "All I know is that he's called the Dancer."

"You have no idea who he is?"

"I was given a name, but it was a lie." The last thing Wes wanted to do was tell Mac what Revis had said. Mac's temper was explosive enough over little things, but what would it be over this?

"What was the name?" Linnet asked.

Wesley hesitated.

"You can be sure it won't go beyond these walls."

"I knew right away it was a lie. When Revis was shot he gave us a name, but none of us believed it. And besides, Mac, you spent two years in North Carolina. It couldn't have been you."

The silence in the room was deafening.

"Me?" Mac said, then slowly he began to smile. He walked over near Doll. "You hear that, ol' man? I'm supposed to be the leader of these outlaws. I'd like to know when I'm supposed to get time what with all the kids I've got, and what did I do with the money? Miranda wants a new dress once a week and I can't give her one."

He seemed to be highly amused by the whole idea.

"Seems mighty peculiar to me that a man that's dyin' would tell a lie," Doll said.

Wesley was sure Mac would start yelling at Doll again.

"That *is* odd," Linnet said. "What do you think, Devon?"

"He was scared," Mac said flatly. "Maybe this Revis has some kinfolks and if he gave away who the Dancer was, this Dancer would kill 'em."

"I hadn't thought of that," Wesley said. "I just never believed what Revis said about you."

"But you did ask around enough to know Mac was in North Caroliny and *couldn't* be this robber," Doll injected.

"So why does the Haynes woman still say Leah is a murderer?" Mac asked.

"Because whoever the Dancer is, he's afraid Leah knows something. Did Leah know Revis very well?" Mac answered his own question before anyone else could speak.

"Not the way you mean," Wesley snapped. "But—" He came off the barrel. "Revis could have bragged to the Dancer. Revis was a loner, skulked about the woods all the time, nobody ever knew what he was thinking, but he liked Leah. From what I gather he killed the Haynes woman's husband just so he could force Leah to stay with him. He seemed to terrify most women and Leah . . . Leah doesn't usually scare too easily."

"I once lived in a town," Linnet said softly, "where if one of the residents had been accused of murder the other townspeople just might have hanged her. Sweetbriar isn't like that," she said proudly, "but even our town can be pushed too far. Some of the newer residents are saying you may have paid those two men to say Leah was forced into the robberies."

"Just tell me who they are and I'll break their lying bodies in two," Wesley said as he spat.

"That won't do any good," Mac said. "I think we've got to find out who the Dancer is."

"Must be somebody pretty close or he wouldn't be so worried about your missus," Doll said.

"So how do we find out who he is?" Linnet asked. "We can't just ask people."

Mac locked eyes with Wesley. "There's only one way: by making him show his hand again."

It took Wesley a moment to understand. "You want to use *my* wife as some sort of pigeon for this Dancer to shoot at? You expect me to expose Leah to the whims of a thief and a murderer? Not on your life, Macalister."

"Nobody's askin' you to—," Mac began angrily.

"I think you should ask Leah," Linnet said. "She should be given a choice. Right now she's miserable because she's been accused of murder and she has no way to clear her name. If the real culprit is found only then will she be free."

"Absolutely not," Wesley said firmly. "I don't care if Leah never leaves my house again. I won't let her expose herself to a murderer. If the Dancer thinks she knows something, he may try to kill her. I will not let Leah out of my protection."

"Then you're forcing her to a half-life," Linnet said with passion. "All the Dancer has to do is keep paying that dreadful woman to spread her stories about Leah, and if Leah merely stays home and cries, never defends herself, it won't be long before people begin *believing* Leah is a murderer."

"Yep," Doll said. "People will say where there's smoke there's fire, and in a few months they'll all agree that there must be somethin' behind your little wife's misery. They might say maybe she's stayin' home 'cause she feels guilty."

"Wesley," Linnet said, her hand on his arm. "You must talk to Leah about this. It's really her decision."

"As long as she's my wife—."

"Hah!" Mac interrupted. "If you want her to act like a wife oughta, you better hightail it out of this town right now. It's my guess that if you won't tell her, Lynna will."

"Is that true?" Wesley asked, eyes wide.

"It had crossed my mind," she said, giving her husband a stern look when he smiled at her.

"Maybe we could go—," Wesley began.

"It'll follow you wherever you go," Mac said. "The only way you can settle this and really protect your wife is to find out who the Dancer is. And the only way I see of doin' that is to have Leah show her face. Maybe she knows somethin' she don't remember. Maybe the Dancer wants her out of the way 'cause of that. Maybe the Dancer lives a hundred miles from here and that Haynes woman just wants to pretend she's important. Who knows? But the only way you're gonna find out is if Leah leaves that house of yours and we see what else the Dancer does."

"Seems to me," Doll said, "that maybe there's somethin' else this here Dancer wants 'cause he could have murdered your woman right away. What's he got to gain if he makes her look like a murderer?"

"Freedom," Wes said slowly. "If he can make someone else look guilty no one will suspect him. Even if he makes a slip now and then, people won't notice because they'll remember Leah as the guilty one."

"Remember?" Linnet whispered.

Wesley's eyes turned dark. "I won't let her out of my sight," he said under his breath. "If I have to take her to France to live, I will. She'll never be in danger if I can help it, and if any of you hint to Leah about any of this, I'll make you sorry." With that he left the store.

Chapter 28

LEAH WAS slowly braiding Kimberly's long hair.

"I'm so looking forward to the dance tonight," Kim said. "I'm going to wear my rose silk dress with the lace shawl. It's the first time in months that I've been anywhere. Except here, of course. John makes me stay home the rest of the time. What are you going to wear tonight, Leah?"

Leah turned away toward a basin of dirty dishes. "I'm not going."

"Not going! Oh Leah, you must go. Everyone will be there. Even Bud and Cal are going." She laughed. "I hear Miranda Macalister has made both of them new shirts and everyone is dying to see if she can dance with both boys at once. It's going to be such fun! I know you have pretty clothes, Leah, so there's no reason for you to stay home."

"I have been forbidden to go," Leah said with suppressed anger.

"Forbidden?" Kim was aghast. "But who—? You mean *Wesley* said you couldn't go?"

Leah's hands clutched a plate beneath the dirty water. "I thought perhaps it was time I left the house and faced the outside world, but my husband wouldn't hear of it."

Kim looked as if she'd just heard the most tragic story of

her life. "But why, Leah? Wesley is the kindest, gentlest, most considerate man alive. How could he forbid you to go to a dance?"

"I have no idea. He refused to discuss the matter. He just said he didn't want me surrounded by so many people."

"I'd rather be surrounded by people than home alone with John," Kim said. "Surely Wesley gave you some reason."

Leah turned toward Kim, fighting back tears. "Maybe a Stanford doesn't want to be seen with a Simmons who's been accused of murder. Perhaps my husband can't bear people knowing what kind of wife he has."

"Oh Leah," Kim whispered as she put her arms around her friend. "Sit down and let me make you some tea."

Obediently Leah sat down, her shoulders shaking with a combination of grief and despair.

"That's not very nice of Wesley," Kim said thoughtfully, sitting down at the table and forgetting about the tea. "When I first met you I dreaded having to travel with one of the Simmonses. Steven kept saying the most awful things about you. He bragged about how he was going to . . . well, do things to you as soon as Wesley turned you over to him. He said all you Simmons women loved, you know . . . sex."

Leah was looking at Kim with horror.

"I believed him," Kim continued, "for a long time, but you were always so kind to me when other people weren't and as far as I could tell you weren't running into the beds of all the men like Steven said you would. I almost understood when Wesley said he wanted to stay married to you. But I was very, very angry." There was an apology in her voice.

"What did Wesley say when he told you he wanted to remain married to me?" Leah asked softly.

"Actually, he was very kind, although I didn't think so then. He said it'd been a hard decision for him to make but he really thought he ought to stay married to you."

"He ought to, huh?" Leah muttered. "That's all?"

Kim smiled. "He said he'd always love me because I was his first love, but he had to do what was right and he'd married you and he planned to honor his wedding vows."

Leah stood. "Those Stanfords are good people aren't they? They believe in honor and loyalty to the core. Even when it means doing something as disgusting as remaining married to a bit of swamp scum who forced him into marriage in the first place. Of course there are compensations. Women from my station in life make great bed partners and farmhands, and if they get in trouble while protecting a Stanford then the women can be hidden away, not allowed to go out in public, just stay home, cook and clean, and warm his bed at night—or in the day. Women from the Simmons family are easy to persuade."

"Leah," Kim said with a frown, "that may all be true, but when Wesley told me he was going to stay married to you, I felt that he *wanted* to, not that he *had* to. Wesley can be awfully stubborn and he won't do what he doesn't want to do."

"Oh, he wanted to stay married to me, all right," Leah said with anger. "Where else was he going to find a worker and a sex partner? He took me to town once to introduce me, but he hasn't let me go out in public since. And tonight he doesn't want to be embarrassed by somebody like me."

Kim frowned harder. "I don't understand. I thought you didn't *want* to go into town."

"For a while I didn't, but for the last two weeks every time I've mentioned facing the townspeople, Wesley's given me a dozen reasons why I should stay home. And tonight he's forbidden me to go to the dance."

"I was so hoping you'd be there," Kim said. "In fact, I even brought you a present." Out of her pocket she pulled a little package wrapped in a scrap of fabric. "I thought it would look quite nice on your green dress."

Slowly Leah opened the bundle to see a brooch, gold filigree, edged with a hand-painted miniature of a woman on the ivory oval. "Who is she?" Leah whispered.

"I don't know. It's very old, don't you think? And the green dress in the picture just matches yours. I so wish you were going tonight."

"I am," Leah said suddenly, astonishing herself. "Wesley Stanford may think he can hide me away, but he can't. He may think a Simmons has river mud for blood, but we don't."

"I'm not sure you should do that, Leah. Wesley can get awfully mad sometimes."

"Wesley Stanford doesn't even know the meaning of anger. I'm not going to sit here in this house for the rest of my life and feel sorry for myself. I didn't participate in those murders and that woman can tell everyone from now until doomsday that I did and it won't make it true."

"I think I'm glad you feel this way, but Wesley said you couldn't go and—." She brightened. "Maybe if you cry and tell him you'll just die if you don't go he'll say yes, then you won't really be disobeying him. Or maybe you could faint! Wesley does love—."

Leah gave her a stern look. "I'll not beg and I'll certainly not faint. No, first I'm going to get Wesley to go, then I am going to turn up at the dance. I can hardly wait to see his face."

"Neither can I," Kim said grimly. "I think I'd fall down dead if anybody got as mad at me as Wesley's going to be at you."

"It'll be worth it just to show that arrogant man that he can't keep me locked away from the world as if I were something nasty he had to hide. And you, Kim, are going to help me."

Kim paled. "No, Leah, Wesley scares me."

"I thought you said he was kind and gentle."

"Only when he gets his way. Really, Leah, I couldn't possibly help you."

Leah sat down across from Kim. "All you have to do is send him a note tonight saying you need help. Lately Wes has been hovering over me, but he'll leave the farm to go to you. You're the only one. And while he's gone I'll go to the party. You can write another note for me to leave Wes saying I've gone to the dance. When he gets to your house he'll find you and John gone, come back here, find the note, and probably come to the dance. Or maybe I'll come home with someone else if he doesn't want to come to the dance."

"Do you think Wesley will beat you when you get home?" Kim asked seriously. Her eyes widened. "Do you think he'll beat *me?*"

"No, of course not. I expect he'll be mad, but I hope to show him that I won't embarrass him in public. Nicole had a man teach me how to dance, and my clothes aren't exactly what someone from the swamps would wear. Maybe when Wesley calms down he'll realize I'm not something he has to hide away."

"Oh Leah." Kim put her head in her hands. "I'm just awfully afraid of doing this. Somehow it doesn't seem right. Wesley doesn't act as if he's ashamed of you, in fact he seems to like you a lot. Couldn't you write the notes yourself and then I could be innocent? I can say I knew nothing about anything. I'm good at lying. It's easy for me."

"I can't read or write and if I have someone else deliver the messages, then they'd be involved, and besides there are only men around here anyway. They'd all take Wesley's side. Please Kimberly. Please."

There were tears in Kim's eyes—tears of fear—when she nodded agreement.

As Wesley rode back to his farm he imagined all the things he was going to say to Kimberly the next time he saw her. What great crisis had happened to make her write that frantic note to him? No doubt John had dared to suggest she get off her spreading backside and do some work, and in anger she'd written to Wesley. And Wes, like a fool, had gone rushing after her, ready to rescue her, ready, if needed, to punch a good man like John Hammond in Kimberly's defense.

Yet when Wes got there the house was empty and a hand said John and Kim had left for the dance an hour ago. All Wes could think of was that he'd left Leah alone in the house, unprotected except for the hands, and for all Wes knew, one of them was the Dancer. Right now he trusted no one. He'd even begun to suspect Bud and Cal. Yet here he'd left his wife alone, drooping about the house, feeling poorly, tired, overworked—and possibly the victim of a plot against her.

"Leah," he called before he'd even dismounted. Slamming into the house he tore through it, shouting, "Leah!"

The emptiness and silence of the place made his heart pound. He ran outside to the outhouse, to the chicken coop, calling repeatedly for her.

"Where's Leah?" he shot at one of the Macalister twins.

"I thought she was in the house."

"Damn," Wes cursed, running back into the house, and there he saw the paper on the table.

Dear Wesley,

    Leah can't read and even though she's telling me what to write, I'm going to tell you the truth. It wasn't very nice of you to forbid Leah to go to the dance. Just before she got mad at you, her feelings were hurt. So, she made me write two notes for her so she could go. It wasn't really my fault, Wesley. Please don't be mad at me.

                           With love, Kimberly

P.S. Leah is really very nice and she isn't at all some nasty thing from the swamp. Please don't hit her.

"Hit her!" Wesley said with a gasp. "Oh Lord, you stupid women. I may beat you black-and-blue, Leah. That is, if you're still alive," he whispered.

Crumbling the note, he left the house in a few easy strides and mounted his horse, setting off for town at a gallop.

Leah was nervous by the time she reached the Macalister store where the dance was being held. It wasn't exactly proper for her to arrive unescorted.

"Leah!"

Justin Stark was standing outside and now he hurried forward to help her from her horse.

"So where's that husband of yours who keeps you locked away from us? He didn't let you out of his sight, did he?"

"Wesley . . . had some work to do. If he finishes he'll be along later." As she spoke, Leah's eyes went to the side.

Justin caught her arm and pulled it through his. "I won't question that. It's Wes's loss and our gain. Come dance with us and let me show everyone I have the prettiest girl in the state on my arm."

The inside of the store had been cleared and was lighted with what looked to be every lantern in town. Four fiddlers occupied one end of the big room and one side had a long, long table weighted down with food.

"I should have brought something," Leah murmured.

"Your own pretty self is enough."

"Leah!" Kimberly exclaimed from beside her. "You're here. Did Wesley—?"

"Would you please excuse us?" Leah said to Justin as she led Kim to a corner.

"Did you see Wesley? What did he say? Was he really mad?"

"Kimberly," Leah said slowly, sniffing. "Have you been drinking?"

"Just a tiny bit. Not even enough to count. Justin's father makes this wonderful stuff that relaxed me with one swallow. I've just been so nervous and John is hardly speaking to me. Don't you think Justin looks nice tonight? But then so do all the men. Every man looks good except my husband."

"Kimberly, I want you to eat something right away and for heaven's sake, stop talking!" With some force Leah led Kim toward the food-laden tables.

"Leah!" Linnet Macalister said, looking at Leah as if she were a ghost. "I didn't think you were going to be here."

"What a pretty dress," Agnes Emerson said. "Is that a picture of your mother?" she asked, referring to the brooch Leah wore.

"It was a gift from a friend of mine. Could I get a plate of food for Kim and maybe someone would see that she eats it? I need to talk to Doll Stark for a moment."

Agnes took one look at Kim and understood immediately. "I hope you say a few words to Doll for me too," she called after Leah.

Doll sat in his usual place before the fireplace, except that now his chair was turned to face the dancing people. Lester Sawrey, sitting next to Doll, punched the older man when he saw Leah coming.

"Yes, ma'am," Doll said. "What can I do for you?"

"I want to ask you not to give Kimberly Hammond any more of whatever you gave her."

"That little lady sure can drink," he said in wonder. "Thought she was gonna drain the jug."

Leah glared at him.

"Where's that husband of yourn?" Doll asked. "I didn't think he'd let you come to this shindig."

Still refusing to answer, Leah just looked at him.

"All right," Doll said heavily. "I won't let her have no more. Sure seems a shame to me, though. That little lady has capacity."

"Mrs. Stanford?"

Leah turned to look at John Hammond. He was a good-looking man with beautiful gray hair. "May I have this dance?"

After a quick look to see that Kim was sitting down and eating, Leah took John's arm.

Her dancing lessons hadn't prepared her for the energetic country dances, and when they were finished she was fanning herself with her hand.

"How about a breath of air?" John suggested, his eyes twinkling.

"Yes, I need it," Leah said with a laugh.

Outside with the stars winking overhead, the cool, fragrant night air about her, Leah was very glad she'd come to the dance. And to think that Wesley had forbidden her to attend.

"Penny for your thoughts."

She smiled at him. "I was just thinking that I'm glad I came."

"I am too," John said seriously. "I've wanted to talk to you for a long time. Actually, I wanted to ask your advice. You see, I know Kimberly is very unhappy, but I honestly don't know why or how to make her happy. I've tried my best to be as patient as I know how. When I come in from the fields, supper isn't ready, and it's taken me weeks to teach her how to fry eggs for breakfast. I've done everything I can to be lenient with her, to understand that she's not used to so much work, but no matter what I do, she still seems to resent me. You must believe me, Mrs. Stanford, I love my wife, and if I could afford servants for her I'd gladly hire them, but I can't. I know the two of you are friends and I thought maybe she'd said something to you. Could you please help me?"

Leah wasn't sure, but there seemed to be tears in his eyes. Damn Kimberly! she thought. Her laziness was causing this gentle man a great deal of misery. "She hasn't said much to me," Leah lied.

"But anything could help," John said in desperation. "She won't talk to me and if I just knew exactly what she complained about maybe I could fix it. I do want to make her happy."

"I guess marriage in general is difficult for her," Leah said slowly. "She's not exactly in love with work."

John smiled. "How kind you are. But there's nothing . . . specific about our lives together that she complains about?"

"John," Leah said, putting her hand on his arm, "I really wish I could help you. Kimberly is my friend, but I'm aware that she must be difficult to live with. I'll talk to her and try to find out whatever I can. I want both of you to be happy."

"Please try to convince her that I love her," John pleaded.

"I will. Now, shall we go inside?"

With a grin John offered her his arm. "You must have heard this a dozen times already tonight, but you look lovely. That green sets off your eyes. Is the miniature on the brooch of your mother by chance?"

Leah gave a little grimace as she thought of her mother's never having worn a silk dress in her life. "Actually, Kimberly gave me the brooch. Perhaps it's a picture of someone in her family."

"Ah yes, perhaps I've seen the brooch before and don't remember it. It was nice of her to give you a gift, wasn't it? Perhaps she'll tell you the history of the woman in the painting and you can tell me. It looks like the only way I can find out about my own wife is through a third party."

Leah's heart went out to him and she felt like smacking Kimberly for mistreating this sweet man. "Excuse me," she said when they were inside, and she went directly to Kim.

"You were talking to John," Kim said belligerently before Leah could speak. "Did he ask about me?"

"Yes he did. That poor man is working very hard to make you happy and you've been very unkind to him."

"Leah," Kimberly began, but suddenly John was in front of her, his hand extended.

"Dance with me?" he asked with longing in his voice.

Kim's face lost some of its color. "Yes," she murmured and took his hand.

As Leah watched they joined in with the others, but every

time Kim came in contact with John, her face fell until by the end of the dance Kim was no longer smiling.

"You can't stay here against the wall all night," Justin said from beside her. "I expect any minute for that husband of yours to come roaring through the door and take you away from all of us."

"I'm afraid I expect that too. Do you think we could get some food instead of dancing? I think my dancing mood has fled."

"Could it have to do with John and Kim? You've been watching them and frowning for minutes."

"I don't guess I like to see anyone unhappy."

Justin snorted. "Kim would make anybody unhappy. I pity John for having to live with her. Uh, oh. I think a storm just blew in."

Coming toward them with the full force of a gale was Wesley, his cotton work shirt damp with sweat, his hair plastered about his face.

Chapter 29

"COME WITH me," Wesley said through clenched teeth as his fingers bit into Leah's upper arm.

"If you'll pardon me," Leah said politely to Justin just before Wesley gave her arm a quick jerk.

All the way across the floor Leah tried to smile and nod at people, tried to act as if she were merely on her way outside with her husband and he wasn't half dragging her. But inside her anger was reaching the boiling point.

"Get on my horse," Wesley commanded as soon as they were outside.

"So you can save the rest of your reputation? Let me tell you, Wesley Stanford, it's too late! Everyone has already seen me, already knows that his majesty, Mr. Stanford of the magnificent Stanford Plantation, has a wife from the swamps of Virginia. And you know what, no one was repulsed, not one person wiped off his hands after touching scum like me."

"Have you gone crazy, Leah? I don't know what you're talking about."

"I'm talking about being a Simmons, that's what. I'm talking about your being ashamed of me and not wanting me to be seen in public."

"Not wanting—." He shook his head at her. "I still don't understand you, but let's go home and discuss it."

She backed away from him. "Go home and no doubt climb into your bed, is that it?"

"I wouldn't mind," he said with a grin.

"You—!" She made a fist and punched him in the stomach.

Wesley didn't move. "What in the hell's got into you?"

"You forbid me to go to a town dance because you think I have to be kept at home chained to your bed and your kitchen and you ask me what's wrong? You may think only rich people have feelings, but I assure you that I have my pride, even if I am a Simmons."

"Women!" Wes said under his breath. "Leah, I'm not ashamed of you. I don't know where you get such dumb ideas. You're beautiful and tonight you're no doubt the prettiest woman here, but right now I just don't want you around so many people."

"Because I don't know how to behave? Because I might not live up to the Stanford name?"

"Good God! It's your name, too. Just one day of my life I'd like to really understand a woman. Just any woman will do. Leah, will you *please* come home with me right now?"

"Why?" she asked angrily. "Why do you want to hide me?"

"I don't want to hide you . . . well, maybe I do." Smiling seductively, he moved closer to her. "I can make our own party at home."

"The only way I'll go with you is if you carry me kicking and screaming, and that could further damage your reputation."

Wesley turned away from her for a moment, and when he looked back his face was a study in confusion. "Leah, I honestly don't have any idea why you're so upset. I didn't ask you not to come to this dance because I'm ashamed of you and don't want to be seen with you. Far from it. I'd like nothing better than having you on my arm. But right now there are reasons why I'd rather have you home where I can be near you."

"What reasons?"

"I can't tell you and for once you're going to have to trust me."

She gave him a nasty little smile. "I don't have to guess why you want me to go home with you. I *know*. You said you hated the whole idea of being married to somebody like me."

"*I* said that?" Wes exclaimed. "When?"

"You told your brother Travis that, and Regan and I heard you."

Just then two overheated dancers came outside, so Wes grabbed Leah's arm and pulled her into the shadows, imprisoning her between his legs. "All right, you little wildcat, you're going to listen to me. First of all, I'm sick and tired of your telling me I'm this century's biggest snob. *You* are the snob, Leah. You're much more concerned with where people grew up than I've ever been. Yes, I did tell Travis I hated being married to you, but not because I couldn't bear living with a lowly Simmons."

"Hah!" Leah tried to look away but Wes pulled her face back around.

"I wanted a woman who needed me and as far as I could tell Kimberly needed me worse than any man's ever been needed. So here I was wanting a woman like Kim and instead I got one who could run a farm, raise kids, deal with a crazy father—you, Leah, didn't seem to need anybody or anything. You made me feel useless."

"Me?" she whispered. "How could you feel useless?"

He put his nose to hers. "Because you never ask me for a god-damn thing," he said with feeling. "You join robbers and never even mention the fact to me. Remember last week when the chimney half fell down? You fixed it by yourself. I wouldn't even have known about it except Oliver saw you hanging onto a ladder and setting stones. You could even take the ugly woman I married and make her into the beauty you are now."

Pausing, he smoothed her hair back from her face. "It took me a long time to realize that you need me more than Kimberly ever did. Kim will always land on her feet, but you, my little wife, can get into trouble on your way to the outhouse."

Leah was trying to digest this information. "But Kim's a lady and I'm—."

"You're my wife and as I've told you, you're a Stanford now, so if I'm royalty, you are too."

She pulled away from him. "Then if you aren't ashamed of me, why don't you want to be seen with me at the dance? Why do you want to keep me hidden on our farm?"

The last thing Wesley wanted to do was tell Leah about a possible plot against her. No doubt Leah would stay up nights figuring out how to get involved. "You have to trust me. You have to believe that I want what is best for you."

Leah walked away into the moonlight. What he said about Kim's needing him made sense; in fact, Kim had even hinted at that. She sensed that Wesley wanted her to faint, wanted her to be helpless, and Kim had obeyed him. But Leah had just done what had come naturally to her. Could it be possible that she also made other people feel useless?

Wesley didn't speak of love, but maybe love wasn't far away if he didn't resent her being a Simmons. What was really amusing was that Leah had worked so hard not to be a burden to Wes. When the chimney had fallen, she'd first sat down and cried. Then with determination she'd repaired it herself merely because she didn't want Wesley to think she was helpless.

She turned back to him. "If I faint for you, will you sweep me into your arms and carry me to your bed?"

The look on Wesley's face was reward enough for her jest. Without a word he came to her, lifted her, and held her close to him. "Sometimes it amazes me how much I've come to love you, Leah," he whispered. "I just wish you wouldn't yell at me so often."

Leah's impulse was to push away from him because she wanted to see his eyes when he told her, this first time, that he loved her. Instead she snuggled against him. "Maybe now that I know you love me I won't be angry quite so often."

He walked with her to his horse and lifted her into the saddle. "I've sure told you often enough. It's about time it sank in."

Above all Leah didn't want to start another argument. "I guess I just didn't hear you say it the other times. Oh Wes," she said when he was mounted behind her. "I have to get my shawl."

"I'll get it tomorrow when I get your horse."

"Good heavens, no. That shawl cost Clay a fortune. It came all the way across the ocean. I'll just be a minute."

"You stay right there," he said down to her. "I'll go with you."

Leah giggled. "Can't stand me out of your sight?"

"Something like that," Wes said seriously.

Quietly Leah stood outside and waited for her husband. It wasn't easy for her to think of trusting him, but perhaps he did have a reason for not wanting her to attend the dance. It could be that he was jealous, which gave Leah a little sense of delight. If it were true that he did love her it would make sense that he was jealous. Leah certainly had been jealous of Wes and Kimberly.

Suddenly she remembered that she'd seen Corinne Stark wearing a shawl very much like hers. Wesley would never find the right one by himself.

Inside the brightly lit store everyone was dancing and laughing. Kim stood against the wall, her eyes downcast while her husband John stood near her.

As Leah searched the room, the music stopped and the laughing dancers halted. It was in this comparative silence that the woman screamed, and when Leah turned in the direction of the scream, the woman, whom she'd never seen before, was pointing at her.

"That's my aunt's brooch," the woman screeched at Leah. "You stole it from her!"

Aghast, Leah put her hand to her breast. "No," she whispered. It was like the repeat of a nightmare.

Instantly Wes was beside his wife, putting his arm about her in a protective gesture and leading her outside. "Leah," he whispered once they were outside. "Justin's going to take you home. I'm going to stay and find out what I can about this. Do you understand me?"

Numbly Leah nodded as Wes handed her up to Justin.

"Take care of her," Wes said. "I'll send word as soon as I can, but right now I want to stop this once and for all." His head came up sharply as Kimberly came outside with John. Kim was crying softly.

"Go on, get out of here," Wes said to Justin.

Leah didn't think much on the way back to the farm and only when Justin pulled her from the horse and led her inside did she realize how cold she was. She began to shiver.

Justin led her to a chair and then pulled her into his arms. "It's all right, sweetheart. Wesley will find out what's going on. No one will believe you stole the brooch."

Leah couldn't cry but just leaned stiffly against Justin.

"Where did you get the brooch, Leah?" he asked, stroking her arm. "Leah!" he commanded when she didn't answer. "Where did you get that pin?"

"Kimberly gave it to me," Leah whispered.

"Damn that selfish little bitch!" he said with a growl as he tossed Leah back against the chair and began to pace the room. "I could see her being involved with robbers. She has the morals of a whore. Pardon me, Leah, but she does. She'd sell herself or anybody else to get what she wanted. Do you think John has any idea what he married? Poor man, he probably thought there was a woman inside her pretty frame.

"Leah," he said, kneeling before her. "I'm going to see what I can find out from Kimberly. Maybe between John and me we can talk some sense into her. Wes'll probably be back soon, just as soon as he finishes talking to that woman at the dance. Oliver's in the barn. Do you think you'll be all right here by yourself?"

Absently, Leah nodded. She wanted to be alone; she didn't want anyone to see her shame.

He kissed her forehead. "Just stay here and wait for Wes. Don't go anywhere, promise?"

Again she nodded and Justin left her alone.

Leah had no idea how long she sat there because time seemed to have no meaning. Her thoughts wandered to the fact that the fireplace needed cleaning. The sun was beginning to rise when she stiffly got up from the chair and began the filthy task of cleaning it and as much of the chimney as she could reach.

Behind her the door burst open.

Slowly, disinterestedly, Leah turned to see Kim, her eyes bright, her hair tumbled about her shoulders, her muslin dress grass-stained.

"Oh Leah," Kim said breathlessly. "It was heavenly, absolutely heavenly. It was the most wonderful experience of my life. What in the world are you doing? Leah, look at you! You've absolutely ruined that beautiful dress."

Kim went forward, but as she reached Leah she pulled back. "I don't think I'll touch you. Stand up right now and get that dress off. And while you're washing I'll tell you about the most wonderful night of my life."

Kimberly gave Leah cold water to wash in because Kim wasn't about to lay a fire in Leah's bare fireplace. "Wash your ears, too," Kim commanded as Leah stood in her underwear. "It was so silly of you to ruin your dress. Oh well, that's enough about that. Leah," she said slowly, "Justin and I made love last night."

That was the first thing that had gotten through to Leah. She paused in her washing. "You and Justin?"

"Isn't it so hard to believe? It seems that Justin has hated me from the first moment he saw me. Men don't usually hate me, but Justin did, and last night he was just furious, but later . . . Oh Leah, it was sheer heaven."

"Kim," Leah said. "Tell me everything from the beginning. Where did you get the brooch you gave me?"

"Well, that," Kim said with a sigh. "I guess things started a long time before last night."

"I have all day," Leah said firmly. "Would you like some breakfast?"

"Breakfast? I guess so even though it's afternoon, but love-making does make you hungry."

Minutes later Leah was washed, dressed, and cooking. "Start," she ordered Kim.

"I guess it started with Steven. He said there were two kinds of women: ladies who didn't enjoy it and women who did."

"Kim, why don't you tell me about the brooch?"

"I will, but everything's tied together. Oh Leah, you have to swear you won't hate me when I tell you all this. You're the best friend I've ever had and some of the things I've done—."

"I swear I won't hate you unless you keep delaying the story."

"As I said, Steven made me think that ladies had to behave all the time so when Wesley and I fell in love—and I really did love him—I never let Wes kiss me very much. You see, I very much liked Wesley's kisses, but I was afraid that if I showed him that I liked them he would think I wasn't a lady and wouldn't marry me. Oh Leah, it was hard at times to push him away. Wesley's kisses are so nice. They're—."

"Could we skip this part of the story?"

"I guess so. Leah, this is the part I don't like. When Wesley told me he was going to stay married to you, I was very, very angry. Actually, I was furious. It seemed so unfair because I'd always been holding back and being a lady while you and Wesley sneaked out at night and delivered food—oh yes, I knew about that. And, too, you'd wrestled in the mud. You hadn't been a lady at all but you'd won the man."

Pausing, she looked at Leah pleadingly. "I was so angry that I stuck a hatpin in the horse and made the wagon fall down the hill. I thought you were inside. Oh Leah," she wailed, burying her face in her hands. "I hated you so much I wanted to kill you."

Leah put her arm around Kim's shoulders. "I had a sudden call of nature and left the wagon, so you didn't hurt me. Maybe in your place I'd have done something similar. Here, now, eat your eggs and tell me what happened next."

"John Hammond saw me stick the pin in the horse and when I fainted—it's the one and only time I ever really did faint—he told me he wouldn't tell anyone. But later . . ."

She took a big drink of milk. "He really is a dreadful man, Leah. He said he'd tell everyone what I'd done if I didn't marry him."

"He blackmailed you?" Leah asked, aghast, as she sat down across from Kim. "But why? Why would he want to force you to marry him? He must have known you'd resent him."

"I asked myself that over and over. I didn't like him much for making me marry him and I did everything I could to make him regret marrying me." She smiled at a chunk of buttered bread. "You want to know a secret, Leah? I can cook. I never let Wesley know because Steven said real ladies didn't cook and when we were traveling you always seemed to want to do everything by yourself."

"I made you feel useless?" Leah asked softly.

"You could probably make any six people feel useless, but anyway, to punish John I refused to do anything at all. He was . . . very unpleasant at night and I didn't really know about lovemaking until Justin—."

"What about the brooch? Doesn't that come before Justin?"

"Oh yes. It was very boring in John's house, what with him gone all day, and since I refused to do anything I was supposed to do, I had trouble occupying myself. Except that John has this study, which he keeps locked, and right after our marriage he told me never, never, never was I to go in there."

"So of course you did," Leah said with a smile.

"Every day. It didn't really matter because I didn't care if he caught me or not because I'd already sworn to spend the rest of my life with him, so what more could happen to me? It took some searching, but I found the key, used it every day, searched the room, and returned the key."

"What were you searching for?"

"For whatever he had hidden in there that he didn't want me to see. I couldn't find anything until I found his hidden closet."

"Hidden?"

"Behind a bookcase. It was all I could do to move that case. Anyway, inside this closet were some very pretty things like jewelry and pretty little boxes and some books. It made me so angry because I thought he was hiding these things so he wouldn't have to share them with his wife."

"You *thought* this? You've changed your mind?"

"Leah, I couldn't wear any of the jewelry, but I thought someone else could. John wouldn't yell at someone else as much as he would at me. And besides, you're so good at yelling back at men. You scream at Wesley all the time. I never could understand that, Leah. You said terrible things to him and I was always nice, yet he wanted to stay with you."

"What about the brooch?" Leah repeated.

"I thought it was a miniature of one of John's relatives and I knew it'd look good on your green dress and it did until you ruined it by playing in the soot. All right!" she said at Leah's narrowed eyes. "The next thing I knew, that silly woman was screeching that you'd stolen John's brooch. John grabbed my arm, said some terrible things to me, and pulled me out of the dance. Oh Leah, I was so scared."

"Then what happened?"

"John didn't speak to me all the way home and at the house he locked me in his study and I heard him ride away."

Kim's eyes turned misty with a faraway look. "Then Justin came to my rescue."

"Rescue?" Leah asked. "Wasn't he a little bit angry at you?"

"Oh goodness yes. He was raging! Shouting all sorts of

things to me and calling me the most awful names. I'd always known he wasn't exactly enamored of me, but I had no idea he detested me. While he was shouting at me, and once he put his hands around my throat, I kept trying to show him the bookcase where the hidden closet was. It took a long time to get him to listen to me, but he finally helped me move the bookcase."

"And Justin saw all the things inside?"

"More than that. While we were inside, John came home."

"Kimberly! Where's Justin now?"

"I'm getting to that. You see, Justin didn't have any keys and all the doors in our house have locks, not like your house at all, and John had locked every door so Justin had to break in a window and the study door to get to me. Justin and I hid in the closet, wrapped in each other's arms"—Kim sighed—"while John walked through the house. When we heard him leave and ride away, Justin said, 'Let's get out of here.' So we went outside, way into the woods, and it was dark and Justin wanted me to tell him everything that was in the closet because he hadn't been able to see anything because John'd returned and we had to pull the bookcase shut. So"—she paused for breath—"I was talking and suddenly Justin got real excited and began to kiss me. I was so tired of holding back with Wesley and even with John that I just let go and the next thing I knew we were making love. It was so, so wonderful, Leah. I never dreamed—."

"What did you say that made Justin kiss you?"

"It was something very ordinary. What was it? Oh yes. At the dance last night John'd said he wasn't a good dancer and I told Justin that was a lie because I'd found a paper in the closet that said he used to teach dancing in St. Louis."

"Kimberly," Leah whispered, "where is Justin now?"

"He said he'd seen Wes and Wes was on his way to Lexington to see what he could find out from the woman who used to own the brooch, and Justin said I was to come to you and we were both to go stay with Bud and Cal, and Justin was going to wait for John to return."

"Kimberly," Leah said with as much calm as she could muster, "I think Justin may be in trouble."

"Probably." Kim smiled. "John's going to be very upset when he finds out I'm leaving him, but now that Justin loves me . . . I did tell you that Justin said he loved me, didn't I? He even said it with a prayer. He said, 'God help me, Kimberly, but I think I'm in love with you.' Isn't that sweet?"

"Get up, Kimberly," Leah commanded. "Leave the dishes where they are. We're going to get Bud and Cal and then we're going to try to help Justin. Wait! We have to leave a note for Wesley."

"Oh no! Not me," Kim said, backing away. "Justin made me tell him all about the last letter I wrote Wes, and Justin said it was his guess that Wesley was keeping you from the dance so he could protect you. If you hadn't made me send for him, none of this about the brooch would have happened."

Leah advanced on her. "If *you* hadn't tried to kill me you wouldn't have been forced to marry John. And if *you* hadn't been so nosy you wouldn't have found the Dancer's cache. And if *you*—."

"I understand, Leah." She brightened. "If none of this had happened, I wouldn't have known Justin loved me and we wouldn't have spent last night together. Oh Leah, marriage to someone like Justin must be heaven."

"You can tell me all about it later," Leah said, removing paper, quill, and ink from a drawer. "Now write what I tell you."

Dear Wesley,

I hope this letter doesn't make you as mad as the last one did, but this time I am innocent because I don't even know what Leah's talking about. She said to tell you that my hus-

band, John, used to give dancing lessons and that Justin, the man I love now, knows everything and since you're not here Leah and I are going to ask for help from Bud and Cal before we visit John and Justin.

I think that if I understood all this I'd be frightened.

I hope you had a pleasant trip to Lexington.

Very sincerely yours,
Kimberly

"Did you write what I said about asking for help?"

"Right here," Kim said, pointing. "Leah, what are we going to do if Bud and Cal aren't home?"

"Justin needs help," Leah said stubbornly.

Kim swallowed hard. "I was afraid you'd say that."

Chapter 30

DEVON MACALISTER helped his wife from her horse. "Anybody home?" he called into the empty-looking Stanford house.

"Wesley said Leah was staying here with Justin looking after her," Linnet said. "You don't think something's happened, do you?"

"Something's wrong," Mac said, looking about. "It's too quiet and why the hell is that cow bawlin'? Lynna, I want you to stay right here while I find out what's happenin'."

When Linnet saw him disappear into the barn, she entered the house. There were dirty dishes on the table and everything looked as if someone had left in a hurry. But there didn't seem to be any signs of a struggle.

As she was leaving she saw the note on the table, half hidden under a plate.

Mac burst into the cabin. "I thought I told you to wait outside," he snapped. "This whole place is empty. None of the cows've been milked, the other animals need feedin'. What you got there?"

"I think Leah and Kimberly may be in trouble," she whispered, then read aloud Kimberly's note.

"So, John Hammond's the Dancer," Mac said thoughtfully.

"Devon," Linnet whispered. "Bud and Cal were coming to our house today. They won't be there when Leah and Kim arrive."

"Surely those women wouldn't go after somebody like the

921

Dancer all by themselves, would they?" Mac asked in disbelief, but he didn't give his wife time to answer. "You get on your horse and ride back to town as fast as you can. Get somebody to go after Wes and somebody else to tend to this place. And *you*—" he threatened, "stay in Sweetbriar. I don't like what's goin' on at all."

"Devon," Linnet began, "perhaps you should get some help before you—."

"No time," was all he said before he gave her a quick kiss and was out the door.

It was just growing dark by the time Kim and Leah reached the Hammond house.

"Are you sure you should do this alone?" Kim whispered as Leah dismounted some distance from the house. "Justin seems awfully strong and brave and maybe he knows what he's doing."

"Get down and be quiet—and I'm not alone. I *did* ask for help," she said defiantly. "And I have you."

"I don't really think it's the same," Kim said as she dismounted.

After tying their horses out of view of the house, they stealthily began to make their way toward it. From the glow through the windows, every candle and lantern in the house must be lit.

When the shot echoed through the cool night, Leah and Kim looked at each other for a moment before Kim turned back toward the horses.

"Let's go!" Leah commanded, grabbing Kim's arm and pulling her toward the brightly lit house.

They ran across the yard to crouch by a window. Inside everything looked perfectly normal, with no one to be seen. "Where's the room with the hidden closet?" Leah whispered.

Kim, obviously too frightened to speak, managed to point to a far window.

Leah, holding Kim's hand, made her way down the side of the

house, crouching all the while to keep her head below the windows. Cautiously she raised herself up to peer inside the house. What she saw made her gasp. On the floor, lying in a pool of blood, lay Justin, dead still.

Leah slid back to the ground. "Justin," she managed to whisper.

Immediately Kim stood up to look, and just as quickly she bent down again. "I think John may have seen me," she said.

"We have to hide," Leah said, looking about the unfamiliar farm. "Where?"

"Follow me," Kim said, standing and raising her skirts, running with extraordinary speed toward the forest.

Leah followed her friend, running until her heart was pounding hard.

Once inside the forest Kim kept going, jumping over fallen trees, pushing aside briars and brambles with ease.

"Wait, Kim," Leah urged. "Stop for a minute."

Reluctantly, wild-eyed, Kim obeyed.

"Where are we going?" Leah asked.

"Into the forest," Kim answered.

"Yes, but where? Surely you have a destination in mind."

"The forest," Kim repeated, puzzled, frowning as she panted from her run.

"But—," Leah began, but she didn't finish because a shot rang out and landed in a tree behind her, missing Kim's head by inches.

No one had to tell either woman to start running again, and Leah didn't care where they were headed.

They ran until their legs and lungs ached, and Leah caught Kim's arm. "We have to stop and rest. We have to figure out where we are and head back toward Sweetbriar."

"I don't know where anything is," Kim said. "Do you?"

"Not until the sun rises and I can find a direction. Kim!" Leah cried. "See that black space up there? Is that a cave?"

"I don't like caves," Kim said, her jaw tight.

"But maybe we could hide in it, get some sleep, and in the morning we can make our way back to Sweetbriar."

"Couldn't we stay here and not hide in that place?"

"John'll see us with our light-colored dresses. We have to hide somewhere. Come on, let's start climbing."

The climb up the side of the cliff wasn't easy, but they made it in record time and when they slipped inside the little limestone cave, Leah leaned back in relief. She hadn't told Kim that her biggest fear had been a bear in the cave, but now she could see it was empty. The cave was about ten feet deep, fifteen feet wide, and eight feet tall.

With a smile she turned to Kim. "We made it."

But her smile was soon wiped off her face, as from outside came John Hammond's voice.

"So my stupid little wife and her stupid friend have trapped themselves," he said with amusement in his voice, his words echoing so they couldn't tell whether he was close or far away. "I gave you a chance, Kimberly, to join me. In fact, I chose you because you seemed to have no useless morals against trying to kill somebody who was in your way."

Kim, flattened against the cave wall, gave a quick look at Leah.

"But my wife," John continued, "disappointed me. Now your lover—oh yes, I know about him—lies dead at our house. What a tragedy everything will seem when the town hears how Justin was killed and two women died all in one night. I'll be the bereaved husband."

"Help me gather rocks," Leah whispered. "Let's make a pile of all we can find. Maybe we can hold him off for a while."

Obediently Kim began to pile rocks near the entrance.

"He can't come in by the side, only from the front. We'll have a clear view of him. If he shoots, fall flat to the floor. Understand?" Leah commanded.

Kim nodded.

With a smile on his face and a pistol in each hand, John stood before the cave entrance, his body outlined in the moonlight.

"Now!" Leah ordered as he took a step forward.

The women began throwing rocks with both hands.

Stunned, John ducked, grunting as stones hit him. When he fired, both women flattened themselves on the ground, bullets whizzing overhead, yet they never stopped throwing their rocks.

Kimberly sent one with force, hitting John on the side of his head, blood running immediately.

Almost staggering, he backed away from the entrance and quickly scrambled out of sight. "So, you bitches think you're smart, do you? Let's see how long you can last in there with no food or water. When you're ready to give up and die a quick death, let me know. I'll be here waiting."

Kim sat up behind what was left of the pile of rocks. "We're going to die, aren't we?"

"Of course not!" Leah snapped. "Kim, you have to have courage."

"Courage?" Kim said despondently. "Leah, I have no idea where you've gotten the idea that I want to be anything but a coward. Your bravery gets you in all sorts of trouble while my cowardice keeps me safely at home."

"Safely at home married to a murderer and thief," Leah pointed out. "You let yourself be blackmailed into that marriage, too, because you were afraid of being found out that you'd tried to kill me. And if you weren't so sneaky you'd never have found out about that hidden closet of your husband's and if you'd never found that out we'd not be here now. And furthermore—."

"Leah, I really think you've made your point. Perhaps we both should change. When Justin and I get married, we'll—."

"Justin," Leah said, putting her hand on Kim's arm, "is dead."

"No he's not," Kim said with simple conviction. "I'd know if he were dead. He may have looked as if he were dead but he wasn't."

There was something in her tone that made Leah believe her. "Kim," she said softly, "what John doesn't know is that we left the note for Wesley. And if Justin is still alive that makes a witness. Even if John kills us he won't get away with his murders."

"Let's tell John," Kim said, rising. "He'll have to let us go now."

Leah pulled Kim back down. "I'm sure your honorable husband will smile and let us go and everything will be solved. Maybe he'll even shake hands with us."

"You're right. John has a dreadful temper," Kim said glumly. "He's already killed lots of people, so maybe he'll kill us just to keep in practice. Leah, what in the world are we going to do?"

Leah stood and walked to the far wall of the cave. There was water trickling down. Wesley, she thought. What would Wesley want her to do? She remembered all the times Wesley had said she just ran off and did things rather than asking for help. At least this time she'd thought of asking for help from Bud and Cal, but when they weren't available she'd just gone ahead, dragging Kim behind her, and tried to rescue Justin and capture a murderer all by herself. And now, because of her vanity in thinking she could do everything alone, both she and Kim might die.

"What would Wesley want me to do?" she whispered.

"Wait for him," Kim answered. "He wanted you to wait for him at the farm until he returned from Lexington, but since you wouldn't, I guess waiting in this cave is the next best thing. Could we please just stay here and not do one single brave thing, Leah? Please?"

"But what if—," Leah began but stopped. "We have water but no food and it's going to get awfully cold in here."

"I think graves are probably colder," Kim said. "Leah, someone's bound to find the note I left and when Justin wakes up he can tell them John is a murderer. Someone will come after us."

"But even if Justin is alive it could be weeks before he can speak. He looked badly wounded to me."

It was at that moment that a rock came sailing into the cave.

"Looking for this, ladies?" John said with a laugh.

Leah could see that a piece of paper was tied to the rock. With trembling hands, Leah untied it. "It's the letter you left, isn't it?" she asked, tears in her voice.

"One of them," Kim said without much concern.

"*One* of them?" Leah exclaimed.

"Leah, you just have no idea how mean my husband is. Someday I'll tell you the things he did to me at night. And, too, I knew that if I was going somewhere with you I'd end up in trouble. If you and Wes go out to deliver food, to do a good deed like that, you nearly get killed. I heard how the dogs nearly got you. And it was your fault, Leah. You collect more trouble than a piece of glass collects dust."

"How many notes did you leave, Kim?" Leah whispered.

"Three. One in plain sight, one under the dirty dishes—I knew John would *never* touch a dirty dish—and one under a pillow in the bedroom."

"But I didn't see you," Leah said. "How . . . ?"

Kim stiffened her back. "As you've pointed out, I can be secretive. Now, Leah, this isn't easy for me to say because I know you can be persuasive, but if you leave this cave, I'm not going with you. I'm staying right here until a real live man, one with muscles and, I hope, a gun, comes to rescue me. If you go, you'll have to go alone."

Leah looked around the ugly, cold little cave. "It could be days before anyone comes."

"I'd rather spend a week in here than arrive dead in Sweetbriar four days early."

"Me too," Leah said, her eyes sparkling.

"You know exactly what I mean. Leah, how long can a person live without food?"

"Maybe we're going to find out," Leah said softly.

Dawn came and with it no sign of help. John Hammond found a perch exactly opposite their cave, across the deep ravine, and at random fired shots into it, making it impossible for the women to rest or even relax.

"Maybe we should try—," Leah began a hundred times, but Kim gave her such quelling looks that she subsided.

When night came they were utterly exhausted. John stepped up his firing and, once, he let go a volley that hit the ledge of the cave.

"Is he trying to shoot it off?" Leah cried out.

"Here!" came a faint voice. "While he's reloadin', help me."

Kim and Leah exchanged quick looks before hurrying to the mouth of the cave.

"Mac!" Leah said, dropping to her stomach to reach out to him. Between the two women they managed to pull him inside.

Mac leaned against the wall of the cave. "It's my leg. It's not too bad, but it's bleedin' a lot so if you ladies have anythin' to wrap it with, I'd sure appreciate it."

Both women tore their petticoats away as they fired questions at him.

"How did you find us?"

"Is Justin hurt badly?"

"Where's Wesley?"

"How are we going to get out of here?"

"Do you have anything to eat?" This was from Kim.

"Hold on a minute," Mac said. "Let me look at my leg. I thought so. Bullet went through. It stunned me so bad I nearly fell off that ledge."

"Does it hurt much?" Leah asked.

"A mite. The worst thing is I don't think I'll be able to walk on it very much. Here." He handed Kim a piece of jerky from a pouch on his belt. "Now, ladies, as for your questions. You were easy to find because you couldn't have left a bigger trail if you'd used a broad ax. I don't know nothin' about Justin. Lynna and me visited the Stanford farm and she found your letter. I sent Lynna back to Sweetbriar to spread the alarm and sent somebody after Wes. I been outside all day but had to wait until dark to get in here to you."

"I don't want to sound ungrateful, but why didn't you go after John?" Leah asked.

"He's holed up in a little cutback in a rock wall across the ravine. To get down there without him knowin' it I'd have to come down from the top with a rope and I ain't got a rope with me, but more'n that I wasn't real sure that maybe he wasn't shootin' at a bear."

"Bears don't live in caves," Kim said, looking around her suspiciously.

Mac only glanced at her. "I didn't figure on gettin' shot while I was climbin' up here. I must be gettin' old."

"I think we ought to—," Leah began.

"Don't listen to anything she says," Kim interrupted. "What do *you* think we should do?"

"We're gonna sit here and wait. Wes and some of the other men will be here soon and I hope they're smart enough to come prepared. I ran off like a—what the hell!"

His exclamation was because Kim had leaned forward and kissed him firmly on the mouth. "I just love men," she said with a sigh. "They're so sensible."

"I'd ask for an explanation for all this," Mac said, "I'd really like to know why two damn fool women ran off after some murderer like the Dancer, but to tell you the truth, I found out a long time ago that women's reasons for things usually make me madder 'n hell, so if you don't mind I'd just as soon talk to John

Hammond as you two. I want both you women to lie down on the floor back there, make yourselves as little as you can, and no matter what happens, stay there. You all understand me?"

"*I* do," Kim said pointedly.

"If you're planning something, maybe I can help," Leah said sincerely.

"The last thing I need is—," Mac began, but a gasp of pain from Leah cut him off.

Kim had grabbed Leah's arm and dug her nails in. "Leah's going to do just what you say, Mac. Aren't you, Leah?"

"I was just asking," Leah said defensively.

"Go! Now!" Mac was seething and both women obeyed his orders.

On his stomach Mac crawled near the opening of the cave. "Come on, Hammond, you not man enough to take on two little women and a wounded man?" Mac shouted across the ravine. "You havin' trouble with us?"

His answer was two shots fired into the cave. Both Leah and Kim covered their heads with their arms as the shots echoed above them.

"That wasn't even a good try, Hammond," Mac yelled.

For hours Mac yelled and John shot into the cave. Leah's ears were ringing and she could tell Mac's voice was giving out. Ignoring Kim's commands to the contrary, Leah crawled forward on her stomach until she was beside Mac.

"Your leg's bothering you, isn't it?" she asked. "Why don't you take a rest?"

"I want all of Hammond's attention on me," Mac said hoarsely. "Look across there."

At first Leah could see nothing, but as she concentrated and strained her eyes, she saw a figure against the lighter rock.

"Hammond, did you kill Revis? I heard how you were there. Is that why the man gave my name?" Mac bellowed.

"Who is that?" Leah whispered.

"From the size of him, I think it's Wes," Mac answered.

"Are you angry, John, because two women discovered who you were?" Leah screamed.

Mac put a hand to her throat. "Don't you *ever* disobey me again. Now get back into that corner."

Meekly, Leah crawled backward to lie beside Kim.

"I saw Wesley," Leah whispered. "He's coming down the cliff on a rope. It'll all be over soon."

"One way or the other," Kim said, burying her face in her arms. "I hope nothing happens to Wesley."

For the next few minutes Leah lay paralyzed with fear. "Please, God," she prayed, "don't let anything happen to Wesley. I'll be obedient from now on and never get into any more trouble and I'll always ask for help with chimneys *and* murderers."

"If we get out of this alive I'm going to make you repeat that every morning," Kim said. "And I'm quite sure Wesley will help me."

Leah had no idea she'd spoken aloud. "If—," she began.

"You two shut up," Mac said. "You're distractin' me."

In the next minute there were several shots fired, then came the awful sound of a man's scream as he fell.

Leah didn't breathe.

"Who was it?" Kim said with a gasp. "Not Wesley?"

"I can't be sure . . ." Mac began.

"Leah!" came what she knew was the sweetest voice she'd ever heard. "Are you all right?"

"Yes," she whispered, then started running, tripping over Mac as he was rising, ignoring Kim's calling her back. She tore down the side of the cliff on the way to the bottom.

Above her came Mac's voice. "Stanford, you better get to the top quick 'cause your wife's comin' after you. And I can tell you she's got no more sense 'n to climb down that rope after you."

"About as much sense as your wife's got, Macalister," Wesley shot back across the ravine. "Linnet's at the top holding the rope."

"Goddamn you, Linnet!" Mac shouted. "I told you to go get help."

Leah was halfway up the opposite wall before Wesley came sliding down to her, pulling her to him.

"I don't know whether to beat you or make love to you. Leah, you almost got yourself killed. Why didn't you stay at the farm?"

"I'm glad I didn't because John came sometime and took one of Kimberly's notes and Justin had already run off and Bud and Cal couldn't have helped me because they weren't there and—."

"Shut up, Leah," Wesley said, putting his lips on hers.

"Yes sir," she said obediently.